W9-BBG-163

IRON
LADY

IRON LADY

A Biographical Thriller

Stephen Forest

THOMAS
DUNNE
BOOKS

ST. MARTIN'S PRESS
NEW YORK

THOMAS DUNNE BOOKS.
An imprint of St. Martin's Press.

Library of Congress Cataloging-in-Publication Data

Forest, Stephen.
    Iron lady : a biographical thriller / Stephen Forest
        p. cm.
    ''A Thomas Dunne book.''
    ISBN 0-312-20466-3
    1. Thatcher, Margaret—Assassination attempts—Fiction.
I. Title.
PS3556.07242I76 1999   99–13784
813'.54—dc21   CIP

First Edition: November 1999

10 9 8 7 6 5 4 3 2 1

For Keller,
a boy who lived it

Whoever would be a creator of good and evil, must first be an annihilator and break values. Thus, the highest evil belongs to the greatest goodness; but this is being creative.

—Friedrich Nietzsche

Author's Note

THE DEEP NIGHT at the Grand Hotel and the ensuing search for the bombers are historic fact, and Margaret Thatcher makes a cameo appearance in these pages, but this is a work of fiction and the usual rules apply. None of the other characters are real. These events never happened. Maggie Thatcher would tell you as much.

FIRST
MOVEMENT

1

SHE, LIKE EVERY woman, was as great as the stories told about her. A women lives, not in her hips or breasts or mind or heart, but in the pith of those stories told about her. There are four clutches to the entourage of a woman's stories: knowing the truth, finding it, telling it and believing it. She had heard most of the stories, and one or two she favored but couldn't afford the luxury of believing simply because she wanted them to be true. She knew no story could be doused, all stories have their own life; each story had a reserved place somewhere. Some were laughter, some told as the crack of the whipping post, most dispersed around her edge, and though the stories might be told for a thousand years, no one would ever get her quite right. Only she knew the truth.

The stories they told about her had an historic ring to them. They tolled as the brass tocsin of bells that hung high about her on center stage. When the bells were rung, their echo boomed over Lake Constance that is a great curving mirror. The lake gazes upon the world like a vast liquid eye, giving off exact copies of all it sees, life reflected in multiples in the water that by day is blue and infinite, a source of peace and tranquility, but after the night has come the water turns silver black, as unfathomable as death. The stories they told were five thousand years old; she neither acknowledged or denied them. They rolled as the peel of bells over her ever changing consonance, like that inspired lake nestled in the low vine covered hills between Germany, Austria and Switzerland. And now she saw her clients arrive, on time.

They came out a Gaelic past. In the year 612, an Irish monk named Gall founded a monastery fifteen kilometers southeast of Lake Constance. The city that bears his name, St. Gallen, is a clean, picturesque Swiss haven of cobbled streets and timbered old architecture not out to prove anything. It contrasted sharply with the limousine that glided like a black liner into dock before the Abbey Library. The driver opened the passenger door, an old priest stepped into the clear October morning. He smiled up at the twin towers of white stone jutting into the blue heavens, the towers as tall as his Cathedral back in Killarney. The towers and the bells they held presided physically and traditionally over the town, they stood as a bastion against the hectic future, gazing down on the folly of man intent on going to the devil.

If Ireland had a face it would look like Father Shanahan's. Deep furrows were cut into hard, gaunt features dominated by black eyes made blacker by long silken white hair. There was a sharp nose, a muscular jaw and a thin slash of a mouth set in an oblong head that protruded from a stiff, Catholic-white collar. A network of veins lined the hollow cheeks that were not those of a saint, but a man bitten hard by the bottle.

Shanahan was joined by his mate since childhood, Red O'Grady; together they been altar boys, only yesterday. Shanahan stayed with the church, while O'Grady built a shipping empire in Boston. Now they ascended to the abbey, the one in a flowing black robe, the other in a hand-tailored navy suit. O'Grady still walked with the sea-leg roll of a sailor, though he was pushing seventy. The once proud body was softened by Parkinson's disease, but he kept the shoulders square and the fine suit gave a youthful quality to the full beard, glowing in the sun like copper set aflame. He had recently lost his heir, a son, to a British bullet in Belfast, and now with the disease, he was suddenly closer to the end than to the beginning. Death was real, definable. Death was what brought O'Grady to St. Gallen, to finish what Michael Shanahan had begun.

"Are ye certain ye want to bring in an outsider?" Shanahan asked O'Grady, who was to preside over this hour of fate, that if it were left up to him, would arrive still-born.

"Aw, cheer up, Michael," O'Grady said, smoothing his silvery hair that whipped thinly about his handsome head.

"I find no cheer in hiring a bloody mercenary," Shanahan muttered. "Why not give the lads a bit more explosive?"

O'Grady grunted under his breath.

"Another fifty pounds of Semtex," Shanahan implored, in another last-ditch effort to fend off the inevitable.

"Michael," O'Grady turned his smile to the sun flecked in red and silver and snowflaked eyebrows taken flight. "I could give you five hundred pounds of Semtex and it'd make no difference. After Brighton, they'll be guarding her like the fucking crown jewels."

Shanahan grunted under his breath. There was a stifling heat in his cassock, the blessed sun, even for this time of year, was formidable. It was the year of tempest, the grand arrival of that time foretold by George Orwell in *1984,* a story so bleak, it could challenge an Irishman's sense of the tragic. And the Brit prophet couldn't have been more wrong. Only a congenital feminist optimist could imagine the rich pickings of Orwell's rat cage terror would come not from Big Brother, but Big Sister. Shanahan turned away from the sun that shone on Margaret Thatcher like a god on her way to stardom in a world gone mad. A woman had tipped the scales of history in a way Orwell could never have imagined, and the world would not be the same. There was one remedy, Shanahan contemplated it as he watched his heavy shadow glide over the walk to the abbey where Man had come to make a stand against that inverse prophesy, Big Sister.

"Fine." Shanahan groused. "But mark my words, Red, woeful things happen when ye put yer trust in those ye don't know."

"Aw, take it easy," O'Grady said, anchoring a curled pipe into his hopeful grin. He straightened the spine of a fighter's frame. His gaze on the holy library was as steady as a marksman's. He had come not to whine about the ornery past, but to address the future for which he had a genuine goodwill. The future could be concocted, not with the brouhaha of emotion, but with money. He no longer wanted money, he would soon happily part with it all.

All morning a precarious hush prevailed the lobby of the Benedictine monastery. As though Brother Francois's were aware of last week's explosion of the Grand Hotel and knew its cause. The obese Spanish monk with the tiny eyes set in oversized lids was manning the reception desk as the guests emerged from the gaudy day. He smiled with the glow of a princess, cheeks dimpled like upside-down valentines, head as hairless as a boiled onion except for a gray fringe around pink little ears.

"Good morning," Brother Francois said, quiet as a nun. "May I have your shoes, please?"

O'Grady's sea-parched face drew into a net of wrinkles. "What?" he said to the sweet smiling monk.

"It's the parquet, sir."

"Parquet?"

It was customary for Brother Francois to greet guests with confusion; the common were unaware of the artful floor, and while his princess smile held them, Brother Francois circumspectly sized their feet for the princess slippers. "We ask our patrons wear slippers to protect the rare woods," he said in English, pleased he had guessed their tongue. "It's the floor, sir," he continued. "The seventh-century floor." He withdrew slippers that would be the correct size. They frowned at them as though the dears were to wear them on their head. Brother Francois' joy was to watch the devastation of confusion rejuvenate to the glow of amazement as the lost entered the sacred library. He offered the slippers, gesturing to the line of chairs before a shoe rack. It was his secret triumph, all would enter the library as a princess.

Shanahan had no choice, those dimples smiled insistently. He accepted the slippers and took a seat. He pulled off boots, the black hide polished over deep scars. The soft, silken slippers were a fit, as a bomb hidden above the Napoleon Suite. He had expected the entire frame of the Grand Hotel to collapse. It was to have buried Thatcher and her cabinet, but he hadn't counted on the gale-force cross bracing; the work of the English Victorians that had designed the hotel in Brighton. The Grand, like Thatcher the Iron Lady, refused to fall, though he had left an ugly scar on its face. Slippers in place, he reached into an interior pocket to withdraw a sterling silver flask. He waited till Red's head was turned to his feet. Crouched in the loose skin of his robe, bony shoulders drawn around him, Shanahan took a quick pull.

O'Grady duteously removed a pair of Johnson and Murphys; they gleamed like a weapon as he put them away. He stood and looked to his feet. Without alligator shoes he felt diminished. Out of his element. Out of control. The stride of the business he had come to conduct was cut to a tacitly decided shorten step, so he wouldn't slide onto his ass. O'Grady preceded quietly, tamely, into the magnificent library, Shanahan at his side.

A month prior to the bombing of the Grand, O'Grady, knowing the luckless proficiency of Irish bombs, had contacted a casino owner who had profited handsomely in one of O'Grady's supertanker ventures. Paolo Vanzetti was bound by honor to return the favor. Yes, the old Italian had said, speaking so softly it was difficult to hear him, he understood O'Grady's dilemma: "Luck is a thing that comes in many forms, and who can recognize her?" Vanzetti said he would do what he could to help his friend. A week later he called to give O'Grady the phone number of a Herr · Saussure, a Swiss attorney who represented Gorgon. Vanzetti had never met Gorgon—he knew no man who had—but he was said to be the best. Vanzetti told O'Grady about the repressible Colombians and the others he had heard about, including a Russian general.

"The work of a true artist," Vanzetti said. "Creative, almost nonviolent. Gorgon," Vanzetti assured his old friend, "is a professional limited only by the size of your ambitions."

O'Grady promptly called the number in Zurich and, after giving a pseudonym, asked to arrange an interview with Gorgon.

"The artist," Herr Saussure explained in a dismissive German accent, "does not do interviews."

"Artist?" O'Grady said, in a rare tone of uncertainty.

"*Ja*. Gorgon is a sculptor, no? He specializes in busts of famous personages."

There was a pause on the Boston end of the line, then O'Grady came back quickly. "Artist! Sure, I get it."

"His work is executed prudently, always sympathetic to the singularity of the subject, and always to the satisfaction of the client. Though the artist is something of a recluse, which is why I conduct the business arrangements."

"And some artists can only work in obscurity," O'Grady offered.

"Just so," Herr Saussure said in his pleasant, cheerful snobbery. "I need only the name of the subject to be immortalized, the location of their domicile and business, and any exceptional characteristics of the individual—times available for a sitting, and so on. Should Gorgon accept your assignment, I will be quoted a fee which I shall relay to you. You shall make a half–payment in advance. Balance to be paid when the work is complete."

"That's it?" O'Grady was baffled in the simplicity of it.

"*Ja*. I need only the name."

"But this sculpture. It's for someone famous!"

"*Ja*. This is not unusual for Gorgon."

"No," O'Grady insisted heedlessly, with a hot pang of grief. "I *must* speak with the man." Nothing would dislodge his heart. God couldn't dislodge him. Fortunately, he had God on his side, in the form of Father Shanahan. "I can't explain over the phone."

"I see," Herr Saussure said. "A most *exceptional* request." He paused to consider his reply. "Truthfully," he said flatly, and Herr Saussure always spoke the truth, "I have never met Gorgon. We correspond by newspaper advertisement; the artist is an obdurate recluse. But an interview *might* be arranged. It is a laborious, time consuming process and will require a nonrefundable retainer of twenty–five thousand dollars."

O'Grady didn't balk at the sum; he asked only where to wire the money. Herr Saussure gave the name of a Zurich bank, and the transaction was concluded in a mundane manner, the nature of all business in Switzerland, whether it be life or death.

Father Shanahan entered the library with God up his sleeve, in the form of a stiletto he normally wore in his boot. It was only prudent to bring experience to the unknown that took the form of the sacred in the hush of the great library. He tilted a gaunt face to the vault, a florid framework of ivory plaster opening onto angelic windows painted in scenes depicting the Scriptures. His eyes followed a winding balcony supported by gold-crowned pilasters. The Abbey Library was the Sistine Chapel of books. Man's greatest printed works were within two floors of burled shelves. A cherished collection of rare books. He knew Yeats would be here. And Joyce. And Shaw. And perhaps a Brit or two. Shakespeare. Conrad, if you insisted on calling him Brit. But not Orwell. George Orwell saw his time for what it was, but missed the turn of gender. The Fall of Man was not in Eden, but in recent times. Fate had placed Father Shanahan squarely inside the emerging world of woman, Orwell's totalitarian nightmare had only begun.

The two former altar boys walked reverently over the lustrous inlaid floor, a magnificent swirl of parquet unlike any art of this world. Shanahan shuffled in slippers through the unbroken silence, studying the handful of patrons scattered about. Which one was Gorgon? He looked to the ceiling again. Saussure had told them to wait beneath an inscription, and now Shanahan saw it in Latin script in a window of lovely scrollwork.

ET ECCE EGO VOBISCUM SUM
Matthevm 28, 20.

The inscription was centered in the library. Below it, a glass case that held the yellowed, torn pages of a remnant by the Roman poet Virgil, who had a gift for turning history into story. The best stories were rooted in history; the great stories made history. O'Grady stopped inside the light that enclosed the glass case. His smile, he established, was still in place. The loud beating of his old heart had not dislodged it. His tie, self–tied, was suddenly too tight, and he pictured a strangled victim sinking to his knees before the Virgil. His fading eyes tracked around the hallowed room. There was only the silence. It endured horribly.

"Now what?" he whispered to Shanahan.

"Red, are ye certain about this? The lads would never approve of bringing in an outsider."

"I am not the *lads!*" O'Grady whispered back.

Shanahan needed a drink, but not take it here. Not in this holy place of the printed word. His eyes cut over the scatter of patrons. Across from them, stooped over the card catalog, was a garishly made-up woman, gypsy black hair teased so it resembled a shrub. Fingers and wrists thick with jewelry, a camera dangled at her heavy bosom. Next to the card catalog a slender, graying man sat a table in an immaculate suit. An eelskin attaché case sat open on the table, an air of gravity about him as he copied text from a faded reference book. He had a feline manner of stroking a mustache as he worked. Shanahan turned to study a silver-haired shapeless old woman rummaging through the stacks behind them, her pale skin so fair it appeared translucent, hands darkly spotted, leaning feebly on an ivory-handled cane. The cord of a hearing aid was noticeable in her ear. Near the doors in a high bay of stained-glass light, a young man stood reading a book. Shimmering cascades of blond hair fell to a Victorian lace collar, the cuffs of his shirt a matching lace, jutting from a plum velvet jacket. A pretty boy as the hysteric annotation of a new feminine world upon them. This one in slippers, like Shanahan's, but that couldn't be helped. Above the darling, a fierce-looking Arab in the balcony. Dark-bearded and black-eyed, swathed in a white kaffiyeh. A hook nose projected above the Koran held close to his cruel face as he read. Shanahan surveyed them all again measuring each against the stature of Gorgon. And none measured up.

* * *

"Good morning, Mr. O'Grady. Welcome to the Abbey Library."

Shanahan was watching the idyllic boy fairy-lit by stained-glass when the voice came from the bookcase. He spun around.

"Father Shanahan," the voice said. "You'll be thrilled to know you're in the midst of the greatest collection of authors ever assembled. They are all turned to dust, though their words live on." Shanahan stared at the glass case like it held a snake, and some kind of fear blew cold on his soul. "But you didn't come to St. Gallen to discuss immortality, did you, *gentle*men?"

"You're Gorgon?" O'Grady asked, feeling like a fool, in quiet slippers, talking to a damn bookcase.

"I am," the voice said quieter still, drawing the old men in closer. "If you'll use the headphones, you can hear me clearly."

Shanahan saw the headphones; they hung from the underside of the case. He looked to O'Grady. They lifted the headphones and examined them. Gray, padded drums with a banding between them; on the bottom side was an inventory sticker, with a number and Abbey Library in small type. On the glass case there was a button for a Virgil audio program that played through the headphones. O'Grady put his on, Shanahan about to join him, till he balked. He stared disapprovingly upward like a man peeing. Breathing heavily, in the grip of a terrible indecision. O'Grady caught his eye and smiled at him, and one could almost believe he was a crackpot, grinning there in slippers and headphones. And now in slow motion Shanahan set the heavy padded drums about his ears. He had never worn headphones, but it wasn't so bad, they fit like earmuffs. He decided he was impressed with this arrangement that had a jeweled brilliance, as the old hag with the cane. She stepped away from the card catalog, muttering to a camera while reloading it. Was her camera a transistor microphone and transmitter?

"The case before you," Gorgon whispered into their ears, "contains a remnant from Virgil's epic poem *Aeneid*. If you'll pretend you're considering the work, your presence will appear perfectly normal." Shanahan peered down at the masterwork that celebrated the dual birth of Rome; the legendary founding of Rome by Aeneaus, and the world expansion of Rome. A precious piece of history, gleaming with mellow color that as Shanahan turned his head seemed to throw off golden prisms in the lamplight. He was awed, but would rather the manuscript tell the tale of Gorgon's founding and international expansion, what darling reading that would make. "There is a transmitter," Gorgon said, "attached to the bottom of the cabinet. I've taken the liberty of placing a mike in your headsets. Speak quietly; I'll hear you."

Shanahan listened close, trying to place Gorgon's accent. His voice low and melodious. A smooth French inflection with a refined quality that sounded to Shanahan like Paris.

"I am watching you," Gorgon said. "Please refrain from any sudden moves. The banding around your skull is lined in Semtex. A small charge. Not enough to damage Virgil's priceless work, but it'd leave a mess of your brains all over the glass."

Shanahan quickly raised his hands, momentarily welded to the headphones. If he yanked the damn things off, he might lose his hands. He turned to O'Grady, giving him a look fit to splinter the glass case. He knew this was a mistake! O'Grady's ruddy face was flushed; his mouth worked silently, wheezing out, "No." Shanahan lowered his hands, leaving the bomb in place. He swallowed and heard a click inside his throat, but that and the voice of Gorgon was all he could hear. He was all but deaf. Someone could approach them from behind and he'd never hear. His eyes cut again around the library patrons. They could all be speaking to each other and he wouldn't hear a word they said! He glanced to the Latin on the ceiling, and read it now as an author's inscription: *Behold, I am with you.* Not the spirit of Virgil. But the spirit of Gorgon.

"Very clever," Shanahan muttered, feeling the stiletto in his sleeve. But who would he use it on? Which one was Gorgon?

"Thank you, Father. I realize how unsettling it is, wearing a bomb, but Semtex is your *favorite* explosive, isn't it?" Gorgon paused, as if to enjoy Shanahan's frozen sneer. Semtex was the explosive he had used at the Grand Hotel, but now could Gorgon know that? "I want you to realize, gentlemen, something of what will happen if you ever give out my agent's number without first requesting his permission. Do you understand, Mr. O'Grady?"

A film of sweat had formed on O'Grady's rumpled brow. His big hands clenched and unclenched into fists. He tried to recall what Vanzetti had said about Gorgon— what was it, something about lady luck?—but it was hard to think with explosive wrapped around your skull. It laid siege to reason. One thing was apparent, Vanzetti had posted Gorgon before giving him Herr Saussure's phone number. Gorgon likely knew everything about him. Where he lived. How he lived. What he had come to live for. Gorgon might even know how long he had to live. The day's good end was in sight, and swaying in satin slippers, nearly swooning as a child in love, seventy years seemed as a day. He did not want it to end in disaster.

"I understand," O'Grady said, forcing calm into his voice.

Across the room Shanahan saw the mustached man at the table raise a hand to his mouth, as if to muffle a cough. There was his open briefcase. Could it contain a transmitter? Was he Gorgon? His elegance fit the voice, but the man seemed too slender, too languid, too delicate, for their purpose.

"Why bring us here?" Shanahan said, watching the man at the table. "To Switzerland."

"I thought you'd find the library a pleasure. And Switzerland is such a tranquil environment from which to work. There is no *carelessness* in this impregnable kingdom of the privileged."

Shanahan's jaw clenched. He tried to imagine the speed with which he could yank the headset off and get away. He saw slipper smooth feet slide over the polished floor, his head exploding like one of his bombs, one of the beauties that actually worked.

"I suppose," O'Grady said, trying to return his voice to its commanding register, "You know why we've come?"

There was no reply.

"We're here about a prime minister," O'Grady added softly.

"Mr. O'Grady, any prime minister is the object of security. But this *particular* prime minister is *particularly* well protected, something you and your Gaelic friends have made sure of with your bungling attempt in Brighton."

"I beg your pardon?" Shanahan snapped.

"It was more like a piece of theater. Quite impressive to drama queens, I'm sure. Astonishingly so. You tried to collapse an entire building to kill *one* woman. What were you trying to do? Bury her? And she escaped without so much as a scratch."

Shanahan's black eyes flashed. O'Grady tried to settle him, waving down his ire with his long, freckled fingers.

"My work, gentlemen, is a *delicate* business. And it's an especially delicate affair when it involves a prime minister who was attacked only last week. The devastating and irrational only complicates things. I like to keep my work *simple*. The greater the complications, the greater the risk."

"Hence, more expense?" Shanahan sniped. He glanced over to the pretty boy, his face bowed in his book with his lips moving. Was he reading? Or talking? Could this sweet thing be the man they were hiring? Shanahan shuddered at the thought.

O'Grady leaned over the glass case as if studying the ancient parchment. "Because the target is female," he began woodenly.

"Gender makes *no difference*, Mr. O'Grady. My method is the same, male or female. I use whatever technique agrees with the subject. There are *so many* ways to take a life. As a rule, I prefer to arrange it so the marks kill themselves."

The self-annihilating method sounded to Shanahan like the devil; a close approximation of life itself.

"Well, that's fine, just fine," O'Grady said, nodding. His back was stiffening up by all the bending at the glass case. He straightened and fumbled in his pocket till he found the cold pipe, needing something in his hands. "Now, you're going to want to know why I want this bitch dead. My son—"

"Mr. O'Grady," Gorgon interjected, cutting him off, "I don't give a damn about tough times, we all have tough times. Tough rhetoric is quite unimpressive in a world that understands only death that we know and do not know. We know death as love; we waste the same frantic devotion on both. We stalk love, imagine it, try to second-guess it. Sheer foolhardiness of behavior leads us to love, and in her arms we are free at last. Love, like death, is not made of what is fair or just. It is a state of union, love and death. If we come to terms, we shall be in union. If we come to terms, I'll kill your mark. Simple as that. I'd kill your mother for the same reason. If it came to it, I'd kill you. I don't work for passion or patriotism. I work for *profit*. So, could we please get down to business?"

"Fine." O'Grady licked his lips and put on a big smile that looked ridiculous on the rugged geography of his face. He toured the brave smile round the room for all to see. Out of his shoes and now out of his face, the smile so stiff, as if wearing someone else's dentures. He turned back to the glass case.

"The job pays—" He hated doing business this way, not being able to look his man in the eye. "We have a million dollars, American," he said.

Laughter erupted in their headsets.

"For Thatcher!" Gorgon said. "We are talking about *Margaret Thatcher?*"

"It's what we have," Shanahan hissed. "Take it or leave it."

"It would cost that much to set it up," Gorgon said.

"All right," O'Grady looked at the yellowed, torn manuscript. Suddenly feeling as old as the manuscript, and as torn. "Make it . . . two and a half million."

Shanahan inhaled sharply. "I could buy the devil himself for two million," he muttered.

"No, you won't," Gorgon came back, cool and confident, and Shanahan could hear the years of training and experience in his reply. "No, the price for Thatcher is *six* million."

"Six million!" Shanahan choked.

"Aw, take it easy," said O'Grady, waving off his tirade. "I have five million," he said to the ceiling of angels.

Hot blood rushed to Shanahan's head. *Five million!* Why, for that money he could take the Houses of Parliament to the ground. He could see it as a Turner painting. Windows blown out, glass dancing in lurid flames! A mass of smoke reared from the ruins to glow a deep red in the setting sun mirrored on the sheets of water so the Thames lay like tidepools of primal blood. The inspiration brought a Psalm up from the heart: *He smote divers nations: and slew mighty kings; Sehon king of the Amorites, and Og the king of Basan: and all the kingdoms of Canaan; and gave their land to be an heritage; even an heritage unto Israel his people.*

Now Shanahan listened as the mercenary asked if there was a deadline. Did Gorgon know Red had only six months to live?

Red said six months, and Gorgon replied, "No, six months is just sufficient lead time for any job."

And now O'Grady offered the appointment calendar; their ace in the hole. Shanahan had a contact within the British government that had given a copy of Thatcher's appointment book. Not a thing that money could buy. If you knew *when* and *where* the PM would be, you could be there waiting. Less risk, less expense—it seemed reasonable, since bloodless profit was the only consideration.

"How reliable is this source?" Gorgon was saying.

" 'Tis impeccable!" Shanahan proclaimed, knowing it was so. And it was a device to keep tabs on the contractor. "I developed the contact myself," he said, feeling the weight of eyes that saw him as a scarecrow alcoholic concealed in the robe of a priest.

"Appointment calendars change," Gorgon countered.

"That's right." O'Grady grinned, placing a hand on Shanahan's bony shoulder. "And we'll give you the changes as they're made."

Out of the corner of his eye, Shanahan watched the fickled hag on the cane, wandering in and out of the stacks. Looked like she was talking to herself. Or was she? Was she talking to the cane that concealed a microphone? He saw the wire trailing from her ear. A hearing aid? Or an earpiece? Was the hag disguised? If so, for what? And now it occurred to him that neither Vanzetti nor Saussure ever referred to Gorgon's gender. Shanahan folded his long arms over his chest. He could feel a migraine coming on, with a kind of delicate horror. Sweet Jesus, were they about to hire a woman? He gave a jolly laugh at the thought, though the inside of him was frozen in alarm.

"Very well," Gorgon finally said. "Have the calendar typed up without mention of a name. Seal it in an envelope. Take it to the Hilton Hotel in central London. Leave it for Dana Jenkins."

Shanahan considered the name. It could be a man or a woman.

"Have it there by Thursday," Gorgon said.

"That'll be pushing it," Shanahan said.

"Then push it, *priest!*"

Shanahan bristled stiffly at the exhortation in "priest." The annunciation was hostile, and set his spirit aflight. It flew in suppressed fury over the splendor of the room, zooming upward to a chorus of angels that knew who Gorgon was. It flew in and out of the thousand-year-old fruit on the shelves, composed by the souls in the jetstream of that divine muse that does everything but write the words. He flew in a winged chariot, back to the age of Virgil, from which issued the far sounds of female singing, and a veritable windstorm of unreason took possession of Shanahan. He had assumed Gorgon was a surname, perhaps German, of or relating to the distant Teutons. But before the Teutons there were the Greeks. In mythology, the Gorgons were three accursed sisters from celebrated monster parents. The eldest, known as Medusa, had serpents locks and a gaze that turned men to stone. And now Shanahan went rigid. Were they actually hiring a woman?

But no woman could do the work. Violence was the way of men; aggression was not a trait of women. This had been known since ancient times, since the Garden of Eden that was part of the male mind. Eve was responsible for man's fall. When Eve was created, Satan rejoiced. Since the banishment from Paradise, Man had led nations and wars; Woman followed as his helpmate. The order of things spelled out in Corinthians: "Neither was man created for the woman but the woman for the man." Woman was created *from* Man. Man created *from* God, in His image. This Creation story succeeded the Assyrian scripture, duplicated it, except in the Assyrian text God was the Mother-Womb, Creatress of Destiny, who made male and female beings out of clay, "in pairs She created them." Thanks to early Christian theologians, like Gall, She was gender-bent to He. The ancient texts were purged, expunged, *She* systemically erased so in the last few thousand years *He* ruled. The corollary of this was real wealth in the absence of a goddess within woman, in the hierarchy of men genetically predisposed to violence. Shanahan had read as much in medical journals, reinforcers of the spectacle of Eden that entitled the creator's gender. A woman could no more be a professional killer than . . . *than a woman could be a prime minister,* a Thatcher-like voice retorted in his head.

By the time Shanahan had returned from hovering at man's legendary tower, all was agreed upon. The job would be done in six months, and due to the time element, the price was now $7 million. It occurred to Shanahan that this Gorgon negotiated like Thatcher. Half payable now, half when the contract was complete. Shanahan stared in wonder at O'Grady as he agreed to it all, his cheeks as fluid as a baby's, the dabs of color very high. It was to all be in U.S. currency, no bills larger than fifties, no consecutive serial numbers, all used notes. There would be no wire transfers that could be traced.

"Mr. O'Grady," Gorgon said, "on Thursday you are to go to the New American Cleaners on Howster Street in Boston."

"Yes," O'Grady replied earnestly. "What about it?"

"Tell them you've lost your receipt, but you want to pick up a suit for a Dana Jenkins. Inside the lapel will be a piece of tape. On the tape will be two numbers. One is my bank account in Zurich, for the down payment; you are to deliver it personally. The other will be a telephone number. It will be answered by machine. If there are changes in Thatcher's schedule, you may leave them on the machine. Make it short and sweet. No clever codes. And no names. Remember that, *no names.*"

"No names," O'Grady repeated. "Dana Jenkins. New American Cleaners. Howster Street."

"Memorize the numbers. Then eat the tape."

"Eat it?" O'Grady's mouth puckered as if at a weird taste.

"Don't worry. It'll taste *sweet*. You'll enjoy it."

The provocative spin put on "sweet" pierced Shanahan with the certainty that they were hiring a woman. He rolled his eyes at O'Grady. How could he warn him? He couldn't remove the damn headphones! If he said it aloud, Gorgon would hear him.

"And one more thing," Gorgon said. "No one is to know about this. Not ever. And you are not to credit me with the hit."

"Fine," Shanahan said. "Our people will take the credit."

"No one would believe it, *priest*. I don't care if you put out the word that the Ayatollah did it. Or Saddam Hussein. Makes no difference. But if there's a leak, *any leak,* before or after, I'll kill both of you. One at a time. And I won't use Semtex. It will be painful and disgraceful and infinitely *personal*."

Shanahan wanted a drink. He needed the flask in his cassock. He allowed his shoulders to slump in a gesture of impatience, but still O'Grady would not turn his head from what captivated him.

"Christ, I'll be glad when it is done," O'Grady said to the glass case. "Maggie Thatcher is a heartless bitch. She proved that when she let Bobby Sands and his mates starve to death in Maze Prison. She's filled a cemetery full of green graves."

"Aye," Shanahan said, crossing himself. "'Twill be an honorable Irish murder."

"Hell," O'Grady groused, thinking of the starved lads, "if it were possible, I'd have Thatcher chained to one of these columns and watch *her* starve to death. Let her die of her own poison!"

Shanahan glanced up at the black-eyed Arab, now behind them in the balcony, the Koran still held close to his face, concealing his lips. And now he recognized the scent of Arabian jasmine on the headphones, and Shanahan breathed a sigh of relief, feeling his world right itself. The balcony was the position from which to control, and a man would know that. The Arab *had* to be Gorgon.

"It's a pleasure doing business with men of such conviction," Gorgon said. "I'll wait to hear from you."

"In London," Shanahan said, smiling up at the fierce Arab.

"In London," Gorgon replied with the extra gruffness that he used when addressing the priest.

Shanahan reached for the headphones and slowly lifted them from his head. He breathed deeply, feeling his thoughts unwind. Sounds returned. The crackle of a page as it was turned. From somewhere came the ghastly creak of a chair as weight was shifted, with the weight elevated from Shanahan's shoulders. The impatience he had felt was gone; he entrusted the job would be done, and owed his allegiance to the competence of Arabs who had no sentimental visions of women. The two former altar boys retreated over the swirled floor, taking their time in all that majesty, leaving the five patrons behind, seemingly oblivious to what had transpired.

"Good God," Shanahan whispered to O'Grady changing shoes, "for a moment there I thought we were signing on a woman!"

"A woman?" O'Grady's face rumpled, lacing up his superior alligators. The damn satin slippers belonged with evening gowns.

"Aye," Shanahan said, smiling now. "Gorgon, as in the myths of the ancient ones. Ye remember Medusa?"

O'Grady let out a guffaw of laughter. Michael always had an appetite for the everlasting cockteaser. The unattainable bitch. Most American men kissed them the way Catholics kiss the crucifix; men had to believe in something, so it was the insatiable bitch. Your skin will never be broken, burned or in any way irrevocably marred. You will simply become an object of amusement. To love them was to be reduced to nothing, to surrender your will, all while believing you are your own man. And the more you loved them and gave them, the less they respected you. Women who were a sort of Moby Dick. A white man-eating whale. But, no, he probably had that backwards, the Medusas were more akin to Captain Ahab.

O'Grady was in a fine mood as they bid the monk farewell, to step into the pristine brilliance of Swiss air. Light flickering like a movie in the alterations of sun and shadow as they came down the walk beneath overhanging oaks. O'Grady lifted his face to the good warm sun, seeing two white clouds pinned to the sky.

"You know, it might not be such a bad thing," he mused. "A woman, that is." He slapped Shanahan's shoulder with a short shout of laughter. "If we don't expect her, the Brits never will!"

Shanahan made it as far as the street, then pulled the flask and took a good long drink. The fiery arrows reflected from the limousine brought the words of Isaiah: "We have made a covenant with death, and with hell are we at agreement."

"Good-bye, Maggie Thatcher," O'Grady said, taking the flask, drinking to his fallen son. "You English whore."

Shanahan baptized his throat once again, allowing himself to be party to mistaken perception. She was said to have once been beautiful. A whiteness against the whiteness of the pure. But she had been raped in a church, by an ecclesiastic, as he recalled. The betrayal turned her ugly; Medusa crawled with snakes, within her, and she had hair of snakes as well. His mild gaze, at odds with a pugilistic Irish heart, remained fixed on the Abbey Library as some jest, he imagined, some merriment if it were the choice of Medusa. The ancient abbey embedded as it were with the history of those standards of a masculine God made with an eraser. And then there was her rape, though she would have to be hanging as a star well above it, to turn it into play, to use angst as staging.

The driver opened the door. Shanahan took the blessed flask with him, vanishing into the dark interior of the fine car.

Brother Francois was waiting for her when she came out of the library with the others. She appeared monstrous in her beard, but now she peeled it away. The hook nose came off next, then the wig. She shook out amazing blond hair that fell in sun streaks to her shoulders. While she took out Arab-black contacts, her beauties pulled off wigs and wrinkles. Gorgeous smiles hovered round him, buzzing like bees at a yawning flower. Taking possession of his space. And now pastries appeared! Where did they come from? Eating in the library was strictly forbidden, everyone knew that. He had told them that, hadn't he? He couldn't recall, all that came to mind was Scripture: *Out of the mouths of very babes and sucklings hast thou ordained strength, because of thine enemies: that thou mightest still the enemy, and the avenger.*

They were not to have food in the library, Brother Francois reminded the girls, with a smile in his voice, playing the humble servant. His appetite taunted him as he scolded them. But it was impossible to be angry with them, so bewitching in their costumes and accents from around the world. One disguised as a boy. Narrow hips and golden hair of an angel in deep purple velvet and lace. His, or rather, her name, was Alexa. She was suddenly beside him and Brother Francois's heart stopped. There's nothing in nature more beautiful than a beautiful girl unless it's a beautiful girl who looks like a beautiful boy, or a beautiful boy who looks like a beautiful girl. Impossible for Brother Francois to escape even for a moment from the spell of this storybook creature at his side. The circumstances of gender lost in his-her blue eyes.

Alexa gave him the envelope of cash. She thanked him for opening the library for their modeling shoot. They had wanted to take pictures of the Virgil, which was against the rules, but he made an exception. Now Alexa was leaving him, and he would have wept, but she was there with her contacts out, smiling into his hardship with eyes as deep and blue as the fjords of Sweden. He told himself to look away from those eyes, but couldn't stop his lust, those eyes so blue, almost violet, but for a blackness at the centers. She thanked him personally, and he assured her the day in library would remain their secret. She kissed him lightly on the cheek, and after she was gone, he could not recall her face or her height or any other feature, only those smiling eyes, and the glistening apple pastry she left behind.

He ate with German gusto, as though drinking what he ate. When he had finished he licked his fat fingers, sucking at the traces of sweetness, as sweet as the serpent's sweetest apple. Kneeling at morning prayers, Brother Francois was still seeing those eyes that turned him hard as stone. He renounced the devil and all his works, the pomps and vanity of this wicked world, and all the sinful lusts of the flesh. He had only just expunged his soul, erasing her from his heart, when the first seizure struck. He sank from his knees to the floor, pastry retching up, swelling his throat and he couldn't breathe. His tiny eyes seemed to fill his face, the rolls of fat on his neck flowered over his hands at his throat. He looked gross and piggish writhing between the pews. In spasms of choking, he saw a vast liquid eye that gave off exact copies of his life reflected in multiples in the water infinitely blue and beautiful. A blueness all around him and soon inside him with his face turning blue as he drowned in those eyes that turned silver black. And as Brother Francois peered into the dark depths of the hereafter, his small pale hands reached up for heaven.

2

THE HEATHROW CUSTOMS officer glanced up from the entry card. The arrival was a computer programmer from Los Angeles. He gave a smile. She was lukewarm. No devil there to drive his smile further. Tall and slender, attired in a suit of the same shade of boring brown as her eyes and bobbed hair. A woman falling out of her thirties toward middle-age; some possibilities in the face, but it had about as much expression as a computer chip. He wouldn't remember the face, only the gold-framed spectacles.

"Welcome to Great Britain," the officer said. "Have you come to Britain for business or pleasure?"

"Business," she replied to the man in the mulberry uniform.

"And the length of your stay?"

"Two weeks."

The officer tapped the name into his computer. Jenkins, Dana S., Los Angeles, California, U.S.A.

"It'll be a moment," he said, watching the blinking cursor.

She rocked in short heels, clinging to her garment bag as if a nagging little worry had set her in motion, as if she didn't know exactly what he'd find on his screen. If asked, she could recite the menu of her favorite L.A. restaurant. She would have been happy to recommend a bookstore, or an English-style pub that played chamber music for Sunday brunch. She could have related how she grew up in a ranch house in San Bernardino with a cocker spaniel named Mandy, in the days before the mountains were gauzed in smog. She would have made it all sound perfectly believable and so utterly boring, you'd beg not to hear another word.

Nudged from behind, she turned to find a freckled-face boy in tropical colors. Face in a grip of concentration as he bounced a blue rubber ball. Another spoiled brat; she could see it in the mother, eyes sheeplike in her adoration. They effaced themselves, these American mothers in their prim costumes that made them look like girls dressed up in Mama's clothes. Living for every last sniveling word of these waist-high dictators who controlled the destiny of a day by their very expressions and manner and mood. Baby pink in the bath. Smelling warm and cuddly as you tucked them into bed. One eye closed, the other taking you in and they know exactly what they're doing, egging you on to stay up another ten minutes. Another thirty minutes. An hour. Parents today so awful ready to please. Weak and tottery, in a subterfuge of passivity that would make one of the most functionless generations in the history of woman. Aspiring children, harboring large ideas, but simply scared to death of themselves. No idea of how to do for themselves. How to succeed in losing. The whole world gone pie-eyed over children, the most talented manipulators in the game, with gumption, but selling out their future every time they win.

Suddenly the ball escaped the boy. It rolled under the door of an empty security booth. She watched the child dash through the line and charge through swinging doors stenciled: *"Do Not Enter."* A moment later, out he came, dribbling his ball.

She turned her chalky, forgettable complexion to the officer. An eyebrow arched inviting response.

"Kids," he mused. "They can get away with anything."

"Really," she echoed.

"Ah, here we are," the officer said as the computer blinked her clearance. He inked an entry stamp onto the clean first page. "Very well then," he said. "May I see the return ticket, please?"

"It's a private plane."

"Well. How nice."

She did not respond to this. Her face welded together without a joint. "And may I ask the name of the aircraft?" he said.

"Pequod," she replied, still with no expression.

He started to jot the name onto the card, then looked up with a slight grin. "I rather thought she went down in the Pacific. All hands lost but one."

"The ship has been resurrected," she said, offering him a passionless smile that flashed briefly, like her spectacles.

The smile was what he really wanted, didn't bother with the plane's name. Sounded genuine. Only Yanks would give an aircraft the name of a sunken vessel. Doomed before it ever left port; even the English had read *Moby Dick.* He returned the fresh passport. "Welcome to Great Britain, Ms. Jenkins. Enjoy your stay."

She slid the passport into a trim handbag and crossed into Thatcher's England, moving through the busy concourse with long, decisive strides. She didn't bother with the passionless smile.

She took a cab to the Savoy Hotel. No need to invite scrutiny at the front desk; her key was waiting with a doorman. The paneled elevator whisper quiet, her ear tuned to the aristocratic accents behind her. So pleasant to be back in the Savoy.

The brass plate on the door announced her assistant had taken the Honeymoon Suite. She acquired a new smile. It had something of victory in it, picturing the lovely bride Kim would make. She entered a lavish room. It did not set her eyes dancing. On the marble entry table, a dramatic arrangement of rare tiger lilies, a note in handsome script attached:

> *Kristian,*
> *I'm at the Central London Library. Research is going great! We'll soon know everything about Maggie; her life's an open book. Picked up the package at the Hilton. What's inside?*
>
>> *Love,*
>> *Kim*

Beside the lilies, a large envelope labeled: "Dana Jenkins." She left it and phoned room service. Then toured the suite noting the windows and doors and the terrain beyond the windows and the fire exits in the hall. She kept it as a blueprint in her mind; it'd be there should the unexpected occur. In the closet, her clothes were waiting, neatly hung. She started the tub; an Arab jasmine scent rolled out on the steam. Only now did she put Dana Jenkins away, the boring suit and wig, contacts, and spectacles all in the flight bag kept under the bed, within arm's reach.

When the room-service waiter rolled the supper cart into the suite he was greeted by a woman who, barefoot, stood six feet tall. She appeared in her late twenties, maybe thirty, hard to tell she looked so fresh and natural in the Savoy's cotton robe, striking against a seamless tan. White-blond hair in a haphazard elegance. Wide lips and high cheekbones and a strong jaw that came with a cool arrogance of dark brows feathered over ice blue eyes. The Irish lad was taken by the eyes, and never noticed the scars.

There was a scar running down her left elbow, from an affair in Moscow that got out of hand; she didn't see the dagger coming, but in taking down the KGB agent so cleanly, she had actually won an endorsement from the Soviets, rather than re-prisals. There was a thin scar clearly visible across the back of her neck just below the hairline, a memento of a car wreck she and Laurnet, the older of her younger sisters, had in Rome, back in the days when they had worked together, before they wrecked each other. And there was a small curled scar on her right thigh, the dia-mond slice of a chandelier that fell in a casino in Bangkok, the only time she had used explosive that was always a gamble, too volatile to control, control the oper-ative word in the dignity of her work. Success never came cheap, but if she were stark naked, the young waiter wouldn't have seen these scars, beauty a mistress that evokes a certain blindness. If the Irish boy had known of the damnation of the jobs gone bad, and of Somberg's eventual salvation, he would have subscribed their success to luck. Most men had no inkling of the relentless effort a woman's achieve-ment requires.

It was indignity, the way the waiter was so stricken with a clumsiness in the presence of those shameless eyes, but he managed to follow her out to the balcony, catching a whiff of some perfume never encountered before. The cart parked, she asked if he would turn down the bed—she wanted to nap after her meal—and as she leaned over the cart to concoct a dip for her oysters, he caught a glimpse of tan breasts straining at the folds of the bathrobe. Her tongue now licking sauce from a sculptured index finger, and he didn't see the strength in the finger, as long as a man's.

He took his time with the bed, not his job but one he gladly did, imagining the job he'd do if she offered an invitation. She did not give orders as some ill-tempered sea captain but rather, everything was a pleasant request signifying nothing, with all the rising and forbearance in you. But she made no other request, and he left, backing out of the room, seeing her through the Palladian window. Dining on raw oysters and a Bloody Mary, one hand keeping time to Rachmaninov, *Rhapsody on a Theme by Paganini.* Watching the ever changing cloud formations. A chilly day, he won-dered how she could stand the cold, half-naked as she was.

The sun was at the edge of the English horizon, but Jessica Moore never saw it. She was inside her four-by-five Hasselblad camera, her whole body, mind and soul, in the camera waiting for the light. The thirty-two-year-old Chicago photographer had come to Warwick Castle to shoot a cover for the Jaguar XJ-6 brochure. The assignment had been a bitch. Rained on the first day. Drizzled on the second. Rained intermittently on this, the third and final day. There was a break of sunshine in the morning, and she had attempted a shot. The Polaroid told the tale: a murky picture of a fourteenth-century castle that looked sour and cruel, beastly, as though some-thing dark dwelled within. Before an open drawbridge was a Jaguar surrounded by six mud-splattered horses mounted by lusterless knights sagging in their saddles, as if the clouds of gloom were weighing on their armor.

The picture was stark reality, and reality was almost always a disaster for a photo illustrator. Reality is a thing we know and understand. Jessica had earned a repu-tation for creating highly cinematic images that made people feel something more than they understood. Any pro with a knowledge of their craft can depict reality, but it takes an artist to depict emotion. The purchase of a luxury sedan, contrary to what most men would tell you, is not driven by reality, but by emotion. Emotion rules.

She made pictures that told a story; she was a storyteller first, a photographer second. She worked in a fictitious framework that resembled reality. She stepped into the framework, often with nothing more than an vague idea of the picture as an end, and she knew the grand theme. She depicted the spirit of humanity, with a true love for people. People were emotion, usually a tangle of emotions, all of them in Technicolor captured by the camera.

It had taken Jessica ten years to earn her name; it took her that long to learn hard work doesn't earn recognition. It didn't matter if a shot took three hours or three days or three years; the time put into a shot didn't make a damn bit of difference. The only thing that mattered was the picture. It must grab people. It had to have spectacle, drama, catharsis, pity, or fear. And to portray these in a picture, you had to experience them, because after the technical was mastered, making pictures was all about instinct. The instinct to make an impact. In art, those who make an impact are rewarded. Those who don't are ignored. Jessica had learned to trust her instincts that were essential to her success. It had taken her ten years and a ridiculous number of failures to learn these simple things, to get the word of mouth going, and she knew it would take only one lousy shot to begin to lose it.

At Warwick Castle, she had spent the budget and come up with nothing, and now decided to gamble. She had one of her knights run her into Birmingham, a British girl who could drive on the screwy wrong-way roads. They rented a pair of fog machines from a film company. A trip to the hardware store produced silver polish, a big block of Styrofoam, and a can of drab brown spray paint. At a toy store she found a cricket clipper and a gift for Danny, her six-year-old son. Jessica bought a set of funky little toy cars. Red, yellow, and blue.

They raced back to the castle, and she put her staff to work polishing the armor; the actors cutting the Styrofoam into booster seats painted saddle brown; the lights were reset for a dusk shot. She waited till the sun dropped to the treetop mark, then called the actors to the set. With Levi's and boots caked in mud, dirt flaked across her freckles, brunette hair stuffed into a cap, she looked more like a pig farmer than a photographer. The pig farmer called for the fog machines. They spewed a fine, wimpish mist that lacked wonder; it offered no mystery. The sun began to sink and Jessica gambled on. She would not allow anything to enter her mind which opposed her goal. She saw an end she had pictured and waited and kept waiting. Until the last of the light fell with romantic affection upon the castle, dissolving cold stone walls, painting the towers and turrets in a cognac light. The temperature dropped; the fog thickened, creeping like smoke from a spent battle through knights riding high in their saddles, lances raised against the travails of life, shards of light glistening off their armor.

The tall, willowy photographer was as calm as a Zen priest. Her mind sharp and clear, as focused as her lens. Jessica saw only what the Hasselblad saw, calling to the actors.

"Knights, keep your lances high . . .

"Square your shoulders . . .

"Look this way . . ."

She raised the cricket clipper and began snapping. The horses lifted their heads, ears pricked. Strobes fired to capture the illustration of a lustrous XJ–6 Jaguar surrounded by shimmering knights ghosted in a fog that licked at the base of the lovely, hospitable castle jutting into a deepening cobalt hue of twilight, as though the sun had been abducted from the sky.

She opened her blue legendary eyes. She lay still in the first waking moments when the oracular qualities of dreams are preserved in their purest form. She saw lush black hair and an Asian face. The perfect symmetry of the bones and sharp-cut eyes, clear and dark, shy as a deer's. His skin smooth, as if waxed and buffed. In her dream, he had feathered wings, as some delicious fallen angel. Kristian Somberg smiled at the thought.

She rose naked from the bed and opened the drapes to let in the remains of the day. A glance to the clock pleased her; she had slept four hours and woke without an alarm. In the robe, seated at the vanity, she brushed her hair loose and free; it rippled to her shoulders. She colored her face; it didn't take much. A trace of shadow on the eyelids, mascara, a dusting of sandstone for her mother's cheekbones, barque beige for the lips. She appraised her reflection, both sides of her face, then full-face in the mirror that was her best friend; it always told the truth. The mirror was reality, the making of which was her career.

She dressed in an ivory bodysuit and gray stirrup pants molded to the muscled grace of a gymnast. An Italian plaid blazer and another glance in the mirror. She was beautiful, and she knew beauty was too highly valorized. Its worth was decided by need. It embodies nothing. It denotes nothing. It suggests nothing. And above all, she knew what most men would never learn, that beauty was not goodness. Beauty was simply pleasure, nothing more.

Satisfied, she left the vanity there, in the mirror, so there was nothing that could be appealed to or flattered or insulted. She took a shoulderbag, the Dana Jenkins envelope fit neatly in the bag, and set out for St. James's Park.

She past the Savoy doorman, denying him a memory of her face. She walked, with a stride that was at ease in the world. It was a world that had not changed since it was made. To know the past is to realize the present. To realize the present is to affect the future. To control absolutely the world in which you live takes an understanding of the past that only fools forgot. If history is forgotten, there is hell to pay; women had been paying for ages.

Before the Greeks there were the Amazons. Herodotus wrote of Libyan Amazons, the first to tame the horse, which would account for their domination of all of North Africa. Contrary to popular belief, the Amazons were not entirely female, there were priests who were castrated and wore dresses, and male warriors entered the service of the Goddess by castration and wearing women's clothes. Medusa was the serpent goddess of the Libyan Amazons, she depicted "female wisdom." In Egypt, Medusa was known as the Destroyer, the Death of the Triple Goddess Neith, "the mother of all gods." She was the past, present, and future. "All that has been, that is, and that will be." A portrayal so encompassing that many thousands of years later the Christians repeated it in depicting Jehovah in the book of Revelations. Before Jehovah, there was Medusa. Medusa of the "wise blood;" she gave women their divine powers. It was not until Christian times that Medusa was blazoned as "the worst woman in the world." She was Death, but she was also Wisdom.

In Greece, Medusa's countenance was given snake-locks that signified female wisdom. Gorgo, Gorgon, or Gorgopis, "Grim Face," was the death goddess. She was a trinity in classical mythology, she and her sisters were: Wisdom, Strength, and Universality. The enormity of the tirade killer sisters grew as their virtues were contemplated. Greeks feared the ghosts of slain Amazons who had worshipped Medusa. They called them Beautiful Ones, built shrines to them, and for centuries to come offered sacrifices, sometimes human sacrifices, beautiful boys taken as bounty in the wars. The boys, usually wellborn and well educated, were seized as slaves, or offered as reparation. And some were tricked into serfage for having injured a woman. Their long hair tied at the nape, hands bound at the back above a bare bottom, the well-endowed boys were stroked until they were stone hard. In such sensual proclivity they were scarcely aware when their smooth throats were cut and they were given to serve the departed Amazons "from henceforth and forevermore." This beautiful, obliging chattel was to propel Medusa and her sisters into the ages, and in the fullness of time, to render the Amazons a flourishing elite once again.

Somberg was in a cab now, her driver a young Arab complaining about the traffic, threatening his anger to anyone who got in his way. Defiant, belligerent, stealing glances at her in his mirror, typically male. Most men lived limited lives, fifteen minutes at a time, empty inside, concealing emptiness by being obnoxious and aggressive and loud. Most women feared or hated men. But Somberg didn't fear men, she knew what other women did not. They knew so much about the power of others and so little about their own.

It's a little known fact that the majority of the world's wealth is controlled by women. It's been a woman's world for some time; the problem is, women don't realize it. They don't think it, so they don't act it. Out the window Somberg saw them examining their flaws in shop windows. Women lived in absolute and utter fear of themselves. Fear and disgust. Only in sleep were they themselves. Only in dream was their heart free of revulsions they accepted. All a woman need do is stop looking at herself and take the day. Take as in Maggie Thatcher.

To destroy Thatcher was natural enough; Thatcher was herself a Destroyer. She had destroyed customs and ideas and labor unions and political adversaries at home and abroad. She had destroyed in war and in peace. She had made destruction her way, and the one she destroyed repeatedly was herself. The classic woman was first and foremost a Destroyer. The good Golden Girl was patterned after the goddess Aphrodite. Myth made her out to be a love goddess, but before the Greeks rewrote her, Aphrodite was the "Man-slayer." The Black One. The Goddess of the Tombs. The Queen Bee who kills lovers as drone bees are killed, by castration and disendowment. Aphrodite was beautiful, but not pretty. Cleopatra, drowning her nighty lovers in the Nile was beautiful, but not pretty. Catherine the Great, who spent the equivalent of a billion dollars on male concubines, men instruments of her pleasure, executed lovers and husbands alike. Catherine was not pretty. The classical woman was always the Destroyer, and her lessons were passion, mastery, self-autonomy, sensual gratification, and power. Thatcher had learned her lessons well; the final one being, Destroyers are destroyed.

Medusa, Aphrodite, Cleopatra, Catherine the Great and Maggie Thatcher were all bitches. In the cab, Somberg smiled pleasantly on the term that was a virtue. "Bitch" was the most sacred title for the Goddess Artemis-Diana, leader of the "hunting dogs." The Bitch was the divine Huntress. In the early Christian ages, a "son of a bitch" was a spiritual son of the pagan Goddess.

Each bitch, by her nature, defines herself; a bitch is never the darling of someone else's decrees. Impelled by a lifetime of bitchery, Somberg had adopted her own code for satisfaction, which was not recited by her two sisters, each had their own sensitive revive of the goddess title. Somberg's was scrawled on a couple of cocktail napkins at a Paris sidewalk cafe when she was sixteen. It had matured considerably, but rendered her existence and she still admired it. It was as follows:

A bitch has skills. Skills are more important than people, the one exception being family. A bitch does what she wants, all bets are off. A bitch does what she wants with her hair, it may look like whatever, but it is her look. Ditto for her clothes. Ditto for her love life. A bitch cares more for her complexion and her skin than she does about the starving children in Africa, the ozone layer, nuclear disarmament, all the dissipated drunkards and vein-dead junkies and homeless God knows what's all put together. As for the whales, whales were meant to be chased. To be hunted. The Great White Whale is pleasure, and the hunt is life.

Nothing feels better than the hunt. In hunting a bitch can go off her rocker and call it "art," and though she may act trashy, she is never cheap. A bitch does not take fatal overdoses; she is the fatal overdose. A bitch gets her way. She gets her way and gets away with it. A bitch, unlike men susceptible to desire, and unlike women susceptible to emotion, is never thwarted by love that is self-asphyxiation. To love is to die. Love is one of the few things more ruthless than the bitch. There is no refuge from love, but should the bitch die she will most certainly resurrect.

A bitch is never sueded, though she is discreet. A bitch's two favorite words are, "Show me." Her mother's motto is, "Dear, you can do it." A bitch never makes a threat, the most foolish kind of exposure. She will not be provoked by man or woman. To be provoked is carelessness. A bitch despises carelessness. She will try to reason with men; she rarely refuses a profitable offer.

A bitch may have a stacked deck of debts, as in the aftermath of the beautiful and the spontaneous, and the debts may surprise no one, least of all her accountant, but they will always surprise the bitch. It is one of the few things that will surprise her.

A bitch believes in Prokofiev and Rachmaninov and philosophy and jive and poetry, and above all, a bitch reads. But you will never see a bitch read. Never. She reads anything and everything while appearing to read nothing. To read is knowledge. Knowledge, unlike beauty, is not part of your genetic code, dear. All bitches begin being a bitch at birth. She knows she's a bitch by sixteen. At sixteen, a bitch defines herself, keeping self-parody in mind.

A bitch has one enemy. No matter what noise she makes about others, the one true, undisputed, but always denied arch enemy is: age. Age has a sign-in sheet. People sign-in themselves. They sign by over-eating. By sleep deprivation. By worry—which is nothing but thinking of others when you should be thinking of yourself. By a lack of exercise. By the use of drugs that is a dependency, and a true bitch is never dependent—not on booze, tobacco, shrinks, or others—the exception being sisters. A bitch may do a gaggle of "crimes" and will escape untouched, but the final, prevailing inheritance of her evils, the moral restitute for all acts, is the heartless, blind, maddening bastard of age. Age is ruthless. The true fear of age breeds ruthlessness. The truly ruthless. Men do not fear age; men don't know what ruthless is. It is the bitch.

Refusing age is the honor of every bitch. There's negotiation with age, and the bitch uses all forms of negotiation, from creams to spas to meditation, each fabula is larger and larger, but the bitch does not believe in miracles. Age is reality. The bitch is always real. The contract with age is the making of the realist.

Anger is sacred to a bitch. A pick-me-up. And anger is always well-spent. The love of anger is self-rape. The bitch never takes anger to bed. She doesn't sleep with anger, she doesn't dream with anger, though she may fuck with anger. Anger is the power that is beneath, but never on the surface. The surface is professionalism. Being a pro is notion, not emotion. Notion is a way of life.

Angels flirt. Women seduce. Bitches sodomize.

Sodomy is the bitch's secret delight, and all bitches suggest sodomy in one form or another. Sodomy is the unstrung male. It is fucking instead of being fucked. It is seduction, then burning him down. It is the sojourn into the male. Sodomy has its own cold comfort, and the bitch's love of it is usually inherited. Sodomy prevails, as in the bitch has balls, and though it is an atrocious ideology, creates quite a commotion, nothing is remotely like it. Sodomy is impregnating him, and the miracle of it is, men can give birth. They give birth to this: the more men are fucked the more they love it, can't get enough of it. Sodomy is a bitch's secret delight and most men secretly love to be sodomized, but the bitch need not hurry, men will fuck themselves, sooner or later.

Somberg left the cab at St. James's Park to stroll the walk bordering the smallish, stately offices and residence of the prime minister. Thatcher's garden was planted in crown imperials. The entrance at Downing Street obstructed by a retractable waist-high metal fence. A child could vault it. Three unarmed bobbies stood outside, chatting amiably with one another. The front door was wide open, workmen shuffling in and out.

Seeing the opportunity at hand, Somberg was reminded of an American journalist who had interviewed Maggie in her study. He said there were no metal detectors at the door, no body searches; he wasn't required to take a picture of himself with his camera. His identification was checked once on the walk and again by a bobby seated just inside the front door. These were the only security checks prior to being ushered into the sanctum of the British prime minister.

Somberg considered the possibilities. The Downing Street security was no more obtrusive than that of her family's triplex apartment atop the Pierre Hotel on Fifth Avenue in Manhattan. Maggie was always receptive to the Americans' media; it'd be relatively easy to arrange for a photography session if you were from an American woman's magazine. One of those four-by-five Hasselblad cameras could be fitted with a .38 Colt special and a Carswell silencer. A hit so easy, a child could do it. Thatcher would be posed, perfectly still, waiting for it. A hollow-point slug driven into her head would throw her back into the wall and expand for an instant kill. A simple enough plan, though it was a bit hot-blooded. Escape would be tricky. There were more effective ways to do a matron of so many accomplishments, who had devoured every vulgar emblem of male hierarchy. Such a Destroyer was worthy of a creative sailing, a female voyagerism, rather than a strike it lucky male shoot-'em-up, *à la* the OK Coral.

A kill was like a suit of clothes, it must be tailored to fit the mark. And if it was the very likeness of the mark, they would try it on willingly, to kill themself. Somberg continued her walk, watching the sun descend, edging the Downing Street fence with a jeweled fire. She had learned her craft from the greatest murderer of all time. One who could strike with the stealth of midnight or in broad daylight. Who took life with no fear, no conscience, no limitations. Who was original, using all the world and its many inventive possibilities for death. *God kills fifteen thousand times a day,* Somberg mused, *and She never uses a gun.*

The park was crowned with vintage trees that like ghosts in a haunted town had anonymously, silently witnessed the great prime ministers. The trees knew they all fell. It didn't require hostile intensity. More often than not, they fell with a whimper, than a bang. One accepted that Maggie would fall; the job was to stay one jump ahead, to arrange the fall. It needn't be bitter; it might be sweet. Didn't have to be a funeral; it might be a carnival.

She passed a couple of girls sipping Cokes at an outdoor table, but this was not a time for collaborations. She chose a stout old tree, a vintage member of the Downing Street surveyors' party, and sat with her back to the trunk, cross-legged in a pile of October's crinkled gold. She looked to a window where she supposed her victim unmurdered and unhunted was carousing in the heaven of her work. Grounded in creation, Somberg closed her eyes. She took in the pungent fragrance of fallen leaves. Tasted death. Savored it. So sweet, nothing bitter or cold about it. She stayed there a moment, suspended in the autumn glow of Death.

She released the breath, and with it every thought, knowing the future existed first in imagination, then in the will, then in reality. Throughout history, from Galileo to Einstein, the most elegant solutions have always been the simplest. Creators know the rules, and each succeeds because they knew *how* to break the rules. Breaking the rules always the key. No greater power than creativity that is wish fulfillment. Now with sharpened senses, she withdrew the envelope from her purse. Inside were the pages listing Thatcher's calendar for the next six months.

From October to Christmas the appointments were scheduled on the quarter-hour, the next four months not so rigidly scheduled. She eliminated the Downing Street and Whitehall dates; they were entirely too hazardous. The Franco-British summit in Paris, the Hong Kong Treaty in Peking, the London conference with the Russians, an economic summit in Bonn, and Thatcher's holiday in Salzburg were also cut. Security would be double on international engagements. From the balance she chose appointments that showed promise. She jotted a listing on the back of one of the pages.

29/10	London: Rodrigo Moynihan portrait unveiled.
9/11	Cenotaph: Lay wreath at Remembrance Sunday ceremony.
19/11	Scotland: Visit Scott Lithgow Shipyard.
3/12	Richmond: Dedicate children's science bus.
24/12	London: Visit children's hospital
22/1	Birmingham: Children's commemoration at synagogue.
8/2	Liverpool: Open shopping mall.

25/2	London: *Daily Star* Golden Awards banquet.
17/3	London: Attend British premiere of Requiem.
24/3	Suffolk: Tour farm.
3/4	Manchester: Speech at aerospace factory.
24/4	London: Open center for Ismaili Muslims.
29/4	Grantham: Her grammar school's one hundredth anniversary.
8/5	London: Escort handicapped boy on walk in St. James's Park.
13/5	London: The unveiling of Thatcher's likeness at Madame Torricelli's Wax Museum.
21/5	London: Dedicate drug rehabilitation center.

Once she had drafted the list in her own hand, it was hers and she would not forget it. She had no preconceived ideas of what she would do and didn't attempt to force a choice. To choose was to think which was counterproductive to creativity.

She closed her eyes again. She drew in a breath. She drifted weightless, hovering a few feet above the ground. She released a breath and rose against the low limbs of the trees, then higher, to where she could glimpse the rooftops of the several buildings of 10 Downing Street. She let go to flight and merged with the sky and the coming of evening, the dreary industry and green gardens of England below; its secret known only to a middle-aged woman who sat alone at a desk on Downing Street. When she died, she would take the secret with her. Lifting higher, she turned back to look across the sea in the direction of Ireland where a dark cloud was fuming like a sullen volcano that cannot quiet make up its mind to erupt. She did not enter that darkness but rose into a canopy of fairy lights; the stars surrounding her and she was laughing in this dark place where there was no time and not a single event was coincidence. God's place. A place of infinite possibilities where gravity does not exist. Where there was no right or wrong, only what could be achieved. Here there was only one evil: the loss of your own integrity. Woman should never do the thing she believes to be wrong. Because to lose your own wholeness is to lose your soul. If she does not believe it to be wrong, then it is right.

She tilted her head back in order to take it all in, and in this wide illumination with stars heaped at her feet, it became her place. Her own place. There was no conscience or conformity or fear of oneself, and here she had no doubts about the rightness of decisions in this place where even the stars died, everything in its season. A place of beauty and harmony with which she was one, all of it as a gift for her pleasure. Pleasure her only belief. Her only ambition. Her only morality. *Pleasure.*

A passing bobby saw her under the tree, legs folded, hands open on her knees in meditation. A faint smile curled on her lips. He grinned. She appeared as a woman in a dream of love.

In the serenity of her place, Somberg reviewed Maggie's appointments, visualizing each as a musical. An Andrew Lloyd Weber production littered with crowds and blinding television lights and raunchy reporters jockeying for position. All in song! Now out of makeup came the self-effacing politicians and the plainclothes security agents, glancing about, looking for a little action. A door opened and out she came, in a burst of song. The star! The self-elected cultural Destroyer. She gave a smile and a wave, sheer flirtatiousness, pressing the flesh of the hoi polloi, basking in fame as all tilted Maggie's direction, everyone doing the big time chorus, a snappy number about an Iron Lady that the audience would take home to sing in the shower tomorrow morning. Somberg saw each gig in this unpardonable parody of Thatcher's England, perfectly conservative, with some pretty bohemians thrown in now and then for color. She watched Maggie work the reception lines. Deliver the speeches. Wave farewell. Singing non-stop, in the key of enlightenment, not to be topped by scrawny Evita who, after all, was never elected to anything and never escaped a burning hotel in the dead of night. In this undemanding, mocking way, Somberg saw the opportunities for a kill in each appointment, watching the show from her place where all things were possible.

With the impressions of the kills fixed in her mind, knowing the possibilities of each episode, she returned from her place. The fragrance of autumn came back to her. And now the damp earth, feeling herself grounded again. This was the very best time, the beginning of a work, and it began as it always did, in *calm.* She would do anything, dream up any clever device to destroy tension that was the culprit of mistakes. She opened her eyes. She rose, refreshed and empowered. Trusting that the line-up of shows would continue to play in their own impulsive ways, the details working themselves out in her place, and the selection of *where* and *how* would come as uncorrupted vision in its time. Across the way, a dark-suited man was being checked by the bobbies before entering Number 10, but what happened there was of no consequence to her. Their power was not what mattered; her power was her only thought. Her power was not violence but creativity. For her, violence was a migration from creativity, as natural as a cherub's smile which would never do the thing she believes is wrong. Somberg pocketed the appointment calendar and left the park as the sun dropped into the clouds. Darkness made no celebration of coming.

3

TRENT STANFORD ENTERED the high altar though the famous front with the lion's head knocker gleaming upon him, only to step aside as workmen came out. One might suppose, looking at their ladders and buckets and hammers and trowels, they had completed another Thatcher facelift. A woman forever remaking herself, and the England with which she was entrusted. He passed through security and went up the long curl of stairs, feeling unseen eyes tracking him as he rose. Perhaps it was the onerous portraits of past prime ministers watching him pass. More likely it was the sweep of a remote camera that guarded the occupant of Downing Street. He made his way down the hall as though he knew where he were going, as though he were not twitching inside his skin. The house was hardly a palace, the carpets, the furnishings, the high, double doors were the regalia of refinement, but hardly luxurious. Though one could not deny the shrine aspect of Number 10; the sense of the divine that awaited him was, Trent supposed, a work of his whinnying male soul.

In the PM's outer office, he was greeted by a plain-looking woman with a frail chin and tawny skin, raven black hair in a bun so tight you could almost hear it scream. Allison Kent, Thatcher's personal assistant, said he was expected. Trent shown to a seat next to his boss. Commander Graham looked up from the Chippendale chair he filled; Graham gave a grunt of welcome. His suit matched the thinning gray hair, in waves around big ears hung on a round, florid face. The old-school tie was held by a stiff Oxford collar that constrained the pink rolls of neck fat. His expression was cemented in the severe; a man primed for battle.

"I'll do all the talking," Graham whispered. "But she may want to speak to you, too."

Trent nodded, glancing up at old Winston staring down with his bulldog scowl above jonquils and hawthorn and plum blossoms. Fierceness and femininity, the Thatcher trademarks.

"You won't advise her about your recommendation, will you?" Graham said very close to his ear. He smelled of mouthwash.

Trent frowned. "My recommendation?"

"To house the cabinet at the Regency Hotel."

"I doubt she'll ask about it."

Graham made a sound, a muffled groan that amplified a million times might replicate the twist of stone and steel that broke the Grand Hotel a week ago. Though Trent had not heard the percussion of the falling hotel; on the sixth floor balcony he heard only the roar of the Irish bomb that had deafened him and seared his face so that now in his pinstripe suit he appeared as if he might have fallen asleep under a sunlamp. His chiseled features were halved, one side paled by the sweatshop of Number 10, the other side shone burnt crimson. His face gave the appearance of the conflict that had summoned him to the PM's outer office. The pale British side blank and cool, the redden Irish side aflame. Split between these sides was a broad forehead and steel blue eyes and the gloss dark hair of a professional of forty-two years.

Now the phone tweaked. Allison took the call from behind an imposing desk that guarded double doors. "Mrs. T will be with you shortly," Allison said to Graham, who she knew. He came twice a month, to pick up a copy of the PM's appointment calendar.

"Ah, thank you, my dear." Graham hoisted a patronizing smile, then muttered to Trent, "She may ask about it, Stanford."

"What possible difference does it make now?" Trent adjusted a crease in the leg of his navy suit. Mrs. T was a closer observer, he had heard. Shine of the shoes, crease of the pants, the curve of the lips, the twist of the face, nothing missed her eyes. Never blink before her. Never swallow your Adam's apple, though you may be swallowing your pride. Never wear your thoughts on your face; keep the face as frozen as a photograph. Never let the chin tremble, not that it would. Never wheeze aloud, even if she has you by the balls. Keep the smile small, don't let her see the fillings in the back teeth, or the dazed look as if you're not quiet sure where you are. Never bite the lower lip. Never allow palpitations of the heart; the woman could read hearts and thoughts. And above all, never, ever sweat.

"Had the Grand covered," Graham whispered, his flaccid face shining with panic. "Spent a half-million pounds! God in heaven couldn't have stopped what happened!"

"Right. But the only thing that matters now is finding the bloody bombers."
"And keeping our jobs!"

There were five dead and now buried, the story buried in the lower pages of the *Times,* but Thatcher's fury would not be buried until the bombers were. The bombers were the contemporary fire-breathing dragon of the heroic myths of old. The morning after the attempted assassination, the IRA dragons supplied the press with a statement aimed at Thatcher: *Today we were unlucky, but remember, we have only to be lucky once. You will have to be lucky always. Give Ireland peace and there will be no war.*

Thatcher responded with a press conference, glaring into the television cameras, looking fierce and aquiline, embracing the tragedy with a kind of pride. She put on her scowling smile and vowed the dragons would be brought to justice, the Grand Hotel rebuilt, the Conservative Convention held there next year.

Trent watched it from the funeral home. But neither the IRA statement nor Thatcher's response answered the question that would not let him go: Who killed his young partner at the Grand, Geoff Duncan? The Irish? Or the English? Why did he feel responsible?

It was a question not easily answered. The undeclared war had been a source of family rows between Trent and his father, forever English, Trent being his mother's son, the blood of a Celtic king ran through his veins. Ireland had been taken by force and held by force for eight hundred years, until 1923, when it was freed by force. A ragtag Irish Republican Army liberated all but the six most northern counties. Through the years England steadily reinforced her position in what was now called Northern Ireland, but the Irish never gave up on those six counties. In the late sixties thousands of Irish and English marched in the streets of Belfast in support of Irish unification. One nation under one flag. A young Trent Stanford watched from his London home, and even his father respected the nonviolent demonstrations in the fashion of Martin Luther King, but on 30 January 1972, the British army fired into a crowd of unarmed protesters, killing thirteen. Bloody Sunday. Birth of the violence to come.

If history were reversed, if the Irish had invaded England, Trent would have been caught in the tangle of his blood. Who would he fight for? His mother's country, where he spent a fairy childhood? Or his father's home, where his ambitions grew up? The battle for his Irish-English heart was a choice made for him.

For Trent it began with Emma Blake. Her elderly mother called her "God's gift," and though Trent never knew the shy little girl, her photo was unforgettable. Made the front page of the *Times,* and for some reason Trent tore it out and kept it—perhaps because the picture tore him out and kept him. Emma had been playing on the walk outside her Hackney home. A girl who played alone, she had chalked a hopscotch onto the walk, dancing repeatedly but always in a different series of steps into and out of the jigsaw islands that were numbered, the total of the numbers kept in Emma's head, so it become a math game. There was a thing fearless about Emma's game that Trent admired. A child's gamble performed before God and all the world, the sidewalk as her stage, and perhaps in her mind it was a floodlite stage, and perhaps Emma dreamed that if she was gallant enough, she might one day skip her way into Number 10. She was leaning against the postbox tying a shoe, when the box erupted in a blast of light and smoke. Trent stood face to face with his father, insisting with competitive firmness that Ireland must be freed, but in the middle of making a point, his treacherous heart would bolt to the picture of a pig-tailed eight-year-old sprawled over her hopscotch game, arms ripped off, staring at the sky with her wide-open dead eyes. Emma Blake rent asunder by the ravages of a prolonged and tumultuous argument that a young man was only just realizing could not be repaired. And still Trent argued on, with a new passion that he not recognize as guilt.

A neighbor knew Mrs. Salomon, who had escaped Stalin's labor camps only to be imprisoned in Hitler's Auschwitz. Anna Salomon, like Emma, knew something of gallantry that had nothing to do with pistols and hand-held rocket launchers and mortars and homemade bombs that were as some wretched game of roulette, you never knew who a secret bomb would kill. The bomb at Harrod's killed Anna Salomon. She had quietly suffered her torments and was suffering as she did her Hanukkah shopping at the department store, arthritis burning with a vengeance, flaring in the joints of her fingers and knees with red fire and blue ice. The silver-haired grandmother was considering a silk scarf when the bomb detonated, pitching her through a window. The *Times* showed her on the walk with the broken mannequins, skirt up around her waist exposing thighs mapped with varicose veins. An outstretched arm displayed a wrist tattooed in a serial number, the fingers turned backward, broken in the same direction. It was the number on her wrist that would not let go of Trent, as though her arm were an article requiring inventory, like the mannequins, and looking close at the photo, he saw they too were numbered. There was a heartlessness in the picture that made no more of Anna Salomon than a plastic mannequin, mannequin and woman shattered by a bomb of plastique. For some reason, Trent had scrawled Anna's number on his wrist, wore it for months, even as he squared himself before his father in defense of old Ireland.

Stevenson was his father's accountant, a formal man, calm and reserved. Trent had met him once when he came to the house to have papers signed. A Friday morning, Stevenson stepped from the train, walking with a slow, stately stride that had always invested him with an impenetrable dignity that Trent found a rare attribute in any man. It was July, but Stevenson wore a waistcoat with his dark suit, a white starched cuff rimmed at the tailored arms of his jacket. He never heard the bomb that shredded his clothes, left him splayed over the rails. Witnesses said he rose for a moment, looked with annoyance at the weeping stump of his left leg, then lay down with a calm orderliness. After Stevenson lost his leg, Trent never again debated with his father. The gallantry had gone out of the debate with the war now in Trent's heart, torn between Ireland and England, pressing for a resolution.

Tuesday, 20 July 1982. Trent cut through Hyde Park on his way home from a long day at M15, where as an intelligence officer he dealt in the souls of men who lived and reported in secret from the Soviet side of the Berlin Wall. A throng of spectators was watching the Household Cavalry pass through the park, riding as if they had no weight at all. Burnished black hides rippling with muscle. Iron shoes drumming the pavement. A strength so deep and sure in the horses, that spectators drew themselves up, fierce and proud. The bomb came as a lightning strike, with the lead horses rearing and screaming and churning about. A riderless mount bolted past Trent and into the park. As the second bomb detonated, a row of horses plowed down into the street. Now he was running through the recoiling crowd with Beretta drawn. Found himself in the street above a horse that lay in a growing lake of blood. Its belly torn open. Lathered and dripping, it was half-crazed in its shriek for relief. It kicked and lifted its head to Trent; mouth foamed pink, whited eyes that would not let Trent go. He looked about, but there was no sign of the rider, the street a riot of madness. His heart ransacked by the bellow of the horse; his hand on its shoulder, its heat and struggle as that struggle within himself. Fighting off a powerful desire to close his eyes, but he could no longer do that for Ireland. Children and grandmothers and accountants and horses, what is to be gained by the slaughter of the innocent? His face smeared with blood, over cheeks and chinlike war paint, as he set the Beretta firmly behind the ear of the huge, jerking, rage-driven neck and shot. At the shot the horse's head fell forward, and Trent's heart found peace. He had chosen.

"She'll see you now," Allison announced.

Graham snapped to his feet. He sucked in his buttery bulk as Trent reluctantly rose behind him. "Thank you, dear," Graham said in a voice of suppressed eagerness, and he started for the double doors where Allison waited as a demi-Amazon centurion.

"I'm sorry," Allison peeped in her perfectly pleasant but nonetheless formal demeanor. "It's not you she wishes to see."

"Oh, that's all right." Trent gave a cheerful sigh of relief and promptly retreated to his seat.

"No. It's *you* she wants to see," Allison said to Trent. He didn't hear her right away, eardrums still torn from the blast. Allison had to repeat herself, and when he heard her Trent didn't respond right away. Needed a moment to believe his ears.

"Me?" he said with a half-laugh. He found his feet again. They wanted to bolt for the door and down the stairs. Graham turned with a glare that Trent would have enjoyed if he hadn't been about to enter the lion's den alone.

"Commander, I have a directive for you." There was more of a soldier's tone to Allison as she supplied Graham with an order. A gust of stupefaction came over the Commander, staring at the red seal of the Queen's First Minister. All dumpy and frumpy, Graham looked back to Trent who opened his hands to heaven and shrugged. How could mere mortal man understand the workings of heaven?

"Special Agent Stanford, do you mind?" Allison said loudly, making a show of it. "The prime minister *is* waiting."

He would much rather take this—whatever this was—as Graham, in a tidy order with a nice blue binding that looked suitable for framing. Allison smiled sweetly, a foot tapping. Why did he feel like she was pointing the barrel of a sixteen-inch fieldpiece at him? He came forward, allowing Graham's hot gaze to flash into his. Doors opened. The unknown awaited. He followed through a hall that wiser men had run from. In his mind he saw them ski, brake, and tumble all over themselves, crawling out the door, not the least bit humbled but grateful for their escape. Allison was humming some lusty tune, the kind of thing they hum when escorting the doomed to the gallows. His conscious mind knocked loose from its perch and flapping in the hollow corridors of his skull like an erratic bat let loose by fear. He saw rafts of them, darkening the air as they rose in their fright, bats leaping up in entire rookeries, swarming the hall that was now the Hall of the Trolls, and Trent was certain he was being taken downward, into a cave.

She stopped before another pair of doors, the place full of them, like the set of a game show. "She's just inside." Allison gave the sweet smile again. "Good luck," she said and vanished.

He did not enter immediately. He counted to three. Gathered his wits about him, overcame the ringing in his ears, and entered with a knock, which made no sense whatsoever. One either knocks and waits to be summoned, or enters without knocking. It seemed in his very first step, the main switch to his brain had failed.

She was on the phone, behind a majestic desk. She glanced up as he entered, and though he had seen her at a distance, he was immediately struck by how small she was at close range. She was taller on the telly. A giant on the campaign trail. A colossus in Parliament. She waved him over, looking crisp and bullet-proof in all black; her creamy complexion ashen, eyes red-rimmed. The leonine blonde hair swept back and he felt, as he quitely closed the door behind him, that he had entered a battlefield.

It was the world's most famous study. Three armoured glass windows in gold-swagged drapery. Behind the lovely wallpaper was battleship steel. There was a Gainsborough. And a Turner. The fireplace formal; sofas cozy and inviting. He was not so lucky. She pointed to the chair opposite her desk. He settled into "the hot seat." He had heard about it. Mildly surprised there were no shackles. No head collar. And no claw marks on the arms. Now she smiled, and he understood why restraints weren't necessary; the gray eyes pinned him to the chair, and above Number 10, Trent was certain the sky was blackening. As black as her suit of mourning.

Her voice seemed to have a sharply serrated edge as she spoke into the phone, but Trent knew this could be his imagination, he could hardly hear her. She sounded muted, though she appeared to be speaking at full volume. He allowed himself to be deafened to her, and took in the aura of history.

This was the study where Lord North had received news of the colonial rebellion in America. It was here in 1815 the Earl of Liverpool had presided over Wellington's Waterloo victory against the little tyrant, Napoleon. David Lloyd George had toiled here day and night as he conceived the triumph at Amiens that led to the final horrors of World War One. And it was here that Winston Churchill had drafted the stirring speeches that forged 10 Downing Street into a shrine of freedom against Hitler's Empire in what were not darker days, but sterner days. "This is not the end," Churchill had declared after the Battle of Egypt. "It is not even the beginning of the end. But it is, perhaps, the end of the beginning." Had they arrived here with the Irish? By Thatcher surviving the attack on her life, on the whole government asleep in the Grand, had they turned the corner on the terror? Had they taken the IRA's best shot? Trent thought of William Gladstone who in this study in 1885 drafted a bill that called for freedom for all of Ireland. And reflecting on Emma Blake, on Anna Salomon, on Stevenson, and the beautiful horse, stifflegged and rigid after Trent's shot, he wished to God that Gladstone had been successful. Now it was left to the woman across the desk from Trent.

On the night of the Brighton bombing, he had watched her work the receiving line at the gala of the Conservative Convention. She was all charm. A woman who had fashioned her own power out of nothing and had steadily increased her power and was not afraid to use her power. The ultimate professional, afraid of satisfaction. Tough to the extreme, details her speciality, the more technical the better. The Thatcher the public saw was always provocative, spellbinding. People were eager to hear whatever she had to say; she used their eagerness to persuade. Behind closed doors she was said to be quick, blunt and to the point. The woman had a magnetic ability to attract the wrong kind. She inspired her enemies with a delicious antagonism. Every speech made her harder to protest. She didn't care. She had no fear.

She was unpredictable, which was why, Trent supposed, most men called her "difficult," and that was being polite. In her sweet-smelling presence, he would not allow himself to repeat the trash said about her. To be in her presence was a confinement, but it was an elegant confinement and he would not betray it. She was elusive. Made of smoke and mirrors. The word was that she made up her mind about people quickly, in about ten seconds, and rarely changed it. Hates owing. Always prefers to be owed. A woman not afraid to collect her pound of flesh. No man alive could keep up with her day-long flow of rhetoric best described as rocketry. Had all the qualities of a great tyrant, rigid and unforgiving, an ego that could not be daunted, driving those around her mad, or nearly mad, or to a degree of scrabbling it was everything but madness. It was said that the walls of the offices in Number 10 were padded, sweat patches on the padding where heads were beat on walls that had more give than the boss. Her staff were not alone in this frustration, it was her arch enemy, the Russians, that gave her the burnished name, Iron Lady. Thatcher wore it like a badge of courage.

But to her credit she had proven herself a healer. A faith healer. Had restored a nation's faith in themselves. Her Special Branch bodyguards were devoted to her. She knew their names, asked about their families; she played them with her meticulous skill, always with an eye on the future. A woman prepared for tomorrow and she expected others to be prepared, and if you fouled up you stood a good chance of finding out what a steak feels like in a microwave. The woman's temper was legendary. Jon Howell, one of her Special Branch boys, told Trent, "We treat Mrs. T with the kind of gingerly respect due a lioness. One admires its beauty, anticipates its desires, and never, never gets it angry."

Now someone had fouled up. A page-one foul up worldwide. The banner headline in the *Times* was 42 point type. How great are the screamers when the C-13 agent fails, though no one knows when he succeeds. He is unseen, unfelt, faithfully yours, until the hotel goes up in smoke and hell comes raining down. It fell from the roof to the basement, right through the laboratory where she had been minutes before. The lioness had escaped, and afterwards her anger was beyond reason. "That bomb really popped her garters," John Howell had said. She was said to be something of a hitter herself. Topping a chap always done in private. Wanted to see the look in the bugger's eyes. Everything everyone said gaining speed as now she rang off and turned to the agent who had been perched above her suite, assigned to the role of guardian angel. It was a known fact that angels had fallen. Some all the way to hell.

"Agent Stanford, how good of you to come." He saw, but didn't fully hear her speak, her hand extended across the neat stacks of papers. It was a feather in his, soft and smooth; her hand felt nothing like iron. "I wonder if you wouldn't be more comfortable across the way?"

He couldn't quite hear her, but saw her glance to the sofas. "Certainly, ma'am," he said, not sure what he had agreed to.

"I trust you've had your burns looked after?" She led the way and he followed close so he could hear, and even as she led, she was bearing down with her inquisitor's smile. "I had a rather nasty burn on my hand last fall. Broiling tuna. It seems we were both broiled."

They laughed lightly at this, as though a week ago she had not been caught in a hotel that blew up like a volcano. She showed him to a sofa. He gratefully sank into its softness, and reminded himself that a cushy sofa was as good a place as any to receive a flogging. The poor bugger was at leisure in a sofa, not pinched into a notorious hard chair used for sundry convictions.

"I learned there's not much that can be done for a burn," she said installing herself beside him, seeming to know his hearing was still impaired. They sat close. Close did not bother her. Close was her way. She sat side-saddle, turned to him, the upper half of her golden lit by a reading lamp, the lower half in shadows.

"They can't do much for a burn, no ma'am, Trent said with his most patronizing smile. "You pretty much leave it to the body to heal itself."

"Yes, and it does that so *miraculously,* doesn't it?" She took a moment to take in his face. Not really looking at the burn but searching for something else. Her eyes shaking him down, turning him to stone, so that even a breath was effort. Now she took in his suit, all the way to the gleaming shoes reflecting the fire flickering merrily. There was a certain romance about the woman; she used it as a song; a sweetheart song. "The cuts," she asked softly, returning to his face. "They're from window glass?"

"Afraid so. Yes, ma'am."

"Remarkable!" she said with a gusto that had made her famous. "How did you ever survive out there on the balcony?"

"I've no idea," Trent replied in perfect honesty. "One minute I was watching. The next thing I knew, everything was on fire."

Her gaze was transfixed upon him in theatrical awe. It was just the sort of miracle she loved, being a miracle herself. "You must have been shielded by the hand of God."

"Yes, ma'am. I must."

"For some *larger* purpose, no doubt."

"I hope so, yes." He wondered what God had in mind?

"Is there much pain?" She asked in a motherly tone. But he felt as though those riveting eyes wanted to sample the pain.

The burn was hot and raw, but he had no intention of letting her into his pain. And certainly he would not confess to it, not to a woman. "It's nothing an aspirin can't relieve," he replied.

His health established, she now launched into his career, and this caught him by surprise. He was prepared to talk shop, hadn't anticipated the personal. But her business was always personal, and so that's where she began. She had read his file last night, "devoured it," she said. She proceeded to recite it. She spoke of boxing championships. Knew the knot on his nose was from a bout that retired him at fifteen. She was impressed with his school record, she too went to public school and thought it wise he took his college work in California. "America certainly broadens one's perspective, doesn't it!'' She continued before he could respond, going into the cold war, his years with M15. She was showing off; the woman had a remarkable memory. She spoke of his runs beyond the Berlin Wall. She was pleased he had transferred to the home front, to the more pressing threat of terrorism, but what the file did not tell was why. He bluffed this, making no mention of Emma Blake, Anna Salomon, Stevenson, or the Household Cavalry horse. That was personal. It seemed his business was personal, too.

"Trent," she said pleasantly. "May I call you Trent?"

"Certainly, ma'am." A thought skipped across his mind: *Does this mean I get to call her Maggie?* He thought not.

"Trent, I'm afraid my time is very limited today, though the Brighton matter is my gravest concern." The softness was already gone, her voice sharpened like a blade trained to probe. "Do we have any leads on those responsible for this *heinousness?*" she asked, making that last word tremble. The trick was to let her words tremble, and not your soul.

"I'm afraid it's not promising," he said, warming up to her, now of familiar ground, though it was a wreckage. "Certainly there are the usual suspects. We're checking on their whereabouts. And we're interviewing guests who were at the Grand Hotel."

"Yes. I read the commander's report. And I hear you ruined a suit the morning after, scavenging through debris."

Graham had sent fifty detectives to the Grand Hotel. All working through the register, calling the guests. Had they witnessed any suspicious activities? Trent knew the boys would hear a hundred stories about characters with hulking bodies and bloodless faces, all of which would amount to the description of an Irish animal dressed in clothes, none of which would furnish a lead. After several fruitless calls, he found himself returned to the sixth floor, a charred shell of brick and timber and twisted steel that reeked of fire drowned in water. He began digging through shattered flooring and broken plumbing and stray shoes, through smashed false teeth and shreds of nightclothes. And as he dug the baked-apple face of Geoff Duncan emerged from the rubble. He had seen it that night as he fell into it. The death of his young partner strictly a commercial venture. Nothing personal.

From the sixth floor balcony, Trent had spent the long night watching in his tuxedo that he wore at the gala the day before. A radio carried the frank and open bullshit of an army of watchers keeping themselves awake. Duncan was in the next room sleeping; he was to come on at dawn. Trent remembered sinking into a chair, and a moment later the heavens were painted whiter than daylight. White as lightning. He was thrown into the banister, and for a second he thought his head had come off. A roar in his ears that started red and went on and on into a searing heat. He saw the windows blown out. They came in a hailstorm of glass. He curled to a fetal position, and after that his memory was not as exact. The balcony was trembling and it felt like an earthquake. He lifted to his knees. He saw the stone columned facade of the hotel cave inward in a surreal silence, though he could feel the air vibrate from the concussion of the blast. He was the sole spectator with a front row seat to what was clearly not an earthquake. And already he was thinking: *Where did the fucking bomb come from?*

He pushed to his feet. White comets streaked through his head. His mouth with a coppery taste and his nostrils assaulted by the stench of high explosive. He staggered into what had been his room and was now a smelting furnace. He tried to take in the enormity of the destruction, but it was a moment before his brain could catch up. The bed was gone. Most of the walls were gone. The floor a chasm of smoke rolling out in all directions with the roof peeled back to the stars. A rafter above broke loose. It fell before him, cartwheeling down, slinging orange-and-purple sparks, making not a sound in Trent's deafened ears. In the rosy dew of the fire, it appeared as if the whole building was caving in on top of the Napoleon Suite where Thatcher was sleeping.

He began picking his way around the hole of his room that was a tangle of twisted steel and broken stone, debris raining down. A screaming in his head, but the hotel continued to collapse into a funnel that plummeted straight down. As he escaped, he looked for blast marks, but all the evidence was collapsing into the fire. A brick chimney let go and dropped into hell. Trent leaped back as a mushroom of red heat rushed up to bloom like a bloody rose into the night. It was then that he found Duncan in the rubble. In the timber and smoke and red flashes, Trent's hand sunk into the goo of what had been a green agent in need of a touch of experience.

Suddenly the air was too hot to breathe; the floor shifting below him and Trent wedged through the frame of what had been the door, and was running up the hall when the water tanks on the roof gave way. A torrent of freezing water spilled through the ceiling like it was coming over a dam, melting the hall, Trent running just ahead of it. He glanced back to see the water slice the hotel wide open; the flood erasing the signature of the bomb. Up ahead, a crowd pushed into the fire escape. He saw a man duck through the door, his arm blown off. The man in shock, he didn't know the arm was gone. He was helping a elderly woman, her face a scarf of blood. Trent ran down a stairwell with the press of survivors in pajamas, most barefoot, all dusted in plaster so they appeared as clown faces tinted in yellow emergency light. Hands bracing one another, moving orderly down the stairs, no demons of panic, and the British half of Trent's heart swelled with pride. Beside him, a woman with no eyebrows was staring at him, and Trent looked at himself for the first time. Blackened head to toe from the blast, his tux in shreds, blood trickling from the slivers of glass that jutted from his skin like a porcupine quill.

By the time he made it to the Napoleon Suite, Thatcher was gone. Jon Howell had rushed her out a side door. In the suite, the ceiling was all over the floor, night burning where the windows had been. There was a great chasm down the face of the Grand that looked like it had been hit by a SCUD rocket. From the one window that wasn't shattered, Trent saw his reflection against the lawn slewed with the red lunatic bolts of emergency vehicles. There was no one to tell his shame, or be ashamed with him; he stood alone and could not bear to witness his failure. He couldn't stand the sight of himself in the glass, and on certain late-night occasions he'd see himself again, standing there with his flash-burned face, the torn sleeves of his rented Moss Brothers tuxedo jacket red to the elbow with Geoff Duncan's blood.

"Mrs. Thatcher," Trent began delicately, skillfully, like an artist creating hand-blown glass. "I don't believe we'll find the bombers ringing up the guests."

"You don't?" she replied baitingly.

"No, ma'am I don't. We'll find the bombers in the hotel."

This set her back, and the brilliance of her eyes darkened. "I don't quite follow."

Trent continued, in a piece of pure devilishness, but then it was that that blew up the Grand. "The bombers may not realize it, but they've left *one* piece of evidence behind. It's been burned and flooded and lies in a wreck. A hotel roasted in hell and from the looks of it, it appears to have been dropped upside down. In that wreck lies a scrap of evidence that tells the tale of the bomb. When we find it, we can establish a forensic trail, and *it* will lead us to the bombers."

He watched her eyes slide out a window into her own thoughts. "You're suggesting handling this like a plane crash," she said to the window. "The aircraft reassembled piece by piece to find the cause of the crash."

"That's about the size of it, yes, ma'am. Unfortunately, it's been raining on the coast. The Grand a mountain of soggy rubble. This is a process that will take *time*." He paused to allow the word "time" to settle on her. "Some of us have been digging," he said, allowing a note of hope to enter his voice.

"Good, good," she said, and eyes returned to him.

"We've detected traces of Semtex in the U bend of a plumbing fitting that came from room six-twenty-nine. There were fragments of lavatory tile in the guest who resided in that room. He was, in fact, a member of our watch team."

"And you believe the bomb originated in room six-twenty-nine?"

"It appears that way. Yes, ma'am."

She went silent again, eyes dull as she bore into the Turner across the room. *Better it than me,* Trent thought. "Did Commander Graham request room six-twenty-nine prior to the convention?" she asked.

Trent assured her that Graham had. Dogs had been run through every room. He assumed the explosive was wrapped in cellophane so it couldn't be detected.

"And the Napoleon Suite," she said, her gaze still locked on the Turner, "was it *below* room six-twenty-nine?"

"Directly below. Yes, ma'am."

Her chin lifted. Her face hardened. She seemed to know more than she was saying, but she didn't offer a reply, so he carried on. "That really is all we have at this point. We need to keep digging. I'm certain we'll find something more." Trent paused, waited through a count of one, two, three, then added, "It will take *time*, but the forensic trail will lead us to the bombers."

He had expected any number of reactions to this hang-in-there approach, like maybe she would fire him on the spot, but what he had not expected was a smile. A faint and secretive smile. Not unlike the Mona Lisa's.

"*We* have a lead for you," she said, turning on him with a brow arched. "Do you recall the Airey Neave case?"

"Certainly," Trent said, sensing a door opening to a larger room with a ghost emerging from that room. Airey Neave had been a influential backbencher in Parliament. He took a young, obnoxious Thatcher under his wing and tutored her. Neave was the one man responsible for her rise to power. After Thatcher was elected PM, she appointed Neave Secretary of Northern Ireland. The IRA saw him as a target. They welcomed Maggie to Number 10 by placing a bomb on the underbelly of Neave's blue Vauxhall. He was driving out of the Parliament underground car park when the mercury switch tilted on the up ramp. The dynamite killed the car but mauled the man. The Secretary of Northern Ireland was trapped in a monstrous snarl of twisted steel that was not unlike the Irish problem itself; Neave forced to witness the spectacle of his raw, disfigured body while rescue workers tried to free him. His last conscious hours were spent in a gallery of blue torch sparks that flew in disarray through his diabolical cell, till the screeching racket of saws gave to the soft rippling notes of Neave's last muttered prayer. In that death lay a dangerous riddle the IRA could never solve, they could only kill, as in the immense bomb in Brighton.

"It was no coincidence the Brighton bomb exploded at two-fifty-nine," Mrs. Thatcher said.

Trent's mind raced. No one had cited the detonation time as significant. He watched a plum coloring rise in a face gone rigid with a ferocity that would never play on television. The gray eyes seemed to darken, and he could swear there were jagged blue sparks in them. Eyes imprisoned in a thing they could never escape.

"That is *precisely* the time they killed Airey," she said. "The only difference being that Airey was killed at two-fifty-nine P.M., and the Brighton bomb exploded at two-fifty-nine A.M."

Was he wearing a look of stupid surprise on his face? He knew it wasn't there, but the feeling was. "Probably the same bomber," he quietly surmised.

"Oh, I hope so!" Hot blood surged into her cheeks. "I truly hope it is! Because *this time* we're going to find him!" She said this as an oath, the spirit of Airey Neave as her witness. She was a woman who never repented. Not she. She brought down whatever tried to bring her down. "Trent." Her voice rose; this was her wartime voice. "You are *perfectly* suited for this undertaking. Your Irish heritage is an asset! An instinct the others do not possess. Brighton is your case. It's to take precedence over every investigation in Scotland Yard. Whatever you need in the way of personnel or funding, you shall have. We've authorized a million pounds for the investigation. Your authority in all aspects of this case is to supersede that of any superior in this government, regardless of rank."

She paused to let the directive sink in. She had, in effect, just made Trent as powerful as herself. He found himself violating all the advice, blinking, swallowing his Adam's apple, wearing his thoughts on his face. Was his chin trembling? Was he wheezing? God knows she had him by the balls. A million bloody pounds! For one case? What would she expect in return? Divine intervention?

"*Use the money.* If you need more, we'll find it!" The woman's fierceness rose into a smile. Trent's Irishness saw it as the dark latent beast of herself breaking into being. But his Britishness admired the smile. The play of 2:59 was sheer Irish diabolical jeering, and Maggie Thatcher would not betray the leprous-white god Airey Neave became in his last hours. She was not a brilliant woman, but she was seductive, a spiritual woman who understood much, and who now brought the full powers of her presence to bear on the half-deaf, half-Irish, half-burned man who sat by her side. There was no falseness in her scarlet fever that was contagious. "When you leave," she said, singing this part, as though it were a rehearsed hymn, "you will receive an order authorizing all that we have told you. Commander Graham is reading it now."

In his weightless state of mind Trent saw Graham reading the directive, face bent down, parenthetical creases around his mouth set like clamps. Graham would be shrieking about chain of command. Since when did the PM assign cases? *Now isn't this lovely,* Trent thought. *I'll still be working under Graham, but my authority supplants his. I'll have a jolly time balancing this act.*

"*Trent!*" She made his name ring. No abbey could compete with the tragic ring of her brave, tormented iron soul. "Nothing is to impede you in this investigation. *Nothing!* No one will attempt to assassinate the head of this government without receiving its most stringent response. Do you understand?"

It seemed an absurd time to think of it, but a line from *Henry VI* came to Trent's mind: *"O tiger's heart, wrapp'd in a woman's hide!"*

"Yes, ma'am," he snapped back.

"I'll expect weekly reports."

"Certainly."

"Call if you need anything, *anything* at all."

He could call for anything, but a way out. He found himself perched atop a scaffold erected from a million pounds sterling, his breath rising as he looked down from that dizzying height. He envisioned the fall, hearing the sickening crackle of bone as his neck snapped, his career left dangling on Thatcher's rope. Buried in a pauper's grave lined with the corpses of the men who had come before him. Cabinet ministers. Department heads. Whips. Many had been chosen, but few had survived. And he, a mere C-13 agent. He thought it wise if he wormed a little grace out of her, before he began spending her money.

"Mrs. Thatcher." He did this bit carefully but forcefully. "You may be assured of my inexhaustible commitment. I want the bastards who did this." He allowed her to see his rage, something he usually kept to himself. "These people will never walk the earth again if I have anything to do with it. I *will* spend your money, and money it will take, because this investigation will take *time.*" Again he paused on that word that no politician wants to hear. Then he blundered on, "What I'm saying is, there'll be no headlines in tomorrow's paper."

He knew immediately he had done it wrong. Her eyebrow arched. The earth trembled, he'd swear it had; the sofa trembled beneath just as the balcony had after the bomb exploded. "I am not seeking headlines," she hissed like a burned cat. *"I want a bomber!"*

At this, Trent came out swinging, as though he had not been knocked out of the ring at fifteen. "There'll be more than one."

"One will do."

"Right."

"We need *someone* held responsible."

"Certainly."

"The public *requires* a manifestation of justice."

Trent needed a moment to get this next part right. He let his eyes take in the citadel of walnut behind which she worked. Behind the desk was a gold framed picture of Airey Neave on the credenza. He had been dead some years, but still stood, right behind her.

"I suspect there will be more than one," he said, praying he could find just one. "And I suspect we won't net them altogether. Assuming we prosecute one. . . ." He waited a beat. She was an attorney, she knew a conviction acquired once would be difficult to repeat. "I wonder what would become of the others—if there are others.

We might consider this now, it would affect how and when we arrest. That is to say, a *conspiracy* could be more difficult to prove than an *individual* act.''

This was met with silence. So pressing, Trent thought the elegant ceiling would crack. She drew in a breath and her voice rose, as if for the microphone, delivering lines from one of her speeches. ''Personally, we've always supported capital punishment. We think the vast majority of the people in this country would like to see the death penalty restored.'' Her gaze fell on Trent, and he saw the bitterness of heart. ''It isn't that we wish to see it used a very great deal, but people who go out prepared to take the lives of others forfeit their own right to live.''

The enormity of her words rolled over Trent like an immense wave. It was, in effect, a license to kill. A bit more than he had bargained for when he shot the damned horse.

''I am half Irish, you know,'' his kicking heart said.

''Oh, I know. That's why you're perfect for the job.''

At this she stood. He rose, shirt cold and damp on his back. As he followed her to the door, he wondered if he was to resolve Brighton? Or the blood of Airey Neave? There was more between England and Ireland than the smashed, squirming, shuddering agony of Neave's murder, but it was a chasm that for this prime minister could never be bridged. Had it spawned a malevolence in Thatcher? Trent suspected there was a guilt in her that slept fitfully and woke way before she did. Hadn't she made her hero a target? Hadn't she appointed Neave Secretary of Northern Ireland? Perhaps this was what he was to resolve for her million pounds, her guilt.

She paused at the door, to have another go at speechmaking. ''Goodwill can never be a substitute for force when dealing with Irish Republican terrorism,'' she said. ''We must use *every* means available to beat the IRA.''

''I understand,'' Trent replied, meeting her guilty eyes.

''Find one and we will prosecute one. But your authorization will stand until the day they are *all* brought to our justice.''

''Yes, ma'am.''

''Agent Stanford.'' She opened the door, giving him one last penetrating stare, the heat of her fierceness upon him as she said, ''Until that day.'' She vanished behind the closing door.

4

THE FIRST THING Danny Moore did was put the tall, skinny bottle of Pantene shampoo next to the short, fat Estée Lauder foundation. Then to the marble edge of his mother's tub he added the Lancôme blush and Clinique Turnaround Cream. The big, wide jar of Skippy peanut butter was situated behind the others, and now the naked six-year-old climbed delicately into the tub overflowing with floral scented bubbles, a few of which washed over the side. He steered an ocean liner and two tug boats into position. The sun was setting through the blinds. He glanced out the window to tiered low-rise buildings with a couple of skyscrapers radiating with light, then back to his glorious feat, a scaled replica of the view of Chicago from a whirlpool tub perched near the top of a jar of Skippy, otherwise known as the Hemingway House.

He did not give himself a bath, not just yet. He swished his hand under the water to inspire the ocean liner on a journey into the glittering sea. It inched along, silent and sweet, slipping through the transparent water as if under its own power; a boy's ear could hear an engine settle into a rugged beat. On the deck, a hundred or so passengers gazed in wonder at mountainous peaks of sparkling bubbles that rose on either side of the rails. No one had ever seen such a sight! A little brown-haired girl in her nightdress was eating a piece of chocolate cake and drinking a Coke, part of her routine before she went to bed. She had good manners and was carefully balancing the cake on a blue paper plate, her eyes fastened in awe upon the froth that heaved itself up into her vision. ''Jeepers,'' she said. ''It looks like a heavenly sea!''

Things were going just fine until the liner wallowed into a snow-capped iceberg, the peak towering above the little girl. The ship was soon eaten by the berg, and everyone held their breath, gazing at a sky of bubbles swirled overhead like an icy fog; like the breath of ghosts, if you believed in such things, and Danny was pretty sure he did. Now a wave washed in and the liner pitched up and down and reared and tried to steer its way out of the mess. But eventually it succumbed and with a sad continuous whistle that only a boy could hear, it submerged into the strange bubbly sea. Then Danny sighed many times from the depths of his soul for the brave crew and captain and all the people, and the poor little girl who at least got to finish her cake before she went down.

Jessica wondered what was taking him so long in there? She was curled in the window seat of her bedroom, painting Cherries in the Snow on her nails splayed over an old copy of the *Tribune*. The headline read: ''Iron Lady's Brush with Death.'' Jessica glanced at the picture of the bombed-out hotel, inserted was a head-shot of Margaret Thatcher. Jessica thought she smiled like a television commercial. Had to be the most distinguished woman in the world. A girl who had what every girl wanted: her own country. The girl with the most cake. Jessica didn't bother with the story, she didn't have time; she had the ADDY awards banquet tonight.

''Danny, are you about through?'' she called, a note of the frantic in her voice.

''I'm brewing a potion for you, Mama!'' Danny shouted through the closed and locked door. He had his beach bucket out, an equal measure of each ingredient from his city now mixed into the blue bucket. He stirred the potion and sniffed it like that TV cook with the giant nose. Then gave it two sprays from the bottle with the big ''*No. 5.*'' Now it was just right; it smelled pretty. A gob of rouged peanut butter was stuck on his thumb. He reached out of the tub and wiped it on a vanity face towel.

''I need the bathroom, sweetie!'' Jessica called. ''Can you finish in your tub?''

''This is a *special* potion, Mama! It cures wrinkles and bad hair days and all that stuff. I learned this on TV!''

Jessica checked the clock. In twenty minutes she'd be five minutes late. She studied her finished nails and tried to suppress eagerness. A minute stretched the limits of her patience.

"Danny, please." She heard a quality of despair in her voice. She waited to see if despair had any effect on a male. It didn't. Now she shouted, "Get out of that tub *this minute,* mister!"

"Okay, okay."

Danny climbed out and dried off, rubbing his blond hair into a spiky bush that looked as if it had dripped sugar freckles over a pug nose. There were the big ears that were his father's, and the eyes set into a light complexion so they shone prominently as two infinitely blue lakes. He combed his wet hair back slick, hung the red towel from his shoulders, and, turning to the door-mirror, scrunched his face into a tough-guy expression. Superman stared back at him.

"D-a-n-n-y!"

"I'm drying off! Can't a guy dry off around here?"

He wasn't quite finished with his potion, but where to put it? He checked the linen closet. The lower shelves filled with towels, but that wasn't a problem. He set his bucket on the vanity and climbed up the shelves, which was a breeze, he was a good climber. He hoisted the bucket, careful not to slosh potion, and slid it onto the top shelf. No sweat. He closed the door, but it wouldn't quite close. The bucket was half-jutting out.

"Are you dried off in there?"

"I'm almost done!"

He stepped from the shelf to the vanity, shoved the bucket back hard, sliding his hand out fast as he closed the door. And that was no problem, the door held by a clasp. He'd sneak back in and get the potion in a minute, after his mom used the bathroom. He was good at sneaking, all boys were.

"Just a second, now. I got to take a leak."

"Weewee, you mean."

"Yeah. Whatever."

He put the bottles of mother's stuff back on the vanity, then ran naked down the hall and into the dining room where three carousel horses on brass poles smiled down on the inventive boy. He gave one of the horses a slap on the butt, and left the Skippy on the counter of the pickled-pine kitchen. That was no problem, he never put the peanut butter away.

A minute later he emerged in his mother's room, in jeans and a Ghostbusters shirt, carrying his favorite yellow rain boots. She was putting another coat of polish on her nails, the smell of it kind of prickly in his nose, he flared his nostrils at it. It was the authentic smell of Mother, and Danny would remember it after other remembrances wandered away.

He had a chance to sneak back to his potion, but imagination led him to the big four-poster bed. An antique. Came all the way from Italy. No telling who had slept in it over there. Might have been a prince. Might have been a pirate. It had drapes you could close so you could sit in the dark to read scary stories with a flashlight. Danny loved doing that with his mom, though it seemed like a long time since they had. They were busy nowadays. He had the books, she bought him plenty of books. He wondered where the flashlight was. He tried to remember.

Pit Martin let himself in using his key. He gave a huge, booming shout as he rolled through the door. But there was no answer and that didn't surprise him, they were both so busy. He wheeled through the living room in a silvery wheelchair, looking like anything but a nanny. Pit never referred to himself as a "nanny;" he called himself "Danny's pal." The man from Texas had a vast muscled chest and bearlike arms, his smooth bowling-ball head crisscrossed with scars from his glory days as a linebacker for the New York Giants. The hands were massive, palms leathered from the wheels that were now his legs. Pit was a man's man, tough as an old saddle that had been on many a wild bronc, but as tender and loving, as instructive and thoughtful, as any iron lady.

He had met Danny while moving into the Hemingway House; the boy was playing in the hall of the high-rise and offered to help. Pit had him hold the elevator door for the movers, and every time they came up he flipped the boy a quarter. And the boy caught the quarters ever time, never missed a one, a fine boy. Jessica was interviewing for a nanny that day, two nice Spanish ladies waiting in the living room when Pit rolled in with Danny, who by then was jingling a pocketful of change. Jessica, Pit learned later, had witnessed one of those macho bonding things, a thing she knew of but didn't understand. Danny was enchanted by Pit's snappy chrome wheelchair, accepting of this man who had lost both his legs, and Jessica found herself asking Pit if he'd like to have the job. He didn't need the job but desperately needed the love, and so she hired him. Or, rather, they hired him. Pit now lived next door, no commute to work, and Danny became the best job Pit Martin ever had. He came to treasure the boy as he treasured another boy, an unmentioned boy far away, and when Pit cared for Danny it was like caring for that boy who was always with him, whose love had never left him, not even when he was taken away.

He found the boy in Jessica's bed, half-dressed, asking for a flashlight, wanted to read a story.

"Good Lord, boy!" Pit thundered. "I don't give a zip-a-dee-doo-dah about no book. Not tonight! We got a hockey game tonight. C'mon. Get yourself in gear! Let's get those boots on."

"Who's playing?" Jessica called from the bathroom.

"Blackhawks and those LA faggots," Pit said, helping Danny pull on his boots. "Should be a dilly of a game!" *Should be a goddamn war*, he thought, and didn't want to miss a minute of it. Besides, his pal Barry Neville was waiting for him, and Pit hated to keep anybody waiting, especially not a friend. But now the boy had forgotten his binoculars and had to go find them.

Pit parked himself by the window bench and read the paper, looking at the picture of the Grand Hotel blown to smithereens. It was crazy that war. All the Irish and English needed was to learn good manners. Learn to share. They were both so damn afraid of the bitterness of an inglorious defeat. But there was a way of winning in losing, the biggest wins came that way, and Pit knew it well.

"Game starts at seven," he said through the bathroom door. "I figure we'll just make it." In his plaid shirt the color of his sun-reddened face, he waited in Jessica's sweet-smelling room, so lovely it looked like a studio set. "I figure we'll beat the hell out of 'em," he added.

He heard Jessica laughing, busying about in there. He tried to imagine what she would wear to the banquet. He figured whatever it was, it would knock the spots off every other woman there.

"Who's on the menu for tonight?" he asked, rolling over to take a little peek through the crack of the bathroom door. He saw her in the mirror, in a black glittery gown that fit like she had poured herself into it. She was as splendid as a dessert; probably had no idea how devastating she looked, and he couldn't stop peeking.

"It's the ass end of Sherwood Pierce Advertising," she said.

Pit grinned. He didn't like that little high-toned snippet. So full of himself, always looked like he was about to deliver a sermon on austerity. He had probably never been to a hockey game.

"Well, ol' Hunter is a lucky man," he said, watching her flip her lovely hair to one side. It fell in a haphazard elegance. Now tweezers patrolled brunette curls for the evil grays. "You must be looking forward to tonight," he said real soft so she wouldn't know how close he was. He had always been close, but didn't want her to know; the dangerous things were best left unsaid.

"Not hardly," Jessica said, finding a gray and purging it. "I'll pick up my award, smile for the cameras, and spend the rest of the night listening to an egotistical jerk talk about himself."

Pit snickered at that, and thinking about that ass, Pierce, he saw himself as some kind of sleaze, peeking in on her like he was. He rolled away, scolding himself.

"Say, Jess." He looked over all that empty room. Not a sign of man anywhere. No cap on the door knob, no muffler hung from the back of the door, not even a copy of *Moby Dick* in the soft window bench. "When you gonna find yourself a fella and settle down?"

"When am I going to find the *time* to find a fella?" she shouted back.

"Yeah," he muttered to the antique Italian bed built for a king. "But how long has it been since you made this bed squeak?"

"How's that?" she called.

"I said, when you're not a photographer, you're a mom. And when you're not a mom, you're on a plane on your way to being a photographer or coming home to be a mom. And when you get home, there's the boy. You never have time for yourself."

"That's it exactly!"

He kept admiring that fine old bed. He could make this bed squeak. Why, he could have it shaking so the screws fell right out of it. Bed and mattress and woman all over the floor. And he'd put it all back together before he left.

"What time will you be home tonight?"

"About midnight," she said.

"Uh-huh," he muttered, considering her framed pictures on the antique dresser, all mixed in with a bunch of pretty knickknacks. There was a picture of a collegiate Jessica in a tight red sweater posed before a Corvette. He'd had a Corvette but never had a girl like that. And now he found himself back at the bathroom door peeking in loyal rapture. She was brushing something iridescent on her eyelids. "Lordy," he breathed, seeing her breasts softly sway outward with her work, and his eyes wolfed her down.

"You know," he said, "there's more to life than money and mommy. There's love. It happened once. It could happen again."

"Who said anything about *love*?" She laughed, adding a trace of gold highlighter to her cheekbones, bringing out the bone structure. Now she paused, looking critically at herself. "Love is giving and love is pain, and most of all, love is *time*. No, I can't afford love!"

Pit's callused hands were gripping the arms of his chair as he watched her slowly outline her mouth with a red pencil. "Well, I think love will come your way again one day," he said quietly. "I surely do. I don't think love can miss a woman like you." He saw her smile, and her smile lit up his heart like a sparkler.

"God knows it's not going to be tonight," she said, filling in her lips with heather rose lipstick.

Pit pushed himself from the door; he'd had enough torture. He was looking at her as if she were dressing for him. How he loved to watch this woman, loved to watch her do most anything. Pit had silently watched over Jessica for years, always there, helping with the little things down at the studio, offering suggestions, listening to her bitch on her crazy days, bringing her a beer, somehow knowing when she needed it. He knew how to read her cycles of stress and lived them with her; she was as much a part of his job as Danny, and he loved them both in the only way a man knows how to love anything, with all he's got.

But as as much as he silently loved Jessica, he feared her. He had loved before, and was betrayed badly. It had been some time ago; he was maybe not the best husband then, but he was the best father. It was the one thing in this world that came naturally, and his eyes would swell with damn tears and he'd turn gloomy as anything thinking about it. In a hellishness of greed, his wife had taken the world away from him, an infant daughter and a boy, same age as Danny. Pit had confronted the loss of the world with the force of all his character, and there wasn't a soul alive who would ever believe all he had been through for his two kids. Only the angels knew. A story that would dwarf fiction. He would lay in bed listening to the insistent comings and goings of his love and anger, a man as beaten as any man could be, and he was prepared to endure it to the end. He would *never* let go of his children that he did not speak of to Jessica. A sorrow beyond words.

Some women thought they had the market cornered on the love of kids; motherhood lived in a highly contrived air of mock civility where men were concerned. Some women didn't know the dawn from the day. They didn't know the day they had waited for had arrived. They were too busy releasing the anger in their souls. An anger that poisoned their nature, so a sweet woman became as the dregs of a fatal wine, and when a man collapsed it was neither accident or suicide but murder. Plenty of men's hearts had been murdered by women, but not Pit's. He had endured the vigil of an angry woman and he was neither exhausted, nor ready to collapse. He would not give up on women or love, despite them both. But he feared a pain that would come in love, and he feared the doom that would come if he was to lose Jessica's friendship. She and the boy were his world. He didn't have to tell Jessica he loved her to love her, and so he never bared his feelings. Pit accepted what she gave and was grateful for it; he drank the sweet wine, careful of the dregs that were enough to kill a horse.

Pit looked around the sweet-smelling room, and wondered what the hell he was doing? Carrying on about women when his pal Barry was waiting, waiting, waiting. Lord, what had become of him? Here he was, thinking about women instead of hockey. He went out and found the binoculars and got the boy moving. "Good times wait for no man or boy," he said. "You got to get after it while you can."

Now he watched as the boy kissed his mother, and she looked like all glory in that dress. The boy scampered out the door and shot down the hall, now thinking right, thinking only hockey. Pit had the key in the lock when suddenly Jessica called to him, and he stopped dead. A prickle went up his back and he could feel his scalp going red. Had she had caught him peeking at her door?

"Why is it the best years," she said, "the pretty years and the career years and the mother years, all come at once?"

She was standing before the door, so close he could hold her. And he was possessed by that old clumsiness he always suffered around women. He fumbled with the damn key, then looked at her, slender and shimmering with all that cascading hair.

"Good gracious, girl," he answered her with words swimming in his heart. "You got nothing to fear. Why, time doesn't touch a woman such as you; don't you know that?" He saw the color rise in her face, about as beautiful as he had ever seen her. "The way I figure it," he said, "your best years haven't even begun!"

He had no idea what he'd just said, couldn't have repeated it to save his life, but it had sounded okay. He grinned and saluted her—now why the hell did he do that?—and quickly closed the door behind him. He raced down the hall, had to hurry because ol' Barry was waiting. Pit was thinking right now. Thinking only hockey.

Jessica floated into the kitchen, wondering how it was that Pit always knew exactly what to say. She poured herself a calming glass of Chablis. Found Danny's open jar of peanut butter and wasn't surprised but wondered what he had done with the lid. She put the jar away and strolled through the lovely quiet. When was she going to find a "fella" and settled down? It seemed there was no answer to Pit's question. You just went on every day and hoped you stumbled across someone. And did she really *need* a man to make her life complete? Didn't she have a man? She had Pit. They had a family of sorts. Wasn't that enough?

Seated at her vanity, she pinned her diamonds to her ears and took another look into the mirror, which like Pit, never lied. She didn't look half-bad. But her blush was a little smudged. As she was reaching for the face towel, she tipped over the Chablis. "Shit!" Now the doorbell chimed. Jessica looked at her mirror. "Count on Sherwood Pierce Advertising to be on time."

There was a peanut butter smear on her face towel, and that didn't surprise her, but she wondered how he managed to color it red. He was adorable, and she didn't know what she'd ever do without him, but Danny gave the devil his due when it came to wreaking havoc on her well-planned life. She used the towel on the wine, reached for another, and as she touched the linen closet door it sprang open.

In the hall, Hunter Pierce heard a chilling scream.

"Goddammit! I'm going to—!"

"I can't believe he—!"

"If that boy ever—!"

The shock was such that Jessica couldn't finish a sentence. Gasping from the cold splash, she looked in the mirror. Her gown, that like the blessed bed had come from Italy, was dripping in magic potion. It was ruined for the night, and this was not the first time this kind of thing had happened. But this was the final straw: she was going to kill that kid. For a moment, she went a little crazy, mistaking parental combat for real life that was simply love. She picked up the beach bucket and threw it in the tub. *"God!"* she shrieked at heaven. *"Save me from this child!"*

5

HE CAME ACROSS the antique Persian rugs, walking with a lot of movement for a male and Somberg missed none of it. Kim Lee, a native Hawaiian, formerly a freshman at Harvard. With a china-doll face and a complexion his sisters were jealous of. Gorgeous wide lips capable of being pouty. Big olive black eyes and lush hair in a swing cut. Thin-hipped with slender arms and wrist and legs; the skin a mellow bronze shade. His buttocks reminded Somberg of the grapefruit she had for lunch. He had a nice boyish sort of cheerfulness that she would be careful not to train out of him.

He stood in a maze of Gothic carvings and books and stained glass, below the sculptured curving staircase of the library in her chateau in Geneva. Her mother had said that libraries were living places. Spirits resided there. The mischievous mien of an author, the muck, the dust, the star turn if they had it in them, the hope and stupidity, the repression, the longing, the intensity and hunger, the blood, the telltale heart, whether it be darkness or light, all came to life in the immersion of the book. To view books as icons was insanity, and mother should know, she was in an asylum. When she was angry with a book, she threw it across the room. Kicked it. Shouted at it. And sometimes she loved it. Books no different than men. But the author's spirit was another matter, and it was not the book. Its swagger came out of the book as it was opened. A library was a place of living souls and if you could see with the eyes of god, you would not see books on the shelves, but the somatic spirits of authors as they were when they wrote.

For this reason, Somberg loved libraries and bookstores. They were akin to haunted houses. A library was a party attended by women and men who knew what others did not. In which voices were pitched at a key higher than the human ear; listen close and you can hear the air live with chatter and laughter and skepticism, harsh and ironic, in a been-there, done-that tone. Introductions can be made on the spot. Passing through the aisles of books was moving among the swirls and eddies of authors all leaning together confidently, you can almost feel heads turning, suggestions gust up and push you along. Somberg's library was roofed in colored glass as the constantly changing light of the stream of history that she had learned to travel easily in. All in the nucleus of a library walled and moated against those who could not, or did not read. This a place of blood, of origin, of experience, of past and future. A tapestry composed of millions of events. Books not of cloth but of the dreams of girls and the sweat of men. So many eyes watching from ages past; the place to take a pretty boy.

She came across Kim in Lucinda Chambers's report to an elite association that Somberg managed; Lucinda a professional with an appetite for tempting, yummy, "fig leaf" boys. Which is to say, he'd look great wearing only a fig leaf. Somberg feel in love with his name first. According to Rudyard Kipling, Kim means: "little friend to all the world." So he was perfect, from the beginning.

Lucinda had supplied photographs of a snooty Ivy League boy, which had a certain reverse appeal, but his odyssey began at the Harvard Library. The whale found him there, the whale of pleasure, with a sudden urge to swallow him whole, he looked so cute tucked into his books. His dark hair down around his eyes. In his preppy sweatshirt. Now a slender idle finger twirling through his pretty hair like a girl, while two girls stole hungry glances at him from opposite sides of the library. Somberg wanted him. Wanted him more than anything, and that's how it must begin. Anything less than that is cheating yourself. You must want him more than anything.

He was so perfectly, typically male, he didn't know he was a three-way target. She swooped down and snatched him up, with him believing he picked her up, while the two would-be Cinderellas watched on in something just short of insanity, the coeds half her age. Silly girls who feared flying. Who didn't know themselves.

She was bewitched that first night, loving him for exactly what he was, a good lay. A beautiful lay. With his little brown beaded nipples and a concave navel like you'd find on the French Riviera. A tiny ripple of an orgasm and a very sore cunt, that was all she got. But there was a kind of madness about the boy and she took him for a midnight swim in the hotel pool with the steam burning up to the stars and the beauty kissing her. Sucking on her with nothing on but water. Her hands slid down his back, cupping and stroking his buttocks. Then slowly parted them, and a probing finger slid gently inside him. She found his prostate and massaged it in a circular motion. And the boy who had never flown before took off for the moon. Now, already, Kim was a great lay. And she was possessed. He smiled. One smile and she was a goner. Or rather, he was a goner. Gone the next day in her Gulfstream. The two sugarplum dears at the library never saw him again.

She called it a "sabbatical." She had used the term before and it never failed her. He had not quit Harvard, but had taken a leave of absence, to expand his education. She hired him as her assistant with a ridiculous salary that meant nothing, he'd never have time to spend it. He was made of privileges, of snobbery, of hypocrisy, of churches and schools, one imperial mother and three neurotic sisters, and this made him perfect in every way. Somberg dropped Lucinda a thank-you note. He was attentive, staring at her every time she opened her mouth, as if he was deaf and had to read lips. He couldn't believe his good fortune, hired by a gifted biographer doing a book on Margaret Thatcher.

His first assignment was to run a research team in London, twenty librarians paid to take a week's vacation to compile an avalanche of data on Thatcher. Kim had the brighter ones cut the avalanche to a fifty-page report reduced to user-friendly notes on Maggie's habits and character traits. He was studying them now. His furrowed brow in melodramatic concentration, and Somberg felt so glowing and intoxicated. Knowing how passionate and tender he was beneath his male act. That he didn't know this made him the more thrilling. He was dressed the part of tender. A lambswool sweater and navy jacket with matching trousers. By Donna Karan. He never noticed he was wearing girl's clothes, cut like a man's. Now looking up with the dark eyes of a very bright child. A tiny millisecond there that she held as if it were an eternity, in this transitory moment in which he was still the composite of his past, softened by a single brushstroke. Somberg made a mental, treasured picture, before the changing future swept him away into dizzying swivel-headedness. A boy beauty to be halved: plain and practical plunged into an abyss, sweet and muted entitled to dreams taken on colored wings, thanks to a hardened hellion. And she smiled into those lovely eyes that suggested the appeal of surrender.

Kim turned intense and purposely to his notes. "She was raised in Grantham," he began drearily. "Grantham is a rural—"

"Don't read to me," Somberg interrupted from her wingback with Kim before a fireplace big enough to swallow him. "Tell me about Maggie. You've studied her, haven't you?"

"Oh. Well. Sure."

"Then tell me what she's like. In your own words."

"Okay. She was, uh, raised in Grantham," he began again, not sure what to do with his pages of notes. "It's total bore of a town," he said, setting the notes down, opening himself to the rich sparkle of the library. It was a bitching chateau, blew him away when he first saw it. Sitting on Lake Geneva. A seventeenth-century palace with twenty-two rooms. The place a jewel. Even the doors. Pebbled glass inlaid in mother-of-pearl. Greek statuary. And flowers. That was the first thing he learned, the names of the flowers. African violets and Oriental poppies, East Indian lotus and birdcage evening primrose. Kristian loved her flowers. Always fresh cut. The house smelled so sweet, filled with sunlight.

"Grantham is about as lively as a graveyard," he continued. "A hundred miles north of London. Maggie's old man ran a grocery. And was mayor. When she wasn't in school, she was measuring out sacks of sugar, getting an earful of politics from Dad. He pretty much gave her permission for her dreams. She was a kid nobody noticed. Showing up at your doorstep, delivering the groceries. Always doing her homework or helping Dad. No close friends. No boyfriends. A goody-goody. Last kid you'd pick to become PM."

"Aren't you warm in that jacket?" Kristian said, as if she hadn't hear a word he said. "Here, let me help you take it off."

She slid the jacket off his shoulders, and that was better because the fire was hot, the heat of it coming up the back of his legs. "Thanks," he said as she took the jacket and folded it and held it in her lap, like maybe it was his skin, or something.

"So, moving right along," he said, wishing she wouldn't stare at him so, "Maggie went off to college—not a place you ever heard of—studied chemistry. Made great grades. And now it's like, hey, check the big brain on Maggie! I mean, she's smart, but totally uncool. Into the politics thing. Goes to the Young Tories, or whatever. Graduates. Gets a job with . . ." He checked his notes, Kristian was a stickler for getting things right. "With J. Lyons testing cake fillings. Can you imagine a more boring job? Testing fucking *cake fillings!* Later, she meets an older guy, Denis. He's divorced but rich. They marry. Then Hillary does law school."

"Hillary?"

"Oh, did I say Hillary? I meant, Hilda. That's her middle name, Hilda. I think she seems more real that way." He gave a bright, ecstatic smile, and wondered what Kristian would give him for doing the report. She loved to give gifts. "After law school, she goes gung ho into politics. Gets elected to Parliament at thirty-four. The kids are packed off to boarding school while Mom climbs the ladder. Made it to PM in ten years. Only female ever elected. But that's no big deal to Hillary, I mean, Hilda, who kicks butt like a man. If you fuck up, you're a goner!"

"Would you mind if I just—" Before he really knew what she was up to, she unzipped his trousers and had him stepping out of them. She took the socks and shoes, too. He was left in lambswool and plum bikini briefs. "There," Kristian said, returning to her comfy chair. "You must feel much better. That fire's so hot."

It was hot. Now he could feel it on his bare legs and on his butt and it felt kind of good. "Gee, thanks," he said, loving her. She was the hottest woman he ever met. They were doing it four times a day at first. Never the same way twice. In fact, it didn't even seem like they were doing it, it just sort of slipped up on him. The intriguing chateau susceptible to sensual possibilities.

"I'd say what made Hilda's career is that she always *sounds certain,* even when she's full of shit. Especially when she's full of shit. Of course, she's the kind of woman who's always on top of things. But I bet she went through the whole insecurity thing." Kim leaped to a high-pitched whine. *"I'm a failure: I suck!"* He laughed at this in a highly contrived air of mock male civility, that paused the erection forming in his briefs. "But hey, she never let on. Hilda has this *huge* self-belief. Super willpower! Either turns people on or pisses the living fuck out of them."

The chateau was full of secrets, and he had begun a secret diary to rid his guilty conscience of its burden. His boss had girlfriends. Dozens of them. He had accidently found pictures in the nightstand. Glossy girls with laughing eyes and boyishly long legs. In lingerie. On the mink throw on Kristian's bed. Kissing and touching. Each wore a gold ankle chain and matching necklaces of diamonds. And what was wild were the butterflies, tattooed on the right check of a perfect ass. Every girl tattooed, but every butterfly was different. There were two small Asian girls, really exotic-looking, with waist-deep hair. A Latin girl, her skin the color of honey. A little African girl, her hair a jungle of curls that fell onto tiny tits and dark, moist limbs. And there were so many other girls, Treasure Girls, that's how he thought of them. Where they came from or where they went, he had no idea. Their pictures were like some pendulum set in motion in his head and he couldn't stop thinking about them. With the music, *Prokofiev's Piano Concerto No. 3* playing all the time. Kristian played it when they were making love, and it seemed to play in his sleep when the treasure girls, like mythic sirens, visited him.

At night he would wait for them, like a good boy on Christmas eve waiting for Santa. At some point, despite all his efforts, he would fall asleep, and then they came. He could hear them creeping through the house and into Kristian's room where he lay sleeping. They came with kisses. One lingering and loving. One playing the tip of her teasing tongue over his lips. Another taking his face and kissing him slow and deliberate and deep. Someone lying on top of him, pressing against him, kissing long and hard. Every time he thought he'd wake and see them in bed with

Kristian, he wanted to see their butterfly tattoos, but he could never wake up in that sleep that did not console. His mouth yearning for kisses that were wet and real, and sailing in sleep he could not distinguish her lips from his lips, as if lips were the same, male and female. He woke in the morning with a beanstalk of hardon that you could climb to heaven, and Kristian did, laughing at his dreams, and the more he dreamed the more he wanted to kiss and kiss and kiss. It was not a thing boys were really into. But he was into it now.

The greedy woman had now taken his lambswool sweater, and his briefs. He was left with only his notes he devoutly held before him, with the heat of the fire working all the way up his back. He glanced to the brass rings in the mantle. What would they be for?

"Tell me about Maggie's personality," Somberg said from her chair, the fire painting his body in trembling yellow shadows.

"Punctuality is an *obsession*," he said, a little hoarse, as if she had taken his voice when she peeled his clothes. "She's compulsive, wants everything now— waiting is *aaagony*." He drew the word out, making a labor of it. "She prefers personal encounters—hates the phone. Distrusts committees—double-checks everyone."

Somberg made a mental note: Low trust level. Impatient.

"Washes her hair once a week, same since childhood." Kim kept the notes before him, so they hid the erection that was getting out of hand, but now and then the head popped up over the pages like a puppet show. "Loves facials and some kind of Italian mud bath. And she's into Hindu electrical underwater stimulation."

Somberg's mind went back to New Delhi, years ago, one of her first assignments. The rotund, bald little don of the India mafia. Wearing only a silk robe as he tested the bath water with a pinky. He dropped the robe, stepped into the water, and switched on the whirlpool. Two thousand volts from the rewired whirlpool slammed into him, driving him up on toes, India's heftiest ballerina *en pointe*. He did a freakish death dance. Hair standing on end. The dark eyes bulging the instant before they burst like grapes in a microwave. Somberg pursed her lips at the memory, nodding her blond head. It'd work for Maggie, but there could be linkage to New Delhi. As a rule, she never used the same technique twice.

"Does she have any health problems?"

"Ah," Kim looked to the stained glass vault, drumming a finger on his bare thigh. "She suffers from hay fever. I hear it can really fuck her up."

"Anything else?"

"No, but you'd think there would be. She works, like, around the clock. But she hardly ever gets sick. It's like nothing can stop her. I guess that's why they call her Iron Lady."

"Turn," Somberg instructed.

"Excuse me?" His eyes came off the ceiling.

"Turn."

He rotated in a sheet of mellow firelight.

"Slower, please. Keep talking."

"Ah. About what?"

The dear was lost, his skin smooth and shiny in the fire, the long curve of his spine and the soft lovely arch of buttocks polished to a warm gleam. Somberg felt a tongue of flame lick in her. The sensual reveals a woman. It empowers her. *This type of enhancement,* she told herself, *is a necessity to the work.*

"How does she relax?" Somberg suggested, watching him stiffen at her stare.

"That's her problem. She doesn't relax. I don't think Maggie ever learned how to cut loose. I don't think she knows how to get down and have fun."

Sitting in the chair, she imagined stroking the gold gleaming flesh that would feel like satin. And the dark eyes with their delicious disorientation at the certainty he was being carried downward into flames with kisses at his shoulders. Just a lovely little sensation, the soft pressure of lips on his bare beaded skin. Nuzzling his heated little neck, feeling his breasts rise at her touch. This boy a succulent blanket of warm flesh waiting for her to wrap him around her.

"She's a loner. Never really *needed* friends. Oh, sometimes she'll have people up to her flat at Number Ten for chitchats. Ass-kissers, you know. They'll tell her what she wants to hear but make it sound like they're being tough on her. Mostly she lives indoors, at Number Ten or in some hotel suite or on the phone or in powwows. Twisting arms. Plotting moves. Living outside normal time. Always *on-stage.* And, really, that's what the real world has become to her, a stage. Everywhere she goes, she's always accompanied by TV lights. I'd say she's *hooked.* A main-liner. A junkie workaholic. Loves to be watched," Kim said, and as he turned the pink-flushed delicately trembling head of his penis peeped demurely around the pages of his notes.

Somberg smiled approvingly, loving it all, instincts at work. They were the most difficult kills, the workaholics. They never exposed themselves. And as she reflected on it, she knew it would have to be done from Maggie's calendar. In public. On stage. The world watching. But every problem comes with opportunity.

She took in this magnificent burnished shell of stolen flesh before her fire. She had stolen him right out of his life. Slowly shaping and training him by the ravish-ment of her senses. She had found first-year college students made for efficient secretaries. They had clerical aptitudes, a fragile confidence, and no fear of death. She picked them up like shells on the beach; they were all over the world. She selected the prettiest; so pretty the boy's features were feminine. So cerebral they were rationally stupid. So vain they craved humiliation. So stricken with the aware-ness of girls, their heads full of girls' imaginings and yearnings, but unaware of how direly they wanted to fulfill those imaginings. And since every straining penis fears rejection more than anything else, they were easily manipulated. Drawn into service with all the hope and expectation of immigrants in some foreign land, and after they were certified, they were sent abroad. The wind was her ally; scattered them all over the world. To a serious, seductive elite that time had forgotten, that some said never existed.

"Tell me about Thatcher's eating habits," she said, rising from the chair, letting her hands travel where imagination had.

"Actually," he wriggling at her cold touch, his voice choked so that it was barely audible, "she's very disciplined about her weight. Breakfast is usually a cup of coffee or a glass of orange juice." She took his precious notes away to expose what they hid. The naked, frantic look in his eyes was priceless; they suggested a wildfire. Now she looked, blue eyes transfixed, Somberg hardly breathed. "She does a vitamin C pill in the winter,'' Kim went on. ''Sometimes half a grapefruit and toast with marmalade—something made especially for her. She eats fish with a cream sauce. And—''

''Who makes the marmalade?''

''Hell if I know!''

''Would you find out, please?''

''Sure. But why?''

She touched a finger to his pretty lips. He kissed it.

''Does she cook?'' she asked.

''Sometimes. Shepherd's pie, mostly.

''Anything else?''

''Mmm—'' He let her turn him. Buns to the fire. ''Muffins.''

''Any sweets?''

''Lemon meringue pie.''

''Anything else?''

There was a slight pout on his face, not much more than a deep thoughtfulness, very sexy, the way it accentuated his full mouth. Her eyes slid down the long curve of his spine where the light lay in yellow tendrils that flared out to shape his downy buttocks, bronze and blushing, traced powder-soft in firelight.

''Well, meringue atop fruit,'' he said with a smile not so certain. ''And chocolate is a weakness. She likes a cookie with her coffee. She's supposed to be crazy about these chocolate mints. Pigs out on them. Like, eats a whole box a time.''

''What type of mint?''

He touched her breasts. It was not what she wanted. She put his hands at his side. Her hand closed round his red-shadowed, sprouting erection. She squeezed, smiling at his dear scream.

''Be *specific*, darling.''

''She loves *Elizabeth Shaw mints!*'' he cried.

''That's better, thank you.''

Finally, she let him kiss her. On the balls of his bare feet he balanced himself to sway forward to graze her lips with all the delicacy of a dreamkiss. He thought he heard voices in this kiss calling from the dark shape of the floor above where the novels of King and Poe and Dante, and other lovesick, hell-bent souls were shelved, and Kim looked up into the glorious, carved library, but the cries seemed to have no origin other than the night itself. He kissed her again, and a light gave warmth and shape to his alien world, and the scuffles in his heart, some harrowed-featured brawny man with despair in his eyes was blown away and transmuted by the light with his mouth open in a kiss and not a word was exchanged. It was, Kim assumed, the light of love and there was no bad that could come from love, so he had been told by his sisters jealous of his lovely complexion, and devilish enough to tell him so.

She must have been reasonably pleased with his research, because now she drew the bottle of 1973 Chateau Lafite Rothschild from the silver bucket that had been waiting by her chair. She filled two glasses. He unable to take his eyes off her panther-print waist-length jacket, black leggings and panther-print boots that made her seem as tall as God striding to the fire to bring him the wine. Moving with the

Breaker's converting ease across the surface of his life, and he really didn't mind a bit. She was a seductive mix of things. Discipline and glamour. Passion and control. A strength to her that was mannish, or maybe he had never really known a woman. Only girls. As in the girls of dreams.

They drank the wine as they did every night, always a sip of wine followed by the good sleep and the sweet kissing dreams, and he assumed they would come again tonight, sooner or later. He told her again, as she kissed him down into a soft chinchilla throw, he was in love—but it sounded lame next to what he really felt that was closer to devotion. As the ancients who if commanded to do so, would sacrifice themselves for the goddess, and count themselves lucky to do so. She presided over the immediate, the ecstatic, and the penetrating modes of dream. And he didn't know how she did that, turning his thoughts to her in lushly textured dreams, so all he could think about all night and at first dawn, was her. It was love. Had to be love. Crystal-headed perfect vision drunk love, and he had a little more wine.

Kim closed his eyes for a moment. And when he opened his eyes again, he found his wrists lashed to the ball and claw feet of her desk. She had bound him with his own neckties! And now she wanted more on Thatcher, an assessment of her popularity, Kristian said with a huge beatific smile. So fine, he played along, why fight God? Maggie was manipulative, he said. Moved people and politics from square to square like a chess game. Communicated directly with the people, unlike anyone else since Churchill, but Maggie's popularity was ebbing. She needed PR opportunities. But she was short-sighted, tomorrow's headlines her only priority.

"She's great at photo ops," he said. "A sucker for every photographer's gimmick. She loves to make mileage with the kids."

"How?" Somberg asked, leaning back, roping his ankles to the brass rings of the fireplace. "How does she use the children?"

"She sets up PR gigs so she'll be photographed with kids. Great image stuff. You know, motherly."

He saw her pause on this, as if to measure what he had just said. To measure it and everything else he had said as a tailor who cuts the crotch and legs and arms out of a bolt of cloth to make a suit that is a perfect fit. And now as he looked up into the fire, Kim saw his legs were spread and tied to the hearth.

"Hey—!" He pulled on his arms, then legs, light-headed as his erection lurched in place. "What the hell!?"

She knelt beside him, laughing at his squirming. A happy laugh, there was a real delight on her beautiful face, and he didn't feel fear, only an elation, for what he did not know.

"Aw, c'mon, man!"

"Man? Do you want me to be a man for you, darling? It can be arranged."

"Please, no!"

"Which is it? Please? Or no?"

She laughed again as he cried out her name to the dark. But the dark answered only with the fire that snapped and crackled and promised life with every high dancing flame. He twisted away from her devilish cold touch, trying not to love it. "Let me go!"

He struggled in his silk ties, and the struggle made him look luxurious shackled to the brass rings with the firelight in his bright face, coloring his lavishly lashed eyes. His nipples, plum brown. She swirled a finger over them. They beaded beautifully at her touch and he shivered. She held his face and kissed him long and hard with his mouth open as if in dream, and when she released him, he gasped for a breath like a boy coming up out of the deep.

She sighed, as if the sight of him hurt her more than it hurt him. "I'm so glad neckties are back in style for women!''

"Come on, Kristian. Cut it out, will you?"

Her fingers traveled over him at will, reducing him to the exquisite torture of anticipation, watching for his slightest change in expression or respiration, the little signals of sexual distress. His distress was her pleasure. Her touch slid down his bronze belly and over a curve of naked hip to where it rounded and fell into a concave that rounded again into bottom. She found his seam. He released a high little gasp as a finger penetrated, just a little, then followed the seam down his legs that elicited the image of a dancer, sleek and languid. How he would dance for her.

He turned his face away, trying to reveal nothing beyond a passive acceptance of punishment, for what he was not yet sure. His squirm slowed to a gentle wriggle as she mounted him, so that it felt like a rocking, a very pleasant wriggle rock.

"Oh, baby." She kissed him and fondled his ass with the touch that he loved so. "You're absolutely delectable. And you know, I'm going to have to kill you a thousand times, over and over and over again, until we get it just right. Until you're born again."

She used the templet of Kim's making, the Prokofiev *Piano Concerto No. 3;* the rabid first movement in concert with his cute struggles. Firelight ignited the beads of perspiration clinging to Kim's skin, the luster of panic. Her clear, short nails traced figure eights in concentric circles over the pebbled nipples with Thatcher's character traits circling in her mind. She was hard at work, this was her job, her duty. She kissed his ears and nose and the delicious curve of lips, while her hand drifted down to his swollen, untouched, unloved, still hardening erection. She asked him to lick his lips so now they were wet and smooth and with his mouth wide open she held his face while she outlined those pretty, luscious lips in Precious Plum lipstick. As she changed him, she could feel the heat coming off his body. She touched a finger to his shining lips and he kissed it, and then she had him suck it, so very smooth was his gentle sucking that hardened him harder. A very sweet boy. This a thing he'd never do for one of his sorority dates; it was they who did the sucking. But Somberg had lost her compassion for gender roles long ago, and her long slick finger kept sliding into the mouth of this overripe virgin never taken as a girl, as though he were only a hard, hard, hardening boy.

"What," he said softly, "are you going to do?"

She smiled down on him, loving his tone.

"There's no escape, darling," she whispered.

Somberg's clothes had been left on the chair and now she rose to her knees over his lovely face that had the lips of a girl, and Somberg felt the virgin girl's warm trembling breath on the smooth insides of her thighs with his lips suspended above his lips.

"You must make me happy, dear," she said to the girl. "And if you make me *very* happy—" Somberg reached back and with calculated cruelty gently ran the cool edge of a nail over the long, swaying, burning erection "—I'll make you happy."

She saw a kind of reason come into his face that had changed with the lipstick. A new intimacy there. A new mystery. It was all Somberg could do not to pluck the brows and shade the dark eyes and highlight those gorgeous cheekbones, to pierce the ears, and to pierce the bud of virginity. The makeup would come in *her* time, the girl within Kim, *she* would do it. As for virginity, Somberg would call upon heaven to restrain her until *she* was ready. Men must die by their own hand, and a girl will emerge in her time.

"Do you understand, baby?"

He nodded.

Somberg lowered her lips to her lips.

Kim did understand.

Now that she had control, Somberg let go. Every muscle in her body lax, releasing the breath she was holding, with a tremulous pleasure flowing through the lapping wetness like a shimmering of waves that carried her beyond her boundaries. The room wavered and blurred in a confection of colors, her mind drifting through the shadows of the library where the witty and overwhelmingly wise, and the wise-cracking and the smug and the smart were all waiting and set free in her seductive, sexy, dangerous mind. A blustery performance of authors that had been real and walked the earth, and now walked with her through the many potentialities of a kill. Among the rehab creators, she was surprised to find Red O'Grady's windburned face. She heard his old sandpaper voice, grousing again about the starvation of ten Irish: "Hell, if it were possible, I'd have Thatcher chained to one of these columns and watch *her* starve to death. Let her die of her own poison!"

She drifted further into the shadowline between what was and what might be with chills chasing shivers up and down her back as Kim touched her spot, a place where there was no time, only pleasure. She found herself at Heathrow, watching the boy in the tropical shirt. Chasing his blue bouncing ball. He ran through the doors labeled: "Do Not Enter." The customs officer only smiled and let the child pass. Quickly, effortlessly, she scanned Thatcher's calendar and abstracted the appointments with children. She re-evaluated each as a maddening hum rose within her, climbing in cycles of intensity, and she let it go without reining it in, the appointments as musicals capsulated as a case history.

She lifted from Kim's devoted tongue, unable to stop her smile as she slid over his hard body to impale herself on his erection. Hands swept over slick bronze skin with a magnificent rocking hardness inside her, growing deeper and deeper with life speeding up in a rocking that became a thrusting that lifted her out of the room and into the limitlessness of her place where she floated weightless. Sailing not through stars, but through small glistening crystal spheres. In each was a miniature enactment of Maggie's child appointments as an Andrew Lloyd Weber musical. Played before her as a silly girl's excessive emotionalism, this collection of perpetual Weber musicals that seemed to have a permanent residence in credibility heaven.

Now the rhythmic rocking became a thrusting that accelerated the spheres into a spinning until the rocking and spinning was a low humming delirium inside her, and she would not stop what was coming. The spheres speeding into an orbiting blur so that all of Thatcher's ridiculous singing speeches ran together as one breath—holding shriek and her body jolted as Maggie hit a high note that shattered the spheres into a blinding starburst. It blew trembling shards of light across the heavens! The light fell over her in a spray like a mist over her naked body, touching the contours of her face and her open hands with a rippling of bells, silvery and insidious, faint but drawing closer on the showering light that was above her and around her, and now she saw it as a sun that opened like a womb to a newborn child. A male child in a fetal position. An eerie luminous blooming as he grew before her eyes, his pulse beat within her, and with this pulse, every detail of a plot turning in crystal spheres in an elliptical orbit around the child that was not the sun, but her son who would kill Thatcher. The plan simple, unexpected, so different from anything she had done before. And she saw it all and felt it all and understood it all with a perfect understanding as omnipotent as God Herself.

The rocking slowed and Somberg descended from her place into a pinkish glow that radiated from the blue steaming mist of her new evolution. She would need child modeling catalogs. She needed only one boy, but would cast a wide net. Better to use the States, not Britain. She opened her eyes to Kim wearing a jeweled crown of perspiration, sweat trickling down cheeks and plum lips and down his neck where it pooled in the cleft of his collarbone. She bent down and lapped him up, everything sharp and clear, certain of the kill to come. And it was as if Maggie were already dead.

6

JESSICA GUNNED THE engine into a throaty roar, and her sleek, low-slung, mean-looking ruby red 1939 Mercury convertible with the wide whitewall tires squealed out of the intersection and went flying down Lake Shore Drive. She let the engine note climb, then slammed the stick into second. The car leaped with another burst of speed, perfectly appropriate for a woman in a changed world, and Danny shouted, *"All right!* I love it when you slap second!"

Jessica grinned and drove faster, crisp autumn air swirling into the open car, Danny holding his New York Giants cap on his head. "Hey, Mom!" Danny called over the wind that swirled between them. "I need to talk to you about some stuff."

"Sure," she said, as an itinerant teacher. She had spent the weekend at Fee Glacier in the Swiss Alps, doing a layout for Saks. Turned out to be one of those career identifying assignments where everything went right, down to the bikinis that fit the girls like a black sealskin that Jessica made look iridescent on the ice. And tomorrow it was New York with diamonds and redheads at Tiffany's. She was a poor creature who had awakened to her calling and was now living her dreams, but valued the simple pleasure of driving her own car in her hometown where she was never lost and never needed a map, with her happy son by her side. Fee Glacier and Tiffany's had nothing as bright as Danny's face as she slung the Mercury around the corner, stirring up a leafy riot.

He had his cap pulled down to big ears, now with a wrinkly seriousness in his face, one of her favorite expressions. She snapped a mental picture for her collection. "What's on your mind?" she asked invitingly.

"Did you know we beat the Mavericks yesterday?"

"I know! Pit told me all about it."

"It was a play-off game, Mom."

"I know. And you won!"

"Yeah, we won. But you weren't there, *again*."

Something squeezed Jessica's heart, and she took a wincing little breath, working up and down the gears. "I know," she said. "I'm sorry I missed your game. But I'll make the next one."

"Mom! You missed the whole damn season!"

It was a career-octopus that had her. Tentacles drawn from the eight different directions her work was going, to squeeze the blood from her heart; it seemed to come like some murky octopus ink, her career like that carnivore that possessed. She tried to deny the pain with a dose of itinerant teacher. "Danny, please." She turned with a quick smile. "Don't use that word damn. Okay?"

She kept smiling as she drove straight on, but what her smile didn't say was that she had missed nothing in ink and she knew it. Every Monday she began the week with her calendar neatly booked by the hour. Then the dizzying, disconnected models wouldn't show up on time, or some prop wouldn't be delivered, or it was raining or snowing or too cloudy. By Wednesday, Juice, her assistant, was rescheduling, erasing all the penciled-in electives, like soccer games. By Friday, the calendar looked like a Picasso, with the weekend caught up in the intensity, until the calendar looked like a surrealistic representation of her life in which there was no past or future. Art and life were one and the same for Jessica.

Danny answered her by looking out the window at a city flying by; he would not look at his mother. "You're always working!" he said to the wind that possessed not a trace of tenderness. "How come you have to work so much?"

"Danny," Jessica started to explain in a measured way, then caught herself making excuses, and that was not what she wanted to teach, even if she was an itinerant teacher. "I'm sorry," she said. "I wish I hadn't missed your game." Now for the excuse. "But, you know, it's not easy to raise a boy when you're a single mom." But he was unimpressed and kept staring out the window. "But I won't work late tonight!" And now for those two words all parents come to regret: "I promise."

They drove on listening to the hum of the car, which was old but in mint condition and ran smoother than either of their lives.

Jessica was the living legacy of the single mother, but not by choice. She was not divorced and had made no victims. She had met Jack in London. He was an art dealer, a man as successful as herself, a thing that was important to her then. He understood her work, and what was more important, he *valued* it. He was straighter and had shorter hair than any man she had ever dated before, and loving Jack had surprised her, surprise the treat of love. There was a trans-Atlantic romance that was thrilling, and costly; the phone bill more than the electric bill, proof of that force so elusive. What woman can recognize love? Most any woman, other than one in love. He was sturdy, handsome, blond with wide-set blue eyes and a square jaw and a great intensity of feeling that people found charismatic. So love should not have been a surprise. Still, Jessica was taken in a tour de force of surprise, and the only thing that ever surprised her more was his death.

He was a methodical man and read Nietzsche and believed in the power of will. It had astonishing effects on his career, and he settled easily into the big time, his strength of will was never compromised by success. Jack used to box. Jessica would put on gloves and spar with him. She was pretty good. Without gloves, they fought over ideas. The silly was a sometimes Communist, only to be closer, to sympathize, to understand people more. They took up residency in Chicago, at Jack's insistance, at the Hemingway House; Jack loved the outdoors; he believed in the physical life. He made money and lost it backing an unworkable personal computer. Still, he managed to support his mother, his mother's adopted son, his estranged first wife, their two daughters, his second wife, and various realities and friends and socialist comrades. Jack was a sucker. Jack loved with everything he had. His last big gamble was a concrete boat, a spiritual denial of the water; it sank in Barbados with Jack and all his love. Jack was a man easy to love and impossible to let go, and Jessica had not loved since.

After Barbados, she fell apart, then slowly put herself back together the way Jack had taught her. She built a high-tech studio in Buck Town from the money he had left that the dear had not managed to lose, adding a nursery to it for their son. The baby carried her through grief, mother and son equally dependent on each other, feeding off each other. One day when the baby scheduled for the Pampers shot came down with a cold Jessica, fighting a deadline, put Danny in the picture, and Jack's son was an instant hit. The baby grew into a toddler who came to think of the world of lights and cameras as play. A natural model, Danny was never intimidated by the direction of others. Soon other photographers were calling for Danny, an agency enrolled him, and they became a two-career family with more money than time. Jessica thought it was a shame Jack wasn't there, he could have relieved them of both problems.

Danny's actor's sense of timing had more than once come to their rescue, and now he waited until he sensed something tight wrapping itself around his mama's heart. He turned, tucking a leg under him. "You know," he said in Jack's practiced way of pitching a thing, "it'd be a lot easier to raise me if we had a daddy."

The carnivore that held the poor creature behind the wheel of the Mercury, cheerfully squeezed the heart tighter and grimaced and risked a sidelong glance to Danny and asked, "Have you been thinking about your father?"

"No," he lied. "But you have."

"Me?" Jessica smiled again, this time as an act of bravery. "Me?" she repeated, her smile growing less certain.

"Uh-huh." Danny leaned over the armrest, in the way that Jack would. "Did you know you talk about my daddy in your dreams?"

She eased the car to a stop at a light. She didn't remember dreams, except the ones she lived.

"You remember?" Danny said, Jack's instinct touching a spot that hurt. "The other morning, real early, when I came into your room, you were shaking in your sleep. Remember that?"

Jessica stared at the light, a memory slowly unfurling. She had wakened to find

Danny in her bed, holding her, stroking her hair. She had wondered then if something was wrong. She had held him and thought he was the one with the bad dream.

"You were whispering about my daddy," Danny said with Jack's gentle diplo-
macy that like many things about Jack was in the blood and would carry Danny far,
beyond concrete boats and fresh-caught single-mama lobster. "I heard you calling,
'Jack!' And you were saying other stuff I couldn't understand. So I crawled in next
to you to, you know, help you feel better."

The light turned green. Jessica glanced at the big truck in her rearview mirror.
Oh, to hell with the truck, she thought, and hugged her son, wrapping him in her
arms, close and tight. The truck's horn spanked the air into a hundred pieces, but
Jessica paid no attention, and Jack of London wouldn't have either. She held
Danny's face and kissed him, and said, "Thanks, pal. Thanks for taking care of me.
Thank you, very much."

"You're welcome," he replied with a small exquisite grin that was also Jack's.

Jessica put the car in gear, proud she had managed all that without any tears. She
drove on with the wind strumming soothingly against the cylindrical pane of the
windshield, everything "all better," as Danny liked to say. She checked her watch.
It was ten minutes until she was five minutes late, and she drove faster.

The son of Jack was telling a dog story when Jessica parked the Mercury in front
of a long, low building lined with yellowing trees, "Birbeck's Ice" written in script
across the brick face. She checked the mirror. She looked like hell, but at least it
was the end of the day. "Danny, I'm *very* late," she said, which was nothing new
to Danny. "I love your dog story—"

"But I'm not finished!" he said, not about to budge from the passenger seat.

"I know. I'm sorry. Really, I am." She took her briefcase and left the car, but
had to wait for Danny. She didn't make a big deal out of it, he was his father's son;
it would have only added that magical ingredient: will. Now he came, slamming the
car door behind him so that the Mercury and Jessica knew of his annoyance. "I
want to hear the end." She tried to sound fascinated in the tale of the dog in the
frozen wild that had a wolf's heart but belonged to a boy. "I *really* do. But the
crew is waiting and—"

"Oh, sure, sure!" He pouted and followed her up the stairs.

"Pit is waiting inside," Jessica said. "This won't take long. Then we'll all go
out for pizza! We can take your friend Joel."

"It's okay." Danny took on a wounded expression. He looked to the sky, where
gold leaves were boating down out of trees. Now his eyes fell to the walk and he
sighed heavily, a routine he had learned in the Sprint commercial. "I understand,"
he said wearily as though it were he, and not the dog, left in the wild.

Jessica assured herself this was an act. She told herself it was okay; they'd be
together tonight. But it didn't feel okay. It felt wrong. Danny needed her and she
was working—again. She'd make up for it. She'd calendar more Danny time next
month, put it in ink so he wouldn't be erased. She walked beside him, dazzled by
the ashes of the glories of Jack in a red sweater and jeans and the favorite yellow
rain boots; Jessica in a travel-proof taupe jumpsuit, her shoulders slumped, carrying
a mother's guilt.

As she pushed through the swinging doors, a forklift whined by, carrying a smoking block of ice. The dock lined with trucks, men tossing in bags of ice. Danny's eyes gobbled it up, ears tuned to the language of the dock, the actor learning new words as Jessica searched for her crew.

Pit's voice boomed out behind her. "Say, Jess! You gotta hell of a night coming your way!"

Danny whirled around, drawing a finger gun from an imaginary holster, firing at Pit in his silver chair. Pit gave a groan and slumped in his chair, as if dying was his vocation.

"Where's the crew?" Jessica asked, chomping on a stick of gum, getting the creative juices flowing. Her eyes cut through the icehouse where men in coats were emerging from freezers as if from a blizzard. Hands in their pockets and their noses red.

"This way." Pit led the way, staying in the yellow-striped alley with Danny beside him, entranced by the blocks of ice and the pallets and the noise. A boy who had inherited the unmerciful methodological supernatural courage of story, images in his mind as compelling as his father's blood. "Here you go, Jess." Pit passed her a fancy topcoat the Birbeck executives loaned them. It was cowhide, with "Birbeck's Ice" in fine script on the pocket.

Jessica took the heavy coat, frowning at it. "What's this for?" she asked. "The freezer's not on, is it?"

"Hoo, boy!" Pit gave a laugh. He rolled his eyes to Danny, a conspiratorial look the boy knew. Pit whispered, "Believe me; she's gonna need that baby." Danny's mouth clamped shut and downward to keep the secret safe. He was often privy to Pit's backstage deliberations, making a game out of his mama's crazy life. Taking what could have been hurt and turning it into fun.

Pit decided to switch to domestic affairs before the work gobbled her up again. "Say," he said. "I got the circus tickets. Sunday matinee. Sure you don't want to come?"

"I'd love to go to the circus," Jessica shot back, chewing impatiently on the gum, looking through the maze of freezers for her crew, "you know that. But I have to *work* Sunday."

"I know," Pit said, watching Danny running ahead. The boy reminded him of a young hunting dog, springy and mindless and full of life, a sense of good recklessness surging about him. "Yes, ma'am," he said, "I know you gotta work Sunday. Why, you've worked every Sunday since Danny's birthday."

"Save it, Pit," Jessica replied, walking faster, eyeing an enormous freezer on the far side of the building. "Danny just worked me over." Cases of camera equipment were stacked outside the freezer, a tall brunette waiting. But where was her crew?

"You know, hotshot," Pit said to Jessica, keeping an eye on the boy. "All that flying around you do—England and Switzerland and New York and such—that may cost you. One day that boy will be grown and gone. He won't make many demands of your time. And you'll be damn grateful for the few." He gave her his eyes that did not ease her heart. "Maybe you should fix your weekend."

"Oh, sure. But how do I say no to Tiffany's?"

Pit took her by the hand. He stopped her charge to the next job, forklifts with smoking blocks of ice whizzing by. "Say no this way." His lips formed a big O. "No."

Jessica smiled very slightly. Pit always made perfect sense. He had brought destiny to the disorder of their lives. And he bore up very well under the rigors of her craziness.

"It's no great shakes saying no," Pit said. "Why, it's the most self-making word in the English language. Learn to say no to yourself, and you can have any damn thing. You can make a million, lose weight, or get over the blues. It's the *Golden No*. Nowadays people have forgotten its power, they're so busy wanting."

She had to agree with him, and Jack would have, too.

"Danny!" Jessica ran after him. The boy dancing in the steam of a block of ice, vapors swirling around him. "I'll make up for the circus!" she called back, taking Danny by the hand, pulling him from the cold tendril that licked out at him, swirling around his legs, like they were going to gobble him up. "I'm taking us out for pizza tonight! Just as soon as this shot is in the can."

Pit rolled up beside her. "Careful, hotshot," he whispered. "There's some things money can't buy. And time is one of 'em."

Pit looked after Jessica in the cowhide coat, hurrying the boy on to the freezer where her crew waited with a lady in what looked like a sharkskin coat. A man had to be careful, tactful how he helped a mother; mothers were akin to those holy cows of India. Only a card-carrying Hindu believes the dour, pious cow is sacred. To the rest of the world it's just a cow, not a whiff of God on a cow. It takes real belief to see a bellowing, stumbling beast moving on shovel feet, standing around all day, chewing as it stares, accompanied by a promenade of black flies, as an animal angelic. The cow has gentle, patient eyes, but try to move one and John Wayne's *The Cowboys* gripe comes to mind: "A cow ain't nothing but a lot of trouble tied up in a leather bag."

A cowboy who works the livelong day around cows would never call their dropping a commission from God, suitable for ceremonial afternoon-tea. A cowboy knows a cow is nothing but a stupid eating machine, not any brighter than a damn shark. Sharks are animals of cravings, an incalculable mass and power, as smooth and concise as a torpedo streaking through the depths. Their brains have the same wattage; it's the mouth that separates shark from cow. The shark rearing up from the surface in a savage grin, with teeth so sharp they can cut flesh as easily as a psycho's razorblade. A man knows then that mouth will reach him, the terror of knowing followed by the terrible pressure at his legs, as if all his guts are being compacted. There's the rank, dark liquid ooze of blood on water, the shark head slides back and disappears, so only the triangle of gray fin is seen slicing through the sea, followed by the scythed tail sweeping left and right with short, spasmodic thrusts.

Only in a world of bonehead human perception could a shark be mistaken for a cow; the shark never to be confused with anything sacred. The mother who straps her two boys into carseats, then watches as car and boys roll into the depths of a lake, is not to be confused with the sacred. Nor is the mother who takes a butcher knife to her two daughters cut to pieces, or the mother who hangs her three young children. All real mothers, none of them sacred. Mothers weren't sacred. Mothers were people. Some people love, and some people kill. And some people are fools thinking killers are cows. Pit Martin had been such a fool. He had believed a shark was a holy cow, and the shark took everything, including the kids. He looked after

Jessica holding Danny's hand, listening to the boy tell his dog story as they walk. That was sacred: the labors and pride of growing up with your child. Nothing was more holy.

"Hey, Danny!" Juice called as he slammed the big door on the gymnasium-sized freezer. "How ya doing, bud?"

Danny started to reply, but Jessica cut him off. "What's going on?" she asked, looking at the cases of equipment around them. It looked like everyone had gone to lunch. And what was Juice doing in that topcoat? It swallowed his compact frame. His smooth, shiny black face white with cold.

"We got everything set up," Juice said, taking her briefcase to help her into the cowhide coat. "That is, everything that don't freeze."

"*Freeze?* The freezer is not supposed to be turned on!" She glanced at the big silver door scalloped in ice and now at the attractive brunette beside it, just as cool. Who was she? Nice enough, introducing herself to Danny, keeping him company.

"I hear you, Jess," Juice said, watching her shift her weight from foot to foot, her creative dance, "but the Volvo folks say the freezer has to be minus thirty degrees Celsius—truth in advertising, or something to that effect." He handed her a blue-line of the advertisement.

"I don't believe this!" She stared at the sketch, and then glanced up to Danny, who had made a new friend. The woman was squatted beside him, taking him in, listening attentively as he told his dog story, no doubt. He was amazing, he could make pals anywhere. Jessica returned to chilling reality. "We can't shoot in freezing conditions! We'll be the ones in a block of ice!"

"Believe it, hotshot," Pit said, rolling up beside her. "Tell you what, I'll go get the pizza, there's a joint just around the corner. We can have dinner right here. Make a picnic out of a tragedy, what do you say?"

"There's this mother of a block of ice in there," Juice went on. "They froze it around the car. Pretty fantastic, but the devil to light. Then there's the cold. Way I figure it, we got enough time to get in a couple of shots, then—"

"The freezer is not supposed to be turned on!" she pleaded, as if it'd make a difference. She made a sharp, exasperated sound.

"Yeah, well, before you get worked up," Juice said, "I got to talk to you about that C-3PO costume for the Calvin Klein shot. The guy in New York wants two grand."

"Two grand!" Jessica started to blow a fuse, but now the stranger joined them. In an iron-colored coat. Very sharp suit. Looked like Armani. "Two thousand dollars," she said softly. "For *one* day?"

"And he wants insurance," Juice said. "A hundred grand."

"Jesus!" Jessica groaned. Her eyes darted back to the woman, and now she knew who she was. She had called about using Danny for a shot. Tan and lovely, she had cat green eyes, her hair a sheaf coiled over one shoulder. A wrist displayed a diamond Rolex and she looked to Jessica like her own ambition incarnate. She could imagine her three-story house sitting on an expanse of green lawn. Her trips to Europe and Tahiti—not really vacations, but part of an inward journey of self-discovery. She was attractive but had chucked the Barbie suit for a figure that looked strong and solid, but at the same time very chic. Her men would have scholarly good looks, Jessica decided, instinctive, experienced, but she wouldn't be enchanted by any of them. She was the kind of woman who never scrimped on luxuries, to whom the whole world existed for the state of her engagement with it. And the image of the woman was as compelling as her dream of herself.

Pit shouted they were going for the pizza and Jessica waved good-bye to Danny. "Okay," she said to Juice, now waving the woman over to join them. "We'll pass along the cost of the insurance."

"No sweat," Juice replied, buttoning her coat. "I'll handle it. Got it set up for November first. The robot suit will be here the day before. I'll do the certificate of insurance, but I forgot to ask if it's plastic or metal. Do you know?"

"Beats me," Jessica said.

"It's a robot costume?" the woman asked.

"That's right." Jessica loved her crisp Australian accent.

"It's probably made of space-age plastic," the woman said.

"I bet you're right," Jessica said. "It's probably made of plastic painted Krylon silver."

"Everything is plastic these days," the woman added.

"Really."

"Especially men."

"*Really!*" Jessica grinned and shook hands with the insightful woman. "Jessica Moore," she said. "You're here about Danny?"

"I'll be with the others," Juice said, headed back to the freezer. Jessica held up a finger, indicating she'd be with him in a minute.

"I'm Jacqueline Sterling," Somberg said, drawing a business card from a lizard skin card wallet. "With Chimera Enterprises, Limited. We're an ad group out of Sydney," she said. "We represent a number of Japanese clients."

Jessica whistled, rolling the sleeves back on the coat that had swallowed her hands. "I hear there's big money in Tokyo!"

"Huge," Somberg said, flashing a magnetic smile.

"And you want Danny to model for a shot? A test shot or something?"

"Actually, it's an *audition*. We're looking for a replacement for the Sony Boy. Testing a select group of boys in three cities—New York, Chicago, L.A. We're *very* interested in your son. He has just the features we have in mind. And he's so adorable! It could be a great opportunity for Danny."

"Really?" Jessica refused to let her voice betray her thrill. Sony was a gold mine.

"I was just talking to him. He has quite an imagination!" Somberg could have made the arrangements by phone, but after seeing his portfolio, she wanted to see the boy. And she could learn so much more about the child by speaking to his inventor. "Unfortunately, we're pressed for time. Our current Sony Boy seems to have sprouted into a teenager overnight."

"It happens," Jessica said, nodding sagely. In her mind she was calculating the television royalties.

"Yes." Jacqueline tucked a lock of brunette hair behind her ear as she smiled, working on a cozy girlfriend connection. "It surprised us how quickly he grew. Suddenly too tall. Too lean. Too gangly. He has the face of a Pepsi ad! And we've several Sony Boy projects next month."

"Oh, that's not a problem for us," Jessica said, drawing Danny's calendar from her briefcase. "I don't think Danny has any commitments we can't reschedule. You need him when?"

"October twenty-sixth."

Jessica made a note on the date, listening as Jacqueline talked about a campaign millions would be riding on. Not only would they be looking for modeling skills, but there would be IQ, aptitude, and stress stability tests. It would all be factored into their decision. As the woman spoke, Jessica glanced at the card again. There was an office in Sydney, another in New York. She had never heard of Chimera, but she was relatively new on the international scene, whereas Jacqueline was obviously a player networked in the global market that was Jessica's dream.

"I wonder," Jessica said after Jacqueline finished, "could you give me some background on Chimera? And an idea of the financial opportunities for the Sony Boy?"

Somberg acquired a new smile. It had something of victory in it. She proceeded to tell Jessica exactly what a concerned parent and an enterprising photographer wanted to hear.

It was a sweetheart of a deal, and it looked like it was made for Danny. Chimera had a $61 million contract with Sony, they were sharks in the Far East, Chimera could really make things happen. They had started in a hole-in-the-wall office in Sydney and had gone global in six years, charging record-setting fees and getting away with it. There was a list of clients that made Jessica's heart sing, the very air in the icehouse rarified by Jacqueline's voice as she gave a sample of the contract, stipulated the terms, all of which they scrutinized together sitting on the pallets used as a table and chairs that gave the deal a Zen righteousness. If Danny were chosen, he'd be a millionaire practically overnight. It was an opportunity on solid ground, that much was clear, but what was more engaging than the money was Jacqueline Sterling.

It was impossible to imagine a more beautiful woman. There was a brilliant summer light in her eyes that Jessica recognized as the generosity of self-belief. A lady of the moment undaunted by any circumstance, you could feel as much in her. She spoke in that fashionable song, that language of the illustrious successful woman, and it whistled to Jessica's heart as a mentor. She had to steady her soul, the drive was so strong in this woman that could teach international lessons that Jessica could learn nowhere else. They just hit it off. The boys came back with pizza and they were still talking. About diving in the Caribbean. About the gorgeous eyes of Arabs. About the Tramontana wind in Barcelona. About a new dark coffee out from Kenya and South African diamonds and how divine J. P. Tod's shoes were and a new facial cream made from herbs from Chiang Mai and all of it was all so necessary, to have someone to share this cycle with, there were so few women at this level. And by the time Jacqueline left, Jessica saw her as a dream realized, a miracle of herself that was possible.

With a new friend realized and the road to the Sony Boy deal mapped out in her mind, Jessica opened the freezer door and caught her breath as cold reality rushed sharply into her lungs. The cold was without mercy, and it took her a moment to comprehend what her eyes were seeing. The white enameled freezer was a scaffolding of lights framed around a red Volvo GL frozen in a gargantuan block of ice. The driver's door standing open. Keys in the ignition. It looked like a Cal Tech practical joke. Her crew in coats, working in clouds of frosted breath. Firing strobes to measure the light, turning the scene into something surreal and silvery. Jessica walked around the car, staring but not believing, the deep cold stinging her face. She looked again at the blue-line of the ad. The hook was: Volvos Start at $16,992 (and minus 30°C). Now she was to supply the picture to prove it.

"Shit!"

Her breath crystallized, then fell to the floor like a broken promise. The staff coming at her with questions. How would they keep the light from bouncing off the ice? How did they keep the film from freezing? They had been there an hour and the shot was impossible. Now someone was banging at the window. She turned to find Danny with Jacqueline, the two of them smiling and waving through a diamond frost, and they appeared as if in another world. In the bitter cold of the gargantuan freezer, Jessica felt as if she were caught in a crystal illusion of herself, she tried to underhand her own disquiet, but there was so much to do and so little time. She began at once, making the impossible happen.

7

THREE O'CLOCK IN the morning, Spenser's sweet Thames was silent and secret in the fog that swirled off the river and drifted in a sprawl down Blake's chartered streets. It thickened and crept over Wordsworth's bright and glittering bridge. Trent breathed in its sticky pall, hand on the damp rail that carried him into the uncharted night. The conviction that he had been missing something had been nagging at him since lunch, when Graham had dropped a report on his desk. The 100 detectives he sent to dig through the rubble of the Grand Hotel had discovered fragments of powerful batteries strewn over the Brighton beach. The bits of battery were of no significance, one of thousands of things they found and tagged, the beach littered with whatever was inside the hotel, yet all day and into the night Trent sensed a revelation floating just beyond his reach. He had escaped the office and entered the mystery of the night fog, not so much to find the revelation, but in hopes that the revelation might find him.

He had been living on catnaps since Thatcher gave him the case; it had become a slow, tedious affair, patience a thing he had to force on himself. He began with reams of computer printouts that gave backgrounds on suspects. Then there was the taped babble of the interviews with the hotel guests. Bringing them in. Using the identikit to make a composite that could be one of ten thousand faces. Prowling through the bowels of London, matching suspects to sketches. Pounding on doors. Hauling the Irish in. Doing the routine. "Where were you on the night of . . . ? Who were you with . . . ? How do you know . . . ? Are you sure that wasn't the other way round . . . ? Yes, but we're just puzzled by one small thing. . . . Would you mind going through it all once more, just for the records?" Graham making neat notes in a little book, smiling at the Irish double-talk. Trent feeling the heat of his ancestors' dark eyes as they stared up from under the glare of the interrogation. He kept at it, with stamina and eagerness, and he shrugged off the stares, he knew what he was about.

Patience, patience, he told himself. *Check it all out, though all of it looks so fucking unlikely.* He was working for a woman who was competent and confident. Whose tough rhetoric was quite impressive. Who believed in individual acts. Whose abilities were superior, and in all these things she inspired. Anyone who worked with her, regardless of gender, was spurred on by her charisma; it was a thing Trent found he could count on. The specter of her was there every day, the seemingly invincible Mrs. T pressing ideas into resolutions. A man was more man when led by the Iron Lady.

He laid out the floor plans of the Grand. Again, he studied the pictures of destruction. He allowed himself to return to the sixth floor balcony where he stood that night looking out over the white columned face of the hotel. All dark but for a yellow square of window in the Napoleon Suite on the second floor, and he knew she was still working. The woman drove herself obsessively, working through two watches, no one man could keep up with her.

"I say, Stanford, is she still awake?"

The voice came from behind him and Trent didn't turn from the night; the bedroom lamp would ruin his vision. He knew the plummy Oxford accent as Geoff Duncan.

"Right." He glanced down to the lone glowing window. "Still working on her speech, I suspect."

"She'll be giving the striking miners hell tomorrow!" Duncan said from the door of the watch room.

"They deserve hell. By Christmas half the country will be freezing while they picket. If she lights a fire under their ass, maybe the rest of us can keep warm."

He gave a wave to one of the boys on the roof. Had one of those new Browning sniper rifles with a starlight scope. And there were stars to see by; it was a shining night.

"Do you think they'll show?" Duncan asked, coming out into the night. He inclined a spindly frame against the banister, a trusting soul. Trent gave a glance, the face smooth and blond, nothing yet written on it. The white turtleneck a lovely target.

"They may already be here," he said warily. He hadn't been out of his shoes in forty-eight hours, since the Conservative Convention began. "But they'll not show themselves. Not quite their style."

Duncan gave a laugh, showing a perfect set of teeth. "The muckers would be stupid to try anything tonight!"

"The Irish Republican Army," Trent said, pronouncing the name with his native Irish tongue, "are many things, but they're not stupid. Lord Mountbatten would tell you that, *if* he were alive."

"Mountbatten? Stanford, I've *read* about Mountbatten. His yacht wasn't secured. But Graham has spent a half-million pounds securing the Grand. We've an army out there tonight!"

"Right. Commander Graham has put on quite a show."

"But you still think they'll try something?"

Trent looked over the sea that shone black and silver in the moonbeams. He took the watch radio from his jacket pocket and propped it on the banister. Adjusted the volume so the banter from the watching army was no louder than the rhythm of the surf.

"I'd say the Grand is too much for the IRA to resist." He stood with his big hands resting easy on the banister, still in the tuxedo he wore the day before. "*Their* political convention is Thursday. They always do something spectacular prior to their Sinn Fein show. And besides, Mrs. T will be fifty-nine tomorrow. They'd love to see the Iron Lady lying in state on her birthday. Then there's the Cabinet, the whole of the British government is asleep under one roof tonight."

"Against your recommendation."

Far below on the promenade, Trent watched a couple take a midnight stroll. He envied them, realizing he had for some time been cheating his rampant romantic who loved to make him a fool.

"But Graham disagreed," Duncan continued. "And Mrs. T went with Graham."

A smile lifted the corners of Trent's mouth. He patted through his jacket and drew a Cohiba from the inside pocket.

"Graham will always tell Mrs. T what she wants to hear," Trent said, stripping a cigar. "It's how the commander runs his department. Cautiously. Tentatively. *By the numbers.*"

"Which means keeping an eye on appropriations."

"Spoken as a loyal corporate soldier," Trent said, returning his eyes to the long shining curve of the sea. He flared a match; drew in the sweetness of Havana. Nothing like the thought of Cuba to help carry a man through a long night. A Cohiba was rolled in the finest tobacco that had the scent of sugar-white beaches set in palms, with dancing bands and rum cocktails for breakfast.

"But what I fail to understand, Stanford, is why are you so uptight?"

"I'm *concerned*," Trent said, turning to young Duncan, who looked corpselike under the moon, "about the possibility of this hotel being brought to the ground."

Duncan laughed. "Not after all our precautions."

Trent lifted a pair of worn nightvision binoculars. "It happened at the King David Hotel." Trent scanned silent shadows below. In nightvision they were green-tinted as though by some spectral Irish smoke. From high above he could see the contrail of history. "It was one of the strokes that won Israel freedom," he said, sensing a knowing without knowing. But in his sleepless daze the knowing of the King David escaped him, lying somewhere at the bottom of his mind, or at the bottom of the Grand Hotel.

"The Jews used a bomb?"

Trent glanced back to the young man who made him feel old. "You didn't *read* about that?"

"Well, yes. Of course! It slipped my mind."

"Right. Must have slipped Graham's as well." He drew on the cigar as Duncan ran on about a war that for Trent held only hollow victories, impossible to separate his Irish guilt embroidery from the whole of his British cloth. On a quiet night, his Irishness cursed. In the white hot minutes after a bomb, in the sizzling flesh, in the stench of burned meat, his Englishness cursed. No way for him to win, short of peace. And if peace came, whatever would he do with himself? Who would devil him along?

"Where did the Jews hide their bomb?" Duncan asked.

"I believe it was in the wall cavity of a room."

"But we checked all the rooms! The dogs sniffed out *every* corner of *every* room. And we vetted all the hotel staff. Made no secret about it. The bloody Irish know we're here in force!"

Trent put the binoculars away. How could he explain it all to this young man from a privileged background? Duncan had joined C-13 with a lofty purpose that endeared him to his family. And he had a promising future. He was ambitious. Energetic. But no experience. Hadn't tagged the body pieces, sealed and refrigerated like cuts of meat in a butcher's shop. He had not yet sacrificed his tranquility that others might have theirs. He turned to the tall, frail, ghostlike outline Duncan made against the dark, some refraction of what was left unsaid, that failure was a thing C-13 agents didn't speak of, showed in Trent's angular face.

"It's hell, isn't it?" Duncan said. "I mean, when it actually happens, when a bomb goes off."

"Can't really say. Never been caught in one."

"Ah, well." Duncan laughed. "Not likely you ever will!"

"No, I shouldn't think so. Though I've dreamt it," Trent said to the dark. "You can't help but dream. They usually come with no warning, you know. First the bombs, then the dreams."

"And is that why you sleep with a light on, Stanford?"

He blew out a plume of smoke and watched as the wind snatched it away. Gone wherever the dead go. Where they stop screaming.

"You'll need your sleep," Trent said, picking up his voice; a shot of Mrs. T optimism in it. "The dawn comes early on the sea."

Duncan stepped back, so again there was only the voice at Trent's back. "Will you wake me for my watch?"

"Right. First light."

"Thanks."

He heard Duncan enter, his long shadow cast by the lamplight Trent would not look upon. He called after him. "Sleep well!" But there was no response and he returned to the night, turning up the squawking radio. There had been a breeze but it withered down to a dead stillness. Somewhere out on the dark water a buoy clanged as it rode the ink-black tide. From where Trent stood, the sound seemed to come from the moon.

The great clock of stars revolved in the sky, and he had been on the edge of sleep for what seemed like a long time when the light blinked off on the second floor. He made a note in the log: *2:55 A.M. Napoleon Suite gone dark.* Mrs. T had put in another seventeen-hour day. He shook his head before her obsessiveness. What was it that drove her? It seemed the more power she had, the more she wanted. He had managed to stay clear of the woman, who had all the glamour and class of a big-time racketeer. She could escalate your career, but more often left victims in her wake.

With her light out, he allowed himself to sit in a chair, taking the weight from his feet. He drew his last Cohiba. Took his time stripping it. The moon was veiled by clouds but the night was black and in the distance he could see a mist that shone against the lightness of the sea; it smudged the warning of the buoys blinking on the horizon. The radio, still on the banister, was garbled with static. A storm approaching. He would watch till dawn, then wake Duncan. And then perhaps he could get some sleep. The cigar ready, he found a match. He tilted in his chair and as he popped the match the night exploded into a hard white flash.

On Wordsworth's bridge, Trent's eyes were again aching for sleep. He saw phantoms swirl over the bridge that reared from the fog that smelled of the sea. Everything blending with everything else, bridge and night and fog, and the concussion of the blast that picked him up and threw him into the Grand banister and for a moment he thought his head had come off. A roar in his ears that started red and went on into a searing heat that cut his breath in two. He closed his eyes against the memory, hand on the damp, cold railing of the bridge. He let the rail guide him as he walked in the night as if in a dream. Not quite there, not quite anywhere, when the fabric of life seemed to ripple and the fog made itself into the smelting furnace of the bomb. The brick chimney let go again; it dropped in a surreal silence. Trent leaped back as a mushroom of red heat rushed up behind it to bloom like a bloody rose into the night. On the far side of the crater that had been his room Trent could see the open hall. The heat so intense he was cooking inside his skin. Climbing a pile of timber, into smoke and red flashes, when his hand sank into a goo. He lurched back to stare at the half-buried, upside-down corpse. A thick soup of flesh and bone and scorched hair. A mouth of perfect teeth open in a silent scream. Eyes baked in their sockets. Duncan's blistered face peppered with glistening chips of bathroom tile. The bomb had levitated him out of bed and through the wall to deposit him in a tangle of brick. And now on the bridge, the apparition of Geoff Duncan rose from the rubble. It hovered before Trent, a scorched havoc of entrails, slathered and dripping. It seemed to speak.

Months ago you read a report about an IRA raid. A cache of weapons buried in the forest.

Eyes still closed, hand on the bridge rail, Trent stopped. His face stony, staring at the phantom of his guilt. It walked on and he followed in its blood-splashed trail.

Don't you remember, Trent? it said, looking back over its shoulder with a sullen smirk. *You read about it.*

The apparition laughed, a screeching racket echoing in the night. Trent's eyes snapped open. The phantom eclipsed in fog.

"Anyone there?" The shamed cry of his voice sped away into the night that was the fabric of life that rippled before his wide eyes. He turned in every direction. Beyond the earth's vail, there was a billion lightyears of darkness, no telling what was in it.

He walked on, then swung around. Not a shadow approached. Not one ghostly shriek came back to him from the fog's gray wall.

"Buried in a forest?" he asked himself, marching on. "What forest? When? And what the devil did the report report?"

He waited, but still there was no reply. He found himself on the bridge, standing there like a damn fool talking to the night. But it was Wordsworth's bridge, and so it would be a courtesan to the night. A corridor of power that served higher appointments.

He pulled his trench coat around him and sprinted from the bridge into the glazed street. Breathing heavily, fog stinging his eyes and nostrils. Street lamps made into gelatinous flame to glimpse corpses, and again he was studying the coroner's photos. Clean, full-color shots. Misshapen naked bodies on a stainless-steel table. A stout man from the third floor, limbs contorted from the heat that had consumed him. A woman once a wife, her pale skin smooth and shiny, glazed by the fire that swept through a fourth floor room. From the same floor, a portly member of Parliament, an outspoken supporter of South African apartheid, straight nose projecting from a charred face, a countenance now black as any African. From the fifth floor, a heavy elderly woman with wounds like a victim of surgical experimentation. And now a face Trent might never stop seeing, the gelatinous horror of Geoff Duncan staring at him with boiled eyes, bathroom tile having been picked from his brain as that hunch of truth that eluded Trent.

A building up ahead, severed in half by the fog, it looked like the Grand Hotel. Now came the echo of feet behind him. He stopped and panting, glanced back, half expecting to see Duncan. Only a shadow waiting. He walked a distance. The shadow followed. He listened to nothing. "Good God," Trent muttered. "I've got to get some sleep—as soon as I find that report." He ran on and the wind got under the fog, and now he saw the building up ahead was the New Scotland Yard Building.

A green canopy cast a wedge of lamplight over the desk and onto a lumpy mound on the corner cot. It slept with a wheezing snore. Trent entered the office and his phantom shadow followed. He shook the mound and called in a voice more vigorous than his shake, "Graham!"

The snoring stopped. Then started again.

Trent gave another shake. "Graham."

The commander struggled like a dreaming dog and muttered, "Be a good chap, Stanford; go home and get some rest."

Sleep sounded idyllic, but Trent knew as soon as he closed his eyes, Duncan would be there in the dark waiting for him. In the dark of Graham's office, Trent leaned on the desk, speaking with deliberate slowness. "Some time ago, prior to my transfer to C-thirteen . . . ." On the wall before him, a shadow waited. Tall and lank, it appeared to be leaning against the banister of the Grand. Trent kept one eye on the shadow as he continued. "I read a report referencing an IRA arms bust. Came down in the country."

Graham groaned and rolled up into a sitting position. The cot sagged and let out a moan. The commander looked almost cute, hair twisted into sleep curls.

"Stanford," he said in a creaky voice. "You asked me to spend the night because you said you were onto something. Jolly good, I've spent the night. Now you've pulled me from a splendid Anita Ekberg dream—"

"Ah! Anita, is it? A Swede. Right, they're brilliant." Trent fought back a laugh, picturing the blundering commander with the erotic movie star. Rather like an elephant mating with a gazelle.

"Indeed," Graham said, fixing Trent's smirk with a bull-like glare. He smoothed back his hair. "We were on the beach. Lying in white sand. Anita glistening. About to kiss when you come along! And for what? An IRA arms bust. *In the country?*"

"Right. The bust was in a rural area, you know?"

"Ah, *rural area!*" Graham bobbed his round head, sarcasm wide awake. "Well, that certainly pinpoints it, doesn't it?"

Trent spun a chair around and straddled it, leaning over the back. "Come on, Graham," he said. "This is important."

"My dear fellow, we've had busts in many 'rural areas.' Any particular rural area you're referring to?"

"A forest, I believe. I was over at M15 at the time. Only glanced at the report. I think it was in January."

"This past January?"

"Right."

Graham rose; the cot sighed with relief. He shuffled around his desk and dropped into a chair. Hands found the glass decanter of port and poured two glasses, steady on, not a drop wasted. He set a glass on a bulletin and slid it across the desk. The commander took his time with the other, sipping and savoring.

"Perhaps," he said, a wooziness still in his voice, "you're referring to the Salcey Forest raid, south of Northampton?"

"Damn. That's it!" The shadow on the wall caught Trent's eye; it was shaking a fist. "What do you remember about the raid?"

Graham's elbows dropped on the desk, port between them, long fingers steepled, dimpled chin perched on the steeple. His voice an automated machine, talking in a half-sleep. "We had twenty-six officers in on the show. Rainy day, as I recall. Commenced on the fourteenth of January?" Graham gazed into his port. "Yes," he said, nodding. "The fourteenth of January. We found four metal drums buried below the floor of the forest. Hard ground out Northampton way, you know. Miserable digging."

"Right." On the wall, the shadow was sitting reversed in a chair, arms hugging the back, as if the chair, like a ghost, might succeed in flying out the window. "And what was in the drums?"

"Explosives," Graham said through a yawn.

Trent waited, giving him time. He sipped the port, glancing at the bulletin. Something about a Tomas Mahoney. Wanted for arms smuggling. "So, what *kind* of explosives?" Trent prodded.

"Plastique," Graham said. "Semtex, I believe."

"And? Anything else?"

"There were detonators. And batteries. And—"

"*Timers!*" Trent leaped as if struck by a live wire; the dark shadow snapped up with him. "Bloody hell! Timers!"

Graham groaned at the display. "Awfully nice of you to wake me for this smashing revelation, Stanford."

Trent paced, following the shadow several steps ahead as the report came back. "They found timer-detonators. A *new* variety. They said they came from—" Trent looked to the commander. "Libya?"

"Yes," Graham said, gazing wistfully beyond Trent to the cot. "We had never seen them before."

"There were three long-term timers, right?"

"Long-term?" Graham yawned again. "Yes," he replied, rocking back in his chair that sang out against the tortuous strain. "Some kind of microelectronic things designed to fuse horrific bombs."

The shadow floated around the office walls, drink in hand. Now the shadow gave up the pacing, Trent watched it drink, and in his exhaustion that did not dwindle with the drink, he saw Duncan in every sway of the shadow. Duncan would be alive today if they had only hand-checked the laboratories. The Grand was a replica of the King David Hotel bombing. Made perfect sense. The King David the stroke that won the Jews freedom. Trent was on the verge of it that night, if he had only pushed on through his exhaustion. If he had trusted his instincts. Listened to the voice within. His Holy Ghost. He listened now as he spoke to the ghost: "The timers were labeled number one, number two, and number four. But the third timer was never recovered." Trent looked to Graham. "Right?"

"Bloody marvelous, Stanford! But what's the point?"

"Don't you remember the report?" Trent spoke faster as he caught up to the shadow, the whole thing coming in a rush. "Our people assumed the number three timer was sent back to Ireland for a hit. Are you with me, Graham?"

"Stanford, it's two o'clock in the—"

"You wouldn't happen to recall the duration of the timers?"

"Twenty-four days," Graham said automatically.

"You're sure?"

Graham stared. Scowling gaze. It was the only confirmation Trent needed. He reached for the phone and rang his office at the Grand, where the scavenger crew was working round-the-clock for the elusive forensic trail he promised Mrs. T. Had he found it? The duty officer answered. Trent asked for Burnett to be called to the phone. He turned to Graham, pouring another glass of port. "What was the date twenty-four days prior to the Grand?"

Graham started at the twelfth of October and ran a finger backwards over the prime minister's appointment calendar lying open on his desk. "Eighteenth of September," he replied.

"Sorry to wake you, Burnett," Trent said into the phone, "but I believe we're onto something. I need you to run the registration cards and carefully—*mindful of fingerprints*—pull the card for Room Six-twenty-nine, *eighteenth of September*. Bring it to the phone. Read me the name."

Trent waited. At the window he watched an Irish fog, rolling down Victoria Street, devouring the Department of Trade, then Westminster Abbey, then the Houses of Parliament, releasing them piece by piece as it drained them of color, altering the face of London in a silent war that Mrs. T insisted was not a war.

Graham watched him at the window, too tall and too stylish and too sure and too Irish. Stanford was Thatcher's New Britain. Lean and fast and aggressive, without the proper respect for the old guard. His PM directive, while it might be efficient, was an affront to the chain of command. What gave *that woman* the right to interfere in C-13? Had she ever conducted an arms bust? What did she know of these IRA animals? What a pity they had failed at the Grand! But they'd have another go at her; he knew they would. He glared at Mrs. T's calendar and wondered what date they'd pick. It was he who had to coordinate the surveillance teams, dogs, rooftop sharpshooters, and minesweepers that would go over the ground before her. The woman was a trouble that never ceased. She was nontraditional. A willful, independent woman. Arrogance would one day do her in, Britain would return to male rule, and the likes of her would not come again for a hundred years. Anything done to hasten that day would be a service to the country.

Burnett returned with the name. Trent jotted it onto a pad. "All right," he said, restraining the thousand-voiced choir of angels struck up in his head. "Bring that registration card to Graham's office. Use an evidence bag. Thank you, Detective."

"Well?" Graham demanded after Trent rang off.

Trent downed the last of his port. He glanced at the pad. "Ever hear of a Roy Walsh?"

"*Walsh!*" Graham exclaimed, staring at the pad as Trent passed it to him. "That's the name on the registration?"

"Right. Why? You know him?"

"Oh, I should say so!" Graham smiled ruefully. "I sent him to Parkhurst Prison in 1973. The bloody mucker is still serving a sentence for bombing the Central Criminal Court."

"Damn it!" Trent pounded the desk, the lamp jumped, and the shadow leaped on the wall.

"It's a bloody tease," Graham sang.

The shadow returned to the window, and Trent saw it step through the glass and into the Irish fog. It hastened in and out of light cones, down side streets, under spiky overhanging trees. Phantoms flittered past, calling from the fog. *The 2:59 detonation time is a tease! Roy Walsh is a tease! We are a tease and we are not imprisoned! We are Irish and you cannot stop us!* Trent saw a shadow's wet tracks over the cobbles, the tracks sucked up and vanished like the tale of the war itself, the murder of Duncan already receding from the ranks of tragedy to become one more ugly statistic. Only the guilt remained as a shadow he couldn't shake.

"I knew it wouldn't be that easy." Trent sighed and turned away from the window to find the shadow waiting for him on the wall. He followed it to the cot.

"It's never easy, old boy," Graham countered archly. "Not in C-thirteen!" Trent heard the chair wail as Graham lolled back. "Did I tell you about the time they went after the Prince of Wales? We ran riot on that one! Daunted the attack!"

The shadow stood over the cot while the chair continued its wailing. In the cry, Trent's gaze drifted back to the mutilated corpses of the Grand. Sliding away to little Emma Blake sprawled limbless over her hopscotch game. And then Mrs. Salomon who had survived the Nazi concentration camps, only to die in a London street with the broken mannequins. Now Stevenson sprawled over the train tracks, his life's blood running into the cinders. Now the great horse of the Household Cavalry lathered and dripping and half-crazed as Trent put the Beretta to its head. The sound of the shot dissolved the horse's head into the hideously blistered face of Geoff Duncan gleaming in firelight. Trent trapped in the cascading debris of the hell that had been his room at the Grand, and for a second he was transfixed, watching as from the pennants of flame came ten men shrunken unnaturally, like vegetable husks in the white uniforms of criminals, and not that of prisoners of war. Ten Irish who had starved themself to death in Maze Prison for the right to be recognized as soldiers. Following them out of the fire, a line of Irish children, each carrying a rubber bullet that Mrs. T said could not kill, in that war that was not a war. All of it so senselessly. The solution to simply *share.* As a divorced family shares the children, so a country could be shared in a thing that is never easy, but is not a campaign of death.

"Had the Irish beggars beat," Graham touted, "till Special Branch got in on the act. Said it was a ruse. Said the business over the prince was Irish feinting for some other show! But it was the prince, I tell you. The *prince!*"

Trent considering the wrinkled sea of sheets, calling him.

"There's the rub, Stanford. You do the job and for what? You get no respect when you succeed!"

The shadow dropped to the cot. Trent followed, slumping like a dead man against the wall, sinking into the shadow. Beyond the window he heard the teasing song of the Irish fog. "The game has changed," he muttered to Duncan. "We've been playing our game, but we must play theirs. We must take what they give and use it."

"What's that, Stanford?"

"I said, at least we know *when* they did it. And *how* they did it." Trent stretched his legs onto the cot, feeling blank inside his head, unplugged, running on bits of batteries. As he lay down, the shadow vanished into the cool of sheets, as though in these words the good soul of Geoff Duncan was laid to rest: "We've the registration card they signed. Maybe there'll be prints."

"Not likely!" Graham gave a laugh. "It's all stage dressing, Stanford. No, you'll find criminal detection is a bit more than handwriting and fingerprints and paint scrapings and microscopic pieces of thread, personality composites, and computer printouts."

"Thank you, Commander." Trent closed his eyes, sinking into sleep, hearing Graham as if underwater, rattling about his battles as he was carried down into the depths. Somewhere from the depths a voice called out, *Wake me when Burnett arrives!*

8

THE PINK-STRIPED WALLPAPER and hooked rug and camelback sofa gave the living room the look of a Norman Rockwell illustration. There was a kingsized recliner in which a Harry Trumanlike father sat, proudly pointing his pipe at the miracle of the century: a square-faced, rabbit-eared television. Mother, all sweetness and light, was in a blue floral dress, blonde hair in a bun, seated on the sofa beside a freckle-faced boy in Oxford shoes. Lying beside the boy on the rug was a pigtailed little girl, the bows in her hair matched the wallpaper, her arm around a collie who lay with her head on her paws, watching the swinging tail and rolling eyes of a black cat clock. Gathered around were neighbors in topcoats and hats, cheeks flushed as if they had just stepped in from the cold, all gawking at the miracle. An innocent scene; the set as a still frame of film from a naïf utopia. On the lunatic fringe of the atom bomb followed by the neurotic: Gandhi assassinated, Kennedy assassinated, Vietnam, Woodstock, King assassinated, then another Kennedy assassinated, the Concord, terror at the Munich Olympics, Three Mile Island, Watergate, an attempted assassination of the Pope, and the IRA's attempt to takedown Margaret Thatcher and the entire British cabinet at the Grand Hotel in Brighton.

Jessica tightened the stocking over the camera lens that would give the picture a faded photograph look. In the camera she saw the upside down image of Jacqueline Sterling. She refocused on the new Sony Trinitron television in the foreground, the screen aglow with the space shuttle blasting-off, the great romance of the wonder of television behind it. She called out to Danny and Jacqueline Sterling.

"Mom, scoot a little closer to your son! . . . That's it.

"Son, put your hand on Mom's lap! . . . Good.

"Mom, let's try your arm around Son . . . Cuddle him.

"Now, Son, look up lovingly at mom . . . Terrific!"

A series of flashes galvanized the scene as the camera whined through a dozen exposures in the space of a few seconds, the light straddling two worlds, between what had been and what is, catching on film this last ancient male bastion, lest it be forgotten.

"Love it!" Jessica shouted. "Only Lassie wasn't quite right."

A chorus of moans rose from the set. The enchanted faces of family and neighbors collapsed into haggard expressions, except for Jacqueline Sterling playing the mother. Her eyes were bright and blue, a cryptic smile on her lips as she gazed at Danny beside her. They looked like mother and son; a perfect picture that did not appear as a fabrication but as a gingerbread model of truth.

The illustration—The First TV as Exciting as the First TV—was the work of Somberg, who had dreamed up and organized the set, and hired the actors and the collie and cast herself as the lily, the blessed mother.

Jessica worked skillfully, shrewdly she thought, to make the most of the Sony Boy opportunity. She had invited Jacqueline to join them for lunch. Jessica sat on one side of the table, Danny and Jacqueline on the other. Jessica told the stories of Danny's life, intimacies shared with only their closest friends, and Jacqueline took in every anecdote. She asked insightful questions with an almost surgical skill, cutting past the cute episodes to find what provoked, challenged, inspired, and revealed Danny, and Jessica was impressed with her thoroughness. It was the work of a professional. Jacqueline never treated Danny as a six-year-old but like a person, and Jessica envied the respect Danny gave her. He was growing up right before her, and it occurred to Jessica, he was going to get old. It was true. No one would make an exception for her. Her son was on his way and the realizing of it urged her not to miss any of it. The hot mass of her feelings for Danny were nearly overwhelming; it had been all she could do to finish lunch, fighting some instinct that wanted to dump the Sony venture. That didn't care about signing bonuses or royalties or stock options. That wanted nothing more than the love of her son.

"Mom?" Danny said.

"Yes?" Jessica answered.

"No, I was talking to my other mom."

"Yes, darling," Somberg said.

"Can I open my presents now?" Danny was eyeing the silvery wrapped boxes on a work table behind the living room set.

"Why don't we finish this shot first," Somberg suggested in an Australian accent, perfectly Jacqueline Sterling. "Then we can do the presents."

"Are they scary presents?" Danny said, grinning at the pretty lady he liked a lot.

"No, they're special gifts. For a *whole new* you!"

Jessica watched Jacqueline run her fingers through Danny's shining hair. She should, she told herself, feel pride, delighted that this powerful, talented woman had found her son charming and attractive. Coaxing herself this in direction, a sense of Jessica's own worth matured in Danny's success. He was entering a glamorous dream and Jessica pushed aside her misgivings, she told herself it was only a fear for the vulgarity of fame.

"Alright, everyone!" she called. "Let's do it one more time. This time with the Lone Ranger. Then we'll all break for the day because *some of us* have a Halloween party to go to !"

Danny spun around and grinned. He cocked his finger-gun and shot Jessica. She doubled over with a dramatic groan. How she loved to die for him, and he loved nothing more than watching it.

She started the video tape. The Lone Ranger came galloping across the screen of the old-timey TV, firing his six-guns. The collie titled her head and lifted her ears, letting out a little worried whine, looking up at the box making the killing sounds.

"Perfect!" Jessica shouted. "C'mon! Faces everybody! Last shot of the night!"

Jessica was having a cool, comforting glass of chablis. She was wearing black tights, her clothes hanging on a peg in the dressing room. Now she spread the twenty-six pieces of the C-3PO suit over the counter. She had rented the suit for the Calvin Klien shot, which was tomorrow, but but tonight the Arts District was closing off the street to turn the whole block into a giant spook house. C-3PO would be the hit of the party! Jessica couldn't wait for Danny to see his mom dressed as his *Star Wars* hero. But now she wished she had asked Juice to stay and help put the damn robot together. At least she didn't have to keep up with Danny, she was lucky Jacqueline had offered to stay. It was Jacqueline who suggested Jessica hide in the darkroom after she was dressed. When ready, she'd turn on the developing light; seeing the light blink, Jacqueline would know to bring Danny around. She'd have him open the door, and C-3PO could slowly emerge from the dark.

She read the instructions again. With the wine, it didn't look so terribly hard. The chrome pieces were numbered, and the instructions went step-by-step; all she had to do was follow the instructions, which was practically impossible for the creative. She laughed at herself, had a little more wine and said, "Hell, even a robot can do it!"

She got started. The two leg pieces snapped together around her feet and legs. The thigh pieces were next. Then the funky looking knee joints. "Easy as pie!" she sang as she put on the trunk that was in two halves locking together around her waist with a sharp *click*! She hoped she didn't have to use the bathroom anytime soon; she'd be sealed up in this thing, no way to escape. What would happen if the parts didn't snap apart the same way they had snapped together? It'd take a can opener to get her out. She was strangely uptight, and that was all wrong, this was supposed to be fun. She dosed the instinct with chablis; did the breastplate and back, the weight riding on her shoulders like a suit of armor. Like one of those knights of old; all she needed was a hero sword. She was surprised the costume was made of steel, but when she took a step she understood why. Her movements were constricted by the heavy steel forcing her into a plodding robotic stride.

She finished the chablis and did the arms and elbow joints, then the neck coupling. The head assembly snapped snugly around her skull. It was dark inside the hull of the costume that fit as tightly as her career, all silvery and shiny. A claustrophobia slithering into her wine-mellow mood, but there was no reason to feel squeamish, and she talkety-talk-talk-talked her way out of it. She wriggled into the jointed gloves. Now she had robot hands. She made a mechaniclike rotation to the wall mirror. She waved at a C-3PO standing in the all-white room; her clothes on a back wall peg, as if the real Jessica Moore had been punctured, all the air let out of her, her skin hanging boneless from the peg. And that was pretty much how she felt at the end of every day.

She worked on her walk. Being a robot was not that different from being a model. Gotta have skills. Gotta sell it in the walk. It wasn't a strut, but a faltering, mechanical pivoting. Speed was everything; couldn't move too fast; didn't move at all but rather creaked, as if in need of a lubricant, or a little more chablis.

She plodded around in her steely suit, robot the essential nature of the full-time career girl, half-dead inside her charm that she had to lay on the gatekeepers and screeners because she was not one of the power-wielding women. One of those women who didn't mince words, who had real proxy and persuasion that was entirely their own and not that of their husband, or someone else's husband. The perfect example was Jacqueline. Never romantic and off-kilter; not pretty and tongue-tied. Nor was she heavy-handed. She was smooth and smart, projecting a solid confidence as negotiable as currency, using sex appeal as wampum and barter.

On a more famous scale, Margaret Thatcher came to mind. She always had Jessica's vote for Woman of the Decade. Maybe Woman of the Century. She had not risen to power on the merits of her cake recipes, as many of her American contemporaries. Thatcher was said to be a scraper. A fighter. They called her the Iron Lady. That would be grounds for a lawsuit in America where *personal style* was the investiture of hopes to rise to the top gracefully. Jessica didn't know much about Thatcher. She wondered, in her shambling robot stride, who had been Thatcher's mentor when she was a girl? Did Thatcher learn her savvy from another Iron Lady? Could a woman only learn her moves from another woman?

She was getting the hang of the robot walk. She did a little box step and made herself laugh; the laughter worked like silicon and the moves came with a fluid iron style. She pivoted to the mirror and, imagining Danny's thrill, said in a robot stammer, "Hel-lo, lit-tle boy. Is yo-ur na-me Dan-ny?"

Somberg was living in the moment. Her face was stunned with rapture, and she was blissfully unaware of it. This was the key to a woman's success. Not found in hardships, or in some favorite stump speech theme delivered to herself. The secret of the player was to never be too self-involved, too self-watching, too self-consciousness. Self-love was the vice that annihilated the moment. The only thing worse was self-hate.

She had dropped the Australian accent, returning to a natural French enunciation that Jessica would have loved. It sounded like Catherine Deneuve, the embodiment of grace and confidence. Somberg was in her own star vehicle, that of the devoted mother, helping Danny change to a Halloween costume. A cowboy outfit of jeans and leather chaps and a crimson western shirt. He had the boots and a blue bandana. Now Danny put on his hat. The straw rim frayed, the crown sat upon once or twice; the hat having withstood the rigors of cattle rustlers and horse thieves and other varmints.

As Danny was strapping on his six-shooters, Kim came through a back door. Somberg introduced him as "my special friend," but Danny paid no attention to the stranger. Somberg helped Danny tie the holster stays at his thighs. She pinned a silver star to his chest. Now Danny was a sheriff, ready to track down varmints.

Somberg had changed to a stone-colored bodysuit with a loose hooded anorak, the stylish outfit made of lambswool and cashmere, soft and warm, motherish. She sat with the sheriff on the sofa in the living room set now lit by an adorable boy ripping into his presents in a giddiness that made him glow. The more time Somberg spent with this gifted youngster, a very bright child, the more certain she was of Thatcher's death.

"Danny," she asked, as he tore at the fancy wrapping, "have you ever flown in a little jet?"

Danny paused half-a-beat. His star map of freckles glowed. "You mean like the one in *Ghostbusters*?"

"Yes, exactly," Somberg replied, laughing at his exuberance. A brilliance in the child, the way he lived in the moment. "Would you like to go flying tonight?"

"Sure! Who wouldn't?" Danny tossed glittering wrapping over his shoulder. He pulled at the darn box taped tight; his face a mixture of trouble and joy. The best presents were always hard to get into, no boy knew why that was, it just was.

"I have a little jet called *Ghostrider*," Somberg said, winking at Kim who knew Isabella was at this moment readying *Pequod* for an overseas flight. "Your mama said we could go flying tonight, if we go *before* the Halloween party."

Danny glanced up from his work. His busy hands stopped. He looked closely at Jacqueline, the way a sheriff looks close at a cool customer. This was strange. Nothing was more important than trick-or-treating. But flying in a *Ghostbuster* jet was just about as big a treat as anyone could imagine.

"We'll be back in time for the party," Somberg assured him. "After we take a tour of the stars on Halloween night!"

Danny's imagination burned merrily. There was all kinds of stuff out on Halloween night. Witches flew on brooms over the moon. And ghosts of dead people turned up where you never expected them, some of them murdered, out looking for their murderer. You'd hate to be a murderer on Halloween night, he had read stories of such things, murderers spooked out of their minds. "Really?" he said, looking hard at Jacqueline. "No joke?"

"No joke. We could fly to a castle far, far away!"

Danny laughed at this, saying castles were only in magical changing places, where pumpkins turned into golden coaches, and maids turned into princesses in high heels and pretty dresses. But Kim assured Danny that such a place existed, he had been there.

The flight was agreed upon, and as Danny pryed open his first present, Somberg had her first parental pang. She wished for a camera. She thought it a shame Jessica wasn't there to take the picture, Jessica loved to take their picture.

"Oh, my Gawd!" Danny held up a golden winged Viking helmet. The name "Eric Anderson" engraved inside. He put the horned helmet on. It slid sideways on his head. "It's alright," he assured his new best friend, patting her on the leg. "I'll grow into it."

"Yes, you will," Somberg said.

He made short work of the second gift, taking from it a sword with a jeweled hilt. He inspected the sword that was not a real sword, like the kind you use to cut off the heads of monsters, but a boy's sword, though it looked like the real thing. He tried the sword out, whacking the sofa so hard it made the bimbo girl jump, and that was fun, boys loved to make girls jump. There was more. He dug deeper into the box and came out with a round shield and a red cape. Somberg tied the cape at his neck as she told Danny the Nordic tale of the beautiful blond Viking queen, the Red Malden, who explored the unknown seas with the bravest and the strongest, Eric the Red. Together they chased dragons and that great white whale that many men would try to kill, but was still swimming in the deep. Danny asked if Eric the Red wasn't like He-Man.

"Oh, yes," Somberg assured him, playing to his speculations, whatever they were. "Eric was just like He-Man, only braver! And the amazing thing is, *you* look just like Eric when he was a boy!"

"Really?" Danny was astonished.

"Oh, I knew it the first time I laid eyes on you," Somberg said, coiling an arm around the soft, hot boy. Gazing into blue eyes that reflected her own blue eyes. Danny took off the helmet and looked at it again, his imagination transfixed, seeing a brand new dream. "You have Eric's sun-blond hair and freckles and big muscles," Somberg said. "Why, you look so much like Eric when he was a boy . . . if I didn't know better, I'd say you were Eric!"

Danny threw his arms around her and gave her a wet kiss, and the kiss surprised and astonished Somberg, struck by the affection she felt for this child. It was something she couldn't quite put her finger on. A fondness. A tenderness. The warmth of a deep maternal instinct that set off a little scramble in her chest. She recognized it as fear and wrung its neck and, having killed it, recovered herself, accepting this natural instinct like a woman.

"While exploring the seas," she continued, "Eric discovered a new country. Do you know the name of that country, Danny?"

"America!" he shouted.

"Very good!" Somberg cheered. He was such a bright boy. He knew things without knowing them; he knew things instinctively, a talent that most men lost along the way and would never recover. But what if a boy were raised in an environment where such gifts were not doomed by male standards? What if he were raised in the secrets of Ishtar? What if a boy grew up knowing God was female. What sort of man would he become? Somberg's mind flew over the moon, speculating on an opportunity she had not considered.

Now from her purse she took a pen and a business card. "This is how you write 'America.' "

Danny watched as she wrote on the back of the card:

AMERICA

"And this is how you write the name Eric."

ERIC

"Do you see the name Eric in *America* anywhere?"

Danny grabbed the pen and underlined the name.

AME<u>RIC</u>A

"That's excellent, Eric! . . . I mean, Danny!" They laughed at the mistake that was not a mistake, but was a critical element in the Thatcher kill some time in the making to make it legible to a child's mind. "Watch what happens," she said, "when we spread the letters out." She wrote the name again and added a letter.

I AM ERIC A

"Let's read that together." Their arms were wrapped around each other as they read aloud, "I am Eric A."

"What's that 'A' mean?" Danny asked.

"Eric's last name was Anderson," Somberg said.

Danny thought about this, then looked again at the name in his helmet of horns. It matched the name on an American passport in Somberg's purse, Danny's picture affixed, a picture taken by the best photographer in town, Jessica. "Not many people know that Eric the Red's real name was Eric Anderson," Somberg added, "but that's where America came from."

"Can I keep this paper?" Danny said, studying it.

"Yes, you may. And we can practice it whenever you want."

Danny stuck the card inside his helmet, put it on, held his sword high and shouted, *"I am Eric Anderson!"*

Kim applauded, Danny's new identity born in his mind, as the affection for Eric was born in Somberg's heart, as a virgin birth. She couldn't help but succumb to this beauty that was simply joy. He had an aesthetically pleasing overtone that didn't compromise her plan, but added to it, and she supposed she had been heading this way all along. The boy had the great look of love.

Danny tore into the last present. He threw the paper aside, opened the box, looked inside, his eyes went wide and he did a little jig. *"Oh, my Gawd!"* It took both hands to lift the heavy silver-plated .38 Colt revolver. "Just like the Lone Ranger!" he squealed. "Is this a *real* gun?"

"It shoots bullets," Somberg said, watching to make sure he didn't touch the hair-trigger. "But they're play bullets. They don't hurt, they just sound real."

Danny held the gun in his hands, entranced. The gun was cold, like a real gun should be. It had a wood handle. And it smelled of oil. He immediately dumped one of his toy guns, but the Colt was too big for his holster.

Somberg whispered, "Would you like to fire the gun, Eric?"

"Sure!" His eyes rolled at the thought of it. "Can I shoot it in the studio?"

"Sure. That's why I gave it to you." She stroked his smooth hair, marveling at the touch of him. He was an extraordinary child who could erect and enter life dramas as easily as other children entered dreams. When your average brat was crawling in the grass, examining bugs, perhaps eating a few, her son was in the studio learning to role-play. He was going to be perfect; she knew it.

"Eric," she said very softly, "you know how your mother loves to play shoot-'em-up." He nodded at this, enjoying the secret that was theirs and always would be and would, in this moment, change the course of both their lives. A secret that would cast a shadow far across the decades. "Would you like to shoot your mama with your new gun?"

Danny's blue eyes flashed at the idea. He grinned at Somberg, pure boy-mischief in the grin, and she smiled back with a cunning that gave no hint of the momentous thing they conspired. He was an innocent raised in a shallow, homicidal society. Violence was play. Shooting mama was play, and the boy sheriff sensed nothing menacing in the warm, fuzzy designer bodysuit he snuggled next to. He didn't know the play would be lived, and so it would be dreamed and would touch the whole system of a boy, heart, mind and soul. There were then no nightmare faces painted on the lady who smiled with him; there was only a deliciously little quiver in the air, like that which is known when making a covenant with the devil.

Danny's glance lingered in Somberg's direction. He gave a low laugh, a sneaky giggle. "Heck, yeah," he said, "Let's do it!"

"Do you think we should?"

"Oh, don't worry," Danny said, swinging the gun around, his voice dropping to a confidential tone. "My mama loves surprises."

"After we shoot your mama," Somberg turned the loaded weapon away from her. Which is to say, she turned the revolver away but not the boy who was to become a weapon. "We can go flying."

Danny couldn't wait. He set the gun down and straightened his horned helmet. Kim took his sword and shield, and Danny lifted the big gun again. "Gosh, it's heavy!" he said, laughing. He held the gun with both hands, like TV. "Okay. Where's Mom?" he shouted.

Jessica stood in the sulfurous yellow haze of the darkroom lamp. Inside the tin-can robot suit, she was coated in an oily sweat and dying to scratch her back. She rubbed against the wall, the suit chafing her shoulder blades, sweat crawling down her back like ants, when she heard them outside. They were giggling outside the door that cracked open. A thin light streamed in to show the narrow room with counters on either side, Jessica feeling like she had been standing in the middle of the dark since time immortal, and behind her, the shadowed shape of the enlargers that made the pictures. The darkroom stank of chemicals, a stench that still offended Jessica's sensibilities, never mind that pros were supposed to be immune to such things. She tried to think about the stink, so she wouldn't think about the itch she couldn't reach. It was crazy the things you'd do for your kid, but Danny would get a charge out of this, and now she powered herself up like she really was a robot, as the door swung all the way open and light ruined her vision. Danny was silhouetted in the glare. Looked like he had on a helmet of some kind. Were those horns jutting from his head? Was that a gun in his hand? And now she saw Jacqueline squatted behind him. They playing some Halloween trick.

Somberg checked her watch. The legless man was coming to take them to the party in twenty minutes, they were doing fine. Kim was in the office, dousing negatives with acid, collecting the prints Jessica had made of her. Eric was adorable strutting across the studio in his cape and boots and a Viking helmet that gleamed like his sheriff's badge. His eyes cutting through shadows, like maybe there were some icky skeletons lurking about. This was going to be the most unusual relationship; where it would lead was anyone's guess. She felt a sense of the aviator about her in the presence of the boy, something within about to fly away to a place that was clear and smooth, with a ticking steady, steady in her heart. Was this love? Whatever it was she accepted it without explanation or any further reflection other than the work that was at hand. They stopped outside the darkroom door, the developing light blinking red shadows over the boy's lovely face. She screwed rubber plugs into his ears, saying, "It's a loud gun, like the Lone Ranger's."

Danny nodded solemnly.

She cracked the door and held the baby close, using a two-handed grip over his hands, her finger on his finger on the thin trigger. With a foot she pushed the door wide open. The discovery of C-3PO came as a musical proclivity, and she saw his bright smile and felt his little coo of joy.

Somberg whispered, "Say, 'Trick or treat, C-3PO,' "

"Trick or treat, C-3PO!" Danny cried.

Jessica lurched forward. She swiveled her head. "Hel-lo, lit-tle boy," she said. "Is yo-ur na-me Dan-ny?"

"No! I'm Eric! And I have a gun!"

"Oh, de-ar. I do not like gu-ns."

Somberg whispered, "Say, 'I want a treat.' "

"I want a treat!"

"Sor-ry. I do not ha-ve any tr-eats."

Jessica took another awkward step into the light so that she shone silvery in the darkroom. She honestly felt like a robot.

Somberg felt the baby's eagerness for the violence that she calmed, whispering, "Say, 'Give me a treat or I'll do a trick.' "

"Give me a treat, C-3PO. Or I'll do a trick!"

"Ho-w a-bout a ki-ss in-stead?"

Somberg said, " 'Say, give me a treat or I'll shoot you.' "

"Give me a treat or I'll shoot you, C-3PO!"

"Ca-n't hu-rt me. I'm ma-de of ste-el!"

Danny threw his head back and laughed, and Somberg, despite herself, laughed with him. The pro in her required a solidarity. A defiance. No self betrayals. There was no room for possessiveness or sentimentality. She understood what she was about, rehearsed and visualized each stage of a job to foresee the complications. But she had not anticipated the joy of the boy now nuzzled against her, his happy laughter taking possession of her, impossible for her to escape even for an instant the spell of this beauty she now smiled upon as she whispered in his ear, "Are you ready?"

Danny nodded, and together they cocked the big hammer of the revolver. It made a distinct click that would be waiting for him in the immense panoramic window of dream that played in that thin line that separates the past from the future. A man may think he is living in the present, here and now, but that is the necessary illusion of every life, of which at least a third is lived in the fullness of dream that is a mastery of time travel. Danny the boy peered into the darkroom and saw only a robot. He felt as sublime and tranquil as his creator intended. A boy in stillness waiting for the imprint of the storm of the man's life.

The arms of the robot opened exposing the chest. "Wo-uld you li-ke a hug, Danny?" Jessica asked in broken robot cadence.

"No way!" Danny shouted. "I want a treat!"

Jessica saw Jacqueline peek around Danny, sighting the gun at her heart. Jessica in the stream of game that came to her without a breath broken, in which she smiled and staggered in her assigned role, though her heart was unbearable, beating like it was trying to escape that tin-can suit. Her heart made no sense, the gun was obviously Danny's, part of some Halloween gag he had cooked up and talked Jacqueline into. Jessica took another step into the light.

Somberg whispered, "Say, 'Good-bye.' "

"Bye-bye, C-3PO!"

The robot started laughing. "No, pl-ease!" The robot held up a hand. "Don't sho-ot!"

Jessica was looking down the black orifice of the revolver, seeing only Danny behind it, when the gun erupted in a roar. A white flame stitched the dark. She was thrown into the wall. She bounced off the wall with the roar in her head and the flame in her side. There was a coppery taste in her mouth, with her stomach rolling, like she was at sea. She took a sliding step, laughing because Danny was laughing, laughing like a loon, then she saw the surreal yellowy blood leaking from the joints of the suit. For a second there she was lost, clawing at the air, trying to keep her feet straight. That seasick feeling all over her. Staring from the eyesockets of the robot at Danny, then to the widening corsage of blood and she was ready to puke, with the burning deep in her side as something awful, when finally it came to her, Jacqueline had just shot her with her own son. It was just a thought at first, accompanied by a swoony horror that turned into a black terror crowding in around her. She reached out to Danny, pulling away. He seemed to be in a space capsule stranded in a storm, and in the middle of screaming and reaching, she fell into a panic that cut her brain off. She dropped slowly past the counter and into the dark, with that damn stink upon her, still reaching for Danny.

The robot did a jingling, shuffling death-dance, then fell face first to the floor with its arm outstretched. Lying there in the yellow dark, so still. *"Great!"* Danny hooted at the freaky outstretched hand, the fingers still fiercely reaching out for him, like the weird hand itself was alive. It was the best death ever; she made it look real. *"Do some more!"* he shouted, clapping for his mama that he had shot. *"Great! Great!"* he shouted again.

Behind the robot face, Somberg saw the eyes spool white, and as Jessica collapsed, the eyes seemed to scream in a spectacle of light, sparkling like an arc-welder's torch. Somberg could almost believe that light would go on into ages to come, so intense was that blaze of rage, that like all things mortal died in its fall. A spinning excitement came over Somberg, motherhood suddenly upon her as though by a magician's trick. But there was no time to think. ''Come, darling,'' she said, taking the revolver, leading her son from the broken robot. ''It's time to go *flying!''* She took him out the back door where Alexa and Kim waited in the warmth of the Mercedes that would sail them away like Eric the Red, into the unknown. The unmerciful lucidity of his mama's death performance replaying over and over in Danny's dreaming mind.

SECOND
MOVEMENT

9

PIT FINISHED WATERING the plants in the kitchen window, and now the kettle was whistling. He took it from the stove and poured it into the tea pot that was some kind of fancy Danish china. Her kitchen was about the nicest he had ever seen. Polished pine cabinets with fluted glass doors and imported wallpaper and a fine wood floor. The counter a green Italian marble, Pit could see his big, bald reflection in the veined surface. A kitchen to die for. Now he took the little sack of green mint tea and set it and the pot on a tray with the deep blue teacups trimmed in gold. A splash of Jack Daniel's into the cups, balanced it all on the arms of his chair, and wheeled through the house in his workout sweats, whistling the last movement of Beethoven's Seventh.

"Say, Jess!" he called. "How about a cup of tea?"

He wheeled past the laughing carousel horses riding their brass poles to the ceiling, through the living room that was a showpiece of charm that without a boy's clutter about felt like a funeral parlor, then down the gallery hall lined in pictures of Danny. Pit was just barely able to balance the tea on his chair in the face of those smiling pictures that paid homage to a beautiful spirit; nothing in this world as glorious as a happy boy! He could see the boy growing up on that wall, a couple pictures of himself there, a member of the family. He glanced into Jessica's room. The big four-poster bed a mess, sheets thrashed about. He found her in Danny's room, in a fleecy jogging suit curled in the window seat, watching a powdery March snow sift over the frozen city.

"I figured you wouldn't eat any lunch," he said, parking his chair beside her. "But a buddy of mine sent you this tea. Thought it might do us some good. Came all the way from *England!*"

She kept staring out the window from Danny's too quiet room, with eyes that were the embers of happiness. Looking at her, Pit would have thought some black sorcery had come over her; she was not the same woman; the youthfulness, the striking gorgeousness of her infectious creative passion, the incandescent vitality, the intrinsic beauty of her smile were all gone, replaced by a damn intractable sorrow. Her hair was in a bun, face sallow and sunken around shadowed eyes. She looked old and hurt old and walked old, her whole torso bandaged from the bullet that had torn through her chest. It had scarred her front and back and deep inside, killing some trusting part of her that would never live again.

"His name's Hayashi," Pit said, pouring two steaming cups. "A little white-bearded Japanese fella. Said this was some kind of *magic tea!* Drives away evil spirits, or something." He laughed, taking two tea bags from the sack, bobbing them in the cups.

Those big baby browns did not budge from staring at their sober reflection, as though they were hypnotized by the factions and themes and scenes and settings of the last months jigsawed together in those sad eyes. Four months had passed since

Danny was taken but it felt like yesterday and it seemed like forever. They had taken her watch off at the hospital, and she never put it back on. She had locked it away, along with the calendars and all the clocks, no longer counting time, no longer feeling the passage of time, but feeling each day as another ache. A thousand evocations had gone up to heaven in those days, and heaven had answered with the spectrum of fine snow sifted from the gray clouds, spooky the way it turned the blooming spring comatose, the cold snow somehow deep and meaningful to Jessica. She saw nothing else.

''I reckon we could do with some magic, so I doctored the Jap magic with a little Tennessee magic!'' Pit offered her a steaming cup of the tea that his buddy had sent express from old England. ''Hell, this stuff would knock the queen flat on her ass!''

The wind rose and Jessica watched the snow lift from the park and spin into a childlike cyclone that twisted through the jungle gym and skipped over the sandbox and whirled up the glazed walk, only to vanish like roadkill into the street. It had been there just a moment ago, a gyrating hipster, and now it was gone.

''C'mon, champ.'' Pit let the steam curl under her nose. ''You look like you haven't got the spunk of a rabbit.''

Slowly she smiled. A crimped, terrible smile that never touched his eyes. ''All right,'' she said.

Pit handed her a cup and hoisted his, toasting, ''Here's to you, kid, toughest mama I've ever known.''

Jessica sipped the tea and watched the snow fall.

Pit had been costumed as Blackbeard the pirate when he arrived to take Jessica and Danny to the Halloween party. The studio lights were on, and all was quiet. He called out and the quiet was pierced by a low mournful cry. Sounded like a prank, and since Pit loved Halloween pranks, he put on his black eye patch and three-cornered hat and wheeled through the studio making spook sounds. The scent of cordite was suspended in the air and that, he knew, was no prank. In the darkened studio his great eyes were pinpoint gleams above the Indian cheekbones, watching the shadows, moving steadfastly through the quiet with an inexplicable feeling of dread. He followed the cordite stench to the darkroom. It was pitch black except for the sickly yellow light. Jessica was sprawled on the floor in the robot costume in a pool of surreal black blood. Pit threw himself down, ripping at the damn tin can costume slick with her blood, fighting the inertia of grief and panic rolling through him, heart in his mouth as he cried out to God! Her face and hands were moonstone. Eyes rolled up in her head, already glazed. A moan, an awful basso sound came not from his voice but brought up from the lungs and he breathed life back into her, calling her from laughing images of Danny and Jacqueline spinning about her head, shooting her over and over again in the blurry preambles of death.

When Jessica awoke in the recovery room, she was told the bullet aimed at her heart had hit its mark but had struck a steel-reinforced crest where the robot breastplate molded into the shape of a muscled chest. The bullet was deflected down, mushrooming as it tumbled through her ribs. They had cut the flattened lead slug from her back. There was a sharp stab in her left side every time she took a breath. The doctor said the pain would subside in a few weeks. She asked for Danny. Pit held her hands and told her, and Jessica soon learned the doctor was wrong. The pain never ended.

It was an insidious murder attempt even by Chicago standards, and the story was front-page news. An impassioned search began for Danny. In the first week they learned Sony was not seeking a new Sony Boy and had never heard of Chimera Enterprises. The police dusted for prints and checked what they found against anyone who had been in the studio, but there were no outstanding prints. The photographs that had been taken of Sterling were missing, and all of Jessica's negatives were destroyed. An artist friend of Pit's, a gray oldtimer named Boz who knew a thing or two about oppressed spirits, worked up a composite sketch of Sterling and the police ran a check. They found a trail of credit card charges and phone records that led in a dozen different directions. The mailing address for Chimera in New York turned out to be a drop box, and the offices in Australia were only a secretarial service.

Pit made a trip to Sydney while Jessica was still in the hospital. He hired a private detective there and another in Chicago. The men worked through a long tangle of addresses and identities, spending all of Jessica's savings, then all of Pit's. They found only what they were intended to find. It appeared Danny had vanished into the mystery of the Orient.

To Jessica, it was as if Danny were dead. The sadness and longing were the same, and the emptiness was the same; only the grief never ended, because hope never ended. She was obsessed with finding him and she knew she would remain obsessed until he was recovered, and she hated the obsession the way a drowning woman hates the sea. She prayed and waited for an answer every day to her prayers, sitting still inside herself, fighting the small gap of not-remembering that had already begun, and that was the most awful part of all. It was terrifying, sheer tyranny, the way a boy's fresh-faced smile began to diminish in the disorder of her lost days. Jessica fought against it, but Danny was fading as some photograph left in a window of sun that over time will dull and discolor until it is all but washed out. She blocked out the fading by concentrating on the inconsequential, the little things that were Danny: the slight curl of his lips when he was plotting something sneaky, the dusting of his freckles and the way his nose wrinkled at a serving of peas, the sweet and direct way he looked at you when he wanted something—pleading only with the eyes, his marvelous glow when he finished a Lego project, the pursed lips when concentrating on a painting, the steady, smooth, slow stroke of his hand as he learned cursive. These things that only she knew were replayed in introspective close-up. And still he faded and she could not stop the fading. He had vanished in a gun flash, leaving only memory that continued to dissolve day by day.

The savagery of time inspired a narcotic that infiltrated the dwindling memories so that the lovely face of a boy was replaced with that of a bone-white killing face whose dull eyes saw only the bitch who had taken her son. The brain of this killing face was that of an animal that had been wounded, and the animal knew that the bitch had made one mistake: it had left the animal alive. Some animals work in obscurity in their stalking that requires no explanation to the mind or the heart that does not know time. Time had been put away and the animal, drugged-out on fury, roughed-up by death, would use the time to become as savage as time.

She held off the animal with belief, with a hope that like the boy, was seemingly drawing further away with every passing day. It was as if she were standing at the edge of some high cliff where the light of the sun stopped and there was only darkness beyond. She waited there. And still there was no sign of him.

"I reckon it's time to call Godfrey what's his name," Pit said, pouring more tea. "You know, that private eye in Sydney."

Jessica stared into the dim whiteness the snow had made of spring. "He called yesterday," she said to the everlasting white. "It's the same old story. He hasn't found a thing."

Pit's forehead wrinkled to the top of his shiny dome; he had hoped for a break somewhere. But there was none forthcoming, and Jessica remained anchored in suffering and despair, seemingly unable to move. Arms wrapped around her knees pulled up to her chin, eyes staring into nothingness. He'd be damned if he'd let her go down this way. He sat in his chair peacefully biding his time, with a bumper crop of hope. He knew better than to rush hope that was a lovely thing, but if you reached sudden for it, why, it'd vanish into the blue. He listened to a little flute playing in his head, the tiny tune a mighty force against the darkness. He waited some more, sipping magic tea, then said, "Don't s'pose you've heard anything from the Child Find folks?"

"They say his photo is 'in circulation.' He may show up on a billboard. A highway toll ticket. A grocery bag. No telling how they'll use his picture. His picture . . ." She groaned and shook her head. "How ironic; my son has been reduced to a *photograph.*"

Pit swallowed hard at that. He glanced around Danny's room, walls as blue as a summer pond hung with Monet's *Water Lilies* and Danny's reproductions. But the pages on his easel were now blank, watercolors cracked and dry. Lego cities stood unaltered on the dresser. Giants cap limp on the bed. A *Star Wars* bedspread lay like a flag over a coffin, not a wrinkle in it. The red, yellow, and blue cars Jessica had picked up in England sat on the desk in the very spot where the boy had left them. Everything just as he left it, as if he might walk in the door any minute.

Pit reached over and gave Jessica's hand a squeeze. "We're going to find him," he said.

She couldn't face him. She turned away and stared at the pale reflection in the window. "I did it," she said to the reflection.

"Hoo boy, don't start that again!"

"I did. I let the bitch into our life."

"Oh, hell. That's bullshit and you know it."

"No." Jessica closed her eyes as if at a bite of pain. "I never checked her out. I should have checked out her company. It's my fault."

"Jess"—he shook a big finger—"should-haves and could-haves ain't gonna find our boy." He scolded her as only he could, a man who had cooked for her and made her eat and made her stay clean and neat and tight and together. Pit would not let her fall apart. He cared for her as he had cared for Danny, and it was never easy, her depression like a damn quicksand. If he got too close, he'd slip down into it himself. Still, he stayed with her. "We gotta keep *believing,*" Pit insisted.

Jessica returned to the window and saw herself standing in the street. Snow flying. As if all of Chicago were snowed in to the roofs. No way out. The horizon so dark and blurred with snow she couldn't make out where she was or where she had been or where she was going. "I neglected him," she whispered to the snow.

"How's that?"

Jessica bowed her head. "I lost him before he was taken," she said. "I traded my son for a portfolio of goddamn photographs."

Pit set his tea down. He swelled himself up. The little flute swelled him; it filled him up. "Don't do this, Jess."

"Is this my punishment?" she asked the cold.

"Punishment? For what?"

"For too many nights working? Too many weekends working? Too many holidays working? And for what? For my fucking *career!*" She was shouting, but she didn't hear herself in the snow, nor did she see the tears in her eyes as she floundered on. "I'm afraid," she confessed to the ghostly woman in the snow. "I was *never* afraid before. Not afraid of anything! But now I'm afraid of the dark and of being alone and I'm afraid to remember. It's like Danny never existed, because I'm not strong enough to remember. I put his pictures away so I won't remember and so I won't go nuts, but at night I bring them out and hang them again because I can't help but remember. Then the damn dreams come."

Pit rested a callused palm on the heat of her neck. He lowered his eyes and listened. It was all he could do.

"The dreams are so bad I'm afraid to go to sleep, so I lie awake, and when I finally fall asleep, I invariably wake in the middle of the night, afraid I'll never find him, and then afraid of what I will find. Imagine that. Imagine what we will find."

"No." Pit shook his head, saying, "No. No. No. We're going to find him and he'll be fine, because you raised him to be fine, and when we find him, it'll be good-bye Charlie to the blues!" He was holding her so tight he was afraid she'd break. It was a fear he had had for months, especially through Christmas. She had been a Scrooge, fleeing from the lights and carols, hiding in her work. Pit knew the hell brewing in her, rather than bury it, he helped bring it out. Gave her a .38 Smith & Wesson for Christmas. They had spent the holidays at the Pickwick Gun Club, Jessica learning to use a gun that was like a camera, required a steady hand and a good aim. She stood on the firing line in goggles, and pulverized one Sterling sketch after another, hearing that automatic ringing in her ears. It rang like Christmas bells! She loved the silvery sound of the bells and kept returning to the range until she was a marksman, always targeting the sketch of the woman whose true name she could not know but whose face she would never forget. And as she shot her face to pieces, she let herself remember what a fool she had been, having seen Sterling as some mentor for her future.

"In the mornings I can't get out of bed," she confessed. "I make myself go to work, and when I work I can't stop working."

"I know," Pit said. "I know."

"I'll talk about anything besides *him*," she added, in a cold strain, "I can't talk about him, but I can't stop thinking about him, you know?" Pit nodded, watching tears fill her eyes. "I can't walk by this room without having a seizure." She looked around, as if only now realizing where she was. "Maybe I should close his door. I guess that makes sense. Just close his door. But I *can't!* I can't close Danny's door! So I sit and wait . . . for what?"

Now something frantic broke inside her and the tears came. She wept nakedly, silently, sobbing with convulsions before the soulless heavens that had taken her son. She would give her life for one hug from him. To hold him. To kiss him. To just sit and listen to him. The scalding tears flowed down her cheeks and down her heart, and she knew she was very near a breakdown. But after a good long, hard cry, she began to settle and find something solid within in her and it was like iron. It had grown up since Danny was taken and she knew that iron part of her would not quit. She took a deep breath and the frantic scramble in her chest subsided. *You're okay. You're going to make it.* It was a voice known only to her ears and Jessica had come to recognize it as the true voice of herself never heard before. The voice coaxed her back from the edge of breakdown; the iron within grew a little bit stronger.

She wiped her eyes with her wrist and looked up at Pit with her face smeared with tears. "What am I supposed to do?" she said with fight in her voice, defying the cringing part of her. "I can't sit and do nothing. If I do nothing, nothing will happen. We've got to *do* something! Something besides believe."

Pit let her stew. Looking right at him with tears streaming down her lovely face, and he let her stew, while he sat listening to the little flute of hope found in Beethoven's Seventh.

The pain throbbed in silence in the pounding of Pit's heart. Jessica had never seen him naked, though he had seen her intense nakedness for months, and sitting there before her pain, he felt as if his pain were clothed in nothing more than a banana leaf. The body of his pain was muscled and golden colored as those who live by the sea, and it wore the bracelet of a Roman gladiator on its wrist, and from its iron neck that could not be broken hung a medal but it was not of a saint. And now he told her what he had hid from her, telling her not as confession, but to help her see her own destiny in the many years that made his pain that stood bare before her, motionless, with nothing to hide.

He had married in a carnival atmosphere, and there was a hint of catastrophe in the beginning. He was not allowed to invite her father to the wedding; he had been gone from her life many years and she thought that he did not love her. And besides, a knot of tears would swell up in her mother's throat if her father was so much as remotely mentioned, and she didn't know what he had done to her mother. So her father was not invited to the wedding and Pit married into a wealthy, politically influential Texas family. Pit was himself a self-made man, by the time the marriage ended seven years later, he had a million. It would not be near enough.

She fled, whether from Pit or to her mother depended on who was telling the story. Her mother was made of a shivering terror. All of her sons and daughters worked in the family business and lived within blocks of her home and she owned the mortgage on each of their houses and gave them each a new car every year. The only child not within mother's reach was the daughter who started her own business and moved away and then married Pit who helped her get in touch with her father. He turned out to be a swell guy and met his daughter with uncontrolled excitement. After that, mother would not speak to her daughter, nor would any of the rest of the family, and the marriage was now in a funeral taxi but Pit saw only the immense sky and the dreams that could be sailed upon it.

They had a son, Jake, and before she left for mother's in postpartum depression, they had Susan, a one-week old daughter. Pit was invited to come see his kids who he thought were all on holiday at mother's. He was met on mother's drive by a guard who leveled a shotgun in his face and told him to "Get." That was the first news of divorce, a shotgun in the face. The family chose the language of violence; it was their formal clothing, they wore it on only special occasions; it was not in their coat of arms, or embroidered on their breast pocket, they brought it out only at the wall of war sirens. A war begun in intimidation can never be resolved in any force less than the intimidation. A family that speaks violence can only be spoken to with an equivalent force, but Pit, dazzled, stupefied by events, turned to the law.

The case was given to a judge fathers called "the Butcher." His court was known as "the Slaughterhouse." "No father has the guts to kill me," the Butcher said in a newspaper story some weeks before Pit's divorce began. Pit and his family were accused of being crazy; they were all dangerous and none of them should be allowed to see the children, mother's attorneys contested on the behalf of Pit's estranged wife. The Butcher honored the absurd charge and Pit had to prove himself sane, and already he felt that he was walking through hell.

After three months and testimony from three shrinks, the Butcher allowed Pit a visit with Jake. The four-year old arrived on Thanksgiving. He had diarrhea. Someone had fed him so many sweets he couldn't hold down food; it ran out his ass. Jake stayed overnight at the home of Pit's mother and the next day Pit's wife picked the boy up in mother's limousine that drove immediately to the hospital where a doctor performed a rectal exam while Jake was held screaming to a cold steel table by his mother. The boy's ass was inflamed. The next day Pit was summoned to the Slaughterhouse and charged with fucking his son. A business as contrived and as premeditated and as cold-blooded as any murder using a child. Now Pit learned from his father-in-law that this was why he gave up his kids, a similar false charge had been leveled at him.

Now Jake was sent to shrinks, and the boy single-handedly beat the heinous false charge, while Pit contemplated the purchase of a shotgun. Instead, he bought a law: House Bill no. 617 had been in committee for years; it gave all parents, regardless of gender, the right to share in the custody of their children. A lobbyist was hired. Contributions arranged. The bill miraculously popped out of committee and was passed into law in the nick of time. Pit was sailing in the sky, the lights blazed on every deck of his ship of dreams! He arranged for his attorney to be on a radio show to promote the new law. A newspaper story featured the attorney in a piece about the new equality. Love would win over violence. Day of the trail, the attorney arrived at the Slaughterhouse saying he "forgot" to file for joint custody. He "forgot" to request a jury so the case would be heard by the Butcher. He "forgot" to file for false sex abuse. Pit, sawed off at the butt, lost Jake and Susan, and the little that remained of his estate. The shotgun beckoned.

In marriage, Pit and Jake were as palm trees and a sugar beech; their love was beautiful. Love slipped into a coma in the divorce. In the visitation erratically honored by Jake's mother, love became a kind of hallucination. On a Saturday at a

Burger King in the middle of lunch Jake said to Pit: "You're not my real daddy. My real daddy is dead. You're just my friend." The boy repeated the lines as though he were a living creature inhabited by a ghost. Then Jake wept. He had terrible misgivings about what he said, didn't understand why he had said it; he was compelled. Pit's heart sank for the boy, his soul longed for a shotgun. He felt something like a man in an elevator that has jolted to a halt; he could wait, in which case he would likely disintegrate, or he could escape. He asked Jake if he would like to go away on a long trip. With tears in his eyes, Jake begged to go. It was a trumpet call, and Pit did not hesitate to his answer.

Pit took Jake to London to a shrink who said the child had been brainwashed. It was an amazing case of hypnotized and dream invention and the shrink filed a clinical report with the *Journal of the American Medical Association.* Father and son stayed away until the boy could put flowers on the grave of dead dreams that no longer touched him. Sea gulls flew on an immense sky of hope and words could no more describe the love of these two than the Sears Tower could touch the sky. Pit couldn't keep Jake from his sister, and when he was healed, they returned to Texas.

Jake was taken away; Pit was locked in the aggravated tank, "Gladiator School." The Butcher appointed Pit an attorney paid for by Pit's ex–in–laws, an arrangement unique to Texas. The attorney met Pit in a visitor's cell. He came with a deal. Pit was to sign a termination of his parental rights and he would walk. If Pit didn't sign, he promised hellfire and damnation: prison. The document was before Pit in a carrier that slid back to the waiting attorney. Pit rose to sign. He left the ballpoint and ripped open the velcro front of the white monkey suit they had put him in. He pulled out his big johnson and pissed on their deal. The black type slurred and ran in a yellowy puddle of piss. Pit shook his manhood onto the termination, then sent it back to the attorney who stared at Pit like he had come from some other planet, a place where men don't give up their kids. Pit gave him the heat of his eyes, then fired the sucker. He rang for the guard, escorted back to his cell, Pit was the only free man in that jail.

Bused to Huntsville, the penitentiary processing center, Pit was called to the captain's office. A barrel-bellied man, looking mighty smart in his starched gray uniform, gut nearly busting out. Looked like a steak gut. Prime cut. No fat on prime cut, except that crinkly little ring around the outside. "We got a call about you," the Captain said in a twangy South Texas drawl. "We was asked to make sure you received"—he paused to deliver a big shaggy grin—"a *warm welcome.*" The Captain rolled back in his chair and watching as the father swallowed his greeting. Pit felt nothing. Not fear, not jubilation. He knew only a strange certain assurance that he recognized as that of a man on a journey.

He was transferred to Ramsey. Like Alcatraz in its time, Ramsey had its share of national figures. Folklore. Legend. Freakish celebrity. The masterworks of personality phenomena kept there in the way one might display a collection of Fabergé eggs under glass so they could be admired together. There were twenty-two inmate murders in Texas that year, eighteen in Ramsey. A vast slab of darkness. In the darkness Ambrose waited. Flaccid, about forty, the close cropped hair thick and graying at the temples; eyelids as pale as the butcher paper on which he sketched as Pit entered his cell, arms full of sheets and mattress and toiletries. The eyes of

Ambrose were sunken into the shadowed sockets of a colorless face that was bloated, gray, mushy; the once hardened killer looked like dog food left in the rain. The sliding door rumbled close behind Pit in an insidious crescendo that echoed through the darkness. Lock-up. The assurance of it gives parents peace when tucking their children into bed, reading a bedtime story, saying prayers, a hug and a sloppy good-night kiss. It was inconceivable to Pit that he would know lock-up for these crimes. He had a sense that everything he had ever believed in was turned upside-down, cascading in tiny flakes over Ambrose's prison cell, like one of those children's snowscape paperweights.

The mind of Ambrose was eaten away, as those holes in a bullet-riddled wall of some inglorious battle. A killer abandoned to himself; he had lived alone in Ramsey for fourteen years, this though there were 32,000 violent felons waiting for a prison bed. Ambrose was a one of a kind. As was Pit, to receive not just a prison bed, but to be given the bunk above Ambrose.

Ambrose's splendid voice, languid, melodious, was compliments of his "happy pills" that kept him from crashing the bars. The day after Pit arrived, Ambrose was taken off the pills. Pit was used in the cabbage fields, hands sacrificed, they bled perpetually. At night Pit lay awake listening to Ambrose shriek at millstone-gray brick walls, as though discovering them for the first time, and it seemed that Ambrose was yelling for Pit. Only now, in a loony bin, was Pit beginning to see in the darkness. He, like Ambrose taken off his pills, was predictable. No one doubted Pit's commitment to his children, they were counting on him to spend everything he had in divorce. Confronted with "Daddy is dead," Pit would leave with the boy, and Pit, the good father who could not deny his son his sister, would return. Then the law that he had passed, that was amended to increase the penalty for violating a custody order, would be used to execute him. In love, Pit had followed his heart straight to Ramsey where hypnotic suggestion was to be translated into truth: Daddy is dead.

Pit was sleeping when Ambrose came in the middle of the third night. Pit heard hooks knocked from an army trunk to the floor. He saw a blur in the night, Ambrose climbing for the top bunk. Pit, in a sheet, was wrapped like a mummy when the killer landed on him in an attack that was not Ambrose. The razor blade bearing down for Pit's windpipe was not Ambrose. The shrieking in his face was not Ambrose. Ambrose was Texas. Ambrose was the family that held Pit's kids. A psycho in the night, no more an accident than the divorce itself, with all its fancy touches. The size and strength of Pit was useless trapped in that sheet. He wanted to rise and could not. He tried to move his arms and could not. He could not so much as turn his head, but try as he might, bearing down with all his weight in his arm, his lips trembling, the edges of his nostrils inflamed and rabbity, Ambrose out of his mind for his happy pills could not cut Pit's throat; his iron hand at Ambrose's wrist. Everything, everything, very real, though in night's black and white where Pit was alone struggling against the state.

Somehow he got a leg under the bastard and launched him into the wall. In what followed, Pit lost the sight in one eye. The eye still pretty, but behind the eye blood vessels were ruptured, his head bashed into the bars, bashed over and over until his head was ringing with the bashing. The blood roaring and beating in Pit's head like the sound of a storm, fighting off a black light that wanted to take him down, swinging blind. Now to open his eyes and find Ambrose sprawled on his trunk, an apathetic pudding, heaving for breath. And it was over, Pit's three-minute dance with the devil. But it was nothing, really. Not a soul in the world gave a damn about what happened in that prison. That slaughterhouse.

The next day, when word was out that Pit had survived, his ex–in-laws rushed to the Slaughterhouse to take possession of Pit's computer. It held a diary, a book that told the hypnotic story. The state, now party to attempted murder, took possession of the computer. The book was not to be published, a father not allowed to rise again. Pit, caught in rage, but with no power, was to be made as purposeless as Ambrose who could not escape his pain.

It was this realization that saved Pit's soul: *pain was the killer.* His first readers were the State of Texas and the family that feared him. After Ramsey, Pit did not buy the shotgun that everyone expected; he bought a computer. He swore himself to the story that would be written with the authority of a shotgun.

He worked in a bookstore among the spirits of authors and the readers, his teachers, who knew what they wanted in a good book. He wrote with the knowledge that the odds of success were like a moonshot, the love of his children so distant, they might as well be on the moon. He wrote for nine years; he could paper the walls of his boarding house room with the rejections: 267 rejections. He wrote in anger paid-for in advance, so the book did not have to pay for it. He wrote with hate. Later, he learned to write with love. He wrote in the magic of beauty that exists in those things we love. He wrote laughing and he wrote crying.

As he wrote, he found his war was not about his children. It was about the making of an independent woman. His wife had made herself, Pit only helped, but she could not stand against mother. She was given a house across the street from mother, and neighbors recognized the child. She had a been a professional, a lithe, free women who had her own business. Returned to the family, her will was fatted into a cow; a safe, demure homebody injected with the gooey shameless steroids of the neurotic and happily beaten. Pit had come to ruin helping make her independence that she gave away, and he would breathe it as fire into any woman with a wanting. This was his revenge. The sharp knife is not dangerous; it is a beauty that the hand respects. It is the dull knife that will cut when a man least expects it. The independent woman is not dangerous, she is the beauty that the hand respects. To this end, Pit wrote.

He had a talent for provoking people, and once accepted, he provoked his publisher who tried to terminate the book that was never to be published. Pit fought off the termination as he fought Ambrose, the best way he could. Author and publisher later patched things up and overcame the irrelevant to find the story which was in the pain, the book soon to be published. Together the woman Pit loved, the law, the state, the psycho killer, and his publisher, made of him a burning bush, and he would never be extinguished.

"I know your hurt, Jess," Pit said, choking back a sob that split her heart. "By God, I do. It's an endless, stupid, grinning ache that goes on and on into a powerful lonesomeness."

The magnitude of this personal history was nearly more than Jessica could comprehend. She had been loud and difficult and sad and impossible, and she did not believe she could be shocked, not by a man. But it seemed Pit had been more of a woman than she had; he had a woman's sacrificial love for children and a woman's pain, and it seemed their emotions were interchangeable. Or maybe pain, like love, was no respecter of gender.

She was drawn from the madness of herself into the creation of the love of a vulnerable man, and as she left the boundaries of herself, telling him how sorry she was for him, telling him that she loved him, embracing him, she was freed from her pain.

"How in God's name did you ever get through all that?"

"Well, I'll tell you," he said, his voice rising as a fighter lifting himself from the canvas. "You got to be better than the worst thing that happens to you."

"I like that," she said, now listening with all her heart. "How do you do that? How do you become that?"

"I had a hell of a time," he replied, "one hell of a time getting there. First thing you gotta know is, we all go down on the floor. Pounded and broken. The going down doesn't make you, heavens, who hasn't been beaten? It's the getting up that makes you. And you're at your best right after you get up."

Jessica thought about that a second. "Okay," she said, brightening. "So, you have to get up."

"Like you're doing right now."

She laughed at that. "Okay," she said, nodding.

"To be better than the worst thing, you gotta find something better than the worst thing. Find it and use it. That's what the best things are for, to be *used*. Books are good that way, you can learn all kind of things from books. But I reckon a book won't do much for you when you're ready to die from miserableness."

"You don't feel like reading," she said.

"Not if you're a-blubbering. And not if anger is gnawing on you. I know all about anger, I've had the brain-fever. No telling but I might come to be a murderer, if it weren't for this." From the pocket of his chair, he pulled out a copy of *Moby Dick*. That was for him, he set it aside, to pass on a gift to Jessica.

The gift was in silvery paper, with a purple bow. Jessica knew Pit hadn't done it himself, the wrapping was lovely. She gave a little smile and, uncorking a breath, opened it. She found a set of CDs, the complete symphonies of Beethoven, all nine of them. She uncoiled in the window with the snow behind her. "The Cleveland Orchestra," she said, reading the cover.

"Yes, ma'am, they're about the finest there is. They're the reason there is a Cleveland."

"Really? I never knew that." She laughed lightly, and it was not easy, she had become a stranger to laughing.

"You'll find Kingdom Come in that box. So many splendors," Pit said grinning. "My favorite is the Sixth. God in heaven, what a lovely thing it is! How Beethoven must have hurt to have found it. It's a soothing for the savage. A fella can be plumb loco, ranting and carrying on, and the Sixth will settle him down easy. It'll lift you out of the royal mess of your life, troubles gone and you won't have the foggiest notion where they've gone to. The sweet peace coming right out of the blue."

"The Sixth." Jessica found the disc. She saw her silvery, shiny reflection in it. "I'll try it."

"Well, you should. But you may want to save it till after we find Danny. What you need just now is the Seventh."

"The Seventh?" she said, puzzled.

"You bet. It's all *hero*. The Seventh is built round a little flute of hope, as sweet as a child. You'll hear it early on—about three minutes into the piece—a rhythmic tune coming back to you time and again, through all kinds of darkness, but nothing can beat down that little tune. Turns into such an energy! How it'll cheer you up. The Seventh is *empowerment!* The symphony that made Beethoven, folks never forgot him after the Seventh."

Pit watched her smile and redden up real sweet to the gift. "Thank you," she sighed and kissed his baby smooth cheek. "You are the best."

"Listen, honey," he said, very still, holding her hands as he held her eyes. "You don't know what's bottled up in me. You can't imagine. A passel of fools, I suspect."

"No way," she snapped.

"Oh, yeah. Why, I've become a lawbreaker for my son. Locked up with the deadbeats. Only to become a damn fraud, nobody really knew who I was. How my soul has screamed and courted the sky! But that's love for you. It doesn't give a damn about laws or your lost pride or your humiliation; it gives and keeps on giving, and it will run you to ground. In love you don't count by what you've gained or lost, or even by what is given—you can't expect a thing for that. Living in love is the whole yarn; it is the beginning and the end. Love doesn't loaf or grunt or whine about, it keeps looking for ways to express itself, and if a man is lucky, despite all his jackass ways, he just might find the great, good peace."

Sitting before him, Jessica saw him perhaps for the first time, as a man fighting for a toehold in a better world. And she had never been more proud of a man, her heart swelled with love.

"Not many folks have time for a whole symphony every day," he said, taking up the box of discs and looking them over like he had never seen them before. "So begin with the first or last movement of the Seventh, do it *every* morning for a couple of weeks, then move on to another movement. Let it soak in. You want it in your blood. Let it storm right along, and it'll carry you out of the woods. I suppose I should know," he said, and gave her a wink, and then passed her the box that had a whole world of sparks in it.

Jessica now knew Pit beyond the normal distrusting bounds of man and woman. It was through the agency of Sterling's appalling actions, the murder contrived with Jessica's son, that an eminence was transmitted and received in the stillness of their eyes.

"My tale is betwixt me and those forces of evil in Texas that believe they are good," Pit said, giving her a keepsake clasp on the thigh. "It's nothing that the truth can't work out. But what matters now is *Danny*. We don't have to just sit and wait. We're gonna do something! And I don't want to ever again hear you use that egg-sucking word, *can't*. You hear?"

"Yes, sir!"

"Now, I've been chewing on a couple ideas, long shots, but I figure it's time to trot 'em out.'' Pit sat up taller in his chair as he announced, ''I'm gonna enroll that bitch in Child Find.''

''Enroll her?'' Jessica frowned. ''I don't understand.''

''They'll publicize a missing spouse, won't they?''

''I think so. Yes.''

''Fine! I got a missing spouse. My pal Boz can print me up a fine-looking marriage certificate!''

A second or two passed before Jessica caught on. Pit would claim Sterling as his wife. The idea staggered her, Sterling and Pit married. In marriage you become one, till death do you part. And wasn't it against the law to dummy up a marriage certificate? How far would he go for Danny?

Pit only grinned and looked at her with untamed eyes. ''I'll just give that bitch a name. . . .'' He gazed into his cup of magic tea. ''Think I'll call her Peggy. Peggy Sue Martin!''

Jessica swiveled out of the window seat, wincing in pain, but smiling through the pain. ''You're really going to do this? Tell them Sterling is your wife?''

''You betcha! And I'll act real sorrowful about it, too. Why, I might even oblige 'em with some tears. And after I do a little boo-hooing, then I'll fix 'em up with a bunch of sketches. I'll tell 'em our house burned and we lost all our pictures. And then, by God, we'll have that bitch's face plastered all over creation!''

''That's great!'' Jessica cheered.

''And that's not all. I got something for you to do.''

''What?'' She couldn't imagine what he had cooked up.

''You're going to London next week, right?''

She shook her head. ''Jaguar wants me to come,'' she said. ''But I'm going to cancel.''

''Wrong,'' Pit barked. ''You're going to London, hotshot.''

''But I can't leave while Danny is—''

''What did you say?'' Pit roared. ''I didn't hear that loser word, *can't,* did I?''

Jessica grinned beautifully. The snow was still falling but she didn't notice and no longer felt as if all heaven had plotted against her, that was now reversed in Pit's insatiable optimism.

''Nah,'' he said, ''that must be the cold wind whistling *can't.*'' He gave her his loving eyes and softly but firmly said, ''That loser word doesn't exist for Danny.''

She nodded, biting her lips, suddenly struggling with tears.

''Now, I got a pal over there in London,'' Pit continued. ''He's the one that sent us this tea. Akira Hayashi. He and my dad fought against each other in World War II. Hayashi was part of that godawful Bataan Death March that led to an imprisonment worse than death. Ol' Hayashi stood guard over my dad and, eventually, they became pals. Dad taught him English, taught him how to read and write, and after the war Hayashi escaped his life. He became a forensic scientist for Scotland Yard—you understand, Hayashi got to know Death intimately in Bataan. He and Dad stayed pals; they used to vacation together. Hayashi taught me how to swim! That was in Maui, long time ago. Anyway, I believe he'll help you, Jess. I want you to drop in on him when you're over there in London.''

''And do what?''

"Well, hell!" Pit threw his hands up. "Do lunch."

"Uh-huh."

"Then ask him to run Sterling's sketch on his computer."

"His computer?"

"Good God, all those Scotland Yard types have computers; everybody knows that! Haven't you ever been to the movies? I figure we've done about all *we* can do. And them private dicks don't know their head from their ass. Might as well give this a try. I wrote Hayashi, told him you're coming. That's why he sent this magic tea. Isn't it fine," he said, taking a sip.

She sat there indecisively, her smile a little less certain, the cold seeping in from the window, chilling her small hope.

"Here," he said, picking up her Nikes, dropping them on her lap. "Put these on. We're going for a jog-spin. Best medicine for desperation is *exercise!*"

"Pit," she whined. "It's snowing out there. I can't—"

He had started for the door but now, at the sound of that word, spun around with a glare.

"I'll be ready in a few minutes," she recanted quickly.

"Fine," he said. "We'll have a good time in the cold. That snow is your friend, Jess; it'll make you feel *alive!* Then tonight you can start listening to the Seventh." He wheeled away calling, "I'm going for my coat and cap and that tartan muffler you gave me for Christmas. It'll look great, streaming out in the wind!"

10

THE ELEMENTARY SCHOOL was integrity. Celebrating its one-hundredth anniversary, the school was the root of respectability and restraint in the quiet English town of Grantham. The school had the town's fastidious, bored look. It didn't lean or slump but stood stone-erect on the crest of a conservative hill. A school of rules, that's what Somberg liked best about it; you could count on rules. Rules do not change. The school taught lessons of control against impulse. Of self-silence for girls. A kind of foot-binding that restrained a girl's strength. The austere face of the school did not recognize the liquidity of hip movement or a come-on smile or flimsy skirts or lavish intelligence. The school was comfy. It was safe. It exercised a kind of pull. The young and beautiful were to accept the captivity of the school. The close observer mastered it all; Somberg saw the school as the garden gate to the town of Grantham, a marvel of survival, at her fingertips.

Room 101 had high plaster walls painted Pink around the Rosey which went nicely with the faded blackboards and frosted domed light fixtures. The tall and airy windows shone on the wide oak floorboards fastened with dowels. On rainy days the floor sighed and muttered to itself with memories of children past. There were three rows of six school desks notched with inkwells; it was said that little Maggie Thatcher had learned her ABCs at one of those desks. Her class's shell collection was still on the shelf above the radiator, and the table in the back still held the

Bakelite wireless that had broadcast dear old Winston Churchill in his famous declaration on the thirteenth of May, not so very long ago: "I have nothing to offer but blood, toil, tears and sweat." These words became the unwritten motto of the school.

The old school was the wearing down and winnowing away of the individual girl into the harmless resilience of the Grantham girl. It was within the precious paradise of a struggle against tyranny that Maggie heard the drum roll of freedom that was not a force of the school or the town, but was found in an England set ablaze by Adolf Hitler. On the table you could almost hear the Bakelite crackle again with the fire of a bulldog warrior, none other than Churchill gave the girl the charge for open conflict: "We shall go on to the end, we shall fight in France, we shall fight on the seas and the oceans, we shall fight with growing confidence and growing strength in the air, we shall defend our island, whatever the cost may be, we shall fight on the beaches, we shall fight on the landing grounds, we shall fight in the fields and in the streets, we shall fight in the hills; we shall never surrender." The words became a girl's battle hymn; as they are for all little people, for whales, and all parents pitted against great odds.

The Bakelite was the voice of history, but the most unique feature about Room 101 was not its history but its glossy young teacher. Had Kea Chieng been as seasoned as her classroom, Somberg would have chosen another site.

She was not much taller then her students, one of the reasons they loved her so. The children loved to touch her soft afro that framed her small, round, forgiving face. Kea had taken her degree at Regent's College but, unable to find a position in London, went a hundred miles north to Grantham. At first she thought she'd die of boredom. A mass lethargy seemed to grip the town. Grantham was a place of impeccable uneventfulness. But after three years, Kea had come to love the quiet life and the noisy children and the old classroom she painted and made her room, though she still spent weekends in London. Nothing exciting ever happened in Grantham.

The pink was to inspire the children; Kea's favorite color was blue, and she was in a blue jumper now, at her desk, talking to her newest pupil. A sweet American boy, pale as the winter months in his gray uniform. There was a lost look about the child. It was somewhere in his eyes. In the way he fidgeted with his hands. In the way he stuttered as he talked about the coming bake sale.

"I made a c-c-c-cake once," he said in stuttering excitement. "I learned to c-c-crack eggs and everything."

"Cracking eggs is a hard job," Kea said.

"We made a *pi-pi-rate ship cake!*"

"Oh, my!" Kea grinned; the boy was such a delight. A real entertainer. "When you say 'we,' you mean you and your mother?"

"Uh, yeah. . . ." A look of puzzled dimness came into the boy's gorgeous blue eyes. "And I think a pi-pi-pirate helped make the c-c-cake. His name was Blackbeard! A f-f-funny guy in a wheelchair. Real strong and real nice."

"How lovely. But we won't be decorating cakes today, Eric."

"I know. That'll be another d-d-day."

"Today we're going to learn how to *bake* a cake. Would you like to crack the eggs for us?"

"Sh-sh-sure thing!"

Kea glanced across the room to Eric's mother helping with the history lesson. Linda Anderson had been coming every noon since Eric had registered in January. She gave selflessly of her time, and the children loved her. She had quite a way with children. A natural beauty, blond and blue-eyed, in a cowl-neck sweater and stirrup leggings. The heather gray color right on target, like a school uniform.

Kea found Linda Anderson surprisingly considerate for an American. She was relaxed and unpretentious. She loved flowers and brought arrangements every day, her most recent contribution a teddy bear cholla. From the sand deserts of California, it had a pungent white flower with a yellow-black eye, the beauties endowed with some power to entrance, but the starburst of thorns was not a genial quality for admiring children. But this small misjudgment was the only oversight Linda had made. She was so serene with Kea, so supple with the children, so subtle with all the staff, such a reliable asset, that at times Kea saw her in the looming specter of a coach that turns into a pumpkin at midnight. Kea had wondered what a woman of Linda's talents was doing in Grantham. She had heard rumors that Linda was escaping an abusive relationship back in Los Angeles. Kea had heard Linda's husband was a wife beater. Had he done something to Eric? Could this be why he stuttered?

In the reading group, Somberg was giving the children a few colorful details on Napoleon that their history books had failed to mention. She had never worked with children before but had found it rejuvenating! The glow and edge of youth was sustenance for the soul. A dip into the sublime! Clusters of jewels in the tiny chairs about her. No guilt. No desperate scurry for power. No struggle within the self. No bleached lies told to a mind trained in disbelief. *Belief!* was the great beauty of children. They still believed in Camelot. In blue dolphins that could talk. In dogs that had thoughts. In Santa and the Easter bunny and the tooth fairy and the first star upon which you may hang your best wish. Belief is the first thing the world kills. And the first belief destroyed is belief in the self. In this death all others follow.

The connoisseur of the nymphet who had trained and refined so many crude, simple, lost male minds was in her element in the sacred kingdom of children. Children still touched each other; a call girl could learn from children. Children marveled! There is nothing as glorious as the wonder of a child, astonished at the simplest of things. In their amazement you discovered wonder all over again. Their hot, soft, little bodies so willing to give of themselves. This instinct is what made for upper-class geishas; be they girl, or boy made into girl. So the lovely English children were in a vaunted position to Somberg, not as kiddie-porn, but as tuition in the female development that can be re-directed; always such fun withdrawing the geisha-instinct from the underground of a beautiful, damned male. This made her time with the children more delicious, which is what a hobby does, be it gender-bending or stamp collecting; it endows motivation to even the dullest days.

Most of the world at large believed real life started at five feet tall. Children were expected to defer to adults, to endure their dribble and belittlement and intimidation until they were strong enough to impose their own authority. Children's powers were their skill at endearment and their mastery of petulance, which was, essentially, the craft of the assassin. Society taught children to become actors. Good children accepted their parts; bad children defied their assigned roles; shrewd ones improvised and learned to manipulate. Somberg understood that she and Maggie both grew up in the improvised category, that teaches invention.

Invention is power. So, children could be bottom-lined into those seductive ones with power, and those without, who just went blindly along. Futures were made not by what was learned, but by what was forgotten. The ones who would succeed were those who would relearn what they forgot, which amounts to *belief* and *seduction*.

She could see the whole world in miniature in the classroom, and in this perspective, better understood her career. Most people were confined to the small space of their life set by their fears. This was equally true in her profession. Men shooting marks from high buildings. Afraid to get close. Brandishing their egos after the fact. Not inventors but mechanics. It was the *making* of a kill that intrigued Somberg. Discoveries, such as the children, gave life. The truth was, most men in her profession were as dead as the marks they shot for a price. Always negotiating for higher and higher prices, but nothing could buy off their fear that kept them at a distance, and so they never closed on life.

Now Somberg heard him stuttering again. It was a nuisance. A glitch in his programing; call it memory regression. It began around Christmas while in Geneva. She had used the drugs and hypnosis in the same manner in which her mother had used them, and everything had worked for her as it had for her mother. Eric had been renamed, and the school and church and family and friends all played along, so Eric never questioned his identity. He preferred Eric to what he could not remember. He would reach back into his mind for a memory, but it was as if it had been rubbed away like chalk. He knew only faint traces of events, and people who he had loved with all his heart were now ghosts. The ghosts were illicit, his mind did not want to go there.

Had he lived in Chicago? If asked, Eric would frown and look blankly with no notion of Chicago. One might as well have asked about Cape Town. Or Paris. Or Banff. Names unknown and faraway. Show him Chicago on a map; it would be void of meaning. It was like his memory had been blown up into an enormous pink bubble, and popped at the top of his head. He held nothing against Somberg for dissolving his historic record; just the opposite was true, he loved her as his mother. His love was real, relaxed, as authentic as anything he knew. A love that shone in the eyes. A laughing love! A blessing. A pretty child's love without question.

A genuine mother might beat her breasts and swear her love could never be deleted, but it was done first by a genuine mother, and a father was lost, and would remain lost were it not for the child's love so critical to Maggie's death. Love begets love, for it is the posterity of love that cannot be erased, not even by the most deceptive mothers, the ones who can take in everyone. Love, apparently dead, will linger and adapt; despite all intentions, it may come together again. It's a bit like earwax. Clean it out, and to a mother's disgust, it returns in an unwashed phenomenon, often in public. But it takes an extra excitement, some provoking of the unsounded depths of the heart to reach the instincts that resist the tactical. An atmosphere of battle may grip the victim. What is suppressed may raise in a massive voice. The voice in the now mature victim may be angry. Even murderous. It is dangerous to hush love, though some mothers have been known to get away with it in the flicker of a candle flame.

The remaking of a boy had gone smoothly and quietly, no one the wiser, certainly not the boy; there was only the stuttering. But that was remedied using a mother's technique, and now Somberg left the children to read their sanitized English history that had lied about brilliant Napoleon.

"Eric has been telling about the pirate cake you made," Kea said as Linda joined them. "And how he learned to crack eggs."

Eric looked up at his New Mama. "Re-re-re-remember that cake?" he asked, hoping she could remember what he could not.

"Of course. I remember that cake! It was such fun!" She had Kea beaming, and Somberg suppressed her irritation, her internal clock ticking. Fifty-seven days until Maggie's arrival. She needed this wrinkle ironed out. "But I wonder, Ms. Chieng, could you excuse us a minute, while we work on our enunciation?"

"Certainly," Kea said. "I'll cover the children."

They retreated to the adjoining music room. A small drab room of acoustical tiles, a single high window, and an upright piano. Somberg had Eric close and lock the door. There was a sharp click as the dead bolt fell.

"I'm s-s-sorry that I'm stu-stuttering again, Mama," Eric said with a sad smile, standing by the piano.

"Oh, that's all right." She pulled out the piano bench and sat down. She gave him a reassuring hug, feeling the weight of his anxiety in his shoulders and back where males tense first, though her geisha femmes tensed first in their newborn nipples. To relax a femme you massaged her nipples, till she was purring sweetly. "It's a thing that will fix itself." Her easy smile led him away from the worry, saying, "Today in reading circle we were learning about Napoleon Bonaparte. Do you remember Napoleon?"

"Sh-sh-sure!" History had become Eric's favorite subject, a way of filling in what he was missing within himself. "He was the l-l-little man with all the power!"

"That's right. Napoleon had a perfect understanding of power. He understood that people with power have the right to do anything that you can't stop them from doing."

"He wasn't much taller than a k-k-kid," Eric added with a thrilled grin. Napoleon had become a paradigm of Eric's new self. "And he wasn't afraid of de-de-death either."

"That's *very* good, Eric," she said, playing on his strings, bringing her lyrics out of him. Seduction was far more effective than grating out orders which is what most mothers did. "Not being afraid of death is what made Napoleon so *brave*. Death was his friend and he often visited it upon others."

Eric's head bobbed agreement. "I know. He was totally cool."

"Napoleon understood life is like a song, only you never know when the song will end."

"You never know when you're closer to the end than to the beginning," Eric recited without stuttering.

"Yes, and the ending almost always comes as a surprise, which makes ending songs so much fun!"

They laughed together as mother and son. But the lesson she had not yet given was that if history has taught us anything, it is that anyone can be killed, including prime ministers who were thought to be made of iron.

"Let's work with the candle, shall we?" Somberg took a small candle from her pocket. She lit it from a match, and Eric stared into the smooth flame. A ring of soft light spinning round the rim of his pupils. Eyes in sync with the steady left-right motion. He became very still, his breath shallow. The pretty light rose into the sprawling roof of his mind and swarmed in glimmer streams into the subdued sub-conscious. Some part of him braced himself and his sad smile widened as the curtain rose on another mythic show where players glistened in fairy lights. His whole mind filled with the gold-lit light, like some wonderful carnival!

"Eric, do you see me?" Somberg said in a low voice, a deep imitation of Pit Martin, who he knew as a father figure.

A door loomed before Eric. He peered into a fish-eye peephole in the door he saw Pit in a pirate costume. "Hi, Blackbeard!" he said with a happy grin.

"Hello, Eric. It's nice to see you again."

"Nice to see you."

"Can you tell me what your name is?"

"Eric Anderson. Like Eric the Red!"

"And who's your mama?"

"Linda Anderson is my mama."

"That's very good." Somberg blew out the flame, leaving him staring into space. Thin light from the window dappled his face, the freckles faded. She ran her fingers through his soft hair, cut Grantham-short. She had come to look forward to their sessions, these loving exchanges of the soul. Her son feeding from her, as though from a swollen nipple. The nurture was as much hers as his and she loved the voyaging. He was shedding one life and growing another, the one she had made for him, and only the elements that she did not shake out remained of his past. He had no recollection of his grandparents, they were not even ghosts, they had vanished all together. All his friends had dematerialized. His experiences were altered, some-times a lot, sometimes a little, so those who remained in memory had only the meaning she had given them; though she was no genius at these things, her mother having done as much for her. The in-depth readings of his mind, the camouflage paint with which she worked, was done in sessions that went on for days on end, with recess time in between. It was bit like plucking the petals from a flower, he lost a little something every time she lit a candle. A rape by voyeurism, the flame immense and tonguing the black night sky of his mind with the house of memory blown to bits, window glass dancing in the air. In time, a new house was erected he could come home to in the mother's pyrokinesis that is the candle flame that no father can overcome, not if he's dead.

"Now, let's open the door into the past," she said.

Danny blinked as if at a sudden bright light.

"Look in the door where your Old Mama is. Do you see her?"

Eric nodded, gazing at a shadowed room in his mind. There was no one there to greet him, nor were there walls as such, just a grayness of shadows that formed the sequestration room. Slowly, out of the shadows, Jessica appeared embedded in one wall, her features and hands faintly recognizable. It was as if she were frozen in the wall that deteriorated her arms and legs so what remained seemed false and pretty strange, no boy would trust it.

"She's Old Mama. We don't talk about her anymore, do we, Eric?"

"No, sir." Eric shook his head. "We don't talk about her."

"And why is that, Eric?"

His face paled. "Because she's dead," he whispered.

"Why?"

His voice tightened and he gave a little sigh. Now for the first time he closed his eyes to confess, "Because I shot her."

"That's right. You're to leave those memories in that room with your Old Mama. Close the door. Lock it. Is it locked?"

"Yes, sir," Eric said, breathing in sips, his eyes wide once more. And Somberg missed none of it, monitoring his pulse at his wrist, watching every subtle change of expression. She waited a moment, letting his respiration settle. She knew his sense of being adrift, in a limbo of your own history, and in times like this she sometimes saw him in a blur, a tall, blond, well-muscled Englishman. Smiling as he opened his arms to his twelve-year-old daughter. Her daddy was the dominant influence in her early life. She had had a messianic adulation for him. The first man she had loved. And he had loved her, more than he had loved his wife. The echo of the shot in the closed space of the barn was very loud and rattled about in her head; in the grayness the sound vanished into an immense silence, and daddy was gone. After that she belonged to her mother. She was hers, all hers.

"Now, Eric," assassin-now-turned-technician, programming her weapon in the environment where it would kill, "I want you to open the door with the picture of that nice old lady."

"Mrs. Thatcher?"

"Very good! You remembered her name. Do you see her?"

Eric nodded. "She's in my classroom!"

"And what's that nice old lady doing in your classroom?"

"Mrs. Thatcher is standing by Ms. Chieng's desk."

"And who is standing there with Mrs. Thatcher?"

"I am."

"And what will you do, Eric?"

"*Mrs. Anderson!...*" Kea called from the classroom. "We're about to step outside for the class photo."

"Thank you," Somberg answered in her sugary Linda Anderson voice. "We'll be right there." She returned to the deep voice: "Eric, it's time to close Mrs. Thatcher's door."

He blinked. "It's closed," he said.

"Lock it."

"Yes, sir."

"When I say my name, open your eyes. You'll not remember what we talked about. But you'll not forget what you're to do."

Somberg waited another moment. He was just perfect here, so vulnerable and trusting. So teachable. Floating in this rarefied air, in this pathway of a new life. She the only possible parent he could see. She loved mothering, the act of making a child by your touch, but it was such a change. A strange turmoil. Every choice seemed to have drawbacks. Every action muddled over by thoughts of consequences, by erratic doubt, by new self-image, by curious feelings of affection and responsibility. There was such an immanence to it, sometimes leaving her feeling abandoned, other times endowing her with power. Amazing the fluidity with which it all moved through her, as though it were love. She hadn't expected this but didn't fear what she controlled, and she was in control, she always was, nothing as flimsy as love could alter that.

"*Blackbeard*!"

Eric blinked at the snap of her fingers. He grinned, feeling all better. Refreshed and happy and very sure of himself as Eric. Somberg led him from the piano and had him unlock and open the door into the classroom that in two months Margaret Thatcher would visit on the school's hundredth anniversary. She paused before they left the music room, squatting beside him, looking into eyes almost as blue as hers. He was hers, all hers.

"Darling, do you know how to crack an egg?"

Eric made a goofy face. "No way!" he said, without stuttering.

"I'll teach you," she replied, please to see the cake memory gone. "I'm an expert at cracking eggs." She kissed his soft cheek and with an arm around him lead him back into the classroom.

11

JESSICA SAT AT a round table by the window in the small and crowded pub. She checked her watch. In ten minutes, he'd be fifteen minutes late. She bristled at the thought and finished her martini, ready to leave. She'd never wanted to come; this was Pit's idea. She didn't know what she was doing here and could barely make herself stay. She could make herself spend years modeling and make herself into a photo illustrator and could make herself endure the loss of Danny, but the self-made woman in her didn't know how to ask a *man* for help. She never needed help from a man. She was a tough mama, self sufficient.

She had talked to Akira Hayashi on the phone, and he sounded terrible, hoarse with the flu, but she could hear the care in his voice. He regretted he could not meet her, he was being reassigned overseas, but had arranged for an investigator to help her. "One of the best," Hayashi said. "A C-thirteen man with many years' experience." He gave her the name of the man and the name of the pub for the rendezvous and promised they would speak again before she left. Jessica hung up feeling abandoned, more alone than ever.

How the hell do you ask people for help? She needed lessons in how all this works. She supposed if she had been flattened by one of those red double-decker buses, she'd peel herself off the street and drive herself to the hospital and set her broken bones and sew herself up and send herself flowers and be sure to call twice a day to cheer herself up. It was not that he was a man. It was that she was an independent woman. Independent a nice word for it. Defiant closer to the mark. Iron-headed perhaps, but she had never been iron-hearted, so she had never been an iron lady. She stared up at the ceiling, disgusted with the strong parts of her that were too strong, and the weaker parts that were too weak.

On the dark ceiling, she created a composite of this cop she was to meet. She pictured a lugubrious build with a slow, dull face stamped with a serious expression and a gut that hung on him like a saddlebag. She dressed him in a cheap navy suit, wrinkled Columbo overcoat, an I-don't-give-a-shit necktie stained with tea, and clumpy black shoes that rustled and squeaked. C-13 sounded like one of America's alphabet-soup bureaus, FBI or CIA. She had called Scotland Yard; they said it was the Antiterrorist Bureau. Now, what did that have to do with Danny? Shouldn't she be in Missing Persons?

All right, she said to herself in the pub, *you might as well go. There's no reason to wait for a guy that's fifteen minutes late. I don't know why the hell you're here anyway. Really, what are you going to say to this Trent Stanford? How will you explain it all? How do you ask a man for help?* But the iron part of her knew she'd find a way to tell her story and find a way to ask for help; she could do anything for Danny. If necessary, she'd ask the whole world for help. She could tell her story one by one to every person in the world, the telling as an extension of herself, and she would kill herself with every telling; in telling a good story one has to kill oneself if one is to accomplish things. She wouldn't tell it as some master, but as a child; the masters all knew that it was the child who was the great artist. She didn't know how to ask for help, but she knew how to make art, and she wished she knew how to kill, because that's really what she wanted to do.

She tried to drink from her empty glass. She glared at her watch. Now it was five minutes till he was fifteen minutes late.

Trent glanced at his watch. Ten minutes late, no big deal to an American. He stepped into the pub, looking for familiar faces, hoping no one he knew spotted him here. He had every government agency and the Garda in Ireland running their networks searching for an employment history, family or friends, any kind of trail they could find on the one warm body they had linked to Brighton. Now, with England on full alert, Trent was now about to have a cocktail. Chat with a Yank about God knows what. He should have passed this to a subordinate, but Hayashi had asked graciously, making a small withdrawl from the favor bank. Trent could hardly deny the request, considering the little man had given him the Fox that was the only lead they had on the Brighton case.

He slid through the pretty crowd and spotted her by a window. Beautifully obvious. Looked better than her blurred photo Hayashi had faxed. She was stunning, though she appeared tense. He took a cautionary glance over his shoulder. All clear. No one from the office likely to be caught in this pond. Too elegantly casual.

As he approached, he tried to recall what it was Hayashi had told him about this woman. She was a photographer? A Yank looking for a runaway? But she appeared too young to have a teenager. She was looking out the window that shone on a beautiful face somewhat sullied. Tepid. Empty. As if there were no passion in her.

"How do you do, Ms. Moore, I presume?"

Jessica was startled out of her gloom. She looked up at a man over six feet. Double-breasted navy suit. Broad shoulders and chiseled features. Dark hair swept from a wide forehead. Hardly her picture of him. In her surprise, her voice deserted her.

"I'm Trent Stanford," he said and offered a hand. "Sorry I'm late. Afraid I was detained at the office."

The blue eyes set deep; he had a strong nose, looked broken, but that was the only thing about him that looked cop. Smiling down on her, and Jessica tried to get a grip on a new sensation. Something as simple as desire.

"Ah, you are Jessica?"

"Yes," she said, "yes," she repeated like a fool, shaking his hand. "I'm Jess."

"You appear somehow surprised," he said as he sat down.

"Oh, well—" A warmth rushed over her face. Why was she in heat? Plunged into man-dismay. She never knew what she wanted or why she was doing whatever it was she was doing with men. Nothing as thrilling as the first eye contact, his gazed dead on her with something going cuckoo, all this reverberating through the back of her brain, while on the marquee, two impossible words: Help Me. "It's just that I had expected someone, oh," she groped like a child, "Japanese," she said suddenly.

"Japanese?" Trent frowned, confused.

She reached for her drink, saw it was empty, and quickly retrieved her hand. "Well, you know, Hayashi is Japanese," she said, as if this would explain her gawking which she promptly put a stop to, though her heart was galloping away.

"He is, in fact," Trent said, smiling now. "Rather a few of them about London these days. But there's still one or two of us Anglo-Saxons left."

"Oh, of course."

"Holding the fort down."

"Uh-huh."

"Until they buy us out, lock, stock and barrel. That's one of my favorite American idioms."

"Mine too," she said, wondering what she was doing talking about this. "I don't know why I assumed you'd be Japanese. I'm glad you're not," the idiot said, climbing in deeper. "Not that I have anything against the Japanese."

"No."

"It's just that, I don't know any Japanese." Suddenly she was a nutcase. Making no sense. "Their customs are so different, you know."

"Right. There's all that bowing from the waist." Trent spun a hand in two hoops, drawing the barmaid. "I'm relieved *you're* not Japanese. Yank is far better."

"Oh. Thank you."

"The Japanese have such a formal demeanor."

"Yes," she replied, wishing they could get off this.

"And there are those accommodating eyes."

He looked right into her eyes, then smiled. Jessica felt as if someone punched an erase button at the center of her thoughts. Why had she come to England?

"There's the essentially passive Oriental character," he said with Jessica nodding agreement. "Which isn't passive at all. All a charade. To make you passive."

"Americans are nothing like that."

"No. What you see is what you get with a Yank," he said with the most gallant smile in London, and for some reason, Jessica couldn't stop her radiance. "And then there's the stately English of the Japanese, never use the letter 'r.' Part of their lull, you see. Draw you in, then conquer you."

"And you like that, do you?" she heard someone say.

"Love it, actually."

He was smiling full-beam, Jessica caught in a sneak attack. In a trancelike state dissociated from the voices and bodies and psyches crowded into the pub, with no one, not even themselves, aware of what they were experiencing. Jessica taken out of her suffering into some ideal of what she once upon a time, before she was shot and scared ugly, wanted to be; a little romance part of a girl's daily living, now experiencing this out of the blue in a wonder that corresponded with the abuse of her suffering. She was no longer rooted in pain but, for a moment, of air without any pushing or pulling of her tired heart and it felt kind of crazy. Then she was saved by the arrival of the barmaid.

"What will you have, Jessica?"

"Oh, it's Jess, please." She started to order a Perrier, but something overruled her. "I believe I'll have another martini."

"And a Black Bush," Trent told the girl.

"You drink *Irish* whiskey?" Jessica asked, scrambling to turn the conversation on him before she started spilling out her whole life story. "I thought you and the Irish don't get along?"

"No truth to that at all. We love the Irish. Fact is, I'm part Irish. Mother's side. The good side. The misty beauty of the land is the haunting character of the Celtic soul. Our family has a thatch cottage over there, in an intoxication known as the Gap of Dunloe. Dates back to 1697. The cottage that is. The Gap goes back to that lace-vailed morning when God made Ireland."

She was beaming and he was talking rot. What had gotten into him? "No, we love the Irish," he carried on. "It's the bloody bombers we can't stand. Hellishness, the terrorism. But I have a theory—if you drink their whiskey it helps you find them."

"That's what you do. At C-thirteen? You *find* people?"

"That's what I'm supposed to do at C-thirteen. But I've had the devil of a time finding one joe in particular." He fell into the Brighton story. Filled her in on the bombing, managed to tell that with integrity, without making it more than it was. Then the Grand registration card. "The lab boys used a scanning electronic microscope, x-rays, chemicals, then a dozen other methods on the card, but couldn't detect any prints. Mrs. T wasn't satisfied. Authorized a miracle. A Spectra-Physics Laser Fingerprinter."

"That's a miracle? What is it?"

She was a miracle. Renoir face. Faint freckles of a girl beneath the features of a woman. Dangerous combination for him, girl and woman. Better it be one or the other. "It's a new gizmo," he said, thinking there was no need for a drink, not with those eyes across the table, "I'd never seen one before. Our mutual pal, Dr. Hayashi, invited me to witness the unveiling. Amounts to a colossal torchlight juiced with eighty thousand watts of power." Trent painted her a picture, Britain's giant of forensic science so dwarfish, Hayashi needed a step stool to elevate him to counter height. He took what looked like a magician's wand attached to a shielded cable that ran to the peculiar looking tube humming with electricity like maybe it might explode. Depressed the trigger. A thin stream of green light, fine as the filament of a spiderweb, beamed onto the card. The light swept around "Roy Walsh" on the name line. Then round the edges of the card. Now fingerprints glowed a radiant green. Trent took them in, heart kicking at his ribs. The miracle was a bargain, and something of a secret, the Irish unaware latent prints could be retrieved from paper.

"It was Allelujah time there for a while! A big break. Our *only* break—other than a bit of battery found on the beach. There were four sets of prints on the card. Two belonged to hotel staff. A palm print remains unidentified. Big Brother—our computer at the Yard, made by IBM, Big Blue, but we prefer an English tag, a play on Orwell's *1984*—made quick work of matching the print of a thumb at the left top of the card."

She leaned forward into the overhead light, something bright in her eyes. "So, Big Brother helps you find people?"

"Right. It's linked to Interpol, and your FBI. Massive data base. Big Brother scanned the print, matched it to a brickworker in Rotterdam, a thirty-one-year-old Irishman arrested by the Dutch police. A known member of IRA, he was held for trial, suspected of plotting the bombing assassination of the British ambassador. But the Dutch, sweating the possibility of a terrorist retaliation, rejected our extradition request. The brickworker was released. But not before a *full* set of prints were taken, sent to Interpol who began a file on one, Dessie Quinn, alias the Fox."

Trent could see the mug shot now. A young, narrow face. Sharp eyes. The hair dark. A pointed nose. The insolent smile looked as if the Fox enjoyed his work. "The Fox had a mate in Rotterdam. He was never identified, gave the Dutch the slip. They were believed to be an Irish assassination team. We have a make on the one, the Fox, all we know of the other is he's known as the Pope."

"You think *he* was the unidentified palm print on the card?"

"Can't say. But if he was quick enough to avoid capture in Rotterdam, he's not likely to leave prints on a registration card in Brighton. I *suspect* what happened is two men checked in at the Grand. They requested room six-twenty-nine—we know the bomb was set there. It was off-season, the room was available. The Fox was about to sign the card but thought better of it. Slid it across the desk to second man, recording the Fox's thumbprint. The second man, an operative, signed and left unidentified the palm print."

Looking across the circle of light into windblown brunette curls, he realized he'd be doomed if he was ever captured by the Amazons. Beauty inspired him to sing. He gave her everything but rank and serial number. Though he didn't tell anything every cop in Britain and Ireland didn't already know. She had the face of a Renoir, but he couldn't recall which one. His eyes came to rest on the gathers of a gray silk blouse. Didn't see the charcoal jacket or the slim wool skirt, though he noted the racehorse legs as he sat down. And he didn't hear what she said just now.

"Pardon me?"

"I said, do you think the Pope was in on Brighton?"

"Oh, I should say. He was in on our Dutch ambassador, he wouldn't miss a go at Mrs. T."

"Your work sounds dangerous."

"Not hardly. As a rule, I rarely see anything more dangerous than a stapler." He had her laughing on that one. And it was true. Most days he could find a stapler. Finding the Fox was something else. "Everything and everyone is on Big Brother, you know. Or, it's *supposed* to be." He went on, sounding like a twit. "It can be a boring business,'' he said, reminding himself he was needed at the office. *Get to the point! Get back to work!* ''One picks up a trip to Ireland now and then.'' *Would you please shut up?* ''Lovely country, really. Have you ever been?''

''No. But I've always wanted to go.''

The drinks arrived. Just in time. Saved him from singing ''Danny Boy,'' or some such rot. He raised a whiskey to the tragic beauty with the soft face and the lovely American accent. Having run his mouth, he was still not quite sure why she was here.

''Cheers,'' he said.

She caught his eyes and took a good slow drink. The martini was very cool and clean, so civilized in Britain. *And very strong*, she thought, and reminded herself not to forget it.

''So, what brings you to London, Jess?''

''Oh.'' She sipped her frigid drink. ''Hayashi didn't say?''

''Actually, we spoke only briefly.'' Trent ransacked his brain, trying to recall what Hayashi had said. ''He rang yesterday. Left a message. I rang him back, missed him. Telephone tag, you know.'' Now it was coming. ''You're a photographer? Here on assignment?''

She took another drink. *Okay, now's your chance. Just tell him. Tell him and keep it simple and don't get emotional.* Her eyes darted out the window. She snapped a picture of a street with bowler-shaped taxis streaming past proud old buildings flushed sunset pink. Walks filled with people, like their martinis, so clean and civilized. She'd always loved London. Once upon a time she'd dreamed of living here. ''I'm working on a project,'' she said, feeling her courage turn to liquid. ''A thing for Jaguar.''

''You must be *very good,* Jess. There are British photographers that would kill for that account.''

Kill! She grabbed the word, turning it over in her mind. *That's what I'm here for! Just explain that. He'll understand; he's with C-13. He knows all about that.*

''How long will you stay?''

''Mmm, maybe a week.'' A hot spot of fear formed in her gut. She doused it with another sip of cool martini. ''Though I finished Jaguar this afternoon.''

He followed her swiveling eyes out the window, feeling a need crouched in her silence, waiting to be stirred. Something iron in her silence. Brought Mrs. T to mind. He now saw her at Number 10, sipping an evening whiskey, glaring at his report. Her short nails tapping. Her clock ticking. Still, he waited on Jessica without really knowing why. Watched as she lifted her glass and drank and kept drinking and emptied the glass but never noticed. *What was it Hayashi said? Something about a runaway? Or was it a child?*

''In Ireland,'' he said, leaning into their circle of light, ''when you come across a wall that you think you can't scale . . .'' He paused as her eyes came back to him. ''What you do is take off your cap and toss it over the wall.''

Jessica frowned. ''Toss your cap over the wall?''

''Right. Then you *must* follow.''

She nodded at this, and he saw the sadness flow from her brow to her mouth, and the color of her mood washed over him and he could not resist it. His voice dropped to a confiding tone. "Hayashi mentioned something about an investigation?"

She reached into her handbag. Took out a sketch of a woman. Laid it in their circle of light. "I don't suppose you've seen this person before?" she asked.

Trent considered the sketch. Guardedly lacking in detail. The work of a police artist? Something for the bulletin board? *Take a look as you file out, boys. Give a whistle if you spot her.*

"I see a lot of faces," he said, looking up into eyes he had seen before. Bomb victims laid open to the bone. Jessica was suffering in the same manner. "What has she done?" he asked, feeling himself being drawn across the table by those eyes.

"I have a son. His name is Danny. He's six years old."

"That's a lovely age," Trent said. "Or so I've been told. The last year before they become obstinate."

"That woman," Jessica said, pointing, "took Danny."

Trent finished his whiskey in a swallow.

"She used my son to shoot me."

He stared at her, not quite hearing her.

"She tried to kill me."

"Good God! This happened in Chicago?"

Jessica nodded, choking back the tears.

"When did this happen, Jess?"

But she would not respond, and he saw the loss flooding into her like water through a broken hull. That, he suspected, was a thing that happened daily. Breaking up and sinking into the deep. "Just talk it out," he said softly. "Talk's the way to numb it. Anything gets old if you talk about it enough. Just keep talking. And keep drinking," he added, calling for the waitress.

"It's been —" Jessica gazed into the martini glass and tried to recount the time. She had a memory of it but no feeling of its passage. "Four months," she said and swallowed hard and found the words that she could not say. "I need some help," she muttered.

"And that's why you're here?"

"Yes," she confessed. "Pit, Hayashi's friend, he's Danny's—well, Pit is our best friend. We've tried *everything* to find Danny. But it hasn't done any good. Or we were terrible at it. Or the bitch who took him is very good. I don't know."

She paused, fighting insistent tears. She glanced at a shadow on the wall and silently called to a boy she no longer knew. He was beyond her. Here, in London, it sank in: Danny was gone and she had no earthly idea where he was. The torment left her dizzy, and at moments like these she became another person. The sort of person who would have no difficulty bombing a Grand Hotel. There was a ruthlessness in the pain that inspired ruthlessness, and you wanted to give yourself to it. You wanted to kill. You wanted to take a sword and shisk-kebab someone through the heart, pinning them like an insect, watching their death-squirms, watching them pivot on the spindle of the blade as you had pivoted on the point of the pain driven into your heart. Jessica had a premonition this very scene was coming. The blade withdrawn to gash through the neck, the force of good fury cleaving through the sinew to make a headless amputee. It wasn't the first time her mind had scampered in the majesty of unfettered rage, seeing a gleaming blood-glopped blade and the gross anatomy of the decapitated pale body flopping ignominiously, life pouring out of the stalk of the neck.

In every replay of the vision, her heart became a bit more like iron. And she knew, sipping the cool martini, where the gory imagery came from. Danny played a game of pirate, she had seen him play it countless times, in which he enacted this scene with his plastic sword. She thought it a shame that those who hold children hostage do not believe in the games of children that in the dark depraved land of heartache become real. Just a question of time.

"Just talk it out, Jess," Trent said softly.

She almost laughed out loud at this. If she let it all out, he'd jump out of his skin. People didn't know, they had no idea what the pain inspired and what the pain could do, how the pain never relaxed and how time made no difference whatsoever to the pain. "Well, we just thought that maybe you could—"

She stopped as the barmaid arrived. "Another round," Trent said to her. "Make them doubles."

Trent straightened in his chair. His eyes narrowed. Jaw set. All business. She was looking into him and already he was entering the black light of her soul. He had been in such places before, but never with someone so attractive. Now firmly but softly, he said, "Jess, tell me every detail of what happened. Beginning with the woman. When did you first meet her?"

She was in silence. On the great wide calmness of the edge of a deep and splendid sleep. She heard what sounded like the lunatic laughter of a woodpecker. It drew her bleary eyes to the window. Was that Kensington Park out there? She didn't remember the park being across the street from her hotel. Jessica sat up. She was in a High Edwardian room of taupe walls and wide dark moldings and a dark wood floor. In a lofty four-poster. This was definitely not her hotel room. She was wearing a man's blue dress shirt. She focused on the monogram on the sleeve: "TNS."

"Oh, God! What have I done?"

She checked the pillow beside her. It had not been used. She breathed a sigh of relief, swung her legs out of bed and stood to a sudden wobbling and immediately dropped back down. She closed her eyes and waited for the wheeling sensation to stop. Now she peeked at the linen shirt again.

"How did this happen?" she asked her bare legs.

Her swaying brought back the pub and her vodka-brave talk. She remembered how easily the heartache had poured out. and she thought it was certainly wonderful what a martini could do. Trent had ordered more drinks that came with his questions, and she couldn't recall her answers or her tears. But she remembered rain dripping from the eaves of the pub. A slow spinning sensation as she rose from the table. Trent's arm around her as if he wanted to waltz. Stepping into a cool, wet night. Odd, it was raining under the street lamps but nowhere else. They walked under an umbrella that murmured softly as she talked, and she remembered the sense of a weight being lifted from her. Featherlight as if she had no weight at all. Was she dancing? Oh, God! Had she actually done that? A heat crept up from the collar of the shirt as the memory unfurled. She had been singing in the rain. Then he was helping her into one of those cute cabs and that was the last thing she remembered, except for the faint sensation of the good, warm bed.

She glanced around the room again and this time found her clothes over a bent-wood rocker. She eased out of bed and shuffled across the room. Her clothes were still wet. So it was true.

"Okay," she said to the rain-waltzing culprit, uncertain whether to be furious with herself or thankful for her binge. "But who dressed me for bed?"

The woodpecker was going buggo drilling his tree; it began to sound as though he were drilling in her head. On a dresser she found a pair of frayed khaki trousers and her purse and a tall glass of water. Her tongue was swollen with thirst, and she drank all the water. The trousers were a little long but fit with the belt that came with them. She cuffed the pant legs, rolled up the sleeves of the shirt. She looked like she was ready jump a train out of town. Now she found her brush and compact and made herself ready for the day, wondering, *Where is Danny this morning?*

Her hair was pinned in a loose bun, wet clothes rolled in a tramp's bundle. She stepped out of the room and into a construction site. On the third floor of a horseshoe balcony in a shipwreck of a townhouse draped in rope and ladders. At the banister she saw an entry hall choked with scaffolding streaked by sun from a skylight. Down there the floor looked as if it had heaved up on itself, loose floorboards about. Like maybe a ship that had been hit by a whale. As in a whale of a story. A whale of a pain. A great whale that roams the oceans, from the Irish Sea, to the warm Caribbean, to the China Sea, attacking ships of state sailed by the civilized hypocrites who terrorize the peace of the deep. The downy sawdust over everything gave a kind of romanticism to the destruction, so it didn't seem so onerous, but only the making of something better. Now she saw the note taped to the carved newel post: *Stay to the right on the stairs! I'm in the study. Trent.*

Now what did that mean, stay to the right? She eased down the stairs, her back to the wall, risers creaking beneath her as she descended into a musty scent. On the other floors, bedroom doors were standing open, rooms in various stages of reno vation. As if some mad Captain had started papering a wall here and run across to another room to begin a wiring job, only to become bored and turn plumber. It seemed that someone's knowledge of renovation was terribly chaotic, and it reminded her of the mess of her own life. Torn from hell to breakfast in the loss of Danny. Speaking of breakfast, she was starved! She crept on, less judgmental about the mess, after all, when did anything ever go as planned? The old house was going to be gorgeous—she could see that—if the mad Captain could stick with one project till it was finished.

She made it to the ground floor, then gazed up the rickety stair. How had she managed to get up them last night? Did Trent carry her up? There was a hoist at the far end of the balcony, a kind of dumbwaiter loaded with bricks. Did he use that thing? She tried to remember, but the last thing she recalled was the cab pulling up to the curb. And now it occurred to Jessica that she could slip out to Kensington Park and hail a cab. She could have his shirt laundered and delivered. She could call Trent from her hotel. They could talk about Danny, but she didn't have to say anything about singing in the rain or the night she couldn't quite remember. She didn't have to face him, not yet anyway. How could she face him not knowing who dressed her for bed?

She picked her way around four great columns lying in a drift of sawdust. Around a wagonload of pipe. A clicking of fast fingers over a keyboard coming from under the closed doors to her right. She tiptoed past, careful not to make a sound, hand on the scaffold to steady herself. She was watching the doors—what would she say if he stepped out and caught her?—when a loose floorboard kicked up with a hollow thud. She leaped back, hoping Trent didn't hear. Her arm was caught in a dangling rope, a snakelike thing she pulled away from, pulling a ladder from atop a scaffold. It came flying down so fast she gave a serio-comic yell. The wooden ladder shattered over the wagonload of pipe, Jessica staring now, vodka-stupid as the pipe came in an avalanche, making a horrible racket, spilling over the floor, taking down a stack of lumber that flew like bowling pins hit by a strike. She blinked as it went on and on, watching with a kind of dazed horror when Trent burst through the doors with a shout, "*WHAT THE HELL?!*" just in time to catch the high, musical jingle of the dumbwaiter chain. They looked up. The load of brick came whistling down. He snatched her back into his arms with the dumbwaiter exploding in a spectacular booming crash that made the whole floor jump, the thunder reverberating throughout the shipwrecked house like artillery fire.

"Good morning," Trent said as the last of the chain rattled down to spank the dumbwaiter, sending sawdust snowing through the trembling shafts of colored stained-glass light. A Kodak moment.

"Good morning," she replied, breathless in her new shirt, but looking around for a hole to crawl into.

"You okay?" he asked, still holding her.

"One minute I was coming down to knock on your door," she said wide-eyed, still hearing the thunder roll of the brick in her ears, "to *thank you* for last night"— Trent steered her through the battlefield, back toward his study—"and then before I knew it, *all hell* was breaking loose!"

"Right." He helped her over the splintered ladder. "And I must say, you did a *smashing* job."

"What?"

"Of redecorating," he said with a perfectly straight face. He noted her purse, clothes tucked under an arm. Was she on her way out? "No nonsense about the way you *attack* your work."

She didn't quite hear him, still shell-shocked. "Trent, I'm so sorry! Honestly, I just never dreamed!—" She lifted one hand in surrender. "Of course, I'll pay for everything."

"Well, there you are, then."

"What?" She stood in the door of the study, staring at him.

"I've one or two things around here that need demolishing, and as I recall, you've a week to spare in London." He closed the doors behind them, restraining his smile.

Jessica didn't hear a word. She was in an English oak study. Tall leaded-glass windows. Oxblood-colored leather sofas before a fireplace. On the back wall, a spiral stair curled into a balcony shelved with books. Her head tilted to view rolling brass ladders. She always wanted a study with brass ladders. Now she took in the partner's

desk before the bay of leaded glass. A laptop computer on the handsome green
leather-bound desk blotter.

"This house is incredible!"

"Thank you," he said as they came down a tier of stairs into the high, rich room.
"I got it for a song—after a stock tip from a fella in a jam in Berlin. Needed to
get on the other side of the Wall. It used to be in great shape, till I started in on it.
Taken me years to tear it to hell, but then I don't have your *style*."

She caught that and gave him a look. It only inspired him.

"A shame we didn't have you in Berlin. By now there wouldn't be a Wall. It
would have all come down."

But she was gone again, this time into the painting above the fireplace mantel.
Madame Monet and Her Son. Madame Monet was in a long white dress standing
in a windswept field, holding a parasol under a blue clouded sky. A boy was emerging behind her, his face just visible through tall spring grass, wildflowers all around.

"Nice copy," she whispered. "Who did it?"

"Ah, well, actually, I did. Used to paint a bit. Something to keep the hands busy,
till I discovered renovation."

The commotion of the morning lapsed into silence. Jessica was lost to the painting,
one of Trent's better efforts, though he had never seen it viewed with such heart
longing. A constant stream of memories, colorful and clear, often helplessly arresting,
flowed through Jessica, she beat on against the current, borne back ceaselessly into the
past as Jay Gatsby of Fitzgerald fame. That self-made, self-invited man who had believed in the American dream of success. He fulfilled that dream, confused it with a
woman, and was betrayed by it. Gatsby, like Jessica, had the capacity to commit completely to a lost love; Jessica believed it was this that had made him truly great. She
treasured the novel, but never saw *The Great Gatsby* as a rehearsal for her life.

"I worked on Danny's case last night," Trent said, a hand on her shoulder,
turning from the painting. "Worked on it most of the night. I have something I'd
like to run by you."

A whirling moment as she was catching up to the present. She kept seeing the
happy boy rising out of the spring green grass behind his mother who didn't see
him coming.

"You didn't sleep last night?" she said.

"Tried to. Found myself at the desk here, linking my computer to Big Brother."
Trent gave his laptop a pat. "We're tied into the mainframe. You can access our
criminal files. And Interpol, too."

"Really?" She was awake now, he was coming in loud and clear. "Great!" she
said, hugging the clothes she was to escape with. "But can you like, get in trouble
for that, using Big Brother?"

"No, I shouldn't think so—"

"Oh, good." Jessica laughed, relieved.

"—as long as I net the Brighton bomber straightaway."

"Brighton?" She was stumped for a second. "Oh, of course," she said remembering, the thing where they tried to kill Thatcher. It was abandoned in her harangue
last night, not that it had a thing in the world to do with Danny. That was Trent's
problem.

"The two cases may seem miles apart. But actually, we, like you, are looking for just *one* person." He reclined against the rope-carved edge of the desk. "I'd say our problems are similar. Our solutions the same."

"What?" Jessica was pierced by the second lightning flash of the morning. "Danny and this . . . Brighton thing?"

"Well, in manner of speaking, yes. You see, your Sterling doesn't realize it, but she's left a trail," he said, delivering the lines he had used on Mrs. T. And why not? Worked for one iron lady, use it on another. "All we need is a scrap of evidence, something solid. Once we have it, we can establish her trail and"—he ran a finger down the gold embossing of the blotter to Jessica's open hand braced on the desk—"follow it to Danny."

They were, he knew, two impossible cases for two women driven by passion and tortured by a past, both tenacious and resolute and perfectly capable of running a man to ground. Only a fool would take them both on. But how could he say no to those eyes that had looked at his painting as if it was the last hope on earth?

"What I had in mind is for you to cross-check your Sterling sketch against our files," he said.

"Great!" Jessica beamed. This was perfect. Better than she had hoped for. "How many faces are we talking about?"

"Oh, about two million in the C-thirteen records."

"Shit."

"Right. But Moby Dick will make fast work of it. I should say it'd take you about two weeks."

"I can do that," Jessica said, feeling a surge of new hope. "I have some obligations in Chicago, but I can reschedule. Does Moby Dick have files on the Orient?"

He reminded himself she was a photographer. She lived in silvered dreams now shattered by the reality of a terrorist world. "Actually," he said, treading lightly on her illusions, "I rather doubt that Danny is in the Orient."

"But all our clues led in that direction!" Jessica squared herself to face him. "The credit card charges, the phone calls, we traced it all to the Orient."

"Right. You mentioned that last night." He paused here and would have liked to have taken this slower, but there was no time. "Jess." He glanced over her shoulder and could almost see her face in the painting. And now he knew, she didn't remember a Renoir, but a Monet. "I'd say a woman who auditions blond-haired, blue-eyed boys in three cities, makes her selection, attempts to murder the parent using her son, is not a woman who makes many mistakes." He let that sink in, then added, "I should say such a woman would leave nothing behind which she didn't *intend* for you to find."

He watched Jessica take this in, wondering if she understood the significance of blond hair and blue eyes and Sterling casting herself as mother in the Sony shot. He was certain of the motive, though he couldn't bring himself to tell Jessica, but he suspected it was a thing she knew but had not admitted to herself. Jessica had been replaced. What's more, she helped Sterling replace her in the enactment of the mother role. Danny was given permission, actually encouraged by his mother to transfer his loyalties to Sterling. A touch of demonic genius to it. It was this touch that dwindled the chances of finding the boy. Sterling was obviously a pro.

"So." Jessica sighed. "We blew it in Sydney?"

"I'm afraid so. I rather doubt Danny is anywhere near the Orient. I suspect he's as far from the Orient as one can be." He saw arms cross, fingers tighten around biceps. A woman in need of help. His mind like the cavalry, clicking through probabilities. What cities are opposite Sydney? London. Moscow. Sterling is tall, blond, blue-eyed. Munich. Stockholm. French accent. Paris. Geneva. Now he saw Jessica again, spinning in the night rain, arms outstretched, head thrown back, letting it all go in a way he never would but wished he could. "Unfortunately, I have the Brighton case pressing."

"Oh, that's okay," Jessica said, "I can come back another—"

"No. I've made the link to Big Brother. You can go to work straightaway. You can work here, from the house. I'm afraid I'm keeping Mrs. T's hours these days—I think the woman has no sense of time, night and day all the same to her. So you won't be seeing much of me. But I'll drop in. See how it's going. How's that?"

"You mean, I would stay . . . *here?*"

"Well, you'll have to if you're to work Big Brother."

"Oh. That's not necessary." Jessica wondered how this had happened? A minute ago she was sneaking out on him. Now she was about to stay at his house? But how could she stay here without knowing what had happened last night?

"We'll want to drop by your hotel, pick up your things. Though the work trousers are a nice fit." Trent admired the way she filled them out, the old pants had never looked so good. He read the tautness in her face, and added, "Glad you found the shirt last night. Looks better on you than it does on me."

Jessica breathed a silent sigh of relief in her gender-reversed clothes. She liked the outfit just fine.

"Are you hungry?" he asked.

"Actually, I'm famished!"

He smiled at that. "Right. I rather thought you would be." He stretched, wishing she'd do the same, give him another view of his shirt and all it contained. He preceded her to the door, blocking her view of the painting. "Afraid the kitchen looks as if it's been shelled," he said. "But it's still serviceable."

"Oh, that's cool." Jessica took in the room again. Forest green drapes. Handsome wing chairs. Gorgeous study, though it stank of cigar. She wondered if he had any scented candles.

"And after breakfast," Trent said, "I'll show you how to work Big Brother. There's nothing to it, really. Just *time.*"

They returned to the entry hall, and under the scaffolding looked out over her destruction. There was hope in the mess. She couldn't have screwed it up any worse, and it couldn't have turned out better. Rather than apologize for the third time, she said, "Thanks for last night. Thank you *very much,* Trent."

"My pleasure." He treated himself to her eyes again, then they started through the brick. "How will you have your eggs?" he said, helping her over the dumbwaiter. "Scrambled, I suppose?"

She shook a fist at him. He only laughed and carried on.

12

IT WAS HER Dark Age. The rest of her life after Danny. Her eyes were stinging after three days of staring at random green faces skidding across the computer screen. Big Brother sorting through thousands of faces that resembled the sketch of Sterling, and Jessica couldn't help but think of Winston Smith of *1984*. Smith had lived in a totalitarian world, believed to be a member of the revolutionary Brotherhood, the state took away his rights in a kangaroo court and sent him to a horror prison for the crime of individualism. Roughly the equivalent of being imprisoned for parenting your child. And Jessica felt like she was in a prison of sorts, worked-over by the Ministry of Love who cooked up the worst punishments imaginable in Room 101, the torture room.

She understood Smith. Caught in a nightmare, she knew vile, relentless despair. She was living squarely inside the absolute power of Big Brother, but individualism was not a crime, it was the computer's meat and drink. Sorting through the faces by nose, by chin, by eyes, by lips, by forehead until all began to look like the one face in the world Jessica hated. Unable to bear it, unable to quit. Too tired to work, too awake to sleep. Trying not to remember Danny but trying to remember how to work the computer that in her bleak existence worked her over. It seemed her chief attribute was helplessness. A helpless heroine with a hopeless outcome. Smith was tortured until the soul was expunged from him and he was able to agree, with tears of love in his eyes for his torturers, that two and two are five. Jessica found she feared capitulation more than anything. She refused to break. In the spirit of Pit, she played Beethoven!

The powerhouse music helped, until she got to thinking about Dicken's novels of impoverished, scorned, mistreated orphan boys, and the Danny inference increased her rat cage torture. In Smith's case, a rat cage was strapped to his face. But rats gnawed at her heart. In old England you were affected, or maybe infected was the word, by those English novels that were not about colossal whales hunts and such, but wormed down deep; you wanted to close the book but could not. Her lost son was a book Jessica wanted to close but could not. *Would not,* damn them! *Them* was good. You could rally a battle cry against *them.* She imagined herself pitted against the state, opposed by absolute forces, in their judicious superiority, with their pleasing contemptuous expressions at her ruin. She'd go down as Shakespeare's arrant kings, in battle or madness! She would either end well, or badly. She'd overcome her oppressors, or she'd die trying. She found consolation in a weirdness that seemed to cloy in the breath of the English fog, and even in the evil world that flashed before her eyes over the face of Big Brother. She was in a forced-labor camp. There, she whistled Beethoven. It drove her captors mad! She kept a diary. A diary was against the law. A diary was Smith's downfall. But she would play out this tune and reverse it, turning her diary into artful construction. Such were her mind wanderings in her Dark Age days, all of it as real as if she were Smith struggling for her son.

Trent worked late every night looking for his joe. Once he returned in the wee hours, Jessica still on the computer. They made dinner together. Eggs and bacon served on buttered toast. They ate in the kitchen at a table of plywood and sawhorses. He was in a tweed suit; the angles of his face filled out by shadows of exhaustion that deepened his features; Jessica found herself showing snapshots of Danny, telling the boy stories of her life. Trent listened with his sleepless eyes half-hidden under hooded lids. Listening with his whole body. He had a way of drawing her pain into himself, taking it in the way a bather takes in the sun, not with clothes on, but bearing his soul. In the clouds of gloom, Jessica's heat had a greenhouse effect, a swelter she lived in. Big Brother went untouched the rest of that night; when Trent left at dawn he took her weight with him to Scotland Yard, and Jessica slept in a deep and dreamless sleep. It was Trent's gift. His mercy. His legacy was not in what he said; he listened. It was his sneakiest skill, he had learned to listen.

The next morning, Jessica's long fingers were flying over the keyboard. Making Big Brother flash and blink. Opening classified databases with passwords she could not try to remember. Searching in files that came up "Classified." She didn't understand all the spy vocabulary, but found some Sterling matches there.

While reeling in the classified section, she came upon a file on Trent. She raided his past like a thief. Found reports on the people he had smuggled out from the Berlin Wall, that seemed to be his specialty. He seemed to go through a lot of wine, there were purchase orders for cases of it; in his memorandums he referred to it as a "lubricant." There were safe houses that only he had the address to and would not give to his superiors, though they sent countless demands requesting them. Jessica knew that she was in one of his safe houses. She felt perfectly safe. Trent always paid in hard currency. A friend of the Russian mafia. In one of the houses, the cellar was awash with guns and Chivas Regal and stockings and American cigarettes and European wines. His memos had a deaf ear to bigotry. He rode out insults. Played court to anyone with a secret. She saw him now, Trent Stanford was the merchant-spy, wining and bribing his way into and out of Berlin, doing it all in the service of a safer, wiser England. She stayed up all night reading his file; never, not once, had he used a gun. Or if he did, it wasn't in the report.

Trent came with Friday's sunset, and they spent the night at the partner's desk reviewing her most promising faces, none of which matched Sterling.

"But I'm getting better at it," Jessica said, showing him how easy she could work Big Brother. "It'll go faster next week."

She brought up the face of a drug addict from Amsterdam.

"Right," he said. "She has the jaw and the lips."

"But the shape of the eyes is all wrong." Jessica pointed to Sterling's sketch mounted beside the computer screen.

"And the forehead's not right," he added. "But I'd say you're onto something with Scandinavian faces. I'd hunt that direction."

They continued through the weekend. Taking cooking breaks—he braved hamburgers on the grill; they went up in flames like some sacrifice to a Yank god. They took destruction breaks; tearing out an Edwardian edifice in the entry hall. On Sunday morning, they did a walk down streets roofed over with trees, the route Trent usually ran. Jessica did her best to keep up, he did his best to slow down. He waved to neighbors who smiled and gazed as they passed. Jessica smiled back, wondering what they were wondering.

"Ever been married?" she asked, a thorn hedge smothered in white blossoms.

"Only twice."

"*Only* twice?"

"Right. Same girl."

"Oh, God!" She stopped. "Really?"

He laughed as the sun washed the empty sky and strolled on. She ran after him.

"How far apart were the marriages?" she asked, breathless.

"Ah, well. Let's see—" Mr. Cool was suddenly walking faster, into a park of stately trees; dew carried their footprints tracked side by side. "We were divorced, oh, two weeks the first time."

"Two weeks!"

"Right. Real depravity, I know." And now with optimism in his voice: "But it's been five years since the last divorce."

They rounded a pond with swans, Jessica's computer-deadened brain suddenly charged by her own spy thrill. A double same-girl divorce? This was so unlike the calculating C-13 agent. But then she thought of his townhouse. A classical exterior, the interior in overhaul. A man not afraid of change. And though the work appeared reckless, there were blueprints about.

"I was moved by irresistible impulse," he said, walking on.

"Twice!" Jessica grinned, proud of him.

"Right." He laughed at himself. "Ridiculous, I suppose."

"No! Not at all."

"Both times I thought I had the girl." He cleared his throat, his face flushed the color of kilned brick. "It wasn't true," he confessed. "The opposite was true. The girl had me."

She pried more out of him, and found how he hated to give up on anyone. But what was wrong in the first marriage was wrong in the second, and he could not make it right. He said he was a fool in the affairs of the heart, and regretted that he, like most men, had never mastered the skill of leaving a woman. Jessica wished the world were made of such fools and thought he was not like most men. She heard the voice of a man who worked at his relationships. They talked about his plans for the house as they walked on, until the dew melted from the grass and the sun was well up in the sky.

She woke to hear the clock chime four. Moonlight spangled over Trent's shirt. No reason to wear his shirt to bed. Except it smelled nice. And the color went with the blue sheets, she told herself. Creaking down the stairs in slippers and robe, on her way to the kitchen for a glass of juice, she passed his room. The door stood open. She tried to picture the girl he married twice. Tall, dark, gorgeous. Probably a model. She made it as far as the ground floor, still on the stair, all quiet in the empty house. Trent wouldn't be coming in for hours. *How tall was she?*

She was drawn to Trent's room, full of fear but compelled to go on anyway. It

was a perfectly innocent snooping expedition, in search of a single itty-bitty pho-
tograph, or so she told herself. She peeked in nightstands and dresser and closet.
Leafed through a box of papers. Found a yearbook. Looked up his picture. Jim
Morrison shaggy hair. Goofy smile. Same great eyes. When had he gone straight?
She started on a third box, no idea what had possessed her, then remembered Trent
talking about fingerprints at the Grand Hotel and how that had put him onto his joe.
She ran to the kitchen and put plastic bags on her hands. But the rest of the boxes
were full of books. She had almost talked herself back to bed when an idea lit up
her mind like a pinball machine. Wasn't there an attic stair at the end of the hall?

A little madwoman had taken over her head. Before she knew it she was climbing
up lamenting stairs. The attic dark as Pandora's box. Her hand found a light switch,
and she discovered a hideaway art studio! A gorgeous mess! Canvases strewn
through alcoves with dusty windows overlooking Kensington Park. In the back by
the window, a table was hardened in paint splatters; there were cigar burns on the
table and jars of brushes and stacks of books. She leafed through them the books,
the pages fell open to works of Degas, Renoir, Van Gogh and Monet. The discarded
canvases were crude reproductions of the pictures in the books, Trent teaching himself to paint by coping the strokes of the masters. He had gone as far back as Turner,
as modern as Picasso. She rummaged through what she hoped were his *early* efforts
at Degas, so terrible they were hilarious! Looked like he had done them with his
eyes closed! She stole through the drawers of an old chest, alive with mischief that
had overrun her misery.

Alone in the early morning when she found a photo album. Flipping through
pictures, faster and faster. Same girl in every picture. Tall but not dark. British blond
hair and freckles and a dreamy smile. She dissected the girl with the ruthlessness
of a modeling agent, some of whom were accused of murder. Some had given the
death penalty; some were due the death penalty; one was an opera unto herself with
a cast of beauties and an assortment of enemies, most of which could be named on
one hand, as her five dearest friends. Jessica couldn't help but think of such stories,
and of perfection looking at the girl, a mix of prettiness and poise. It was nauseating
how great she looked in every picture, and Jessica was hoping she had had a breakdown, or perhaps had driven her car off a cliff, so she wouldn't devour Trent again.

She studied the pictures again, seeing spontaneity in Trent's poses. His boyish
grin. The concentrated set of his eyes, then the adoration in his eyes. The way he
held the girl's hand inside his own, touching it with his fingertips. Downstairs the
clock was chiming six, and she put the album file away, no idea what she was doing
or why. She heard a key in the front door, snapped off the light and flew down the
stairs. Heart in her throat as Trent lumbered in from an all-nighter. She let the attic
stairs up. They ascended with a ghastly creak, but he didn't seem to hear. She ran
for her bed, dove in, wondered if she had lost her mind. Then she remembered the
plastic bags, still on her guilty hands.

There were only shadows in the study. A flare of a match and the kindling in the
fireplace grew to a flame. Now she could make out Trent squatted on the hearth,
working the billows. It was a wonder what billows could do. The flame spread out
delicately, a kind of corona with something of Jessica at its center.

"Sorry I keep coming in so late," he said, feeding twigs to the hungry flames.

"Our joe moved from the south up to Belfast. We had to follow. After he settled, I took the last flight home."

"I understand," she said from the tufted leather sofa that had begun to feel like her sofa. "Besides, the hour on a clock doesn't make any difference to me."

"You work all the hours, don't you?"

"Sure. I don't have anyone to put to bed."

"You will."

She saw him in the new light with the dark behind him and his color deepening as the light grew, dissolving the shadows.

"You will," he insisted. "I have a lead for us."

"You do? So do I!" She grinned, then gave in to a sad sigh. "My last night in London and we both have leads. Figures."

When the fire was burning bright, Trent, in jeans and a cable sweater, moved to the sofa where Jessica was curled in a sherpa sweatshirt and tights. Next to the sofa was a bucket with a bottle of Bollinger and on the side table a silver tray with two crystal glasses and a bowl of strawberries.

"When I was in Big Brother this week," she said, turning to face him, going straight to the business, lest her heart sell-out to this spy-merchant, "I found a little file called Night Owl."

"Night Owl?" A frown of perplexity creased Trent's face. Then he gave a wry laugh. "I doubt it. That's *classified.*"

"I know, but—" She tried a strawberry. Wonderfully sweet, like her thoughts. "I was curious about your role in the cold war, so I sorta tried some passwords I dreamed up." He looked aghast, but she touched him lightly on the arm as if to say, "It's no big deal." "Anyway, I think I found something on Sterling."

"In Night Owl? My God, Jess, you're not—"

She popped a strawberry into his mouth, silencing him as she slid an East German police bulletin from under the tray.

Trent ate the yummy strawberry, staring at a sketch of a woman. "I can't believe you got into a cryptographic file!" he said with his mouth full. "*I* don't have clearance for this!"

"I swear I won't tell a soul," she said playfully, enjoying his transfixed gaze. She was grateful for the file, if he looked at her that way, she'd be a goner. That was at her fingertips, but she was not quite ready. "It's all in German," she complained. "Do you know German?"

"Oh, a little. I can just manage to order lunch in Berlin."

"Lunch, huh?" She knew he had ordered more than lunch on both sides of Berlin, he could probably speak German in his sleep, but she'd let that go, for now. "Can you read this?"

She handed him a supplement. Two pages of small German type.

He was fluent in German, but this tiny lie wasn't deliberate; he lied instinctively about things related to MI5, professional precaution. He reluctantly looked at the file, but it was not why he built the fire, he had other things on his mind. Night Owl was code for Hans Rudolph Vogler, a charming creature of the KGB. A high-level agent cloistered in the East German State Circus. A Russian spook. One of the best, though he had become a bit of a cowboy, too many independent deals with his South American drug partners. Trent had met him once, at a London pub of all places. Said he came over to pick up a tailored suit. More likely he had come over to snatch English secrets, perhaps behind those four cigarettes, half concealed in his suit pocket, and protected by its own skin of cellophane, how you hide the microfilm. A short, bull-shouldered man, muscled like a gladiator. Expressionless, animal-like eyes in a flat face slicked with coal black hair. A thread of violence ran through Vogler's dossier, and Trent wasn't surprised when someone took him out. He suspected it was Moscow, perhaps London, but never knew how it was done.

Now he read quickly, in phrases and between the lines, as he was trained to read. Dear Vogler had died after drinking a frozen margarita at a party in Rio de Janeiro. The sketch was made from a waiter who had seen the female bartender who made the drink. The report cited the boys in the German Circus who believed the woman was a seven-figure hitter. Rather rich for Vogler. He must have been deep into someone's pocket.

"They look *a lot* alike, don't they?" Jessica held Sterling's sketch next to the Argentine sketch.

Trent studied the pair of sketches.

"Same knife-shaped eyes," Jessica said. "Same nose and chin and forehead. Same cheekbones. Wish I knew German!" She watched Trent's eyes dart from sketch to sketch, his face a mask of calm. "So? What do you think?"

He took a Cohiba from his briefcase, igniting it in memory of Vogler, who had had a passion for anything Spanish. He read about the elaborate formality of a Brazilian cocktail party, a living screen behind which only God knows what deals were coming down. A fair-skinned tart in a resplendent pink linen gown on Vogler's arm as they tangoed. Trent could picture it, Beauty and the Beast. But Vogler would play the part well, turning routine into performance art. After the heated dance, Vogler had taken a margarita, to add to the ice in his veins, no doubt. The coroner reported that the ice in the drink was made of an odorless, tasteless acid. The crushed ice melted in his stomach, took the beast to the floor, Vogler screeching like a rabid animal. Horrified guests watched on helplessly while the acid boiled away the belly and throat and the mouth of the face. Nothing left on the dance floor but a bloody tuxedoed monstrosity of arms and legs in a twisted deformity.

Cold kill, Trent mused, *but clever* And most definitely not the work of one of Moscow's death-or-glory men. He considered the moves, a hit something of a dance, Vogler tangoing with a woman he likely never saw. Trent glanced at the sketch again. She had the time it took to serve and consume the margarita, better odds for an escape than a handgun or rifle would have given. But she had to *know* Vogler. Know that he drank margaritas. Had to know that well in advance of the hit. Trent recalled the floating trays of cocktails at the Grand Ball prior to the Brighton bombing. He dismissed the thought. Thatcher never drank anything in public without it being tested first. Still, he checked the report for a name. *Dicentra spectabilis*. Latin, named after a flower, the bleeding heart. Trent had never heard of an acid named after a flower; seemed to be almost a pun. One of those new acids, it'd take a chemist to keep up with them all.

Tomorrow he could check Big Brother for supplements, though he'd have to finesse it. Night Owl *was* classified. No idea why. Perhaps the savagely unprincipled Vogler had been working for MI5 as well? Was the Office his "tailor"? The sketches were similar, but it seemed highly improbable Sterling was related to the ice woman. Assassins are not known for their maternal impulses, and that was the only logical motive for Danny's abduction. Besides, Trent thought, eyeing his briefcase, what he had to pass along was disturbing enough. He looked at Jessica again, very conscious of her fragrance, of her colors, of the shapes beneath her oversize sweater, his hands with the memory of the night he had dressed her for bed. It was the gentlemanly thing to do. Couldn't very well leave her to pass out in wet clothes. Catch her death of cold. He had hoped they could do that bit with the shirt again tonight. With her eyes wide open. "Sketches are only guesswork, Jess." He set the sketches on the table, hoping he could find a way to dance around the bogey of Vogler's monstrosity, to make for a memorable finale evening for them.

"But they look so similar!" she protested.

"Look at the date." Trent pointed out the date in the upper corner of the bulletin. "This occurred twelve years ago."

"Really?"

"And the sketch is so crude. It could be almost anyone."

"But it's all we have!" she pleaded.

We, he thought. He rather liked the sound of that.

"The others didn't work out?" Trent asked.

"No! I've beat my brains out for two weeks! This"—she shook the ice woman bulletin at him—"is the best match I've found!" But no sooner had the words leaped from her mouth than a little voice asked her, *Isn't he the best match you've found?*

Trent glanced at the Bollinger, ice melting around it. The fire was going great guns now. Fire, strawberries, champagne. The interruptive possibilities were enough to make a man hysterical. He calmed the savage. "Jess, it takes *time* to find a fugitive."

She rolled her eyes.

"Look; the whole of the British government is mobilized to net *one* bloody bomber. We have his name. His picture. His prints. And we still can't find him. But we're *getting close.* And you're getting close. Problem is," he said, looking into her eyes, "one never knows just how close one is getting until one is there."

She turned away to stare at the busy fire. There were times when she sensed herself about to slide into Trent, the way she slid into his shirt every night. She didn't know what she was doing. She hadn't come to London for Trent. She came for *Danny.*

"You mentioned something about a lead?" she said to the fire.

This is going to ruin the evening, he thought. *And that's a shame. She needs tonight more than I do.* He dropped the Cohiba in the ashtray and took the file from his briefcase.

"Jess, I'm afraid this is a bit irregular."

"What do you mean?" She turned with a frown of perplexity.

"Well. I'm afraid it's a bit . . . *twisted.*"

"Oh." She settled back into the sofa with apprehension. She understood twisted. Might have missed its meaning last year, but was up on it now. There was a certain cinematic treatment to it, the way her son was used to kill her. Then there was the bullet itself, twisted as it tumbled and tore through her body and lodged in her back. Twisted is as twisted does. Problem is, saving your soul from becoming twisted.

That was the death-defying trick. It was a trick poor Winston Smith never mastered. It was cruelty, once you were in the hands of the Ministry of Love. And it was that that twisted and twisted, the thwarted love for Danny.

He tried to explain it rationally. He had recently worked on a case where a racketeer, gone missing for years, had "turned up rather dead as a female. That is say, he had had a sex change. *He* became a *she*. So, with that in mind"—Trent opened the file, watching a faintness come over Jessica—"I scanned Big Brother based on the premise: What if Sterling were a man?"

"No way!" Jessica snapped.

"Well, Jess, sex changes are not *that* uncommon. And we've come up short using the conventional approach."

"Trent, she was in my studio! She's *not* a man! Okay?"

"No, of course not. But she might have been, *once*."

Her face went crimson. She stared into the fire. "I can't believe *you* would come up with *this*," she said, and it occurred to her that classified files do not have all the secrets about a man. Nor will you find them in his closet. Or in the attic. Or in the dusty—thank God it was dusty—photo album. There are some things that some men keep to themselves, and no matter how devoted you are at prying into his secrets, you will never find them all. And just now, Jessica was grateful for this. Some men had to be known. The best men were known to themself. That was enough.

Trent glanced mournfully at the Bollinger. And it was such a good year. But now he told her of Peter Julius Nordstrom, arrested in Stockholm on drug charges in 1969. Big Brother had matched Nordstrom with Sterling. The tidy computer did a composite from Nordstrom's mug shot, as if the Swede were a female with Sterling's hairstyle. Trent took the sketch from the file. It showed high cheekbones and knife-shaped eyes and wide lips.

Jessica looked briefly at it and turned away. "This person," she said in a clotted voice, "has had a sex change?"

"No. Not exactly. He's a man with features like your sketch, and he had a run-in, as you Yanks say, with the law. Add to that he was something of a cross dresser. Dresses as a woman, you know. In London these days, well, I suppose that sort of thing happens everywhere. Even in Chicago."

A log exploded in the fire. Sparks spiraled up the chimney. Jessica began to slip away. The worst hell is not what you know, it's what you don't know that your mind, twisted by bullets and whatnot, imagines. A woman who imagines the pornographic will see it in others. Hate will see it, it will insist on it, and more, turning reality into a freak show. Her gut dictated what she knew of Sterling: she may be the coldest thing God had ever made, but she was not yucky. Yucky was beneath her. Still, Jessica glanced fast at the sketch again, something twisted couldn't help it. "Do you know *anything* else about this person?" she asked.

"No. But I have the time now. I'm looking into it first thing tomorrow. Unfortunately, Nordstrom seems to have evaporated since '69. Of course, Nordstrom is probably nothing. But—"

"But you thought it was *something*," she said quickly, "or you wouldn't have shown it to me."

"Well, we have to consider all the—"

"Would you do me a favor?" she said, cutting him off.

"Anything."

"Would you make me a scotch, please?"

He waited, looking at her with suppressed eagerness. But the Bollinger would be a waste now.

"Certainly," he said.

He returned the file to his briefcase, dropping the sketch on the side table. He tried to pinpoint exactly when he started caring for this woman. There was no real decision. He had lost touch with his own volition in being drawn into hers and now was well on his way to—what? Wasn't she leaving tomorrow? And besides, how could he compete with a lost child?

"Trent!"

He whipped around. She was staring at the Sterling sketch and the ice woman sketch and the Nordstrom sketch. All lying side by side in a circle of lamplight.

"Look!" she said, pointing. "They look like sisters!"

He stepped back and looked speculatively at the sketches.

"Could they be from the same family?" she asked.

"Highly improbable."

Her mind was gibbering, as if trying to collaborate with the sketches, but she was too sickened and annoyed to hear. Her center knocked ajar. Sent one way by perversion. Sent another by love. For the first time she thought of herself, not Danny, as lost. "God," she said, staring, "they all look alike, don't they?"

"Yes, well, composites are nothing but guesswork, Jess."

She turned her head more sharply to the sketches, studying the trio as if it were all going to come to her suddenly. On the edge of something terribly important, she knew it, the confusion running riot in her head. Everything tangled up with everything else, and she could hardly think. But nothing came and she shut her eyes, wondering if she were going nuts. When she looked up again, she was staring at *Madame Monet and Her Son.* That was one tough mama in that painting; it barely showed, but it was there; she had to be to put with him, Claude Monet's natural habitat was obsession. Studying the picture, an uncanny sensation stole over Jessica. She was on to something. She knew it.

"Trent, what if . . ."

He turned back from the bar again.

"What if they're all—all three of them—the *same person?*"

He saw her eyes pale and watchful. Needing so much, but so lost to herself he couldn't reach her. "Jess," he said softly, "I'm afraid you've too much imagination for this work. It's a bit like copy painting. Slow and tedious. Damn few surprises."

The three sketches seemed to be spinning. Spinning into one face. "This is *so* spooky! It's like we're onto *something!*"

"Right. Let me get you that drink. Then we'll take a walk. It's foggy out. You could take some pictures. Might do Piccadilly Circus. Bright lights smudged in a watery cloud. We might find a surrealist in you." He turned to the bar, then asked, "By the way, how *did* you get into Night Owl?"

"Oh, well." She shrugged and smiled innocently, with no sign of the tough mama in the smile. "I noticed when you opened one of your files, you used a dictionary. Used a math term accompanied by a formula. Right? The formula is the password to get into the file. And I guess that makes sense; that way you just remember the term and don't have to memorize all the confusing formulas. Anyway, I just flipped through and looked up, well, quite a few math terms, most everything I could think of, and when I tried the formula for a definite integral . . . *bingo!*"

"And that got you into Night Owl?" he said, astonished.

"Yeah. It kinda surprised me. It just popped right up! A whole mess of files, in some kind of code. You want the formula?"

"Jess, I'm not supposed to have the formula. I don't have clearance for Night Owl."

"Here." She grabbed pen and pad from the side table, Trent's gaze transfixed as she wrote it down. *f(xi)@Xi*

She had penetrated what he could not know for sure, though he half-suspected it was a covert operation within the intelligence network, what he had heard existed, but only in rumor. One didn't ask about teeter-tottering rumor. One played along. He considered the term. *Integral* implied completeness, entirety; one having everything required. *Definite* was to be certain, precise. He wondered if it was a code for Vogler. He thought not. Vogler's slam-dance approach to his work was anything but precise. But could the term be related to the hitter who did Vogler?

"Right," Trent said, peeling the page from the pad, only to drop it into the fire. "Thanks. I'll get us those drinks."

13

THE FIRST PRICK of dawn penetrated the darkness and fanned over the elms, spraying through the treetops onto a rolling lawn. The light grew brighter, sketching the manor house, probing the high brick wall that encircled the estate, igniting gold-spiked lances atop the iron gates spangled by gas lanterns that flickered as dying stars in the dawn. Below each lantern was a bronze crest cast in a florid script: "Warnock Manor."

The black-and-white Tudor was on the northernmost perimeter of Grantham. Together with the walled garden and the adjoining art studio it occupied a city block. The largest private residence in Grantham, it had served as the home of the Warnock family from the fifteenth till the nineteenth century, but had fallen into disrepair. It had in years past been a retirement home, then a haven for unwed mothers, then a sanctum of meditation for a Muslim sect. The dissipated family trust sold it to Arab investors who faithfully restored the house recently featured in a book of the world's greatest houses, six pages devoted to its halls of walnut paneling and polished marble floors. Its spacious rooms of matte gray walls framed by elaborately gilded moldings and coffered fresco ceilings. An executive retreat, the estate was two hours from

London, it was leased by an heir of the Victoria's Secret fortune. He gave a list of prestigious references which were verified. Paid a year in advance with a cashier's check. It was all "cricket," as they say, the great old house given new life by the stewardship of its youthful tenant, Kim Lee of Honolulu, Hawaii.

How the Turner Studio received its name was a question of debate tangled in the mongrel history of the Warnock family outlived by the celebrated house. Legend has William Turner painting there for a brief time. The beamed and skylit studio, built in 1802, held a balcony with a bleacher where Turner's students were said to have sat in reverence, witnessing the creation of masterpieces of light that would dazzle the world. Legend wears a brave face. Turner, had in fact, stayed a weekend and dabbled on a trifling that for a period hung in the gallery. The studio now a catch-all for the renovation, the many pigmented lacquers for the woodwork stored there, and the thinners and scaffolding that went with the splattered state of the walls. It was this fertile air of creativity that drew Somberg to Turner's studio of light. What the renovation had neglected she prized.

She had saved the scaffolding, racked with the garish slopped cans of lacquer amid the high walls. To this was added books and a symphonic-quality sound system, music the vernacular of genius, overstuffed Venetian sofas found at Sotheby's, an elegant curving chaise from the Newel Art Gallery was grouped with a Louis XV desk snatched up in auction at Christie's. All this before a massive fireplace one could walk into, as though it were a furnace. There were other various pieces, circa chairs and sculptured tables that together had an eclectic effect, an orchestration of color without the push and pull by the demands of a style that can inhibit, one ends up with the same results regardless of failings or success.

Somberg was working now at the desk, peering through the lens of a magnifier-lamp at a brass belt buckle that housed a microchip detonator. With the dexterity of a jeweler she adjusted the timing delay using a pick, then clipped the brass face over the buckle. It was not the work of a madwoman, but very exacting work, though she would allow herself to be portrayed as mad when it was over. When accused of monstrous things, nothing sounds so feeble as the truth. No one wants to believe the truth, regardless of what they say. People prefer a mixture of truth and lies and guesses, all of which would be supplied, so the affair in Grantham would be blown into a masterpiece of duplicity aimed at overwhelming all with the Medusa legend. The bigger the lie, the more people believe it. And the best fabrications are only an extension of the truth.

She had, in the pre-dawn hours, resolved the complication of the American vice president who potentially could have accompanied Thatcher to Grantham. Devastated causalities were one thing, but to invite the pre- and post-scrutiny of the agencies that would accompany the death of an American figurehead was an extramural affair that was simply not necessary. To indiscreetly take down the good soldier vice president would be madness, if not suicidal. And so arrangements were made, and it was not so difficult. There was a hotly contested farm bill pending in the Senate. Katherine Klein, like Lucinda Chambers who had nominated Kim, was a member of their enlightened elite group. Best dressed addicts to history. All of which sang, played an instrument, acted, or painted in the making of the present from the past affecting the future. Mostly gals of brute loveliness, though there was the occasional male. All with the taste for a hot tomato. A love for the striking, the glamorous, the rarified, the priceless, the obsessive, and the adoring. The soul escape and the soul expansion.

Senator Klein had made the arrangements, the farm bill would be called to the floor for a vote, giving the vice president just enough time to return from the British Summit with Thatcher. He presided over the Senate. He would have to be there to cast the deciding vote, so there was no chance he would be in Grantham.

Katherine was unaware of why Somberg had made a withdraw from the favor bank. Didn't want to know. Was happy to be of service. Personal services was what their group was all about. It was not pulling the string that was difficult, the strings had been strung, something like a concert piano, some years ago. It was imagining how the vice president problem could be resolved, and choosing the rational that would best meet the need.

Now she had the detonator belt buckle ready to test. She began another, she would have several backups and test them all. Art could be left to chance, but not murder, and never beauty. And now she looked up as beauty came down the stairs from the gallery into the master's studio.

"Good morning," she said, without looking up, "Is Eric up?"

"Not yet. He's still in the sack." Kim came bearing a gift. Meticulously peeled slices of orange arranged like blades in a wheel round the perimeter of a blue china plate, the deep blue a lovely contrast with the orange, a sensitivity to color part of the new song within him. "Want some orange for breakfast?" he asked offering his gift.

"Thank you, dear. That was very thoughtful of you."

"I'll make some coffee, if you like."

"Not necessary. I've already got it going."

"How's the detonator? Is it working out?"

"Oh, it's going beautifully. We'll try one out, but give me a few minutes, I want to finish the rest of them."

"Sure. I'll do my warm-up stretches," he said and stopped to the desk to plant a long, explicit kiss on her lips.

Somberg felt a tingle, like maybe an electric shock had come through the magnifier-lamp. She reached to kiss him again, but he slipped out of her grasp. He retreated, smiling over his shoulder with such triumph and sensual promise in his gaze, in his flirt, in his hip movements calculated to solicit, that he appeared as nothing less than a polished seductress.

"You despicable monster," she said to herself as she watched him go. She bit into the orange, juicy and fat and sweet, and not one single calorie. He kept going, waving back, the tease. Wearing the countenance of an angel. With a playful expression. Taking his trench coat off before a wall of mirror with a dance rail. She watched his reflection in the glass, rotating his lower body slowly and sensually, warming up both of them. In grape leotards that clung to his every curve. So lithe. So limber. Swingy hair at his shoulders. The soft mouth and Bambi eyes was that of a hip young boy, or a lankish girl with boyish charm. From the rear, the beauty's gender was anyone's guess. The dancer looked madly exhilarating. More alluring and more dangerous than she had ever dreamed. Dangerous because he took her from her work. Her cheeks aglow with hectic color, Somberg returned to the delicate work.

* * *

Kim stretched his head to his knee. He rose, flung his hair back, and checked his figure against the wall mirror the same way a girl would, staring intently, seeking a flaw. There were none. That brand new boy was looking gorgeous today.

His new super willpower had taken his waist to twenty-four inches. It was amazing, he could have never done that before. His bottom was somehow rounder, fuller. And his hips were fuller. Or maybe that was the way he was always standing these days, with a little hip. He had the hair he always wanted but didn't know he wanted. He had been growing it longer and it just took forever, but was just right now, and he loved the conditioner he was using. He had great skin. Smooth, clear, perfect. But every time he shaved his legs he cut his skin. He had learned to shave the flat sides of the bone, using a thick shaving cream, then get as close as possible to the edge of the bone; Kim was living on the edge now. And he had learned to shave in the direction of the hair growth when doing his bikini line so he wouldn't get those little red bumps. Shaving legs was natural for a boy, if he was a swimmer, and Kim had learned to swim with no fear of the deep.

What he saw and didn't see were the gourd-like breasts that were very perky in his leotard. They looked like the nibblings of a young girl's bosom. This, he understood, was a reaction to the vitamin pills he was taking. It was a thing that sometimes happens on those vitamins; it would correct itself in time. Kind of spooky how super sensitive his nipples had become. A feather's touch could send him. A source of embarassment, and secret pleasure.

It seemed that Kristian was provoking him deliberately with himself. So it was hard to stop looking at himself. Hard to stop touching himself which provoked Kristian because that hardness was hers. She had gradually replaced all his clothes with new stuff. There were chenille scrunchy, Ellen Tracy neck sweaters. And Versace tops in velvet and velour. An Isaac Mizrahi suede wrap jacket, and a mink trapper hat that couldn't be more macho, but somehow looked feminine on. Beautiful DKNY scarfs that made sense on a cold day. Calvin Klein black leather jeans that went with a purple cardigan, one of Kristian's favorite outfits for him. And a totally cool Ralph Lauren pin-striped suit, the coat cut to the thigh. A sleek Moschino lizard jacket and skinny jeans that had matching pointed zip-up ankle boots. A metallic Christian Francis Roth silk shirt. Emanuel suede pants. Shoes, shoes, and more shoes! By Gucci and Yves Saint Laurent and Bruno. And what looked like a girl's purse but what was really a boy's leather hobo bag by Anne Klein.

That it was all from girl's designers was a bit unnerving, but it was all cut in a male tradition. Very elegant and chic, and Kim could hardly protest, though every morning he secretly knew he was putting on girl's clothes—a secret he didn't tell himself. The clothes seemed to come with a new sexiness. A new energy. He had reservations about clothes and other little things, like his super nipples, but he couldn't deny their sex was incredible.

They were making it constantly; he was always hard, thanks to an exercise he did every morning and evening. He would contract the pubococcygeal muscle, as if holding back the flow of urine. He did 36 contractions at a time, rested a few minutes, then begin again. It was like weight lifting for the penis. He could hold an errection for an hour or more, like he was petrified, or something. And the nights went on and on, gamely. It was strange, he had never loved more feminine, and had never fucked more like a man.

He felt as if he hadn't changed at all, but what brought out the barbarian in him were the disco girls. That was now his name for them, disco girls, whose pictures he had swiped in Geneva. The girls with the pretty butterflies tattooed to their bottoms, and knowing that drove him batty.

They came to Warnock two or three at time, and he didn't see much of them during the day. But when nightfall came, the house filled with them and the friends that they dragged in. Then the music started, and the dancing. It freaked him a little, the way some of them came on to him. Like they knew him from head to toe. And he wondered if they knew that he had dreamed of kissing them?

Their boldness made him defiant and independent. It didn't last. They hovered around him like perfumed angels. Asking all kinds of questions. Most of them intimate. He answered them and didn't know the sound of his own voice. Why did he so carelessly reveal himself to them?

He learned they were in apprenticeship to Kristian. In some network that placed them with Kristian's friends around the world. They were not self-nominated to this group, but hand-picked by one of the three sisters. Most in their 20s, knockouts with disarming smiles that tortured and lured him. Not into their bed, but into superior, gentle, amusing girlfriend confidences that possessed his mist-filled mind like midnight kisses. Girl talk. Letting him into feminine secrets that burned and tingled like a whip.

He wrote about them in his secret Casanova diary, and it seemed to him the beauties were in three ranks, or levels: *The first level are girls easy to spot with their schoolgirl charm. In pleated skirts and puffy blouses that revealed nothing. Demure. Almost voiceless. Quiet and shy. Good girls*

The next group you can't see as much as feel. The cool ones. The detached girls. Social pretenders. Swingy bobbed hair flung back, tits jutting out. There are more in this second class than in the first or third.

The third group you don't recognize by what you see or feel, but by how they draw you. The magnetic ones. They know how to use their erotic muscle. In androgynous clothes. Most with short boyish hair. A sense of freedom and unpredictability about them. They're dangerous. They're the best, both female and male.

There had met twenty-six girls and made notes of their names and where they lived and who they lived with and how he would fuck them if he only could. But in sleep he did not fuck but worshipped them, and it seemed they had all come from another place and time, though he knew this was not true, for he had gazed into their eyes with the awe of a boy who has looked upon the forbidden. In this infancy of carnal play, the drugged-out roughed-up babe, drugged on femininity, smacked about by desire, could not know that he, the somber baby, was on his way to becoming one with them. One in the flesh, one in bondage, and one in spirit. As that dazzle of diamonds at their neck, as the fine gold bracelet at their ankle, and the glory of the butterfly that flickers on the morning sun.

The glass of the pinnacle skylight caught his eye, to return him from angel chic to the brooding, bored, slouched life of the world-weary male. And now the glory of the girls was nothing more than babbling inanities. He followed the sunlight that fell on the burled rope of a hoist suspended above a marble sculpture, a work in progress, of Maggie Thatcher. There were, Kristian had taught him, two sides to every face. You could take a picture of anyone, cover one side, and see a somewhat, often totally different face in the other half. In sculpture, Kristian always did a bust one side at a time, which was why her work appeared so lifelike. The left side of Maggie's face was smooth, regal, the judicious visage the world knew, the smile a little reproachful. But the right side wasn't finished and roughed out into a patchy complexion. Like she was wart-covered or pock-marked. The nose, at this point, was like a snout, the brow misshaped, as if overgrown with bone that gave her the look of a beast, pretty damn fierce. Studying the finished half of Maggie, and then the bestial half, Kim wondered if maybe the bust wasn't finished?

"Was you give me a hand here?" Kristian called from the far end of the studio, her voice slightly echoed in the high walls.

Kim ran up to the back where his boss was waiting beside two boxes that had the look of caskets.

"What's in the boxes?" he asked.

"In this one," Somberg ran the blade of a jade letter opener up the seam of tape that sealed the long box, "should be Maggie."

Kim laughed aloud at this, in the glitter of her cunning and decadence as he helped rip the box open with the thrill of a boy on his birthday. The lids opened to a thick foam padding molded to a human shape. The padding discarded, a body lay in the box before him, wrapped in strips of protective gauze like a mummy. Together they stood the mummy on its feet. It was as tall as Kim and nearly as heavy. It was all somehow illegal, Kim knew it. He knew it the same way he knew Kristian was going to destroy Margaret Thatcher. He knew it and did not know it, and the knowing did not trouble him, only the glory of girls troubled him, as it did every man.

He went to his knees, as in worship, to began the unraveling of the gauze of what his betraying mind imagined was an idol of Thatcher. The gauze was rolled away to reveal an anatomically correct genderless dummy, neither female nor male. The body of the plastic dummy was numbered in sequence, beginning at the skull dissected in ink in quadrants, the numbers continuing over trunk and abdomen and crotch, dividing the back into quadrants, and each limb was numbered at the joints, with numbers on each finger. The dummy had no eyes or expression, its features blank, fascinating, part of the lie that was truth Kim knew and did not know.

"It's a crash dummy," Somberg offered. "Used in safety tests of cars, to keep drivers out of the graveyard."

The graveyard. Kim had an image of Kristian's bedroom. He was to be burried there, he knew it and didn't know it. "What in the world is it for?" he asked.

"You'll see. Give me a hand, will you?"

Somberg took the head, Kim the feet, together they carried it to the back wall where there was a blackboard Somberg used in her imagining. Blackboards could be erased as easily as minds; it was amazing the things people forgot.

"It's the same dimensions as Maggie," Somberg said, carrying the body. "She's an amazing woman. Changed so many things."

"I'll say," Kim replied, and earnestly started rattling off numbers, like a guy. "When she became PM, England was on the verge of economic collapse. Inflation was twenty-seven percent. Income tax eighty-three percent. Unemployment seventy percent. There was a strike every other day. The unions had England on a three-day work week, because there was no work.''

Somberg smiled proudly into his gorgeous eyes. With just a touch of mascara; enough shadow to make him look dreamy. ''And Maggie changed it with seduction,'' she said.

''Yep. She used America's entrepreneurial formula. Broke the unions like it was her mission. Inside a year, inflation fell to twelve percent. Unemployment to nine percent.''

Somberg listened, not to words, but to rules. ''The rational structure of the male-driven world is the best friend a girl has,'' she said, sitting the dummy down before the blackboard. ''She can count on it to never change.'' She positioned the dummy's back to the blackboard. ''The answer for women has been sitting there all along, waiting to be found, in a future that belongs to change.''

Kim stepped back to consider the dummy before the blackboard, seeing it as an earnest dreamer. ''She made all kinds of enemies,'' he said of Maggie. ''The unions called her Attila the Hen. Then there was the old guard. The corporations. The Establishment. The intellectuals—they didn't oppose her, they *abhored* her. I'd say Maggie has a way of pissing people off.''

Somberg smiled on the sex-neutral dummy painted in numbers as the numbered step-by-step stages of woman's prosperity. It was all there, in the Thatcher image.

''Men believe in experience,'' she said as she led the changing beauty back to the boxes. ''Experience is the worst teacher in a world constantly changing. Men suffer the crippling delusion of loyalty. But there is no loyalty any more. Whereas a girl acts in concert with chaos that *is* the future. Reality is nothing but a hunch that is wide open to change that is the nature of a girl and the fear of men. The future belongs to change, and a girl's success with men lies not in appeals to reason, but in the appeal to the self that does not change.'' It was Somberg's secret power, the changing of men. Done not so much by the drugs and beatings of femininity, but by sexual rapture, the way every man wishes to go. ''Men shut their eyes to change for fear the winds will sweep them away,'' she said to the primal boy strung-out on girls, ''It makes it such a pleasure when experience unhinges them from the outcome of their rules, in a future that belongs to change.''

Kim didn't want to hear any of this. He tried to ignore it. He thought only of Thatcher. ''She has a closetful of personalties. Changes personas like other women change clothes.'' He watched as Kristian cut open the second box. ''Maggie can be a screamer. A sweet-talker. She can be gracious or bulldoze, rationalize or flirt or beat you silly with the facts. I'd say she's into head trips.'' He helped remove padding to find the form of a child dummy in the second box. ''She was a little brown-haired girl that became a blond. She was a bore who made herself *cool*. Made a new media image. Did herself overnight. Then started in on the country.''

They unraveled the mummy like gauze, and the child dummy was like the adult, divided in various stages by painted numbers.

''A man focuses on a strategy of how to get there,'' Somberg continued as they carried the dummy across the room. ''He lives in a world built on predictability that no longer exists. But a girl counts on the certainty of uncertainty.''

Kim looked up at this, with a faint understanding of it that curled tenuously into a smile, lips a shade darker than natural, glossed in Hip Honey, not loud, but it was nevertheless lipstick.

"A girl," Somberg said, speaking to the girl that could be seen whenever he was bedazzled, "focuses on being the best at what she does, starting with hair, makeup and clothes. Begin with the body and the mind will follow. A girl ignores strategy, to focus on the *process* that is *discovery* that will make the outcome."

They sat the child beside the adult dummy. Somberg positioned the child so it slightly faced the adult, shoulder of the child to the blackboard.

"A girl can remake herself whenever and in whatever ways she chooses," Somberg said, strapping an explosive belt round the waist of the child dummy. "In learning to remake herself, she learns to remake others. When she begins to change herself, a country, the world, she has no idea how it'll come out. She trusts in intuition; she trusts in self. True self-reliance is true independence."

She said this with the certainty and wisdom of Death, and Kim did not doubt her and loved to listen. Her words as a templet that a part of him was using to make a new suit of clothes for herself. Was it a suit? Or was it a dress? Kim shuddered at the thought.

Somberg released the tiny safety on the brass belt buckle detonator. She took Kim by the hand, retreating to her desk where a video camera was mounted on a tripod.

"Maggie is not really into the women's-lib thing," Kim said, denying to himself any possibility he was changing, and in this way he was so easily changed. "She just *expects* to be treated like an equal. And it's kind of funny, American women raising all kinds of hell about equality but none of them has come close to what Maggie has achieved. She's the most powerful woman since . . ." He looked to the glass skylight, and was lost for a comparsion. He thought of Catherine the Great. And Cleopatra. He looked to his beloved and thought of Medusa. She was in jeans and sneakers and a cool navy military jacket. Gold braid on the sleeves and collar, gold buttons embossed with a crowned eagle, claws embedded in the world. "She's naturally impulsive," he went on. "What's more, she believes her impulses are right."

"Is that so?" Somberg smiled, sliding a remote detonator into her jacket. She turned on the video camera, focusing on the pair of crash dummies. From her desk she took a hand-blown glass vase so it wouldn't be shattered by the coming blast. The delicate vase had torch gingers; the flowers looked like huge pink penis heads.

"Maggie's sorta psychic," Kim said, following to the front of the studio. "It's a joke around Parliament. I mean, here she is, overhauling the economy. Fights wars. All the time she's kind of watching the stars. Makes a guy wonder how smart she really is."

"She's a woman of middling ability," Somberg replied. "Not particularly intellectual. She uses her *will* to overcome hostile forces, including herself."

Somberg placed the fragile vase of pretty penis flowers on a scaffold shelf, wrapping Kim's coat around it so it wouldn't break in the forthcoming changing blast. The ancients had used castration, but the Amazons didn't have estrogen. Her belief was pleasure. A penis was pleasure. It was feel-good. Why do without? Why break what you could change?

She asked Kim to play Prokofiev's *Piano Concerto No. 3*. The music a rhapsody that when taken in regular doses leads to a ravishment of the senses. She skipped the first movement, a modified sonata, and went to the guiltless innovations of the second movement. It was suspended fire. Bold but subtle. A thirst for the atrocious made perfect and respectable. She took up the detonator.

"Maggie was a girl on the outside," she said before putting her work to the test, "and it's only from the outside that you can truly see the world for what it is. You can escape the illusion of reality that holds others, to meet reality and *use* it. In this way Maggie became the future that arrived at lightspeed," Somberg said to Kim who she would take in this same way.

She waited until the music reached a crescendo, not wanting the blast to wake Eric, then flipped up the protective shell on the detonator button. She pressed it. There was a ten-second delay, followed by a thunderous white-hot explosion of the child dummy.

Kim leaped at the bang made by a two-ounce wafer of Semtex in the belt lining. He saw a shrapnel of arms and torso exploded into the adult. *"Far fucking out!"* he shrieked in boyish glee. Smoke hung over the blackboard embedded with white chips of dummy, the adult broken on the floor where it had landed. "God! Think what it'll do to Maggie! There'll be blond hair all over the walls!" He saw her in several large wet, pieces. He looked for the child. The floor was blackened, but there were only fragments of legs left.

"I think the charge is just right now," Somberg said, turning down the concerto but letting it play to live in Kim.

High on a whiff of explosive, he was twirling to the concerto seen in the mirror as a myriad of reflections. Boys and girls, impossible to tell them apart in this Age of Possibility in which there are no rules. He saw only a beauty spinning. So graceful. So absorbed. "It's the shrapnel that does Maggie, isn't it?"

"That's right, dear. The explosive elevates into the trunk region, detonating the chest and arms like a Claymore mine."

This worth an entry in his diary. Kim wondered where he hid it last? He kept moving it so Kristian wouldn't find it.

"But, unfortunately"—Somberg let a greedy hand glide over his sleek, tight, twirling ass—"the belt would cost me Eric."

Kim allowed himself to be caught gently against her, in her arms, loving the gentle pushing against his pelvis. "But the belt is just, like, a backup, right?"

"That's right," she said watching them in the mirror as she turned his head to take his lips with her lips tight against his open mouth, caressing his nipples which went erect together with his penis. She could feel his craving and it gave the pleasure of generosity to change him at her touch, the estrogen pills returning him to his true nature, that of God Herself. Softly, softly, she stroked the pretty baby, with infinite soothing and assurance, and as they kissed she rocked the beauty being born within, teaching hips to roll to her rocking, and he grew soft inside and hard all over, while she turned hard inside and remained soft all over.

"The belt is, like, an insurance policy," he said, seeing in the mirror some perfect girl he had always loved, smiling at him in the mirror. "Like a death insurance policy, right?"

"Hmm." She stroked smooth spandex that clung to his buttocks as a second skin.

He was on his way to perfect, with the bottom of a girl and the hips of a girl and the nipples of a girl and all the sensitivities of a girl, but a penis that, on her estrogen, was more responsive than ever. "But I doubt I'll need the belt."

"Yeah, good! 'Cause it'd be a bummer to lose Eric!"

"No, I doubt it will come to that. Losing is not my way."

Kim gazed into the mirror, hypnotized by his own lush eyes that were no longer his eyes. In the mirror he saw the imaginary girl who lived inside his head in a cast of perfect light. Melissa Brooks. A model he had chased after and never caught, and now it seemed as if she had caught him. His hair as long as Melissa's who had his features and whose fashion-model breasts were not much larger than his were now. Wearing Melissa's male-chick styles in Donna Karan and Ralph Lauren and Christian Francis Roth and all the rest, in Melissa's colors of black and jade and amethyst. The pretty eyes in the mirror knew and didn't know this, as an elusive rhythm, an undeniable orgasmic sensation, a name that for a moment tried to take shape and his lips that parted in a gasp, but they made no sound and what he could not believe slipped away.

He had been with Kristian for what seemed like forever, and had come to understand men were more susceptible to seduction than girls; that was pretty straightforward, most people agreed with that. He agreed with it. Girls were more swept up in romance; he had counted on that when he was a Romeo. But now at every kiss he was so wistful and wondering, revaluing everything according to the measure of response it drew from Kristian's eyes. The sort of thing Juliet would do. Both Romeo and Juliet lured into tantric drives that were two parts of the same thing: love. He had never encountered both parts simultaneously, not many people did, and he was surprised and overwhelmed by it all, seduction and romance.

He thought he was just a little in love—might be related to the vitamin shots and pills he was given. In love with Kristian. With her girls. And in love with someone best described as the dream of himself. It was the nature of love to give all, to obey the heart; his heart uprooted, driven into a sexual exoticism of unknown origin. Caught in tantric trickery so disorienting he sometimes thought was going nuts. A whisper was urging him to let go. To go right out of his head! All of it happening in such fine graduations of love and need and desire and lust, but he was not obsessed, and he was running his life, though the idea of himself was evolving. He listened more with the heart than the ear. Listening for a secret rendezvous, part of the long delayed rendezvous with himself, his obedient heart enamored in hopes and heavenly fire. A boy being prepared to die of his own dreams.

"Something's happening but I don't understand any of it," he said to the girl in the mirror.

Somberg kissed his heated neck. "At some level it'll come to you, dear. As lyric. As wisdom. As a power of revelation. Time's gift to a maturity you're rapidly approaching."

"Will I stay like this?" he said, a little wildly.

"Like what, darling?"

"You know. Sorta feminine."

"What's feminine? Hmm?"

Somberg waited, but he didn't answer.

"Girls today are wearing their hair boy-short. Wearing boy's blazers and shirts and ties. Playing boy's games and doing boy's jobs. Does that make them any less feminine?"

"No, ma'am," he said, knowing better than to say anything against the autonomy of today's woman.

"Now your hair is longish and lovely." Fingers ran through a lush, silky, swinging cut. "You're wearing girl's clothes, doing girl's work as an assistant. Kissing as a girl. Loving as a girl. Does that make you any less of a boy?"

He hesitated, confused. "No, I guess not," he said.

"Really, darling," she said, wondering what William Turner would say of her sumptuous art, "there's nothing feminine, nothing masculine but that *thinking* makes it so. The world is changing. If you want to be pretty, you don't have to be female. If you want to be strong, you don't have to be male. If you want to be both you can. We make our own rules. We live our dreams."

Traveling on the voyeuristic powers of the Prokofiev that knew no bounds, Kim was taken beyond the narrow that confined most people's lives. Changed in some provocative way he could not yet understand. Drenched in eroticism. Needing to touch, as much as wanting to be touched. Feeling like sexual plunder, and he didn't mind at all. He didn't mind not being the aggressor. Didn't mind being the captive. Very still in her arms, in a sort of sleep, in a sort of dream with a new nakedness emerging, and he didn't mind.

"Just look at me," she called from a mirror Garden of Eden. "That's how you are and I did it and there's nothing you can do now. You've been changed."

"No," he muttered, shaking his pretty hair.

"Oh, yes. You love that Beauty. You've *always* loved her."

"No," he repeated to the skilled killer.

Somberg watched the spandex swell between his legs.

"Your lie detector says you're lying!" she said, laughing.

He closed his eyes and leaned back against her, letting her take all his weight. Now lifting shoulders, beaded nipples pressed hard against the spandex with a slow girl shudder spilling through him while hands explored his smooth belly and slid down his sides to slow rolling hips and dipped down to take his breath away, and he could almost live without breath. He needed only Kristian.

"I'll review the video," Somberg said, witnessing his first female orgasm. "Analyze the scatter-pattern of the body parts. But I'd say the belt is finished. Lovely art, really."

"Oh, it's tip-top," Kim said in a softness he seemed destined to endure. "I think it's a great invention. The *belt,* I mean."

"Mmm. It's *gorgeous,*" Somberg soothed, and took his hand. Kim let himself be led up the stairs, a boy about to ravaged, and already he was as large as the pretty penis flowers. He would do it all, and Somberg would do it all to him, but that one thing that would have to wait; it would only come as the overture to that actual moment when his male heart ceased to beat. And she could hardly wait for his romantic reunion with Melissa Brooks. The Amazons had nothing on Somberg who loved sacrificial rituals.

14

THE RING OF Kerry shaped itself out of the delicate beauty and hard, rugged realism that could only be Ireland. They came along the road that twisted with the fickle sea, driving through the mist that veiled sheer rock cliffs God forgot to finish. From the wheel Somberg watched Eric cock his head and take in the high, hushed drama. Through his eyes she saw the gray, ghostly light, now drifting up the cliffs, not quite reaching the sky, the light changing to topaz and golden so the cliffs glittered as the walls of some fabled bastion set on the foamy shore of forever.

It was a game she played, to slide into supporting player so the world revolved around the star. It was a symptom of what she had come to think of as "mother sickness." The child's life was the perspective. You forget about your own. You spent most your time arranging events for the sheer whimsical amusement of the one and only. She could see how this self-involvement with a boy could be parlayed into addiction. Damaging to any career. Damning to one who worked in the realm of death that was a common circumstance of business. Still, it was fascinating and irksome how often she had found herself living in Eric time. Such a pleasure to indulge him. He begged to come to Ireland with her, it was not the professional call, but she found herself buckling him into his co-pilot seat on the Gulfstream that when he flew was not *Pequod* but *Ghostrider.* She made sure he had his crayons and Game Boy and chilled apple juice. There were chocolate grahams, all natural, organic whole wheat, only the best would do, but the grahams couldn't be had until he had colored a map of their flight from Grantham to wee Killarney. She had stayed up half the night doing the map that was a pictorial of a gender-reversed Thatcher as Lord Cromwell invading Ireland with her ships of bloodthirsty Saxons. By the time the grahams were finished, he understood the whole ridiculous 800-year mess that could be summarized in one word: greed.

She found a brilliance in explaining the world to him. He was a pleasant interlude in her life. Her only idealism. A new sense of personal style. Such a gifted boy. So bright. So beautiful. So hers. Or was she his?

They came into Killarney and the mist had turned to rain; a sudden downpour. Somberg pulled into the car park, squinting out the window as a rolling crack of thunder let go and came peeling down the sky to the high, pointy towers of St. Mary's Cathedral that jutted into a sky dark as sin. She sat there a moment, an eyebrow raised at the pelting storm, her son watching the shadows ripple over her frown. And she knew he knew she was displeased with the Goddess; they talked about Her often, how not a single drop of rain missed its mark. The Goddess never missed.

Every job had its complications, and Somberg had known when Shanahan walked into the Abbey Library with O'Grady that he would be one. She understood men like Paolo Vanzetti who had recommended her to O'Grady. Honest crooks are motivated by cash, and they are by a damn sight more reliable than politically inflamed zealots. A political zealot was half sister to a first-stage femme caught in the "bimbo eruption." Obsessed with herself. With her style. With her name. Her hair. Her dreams. Her horny, nagging eyes that pleaded, "Do me! do me! do me! I can never get enough." The first-stage femme was doom. Overwhelmed. A chatter box. They and zealots were thwarted, frustrated and neurotic. An act in the invention. The difference between a femme and a zealot was the femme became another person, they expanded to serve the leisure class, whereas the zealot was uncompromised, on the edge, always overworked and underpaid, capable of anything. They were not professionals.

Two weeks ago Shanahan had left a message on her machine in Zurich. "The lady has had a change in her calender." He called for a meeting in Killarney. He was probably overreacting to some entanglement; part impulse, part contradiction, she knew Shanahan. She had trained the type, from newborn femme into second-tier. The male muted, muffled, the emerging female practical, aware of her sensual possibilities, composing desire, to become everyone's best friend, to make bonfires out of other people's desires. Any of her sweet and severe second-tiers, graduating to the electric, could take Shanahan to his knees; the only fight would be in his soul. She would meet in Killarney, but take appropriate precautions.

Her "eyeball" van with the one-way glass was at the corner. From there the front and side entrances were covered, the five assets inside the cathedral monitored by the "baby," Somberg's youngest sister, returning from a job in Helsinki. With a root derivative from her garden, she had baffled the chief Norwegian pathologist. She was on her way back to Chiang Mai to her village compound descended from the ancient kingdom of Lanna, that means "a million rice fields." The main house, a high sloped roof affair decorated with winged *kaelaes,* was of the Thai tradition enhanced with space age technology; it extended to converted rice barns that served as guest pavilions, lined by garden pathways of sandstone and laterite. She lived in coconut and rattan and wicker and all-natural fabrics set in great sliding doors with mountain views all around. Ceramics were made by her villagers, along with sacred decorative pieces like the carved wooden elephant head above the fireplace, and the living room carpet that showed the phases of the moon. She read in the cool of a rice paper umbrella on a teak veranda to the flowering lotus pool; the lanterns carved into the railings served as miniature spirit houses. It was a quiet setting, one with nature; as peaceful as the song of a bird.

Somberg and Eric ran into hurtling rain, splashing through stained-glass light bleeding in pools on the walk. Up gleaming marble steps. Somberg heaved open a paneled door, rain pelting their backs. A billow of a woman was just inside the door, loading a camera in the vestibule. Her girth was tented in a dress of such gaudy floral glory, she looked like a tree-size bouquet. A round, pink face was framed by a plastic rain scarf tied in a mule's-ears bow beneath a portly chin, red curls corkscrewed out the front of the scarf, their coils as bouncy as pasta rings. Somberg pushed Eric inside and the woman recoiled, but not before the camera fell from her hands. It hit the slate floor with a sharp crack.

"Uh-oh." Eric stopped in front of the camera.

"Come on," Somberg said, taking him by the hand.

"Now, wait just a minute!" the woman cried.

Somberg spun around to give the frump darling a dose of her hot eyes. The accent was American. Midwest. Perhaps Ohio. Maybe Illinois. "What?" she snapped. The woman's mouth opened, but no sound came out. The fillings of a little girl who loved sweets were displayed. Stared at those sharp blue irises, she backed into the slowly closing door, rain prickling down her spine.

"What?" Somberg repeated.

"He just!—" The woman paused to catch her breath. "Your son just knocked my camera to the ground!" she protested.

"I believe you just dropped it," Somberg retorted, shooting the woman a quelling glance. It snapped her head back as if she had been slapped. She took Eric's hand and started inside.

The woman shrilled after Somberg, "Well, I never!" She picked up her camera and it went off in her hand; a strobe flash tattooed the floor. She shook the camera next to her ear. Her soft face rumpled as she took in the dent on the nose of the camera's lens. "Back in Waterloo," she shouted after the rude woman with the beautiful, brutal face, "we apologize when we knock someone's camera out of their hand!"

"You're not in Waterloo," Somberg jeered, and tugged Eric into the sanctuary, leaving the American in the rain.

She reached into her handbag and flipped on the receiver. Kim's breathing came through the wireless earpiece in the shell of her ear as she and Eric walked slowly, reverently, up the aisle and through the Gothic shadows. Eric's eyes ran over the beams way up there. He liked the tall pointy windows of colored glass. And he thought the shiny organ pipes in front were pretty. The piano was bigger than the one in his school's music room and he pictured an angel playing something very softly as they came into the quiet that was kind of spooky. It was a nice, huge church for such a wet country, and he wondered if they had Froot Loops in this country? For some reason the organ pipes made him think of Froot Loops. And the more he looked at the organ pipes, the more they reminded him of a spaceship to the moon. Now he saw the altar candles. That was the best thing. He stared at their silent glowing light, and Somberg stared with him, feeling their glow that filled the eyes and was inhaled, so the light was inside and behind the mind. This was how it worked, if you stared into candles.

Somberg noted the high pulpit, it jutted like a ship's bow into the cathedral. From the pulpit a needlepoint tapestry hung; it portrayed a ship beating on against the terror of a storm that lashed at a rocky coast. Above the dark clouds, an angel's face sent a ray of hopeful light to the deck of the troubled ship. The inscription below was from Psalms: "Thy word is a lantern into my feet: and a light unto my paths."

Two nuns were polishing the pews with lemon oil; they looked like the real thing. Six patrons scattered about, five of them hers, they appeared like tourists stepped in for a whiff of God. Their outfits were the real thing, copied from the photos Alexa took last week. Five pairs of eyes looked nowhere and everywhere. Trained to move like smoke, to confuse, to drive, to intervene if necessary, to annihilate if ordered, though only two were armed. Alexa carried a Delta Elite, the 10mm rounds were interchangeable with Nicole's Spanish Star Ten, Isabella's gift, and one of the few

European 10mm Auto caliber pistols. Each was a qualified marksman and had fired at least 1,000 rounds with the weapon they carried that blindfolded they could assemble in under a minute. Backing up the fireteam was Isabella fresh from Madrid, and Natasha scheduled to return to Moscow next month, and Anna who was tutoring Kim, since Kristian was so occupied with her son.

The alligator bag in Somberg's right hand said it was safe. If moved to her left, smoke would be set in motion. She and Eric would vanish into the smoke that would surround them and move with them to the car that would be at the door, the baby at the wheel.

Somberg passed her newest devotee on his knees in a pew. Long lashes darkened in mascara, lustrous hair to his shoulders. He was not considered an operative, he had not been broken, but the look of him suggested it could be done any time. Kim swaying in a new moody nature, on estrogen pills; a flower of femininity blooming within. A perfect head number being done on him. Tutored in an exclusive girl's school, being remade into the likeness of the Goddess, and he was already unspeakably, devoutly possessed.

It was such a gorgeous sanctuary, and if it weren't for the business at hand, Somberg might ask Shanahan to conduct a wedding. Each beauty was in their way, secretly, sincerely, wed to her, and Kim with those beguiling cheekbones and rosebud lips was going to make a sumptuous bride. The enormous smothering, tormenting wealth of his training had made him salubrious, on his knees, very quiet, very delicate, almost as in a sleep, as if praying unconsciously for those pretty little cries of the wedding night. Somberg's lips curled at the thought of it. Such delicious thoughts in the dark, holy house. She would swallow him alive. And after the bride was sent out to the world he, like the others, would come back to her more hers than when he had left. Hers to renew and counsel and inspire, hers to nurture and complete and own. Hers to use till death do him part. A work of the lust of love that is the desire to possess, or be possessed. Therein lay the difference between the belied armed beauties now moving mechanically into position, in a mental state of warfare, and the devotee on his knees.

Kim rose on cue, feeling more than seeing. With his Bible he glided through pews, making his way to the back of the cathedral.

He entered the confessional, a dark phone booth to God. A latticework made for a nursery window. A panel slid back and he saw the murky shape of an oblong head. He touched the transmitter on the back of the silver cross that hung from his slender neck, now Somberg in the sanctuary could hear the priest say, "God bless and keep ye. Tell me yer sins, child."

"Cut the shit, Shanahan," Somberg replied from a distant pew, speaking into a microphone in her purse, Kim's lips pantomiming her speech that came from a speaker concealed in the Bible. "What the fuck do you want?"

"Ye surprise me, Gorgon," Somberg heard Shanahan say in her earpiece. "The enormity of yer reputation dwarfs the edifice of yer physique." He paused, but Somberg did not reply. She was watching Eric accompanied by an old nun, mounting the stairs with an altar candle. "All is going well, I hope?" Shanahan added.

"All is none of your business." Somberg's eyes cut through the sanctuary shadows that held illicit memories long since past. They had flown away on a candle flame, but were now returning on the flickering points of the altar candles. "What do you want?"

"I was merely inquiring—"

"What . . . do . . . you . . . want?"

Shanahan whispered, "The lady's visit to the aerospace factory in Manchester has been canceled."

Somberg grimaced. "You could have put that on the tape."

"Aye!" In the confessional Kim heard the laughter of the priest, though there was no change on the shadowed face in the window. That was weird. But then everything was weird, since he fell in love with Kristian. "But I couldn't leave this on the machine. About the visit to Grantham. The lady won't be alone."

"Go on." Somberg's eyes swept the east wing where no one moved. Now over the organ pipes that gave back a gleam and her eyes did not purse past the gleam. She smiled on the flowers on the altar table, the stalks of Canterbury bells such a brilliant blood violet. She stared without focus at the polished walnut crucifix above the table. Christ pinned like an insect, hanging on the spindle of bloody nails. She smiled seeing him in his death squirms. Flies at his bubbling wounds. His hung body stiffening and heavy as the last breath emptied out, his face evolving into that of the goatish, sloped-forehead priest of her youth.

The culpability of a young girl was what he was counting on; she knew that now. She had, even as it was happening, believed she was at fault. She had done something terrible, she sinned and was deserving of what a girl's mind could not comprehend. He entered her side of the confessional with a desperate lunge. Lifting her knees high and driving his whole body forward with his hand at her mouth, and she twisted as he pinned her with a spindle. The pain in her uterus reached her throat; a blinding, ripping agony. She had forgotten the burning in her lungs; she couldn't breathe for his hand at her mouth. Leaning drunkenly over her, big and clumsy in his grunting breaths, a searing piston in his pounding, driving her to a corner where shadows were ubiquitous and with her still. Blowing and heaving into her squeezed face of pain. She saw the cords of his reedy neck bulging with the strain. "Life is short," he had gasped in his insatiable appetite, "but pain is long."

"The vice president of the United States may be in Grantham," Shanahan said, jolting Somberg out of the rape.

A few seconds there before it sunk in. "How do you know?" she asked with a cool Novocain numbness.

"How do I know anything?"

"Your source is?"

"The intelligence is accurate, I can assure you."

The cathedral was ill-considered, she could see that now. She had constructed her career in terms of certain assumptions about the past that were not susceptible to the acts of men. Her life had proven it was far better to make victims than to be one. She could sense the past filling the sanctuary like an odorless gas, a technique she had used on an ancient Islamic society that held certain traditional views of women. Perhaps the raping priest was the inspiration for accepting the contract in which she took out twelve holy men, though it was idiocy to scrutinize pleasure.

Your happiness should never be betrayed with analysis. Happiness should remain unexamined as long as possible. She saw the holy men again. Some in their chairs jerking as if with epilepsy. Some brought to their knees, backs bowed, buttocks up in the air as if kissing the floormat, faces taking on a bluish color. The mouths of each were open, the veins in the temples stood out prominently. Choking to death right in front of her eyes. In a gas mask she stood above a collapsed elder; his feet began to rattle a mad tattoo against the floor, a harsh, rattling sound in his lungs, like the breathing of an old man with emphysema. She watched him die. It was pleasure. Always replace a vulnerable memory with a competent one.

Returning to the cathedral, she blinked and glanced about, the signal causing her people to rotate.

"I'm telling ye," Shanahan said, peering from the shadows behind the rampart of organ pipes. He was speaking into his own remote transmitter, Kim listening to an amplified voice, a mask in the lattice window opened by remote. "The vice president may come to Grantham. Part of a Brit-American summit. If the school—"

"*'May,'* you say?" Shanahan watched as the lad and the nun lit a candle. The other nun still polishing the pews. The tourists were scattered about the sanctuary, in a state of flux. "I thought you *knew* her schedule?"

"We know it as soon as it is known. If the school in Grantham is yer design, then ye *must* select another location." He studied the faces in the sanctuary. Which was Gorgon? Obviously not the queerboy in the confessional—or she might be a girl, she was so lithe. He studied each tourist in turn, but there was not one with a feature of power. Each was perfectly appropriate, their faces quiet, sending no threatening messages in their manner or mood or the language of their body. There was the mother in the front pew, chin in her hand as if in thought, fingers concealing her lips. A low-grade panic rose in him. Had he been right in St. Gallen? Had they hired a *woman?* "If ye forsake the job, Gorgon, then ye must return the three and a half million," he said watching the mother, her lips still concealed by her hands.

"The change will have no effect on my plans."

"*Are ye certain?* To hit a Yank would be our death. The entire American patriot network would collapse." Shanahan's eyes widened as he saw the mother's lips respond.

"I don't give a damn about your network," she said, glancing back to the confessional.

"O'Grady was adamant!" Behind the organ pipes, Shanahan was on his feet, staring at the fetching blonde speaking into her handbag. His pulse shot up to a giddy plateau, nerves singing like the pipes around him. Gorgon was a woman! "If Grantham—"

"I'm returning *nothing*," she snapped. "The change has no bearing on my plans. And as for Mr. O'Grady, you may tell him to deposit fifty thousand in my account for the expenses incurred by this meeting, which could have been avoided if you had used the tape *as instructed.*" He watched her take another quick glance about the sanctuary. She froze, like a animal in the wild. Did she feel the heat of his eyes upon her? "Do you have any *pertinent* information?" she asked, transferring her handbag to her left, moving quickly up to the altar to fetch the lad. In the sanctuary, tourists were withdrawing from the pews, all blown into motion.

"One thing," Shanahan said. He watched her take the lad from the old nun. A lovely lad. Looked just like her. "Sin not against Ireland, for the wages of sin is death!"

She hissed into her purse, "I am death, *priest*. Don't fuck with me again."

Shanahan saw Gorgon and the lad start to leave, the tourists converging in their direction. He ran down the back hall, his brain on fire. He damned himself. They had hired frailty, a *woman*! God's anger lashing at the windows; the storm as thunderous as the one in Shanahan's heart. Panting, he paused to peer from the east vestibule. She was hustling the lad at escape velocity. He saw the queerboy step out of the confessional. The nuns were detained by a silvery retired couple. An Oriental girl now headed his way, coming fast. He snapped off the vestibule light, Proverbs coming to him in the dark. *For the lips of a strange woman drip as a honeycomb, and her mouth is smoother than oil; but her end is bitter as wormwood, sharp as a two-edged sword. Her feet go down to death; her steps hold on hell.*

Somberg had read the signs of an imminent reckoning and was prepared and relieved when a figure stepped out of the darkened vestibule. It was only Shanahan, his thin lips compressed white, wearing a terrible face, all wrong for the cathedral. She smiled as he approached, drawing him even with the last pew, glancing to the trim, elegant Spanish man with mustache and goatee trailing her. Isabella leveled a briefcase at the priest. Alexia, as the female half of the elderly couple, was now circling behind, a big baggy purse in both hands. In this world women have very little recourse, if provoked, they must be prepared to engage.

"Well, now," Shanahan said, reaching out to stop the lad, "who do we have here?" He squatted down beside the angelic lad, his white hair and black robe and purple sash a contrast to the bright colors of the child. "What is your name, lad?"

"I'm Eric!" He spoke with authority, the glitter of blue eyes the document of the truth, Shanahan did not doubt him.

"Eric, is it?"

"Yes, sir. Like Eric the Red!"

"If you'll excuse us." Somberg stepped around Shanahan. He countered, holding the lad's hand, his oblong head now alongside the carved facing of the pew.

"Eric what?" Shanahan pressed.

"Eric Anderson."

Somberg had him positioned now, but it wouldn't be prudent to kill him in front of her son, though she was tempted. One kick. She could hear the crack of his skull against the oak pew. But then there was O'Grady to consider. Would he pay in full if she had taken out his old crony? Shanahan would have to wait.

Shanahan gave his crooked smile. "I saw ye light a candle today, Eric. Ye looked as though ye'd never done that before."

"Oh, we know all about ca-ca-candles! We use them all the time back in Gr-Gr-Grantham."

"Grantham, is it?" Shanahan's eyes flashed up at Gorgon with a sardonic brilliance. "And do ye go to school in Grantham?"

"Yes, sir. That's where my mama and I live."

Shanahan released the lad's hand and searched his memory, going back through the mournful gloom, the eight hundred years of British occupation, and beyond those dark ages to the medieval, ancient, even prehistoric times, all of which had played on the Irish stage, only yesterday. In that time, had there ever been a woman such as this? One who would bait her own son in a kill. Was the lad in some way her weapon? Shanahan feared he was. What kind of woman would use a child in a sadistic way? Then claim she loves him, no doubt. He knew as he rose to take Gorgon in, who he was facing. Stained-glass light rippled over the exquisitely boned face, wide red lips, tall, ripe body in silk black as the darkness at the center of the violet eyes as foreboding as that sea at the edge of the world. The maps of the ancients had warned of it: "Beyond here lies the Unknown." The sea that swallowed men whole. To enter it took great daring; it was another cosmos, as that of woman herself, to be feared, fabled in libations and mermaids and dragon queens and other monsters of the deep. It was from such a boundless sea came the whale that swallowed Jonah, and a sermon returned to Shanahan that he had delivered in this very sanctum, from the lofty prowl of his pulpit less than a week ago.

"Jonah was swallowed as many men are swallowed by something, whale, elephant, wolf, beast, woman or prison. The whale is a form of annihilation. And God love us, 'tis usually self-annihilation. The hero inside the whale may be said to have died to time, and some may falsely sing of his death. His passing into the great whale is a metamorphosis; the secular skin shed in this trail in which the hero must fight the awful monster. But Jonah, ye say, was *within* the beast. Right enough. And so the monster the hero must face is none other than himself."

Shanahan knew as he was preaching that he was preaching to himself, which made for the best sermons. He preached in a rich and ripe philosophy, that had the body and tang of good homemade stout, and poured as clear as a stream from great granite terraces of sun and shadow in the Gap of Dunloe, the first place God made.

"If anyone undertakes for himself the perilous journey into the dark by descending either intentionally or unintentionally into the whale of his own spiritual soul, he may, as lost Jonah, find himself in a tangle in which it is difficult to know the way out. We know not what ails us, nor of the danger burning within. For if we stare too long into a fire, that fire stares back from our eyes. The way of man is doom! Ye cannot live long without knowing it. But it's a terrible liar who would tell ye there is no passage out. We need only obey the voice within. To obey the quiet inward voice is to obey God. It comes as good instinct, as the pealing of church bells that herald the hero's hour who will give the soul a ride! It takes only reading the handwriting on the wall."

He now peered down at the wall hanging with the inscription: "Thy word is a lantern unto my feet: and a light unto my paths." Father Shanahan knew this was true, and there would be other words written on other walls that would light the way.

"The force of the terror monster is phenomenally dispelled in the inward voice, that is a letting go. Getting off it. Therewith, the situation is changed. Our hero is no longer caught, but set free. Free within the monster, ye ask? Aye. For that which the hero remembered as himself is forever freed. He is rendered self-denying. Self-denying he becomes spirit that can enter the stories of others, to travel beyond the paranoidal self to offer his soul to the world. Not as a mere name or form, but as that which is eminent within us all and transcends all names and forms. In the great, good *love,* the annihilated hero is spewed forth to return to the world's womb to tell of the terror of the whale. He'll never grow old, that one. Follow the thread of the hero path, and where ye had thought to find an abomination, ye shall find God. Where ye had thought to slay another, ye shall slay yerself. Where ye had thought to travel outward, ye shall come to the center of yer own being. Where ye had thought to be alone, ye shall be with all the world. Glory be to God!'' Shanahan said, crossing himself.

He spoke to that place where he was headed, though Shanahan himself was not there yet. Anyone unable to understand a god sees it as a devil, and is thus defended from the approach. Knowing beauty as a god, Shanahan now saw the woman as an incarnation of Lucifer. He was breathless before the beast in whose blue eyes the whale swam in the deep, and peering into them, he turned to stone. It was damnable, to go hard for a demon in the House of God.

''I'm Father Shanahan,'' he said, refusing to extend his hand to the unclean woman. ''I believe we've met before, haven't we?''

''No.'' Somberg smiled, watching Alexa circle in behind him. ''You must be mistaken. I've never been to Ireland.''

Shanahan saw the Spaniard take up a position in the aisle before him, the man with his legs in a wide stance. He glanced to his back to the silver-headed old woman. ''In Ireland,'' he said in a low voice so the child couldn't hear. ''Our women make our tea. Warm our bed. Nurse our children. What do ye do?''

''I kill men,'' she whispered, still smiling.

''Ah, the contemporary woman!'' Shanahan laughed aloud and the lad laughed with him. A smart-looking lad, Shanahan shuddered at the thought of being raised by a bloody murderess. ''Come over from Grantham, have ye?'' he said to the infidel.

''Hmm. Came to see the sights.''

''To see. And be seen.'' Shanahan grinned his skeletal grin.

''Yes. But you mustn't forget the Scripture, Father.''

''Oh? And what would that be?''

''Those who look upon the face of God are blinded.''

A scalding tide rose up Shanahan's neck and over his gaunt face. It was just like Memnoch to quote Scripture. He tried to wrench his gaze from those eyes. In her presence his soul seemed to shrink, lost in the loose skin of his robe as the frame of a dog in a napless hide. And he hated his desire for her.

Somberg beckoned Isabella with a finger. ''Would you take Eric to the car, please?'' And to Eric: ''I'll be out in a moment, dear. I'm going to have a word with this nice *man of God*.''

Shanahan watched as the lad was led away, and the words of Isaiah came to him as he cut his eyes over the woman. '' 'And a child shall lead them,' '' he said to her.

''Not hardly,'' Somberg sneered, waving good-bye to her son.

The hands of the priest that had prayed and baptized and had given God's holy sacrament, curled into the fists of the patriot that in the name of Irish freedom had killed. Large, bony, darkly spotted and prominently veined hands, that like a jeweler's hands had constructed bombs. It was the patriot who spoke. ''Ye've taken our money. Now take me advice. Leave Grantham. Pick another site. Or forsake the job.''

Somberg waved again as Eric glanced back from the vestibule. Her gaze returned to the priest and stayed there. "You came to me, let's not forget." She gave a smile that stretched into charm. "You do recall who was wearing the explosive about his head that day, don't you, dear? It's I who *command*."

Shanahan's jaw muscles bunched up. "I've half a mind to kill ye right here." He pretended to scratch his calf, fingers groping for the handle of a stiletto strapped to his ankle. He hesitated, caught between patriot and priest.

"I doubt you could do it," Somberg jeered, still smiling. "I doubt you have enough explosive to blow up the whole cathedral. And that's about what I'd expect you to try. That's what you did with Maggie, isn't it? Blew up the Grand Hotel to kill *one* woman. Really, Father, are you that terrified of women?"

"You—!" Shanahan pulled the knife with the intent to march her to his office to call O'Grady, but Somberg moved as if in his thoughts and Shanahan couldn't believe the woman's speed. Like an animal in her quickness. Her left hand shot out and dug a thumb into the space between collarbone and shoulder. A foot swept into the back of his leg, and his knee buckled. A fury shot through him, and the patriot wanted to kill her right there, in the house of God! The blade flashed in the colored light, but her right hand grabbed his wrist and twisted the knife from it. He let out a cry as the blade fell. She spun him downward, as if it were the next step in a dance, jamming a knuckle into the fleshy web at the base of his right thumb. He moaned, sinking to his knees. She lowered him into the shadowed pew as if in prayer.

"I have my thumb on your carotid artery," she whispered. "If you make a move, I'll put it out and strangle you with it."

"God-d-d Alm-m-m-ighty!" Shanahan stammered. "What manner of devil are ye?" Her heat was at his neck, her solid weight on his shoulders. He was curled in her taut stomach and soft breasts. The hard muscle of a man but the flesh of a woman, and for a moment, he found himself inside the whale. He stayed there face down, with thoughts of a clumsy punch, and thoughts of outraged love.

"Not a devil, Father. A *professional.*"

Shanahan felt himself in a burial, in a grave, certain of the woman that held him down. "You have been known for a thousand ages under a thousand names, the incarnation of evil, the emperor of the realm of grief, Lucifer! The angel of God whose pride sparked a war and rent the Heavens and caused no end of misery—"

"It's all right," she cooed, stroking his hot face as she would a child. "You were too angry to kill me. In a sense that's the whole trouble with the Irish. Too many angry people. Anger isn't efficient. But I'm not angry. I don't give a damn about Ireland or Britain. I kill efficiently. You can count on it."

"When O'Grady hears of this!—"

"You'll not report this to O'Grady," she said, increasing the pressure, veins in his forehead popping out. "If you do, I'll know about it." She saw the long curved blade of a sword polished to a blinding shine. "You will forget everything you've seen here today." The blade thrust through the window of the confessional. "You will forget my face." She saw the raping priest skewered through the neck. There was a gagged cry. A door closing. And now another opening. Three gashing strokes over the groin of the raping priest. In the name of the Father, and the Son, and the Holy Ghost. Through the shattered lattice window she saw her mother as a bloody maniac's portrait. Unskilled. Unprofessional. All passion. The sword rose and cleaved his skull in two. It rose again, came down in a whistle and she saw the head of the priest roll free. Mother wiped the sword on the robe of the headless priest. She couldn't take her eyes from it. She was sixteen, breathless with the fascination of violence. *"Come, Kristian!"* Mother had called. *"Confession is over."*

"If I hear you've spoken to *anyone* about what you've seen here today," Somberg said into his burning ear, "you will never speak again. Do you understand?"

Shanahan groaned an acknowledgment.

"The whole problem with men is your angry male God," she said in a very quiet voice. "But the Goddess is not given to anger but to precision. All dogs can be trained, once you overcome their miserable habits and teach them the natural things." And now she lifted his gaunt face to hers. She kissed him full on the mouth, branding his lips with sacred red lipstick, smiling on his horrible face. "Murder," she said in a mind game, "like love, is blind."

It would be no good to kill him outright. It would not be enough. But in walling-up her enemy in lust, she could devour him utterly. She sought to bring about the indiscreet capitulation of his soul. So that she could possess him in bonds that he could not break, and collapse into nothingness. Then to become a monster. It was her way. The very way in which she made the femmes.

She released him with a smirk, picking up his knife, showing it to Alexia covering the aisle. "Japanese," she said with a frown. "Not much tungsten in it. Sharp, but it won't penetrate bone." She spun it quickly through the air to the far end of the hard oak pew. It stuck there, quivering. "Amateurs," she said, shaking her head as she and the disguised old woman walked away.

Spikes of migraine pain burst into Shanahan's brow. A muscular tremor fluttering in his cheek as he pulled himself into the pew, breathing hard, wiping her red smear from his mouth. He could still hear the deliberate calmness of her voice, uninflected beyond the natural rise and fall of her compelling French accent. Her face blank as a page, staring at him with those blue killing eyes that would come to stalk his dreams. Her words came back to him, cutting across his tormented rage with an incisive clarity: *"Murder, like love, is blind."*

Shanahan stood, rubbing his shoulder. He saw the pestilence walk into the darkness. He recited Exodus to his bruised soul: *" 'Thou shalt not suffer a witch to live.' "*

15

IT WAS NEARING the end of the day at the end of a long week that came at the end of a month of heartache, and Jessica tried not to think about it all. She had gone to London to find Danny and had found Trent instead, and now she was missing Danny more than ever because she was missing Trent. When she wasn't thinking about Danny or Trent she was thinking about the three sketches. It seemed they were somehow related, in dream she viewed them as body parts that were all interchangeable. Her only escape from love and mystery was the work. She had worked continuously since returning from London, and the work was good. It wasn't confusing and it gave no pain. The only thing that mattered in photography was focus, and now she put all the distractions behind her and kept her mind sharp and clear, and she was very grateful for the work; it was the best thing in the world, other than your children.

Jessica peered into her Hasselblad at the upside-down image of Charlie Chaplin in a black suit and derby hat seated before a white computer table that held a box of IBM software and a single red rose. She focused on the lopsided grin of the famous little sad clown that looked like the fool she had become. The fool had been something of a robot that loved the work more than Danny; it was ugly, but true. The work had become a self-inflicted wound of the soul that objectified itself in the shooting. Her own son had shot her. In this hothouse in which her personal woes flourished, she added the feeling of dehumanization. Danny was taken away; it was agony and felt like shame, like punishment, like maybe she had deserved it. Left naked and broken in a damn C-3PO suit all over the floor. And wasn't that just perfect? She had been dying ever since, though once upon a time, not so long ago, she had it all. Only a fool could loose it.

"Charlie, tip your derby to your left ear . . . that's it.

"Lean your cane against the table. . . .

"Lift your eyebrows. . . .

"Big smile! . . ."

Her finger was on the plunger of the shutter cable when the calm of the studio was suddenly shattered by a savage cheer. It sounded like the blood-curdling cry of an Indian on the warpath. She looked up as a wheelchair flew out of the shadows and knocked a reflector wobbly. Pit roared onto the set, sliding into a wild power turn, sending Loric, the actress playing Charlie Chaplin, tumbling into the seamless white backdrop.

"Jessa! He's been spotted!"

The moment seemed to crystallize itself. It hung before her eyes, a gorgeous hope trembling. She, the star martyr, stared, too afraid to speak or move or allow herself any sense of joy in this punishment role of the fool in which she had conscripted herself.

"Somebody spotted Peggy Sue!" Pit bellowed, shaking a fist at the wide snout of the camera. "And our boy was with her!"

Jessica's breath was cut in two. Her heart jumped up among her lungs. "Peggy Sue?" she said, not quiet coherent, her voice very thin, far away. As though she spoke from that unknown place where Danny lived, and that he was alive she had never doubted. Spotted? He had been spotted? Dare she believe this?

"My missing wife!" Pit thundered. "Remember?" He grinned with his big beefy face, waving the red rose like a flag of triumph. "Somebody spotted the friggin' bitch and called her in!"

"Danny?" Jessica's mouth felt numb. She took a staggering step toward Pit. "*Danny* was with her? Someone saw them?" She was suddenly choking back a sob, the ache awful and already she had downgraded herself from "fool" to "victim." Something in her that had been dead, frozen, stony, petrified by the cruel irony of her loss, was now brought back to life. A heart transformed, pulsing once again, though the blood vessels were broken. It was pink, the color of salmon flesh. Her face flushed the same color. Her mouth opened in a silent chorus of praise to God! "How?" she stammered, still not quiet believing. "When? *Where?*"

"They called just now! I drove right over!"

Jessica allowed herself a smile. A small one. It grew. Pit was glowing. His head reddened, it looked like a shiny apple.

"And *Danny* was with her?" she repeated.

"Damn straight! The woman that spotted him has got a picture to prove it. It's a blurry picture . . . but it's our boy!"

Pit couldn't contain himself. He threw his head back and uttered a raucous cry. Lorie, peeking from behind the computer, her Charlie Chaplin mustache cocked sideways, stared at the crazy spinning in his chair, whooping and screaming. Jessica danced with him. She threw her arms around his great mountainous shoulders and kissed him with the depth of feeling now fully resurrected in the miracle that was momentous. In a minute, she'd need air. Wild, surging rivers of love undamned. A love desperate and obsessive and willfully blind to the unasked questions. He had been spotted! Someone had a photograph of him! She would move heaven and earth to get her hands on that picture. A picture. A little respect, a little integrity returned to her work. She had paid an inflated price for her pictures. Love was cheated by her pictures. Her son reduced to a picture in her search. Now found by a picture.

"Where?" she said, not in tears, but in fury. "Where is he?"

Pit made a gentlemen's show of handing her the red rose that had become a monument to such a variety of meanings, among them a little town tucked between mountains and lakes, the red rose of Ireland. "Pack your bags, hotshot," he said with a broad grin. "You're headed for Killarney."

"Killarney?" Jessica tried to place the name, but couldn't think over the chant that spun from the name, *Kill, kill, kill.*

"It's in Ireland," Pit announced. "The boy is in Ireland."

"Or *was,*" Jessica said, coming down to earth.

It was a quiet Monday after a busy Sunday. Shanahan carrying a dog-eared Bible as he passed through the corridor that linked the abbey with the cathedral. He was coming from his rose garden, his heaven on earth; as he walked he silently repeated the morning meditation, the tranquil Psalm an insight into his condition: *"O Lord, my heart is not proud, nor my eyes haughty; nor do I involve myself in great matters or in things too difficult for me. Surely I have composed and quieted my soul; like a weaned child rests against his mother, my soul is like a weaned child within me. O Israel, hope in the Lord from this time forth and forevermore."*

He entered the church offices. Marline Ryder, his secretary, gave a trilling wave. Pink cheeks and auburn curls. A switchboard unto herself, the gossip nonstop. She was on the phone which she likely would be when called to heaven, though the angel would be put on hold while dear Marline passed along one more scintillating scandal. Now she cupped a hand to whisper, "It's for ye, Father. A Yank. She called *twice* this morning already. Seems—"

"I'll take it in me office. Thank ye, Marline."

He entered his sanctum rippled in ruby stained-glass light. Didn't bother with the light, he took the call at his Gothic desk. "This is Father Shanahan," he said into the phone.

"Father, I'm Jessica Moore. I'm calling from Chicago."

"Ah, top of the morning to ye, Ms. Moore! 'Tis morning there, is it not?"

"Actually, it hasn't been morning for me for a long time. Father, I'm looking for my son. He was kidnapped last November."

Shanahan assumed an air of clear-eyed order. He pulled out his chair and settled in. His hand found a pad and pencil. He made a note of her name. He searched his memory and it did not surface. "God bless ye, child. How may I help?"

"Well, I was hoping that maybe you had seen him. His name is Danny. Danny Moore. He's six years old. Has blond hair and blue eyes. He was seen at your cathedral on Saturday, March ninth—"

"Seen *here?*" Shanahan sat up alert in his high-back chair. "Seen in wee *Killarney?*" he said, feeling certain this was a mistake. "Are ye sure?"

"I'm *certain.*" Jessica was in her living room, Pit listening on the extension. In her hand she held a photo that showed mostly floor and part of a door, in the upper left-hand corner was the startled face of a boy, his features blurred, but distinct. The jug ears alone were enough to identify him. "We have a picture of him," she said to the Irish priest. "It's a freak thing, really. Danny and Sterling—that's the alias of the woman who took him—bumped into a tourist in your foyer. . . ."

Shanahan held his head against a migraine's warning pulses, that was as the pulse of the air. His heart jumped to the poetic despondency in the woman on the other end of the line.

"It seems Danny knocked her camera out of her hands when he ran in out of the rain. So she *remembers* him. Plus, like I said, we have the picture. When she picked up the camera, it went off in her hand. After she got back home—"

"Home," Shanahan said with alarming determination. On the lunatic fringe, playing on-line sleuth. "Where would that be?"

"Oh. She lives in Waterloo, Illinois."

"The woman with the lad?"

"Oh, no. The *tourist.* The woman that Danny ran into."

"Aye. I see." But he saw nothing. Only ice blue eyes bearing down on him. She had jumped him again and all he could see were those eyes that turned him to stone. Temptation in those eyes. A manifesto in those eyes. He helped put it there. The procurement of murder, his soul could not deny it. *Necessity,* the patriot called it. *Wickedness,* the priest moaned. "Carry on, child."

"Well, anyway, she, the tourist that is, identified Sterling from a flyer she received in the mail. She called her in. And then she checked her pictures and found the one of Danny. I have a copy of it. Not a very good likeness, but it *is* him."

"A flyer?" Shanahan said, feeling the bloody migraine coming on fast. "She identified the woman from a flyer, ye say?"

"Yes, sir. A missing-children's flyer. They're quite common in America nowadays. They have advertisements and coupons on one side, and pictures of lost children on the front."

"But ye say the kidnapper's picture was on the flyer?"

"Well, it wasn't a picture. We don't have a picture of *her.*"

"Ah, what a shame." *Thank God,* Shanahan thought.

"It was a sketch."

"Ye have a sketch?" Shanahan snapped the pencil in half. The headache settled in at once. "Of the woman? The kidnapper?"

"Yes, sir. An old friend of mine, his name is Boz, but that doesn't matter, anyway, he made up what's called a composite. And Pit, another good friend"—Pit beamed and made Churchill's "V for Victory" sign—"well, it's a long story. Anyway, we managed to get her sketch in circulation. So, that's how the tourist saw it and reported her."

"I see." Shanahan's voice fell. Conspiracy theories spun, as if his mind were akin to Marline. There was more than his hide at stake, there was O'Grady. "Sounds like the hand of God at work," the priest in him said.

"I hope so, Father! What I need to know is do you recall seeing an American child? Six years old. Four feet, three inches. Blue eyes. Blond hair. Freckles. Really cute."

The line went silent and for a moment Jessica thought she had lost him. But Shanahan was only praying. In the dark of his appeal he saw a light at the end of the study. Was it an oncoming train? In the dark there were models of efficiency in death, none more fetching than Gorgon. But the bitch had botched up. There were only two options for the patriot, but the priest bore the pain a bit longer, opening himself to it, to look for a way out.

"Are you there, Father?"

"Aye," he said hoarsely, head throbbing like a rotten tooth.

"I'm sending Danny's picture." Jessica glanced to Pit feeding her fax machine. "It should be coming in on your fax now."

"Me fax?"

"Marline gave me the number."

Shanahan spun around to his credenza. He stared at the fax as if it were a damn snake. *But there are no snakes in Ireland,* he reminded himself. *There are now,* he thought. *A blond viper! Brought her venom to the very door of the church! She is evil incarnate. The iniquity of woman. A tart tort. A transgression against God. She is demon. Only demon would bring murder into the church.* But hadn't *he* called *her?* He quickly banished the thought. "There's no fax," he said, breathing a little easier. Now he took up the role of performer: "I don't know that I've seen such a lad. Did yer tourist recall seeing him with any of the *sisters?*"

"No, sir."

"How unfortunate." *Thank God,* Shanahan prayed. But to be on the safe side, he'd be asking the bishop to send the two nuns on duty that day to the convent in Dublin straightaway.

"Well—" Jessica looked to Pit. He banged on the fax machine. "I guess the fax must be lost in the satellite feed or something. Anyway, I'll bring plenty of copies when I come."

"When ye come?" Shanahan bowed his head in pain. A headache of such saber-toothed intensity that it made his eyes tear. Caught here, between two strong, modern, willful women. Or was it three? He silently called out to the Almighty! Now his fax machine was chirping. Shanahan turned to find Danny's smiling face sliding into the pickup tray. "Ye say ye're coming to Ireland?"

"Yes, sir. As soon as I can. Tomorrow, I hope."

The machine started sending out a second page. The arrogant chin and wide lips and knife-shaped eyes of Gorgon sent a gleaming spike of migraine pain through Shanahan's ears and into his brain.

"Yer fax is arriving now, Ms. Moore."

"Oh, great!" Jessica joyously applauded Pit. He took a bow. "I can't wait to get there!" she said. "I'll be taking copies to the police and the customs offices. And all the schools there."

Shanahan took a moment to think, fist curled around the stub of broken pencil. Fate was advancing, but he claimed the right to self-determination. He gazed at Danny's fax, such a lovely lad. Looking upon the picture, he knew that if this were his lad, he would as Daniel enter the fiery furnace; the great burning of the soul where flames are tall and furious. Where the very sound of the wind is as the devil laughing. On a wing of love he would fly through the dark satanic, red-shadowed war of the lad's search. In a vertiginous energy he'd exploit the acrobatic possibilities of love, to sail out of the trial unscorched by what would claim him. He would survive to tell of it, the telling as an evolution from the mayhem he now heard in the voice of the mother.

How different was a mother from a father? Did a mother dream like a father? Did a mother weep like a father? Did a mother die like a father? If a mother did these things like a father, then a father did these things like a mother. And so he knew her pain.

In an attempt to forego any confrontation, he spun an idea, to blow her away. "Ye know," he said, piecing the lie together as he went, "Looking at his picture, I do remember yer lad."

"Really? *Oh, God!* Really!"

"Aye, I feel sure of it. They were in me tour. I frequently take tourists through the cathedral. Aye, I can see him now!"

"Oh, God! How did he look? Did he look . . . okay? The tourist said he seemed . . . almost happy."

"Oh, he looked fine. Just fine! Healthy. Alert. Ye have a fine lad there, Ms. Moore. He's built strong. And the woman with him, it seems she was tall. Very striking."

"That's the one!" Jessica shouted. Pit shook a fist and growled. "This is *fantastic!* I can't wait to get to Ireland!"

"No," the patriot said quickly. "I fear that'd be a mistake."

"A mistake? Why?"

"Because the woman ye seek is not in Ireland."

"She's not? You talked to her?"

"I did," Shanahan lied, and saw the crucifix on the far wall double, then triple in size. For a moment he thought it would fall and crush him. He said, "As I recall, she said they were tourists. Going to Europe. Then back to their home in the States."

"*Where?* Where in the States?"

"I don't believe she . . ." He paused for effect. "No," he said. "I'm certain of it. She never said where they lived. But I believe yer time would be better spent in America, Ms. Moore."

"I don't know—" Jessica turned to Pit. He was pumping a long finger, pointing to Ireland like a referee signaling a first down. "Father, I just feel like I should come."

"Aye. But ye could net her as she enters America. She must come through customs, ye know. I'd get onto it straightaway! Ye need to be where's she's *going,* not where she's *been.*"

"Well . . . that's a good point."

"I'd suggest ye coordinate the search at yer end, and I'll do yer bidding in Ireland."

"You'd do that?"

"I'll begin today. I'll make copies of yer lad's picture and circulate them." *Like hell I will,* the patriot thought. "Take them to the *proper* authorities. After all, I know them *personally.*"

"And the sketch. Don't forget the sketch of Sterling!"

"No, no. I'll not forget the sketch." *I'll be seeing the bloody sketch in my sleep,* the patriot thought. "I'll take special care with her sketch; ye can be sure of that."

Jessica paced before the grinning carousel horses on their brass poles. They served as a divider between living room and dining room. The horses like the story of her and Danny's lives. Going up and down and round and round, in a merry whirl until Danny was taken. But more than Danny was taken. Everything was taken. Her sense of purpose. Her pride, her career, her honor and self-respect, and, most important, her belief in the future so grandly dreamed. You lose more than a child when someone takes your child. Left with depression. And crushing fatigue. And the rage. But more than anything there was the emptiness. Now holding onto herself, trying to suppress a giddy, spinning excitement when Father Shanahan recalled Danny; she was going up and down again, then crashing and sinking as he told her not to come to Ireland. The lovely, lonely carousel horses, they were the creating of herself. She sat down, dizzy from the round and round.

"I don't know." Jessica closed her eyes. "I was so pumped! I thought we found him! Or found something." The shakes set in. She couldn't hold the phone still. "Guess I was dreaming," she said, a knot of tears in her throat. "Dreams are as close as I can get to him, you know. He comes every night. It's wonderful and awful. Sometimes I don't want to wake up. And when I wake—"

Shanahan heard a static on the line, then realized the static was the mother weeping. In the crimson dark, he bowed his head, burying his face in one hand. "I ache for ye, child," he said with woe. "Ye must have known a world of suffering."

"It's like he's dead. But he's not! We have a picture now. So we know he's alive," she replied woodenly. "But the pain is like he's dead. Maybe worse because you can't let go, you know?"

"Aye," he said, fearing what he would become in all of this, his heart torn asunder. He reached through the long-distance line to hold her hand. "Do ye feel like ye've squandered yer mothering years, Jessica Moore?"

"How did you know?" she gasped.

"I've known many a soul afflicted with grief," Shanahan said, now seeing only the cross. "We always look back and wish we could live again what was lived. 'Tis especially true of parents."

"Yes!"

"Children are like the flowers," he said softly. "They bloom for a season. A short season. God's golden season of delight! 'Tis glory when they are here, sweet memory when they are gone."

He heard her breaking up, and her tears washed through his soul and burned as a fire. How could the Irish patriot tell her where the lad was? But how could God's priest not tell her?

"Faith, Jessica Moore, gives sight to the blind, speech to the deaf, life to the departed. Keep believing—*don't lose yer faith*—and ye shall see Danny; ye shall hear Danny; ye shall mother Danny again. All is possible for those who believe."

Jessica felt Pit's arms around her. He was holding her, and only now did she realize how terribly she was shaking. In a storm, blown inside out. "Thank you, Father," she sobbed. "You can't know *how much* this means to me. What you've said helps. You're a wonderful priest! I hope we meet one day."

"If it's God's will," he replied, and closed his eyes so he wouldn't have to see the picture of the lad. He couldn't bear to hear the mother's tears and see the lad's smiling face.

"I'll send the photographs and sketches today," Jessica said, getting hold of herself. "I don't know if I'm coming, not yet. But if you hear *anything*—"

"I'll call," he promised. "Ye may be assured, I'll be giving this matter my *immediate* attention."

"Thanks again. Good-bye, Father!"

"God go with ye, child."

As he rang off, the migraine settled over the back of his head like a black widow spider, spreading her web, closing around him, the killing agony sinking in. He dropped the faxes in a drawer, locked it, and escaped out the back door.

He went out from the cathedral along the steeply slanting road, long legs striding in his black cassock powdered with dust. His guilt carried him up the hill to the flat summit where he had a fine view of Killarney shining in the sun, blue lake and purplish mountain all around. With his misery he descended into a thicket and along a stream flashing with speed and song. Down through the ancient wood where the trees were old and the roots bulked and twisted above the ground. The air cool and damp here with the smell of rot in the tangle of light, moss growing over roots and rocks and up trunks of trees. He found a shrunken husk of a fallen oak, and there he rested, holding his head against the thoughts chasing one another like weasels in the dark. The chase brought a Psalms: *I am become like a pelican in the wilderness: and like an owl that is in the desert. I have watched, and am even as it were a sparrow: that sitteth alone upon the house-top.*

How could he not save a child he knew was stolen? But how could he interfere with the death of that British Jezebel who had filled a cemetery with green graves? The patriot knew if Ireland was to be free then Thatcher, the great hater, must die. Was the lad the weapon? Or was he merely Gorgon's cover? The mother could be told where the lad was after the kill. Or would it be too late for the lad? But how many children had died in Ireland? How many laid on the altar of freedom? What was one more nameless child? Two faiths struggled for his soul. The oath the priest had made to God and the pledge the patriot had made to the IRA.

He was divided in himself, against himself. And wasn't that the meaning of the cross? He felt himself there, on the cross of his own divided psyche. His own Holy Ghost enjoying the pain. He wallowed in it, this battle of wills. It was more than the child. It was made by Woman! The fraught, the slings of heaven's arrows, the revolution of this age, was Woman. Once they were but sewing needles and tongues that ran until they were out of breath. Now the blinding agony in his head was as much woman as migraine. It was ghoulishness! Not one woman. Not two. But three! As nails in his palms and through his twined feet. God in heaven, what had he done to merit this? You set out to dispatch one hussy, and you're caught in a triangle of unreason.

The brutal truth was the ancient bastions had fallen. All of Shakespeare was but a tragic wail against the downfall of man. Male authority descending with Elizabeth. Then Victoria. Thatcher who was the worst yet. Her belief was in neither man nor woman but in herself only. As though there were no gender. As though wielding power was the only gender. These crossed beams, man and woman, began with that first hissing snake and now here he was in the grapple of the age and his instinct was to solve this like a man, kill all three women and still the clawing within.

It was a galloping venture, to kill a PM, a British PM, so it was an honorable murder with a passion neat and simple. But hire a woman and where it does it lead? To a discord of moods and tempers and too many outlooks, to a heaving this way and that, to the cold shudder up the spine, the ticking of the soul, to the bloody pinch of guilt with the good, calm mind eaten to a honeycomb in the sea-churning of it all. The honorable murder come to ruin by Woman! Irresistible impulse lost in a knee-walking quandary. In the lace of ferns Shanahan saw the soft, freckled face of the lad. Blue eyes and a smile of such faith! The lad waving to him again as he left the cathedral to vanish into the dark. And now for the Yeats, "The Stolen Child." *Come away, O human child/To the waters and the wild/With a fairy, hand in hand/For the world's more full of weeping/Than ye can understand.*

The patriot reached into the robe and withdrew the flask. The priest lifted it to his lips and prayed for the burning fire to silence his quarrelsome heart. He would have to warn Gorgon of her exposure, while keeping her in check, to save the lad and the mother. He took another pull at the flask. He dare not approach her, Gorgon might ply the wares of her sex trade. He drank and kept drinking, thinking of the pretty slave boys she must have; she was such a woman, from whom there was no escape. A Psalms rose up, that of the father to a woman's world: *I labour for peace, but when I speak thereof: they make them ready for battle.*

16

IT WAS A windy day in Grantham with the sun coming out from behind gray clouds, then going under in sprinkles of rain. There was a false sun now, streaming through the classroom windows and onto Mrs. Anderson. She and the children were gathered at a table decorating four sheet cakes for the library bake sale that was Linda's idea.

Kea loved it and thought the bake sale had a flair of the surreptitious. To sell sweets for meat. How Linda loved her books. "Books are mirrors," she had said, "you see yourself in a book. Great books are those mirrors in which you see something of yourself that was not there before." Linda had so many clever things to say. She was now using an opaque projector to cast cartoon characters onto the cakes, so the cake became something of a mirror, giving back cheery images. The children traced them using an airbrush that sprayed colored icings. They had made a Mickey Mouse cake. A Casper the Ghost cake. Their cake-decorating skills improving with each effort, doing a Thomas the Tank Engine cake just now; it looked like the work of a professional.

Linda was thoughtful, she had been bringing the children snacks for months. Chocolate chip cookies one week, brownies the next. A treat every Friday that the children looked forward to. It was only by chance that Kea learned several of the children had become ill over the weekend. Stomach spasms. Mild nausea. It was almost as if the children had a mild case of food poisoning. At first she thought the four children murmuring about upset stomachs had eaten too many sweets. But the following week when two more children came down sick, she mentioned it to Linda. They decided it was the American baking ingredients imported for Eric's behalf. That was easily remedied, and the next Friday when gingerbread men were made using local flour and sugar from Mr. Robert's Grocery, Mrs. Thatcher's father, there were no reports of upset stomachs. This was as it should be. Certainly nothing bad ever came out of Mr. Robert's Grocery.

Linda was so thoughtful, so helpful, so well loved—something of a pied piper, not that the children were rats, but they did follow her—that she was almost *too* good to be true. What with her luscious, lustrous golden hair, skin as smooth and alabaster as new fallen snow and those immortal eyes, or so they seemed, no one in Grantham had ever seen orbs so purple, so blue, so violet. Men turned to stone before her eyes; it was amusing to watch. It seemed there was something infallible, or perhaps the word was *inevitable*, about her eyes. You could carry on about them and make them something they were not, which people were inclined to do; her eyes were that striking. The fact is, women were not immune to them either. On more than one occasion Kea had been touched by a direct hit, you might say. It was not a thing she would confess to anyone, but she had felt a certain blushing in the way Linda looked into her. Linda aware of her blushing. That was exquisite, in a strange way. But it couldn't be helped, Linda had a way of possessing the moment. And you didn't mind, really.

All of this goodness led one to wonder about what was bad and crazy, and it seemed those things must exist if you were *that* good. After she became PM, people spoke of Mrs. Thatcher in the same vein, as though she were for all-time, awe-inspiring, and you knew there must be something else behind her famed resilience.

Linda had been understandably reluctant to talk about her past, but when it finally came out, it was as Kea had suspected. Eric had an abusive father. One of those violent American men, their ugliness well chronicled. It was hard for Linda to admit she had been abused. He had said terrible bruising things to her. And he had smacked her. Linda shared a picture and it was ghastly, the bruise on her upper arm near the shoulder. Was there anything more repulsive than a man who committed family violence? Thank God she divorced him when she learned he had sexually abused Eric. The trauma of that was the root of his stuttering. "American fathers are beastly!" Linda said. "Children must be protected from them."

Certainly Linda had proved her mettle by escaping the ordeal. But why Grantham? She said she came for the calm of the English countryside. And wasn't that what Kea loved about Grantham? They had spoken of it so many times, both of them outsiders to these solemn people who missed nothing in their little community and could not be fooled for a minute. Kea helped Linda fit in. She could be so amusing! Her observations on school life wonderfully cheeky. Always giving of herself. Kea gazed upon Linda's most recent gift that sat on her desk, an extraordinary flower from the States, Venus's flytrap. She had given one to Mr. Higgins as well who was taken by her. Linda so thoughtful, like the best child, with flowers for the teacher. Schools had a predisposition to the child mindset. Teachers as children to the principal, the parent volunteers as children to the teacher, the children as themselves to the parent volunteers. It was difficult to be your adult self in a school where you were either parent or child, everyone in need of attention. An environment conducive to cultivated magnetism that in Linda was electric, whether as parent or child or adult.

From her desk Kea watched the children huddle round Linda as she slid the last cake under the projector. It was a secret only Kea was privy to.

"This," Linda said to the children, "is a *special* surprise!"

"I bet it's Su-Superman!" Eric shouted.

"You almost guessed it. He's like Superman."

The children could hardly contain their excitement as Linda slid the photograph into the projector. The image of Mr. Higgins was suddenly cast onto the cake; the class erupted in hilarity! Linda had drawn the principal as a caricature of Santa Claus, a jolly little man with rosy checks, white hair and a round belly. The children were in tantrums of delight! Kea couldn't stay away any longer, she joined the children around the cake and couldn't help her laughing. She had never thought of Mr. Higgins as Santa, but he did have the look when pictured in that red suit. And she knew Mr. Higgins was going to be absolutely in love with Linda, seeing himself mirrored as the beloved St. Nick.

"This is going splendidly," Kea whispered as they queued up the children that took turns tracing the portrait onto the cake.

"They've certainly taken to the decorating," Mrs. Anderson said, so chummy. "You'll never know what a pleasure that is for me. And think of the money you'll raise for *books!*"

"Oh, your bake sale is a smashing idea!"

"But it's not *my* bake sale," Mrs. Anderson corrected. "*You* drummed up the support from the other teachers. Remember?"

"Well, *you* gave me the idea. We've never had a bake sale before. But I think it's going to be grand!"

"I hope so," Mrs. Anderson said. "I've a lot of riding on it."

Kea gave Linda a reassuring pat on the arm, as you would a child, knowing how anxious she was to fit in. "Don't worry," she comforted as the wise, good mandarin watching over all. "Our cakes will be the first to sell. Everyone will just love them!"

*   *   *

Somberg watched the little brats fight over the airbrush, was there anything more toxic than greed? Greed was the very best of friends, you could always count on it. As the children did the work, they munched on a slightly toxic cake made just for them. The last installment in her escape plan. The groundwork for the Thatcher kill that was going smoothly, though every job came with little complications. Like Eric's stuttering. But even it was reduced and he was more comfortable in his role, in part because she was more comfortable in her role as mother.

Motherhood was rebirth. You became someone else. Part child, part tyrant. It was an indulgence, with some element of contempt, especially for men who could never biologically match women, so all mothers shared this certain universal presumption of parental superiority. That too you count on and play to. It was a club, motherhood. Some of the best of women were not members. She had never been a member and never knew what she was missing, until now. A gentle whirling in the steadily increasing devotion of the child, the child to you and you to the child, and this last part she had not counted on. She had assumed she would dispose of the child when the job was finished, but had begun to entertain the idea of a future together. She could transfer her business to her sisters and retire to Eric. In pastoral Provence. Or perhaps something more urban and intriguing, like Vancouver. So many fascinating flesh tones in genial, multinational Vancouver. There was more to life than just killing men. There was motherhood.

She now had an opportunity to *make* a man. To build one from the ground up. An achievement her mother never aspired to, never attempted in their all-female world. Without a wedding ceremony, without the pangs of birth, she was suddenly, unexpectedly, on the cusp of a new life! Pendulous, but intrigued by this state of pampered captivity that all devoted parents are born into, Eric such a gentle captor. Happiness threatening to spill over like water from a too-full glass. It was all a bit too saintly for her, perhaps nothing more than a whimsical amusement, but she wondered about its possibilities. She wondered if she had changed since Chicago, though only the boy was to have changed.

"I wonder," Mrs. Anderson confided to Kea's ear, "what would you think about the children taking their Mr. Higgins cake down to his office? They could present it to him."

"Oh, my! Mr. Higgins would be thrilled!"

"Do you think so?"

"Oh, he'd love it. Let's do it!"

"That's a good idea," Mrs. Anderson said, guiding Kea as they strolled behind the exuberant children, busy little hands trained for a kill. There was no white hot explosion, no spatters of blood and guts of flesh and hair clinging to walls, nor the stench of burned meat that accompanied most Irish kills. No heads were caved in by war clubs, the brains bursting forth through the skull in a bloody spew and shrieking so typical of male berserkers who through the ages had made such a mess. No one hacked down with enormous knives, waylaid and slain, all disgustingly male. No, this was a kill made with precision, and in their drawing it was as if the children drew a blade with no hesitation across the exposed neck of Maggie Thatcher, just below the jawline, the thread-thin lip of blood slowly widening to a smile. The smile of the sublime! This is how a mother would kill. As beautiful and professional as a job as could be, using children. "I wonder," she confided to Kea, "do you think Mr. Higgins would mind if I rang the *Gazette?*"

"The *Grantham Gazette*?" Kea said, astonished.

"It might be fun to have a photo of the children giving their cake to Mr. Higgins." Mrs. Anderson smiled hopefully, knowing Alexia had made the arrangements with the help of a 100-pound note. "What do you think?" she asked the teacher.

"Oh, my! Call them!"

"Really?"

"Mr. Higgins would love to have a picture!"

"All right. That's a good suggestion. I'll call them."

"Who knows?" Kea gave her volunteer a gentle nudge in the ribs. "The *Gazette* might print the picture in the paper! There's no telling where this cake decorating will lead to!"

"No telling," Mrs. Anderson echoed, smiling as brightly as the sun now streaming through the windows onto her son, the light transmitting a gleaming assurance of what their future could be.

They came out of the school to the car park to find a note fluttering under the windshield wiper of the Mercedes. Somberg told Eric to wait in the car as she read the scrawl, as craggy as the Irish coast.

> *Someone is searching for you, Mrs. Anderson. The one who seeks you, hates you more than I. I shall give her to you, but you may only detain her. If she is harmed, you will not be paid. Should she or her son die, you will follow. "The Lord executeth righteousness and judgment for all those who are oppressed." —Psalms 103:6*

She was not surprised Shanahan had found her but for a moment was stunned as she read Jessica's name and address. Suddenly she was back in Chicago with Eric in her arms. Outside the darkroom, in the thrill of virgin birth. She felt again the kick of the revolver and saw the spectacle of Jessica's eyes that spooled white, but she had not died and now Somberg knew the robot suit was made of something other than plastic. She couldn't believe it; she had left a mark alive. What had come over her? That wasn't like her. That was like someone else.

She slid into her Mercedes with this small complication that was not without solution. She understood the burning agony of the pain she had inflicted on Jessica by leaving her alive. And she understood the true marvelous transforming effects of pain, how it can shatter and heal and strengthen, and how relentless it was in extreme cases, how it can rob mind and soul of the will to live. Pain could kill as surely as a bullet. She understood all these things, surprised Jessica had endured it all, and this perception had no effect on her. Somberg had in many years past taken small toxic doses of suffering that had spread and deepened and ravaged through her, building an immune system against the poison pain, to fend off any further vulgar attacks. It was unsightly what the pain could do. Somberg had come to live in a calm far above the hot struggles of the weak, and now she smiled down upon her new surprising pleasure, kissing his soft cheek, thinking how she hated to leave him for the sake of a business trip to Chicago.

17

PIT SAT WITH her bag on his lap in the Aer Lingus terminal just out of earshot of Jessica on the pay phone. He knew she was talking to Trent, and knew she was going to him and knew he would lose her to Trent and that knowledge had no effect on his love. His love was not in need of confession; he didn't have to put it on the air, didn't need proclamations or exhibitions—life had taught him to leave the dangerous things unsaid but not unfelt. He didn't want vows that were always broken, and he had no need of ownership or possession or conquest or manipulation. His love was not given to presumption, to sentimentalism; it wasn't in need of comfort; it was the authority of love, it stood on its own, and in it Pit felt as free as if he had escaped something.

He knew Jessica loved and appreciated him, and it was enough. He only wished he could spare her the misery she was living. She finished the call and came through the crowd in her khaki trousers and matching wool trench coat with the collar turned up to her new boy-short haircut. Pit started them toward her gate.

"Trent's going to meet me in Dublin," she said with a lyrical tremor. "He has a plan! Something about entry cards. I want to go to Killarney, but he says we should try this first. He found his joe and has the time. I guess we'll see, after I get to Ireland."

"Oh, he won't steer you wrong," Pit said, rolling beside her. "I don't believe he would. Trent's a fine fella." He was pretty certain of this, and he was not going to let his greed get in the way of love. He'd keep everything square and aboveboard.

She smiled very slightly, as if trying to deny herself the pleasure. "Well, I think Trent's going to help."

"Shoot, he's already helped!" How could he fault the man for wanting to help her? What man wouldn't want to help her?

She walked on. Now her smile shone down on Pit's blue plaid shirt. "I guess I'm just lucky," she sighed. "To have you both."

"Boy, now that's the kinda talk I wanna hear. *Lucky!* Talk like that draws good things to you." He had kept a powerful secret from her, how he had learned to center himself, to let go to find peace. That had begun with the Beethoven which she had started and with it would come the shedding of shame. He would tell about the centering another day, when she was good and ready, for now he'd talk around it. "Why, you grow positively *magnetic* when you get to thinking you're lucky. Look at you, new boy-haircut and all. Traveling again! Jess, you never looked better!"

He had her smile shining full-beam, the best gift she could leave him. He waited as she checked in. She had surprised him with that haircut, surprised herself, and he figured it was important to a woman in a way a man didn't know. Must have been a fright, to hear those scissors around her ears and see the shocking piles of hair dropping on the floor. It was bravery and now she looked brand-new. In the wind, her hair fell to her lips, but she wore it swept over her ears and tapered to the nape of her lovely neck. And as he looked at her, he saw her deep brown eyes and the high round cheekbones, then the smooth, elegant lines of her chestnut hair. It was a fine haircut; you saw Jessica, and then her hair. It was the way it should be, putting the woman before beauty.

He pulled a book from the pocket of his chair and commenced reading action and betrayal, from head to tail, *Moby Dick*. He wasn't reading long before he disappeared into the story with the tortured whale, dropping down into thought. All he ever wanted was to share in the love of kids; it seemed such a simple, fair thing, and had made such a mess of his life. His greed-afflicted in-laws had come after him with the meanest, most treacherous attacks. The fuckers couldn't get enough of killing. Every time Pit came up for air, they had to try to kill him again. They had to kill the boy as well; and Pit's daughter; they had to kill the love. They had a very great fear of his love, their hounding relentless, driving him into an awful pack of trouble, but in a starlit way, Pit felt he had made no mistakes. He looked up from the sea yarn to the big window where planes were rushing down the runway and soaring into the sky, in that same way that each of his errors had opened into a discovery. What the hell was life if it wasn't discoveries? This was the assurance, that he had made no errors. Now he was helping a mother in a search for her son, though he had taken his son, and it didn't feel like a contradiction. Funny how life can turn you round and round, in the great roll of love.

Beyond the planes the sky darkened with a cloud, the sun shut up behind it with a deepening around Pit. He and the boy had sat before a window such as this, waiting for a flight to London; it had been an easy decision to make, but a hard thing to know. How can a man be free if his boy believes he's dead? How can a boy be free? Men and boys are less free than they might imagine. Most men are held by the spell of rules. And fear. No man is free if he's separated from the love of his kids. Men are free only when they obey some deep, inward calling, like Jessica just now, on her way to Ireland. Not doing what she wanted, but what she *must* do. Fulfilling some unrealized purpose. Have to do it, no matter the cost. You don't worry about being naïve or foolish—which Pit had been repeatedly—you have to drop down into the deep, and you have to be powerfully optimistic to enter the darkness of the unknown. To obey from within, this is freedom. Pit and the boy boarded the plane. The bravest and best thing he ever did.

He and the boy took a spiritual retreat. On two strong legs, Pit carried his son on his shoulders into the unknown. It might have been wrong, some had judged it so, but in those days their love grew to a beauty, so vast, more than most folks know in a lifetime. Pit had never been closer to heaven. Now, sitting in his wheelchair, smiling down on a cheeping cricket by the window, Pit smiled remembering it all. Only he and the angels knew the great high of that love. Little snippets of words could no more describe it than the Sears Tower could touch the sky.

The divorce decree had been altered. Pit still had visitation rights—about the cruelest thing ever devised—but the rich Texans wouldn't honor the court order that Pit had been sent to prison for breaking. To date, they had broken it 156 times. His children were about as far away as the moon. He was still writing, and knew the odds of success were like a moonshot. He had a powerful lot to say. He'd like to get at the combat between men and women, raise a little hell, but what he had to do was jump the possessiveness of those who refused to shared the kids; it was a torture to love.

Torture is akin to murder. It cuts to the very center of the soul. Men and women needed to find more subtle ways of torture in which children were not used. But the longing for torture was so great, because the burning hate is only the inversion of yearning love. Folks get walled-up in their possessiveness, that turns them to monsters. Strange how monstrous greed will persist evilly, and the thwarted spirit of love will persevere through torture and even death. Men must learn to hold out for love, and to laugh at their fool selves. To stand alone, and listen to the innermost voice.

His eyes scarcely left Jessica as she came striding through the crowd to where he waited at the windows. She was in her story and he was out of his, and they were not the same but similar and opposite in the way men and women are opposite and at war. This was the supreme crisis repeated in glorious series throughout all time, with the fullest development of it in the murder theme; Pit knew it well and would not inflict a defeated man's retaliation on Jessica. The ability to commit atrocities of the heart was in the strain of both genders, as was the fever of high-toned bitchery. Women and men both had a gallery of macabre troubles blamed on the other, watching each other with all their might, caught in a kind of stand-off. Man, the mechanical, lustful ego succeeds for ages in killing Woman, the living self. But Woman ain't no slouch, to keep herself intact she seeks to bring about the capitulation of Man's soul. The only victor is he who breaks the bonds of his own identity, to kill his own miserable self, to open to others. This was how he welcomed Jessica, his arms wide, face full of light. My how she smiled, what a wonderful smile! And Pit felt lucky.

"This flight's gonna be a dilly," he said as Jessica joined him. "Long way over there!" He glanced out the window where the planes were roaring down the runway. They rose into the sky and shrunk, and then they were gone.

"I've been up all night," she said, yawning audibly, "but I'll sleep on the plane."

"Well, you're an old pro at that. You'll do fine."

She took the end seat in a line of seats with Pit in his chair beside her and the passengers milling at the gate. She was so tired it was almost exquisite and she felt vulnerable without sleep, her heart crowded with emotions. She had lived out her days between mood swings and crying jags and the cheap tricks of the dreams that became some exposé of the madwoman no one had met yet. This was another whole woman held hostage by Danny's loss and she appeared in tempers and turns, and Jessica supposed she had always been there. She was a girl whose hair was on fire and the dreams indulged her, they catered to her; Jessica resented their revered, adoring, painstaking attention to this dangerous nutcase. She manifested herself in scenes so inexplicable, they could not be recalled by day, the girl on fire vanished as soon as Jessica opened her eyes, taking with her the whimsical episodes of violence and self-destruction.

The gargantuan dichotomy to this frantic web was the cream puff. A child who made no attempt to run from the lizardly things that haunted dreams. She cringed before them, raising one shoulder and tucking her head behind it, screwing her eyes in anticipation of a blow. She had small eyes in a great naked face. Spiritless, anemic, a pale, feminine, despairing figure, she was reduced by her wounds; the dignity was gone out of her. She lacked the looks of her fiery sister, her faint voice faded into dawn. She wept but not from wrestling phantoms, the cream puff wept simply because nothing was bearable. Jessica knew this sister better, she was a girl content with too little, and so she was doomed to fail.

She was totally subject to the power of dream, hapless before the reinventing, reassessing, redeeming aspirations that played out a woman who was, and was not. Were the dreams true? Or were they false? That they were often illogical didn't bother her—the one sister burning down a skyscraper, the scene shifting to the other, hypnotic and paralyzed by the flames—what was wearing her out was waking in the burn of guilt. She had not admitted it yet, but she could not avoid it: hadn't she helped Sterling take Danny? It was Sterling who set her life ablaze, while Jessica gaped on, but Sterling could not have done it without her, and Jessica was coming to realize guilt had no solution. It was false-bottomed. It was the trapdoor of dreams. Each night she waited in a fiery pit of shame tears. Each morning she woke with her heart squeezed.

"Got a stick of gum?"

"You bet." Pit fished into the pocket of his chair. "Here," he said, coming out with a pack of Trident cinnamon. "Take it to Ireland. Set the place on fire, you sensitive artist."

She laughed at that. Peeled a stick and dropped the rest into her purse, something for a rainy day.

"What's so funny?"

"Oh, what you said."

"What? About the gum?"

"No. About the fire. It's become a prototype dream."

"Doing a little barbecuing in your sleep, are you?"

They sat watching the planes take off, not talking to each other, but talking to the planes on their way to God knows where.

"I'd say I'm the one barbecued . . . when I sleep."

"You having trouble sleeping, kiddo?"

"A bit."

"Well, hell, Jess, it's is the easiest thing in the world. You just close your sweet little eyes. Nothing to it."

"Yeah? And what does the 'sensitive artist' do with her not-so-sensitive dreams? I'm feeling a little like a victim here."

"I don't know much about dreams. I learned a few things when my son had trouble sleeping, voices talking to him in his dreams." She watched him fold a page and close *Moby Dick*. He held onto the book, directing his gaze out to the runway, studying it a moment. His shiny skull somewhat rippled. "Whatsya got to know about dreams is they *rule.* We think we make our dreams. We got it backwards. Our dreams make us.''

Jessica nodded to this. ''I'd say that's true.'' She checked the gate, there was a line but it wasn't moving.

''Dreams can be oppressors,'' Pit said in his big, husky voice that went well with the *Moby Dick* he was frowning upon. ''Like some Texas kangaroo court. Offers facts of stuff you did in the past, like yesterday, or your childhood, to the witness of imagination, putting a false spin on it, and then pretends they're real. They can dump you into spiritual denial. In jailhouse wailing, all dreams a form of jail. And like jail, they can leave you feeling like a loser. Using voices of the past rising from their tombs in some robber-baronial thinking of the negative.'' He glared up at Jessica with fight in his beefy face. ''Dreams are mighty, you bet, but you can sic a dog on the bad ones, turn 'em around.''

''How do you do that?'' She checked the line. They were taking tickets, but there was still time. ''How do you turn them around?''

''What you got to remember about dreams is, they speak from the past to the present and into the future.''

''Scotland Yard has this computer, Big Brother, they call it. Comes from Orwell's *1984.* You remember *1984?*'' Pit gave a nod, but she went on. ''Winston Smith accused of being in the Brotherhood, tortured for writing a diary. The Party's slogan was: 'Who controls the past, controls the future; who controls the present, controls the past.' ''

''That's right on,'' he said as defiant as Winston Smith wished he had been. ''You want that evil slogan reversed into the positive. Dreams are complex little shits, but you don't have to understand them to inspire them in a long-standing campaign to overthrow the oppressors. *You* can rule, I know it for a fact. There was a time, not so long ago, when my mind was never far from killing the bastards who took my kids.''

''That's all I've been thinking about,'' Jessica confessed. ''Killing her.''

''Well, good gracious, dear heart, you need to do something about that. Killing is one thing—I bet Trent would tell you there comes a time for it—but thinking on it is no good. And dreaming about it is worse. Dreaming about it is *deadly.*''

''I had the impression,'' she said, hurrying along, glancing to the line vanishing into the jetway, ''that we're more or less subject to the powers that induce dreams. The subconscious.''

''Yes, mama, you got the *induce* part right,'' Pit barked. ''But dreams are a *free market.* They don't have to justify slavery, or child labor, or those heebie-jeebie things brought up from the deep. You can turn such dreams around.''

''*How?*'' she asked again, pressing with time running out.

''Why, I already told you how.'' She stared at Pit a second, as if she were in *1984,* or in a dream in which she didn't have the right to speak freely or hold an opinion. He waited her out, and when she didn't respond, he said, ''You got the answer right here in your carry-on, I saw you put it there.'' Pit picked up her bag. He opened a pouch. Pulled out a CD. Handed it to her and she looked at Beethoven and grinned, as if at a forgotten friend.

''Dreams are cause and effect, and the mind always *gives as it receives,*'' Pit said, his eyes bearing into her. ''Dream is nothing but a showcase for what the brain receives. You overcome the defeatist dream same way you overcome the defeatist life. You can evoke dream from music, just as you can evoke life from music. You can take what's fervent and joyful and beautiful and blessed, all of which is rightfully *yours,* all of which you'll find in Beethoven, and release it into the soul.''

''And that's it? That's all there is to it?''

''Sure. It's no great shakes. Bug out on a little Beethoven, and you can crawl out of any shitheap.''

She laughed at this. There was nothing about Pit that looked like a labor camp, and the state that had tortured Winston Smith would be disgusted. What was worse, Pit was still writing, though the state had suppressed his diary—Winston Smith would be elated. ''So it really works?'' she asked, an eye on the diminishing line.

''Shoot. It's true and you know it's true, you've seen it work in my sorry life.'' Pit met her eyes and held them, imparting these words as though they were his last. ''I wouldn't pass it off as a cure-all. *You* are that. Music helps make you the cure. There's a million different kinds of music out there. Whatever you choose is what you become. I've found Beethoven works best in the morning, introduces my day to my chosen thought-speak. Carries into the night. You can give yourself a dose before bed, but you might get looped on that high-flying Seventh. Point is, commit to the music and your dreams will hitch themselves to the tunes. It's an uprising against what you don't want to become. A sneak invasion! Keep it going. It becomes resolution. Confronts. It constructs a way of seeing. Forms a consciousness of thought. Happens automatically; you won't know it's happening. The mind is an instrument with no limit to what it can do. The wonder of it is, it's all *yours.*''

He leaned back in his chair, smiling at the ceiling, like a concertgoer who knows the music well. ''I believe you,'' Jessica said and reached across the chair to kiss his ruddy cheek. He blushed at the kiss, the color rushing up his neck and into his head that glowed like Rudolph's nose.

They waited together in the line, Pit looking out the window at the planes with the light in his face and Jessica shot a mental portrait just for herself. She loved the faint white wrinkles at the corners of his eyes that grooved merrily when he smiled. And those bear-like arms wrapped around her bag, as if it might jump out of his lap and run away. She owed him so much. How could she ever thank him? She never had, but now something in her knew she had to try. ''I don't know what I would ever have done without you,'' she said, standing beside him. ''You were always there for me. I guess I went kind of crazy the last few months. I know I was a bitch sometimes.''

''Ah, hell.'' He dismissed the past with a wave of his hand. ''We all get into a royal mess now and then, without the foggiest notion which way to go. Gotta rant and carry on some. Try to make things happen in our own harum-scarum, klutzy way. The important thing is you're obeying that deep, inward voice. Obeying from within. Can't go wrong doing that. I'm proud of you, dear heart.''

''Thanks,'' she replied, a sudden tautness in her throat. The hope had come back into her. It was shining in her face and she could hear it in her voice and she recognized it as his gift.

''I want you to call every day,'' he said.

''I will.''

"I'm going to plot a map of your bird-dogging."

"I like that! *'Bird-dogging!'* "

"That's *exactly* what you're gonna do. You're gonna sniff out that bitch like a hound. You're gonna get on her trail and stay on her trail until you find her. I'll take care of everything back here. Don't you worry about a thing."

"I won't," she promised. "I'll get down to business."

"I'll check in on your staff, be sure they're not sleeping on the job. And I'll catch the mail and water the plants. You just get out there and get on her trail."

"I will and I'm going to listen to the Seventh," she said, hearing not her words but the things she hadn't said.

"I know you will. And I know you'll find him."

Jessica gave her ticket to a flight attendant, a girl with long dark curls, and for the first time she sensed she was really on her way to Ireland. But she couldn't leave just yet and told the girl she needed another minute before boarding. She stepped to the side, letting the others pass.

Standing under a sputtering fluorescent light, she tried to find the words for all she felt when he set her bag down and took her hands, and he gave her his eyes and all they held.

"I'll tell you something," he said. "It's not pretty, but it's true. Long after they take your legs, you can still feel your feet down there. I swear, there was a time there I could feel my toes wiggling. But that went away. I don't feel that anymore."

"Pit, I—" Her voice suddenly broke as love washed over her in a tidal wave, and she hadn't realized till this minute how much she loved him. How much she needed him. How much he needed her. "I never told you how sorry I am," she said, "about your legs."

"Well, hell." He waved it off. "Accidents happen. No sense boo-hooing about it now. Point is, I suspect you know what I mean about feeling the foot after it's gone."

Her face buckled. Tears swarmed in her eyes. "I can't imagine not being able to feel Danny."

"That's good." Callused hands squeezed hers, so tight. On the verge of tears himself. "You know, Jess, sometimes you have to forget your personal tragedy for the sake of a clear head." His big Papa Bear face filled with a grin, and he drew on the man in whose house he lived. "Hell, we're all bitched from the start, but once you get a hurt you want to *keep* the hurt. *Use the hurt.* Be true to it; don't cheat it. That hurt will keep you going; it'll give you courage." He lifted up these words and nodded at them. "That hurt will take you places you'd never go on your own!"

The last of the passengers vanished down the jetway, and in a rush she said, "Thank you! For *everything*! For the darkroom and the hospital and the love and all your patience, and mostly your *belief.* You saved me! God, you saved my sanity! You never gave up on me." She couldn't see for tears, and now she was shaking like a child. It was crazy, she was only going to Ireland.

He gripped her hands and, in a low commanding voice that she would never forget, told her, "Don't you ever give up on that boy. No matter the hurt. *Don't you ever give up.*"

"I won't!" she said, and threw her arms around his bear neck and kissed him and in some small way tried to make up for the tenderness and affection that the world had cheated from him, that she herself had cheated from him. And he felt it all and cherished it all and wrapped her in a massive hug that would keep harm away.

"Be careful of the hate," he whispered.

"I hate that bitch!" She was astonished at the way it blurted out. The force of it. The heat of it. The blood lust in it.

"I know it," he said. "And nobody would fault you for that. But be careful of it. Hate is a mean-spirited ailment. It'll eat you up." He glowed as he looked upon her. "And don't forget, hate is a *power*. Use it! But keep it locked away till you need it."

The stewardess touched Jessica's shoulder. Now Pit saw the others had left. He stroked her smooth fingers and looked at her slender hips and at her tear-smeared face that said everything he ever hoped to hear. He slipped the image of that face into his pocket for a future lonely hour and released her hands. He put her carry-on in her arms. "You know," he said, holding her in a gaze of fearless love, "most folks are bored shitless with their lives. But you got an opportunity here. Meet this awful thing and beat it—don't let the sorrow waste you away—and it'll make something of you that's stronger than you ever dreamed you could be."

She tried to speak, but words wouldn't come. Only tears.

"Now you go on, champ," he said and gently pushed her away.

"I love you, Pit!"

"Go on," he said, big tears streaming down his heavy face. "Go on and find our boy. Find him for both of us!"

Jessica started down the walkway in a wreck, trembling, the sting of tears in her eyes. She waved. "See you in a few weeks!"

He returned her wave, sitting in his chair alone, under the sputtering light, a broken man converted by love. A true believer. Pit kept waving until she turned the corner and was gone. Then he rolled down to the window where he could see the plane. He would wait and watch it till it rose up and vanished into all that sky. He pulled out *Moby Dick* to keep him company.

18

HER FACE WAS shining as she came out of customs. Her stride full of fight and determination. Her light and energy made Jessica more beautiful than ever, then there was their time apart that had felt like forever. Watching her approach, smiling now, Trent was astonished at the effect she had on him. Rather like spiritualism. His spirit raised! Or was it witchcraft? Did it matter?

They embraced. Then came the kiss. A thrilling voltage. He took in her new haircut, but only with the eyes, though his hands were moved to do profound things. The cut chic and smooth, just right for bed. A khaki silk broadcloth shirt an inspiration. What would she look like wearing only the shirt and her new hair? And that

smile. And those glossy lips. And the color in her cheeks. On a cloud, till he retrieved her two-ton bag, brought him straight to earth. They started down the Dublin
concourse.

"How was the flight? You must be exhausted. Are you ready for bed?" he asked
hopefully.

"Not hardly. I'm ready to go to work!"

"Ah. Well. So am I." He groaned lugging the bag. Brute labor. Bedeviled by
brute beauty. That longish, tapered boy-hair unhinged erotic drives. Cruel, actually.

"You're free? The thing with your joe is really over?"

"We've two or three problems to resolve." He steered them away from a newspaper stand, his scowling picture on the front of the *Times*. Taken outside Number
10. Had a lurid, tabloid quality, like the accompanying story. "But I've taken some
vacation time."

"That's great! So you can go to Killarney with me?"

"Killarney? Actually, I thought—"

They were split by a stream of Yank tourists decked out in leprechaun green.
Singing "Wild Rover" like happy fools. Gave him a chance to recover. Reminded
himself that beauty was skin deep. Being a simple soul, a man, he repeated it three
times. Then he glanced her way, through the Yanks. She smiled. His heart jumped
inside his chest. He repeated it all again. But it was useless.

"Just now," he said as they teamed up again, "when you came through customs,
you gave an entry card."

"Name and address, all that stuff?"

"Right. And you had to list your passport number."

"Uh-huh. And they stamped my passport."

"Right. They stamped *everyone's* passport as they enter Ireland. And *everyone*
fills out an entry card. Including Sterling."

"She did?"

"She had to."

Down the corridor, one of the tourists burst into melodic song. A beautiful tenor,
full of brooding, the high, clear voice flowing through the crowd like a pulse in the
air:

> *"Oh, Danny boy, the pipes, the pipes are calling,*
> *From glen to glen and down the mountainside. . . ."*

He watched Jessica's glossy lips tighten. She gazed wistfully over her shoulder,
besieged by song that cut to the heart.

> *"The summer's gone and all the flowers are dying;*
> *'Tis you, 'tis you must go and I must bide."*

The squeeze of pain was in her eyes, the singer gathering an audience with the
old tune, profound in its subtle magic. Trent walked faster to aid her escape. Wasn't
easy with the bloody bag. What had she packed? Heavy as the weight of all the
world.

"But come ye back when summer's in the meadow,
Or when the valley's hushed and white with snow.
'Tis I'll be there in sunshine or in shadow.
Oh, Danny boy, oh, Danny boy, I love you so."

The beauty went from her face gone pale. The bard bringing out a meaning in each word that it never had before and now, for Jessica, would always have. She was in overdrive, Trent racing to keep up. She hadn't expected this. Been in Ireland ten minutes and already she was caught in the Gallic sense of the tragic and beautiful. And she hadn't even seen the countryside yet.

"Could Sterling have snuck into Ireland?" she asked, face now uptilted slightly, expressionless. The click of her heels was that of special forces. Caught in a snapshot engagement. The song like tank fire to the heart, air and earth commenced to vibrate in unison. Trent's Hopeful Reunion retitled: Operation Urgent Fury.

"Not likely," Trent said, struggling with the damn bag. "Not with a child. Problem is, we don't know *when* they arrived. But we know when she was sighted. And she came with a six-year-old boy under her wing. And *he* would have an entry card, too."

They turned a corner and were out of earshot of the singer, but the soul-beating of the song could not be escaped. It had a permanent love affair with the heart. Its permanent ambition to send you to heaven, where hope resided. The tenor would continue singing in a place beneath the waking world, deeper than a dream.

"As a rule," Trent slowed their manic pace to something just shy of a march, "the Irish wouldn't show us their entry cards. The Irish and British are not exactly mates, you know. But I've a letter from a friend. They've agreed to let us take a peek."

She swiveled to give him a look. Same look as those marksmen who shoot prey such as mink and beaver through the eye, so as not to ruin the pelts. "I don't know about this, Trent," she said very precisely. "I came to Ireland to go to Killarney."

"Right. But if we can find Sterling's entry card, we'll find her name and address. And a *passport number.*"

"*Killarney,* Trent. That's where Danny was sighted."

"Once we have a passport number," he continued, "Big Brother can check the entries and exits into Heathrow. It's the hub of all Europe. Might turn something up. Might be on her trail in days."

She marched on. The color elevated into her cheekbones. She was beautiful again, but in a different way. A certain hardness to her features. As those beauty carvings seen on the prows of ships breaking gigantic ice floes. A singleness about her. A wholeness. Was that a devil lurking behind her? Could this unity be a thing picked up from Sterling? A ticklish question. He passed on it.

"We can begin around March ninth," Trent said, "when Sterling was seen at St. Mary's Cathedral."

She consider this. "How long will it take?"

"Ah, difficult question, that."

"A day? Two days?"

"I should say it would be more like two weeks."

"No way."

She walked on, faster. He trudged after her.

"I've *got* to get to Killarney," she said with a tenacity that would plow through all obstructions. "That's what I came for. I don't have time for Dublin. Dublin is for the singing tourists."

Was she afraid she'd hear the tenor's bittersweet song again in old Dublin? "Right," he said, playing his part. "I understand. Makes perfect sense."

It was a long concourse, in this he was lucky. Gave her a chance to persist, right through the big middle of everyone, with Trent keeping pace, barely. She stared at some imaginary point beyond the crowds. That distant region where the existence, or nonexistence of the lost is inconclusive. By the set of her eyes, it was difficult to tell who she searched for. Danny? Or Sterling? He stole a glance; knew the face. That she had slipped seamlessly into a cool, no-nonsense demeanor was proof enough, and the face confirmed it. She was, for the moment, of that constituency that could always raise a logical reason for doing what they wanted to do anyway. In his cold war years, he had nursed similar possessed souls through loves and hates, through fits of despair and wanton malice. He had learned to translate emotional logic, how to hold a hand and read the palm, to distinguish between histrionics and the real thing, to take a joe through boredom, beyond the places where nothing happens, only to send him back over the Wall to sleep with the enemy. It was instinct mostly, some of it schooled, some of it coerced, always a thing of *timing*. Agents were like watches. They called for a jeweler's precision, and the patience of a saint.

He stayed with her determined strides that overtook even the gray worsted businessmen, anger pumping her legs. That and likely fear. He selected a dispassionate, rational tone. "She *did* enter Ireland. And she *did* fill out an entry card, had to, you see. The card is here, in Dublin. All we have to do is find it."

"I heard you before."

"Why not give it *one week*, Jess?"

She shot him a glance, madly exhilarating. Cheeks aglow with hectic color. "You're going to try to get me for a week," she said curtly, "then try for two. I *know* you, Trent Stanford."

She walked on, the window light in her hair and in her eyes, so she had the look of the truly heroic and beatific. And in that silk shirt showing the shape of her, he was reminded of her in the rain, and after the rain, when he had undressed her. Suddenly a reckless demon chucked all the training. Moved by irresistible impulse, he dropped the ball-buster bag. She turned, startled. He kissed her with the crowd streaming past. A long, explicit kiss. Slow and soft. He kissed her until something within her had surrendered, then he released her from his clinch to say, "I hope I get you for a week. Then I'll do my damnedest to get you for two weeks. Then another two weeks. And another and on and on till I finally have all of you."

People were passing with open grins on their faces. All the world loved a romance. Her tough-guy expression melted. A small smile curled, but almost as quickly it grew to a sadness and she said, "You can't have all of me. Part of me is missing."

"And we're going to find that part."

"We?"

"*We.* Together. That's why I'm here."

She gazed at him with everything turning over inside her.

"Love the haircut," he whispered. "It's you."

She turned away. She grinned despite herself.

"Two weeks," he said at her back.

"One," she said, and grabbed the big Samsonite loaded with Danny photos and sketches of the bitch. She labored with the bag, walking heavily, bent to one side. Trying to escape. No idea where she was going. She was, he knew, going in a multitude of directions. Behind every great woman there is a madness. A suffering.

"All right!" he called, catching up to her, taking her bag of sketches and dreams. "We'll begin with *one* week." He held the door but not his smile. She stepped out to greet Ireland with her face that reflected its haunting beauty. A newsstand was before her, he dropped the bag to cover his blasted picture. He hailed a cab.

The ten point type on the front page of the *Herald* blared: "BRIGHTON BOMBER ARREST!" with all kinds of kickers and subheads. The picture was taken before the door at Number 10, Trent's face as rigid as concrete, lion's head knocker gleaming over his right shoulder. Pure Thatcher melodrama. Blinding, the flashes firing in his face. Turning a quiet arrest into fairytale. "Our lives were suspended until the resolution of this awful bombing!" Mrs. T had said. Then introduced the man of the hour. The flavor of the day. Graham forced to watch on from the back of the pack, glowering as Trent took the bows. The tale of the arrest was mother's milk to the press, fed by the bully mother herself, though any arrest was yesterday's news in the pulsebeat of Mrs. T. She would wait a few days, then gather the hounds again. For another showy revelation. A new face before the firing squad. Some blameless soul, touched by the Holy Ghost, saving all England from doom. Doom a favorite media word. Saving what we all need. But the world should beware of saviors, they are rarely what they're cracked up to be.

Trent had spent 162 days and 700,000 pounds hounding the Fox who did not exist to the media. His name never mentioned. He had slipped the relentless manhunt that had uncovered another beauty, a man informants fingered as a mate of the Fox: Patrick Magee.

They found Magee in a tragic Belfast flat, his family living in pinching poverty. Three children in shoes rundown at the heel, though from the way they played with their father it was evident they were not rundown at the heart. Trent followed Magee through the steaming bowels of the war-torn city. Up smoke-grimed alleys glittering with broken bottles and coiled razor wire. Down cobbled streets patrolled by small, ugly armored vehicles the Irish called pigs. The pigs carried British soldiers in full battle dress. On the streets the boys patrolled back-to-back as if joined at birth, automatic weapons trained at the stacking rooftops like foothills in some enemy-infested jungle. The date and time hardly mattered. A scene that had played, in one form or another, for eight hundred years. And would play for another eight hundred years if left to the lust for the Irish that gave Mrs. T that front page image so gloriously alive.

Trent followed into tired old pubs, a form of a life-support system; decaying establishments where pity evaporates at the door. Into the genteel squalor, in a shabby coat, looking hollow-eyed and sad. Lifting a mug while Magee sat at a back table and told a tale to the lads, a full moon smile on him. Now shaking hands as if bidding farewell. Then home to the kids for another roll on the floor and a piggyback ride to bed. Trent saw his own silhouette in the glass as he watched the father read a bedtime story to his angels. A round of kisses, finally turning out the light. Only darkness in the flat, and then the brief, intense beam of a torch light that seemed to probe Trent's Gaelic soul, stabbing with guilt, magnifying what it touched; showing the contours of Magee's wife. A parting kiss at the door. Trent followed him out into the night from which father would not return, Trent aware of this even as he followed, hating his knowing every step of the way.

Magee smuggled aboard a coal freighter. Trent and Graham followed by helicopter, waiting when the boat docked at Ayr. The crew took leave. An hour later, Magee swam to shore. He came out of the sea shedding water, entering Scotland a squat, dark shadow darting through the dock and up the street. Spray of moonlight on his back, walking in shadows to a quiet Carlisle hotel. The next morning he went shopping, and in the afternoon he strolled up to the train station, pacing at the gate. Trent's surveillance team waited with him. A dozen pairs of eyes watching the moon-face that had a full dark beard. Silent cheers went up when the long-awaited friend arrived. A short, sharp-featured young man. Trent followed Magee and Dessie Quinn to a Glasgow flat. Only then were the Strathclyde police alerted, that they had found terrorists.

Trent and Graham had waited in a car on Langside Road while the local boys raided the Glasgow hideout; C-13 didn't have the authority to arrest, but that was a moot point to the Thatcher media juggernaut. In the car, Trent saw mist spilling through a yellow cone of street lamp. Light glinted off stock extensions of Uzis. Off round stun grenades hung from belts. The men dissolved into the night, moving toward the line of houses. From the radio, he heard the sharp crack of stun grenades and saw curtains thrown back from the windows. Front and back doors knocked off their hinges in explosions, shouts of *"Police!"* as they burst into the living room and kitchen simultaneously. Minutes later, they emerged from the house with Magee, the Fox must have smelled them coming, he had left moments before the cops arrived. That was the truth of what happened, the Strathclyde lads made the arrest, Trent got all the glory. But if Magee had never been found, and an arrest never made, Trent would have received the hell. There is no hell quite like that of a mother's stewing soul, Mrs. T damn near medieval in her craving for a Brighton bomber that became Patrick Magee.

His fingerprint had been on the Grand registration card, that would be enough to convict. Magee had entered the great night, not to see the light of day until turn of the millennium. In the bust, a bombing calendar was recovered, names of hotels scrawled on the back of an envelope. Trent found six bombs had been planted, and in disarming them, the chaos of his investigation that threatened to be a disaster turned into brilliance. Suddenly he was a beauty! Mrs. T extended his unprecedented authorization until the Fox was brought to justice. In the charm of these momentous events, Trent asked the PM for a letter requesting the Irish participation in an entry card search to be conducted at the Dublin Custom House. The Avenger was happy to comply, one mother simply helping another.

The only question was, how did the Fox know to escape? Had he been tipped off? If so by whom? The cops were unaware of his name until moments before the arrest. Only two people knew they were coming, Trent and Graham. With the notorious Fox at large, the greater glory was still to be had. It was very likely instinct sent Dessie Quinn running, but there was another somber, nebulous possibility. Graham had been trodden underfoot. He cherished the recognition to amend the Brighton bombing. Could he have tipped the IRA to save the grand prize for himself? The bent of a darker philosophy led Thatcher's direction. She was still a prime target with a young, aspiring terrorist. Thing is, Graham had access to the PM's appointment calendar, passed to him by Allison, Mrs. T's aide, to coordinate security. Trent pondered the mystification of the Fox's flight, within his cocoon of dark thoughts suspicion loomed and faded, like the passing of tumultuous storm clouds.

They worked in the basement of the Custom House scented with mildew and mice. Going through a tomb of boxes lined in cemetery-neat rows. Reading under a wintry glow of strip lights. In the first week they went through six thousand cards scribbled in six thousand different hands. None had the surname of Sterling. But they found twenty-seven mothers who had entered Ireland in March with a young son. Trent faxed each mother's resident country to request a copy of her passport, Thatcher's Brighton authorization inspiring participation, the local boys thought they were after big game. As replies came in, intrigue dissipated to discouragement. One glimpse at the photo was enough to eliminate most prospects.

Jessica read as she had never read before. Through suppressed eagerness that grew to impatience that made her testy. Never quite still. Chomping on nuts or gum. Foot always tapping. Trent tried Mozart, but that soothing theme was for another day, she was not in a Mozart mood. She insisted on Beethoven, the drama of all his symphonies as her collective memory of the struggle. She was a fascination to watch. And the struggle would make her great.

She didn't remember their rambling conversations and scarcely noticed when on two occasions they didn't return to their hotel but slept on the lumpy divan beside the square porcelain stove. She didn't recall those nights because in her mind they were the same as the days, though she did not forget Trent's patience, and recalled their sense of fitting, arms and legs twined as one. He remembered everything. Her quiet, determined face finally at peace in sleep. The slow rhythm of her breathing beside him. Her long dark lashes curled against her smooth skin. The shape of her and the scent of her. Their closeness and her uncertain distance. He witnessed her voracious work habits, listened to her mutterings, then listened to her silences. She told the stories of Danny, who now lived in a world of dreams that walked and talked in her head in the night, clouded her eyes, and etched her face by day. Every morning she awoke with the wound fresh in her side, that wound her son had made in the hands of the bitch, unable to fully grasp or believe that he was gone, these dream-ghost hauntings in the slow, repetitive work, in the privacy of her torment that was the ravage of dreams, threatening her very survival.

She tried to counter dreams by thinking, thinking hard about what she really wanted before she went to bed, thinking even as she went into sleep. There, Pit's voice returned to her. "Dreams, dear heart, don't give a tinker's damn about your great ambitions. Ambitions aren't worth doodley-squat. It's not what we think about ourself that counts, it's what we *believe*."

With her eyes closed she listened, absorbed in the blackness of pre-sleep that was not a color but an atmosphere as thick and suffocating as a steam room. This cloying mist enveloped her, and she breathed in its sticky pall. An echo in the mist. Inside the echo there was a voice not quite Pit's. It came from somewhere far away, as if lifted from her body, unattached, not quite authentic. "Dreams are those hierarchies as cruel as frauds, but in music we redefine the self, and distribute that heavenly source of power to those provinces that rule sleep, and in sleep make the day." The echo of that voice sped away into the mist. Only then did she turn to that genius of survival, listening to Beethoven before sleep.

She lay still with herself until the music had taken some of herself away. At first, she got looped, as though she had rifled a great drink down her throat; it was performing acrobatics on her nerves. At other times, she felt the desire to weep, but not the need. In this stew her dreams were not dulled, but brought to a sharper focus. Eyes blasted and her thoughts slurred, in a smiling tipsy dreaminess of sleep, the Beethoven dancing in her head.

Her dreams were complex and she didn't have to understand them or even remember them. She had this new wealth of assertiveness, the Seventh Symphony, that became her own natural resource, rising appreciably Jessica's psychic standard of living. To lead to new dreams that were as prophetic acts that were rarely remembered. A brightness seeped into her sleep and sped her forward, so she had the sense of a magician on the verge of discovery. Jessica felt herself closing on this discovery without knowing what it was. Beethoven was her weapon against the darkness.

The flickering point of the candle was a silent metronome to the Brahms Waltz No. 15 in A Major. Serene. Tranquil. Soft as the candlelight that framed Danny in his Thomas the Tank Engine bed. Drifting through sleep that wasn't sleep, through a dream that wasn't a dream. Somberg played the waltz every night as he entered REM sleep, the dream state, but only every third night did she add the narrative that Danny heard in sync with the music, as though the dream were the music. And though it would seem to last all night, the dream would run only the length of the baby waltz, one minute and forty-six seconds.

"Eric," she called from his bedside, "it's time for the party." His face puckered slightly; she knew the slow, ponderous waltz had transported him into the experiences erected in his subconscious. She whispered in his ear and into the vast inner chambers of his mind, "It's a happy day in your classroom. . . . Everyone is there . . . all your pals and Ms. Marten . . . and that very special person, *Mrs. Thatcher!*"

Somberg holding his wrist, monitoring his pulse, moonflowers blooming on the nightstand in the haze of the smoky candlelight. When his pulse quickened she continued.

"You're beside Mrs. Thatcher . . . your new special friend. . . . There are TV lights like stars . . . and newspapermen taking pictures." A ghost of a smile came over his pale freckled features, seeing it all in the wide-open gaze of induced dream. "Ms. Chieng is cutting the cake. . . . mmm! . . . It's Elizabeth Shaw chocolate mint icing!"

She waited, watching the waltz do its work, carrying him into a future that he experienced as the present. She had postponed her Chicago trip so the critical repetition would not be broken.

"If Mrs. Thatcher doesn't eat her cake . . . tell her that it's an icing you made especially for her!" Somberg paused again, faithfully following the seductive rhythm of the music. "Watch her *very* carefully . . . counting her bites in a whisper . . . but if you should hear a whistle . . .'' Somberg pricked the transmitter in the brass belt buckle. A low whistle erupted to fill Danny's dream. ''Quickly! Give Mrs. Thatcher an I-love-you hug . . . and then the party will end in a happy white light!''

There was only peace on his face as he traveled in her dream that he had come to love as he loved her. And Somberg loved the feeling of remapping his mind; it was sensuous, truly sensuous, to remake the mind; it was an act of God. The waltz played in sub-memory, in a place where logic dissolved, Somberg caught up in layers of music, feeling the soothing of soft, smooth hands. Deep blue eyes seemed to draw her out of herself, ah, the delicious disorientation of lips on her bare skin. Nuzzled next to Mother's breasts. A young girl sinking into the mesmerizing sensation, drifting on the waltz away from Father hurtled back in a roar into the barn hay with the sudden blood erupting pink and frothy from his wide-open scream. But mother had made everything all right and now the waltz glided to a close and Somberg slipped from the memory and from the room, Danny drifting deeper into the sweetness of the dream that cycled over and over through the honeyed middle of the night. His dream propelled by her mother's hypnotic waltz, which Somberg used on all her beautiful dreaming boys. Boys made into girls as her father was remade into death. Pretty boy-girls as the walking dead, as that father in the wasteland of dream.

It was their tenth day in the Dublin Custom House, long past evening tea, when the fax chimed. Jessica continued reading entry cards while Trent checked to see what had come in.

He spent a moment studying a satellite-blurred photo and U.S. passport application for a Jenkins, Dana Sue. ''Hullo!'' he called out to the mice scrambling in the walls. ''What do we have here?''

''What?'' Jessica looked up from a box of cards.

''Damn,'' Trent said, and read further. ''Damn, damn, damn.'' He dropped the transmission in the reject pile.

''Who was it?''

''Take a look,'' he said and shoveled more coal into the stove.

Jessica marked her spot and joined him at their headquarters. A folding table held a graveyard of chicken bones, Finn Crisp Lite Crackers imported from Chicago, a molding loaf of bread, and some lunch meats. Jessica dropped onto the coats on the sofa, studying a file that had the U.S. passport picture of a woman with a chalky complexion, lips pale, chin tucked into her neck, dark hair in a pageboy. The eyes hard to make out behind the gleaming glasses.

''It *almost* looks like her!''

''Right. And she entered Ireland on March ninth with a boy.''

Jessica took up his entry card that accompanied the mother's. '' 'Jason,' '' she read. ''Six years old!''

''But note the FBI ran a cross-check,'' Trent said, pointing at a fax transmission with a fireplace poker. ''They confirmed Jenkins is a bank teller in Los Angeles. Owns a house. Widowed. The son is for real. Enrolled at Alex Sanger Elementary.''

''But she has the look of Sterling!''

''Right. But she can't be.'' He dropped to the arm of the sofa, took the file from her, and flipped through the pages, showing her the FBI report and the copy of a birth certificate. "You see?" he said. "She's lived in San Bernardino ten years. Teaches Sunday school. In a Tuesday night bowling league."

Jessica took the file back; the loose pages fell out. She put them back, careful to keep them in the order Trent insisted on. He was such a stickler for order. Now she noticed a page missing. "Where's *his* passport?"

"Pardon?" Trent glanced back from the fire.

"The boy's passport. I want to see his picture."

"Right. Yanks said they were still searching."

"Searching?"

"Hey, babe—" Trent assumed a Yank accent. It fell somewhere between Big Sur and Soho. "You gotta be cool for this kinda deal. There's, like, a million missing American kids out there. And no cop gets a medal for finding a missing kid. You hip to where I'm coming from? These things take time. Can you dig it?"

Sure, sure, she thought savagely, *and the time it takes is killing me.* She dug in the Finn Crisp box and came out with a cracker, only one thin calorie per serving. She gnawed on it as she studied Jenkins's entry card. "Look at this," she said, tapping the card. "When Jenkins arrived in Cork, she said her length of stay was *one week.* But she left the same day."

Trent frowned, stirring the fire. "Curious," he commented.

"What if . . ." Jessica frowned at last week's sliced ham, which had a sickly yellowish color. Under the fluorescent light it looked chartreuse. "What if Sterling applied for Jenkins's passport and Jenkins doesn't know it?"

Trent turned from the stove. "I'm afraid that's not likely," he said to a row of high windows painted black. "Rather difficult to slip one by the U.S. Department of State. They have some of the most stringent passport controls in the world. The Yanks, the Brits, though the Canadians are actually tougher. Their passport is damn near impossible to obtain under false pretense."

"But an *American* passport can be had, right?"

"Oh, it happens."

"And how likely is it that an LA bank teller would need a *passport?* I mean, you don't need one to enter or exit Mexico."

"Jess, you can't—"

"Or that a bank teller would come to *Ireland?* It's an expensive trip! We're talking a month's pay."

"Right, but—"

"Then *leave* the same day?"

He nodded. "Now, that part *is* odd."

"Trent, none of it makes any sense!"

"Yes, but people often don't, Jess."

"Tell me about it! What the hell could be more senseless than taking a child?"

"Right. But there were a lot of moves behind that taking. There may actually be reason behind it we don't yet see."

He played the outside man. Innocent bystander. Blind logic to her frenzy. Experience to her overactive fantasy. "People will surprise you, Jess. They'll have a million odd reasons for doing things. One mustn't leap to conclusions."

She rose from the sofa. Spurned the Finn Crisp for a stick of spearmint gum. Her jaw working as she spread the photos and sketches over the table. Jenkins next to Sterling next to the ice woman next to Nordstrom next to the clammy chartreuse ham. "This is spooky," she said, staring.

Trent glanced over her shoulder. "Jenkins looks like Nordstrom to me," he said casually.

"They all look alike to me!"

Trent ignited a match and held it to the Cohiba. He took a moment to consider the possibilities. "Shapes of their faces are the same," he said, igniting the cigar.

"And the eyes!" Jessica added, a suppressed excitement in her voice. "And the forehead and jaw and, well, maybe the nose!" She looked up to Trent wearing the expression of someone expecting a firecracker to go off. "What do you think?"

The cigar traveled from the left side of his mouth to the right. A wreath of smoke ringed his head. He appeared gray, years older, as though smoke had advanced him into the next millennium and he was still looking for the same vanishing, eccentric woman. "There are any number of ways to alter one's appearance," he said. "The rule of disguise is to use as little of it as possible." He looked closely at Jenkins's dark bobbed hair, which contrasted with her pale skin. "Of course, one can do most anything with a face, given time, and the proper makeup kit." He wished he could take the spectacles off her. Hard to see the eyes beyond the glare of the glasses. Quickie passport photograph? Or was the glare the artistry of a pro? He rummaged in the files scattered over the table. "Have a seat," he said, passing Jessica the Sterling, Nordstrom, and ice woman files. "Let's check their height. It won't validate duplicate identities, but it might refute them."

She dropped onto a stack of boxes that served as a chair and, dumping the ham into a bin, she spread out the files that seemed they ought to have meaning; a feeling so perfect in her, it was as though it rose from a dream. A dream came back now. Seeing Sterling through the camera lens, her face upside-down in the Hasselblad, in the way which Jessica's life would be turned-upside down. In the camera Sterling was an actress playing the role of mother on a stage. There was a sense about her in the strong way in which she played the part, that she had played such strong difficult parts before. A perfection in her technique. Nothing superficial about her, sliding casually into the role, and one could almost believe it could swallow her, she was so good at it. Wasn't that a symptom of stardom, its initializing privilege? To be lost in the role. A prickle of hope ran up Jessica's spine. Her glance faster over the files; her voice harder, clotted as she responded to Trent.

"How tall is Sterling?" he asked, pacing at the stove.

"About an inch—maybe two—taller than me," Jessica said.

"Right. Call her six feet. How about the ice woman?"

Jessica checked, chomping furiously on gum. "One hundred and seventy-eight centimeters," she said.

"That's five feet, ten inches. Close enough. What about this Jenkins woman?"

Jessica scanned the report, her hands shaking slightly, and it took her a minute to find the little box that gave the height.

"Five feet, eleven inches!" She looked up, face aglow. They were the same! She knew it. They were all the same woman. How did she know it? Had she dreamed it? Hadn't she been dreaming it all along? Seeing Sterling in the camera lens, the face of the ever-changing actress. Jessica taking a picture of each face, same as the pictures before her now. "You think they're the same person, don't you? Didn't I tell you that! Remember? Back in London?"

"Right. And Nordstrom?" Trent waited. The cigar smoke rose in ghostly spirals that unfurled below the dark beams of the ceiling. Then the smoke vanished, as though through the ceiling, as if the Cuban smoke were carrying the mystery into another place in time.

Jessica found the Interpol fact sheet. Read it and looked up with disgust. "One hundred and seventy-two centimeters."

"Five feet, eight inches," Trent said. "Sorry about that. They can't be the same person."

"Goddamn it, Trent!" She beat on the flimsy table, knocking the Finn Crisps over the sketches and photos. She might as well eat the damn pictures for all the good they would do. She lost the magnetism of the dream, fleeing from the scene that played beyond the upside-down pictures of Sterling. It came every night in the dream. It played in a hugeness of need, in an enormity of appeal she could not face because she hadn't the strength. The darkroom scene of Danny shooting her. The quotidian tragedy replaying in the high-powered vacuum of dream. Why? Why must she face the worst again? "I'm sick of this research shit!" she blurted out. "I didn't come to Ireland for this. I want to go to Killarney!"

A moment of silence. Trent regarded the red embers of his cigar. Neither surprised nor disturbed by this announcement. She had been on the verge of quitting for two days now. He glanced at the sketches, trying to resist her fantasy, which was infectious. The faces *did* have a certain similarity.

"You *want* them all to be the same person," he said, setting the cigar down. "But you can't *want* in this business. Want gets in the way. Want can't be trusted. It will sell out reason."

"It just *feels* like . . . I don't know!"

She threw her gum into the bin with the ham. What good was gum? Why had she taken up chewing gum? Always had gum with her. Always chewing it. Even in the dream. She dug into the box of Finn Crisps and came out with a fistful of crackers.

"You want it so bad," he said, working the knot of muscle in her shoulders. "Looking at those faces with your gut. Needing as much as wanting. Soon everyone's face looks the same. You think you've got it . . . then it turns around and bites the shit out of you. Hope is a bloody cannibal. It can eat you heart and soul."

She chomped on the crackers, staring at the windows painted over black. Black as a night without dreams. But there was never such a night. We all dream. It was one thing to use the Beethoven to empower dreams. But it was something else to recall the dreams, even create dreams that she sensed she could do. Pit had not told these things. It would have to wait for another day. She wafted at the Cuban smoke. The smoke that got into your body, that tied you in to what floated on the air. "I've had enough of this research," she retorted with her mouth full. "I'm going to Killarney!"

He would have preferred to stay with the entry card search and explore the similarity of these faces. The big break often came just beyond the point of exhaustion. When you're dark and blank inside. He wanted to check these sketches with whatever was in the Night Owl file Jessica had unearthed in Big Brother. But the poor soul had a suitcase full of Danny pictures, anxious to canvas the Killarney streets. It'd be a waste of time, but she'd feel better. He gathered the files into a tidy pile. The Night Owl work, and the unearthing of Definite Integral, would have to wait.

"There are a few cases outstanding," Trent said. "Pictures we're still waiting on."

"I'm going!" she declared.

"Right."

She looked up at him. "Are you coming?"

"You bet," he said, glancing at the sofa, remembering nights by the fire. The work had been his best friend. It had worn her out and given them a few lazy hours together. And it had made his wanting maddening. "It's a good time for Killarney," he commented sunnily. "The photos we're expecting will be a few days yet. I'll ask someone to verify Jenkins while we're out."

"And her son," Jessica said. "We need *his* passport picture."

"Right." Trent made a note.

"And can the FBI call Jenkins? Ask if she's been to Ireland?"

"We'll give that a go." He made another note.

"And ask why she left Ireland after *one day*."

"Sure. Our man can do that."

"And maybe someone can take a *fresh* picture of Jenkins?"

"Right." He made a point of writing it all down so she could dismiss it from her relentless mind. Would have done it without her prompting, except for the fresh picture; the FBI wouldn't go that far; though it was encouraging to see she had the instinct of an investigator. She had a *feel* for his work. People with such sensitivities often understood when the work kept the investigator out till hours. Took them to other places, to other times. The unraveling always an intrigue, otherworldly. "I'll just tell the chaps upstairs we're finished here. Thanks ever so much, all that sort of thing."

He started up creaky stairs. Jessica attacked the crackers, glaring at the files, as though she were about to devour them. Maybe it was crazy to think they were all the same person. Was she finally cracking up? But the idea kept turning in her head.

"Trent!" she called out.

He glanced down. She was holding her arms over her stomach, rocking back and forth on the box chair as if she were cold.

"Nordstrom's wife was killed in a boating accident, right?"

"Right."

"I wonder, could we get a picture of *her*?"

"Of who? Nordstrom's wife?"

"Yes. Or at least some kind of description. We should check *her* height, don't you think?"

"Good idea." He did not think it was a good idea, just the same, he wrote it down. And he'd follow through on it, for the flamboyant, pretty Yank child that had his heart. He'd play all her long shots. "I'll buzz the Swedes. Insurance records will cover that. What was her maiden name?"

Jessica dug through the Nordstrom file, something grinding in her head, an idea trying to take shape. Finally she found a copy of the marriage certificate. Had to squint to read tiny Swedish print. "Somberg!" she called out. "Kristian Mary Somberg."

"Right. Got it. Be right down."

19

SHE HAD SLEPT through the gorgeously empty country that from the train window was gauzed in curtains of mist. She never saw the great buttresses of purple cliffs or the mosaic of overgreen hills or the dark, loamy plowlands treaded by little rivers of tarnished pewter. She saw only Danny in her sleep. Trent gently shook her as the train came huffing into the station. Jessica peered out to a Disney soundstage. Cobbled streets lined in shops and pubs and restaurants painted in sunset colors. The good folk sauntering down the walks in oatmeal tweed. No sense of hurry in this town, as quiet as if the last century had passed it by.

They left the steaming and shuddering train behind to rent a car. As they walked to the car park, Jessica's emotions began to swarm. Hot snakes from head to toe. Unbelievable Danny had been here, in this little town tucked into Ireland's big toe opposite America. A sense of the frantic in the fear that could ripen and fester and was now upon her, motivating her to action. To do! Do something. *Anything!* If only she had the gift of second sight, she could follow his spectral footprints. She could see him in the spectral fog that hung here and there like angel mist. She could make out the contrails from his hands, the fantails of his little fingers; she would know what corona had encircled his head. Where was he today? What was he thinking? Did he miss her?

"Can you manage a right-hand drive?" Trent asked when they found the sky blue Volvo.

"No problem," she replied, unlocking the driver's door.

"You're certain?"

"Sure. I want to drive."

"Even if the other cars are going the 'wrong direction'?"

"Stanford! I paid for the rental. Get in."

Without a word, Trent slid into the passenger seat. Behind the wheel, there was hope on her face and determination behind her face and fear slipping out around the edges. The car had a stick; it was at her left elbow. Took her a moment to find it. Trent quietly strapped himself into the seat, as if to be launched. She turned the key and shoved the awkward stick into first, sending them bucking into the wrong-way streets. Trent cupped a hand to cover his grin. The Volvo gained speed, she fetched second with a shriek and a jerk, and the Volvo leaped forward; wheels slammed into the curb, knocking a hubcap loose. He glanced back at the clanging, spinning hubcap. She drove on, in the wrong lane.

"Don't say a word, Stanford!"

She swerved before colliding with a wrong-way bus.

Back in the correct lane, he said, "Sorry to bother you, but I wonder, do you have a pencil handy?"

"For what?"

"Thought I'd start adding up the damage."

"Trent!"

"Let's see. Hubcaps: fifty pounds apiece. A new transmission: that's fifteen hundred pounds . . ."

She soon got the hang of it on the straightaways. It was the turns that were wicked. Turning the right way into the wrong lane. She was already searching the walks for Danny's face among the fat children they passed, as if by an Irish miracle, he might still be here. Perhaps enrolled in school, perhaps learning an Irish jig, learning to speak Gaelic, just waiting for something to happen. Her need for something to happen was so great, Killarney was not safe when she drove. Sterling was not safe, wherever she was. Jessica had the scent. On her trail. It was only a question of time. She told herself this; she made herself believe it. She sank into the belief. The belief was in rapport with her need and she would not doubt it. Now she let herself get worked up a little. If necessary, she'd turn all of Killarney upside down! She whipped around a corner and sent a newsstand spinning.

"You can't get lost here," Trent said. "To find any place in Killarney, you stop at one of three traffic lights and look in all four directions. Everything reveals itself in a glance."

Jessica passed a Victorian hotel with original woodwork and gables, jaunting cars parked at the curb. A cute gingerbread store was to her left, hardware in the window; next to it a giant goose dangled in the butcher's window. Now it was not a goose, it was Sterling hung by her beautiful neck. A light stopped her, but just barely. She waited. She prayed. Across the street in the open door of the bakery she saw Danny in yellow rain boots with his hands full of pastry, sharing a laugh with Sterling, who smiled right at her, but in a blink they became just a local blond mother and son on a day of shopping. The trouble had begun. She was lovesick. She was taunted. The light changed and she drove on and saw him again in the rearview mirror, Danny holding Sterling's hand and waving good-bye. Memory, it seemed, had become a form of emotion.

She had to think of something else. She thought of violence. "So, is the IRA a big deal here?" she asked Trent who hadn't said a word. "Or is it all hush-hush?"

"Well, now," he said in his mother's fine brogue. "One nation under one flag is mostly a dream. Bitter illusion. Mind ye there are those who *truly* believe, though t'IRA is unlawful in Ireland."

"The organization is unlawful, you mean?"

"Right."

"Not the belief."

"Right. Belief lives."

Jessica stopped at a light where a fat-faced cop was telling a story to a group of men, hands swirling before a picture window lettered in gold and green: "O'Flaherty's Pub." Crossed flags, the Irish Republic's tricolor and Old Glory, were painted above the door. "So you never know," she asked, looking at the jolly cop, "who is and who isn't?"

"Oh, *they* know, but they're not known. And they'll call upon yer services without warning. A late-night ringing of t'phone. A burglar alarm in yer heart. And ye'll come and do as ye're told, t'lads real sticklers for rules and regulations. Woeful things happen to those who disobey. Ye'll don yer black ski mask for a hit-and-run across t'border to t'North. And when t'bloody work is done, ye'll return to entertain t'fat Yank tourists with harp and accordion. Hoisting t'rounds! Raking in t'riches. And no one will be the wiser, 'cept yer soul, mind ye. Waiting it will be. As it's waited for t'blessed day, eight hundred years in coming."

"Freedom, you mean?"

"Wholeness, I mean. *Oneness*."

"I hear you."

" 'Tis me mother country torn in two. At odds with herself."

The light changed. She drove on in the affinity she had with a torn nation. "You sound like you almost support them—the IRA."

"Do I now?" Trent acquired a smile she hadn't seen before. A shaggy, cocky grin. "Well, now, some say they're patriots and some say they're devils. 'Tis in t'eye of t'beholder. Decent men, even disciples of God, disagree on it. But no matter how many soldiers are sent, and how many pathetic victims the lads make, t'Brit will never win victory over Irish nationalism that lives in t'heart."

Her heart was aching. She turned onto New Street. Passed the Bank of Ireland and the Post, the town tapering into row houses. Driving slowly and looking at all the windows. No pictures of Danny on display. Had Father Shanahan received her package?

"This seems the most improbable place in the world for Sterling to come!"

"Right," Trent said, returning to the Queen's English. "I was going to bring that up."

"I mean, *this* doesn't looked like Jacqueline Sterling. I could see her in Paris! Or Milan! Tokyo or Bangkok! But *here?*"

"And she came in the *dead of winter*. When only those with Celtic blood tour Ireland. No other fool, other than maybe a writer, would mistake an Irish winter as beauty."

"Sterling is *not* Irish!"

"No. They wouldn't have her."

"And why come for only *one day?*"

"Yes, but the question that's been eating at me," Trent said as an expanse of lawn appeared, the sky suddenly filled with the spire of a cathedral, "is why *St. Mary's?* Hardly the place for a woman who would commit murder to steal a child."

She parked in front of a picket fence and gazed upon a sight seen in dreams. The dreams were so vivid, they rivaled reality, and it was difficult to separate the two. It was an internecine warfare fraught with the worst consequences. The dreams silent, but acting out in screenplay jargon what cannot be forgotten. In dream, her spirit was loose, unclaimed, unprotected—basically asking to be raped. It was confounding how dreams took a trivial item, such as a household item, such as Danny's favorite yellow rainboots, and gave them a value they did not have in the open market of reality. The cathedral was like that. Though it was grander in reality. The pointy edifice seemed to her to be more a monument to a God that smites than a God that loves. And Jessica asked Him again, for the millionth time, *Why my son?*

* * *

"Are you all right, Jess? You look flushed."

"I'm fine," she muttered.

She was sitting very still, gripping the wheel with both hands. It seemed to Trent that eyes had lost their hold on the present, staring at the immemorial where Danny had been spotted. Killarney, for Jessica, was a loaded gun. And she knew what it was to be shot. But she was holding it together, a tough mama.

"While you're with the priest, I'll call the office."

The prospect of entering the cathedral alone only seemed to deepen her despondency. "You're not coming in?" she said, suddenly neurotic, a quality of ghastly surprise on her face.

"I think it best if I don't. I've found it helps to have a man on the outside. Someone your contacts don't know. I'll be that man for you." He offered a winning smile. "Okay?"

She didn't hear a word of it. She pulled her herringbone blazer over the sweater she had bought in Dublin. She took a breath and stepped out of the car, then looked back and said, "Shit."

He watched her go up the walk and wondered if the church was nothing more than a rendezvous. He had used churches. Warm and dry. Anonymity guaranteed. A conversation in the midst of many people is often the safest. And the Gothic dark added a certain sense of menace. Scared the hell out of some people. A natural habit for spooks. A quiet place to transact business. Neither here nor there. Close to home. And where would that be from Killarney? London? Paris? Madrid? The nature of Sterling's business was impossible to know—was she a spook? racketeer? child merchant?—but that Sterling was a businesswoman there was no doubt. Efficient and systematic. International, not afraid to expose her face in the States. Sterling was not the burnt-out buildings, crumbling edifices, detonated bombs, dead bodies and other assorted memorabilia of the postmodernist Irish war that was, if one was to believe Mrs. T, not a war. So why Ireland?

"Some things are better lost than found," he whispered after Jessica. "Danny you want to find. But Sterling, whatever she is, may be better lost."

He wished he could go with her, and certainly there weren't any Brownie points in staying behind. It pissed her off, adding to her hell. What was difficult for her to realize was her complicity in her own undoing. She had actually aided Sterling in taking Danny. That had to drive her mad. But the teeter-totter on which she lived, between memory and reality, limited her effectiveness. It weakened her in this new territory with no boundaries and no ideologies. Sterling was that territory, and Jessica had entered it when she entered Ireland. Her sanity, whether she realized it or not, was up for grabs. She was on the edge. She never left it.

He suspected she was something of a call girl to her dreams. He experienced similar symptoms at the behest of the Grand Hotel that burst open under his feet every night. Top of the building collapsing in red and white and golden sheet lightning, bowels of the structure convulsing in the odd deafness that came to him in the explosion, so the night smoke hung in a gray, quiet shroud in dream that was difficult but not impossible to manage. The visual he had come to dismiss as an air attack; somehow that helped, to see it as war; it was the smell that stayed with him and that he, without any trouble, could smell now, here, in the car. The smell of charred flesh. Nothing like it. Jessica had that smell about her. He watched her take the slate steps. *Nowhere to look but ahead, Jess. Take whatever you can get your hands on, but don't expose what you've got.* He saw her vanish behind the closing door, knowing she was not alone, memory and fear right beside her.

She paused in the foyer. It was here Danny had knocked the camera from the tourist's hands. *He was right here!* She could have kissed the ground, and she was tempted to, such was her despair. Into the sanctuary. Dark pews polished to a soft sheen. Stained-glass windows rose to a high vault. The air a tapestry of odors, lemon oil and incense and candle wax. Up the aisle as if plunging into a dream, sensing Danny's presence, but with control over her impulses. She did not shout his name. Didn't shriek at Sterling. Didn't cry out to God in His house in complicity with her pain.

She found the church offices. The receptionist on the phone. A big woman like Sterling. Long-armed and big handed. Big voice but small mouth that couldn't stop talking. Exchanging the latest, tsking in amazement. A desk name plate read: "Marline." Jessica waited in a chair under a gaily decorated bulletin board that did not have a picture of Danny. When Marline finally hung up, she introduced herself.

"Heavens!" Marline exclaimed. "I remember ye; searching for yer son, ye were! I know Father would want to see ye."

"Is he in?" Jessica asked.

"No. He'd be in Belfast. Attending Tomas Mahoney's funeral."

"Oh. I'm sorry."

"Aye, 'twas a terrible tragedy!" Marline told the story of Mahoney found on the Belfast tracks. "Run over by a train he was!" Marline lowered her voice, leaning over her desk to confide, "He smelled of drink. That one could never stay away from the drink. But what the train did to him!" She shuddered and crossed herself.

Without even trying, Jessica could see the havoc of entrails, splattered and mashed on the tracks. She shut off her imagination and asked about her flyers. No, Marline hadn't seen any flyers. By now Jessica wasn't surprised. She stared severely at the ceiling in an obsession in which there was no Mahoney, no Belfast, no funeral and no cathedral and no Ireland. There was only Danny.

"I'm staying at a place called Cullinane's Thatch," she said, glad she had come to Ireland. Father Shanahan obviously forgot about Danny as soon he hung up the phone. "It's—"

"In the Gap of Dunloe," Marline said, and beamed and added, " 'Tis God's own resting place!"

That struck a note with Jessica. "Really?"

"Aye, 'tis a heavenly spot." She finished her message to the Father, then looked up, puzzled. "There's only the one cottage in the Gap," she said. "I wonder, how could ye know to let it?"

"Oh. I have a friend. In England. He made the arrangements."

"How nice. Well, I'll *certainly* tell Father Shanahan." And tell she would. Minutes after Jessica left, Marline's switchboard of gossip would be lit up, the rumor return rate in Killarney was about ninety minutes. Before Jessica ever met the good folk, her tale would be spread, told in snatches and exaggerated narratives, the mystery Englishman growing with every telling.

"When will Father Shanahan be back?"

"In a day or two. How long will ye be staying, dear?"

"Until I find my son," Jessica said, more shrill than she had intended. But why had the Father not posted Danny's picture? She felt terribly neglected. How could a priest forget Danny? Wasn't a priest a shepherd? Weren't they to look after the lost lambs?

She returned through the sanctuary, and as she entered the sun came out from behind clouds and streamed over the vault in waves of scarlet and green, burnt gold and shadows of misted blue. Down the aisle and through the hush, need and anguish tumbling over inside her, she succumbed to the mania that was in her bones, and now in the shimmer of colored light, as though swarming out of a dream to spill forth horribly into reality, she saw Sterling. Smiling up from a pew, long arm and big hand around Danny.

Sterling's sardonic laughter echoed in her head: *Look, Danny! It's Mommy! Remember her? She looks different now that she's fucked up. See her slumped shoulders and her stooped back? Looks like she's carrying something heavy. Why, I think she's carrying a cross. Yes, it's the old rugged cross! Look at her, staggering around the world. Selling everything. Spending all her money. Hoping for what isn't there. Seeing what isn't there.*

Jessica rushed down the aisle, the taunt trailing after her.

Run, Mommy, run! But what are you running to? I have Danny. I have the business you left behind. I'll soon have your home and everything else. Keep this up, you'll have to sell it all. I've got it and you're falling apart! Coming unglued, dear! How long till they strap you into a straitjacket? A month? Two months? Why not go back to the Hemingway House, buy yourself a silver-inlaid shotgun, stuff the muzzle into your mouth, and pull the trigger?

Jessica burst through steepled doors, into the brightness. Running down the walk, hearing Sterling call after her.

Run, Mommy, run! But where are you running to?

She came out of the glare to find Trent behind the wheel of the Volvo. Calmly jotting notes onto a pad, the notes set in boxes as if it were a sketch. In a cloud of toxic smoke. She dropped into the passenger seat, slammed the door. "So," she said, "you don't *trust* my driving?" She rolled down the window, fanning at the smoke. "This car stinks to *high heaven!*"

He heard the pain. It had turned ugly. He mournfully stubbed out the fine Cohiba. His thinking was over, her emotion had begun.

"Driving is easier than giving instructions," he explained and switched on the car.

"Oh, sure, sure," she said, and stared out the window.

They started down the road in a close silence. Like being in a cage with a bruiser aching for a fight. He remained impassive.

Finally he asked, "Did you see the priest?"

"No. He wasn't there."

"Oh? Too bad. Where was he?"

"At a funeral. A Mahoney something-or-other."

"Right." The name rang a distant bell. Trent saw a bulletin on Graham's desk. A burly, thick-eared youth with a rough beard.

"Cathedral was rather rough, was it?"

"No," she said severely. "It was empty. Full of shadows."

"Did you see Danny's picture posted?"

"No! Marline hadn't even seen it!"

"Marline?"

"Marline, the damn secretary," she said, ready to flare at anything. "Pisses the hell out of me! Father Shanahan *said* he'd post Danny's picture. Why would he tell me that but not put one on the church bulletin board? A photocopy and a thumbtack, that's all the effort it'd take!"

He loved her. Couldn't help it. But could he spend his whole life listening to this? Trent thought not. He followed the road that led them out of town and grew steep and narrow, enclosed in stone. Beyond the walls, lush rolling valleys patched with sun and crossed with streams. He knew these colors, painted on the canvas of his soul. He had run these fields, forded these streams, and climbed these walls. Hope and despair rose here. Now he saw the bulletin more clearly. Tragic nose on a patchy, reconstructed complexion, as if someone had smashed a broken bottle into him. Mahoney. IRA? Wanted for arms smuggling?

"The priest will likely be back in the morning," he said. "Irish funerals have a way of leaving one with a hangover."

"No. Marline said the funeral is in Belfast."

"Belfast?" Trent glanced at her. "Belfast? You're sure?"

"Yes. Why?"

"Well, Belfast is to the IRA what Rome is to the pope."

"Oh, God!" She rolled her despondent eyes over the ceiling. "You're always so damn C-thirteen suspicious!"

"Right."

He drove on, seeing not the road but the fingerprint report on the Fox. *Arrested in Rotterdam. Had an accomplice. The Dutch never apprehended him. He was not identified, but believed to be part of an Irish assassination team.* Trent stayed with the turning road through broken light and shadow. Now the bottom line of the report came back. *His accomplice was known only as the Pope.*

"I wish I knew why she came *here*." Jessica let an irritated sigh escape through closed teeth. "I wish I knew *who* she was!"

"The devil you know is sometimes better than the one you don't know," Trent muttered, eyes fixed on the horizon.

Jessica whirled around and glared at him. "What?" she said.

"The priest. What was his name?"

"Father Shanahan. Why?"

He nodded agreeably. "Slipped my mind," he said, and drove on. It was probably nothing, coincidence, pope and priest. What kind of priest would be IRA? What, God on their side? Mrs. T would never allow it. She would talk God out of it. She'd invite God to that hot seat opposite her desk, stare at Him with those eyes of hers that could burn to the heart, and she'd set God straight. Being God, He'd get the royal treatment, not subject to the mix of lust and loathing she displayed to Trent.

Mrs. T had a hard on for the IRA. The Pope an IRA operative. What kind of priest would be codenamed the Pope? It'd be something akin to blasphemy, not to speak of murder. Now, "Did Marline mention Mahoney's first name?"

"It was—" Jessica frowned into space. "I don't know," she said curtly. "Marline may have said it, but I've forgotten it. I've had other things on my mind."

He asked her to reiterate her conversation with Marline. Jessica rattled it off. He turned with the road that took them along a meadow that held a lake blazed with light, Trent's heart beating faster with a turning idea. The Fox had an accomplice. Mahoney was IRA, wanted for weapons smuggling. The priest was at the Belfast funeral of a Mahoney. They rounded a forested curve and the road slanted up and there was another curve and now the lake was not where it had been; he saw it through the trees, turquoise and jeweled with sunlight. The priest. The Pope. Sterling at the cathedral. They crested the hill, and the trees opened onto squares of field stitched in stone, and in the distance jagged purplish mountains rose into veils of tenuous cloud, a thought emerging to slowly take shape. Could the two cases be related? Brighton and Danny?

The light ran before them over the road that loomed and faded in shadow, the scene changing before Trent's eyes. Could he trust the instinct that would link Brighton and Danny? Or was this some lover's tune played by the heart, he listening in loyal rapture? The pretty-pretty sensation of love! It was in the beauty brooding beside him. Something in him would be her darling! Give the show away. Give himself away. Not what Jessica wanted. Not what any woman wanted. They loved the chase. Needed it. All of it, woman and Ireland and the Brighton bombing singing of destiny. Told himself he didn't believe in destiny. He believed in *facts*. He'd find out if the Mahoney on the IRA bulletin was the Mahoney who died in Belfast. Shanahan's true colors could be established with a few days' work. If he was IRA, he might well be the Pope. That could explain what had never added up, not since Danny's sighting. Why would Sterling go to a cathedral in Killarney? A rendezvous with the Pope? But it was too fantastic to believe—the bitch who kidnapped Danny had met with the bastard who tried to do Thatcher. What kind of priest would incinerate an entire hotel to off one woman? A priest who fucking believed he was God, or the next best thing. This Pope and Mrs. T something of a matched pair.

They drove through a tunnel of trees overhanging the road in shadow and sunlight that gave the appearance of a piano's black and white keys. The car ran down the keyboard that in Jessica's mood played as a frantic concerto with the notes of the Brighton and Danny cases, as opposite as black and white, blooming and resonating within Trent. A previous theme was repeated, Definite Integral. A naïve Jessica balls-up that could be something more than ineptitude. Might it shed some light on the Sterling-Jenkins-Nordstrom-Somberg-Ice Woman enigma? Was this a single beast with five heads? Or five separate creatures? The classified spook operation, Definite Integral, inspired professional curiosity. Had a sharp, brilliant tone. Worth looking into. He could beep himself as an excuse to return to London while Jessica canvased Killarney with Danny's photos. Or, instead of lying, he could tell her the truth; some men did that, now and then. Jessica might join him. Bit tricky though, breaking into the Yard to go on-line with Big Brother, which was the only way to find the under-meaning of Definite Integral. Would Jessica be game for a little stealth?

It would take that, he could hardly ask the Yard to enter a search for a *Yank* child. His entanglement with the mother would surface. Graham would make a production number out of it. But Mahoney *was* C-13 territory. If Shanahan proved to be IRA, then a whole team of investigators could be justified for Danny's case, under the guise of Mahoney. And there was no need for Graham to be appraised of Definite Integral, since it was super hush-hush, and could only be found by those touched by the angels.

The Volvo rumbled over a bridge, through a series of turns, past signs pointing every direction. Was Dana Jenkins' arrival in Ireland coinciding with Danny's cathedral sighting a coincidence? Could Sterling and Jenkins be the same? He could put people onto the Swede, Nordstrom, whom Big Brother *had* matched with Sterling. Was that a fluke? *Who* was Nordstrom? *Where* was he? Then there was the ice woman that Jessica had uncovered in the Night Owl file. It was time to take a peek into those secrets. And he wondered, as he came to the cliff edge of the Gap of Dunloe, where Kate Kearney's Cottage sat overlooking heaven and earth, had Jessica been onto something with all the sketches looking so much alike?

"That's the home of a first-class fiddler." Trent nodded at Kate's pub. "Plays for a pint and a jingle of silver before a fire surrounded by the greatest storytellers since the Greeks!" He pulled into the car park. "And this," he announced, pointing to the great primeval chasm beyond the cliff edge, "is the Gap."

"So?" Jessica released another heated sigh. She looked at the road twisting down the mountain. "Why are we stopping?"

"Thought we'd walk in this first time." Trent climbed out of the car to strap on the pack loaded with their provisions. "The road is rather steep," he offered. "Tricky driving."

Jessica stepped into the wind that took her hair and swirled it about her head. "I'll drive!" she shouted across the car.

"Yes, well—"

"Trent, I'm not afraid of this road!" She looked down over the dusty snake treading down on top of itself. In her hell-bent mood, spoiling for collision, she was not afraid of anything. Not Trent. Not herself. And mostly she was not afraid of Sterling. She told herself that, but the taunting in the cathedral would not go away. She pushed it away. She reclaimed her mind. "I'm not afraid to drive anywhere in Ireland!" she announced to the wind.

"Right. But I need the exercise."

They followed the dirt road that coiled down through high walls of black knotty rock, their feet sliding on the steep grade. Down there somewhere they could hear the wind strumming through the rock, but there was no music between them. She felt all black-and-blue inside. She walked in a stoop, as though she were the one carrying the pack. They rounded a cliff wall and suddenly the hard wind slammed into them and snatched her breath away as the wonder of God revealed itself. Jessica stood there, pants lashing at her legs, hair flying about her head, in the grip of an emotion that for a thousand years the Irish bards have tried to capture.

The Gap appeared as a mountainous curled hand that held a golden glen in its palm, the black fingers of MacGillycuddy's Reeks rising on one side, and across the way, the heather-terraced slopes of Purple Mountain. Four lakes lay in the glen, silver waters wrinkled with wind, and far in the distance, on the shore of the farthermost lake, a white-faced thatched-roof cottage.

The wind came out of where no one knew. It blew down through the empty glen that it swirled in a scheme of secrets, to come in a whistle up the twining road, nipping at the lovely American, blowing her all sideways, ransacking her heart, working at the darkness there. The Irish wind seemed to whisper, "All is well." Jessica rested her head on Trent's shoulder and opened herself to the wind, letting it take her, the wind something of a carnal act. The haunting Gap before her eyes spoke to her ruthless misery that laid down quietly. Her hand found a friend.

"Trent."

"Yes?"

"I owe you an apology."

"Oh? Whatever for?"

"I was a shit in the car."

His arm closed around her in a fit, and she remembered the nights spent on the sofa in the Dublin Custom House basement.

"Cathedral stirred you, did it?"

"Yes, and I'm sorry." Her restless, questing eyes met his. "Sometimes I get a little moody," she said, grateful for the small smile curling over his lips.

"I'd worry if you weren't a little moody sometimes."

"It doesn't last long," she said with promise in her voice.

"Right. And now we're going to have to make up."

They kissed in the wind that would not let them go, and when it was done and they had begun they walked on. Down through the constantly filtering light, over an arched stone bridge, and into the glen, skirting the prehistoric lakes, gold grass bending and flattening before their thatched cottage in that wild ravine.

Trent built a peat fire while Jessica put the groceries in the cupboard, eggs, butter, and cheese in a net in the brook. She swept the plank floors, and he beat the dust from the living room rug. Together they made up the one bed in the one small bedroom. They tramped up winding mountain trails followed by the nosy sheep that watched her pick heather from their mountain. He bellowed to the Celtic gods from a rocky peak. Below she could see tourists coming on jaunting cars down the road, horses lifting a trail of dust that moved slowly with them. And now with the long shadows came sounds of the shepherds from high above, harmlessly insulting the flock on their way home, and Jessica took no pictures; she knew what she saw and what she felt, and it would always be hers. They were neither tourists nor shepherds but travelers in a thing gone well beyond want and need, which had carried them past their guarded limits, surprising them both. They descended the mountain holding hands, her arms full of heather with the blowing country spread out before them, and it was theirs for the night.

Dinner came from the lake. Trent fly-fished with his trousers wet to the knees, Jessica watching from a ledge suspended over the water, with everything behind her, the need for ambition and the need to imagine and the need to fear the future. It was now all behind her and there was only Trent and the eroded mountains and the sun that lay long in the grass that scissored in the wind that carried everything away. As the trauma left her she realized her obsession was false, a mistaken belief she was thinking of Danny when she was really thinking of herself. Obsession was greedy and always lonely; it made no room for others. It is self-perverse.

"Hungry yet?" he asked, still waiting.

"Famished!"

"Really?" he said hopefully.

He was looking back at her when the line popped.

"God, I feel like I haven't eaten since . . . I can't remember when!"

"Dinner is on its way," he said, reeling it in.

The trout was buttered and seasoned and grilled over the fire that had roasted the potatoes. And after they set the table, they surprised themselves by carrying it outdoors. They sat together on an open porch eating like a couple of shaggy beasts, savoring the wine and saying what they could not remember. And when the food was finished they rocked in twig chairs and looked out over their lawn kept by the sheep, watching the western reefs of cloud bleed pink and rose and crimson. And now she knew she was in Ireland.

"It wasn't much of a place to come," he said. "Rather rough. I didn't know if you'd like it."

"Oh, I love it!"

"Do you? We could always take a couple of rooms in town."

"No. I love it all and I want it . . . just the way it is."

"Really?"

"Wouldn't change a thing. I feel good here. I feel safe."

The long evening light turned the waters to a swirled violet, and when the sun dropped under the rim of the mountains they were some distance from the cottage, kissing in the road, their mouths wet and sweet with wine. He led them to the lea of a stone wall centuries old, pinned there Jessica watched the darkness deepen as his hands explored her body while thunderheads reared and quivered in an electric sky and then were sucked away into the blackness again. He had no thoughts; she felt only pleasure. They talked about what only the mountains could remember, enormous around them, hugely black, like high castle walls holding back invading hordes that tonight could not touch her. His hands as smooth as feelings, exploring her dark shapes and moods, to become their polite masters in his touching, while she listened with her heart to the emptiness and watched transient stars burn down the sky, burning as a witch's signature over the black face of the waters.

They heard the rain before they saw it, coming out of the gap between the mountains like some phantom migration. They made a run for it, laughing and racing, her heart in her throat when the rain took them in a cold sudden sweep. The road shining in the dark. Squeezed together in a shivering run. The rain aimed, so it seemed to be punching tiny holes in her skin, screams releasing all that was pent up inside, cold bringing every nerve in her body alive.

"You always seem to come to me rain-wet!" he shouted.

"I know. Why is that?"

"Won't go to sleep on me, will you?"

"No. But I didn't bring that shirt!"

"You won't need the shirt. You've got the man."

They burst into the cottage. One lantern gone out, the other casting the shadows of two wriggling figures dancing with cold, twined together, frantically stripping each other. Her teeth were chattering, his eyes shining and his hand crooked at her beaded breasts bursting through her shirt, her cry whittled small by the cold, now whittled smaller by his touch. He peeled her clothes like a skin dropped steaming before the fire with a warmth already flowing through her. His hands with a mind of their own, slowly traversing pebbled flesh, arms, now shoulders, gliding down her back followed by lips followed by his tongue. She was gone, to where she did not know, perhaps to that place where the Irish wind came from, waiting for exhaustion so it could sing a new song.

Two silhouettes before the fire sank to the floor holding each other, now knee-walking and laughing closer to the red flames with everything slipping perceptibly out of her control. Gathered into a wool blanket toasty from the heat so she felt prized and something like a dish, a golden treasure garnished and glistening before the fire that spit sharply near where she lay. He devoured her first with the eyes, hungry as that terrible wolf that ate Red Riding Hood. Her nipples like strawberries. Jewels of sugar, sweet orbs that had the look of succulent rubies. He bent down to her, the door blew open in a little gust of panic and the lantern went out. He closed the door, left the lantern dark and lit another.

Jessica woke in the night to find Trent beside her, sleeping the good sleep of the dead. She lay in the dark listening to the lapping of the lake that called her from the bed. She slipped away from its warmth, wrapping a blanket around her, walking barefoot on the cool stones that lead to the black waters glimmering with a wonder. Above her, the Irish sky was stretched enormous, hugely black, splattered in a profusion of stars, jagged mountains cut into the glitter. She stared up until she was dizzy, overcome with the song of the tourist in the airport now on the very gentle wind singing "Danny Boy" to the night.

She stood and listened to this anthem of a lost child, and the rush of emotion that flowed through her astonished her, and she did not try to stop it. The flood-gates of love opened under heaven's lights, fattening her heart. She knew Danny as a hot mass of feelings, but knew him now as something more, something that was not mother or father, but the tie that binds that is universal and she shared it with every parent that had ever lived. A love so complete; it was for once not a remix of anything. Not neurotic. Not dependent. Not addiction. It was the crystal-headed perfect vision and she curled on a rock to drink it in. Stark naked inside her wrapper, very little else of consequence to her. She watched stars swing counterclockwise in their course, and the Great Bear turned and the Pleiades winked in the very roof of the vault, winking on her as they had winked for millenniums, and she could not help but feel as though all her life were a journey work of stars. And she knew then that Danny was not lost. Nor was she.

She returned in the dark that was not dark, there were stars to walk by. Trent lay very still as she slid into the sheets, her bare skin cool and damp, fragrant with the night. She curled into his arms with his warm breath on her neck and now at her lips and after a while she returned to sleep where Trent was waiting in a powdery swarm of stars, whistling Danny's song.

20

TRENT CLOSED THE door behind them. It locked automatically. He groped in the dark for the light switch, and found Jessica's breasts instead. He saw sparks in her eyes, and if it weren't for their security breach and the guards roaming the halls, he would have taken a fondling moment before he switched on the lights. But the dark was enthralling, and they'd be safer in the dark, so he lifted his hand from the light switch. They stood together in the dark listening to the soft whirl of a computer left running. The only light was from a street lamp that shone through the far back windows, the golden glow radiating over the half-acre of open-plan offices that comprised Scotland Yard's accounting department.

"This way," he said gallantly, and took three steps and ran smack into the corner of the reception desk. *"Shit!"* He grabbed his shin, let out a low groan, Jessica behind him giggling like a minor. Now the former spy, once a prima donna, like all agents, walked as though his joints were backward, down a dark corridor, taking Jessica by the hand. Through acoustical panels, tops of the walls at eye level. Found what he thought was Edmund Spenser's cubicle. Ducked inside, opening his eyes wider, trying to scavenge light. The work space a slew of papers. Couldn't be Spenser's place. He backed out and into Jessica. Tried the next hole. Three neat piles on the desk. It could only be Spenser. Found his folder in the second stack, tucked it under his arm. "Just stepped in for a file left on Spenser's desk," he'd tell security if they happened by, though they weren't due for another half hour.

Towing Jessica by the hand, he moved down the hall, the dark as their accomplice, hiding them. They took the second left, and then the next right. Trent moving silent and swift. Going as he had rehearsed it that afternoon. Now the back windows came toward him, and the room grew brighter in the street lamp.

"Some kind of rat maze," Jessica whispered at his back.

Trent gave a jolly laugh, though the insides of him were frozen in alarm. It was one thing to send joes over the Wall. It was an entirely different matter when you were doing it yourself, within your own agency, with a lover. He was the proverbial agent turned fool for love. A tale as old as the history of fools. The only surprise was that it was the hard case who for years had kept his heart in a box. Perfect, really; no one would believe it.

The hall opened into a wide common space. Around the potted ficus, Trent went immediately to a birch table. He dropped into a chair in front of the terminal, flipped the switch and the screen came to life. The concentration of his features was now painted in a radium green. Fast fingers played the keyboard while Jessica stood lookout behind him with the street lamp pouring in at her back. Over the walls of open-planed panels, her night eyes were seeing more. The typing pool in the next bay over, the day's two bales of paperwork stacked high. She mapped the corridors in her mind, noting the red exit sign aglow above the distant door. She imagined the place shot in a slow shutter speed and a flaming-flash technique. Artful black-and-whites that would look scared and sad. But she didn't feel sad, she was a little drugged on an adrenaline high, and roughed-up from their Glasgow affair. Would there be shooting tonight? It seemed unlikely. But then she didn't expect it in Glasgow. And neither did Trent.

"I'm not *supposed* to know these codes," Trent said, glancing up. "Just a thing one picks up through the years."

"Sure," Jessica replied agreeably.

"Don't remember anything you see."

"No. Of course not."

"Don't know how you came across 'Definite Integral.' "

"Women's intuition, I suppose."

Letters skidded across the screen, Trent entering codes that accessed Big Brother. As it was a communal terminal, there was no way to trace who used it, by day or in the middle of the night.

"We're just searching for a lost lamb." Trent spoke in tender tones of reassurance to himself. It came out sounding like guilt. "I'm sure the top-floor boys would understand." Would they call this a treasonable offense? He thought they probably would. "It's not as though we're at work for the invading barbarians."

Big Brother blinked up and Trent accessed the M15 directory. "We'll take a look," he said. "Maybe we can find a lead on Danny." He entered the formula for a definite integral: $f(xi)@Xi$.

The screen went dark for a moment; then two columns of coded names appeared. Trent read quickly, a laundry list, a bumper crop of code names, all retired. Good double agents don't act their parts; they live them. The best doubles die. This was a list of the best. He pointed to the second name in the first column: Night Owl.

"Right," Jessica whispered, reading crookedly, head cocked, one eye on the front door. She'd be curious to take another look at Night Owl, now that she knew it was top secret. But Trent slid the blinking cursor down the list. It stopped at Laundryman.

"Let's give this one a go. I think that's Heydrick. Ran a money game out of Frankfurt, played both sides of the Wall."

Trent's swift, light fingers on the keys. A report flashed onto the screen. Six pages. The hum of the terminal was a roar in Jessica's ears straining for the sound of the door, her face lit in a pale glow, leaning close to Trent, hand on his shoulder, her heart lit with a certain inner fire. Didn't catch it all, Trent was such a fast reader, flying through the pages. But she thought that he might be doing that on purpose, as if incoherence could save her from what she was not supposed to see.

The file, with the damnedest pictures, portrayed one Rudolf Heydrick, President, German Federated Bank. Worked for the CIA and KGB. Had a covert network of chic corporations in West and East Germany. Spread grease up and down the administrative ladders, moving assets, not people, over the Berlin Wall. But as a new German alignment came in the wind, Heydrick's heavyweight network was viewed as an obstruction itself and someone opted to take him down. An obese man, Heydrick was a carnivore with an appetite for well-seasoned beef. Bulldozing through a thick porterhouse at his favorite Munich restaurant when in the middle of his gorging he was blasted out of his chair "as if shot," the report said. He climbed to his feet, holding his belly, shrieking "as if he had swallowed ragged glass." Staggering, he took out serving carts and waiters in a blinding agony, hands at his throat in "a hideously hoarse scream." Restaurant in an uproar until Heydrick collapsed over a table. There was an accompanying picture. Jessica stared at it, her exuberance in a downward spiral.

Trent took a moment to consider the report. He was told the laundry artist had died of indigestion. Laid quietly to rest. No headlines. No pictures. Dignity of the banking community intact. Obviously, it was something a tad more severe than indigestion.

"The autopsy said it was Brilix," he said softly, reading the screen.

"In his saltshaker!"

"Never seen Brilix used that way." Trent now frowned at the ceiling quilted in shadow. "Makes sense. Ground to fine crystals, the glass compound would look like salt."

"What does it do?" Jessica asked, eyes fixed on the graphic picture of the man once so hungry, made into a shrieking inanity, then your ordinary corpse in a tux, face down in a Grand Marnier souffle, his favorite, the report said.

The phone on the desk suddenly rang. It made Jessica jump. The concussive noise of it in the dark as loud as gunfire. Trent quickly stood and scanned the room. All the shadows still. But the phone went on ringing, loud as an alarm.

"Cut through his stomach like Drano," Jessica said, reading the report over the annoying ringing.

"The hell of it is, it's so *simple*. All it took was a damn saltshaker."

"Like Night Owl, don't you think?"

Trent nodded. "Right. Horrific."

"No. I meant—"

"Shhh!" Trent held up a hand, cutting her off, listening. The phone kept ringing, forever in the chronic suspicion of Trent's existence but five times in the rest of the world. Now it stopped. Trent tried to fathom its purpose. A warning from a silent friend watching on? Perhaps through the window? Or via a hidden camera? Or was it only a wrong number? Some things you never knew.

"No," Jessica said insistently, realizing now her hands were clinching Trent's shoulder as tightly as if they were on a roller coaster. She let go of him. She allowed herself a deep breath. "I was referring to the *technique*. I mean, all photographers have a technique. You know their work by their style."

"Right. I see what you're saying. Acid made into ice, as glass was made into salt."

"Yes. Wouldn't you call that *style?*"

Trent read the footnote. "The suspect was female. Served as waitress. Tall, Caucasian, brunette. Vanished without prints."

"No photo," Jessica said, rather bitterly.

Trent turned back to the bit about Heydrick's chic laundering operation. There was a reference to three sisters who worked both sides of the Wall, and that rang a bell, loud as the grotesque phone. He had heard something about the dark art of a team of sisters, doing the Yanks and Ruskies. Now the damn phone started up again. Trent and Jessica both stared at it. It rang and rang. Then it stopped. The quiet was thunderous.

Returning to menu, Trent pointed to Fag Tag, near the bottom of the second column. He brought it up. A report like the first, a composite of classified police records and unnamed sources.

The glamorous glum tale of Christopher Taylor, geek attorney in Toronto, and a lover-partner, Oscar Jimenez, son of a Colombian drug lord. Through sheer, manipulative terror, the enterprising young men had systematically squeezed out Jimenez Sr., who had controlled the consortium of drug trafficking in Ontario. Taylor and Jimenez, expecting a retaliatory response, were held up in a fortified estate in Bermuda. Killed simultaneously in the living room, bodyguards stationed outside the door.

"It's truly a momentous thing when the money stops flowing into Colombia," Trent said, his voice dropped to a mutter.

" 'Regurgitation overcame the subjects,' " Jessica read, " 'when they inhaled smoke from a Marlboro cigarette.' " Jessica scanned and summarized. "The cigarette filter was treated with fibers believed to be an extract from the root of a woody plant grown in the Burma mountain region."

"Jesus!" Prickles rose up the back of Trent's neck, thinking of his cigars. One dismissed all warnings of death when smoking. Lighting up a ventilation of stress. In the calm. The glide. The pleasure. And weren't they all in a pleasurable activity at the time of their death? Night Owl, Laundry Man, now Fag Tag.

" 'After inhalation,' " Jessica read, " 'the victims became nauseous. Stomachs erupted in bile that obstructed the throat.' "

Trent scrolled to a photo of the two guys with acne scars and matching tropical shirts. Slumped in cane chairs. Looked like they were strangled by invisible hands. "Each hit degrades the victims in the act of death," he said, staring at faces stretched hard, chins bearded in a froth that bubbled from hinged-open mouths onto their sweet shirts.

" 'Attributed to a call girl,' " Jessica read. " 'Oriental. Blue eyes. Early twenties. Close to six feet. Short hair. Looked like a boy.' " Jessica gave a grimace of disgust. "Not your typical big-haired whore. But being gay, I guess that wouldn't do."

"One wonders what *her* duties were," Trent said absently, "the boys being gay."

"Really! What could she do for them?"

"*To* them, is more to the point." He thought about Jessica's new haircut, rather boyish. "And the sexpot-as-girl-next-door has a certain animated quality that excites a lot of men mightily."

The kills had their own dark undertaste. It tasted bittersweet to Trent as he stared out into the dark, lost in thought for a moment. The priest. The Pope. Sterling at the cathedral. He saw Mrs. T on the phone, behind her desk. Crisp and bullet-proof in a navy suit. But bullets didn't play a role in these hits. This contractor didn't caress the blue steel of his weapon. Cracking the breech. Unable to resist peeking inside. Fondling the gun as though it were a sexual object. No, it was more like the men were objects used as weapons on themselves. The hits sensory in nature, but not about guns. Or explosives. He checked his watch. They had fifteen minutes till the guards made their rounds.

"Young, Oriental. Couldn't be the woman who took Danny." Jessica's voice slipped a moment, she straightened herself and seemed to regroup. "I don't see how Sterling could ever pass for an Oriental."

"An Oriental with blue eyes," Trent said in wonder, thinking of Nordstrom who was Swedish. His eyes went out the window to the insect-swirled blaze of the street lamp. Vogler and Heydrick were likely MI5 shows. Someone on the top floor doing housecleaning. Maybe Ridley. Though Parkinson was the real expert at this sort of thing. Trent returned to the menu as Jessica's hand settled on his back. But the Colombian thing had *nothing* to do with any home office operation. He considered the menu. *Someone is monitoring the repertoire of a contractor. Code name Definite Integral. Though that's a name our boys devised.* He thought about Parkinson, a mathematician filled with high-tech piss and vinegar. The code was like Parkinson. Might that have been him just now? Traced the computer feed? Ringing the phone? Playing games? There was, as Jessica noted, a certain style to the work. A creepy, almost naïve style. Nothing ordinary. Sometimes suggesting an earthiness.

Trent smiled dryly and pointed to the second column. Ursa Major. "That one I know. Code for General Nikita Rostov."

"I think I heard about that!" Jessica gave a little twitch inside her skin. "The Russian? Eaten by dogs?"

"Right. Beastly killing."

Trent brought up the file. Rostov had taken his Dobermans for an evening stroll in the forest outside Kuibyshev. But on this evening, the dogs' food had been spiked with gunpowder.

"That's an amusing twist," Trent muttered. "Gunpowder for a rogue munitions merchant! Someone has a sense of humor."

" 'The dogs became deranged shortly after the gunpowder entered their digestive tracts,' " Jessica read. " 'After they killed the general . . .' "

Trent flipped to the accompanying photo. "They played tug with his remains," he said as they gazed onto a picture of six wild-eyed hounds dripping blood, seated beside a mutilated corpse in a Red Army uniform. In the foreground, mauled limbs half-buried in snow. Cords of intestines were strewn through dark pines.

Another impossible hit, Trent thought. The victim engaged in a pleasure, years of training disarmed Rostov, like the others, was relaxed in high security. No make on the hitter, but the report cited an unnamed source that divulged a name, Gorgon, said to be in the service of the KGB. Trent considered the code as he flashed through files at random. He had never heard of a Gorgon. Might be a ruse. Probably genuine KGB. Sounded like them. He checked his watch, they needed to be on their way, but the cases were fascinating. Rather like a stroll through a Dali exhibition.

Avery Augustine, American corporate raider, went in to get a tooth capped. Three days later he died from a slowly dissolving filling laced with *makalu,* a lethal plant grown in the Himalayas. Soichiro Tanaka, after expanding his Tokyo drug territory, took a skiing holiday in New Zealand. Wiped out at the top of Mount Cook, poisoned by his lip balm. Haroun Rashid snored in his sleep. On the night of his seventieth birthday, black Kenya spiders crawled out of his pillow and into his open mouth, paralyzing him, then killing the oil sheik as they fed on his candy-sweetened gums.

They printed out the reports, though they had only covered half the list. "They all *appear* to be the work of a female." Trent paused to consider this, again seeing Thatcher at the throne of her desk. Was this Graham's prejudice betraying him? Associating Mrs. T with a killer? Or was this something else at work? "Appears the work of a female, but always a different description. Victims all *men*. Code name Gorgon referenced twice.''

''You know what?'' Jessica gave a little gasp.

Trent looked up at her, she was colored with tension.

''They all suggest an oral gesture. *Oral kills,*'' she said with something leaping in the inflection of her voice. And she stepped back to watch the astonishment on Trent's face.

He checked the printouts. ''Right you are. I missed that.'' A dazed look came over him as he thought how that must complicate a contractor's job. ''Rather amazing, isn't it?''

Jessica looked vacantly around the office, she stood in a labyrinth of uncertainty. ''How does all this help us find, Danny?'' she asked the dark.

''Hard to say.'' Trent glanced at his watch again. *Time to go.*

''Could this killer be Sterling? You don't really think so, do you? I mean, how could it?'' There was something of a real soldier in Jessica's tone, something made of iron holding back what wanted to scream. She had learned some time ago that shrieking and tears all the rest of the mess she had been achieved nothing.

Trent did not reply right away. His eyes settled on a plant blooming in the window, like those exotic flowers that shrink in the dawn and come forth again at the moon's rising. ''*If* it's a woman—though I can't imagine how *one woman* could do *all this*—then she has one hell of an oral fixation for men.'' He thought that Parkinson must be having a jolly time tracking these female kills. Certainly knows who to ring if he has a male contract.

''But if she has *Danny?*'' Jessica was keeping a flood of memories at bay. Just saying his name brought choking tears to her throat, and scenes of what was meant to be her dying, and perhaps was her dying in Danny's eyes. ''My death,'' she said as the dawning came to her, cold and fog gray, ''was intended to be something more than homicide. It was the *murder of love*. A thing that maybe only a woman can grasp, and how unmerciful it is to kill you with your own son. Though Pit was killed in a divorce in the same way, his son used in a false sex abuse charge. Pit would understand.''

''Pit sounds like a good man,'' Trent said, holding her hand that was as stiff as a corpse. ''But we need to be on our way.''

''That revolver was not oral, Trent.'' She looked hard at him, and at her reflection in the screen behind him. ''But it was a kill made by a child from my womb, *my creation,* in the way each man was used to create his own death in this, this, whatever this is that we've found. The thing is, these are all megabucks-type people! I'm only a photographer! Why me? What's the point? Really, I don't see how this is related.'' She wished she did not think so quickly. She had entered a netherworld of double-speak and spying and murder and she was in over her head. In deep water. In water where she did not belong. Now she wished she had never come back to England. What the hell was she doing here? Danny had been seen in Ireland. Ireland was why she came. ''I have to go back,'' she said suddenly. ''To Killarney. I have to go back first thing in the morning.''

''Too early to say what this means, Jess,'' Trent said, as if he were responsible for the ills glimmering on the screen before them. It was the dead flowers in the vase, the rotting fruit in the bowl, the dried tears of his past, and he still loved it. "If it means anything. Have to see what turns up on Father—"

There was a rustle at the door. Trent looked up. There came a sound of a key being turned in a lock. Snapped off the computer. He stuffed the printouts into the file. Took Jessica by the hand, now rushing back through the maze with the door slowly opening and light streaming in over the tops of panels that hid them. If it was security, and they were caught, the left-a-file-on-Ed's-desk story would likely work, but security might want to peek at the file. And the terminal behind them would be hot to the touch.

They made it to the reception desk, hiding behind it as a man in a uniform entered the office. He peered into the dark. Trent tapped Jessica's shoulder and she looked back to a face as cool as a player at a blackjack table. He gave a wave of his hand, that said to her in the blandness of its sweep, No sweat. He prepared his face, the story ready behind it, while ducked behind the desk, readying them both for a run. Story or run. Depended on the play.

The silhouette in the door left; then returned with a trash bin that he rolled on chattering wheels. A rotund middle-aged man with a cherubic face and a rumpled thatch of hair. Moved with a lazy speed, whistling "The Rose of Tralee." He rolled his bin before him, and as he turned to bring up the lights, Trent gave Jessica a push. Longest ten yards she ever ran in her life. They darted out the open door that closed behind them as the lights came up in the office. Once in the hall, Trent pulled her into a fire escape. He abandoned himself in escapist reality, pinning her to the wall, kissing her open mouth with their hearts pounding. Jessica glowing. She could light a city with what was going on inside her. She could get used to this life. The kissing part anyway. Was this how agents were rewarded at the end of the day?

"Before you leave for Ireland," he said to the pretty Yank sexpot-as-girl-next-door, "let's go back to my place. We should have a nightcap. Or breakfast, as the case may be. Perhaps brunch, by the time we're though."

They ran down the stairs, one of them laughing, two missiles racing for their mark. In joyful fruition, they would not miss.

21

THE HUGE WHITE sperm whale was old and hoary and monstrous. It swam in the deep, illusive, damn near impossible to kill. It was strangely fantastic, this great white whale. A great vision! A vision needed for a man was the self-declared master of his fate. The captain of his soul. And at the bottom of it, fear. The whale lived at the bottom and the great whale must be had or old, hoary, monstrous Ahab couldn't live. *"Moby Dick must die!"*

Pit woke with a jolt, Ahab's oath ringing in his head. He had fallen asleep in his La-Z-Boy recliner, morning sun coming through the forest of high-rises to turn the Hemingway House to gold. On his lap Melville's *Moby Dick* lay open. In the bedroom an alarm was ringing, Pit fuddled in sleep in which the phantsmagorical sea yarn had swum from book to dream.

He had dreamed he was on that mad ship. In that frantic hunt. In the mind of that maniac captain, spell-bound by the slidings and collidings of the ship with the heaving sea. Sensing Ahab was almost over the border: ready for a crack-up. Ready to sail off the edge of the world. Heat and tension in his fists and forearms, with the prickly heat pressed against his face. Ribbons of time went by, which he would not remember. By and large he was able to avoid the sickness down below, moving with determination across the surface of the sea. These sensations mixed with little dream fragments of Danny, seen in the mad light in Ahab's eyes, that strangely were not Ahab's eyes, but the bitch's who took Danny. And as he looked at Ahab again, Pit saw the features of Boz's sketch, the beautiful face and rippled hair, blended together into a soft, suffusing, seething Ahab. Hunting down the great whale.

The dream-experience would not be suppressed, so strange, the impression of that manic captain merged with that beautiful woman. And the great whale suspended in those watery vaults. What was her Moby Dick? Was it Danny? But didn't she possess Danny? Could it be Jessica? Or was it someone else? Who could it be? Maybe it wasn't a person at all. A whale in a shell. In a shell game.

Pit closed *Moby Dick* and put it away, that great sea yarn. Like most great American stories, it was over-the-top, superhuman, bigger than life. Something of a children's tale. He'd have to tell it to Danny some time. But he'd begin it at the beginning, years before Herman Melville's big book began, in that first hunt when Ahab lost his leg. Moby Dick took Ahab's leg off at the knee when the crazy man attacked him. It was the whale's only mistake. Should have taken both legs, and the arms and head. Ahab stumped around on a limb made from sea-ivory, never got over that wound. The wound that infected his soul.

Pit shook off the damn dream, like a dog shaking off water, and slid into his chair. Navigated around the stacks of books to the bedroom to kill the alarm still ringing. Paused at a map of Ireland pinned to the wall. Jessica had called last night to give him an update, now he drew a red line from Dublin to Killarney to a place in the mountains called the Gap of Dunloe. Looked like a real pretty spot. That was fine. She deserved as much. That was his hope for her, that she'd always be in a pretty spot. He pulled into a Giants workout shirt, hit the fridge for an apple, a big red delicious, then wheeled out the door, a man on a mission.

He let himself into Jessica's condo. All quiet, like his miserable heart. It had been seven years since his ex-wife took their son and daughter and renamed and remade them in a thing she called love that if it weren't done by a mother would be called greed. A mother could get away with murder. And he surely had been murdered but his hope still lived. He laughed at himself, at the fool he had been, slapping a grinning carousel horse on the butt on his way to the kitchen. Finished the apple; dropped the core into the disposal. Hit the switch. It was a comfort sending no-good trash down the disposal. A miracle, really, the way things just disappeared down the drain. Like fathers, disposable.

He filled the watering bucket. Making his rounds like a good mother—who said a father couldn't be a mother?—started with the African violets in the kitchen window. Then the ivy climbing all over the china cabinet in the fancy pickled-pine dining room. The place looked too nice to eat in. And wasn't that like a woman?

He did the ficus trees in the living room, and by the window, the philodendrons growing wild and reckless like his heart, an eruption of lush leaves and hungry roots jutting out of the pot. Like those harpoons, growing out of Moby Dick's back. Every time he came up, here the bastards came again. So he lived isolated, the far-driven soul that tried to escape the pain, alone in the deep, only human contact were the hunters. Renegades, castaways, cannibals. With their gaming harpoons. Folks would get together to save the whales. But people didn't gave a damn about fathers. His son was a gifted youngster, a very bright boy when they were last together. Didn't know his daughter. An infant taken away in the wisdom of a mother. In a plan that couldn't fail. A girl can't love what she doesn't know. Pit figured he was some skeleton in a closet to his son, but his daughter didn't know he existed, though he gave everything he had in a fight he never wanted. Like that poor son of a bitch whale, confined to living in the depths.

Moby Dick had been a boiling, surging monster in Ahab's eyes. But Pit saw him as warm-blooded and loveable. He wasn't vicious. He didn't bite. But they hunted him down. Caught hell every time he came up for air. Swam half way around the world to avoid the killing. Wasn't looking for trouble. He was a lonely, harmless white whale. A love-maker. Did it on the surface under the sun, and in that wonderous world of the deep.

Pit reflected on it, the great whale living in muted misery, a thing hunted. Didn't he know that misery? The only thing in this world that he wanted was for those children to know he loved them. That his heart, no matter the pain, never gave up on them. God damn those mothers who held the children from their fathers. God damn every last one of them to a fiery hell.

"Good morning!"

The voice spun Pit around. He saw the gun first, the sausage-shaped silenced barrel of an automatic leveled at his head. Then the black jumpsuit that clung to her generous curves. Now his eyes rose to the face. He tripped out a little, for a second there, he saw old Ahab's mug. He blinked. It was like his dream; Ahab's face changed to Boz's sketch. Only this wasn't a sketch.

"Did I frighten you?" she said, as though she were his best friend. Where had she come from? Had he left the damn door open? Or was she in the house when he came in? "I feel like I know you, Pit. It is Pit, isn't it?" He watched her lock the door. So, she must have come in that way. Must have picked the lock. He took her in again, speechless in shock. Wouldn't let himself look at those eyes, he had a feeling about those eyes and wouldn't look at them. Looked only at the damn gun. He felt the presumption behind it. "We've never actually met," she said, sweet and severe. "Allow me to introduce myself: I'm Danny's new mother."

There was a whirling in his head, so confounding, Pit wasn't sure this wasn't another one of his unmerciful dreams. Only she was very clear and sharp, and as he struggled for breath, he bit into lip and tasted coppery blood and knew this was going to be a fine day. A glory day. And already the one thing in the world that he wanted had changed. *"Where the hell is he?"* His own bellow was the final proof, this was no dream.

"No. The question is, where is *Jessica?*"

He rolled back as she approached with that menacing smile. That smile so damn perfect. What a voluptuous hellcat. How long did it take her to evolve? How many men did she lay to rest? Pit wondered. They did not go down prettily, you can bet. She circled to the windows. That damn gun motionless, never wavered from his head. He figured she was putting the glass behind her, in case a shot shattered a window, might alert someone down below. He was alone and he fought off the monstrous fear and found his voice.

"What have you done with our boy?" he shouted, wishing the condos weren't sound-proof. He could yell his head off, nobody would hear him. Like nobody heard him yell for his kids. Yelling as silently as Moby Dick, with every harpoon they drove into him.

"He's my boy now," she said, so cool.

"Not in ten fucking million years!"

"You'd be surprised," she said. "He has a new name. A new home. A new school. A new life. He's all but forgotten his past. It's as if it never happened. I can assure you, he's *mine*."

She held that gun as if it were an extension of her hand. It did not waver. The holding of it was routine. Taking possession of the house with the mastery of an expert, as though she owned the joint. That voice of hers, serious and seductive. Especially with the damn gun. Now he let himself take in the rest of her. The loose white blond hair to her shoulders. Her beautiful face set in playful provocation. Now those grape-colored eyes that were pure sea-motion. As blue as the depths where the great whale lived in peace, and Pit saw himself swimming in the depths of those eyes.

"Lady," he said to the strange world met in those eyes, his gaze unable to break away. "You've walked into the wrong house. You took the wrong boy. You got mixed up in the wrong story."

"What story is that, Pit?"

He didn't answer. He saw the black kid gloves. Gloves of a pro. Again he felt the cold death in him, and the hopes for Danny pinned to his heart working hard in his chest. If he couldn't save the boy, why not kill the woman? Wasn't that just as good? Sink the bitch. He glanced about for a weapon. There was the feathery sofa and book shelves and the coffee table with dream magazines. He felt himself pale, as pale as a redhead's bosom. A putrid nausea rising from his depths. He surfaced with a deep breath and controlled his panic, looking into those eyes and the strangeness of their luster. The stark bewilderment of death left him in the conceit behind those eyes that believed they had him. She had him all right, and he'd give real value. She'd get more than she ever expected. He'd give everything he had. Always did.

"I've searched the house," she said, following as he rolled back to the dining room, his eyes on the gun. "I know she's left town. But she's not using her credit cards. Why is that?"

Pit's smile flashed in triumph. Jessica was using his cards, her cards were maxed out. He hoped she spent a damn fortune, if he was going to die, he wouldn't have to pay. He hoped she would buy herself a fine castle over there in England, put it on his card, settle down with that fella. He spun around the dining table and glanced to the kitchen. A block of knives on the counter.

"Where is Jessica? I can see you know where she is."

"Why, how you talk!" Pit gave a laugh, edging for the kitchen as she moved up to the grinning carousel horses. Left over from one of Jessica's shoots, but she never had a model with the looks of this one. Where do you get eyes like those? Gorgeous eyes. So damn smart and self-assured. He hollered at those eyes. "You think you're the meanest, most treacherous thing around, don'tcha?"

He waited for her to reply, hoping to distract her, but she said nothing. Taking her time, terribly calm. She did everything in a methodical way, as if nothing unforeseen had happened to her since time immemorial. How old she was was anyone's guess. Looked thirties, but she had a courtship with evil that was eons older.

"You may think you're something original, a real bully circus, using a boy to kill his own parent. But it's nothing new. I've seen it done before." He rolled back into the closed kitchen. "You don't have the foggiest notion of what's coiled inside me."

He felt his guts tight as a coil of copper wire, the feeling a life force, like electricity. The alarm in his bedroom ringing again, this time in his head. Heat and tension in his fists and forearms, with prickly heat pressed against his face, like that damn Ahab. Ahab the master of the violent. Master of the chaotic motion, caught up in a wild chase. Ahab was Quaker and nothing like this woman, if anything, she was opposite of Ahab. She was exquisite and chic. All charm and style. A goddamn seductress. A songbird in the way she had enchanted Jessica and Danny. But, by God, she would not enchant him. He looked away from those eyes.

"I don't know how you know my name, but I know your face," he said, with fight in his thundering voice. "Or, rather, I know the look on it, bitch."

"Pardon me. What did you call me?"

He grinned. Now here was the hardened hellion. That was what he wanted. "You heard me, *bitch*. It's a tiresome title, used too much these days, lot of punkin-heads out there cavorting around, laying claim to a title that they have a crush for but will never earn. But I reckon you're the real thing."

There was a moment there, brief as it was, when they shared a kind of understanding. A true respect. She had not come from the domestic realm, hanging around the house, waiting for something to happen, waiting for a Pit to marry so life could begin. She had the type of direct energy he admired. Energy crackling with sex. It inspired. He was about to make a move for the knives, but she was there and he spun to the back of the kitchen. Trapped. Fine. That was just fine. He loved trapped. Did his best work trapped.

"Where is Jessica?"

He ignored her question and went on about the Hecate he had loved with his heart and soul. "You know what you are and that's to your credit. But she didn't know. Wouldn't believe you if you told her. Problem is, I didn't have the foggiest notion of what she was either. I was a blithering idiot. Didn't know till she took my kids. Till she used my boy in an attempt to kill me. To gun me down with that false sex abuse crap. Shot me in the heart and left me for dead. Same as what you did to Jessica. Makes a man want to *kill* somebody. But how do you kill your son's mother? How do you explain that to your daughter? There's the bind, you see. That and I loved her."

"No. *That's* the bind."

"Well, I'll be damned. You don't fool easy, do you?"

"A man like you doesn't kill love."

"I don't, huh?"

"No. A man like you is killed by love. That's the way it is. It's kill or be killed. It's why I *never* mix love with business."

He was crouched in his chair, peaceful, chewing on himself, waiting. "Love will getcha in a dilly, won't it?"

"Oh, it's a pleasure. Strange and fantastic. A voyage of the soul. Like a child. No telling where it will take you."

Seeing a twinkle in her eyes, Pit wondered if she wasn't in love with Danny? "I guess you're right," he conceded, eyeing the butcher knives. "I was killed. You can bet she's been dancing a witch's jig of triumphant sense. But you know what? You live with it. Unless you become what she is, a damn killer. That divorce smashed me all to fenders, lost my kids, happened years ago, but time makes no difference to a father's heart that won't let go."

She blinked at that, and he saw the bloodlessness drain out of her at the mention of father that for some women was synonymous with *The Big Sleep.* Daddy gone away, but never gone.

"That's the problem with men," she said, returning to smart and self-assured. Taking in the pine cabinets with glazed-glass doors. Emerald wallpaper. English pine floor. She admired the green marble counter, as though she might linger here for a year. She slid the block of knives away. "Men won't let go of the past. You have to let go, dear, and *move on.* Now, where's Jessica?"

"I like jabbering with women," he said, eyeing a big marble rolling pin on the counter behind her. "I don't know why. They have a way of talking around things, like *murder.*" Jessica used that rolling pin to make candy. Sweets for the sweet. "But what I can't stand is those whiners who say men don't know how to make a commitment. Hell, most women got no idea what a commitment is. They play at love like it's a pie-in-the-sky dream. A man may not love well, but when he loves, he never lets go. No matter what."

She smiled at the burners on the gas stove. She lit one and watched its blue flame burn upright and still. Like a very bright candle in which you could lose yourself. Her cool smile raked over the father as she said, "You Americans have more torture devices in your kitchens than the Spanish Inquisition."

"Go fuck yourself," Pit said, his polished dome a howling red. Motionless in his chair, he waited like some huge white sperm whale, unspeakable in its wrath, having been so often attacked.

"Where's Jessica?" the woman repeated in a toneless voice.

Pit only smiled at her, the way he figured ol' Moby Dick must have smiled as he let himself loose. A great whale with all that power and patience, all turned out on that fine, bloody day that must have felt like something wonderful! Pit could feel it coming over him in a powerful fine sight. Coming up through those black hillsides of water with streaming sunlight glinting through the surface, to show the dark shape of that killing boat. Like those courts of father killers, all thinking they're in the right. Once Ahab's boys got their hands on a whale, they stripped it, cut it up in a way that wasn't magnificent, only Melville's telling made it so. Taking the sperm oil from the head with its tiny little brain. That could characterize a man, Pit never fit into the lunacy of academics. A man who was all feeling. All instinct. All backbone.

"When I finish with you, half-man," she said in a promissory tone, "you'll be screeching and gibbering like an ape."

Still Pit said nothing, staring at her, seeing her through the red mist of his past. In the sink the faucet dripped. The drip like thunder in all that quiet. He and the woman turned to watch the water fall and drain into the garbage disposal. Her face tightened with interest. She lifted the rubber sound baffle. She considered the mouth of teeth. They could tear, they could shred, they could swallow. Mechanical teeth. They automatically churned and devoured. This too was like a divorce court, pain coming back to Pit, not in his missing legs, but in the loss of two children.

"I'll ask you one last time. *Where is Jessica?*"

He wheeled back to the wall as she came forward. She switched on the disposal. She smiled at the effect. The roar a screeching racket as loud as the fury in Pit's heart that broke from the depths that for all the darkness there was transparent, filled with spiritually feasting life. Pit saw his fury as Melville's whale that broke as a great white mass that lazily rose, higher and higher, clearing itself from the azure, rising "like a snow-slide, new slide from the hills. Thus glistening for a moment, as slowly it subsided, and sank. Then once more arose, and silently gleamed. It seemed not a whale; and yet, is this Moby Dick?"

She shouted, "One last time! Where is—?"

"Can't hear you!" Pit yelled.

As she reached to switch off the disposal, he whipped his chair forward. She turned just as he launched a right hook that caught her in the gut like a wrecking ball and threw her onto the counter with Pit coming in a quick, powerful rush, into thrashing legs. Two sharp spits exploded the light fixture. Pit went for the gun before it turned on him. They held it together. The gun made a short, hard circle in the air above his head, Pit holding on for life, using her hand to pull himself closer. She yanked down on the gun and it hit him in the bridge of the nose with a hard, toneless crunch that Pit never felt, prying at her fingers on that damn gun. Get the gun and it was over. Get the gun and he'd be asking the questions, and he knew what the first one would be. His eyes with the demons of a man who had never abandoned the fight, never surrendered so he had never lost his children that were nothing less than all the children of the world held hostage by this bitch who was all the ugliness and illness of the women who had turned fatherhood into sorrow. Who in the name of greed created a fatherless generation that would become troubled teens lost to themselves, mistaking heaven as earth, in a world where a mother could never be both. This was the marvelous piece of fury he drew on, to become a boiling, surging monster, rising now, into the madness that possessed this murderous Ahab.

A foot caught him in the jaw, and he felt a tooth rattled loose but managed to hang on to her wrist, pulling into her to windmill a big hook that missed. Another coughing spit and he heard glass shatter in the cabinet at his back. She hit him with a flattened chop to the neck. Like hitting a tree trunk. He grinned and saw blond hair and those wicked blue eyes and, holding the wrist of this grade-A bitch, he drove a twisting uppercut to her chin. Her head slammed into cabinets. Doors flew open. China belched out. Looked like Christmas, everything coming unwrapped! So, she was only human after all, and in a matter of seconds, as soon as he got that gun out of her hand, he'd use the floor to make an eggshell out of her pretty skull. Then she'd be telling him where Danny was, and after that they could set the rest of the father-fucked world straight, beginning with his kids.

"*You legless sonofabitch!*" she screeched. She tried again to turn the automatic on him, fired, and the pine floor splintered. And again she chopped at his neck, but he kept coming, the huge bulk of him all over her, pulling on her legs, reeling her into him. Gloved fingers jabbed into his eyes, leaving a foamy wake in his vision that was blood that Pit saw as the wake of a ship closing back on itself. She kicked him in the ribs, and then in the head, and he dove under those legs and came up, his whale head swimming. Trailing the little ship inching along, through the transparent still water, seeing it as the whale now, moving silently through the cool water, with an invalid's labored breathing. And here from the ship came the tiny boats with the even smaller men with their intense countenances, the oarsmen with their faces of life and death, the killer, his wicked harpoon raised, standing in a flimsy, flea-speck of a boat wallowing in that enormity in which all the world was water, boiled up green and luminous against the darkness washed away in the phosphorescence of one that could rise with the force of a watery earthquake. Only now did Pit realize what a fine soul was Moby Dick. Why, he could have drowned that damn Ahab any time he wanted to; in the same way Pit could have killed the woman who held his two kids.

She seized him by the throat, and it felt like the false sex abuse charge of that mother, once wife and lover, who feed his boy sweets till his buttocks ran red with diarrhea. Took him to his father's for Thanksgiving. The boy spent the night with Pit. Next day, she picked him up in her mother's limo, went straight to the county hospital. Held the boy screaming to a cold steel table while a doctor performed a rectal exam on his diarrhea-inflamed buttocks. Then she marched into court with a mess of attorneys and charged Pit with fucking his beloved four-year-old son. But it was she who did the fucking; guilty of the very crime she charged. Like Ahab, the great whale was old and hoary and monstrous, but it was Ahab who fit that bill. ''The cheap nickle-plated cold-cunt bitch!'' Pit choked, sinking into his chair as he was strangled, a thumb boring into his windpipe. Pit's great eyes bulging out of his head as if in the utmost surprise, and this surprise was as that in the court room that day. ''That murderous mother!''

The wonder was that she was snow-white and blameless. As meek and good as gold. The dutiful mother. All of it coming back to him out of the blue, in this struggle with a man-eating woman that he could not extricate himself from. And now, again, they were before the judge, his wife and her attorneys, and as Pit was accused of the most heinous crime man could commit, she leaned back to smile at him. A grin of sheer diabolic jeering. An unforgettable grin. There in that grin was Woman. Took him years to see it. Perhaps he was only seeing it now, in his own merciless strangulation. He couldn't get a breath. Wide flared nostrils and bloody eyes and a wide-open mouth gasping for air like a beached whale. What would Moby Dick do? Why, a whale would go down! Down! Down! Down to the depths! Pit pulled down and out of her slick grasp, leaving claw marks on his neck, to come up laughing between her thrashing legs. It was a good fight. A long time in coming.

She had been his Savior. Saved him from himself. He loved her with all his heart, but not quite as much as he loved himself. The Savior made the innermost fool of him. A fool of love. Beware the woman who offers love. Beware the understanding woman. Pious as pie; she is as false as hell, all for your sake, boy. He wrestled now with a candid devil, twisting his head so far around, he might be able to watch when he wiped himself, but he fought then with a gentle devil. She couldn't bear to see anything *physically* hurt. Subtly diabolic. It happens, happened once she stopped believing in him. Turned devil. The unconscious spirit of the new woman. Maybe the old woman, too. This revolt against the spirit of man. To continue until she finds her own spirit. Does woman have her own? Or is her only belief man? Without him she is a devil.

He took a kick to the groin that caught his testicles. His spirit faltered in another gasping. Is there ever an end to the struggle? In the getting and being got it was hard to say, one hand on the gun, the other stretching out for her lovely neck, but Pit knew this: there is only doom for the weak-kneed man craving to be understood. To be loved. Man's only hope against Woman is to believe in himself. Love her and she'll booster that belief; give her half a chance and she'll tear it down. She can't help herself. It's the devil in her. Love makes her indignant and makes you the fool and makes her want to wring your neck. It's all the nature of love. Man must save himself or Woman will take the whale in him, to leave him cold and skinned and drained on the deck.

And now he saw the marble rolling pin; it was right behind her on the counter. He gave up hitting her, let her hit him while he put a ton weight of both hands on her hand that held the gun. He brought it down on the counter with all the force God could give a man, and the damn gun came out of her hand. Her howling was a fine thing and he listened to the effect while he went for the rolling pin to her right, she scrabbling for the gun slid down the counter to her left. A beauty of a rolling pin, and its gleam, as he picked it up, he could hear water rippling in the Sixth, the songs of the nightingale and quail and cuckoo which Beethoven had put there, now accompanied by a woman's tirade.

He had the heavy hard pin coming around backhanded to smash her spine, the vertebrae exposed and taut and arched from her now twisting for the automatic. He was pretty certain he could break her back with the first blow, and the cheering in him as he swung that beautiful pin of marble was enough to almost make him laugh. His mouth opened in a shriek of joy as he brought that baby home, and before his wide eyes was a whale swimming smooth and easy in dark waters with a wreckage behind. The great tail powering in time to the tranquility of the Sixth, in the deep where confidence and force resides, in the quiet deep of the soul. And as he busted her back, he saw the fat black bore of the silencer and there was a white-hot blinding flash, and that was all he ever felt.

22

SHE TOOK ANOTHER cooling sip from the clouded yellow-tinged absinthe and sank deeper into the suede of her Gulfstream. The agony in her back from Pit's marble rolling pin had deepened and spread to her perfect face and she refused the pain her thoughts. She looked to the Atlantic night, immense and transparent, and the

Pequod seemed motionless among the stars; the wings silvered in moonlight that soaked the clouds so they appeared as lurid as the absinthe. The moon was not soft but harsh, hot and intense, her eyes wide and dilated like the eyes of some nocturnal animal.

"Finish a problem quickly," Isabella said over the drone of the engines. "That's what you *always* told us."

Somberg pressed her eyes shut, remembering some dream from ages past. A little girl in a wedding gown clutching babies to her bosom. How old was she when she had that dream? Six? Seven? And hadn't she made it come true?

"When you have a problem, return to *basics*," Isabella said, repeating what had been taught.

Somberg gazed into the haze of her pain-killer drink. She seduced them out of the world that taught them to keep themselves small, to lower their voices, to shorten their steps, to remain utterly passive and press their emotions into the stereotypical girl. It took time to transform them because it was hard to learn to think for yourself without the rules thinking for you. It had taken Isabella five years. In that time they had hunted together, and it was a predatory pleasure. Isabella could naturally kill a boy into a girl, as velvet-clad and delicious as Kim, but Jessica Moore was not about decadent sacrifices. This was business. An indisputable territory, Isabella learning by emanating.

"I can do her," Isabella insisted. "I'd *love* to do her. I think I'm ready for the assignment."

The terrible paralyzing pain delivered by the legless man was excruciating in her back, drinking her senses as greedily as some vampire that would rupture his victim's heart in his great thirst. Somberg herself had done as much on occasion, in an orgy manner of speaking, and now drank down the sulphurous moonlit absinthe that tasted like the tree of knowledge. The ghost of a smile curled on her wet lips as she focused on the Barcelona beauty illuminated by a pinprick of light. Dark Spanish hair curled over a shoulder; the eyes cool green, clear tourmalines, fringed with thick lashes. Her olive face made so enticing by those wide Cleopatra lips.

"Return to basics," Isabella repeated. "I'd follow her to her car under the cover of night. Being American, she'll strap herself in place with a seat belt. I'll act like I'm about to enter the neighboring car. Then turn to her with an automatic in a folded newspaper. She'll never know. Double tap to the skull, above the ear and in the temple. The only sound the splinter of the glass."

Women have a profound capacity to be still and find their quiet center. A place that is like the mystery of personality. A place of desire and love and the creation of life that cries forth a new child into the world. It was there they found some concept of themselves besides that of a space decoration. It was there Somberg taught them: women have the power but can't act on it.

"We know *he's* not there," Isabella continued. "He's in London. *She's* in a cottage in the middle of nowhere. A sitting duck! I could do her tonight. Really, it'd be so simple."

Somberg drank in the beauty beside her who was a monumental feat. A teenager who had been a subhuman slave, to become a girl sadist, then discover herself and become family. There were odd intensities and spiky moods, part of the complexity of Isabella. And there was the Giuseppe charcoal gray striped jacket that was the style of the reckless sexually obsessed drug lord who still owned her. How easy it is to become that which we oppose. The girl a magnificent drug, and the sensual Mediterranean glow of her heavy and loose breasts brought Somberg back from the pain.

"Do you recall Nicole finding an automatic in her closet?"

"Yes, but that was back in *Chicago*. She can't be armed in *Ireland*."

"And didn't Alexia follow *him* to Scotland Yard yesterday?"

"Yes, but—"

"He works in antiterrorism. What if he left her a weapon?" Somberg watched the intelligent eyes widen with receptiveness. "Besides, it must appear as an *accident*. She's in Shanahan's town. Shoot her and he'll raise holy hell with O'Grady. I want to collect on the *balance* of the Thatcher contract."

"I know; I know! But, really, you don't *need* the money."

"That's beside the point. And three and a half million is not small change." Somberg drank deeply from her cool absinthe. "Money always matters," she said to the twenty-one-year-old who mattered a great deal. "Money, like paint to Picasso, is the medium in which I work." She smiled upon this child born by the power of imagination, both hers and Isabella's, now with a serene olive face capable of so many expressions. "But what matters most is the *creative act*. That's the dangerous beauty of the game."

"That's why we're doing Thatcher?"

Somberg raised a lofty eyebrow. "How could I resist her?"

This was greeted with an irresistible smile; devotion in that smile. "Okay," Isabella said in a soft, rhapsodic Spanish accent. "I see your point. Just let me do it. You know I'm *there*."

"Darling, professionalism is a journey, not a destination."

"But I've never done one all by myself before." Isabella's breasts peeped through the division of her suit jacket; she could speak without words. Then she ruined it. "Please," she begged.

"Let me think about it," Somberg said, the graceful signal for, Leave me alone for a while. And before she left, Isabella made certain the pillows were just right for her tormented back.

Somberg took another good long drink and gazed out the port window. The moon shed a blue, unearthly light over the feminine air, and below in the deeps, far down in the bottomless blue, rushed a mighty leviathan of pleasure. Somberg first caught sight of the wonder when she was a girl, her mother having chased it over the waters of the world. There had been scandalous affairs on the Continent, in Africa, in the Far East. From this breathless flight were three daughters, one blonde, one black, one Asian, all with mother's blue Swedish eyes, as blue as the feminine air, as blue as the masculine deep. Mother always in the steady wake of the musical rippling playful whale, a woman possessed, in fitful flights, dragging three stunning daughters along, and Somberg soon learned one rarely saw the entire dazzling white hump of the great wonder sliding along in the deep, but caught only snatches of joy, now and then glimpsing the broad milky forehead along the sea as though pleasure was an isolated thing in the mystical waters of life. The fruition was in the chase, Somberg learned it young. It was often far ahead, not to be seen at all, but once on its trail, from either side bright bubbles rose from the wondrous world that were nothing less than the sparkling champagne that accompanied mother in her endless chase of the great white whale of pleasure.

There is something overwhelming in whale-hunters, some might say superhuman, others would insist inhuman, certainly bigger than life, the chase more fantastic than any human activity. It is so curious, so real, so unearthly that it attracts the young, yet so illusive that most give up and settle for whatever glimpses of the great good pleasure comes their way. To chase is to know the rush of all heaven. It is the voyage of the strangely fantastic soul, and has been known to leave one wounded, to make one ghastly, to compose such startling experiences they can only be understood by those who reside in the nuthouse. To chase is to risk, always. To chase is to commit, always. To chase is to turn the head sunward. To breathe and to surge and to shout mad. To live from the center, terrified of the herd, seeing only the eyes of the whale.

The whale's eyes are on opposite sides of the head, and at any given moment the whale will see two images, as those genders that make up the world that never see the same thing the same way. It is a vision that is known only in the whale that may swallow the hunter, and will annihilate the hunter, and Somberg knew this annihilation. When the hunter is swallowed by the pleasure chased, the dream-experience becomes the soul-experience. The hunter is water-born. A thing wonderous steals over the lost hunter that has entered the strangeness of luster that is in the whale. The hunter may then return to the world womb to tell the wonders of the dual vision, in which the integral hunter may pass back and forth, as across the horizons of the world, in and out of the dual vision, as easily as a monarch through the rooms of their house. Therein lies the hunter's power to save. In the knowledge that there is nothing to fear. The vision is dual, but universally united.

Somberg was a hunter, and a savior. She saved her two sisters first, from their mother's despair and collapse, and from her own annihilation. She taught her sisters how to chase pleasure without being swallowed, but with the great knowledge that came from being swallowed. She saved the deadly faint, and bowed, and humped, the babe girls who felt so old, like Isabella. And she saved the lucky few, those poor imbecilic males who were adopted to the worship of feminine thunder-fire. That living sundering fire which they would bear the brand, from head to toe. The electric storm of a Goddess. When the corposants burn the pretty boy in high, tapering flame of the supernatural, when the compass is reversed, when life itself seems mystically reversed. After this there is only madness and possession, a boy taken from the vast sea into the feminine air.

She sailed with a renegade crew: African, Indian, Polynesian, Asiatic and American. All were girls, in the rap of girls who call each other ''girl,'' so they were all true girls, whether they were born girls, or born-again girls. Girls who would learn to see in dual vision. Some were sweet lambs, cozy and loving; some self-absorbed and sparkling; some strange and secret hipsters, black-garbed fire-worshipers; and now there was a child aboard. A boy child in keeping with the great whale chases. A child of the sun who went on the chase hand in hand with the captain and master.

To each rare member of her crew, Somberg gave a piece of her heart; giving the quantum longevity. She gave to them alone; there was an invisible hand that grasped her heart and prevented it from opening too much to strangers. They lived with the world, but in a *cul de sac* of each other, their aroma, their fruits and flowers shared with a select few. They had each at one time or another stood alone, and each knew the yearning of love and the burning hate, which is only inverted love. In full maturity, they possessed a feminine violence, the brave soul of a man stood not a chance against them, they could pierce to the very quick of the soul. Among themselves they were beautiful like children, and mostly generous and always graceful. They were elegant because they had all been saved; they knew the darkness.

They sailed in the feminine air on a mad ship, the *Pequod,* in which they sometimes saw stars. The ship a loony-bin trip; each girl, whether born or reborn, changed in some way in which none could have predicted, not even the captain. Taken far away, on the wild and fitful air, so they had to depend on the sometimes dark, sometimes brooding, and sometimes maniac captain. The awful hunts consumed more than they gave; they detracted and compelled; they went on undiminished and were often deep and meaningful and came with touches of pure beauty. All in the blood of dreams made real. In the light of the selfsame wondrous eyes that had saved them, there was something of the terrible tyranny of a mother's neuroses that the absinthe did not help. And now Somberg killed the drink along with the ache and she felt dangerous again.

Pit Martin had cracked two of her vertebrae, but she didn't resent the man who had a certain style and glamour in his self-destruction. It was never her intent to kill Pit outright. Her mother believed if an innocent man is killed outright, his soul remains integral, free to return into the bosom of some beloved, where it can enact itself. This was not the case with the punk-deserving and she gazed out at the moon to see a badly decomposed body lying in a sewer near the harbor section of Barcelona. The heavy rains had belched it up into the street. The sadist had been shot, though the gunshot was just for effect, the cause of death were the hands chopped off along with the testicles. He would not inflict himself on Isabella again. Such a death was pleasure but it was far better to bring about the indescribable capitulation of a male soul, to break the bonds of his identity, to take the lustful ego to yourself and take him into the infinite. She preferred the pretty death of Kim that was artistic, a study in psychological reactions, over that of Pit that was morbid. Though the filth in the Barcelona sewer was a kind of barbituate in which she could overdose. His corpse inspired evocations of goddess ideology.

It was the work of God Herself, to change hate into love. But with the pretty boys Somberg often had to kill the hate to change them, so of course she killed them, but there was no rush, she took her time, and in good death they were given new life. She, as their God, had created a third sex. She called them *femmes.*

The fine and gentle organza of creativity rarely endows the creator with the gift of perception of her creation. But from the beginning Somberg knew the value of what she had made. A femme was an *objet d'art.* A one of a kind. A mosaic. A functioning female in every pristine, delicate way, who fucked female, was fucked as a female, or fucked as a male and loved it all. A muse postmortem boy-girl beauty that tiptoed through the shadowy house of gender like a siesta dream. Walking with a leggy stride, light-skinned, sometimes dark, or exotic caramel skin, Somberg's favorite color.

Childlike in their early years with a clearly unconscious loveliness, their voice was tinged with a elegiac poetry of boy sadness. Mesmerizing in their ability to attract girls and men, given delicious value by their transgressive birthright. Femmes were sin. Strictly taboo. Black magic. So they were compelling. Created by seduction, prone to seduction; they courted pleasure. Switched on to both genders, their erotic capacity was virtually unlimited. A luscious game of exploration, they knew the oral histories of men as men, and girls as girls. They knew everyone's secrets. A busy, jumbled, ridiculous, aesthetic Somberg signature frivolity of androgyny just in time for the Age of Possibility.

Power and sex, Somberg knew, were intrinsically intertwined. Which is why those with a driving libidinal force are invariably in positions of authority. A worldwide network was formed. CEOs of industry, politicians, entertainers, money managers, and those centrally situated in the quiet of long-term success. A doll could not be bought, but given in exchange for favors. Insider tips on markets, forecasts of multinational corporations, confidential government reports, lucrative property deals. Somberg accumulated a fortune in near miraculous fashion as the purveyor of what stood to go crazy without her. She was idolized. Worshipped. Adored. It wasn't a bad life. Among a chosen few congregated in London, New York, Los Angeles, Paris, Tokyo, Monaco, she was a fashion icon.

Men used femmes to discreetly practice a gay life. But the femme was principally created to serve women. They were received as secretaries, sometimes as a niece, spouses unaware the dear was anything other than what she appeared to be. The femme confronted the limits of a woman absolutely awestruck by these wunderkind lovers that yearned to please. They were educated, polite, gentle, sympathetic, and naturally responsive to a woman's needs. With a femme, life was redefined. A woman who thought she needed the whole story suddenly found she didn't know herself. Fear of conformity that was nothing but a woman's fear of herself was now negated by passion confined only by appetite, imagination, and a goddess's ability to entrance. Relationships were cultivated. Femmes were vulnerable. Delicately calibrated. Temperamental. Moody, often needy, a mystery to themselves. Their complexities added to what became deep pools of togetherness, a woman elevated to a deity, and new limits were set. Many women found femmes an inspiration unlike anything ever experienced; power the ultimate aphrodisiac, sex the creative energy of all genius.

Somberg did not accept. It was the unilateral feature of her character that permeated all the gosh golly gee of her pursuits that were part hell, part heaven, shot full of discrepancies. She saw modern woman rendered, despite feminism, or because of it, as overbearing and crazy, or submissive and depressive. Woman in need of her past to make her future. Somberg was quietly using the present, a jigsaw of femmes and patrons, to recover the past and the future by way of those victims of history that were modern woman's salvation, whose life force was still within humanity.

Suetonius, the Roman biographer, said they once ruled over a large part of Asia. As late as the fifth century A.D., the Black Sea was still known as the Amazon Sea.

Diodorus, a first-century Greek historian, referred to them as the "warlike women of Libya." To this day, North African Berbers call themselves Amazigh, though they are known by their common name, Berber, from Latin *barbari,* "barbarians." The Greeks feared them, and in the many references in ancient text, the Amazon women were never once characterized as overbearing, crazy, submissive, or depressive. They possessed a quality that seems to have eluded modern women: aggression.

The Taurus women sacrificed to the Goddess all men who landed upon their shores. In Lemmos, women rose up against their husbands overnight and murdered them all, dancing in the dark light of the moon. The Greek historians left no doubt: women could annihilate entire populations of males; so fierce and sanguine, their battle cries terrifying, there was no effective defense against Amazons. The early Christian clerics tried to erase them from history, they called the Amazons myth, and in Northern Europe some were, such as the legend of the Valkyries. But there were many true tribes of Amazons, in Libya, Russia, and among the Vikings there were female captains. One of which invaded Ireland in the tenth century A.D., a warrior queen, the Red Maiden. As late as the eighteenth century, those women in the Amazons' territories around the Black Sea still wore trousers and rode horseback astride, fighting beside their men in war. They were not angry women, but women at peace with the past. They have come through the ages, in the meted out tales of life and the fickle fireside myth, a supergroup of women with faraway searching eyes. Those men who survived the custody of Amazons each sang the song, destined to become a big hit: Handle With Care.

A legacy is a powerful weapon for change. What Somberg had in mind was a return of the ancients. She worked quietly, building a network, enrolling hot-blooded women in a future begun the way a woman makes change, not focused on a strategy of how to get there, but on the process that is discovery. As the discovery of the self in the gift of a limitless femme. They were not a condition of the pantheon, some women had femmes, others didn't, but it was through discovery that a country founded and administered by women would be made. An American Monaco. A Corporate Olympus. Inspired by the Amazons. A future not based on predictability, but counting on the certainty of uncertainty. Inviting ambiguous circumstances. It would take time, perhaps to the new millennium, but Somberg had her blue eye on the dream: The Garden of the World.

If Maggie Thatcher could do it, any girl could.

Alexia came with a fresh absinthe, but she could see Kristian was meditating, and took the seat across from her. She was spaced out, face blank as a page, hair in a bun, in Jessica Moore's gray fleecy jogging suit, staring out the window, watching the powdery stars sift over the frozen dark, as though it were her son lost. The absinthe didn't help. But maybe the wormwood toxic was in keeping with Thatcher, who Alexia had never been impressed with. She was an unaccountable cognitive dissonance of at least two people sharing the same body forever shifting and rearranging her image in the mainstream as if she had committed some kind of crime.

The legless father had busted up Kristian pretty good, and the only sign of life was the pain. They were all bummed out over Chicago, which had been a mess. She and Isabella were searching the man's condo, found a map of Ireland, Gap of Dunloe circled, when things got out of hand next door. Someone had to toss the monkey wrench of violence into what should have been the simple. But then Kristian, for all her strengths, could never master the mundane.

By the time Alexia got over there, into Jessica Moore's place, Kristian was glittering with a calm orderliness in all that mess of blood. Her hair splattered, dark tendrils down her breasts. A totally reeking scene in the kitchen. Kristian had tripped out, shot the man in the face so many times, he was unrecognizable, his face splattered all over Kristian, as if she now wore his face. It was at times a raunchy business, no way to avoid it. Chicago was bad, but Alexia had seen worse, after a while you got used to it. Blood like oil, just part of the way things work.

She cleaned the place of forensic evidence while Isabella helped Kristian change into the jogging suit. The pain then was excruciating. A suffocating, throbbing band of pain had cinched itself around her middle like a girdle, and that was bad, but what was worse, she couldn't feel anything below that girdle of pain, nothing at all. She made it as far as New York, then collapsed.

On their way, Alexia started looking for the sisters. The youngest was not in Chiang Mai, where she was was anyone's guess. Alexia figured she was in Tibet connecting with metaphysics and reincarnation. She found Laurnet at her animal sanctuary. The older of the two younger sisters lived in a park-like country of the foot-hills of gray-green Kenya with the forest behind her, and it was a great place to visit. What with its big peaceful animals; the massive, iron-like elephant, the snorting, sniffing rhino, the strange, graceful giraffe, and the royal lion seen before sunrise. Laurent, like the animals, had a talent for evading strangers, not many people knew the way to her eight-story pagoda-like tower made of a steel rib cage finished with cypress; as delicate as a carved wooden toy, engineered to sway in the wind like the yellow fever trees filled with laughing monkeys. Alexia knew it took Laurent years to build that tower, it wasn't easy to create structure that would give. From high in the tower it seemed as though you lived in the air, the interior panelled in mahogany, the windows with views immensely wide. The main feature of the African landscape and of Laurent's life was the air, and from the topmost room there was a great view of the western summit of the snow-capped peak of Kilimanjaro usually ringed in clouds as the "House of God."

On her game reserve was a tribe of Masai, an intelligent and betwitching people who could be bewitched—they had very great ideas of queens. Silent in their dignified, gentle ways; their laughter was like silver bells. To the Masai, Laurnet was *Jabilo Jeri*. They believed her to be a witchdoctor; she did not deny it. The natives, who had a strong sense for dramatic effect, were the philosophy and fortitude of Laurnet's soul, that Alexia knew had a love for danger. Killing was natural to the animals, and it was both natural and art to Laurnet. Her attitude to her art was that of the master and she traveled far, but always returned to Kenya. There were no fat and no luxuriance there. There were only the blue late afternoons, and high above the Eucalyptus trees, the peace that hung in the great African night. Laurnet was Kenya. She knew the music of its birds and its colors and its smells, and it was something else listening to her talk about it all. Laurnet sang her stories; it was song whenever she spoke of Kenya, singing as if around a fire, the queen imparting wonders to the tribe.

She came from the forest and highlands to heal big sister, and it wasn't the first time. Laurnet was a slender, exquisitely tall, light-skinned black woman with an oval face and high, round cheekbones and her mother's knife-shaped eyes that were blue, but Alexia saw them as a blue of a deeper hue than Kristian's. Laurnet had been raised by Kristian in Paris where she had acquired big sister's professionalism; her killing skill with reptiles and insects and birds came from her father's native Kenya.

There were rumors, so many rumors about Laurnet; the family loved to talk about her. It was said Laurnet made love with an animal-wild passion, those who came under her spell were unable to escape even for a moment her presence. Alexa couldn't speak from experience, but she had seen as much. Laurent could fix you in a mess. The girl was fire to the heart. It was creepy. Like you were dusted with her phantom presence. Lovers said there was voodoo in her black soul. And Alexa figured there was some truth to it; she had a necklace of bones, feathers and animal skulls that when shimmied before the eyes could trip you out like hypnotism. She was a blend of tribal and contemporary. A superbly educated mind, she possessed the rarest quality in intelligent people: happiness. A woman happy with herself. With life. With her work. And with her companions, though those poor devils were rarely happy.

She treated Kristian at their penthouse at the Pierre Hotel that had a living room the size of a tennis court. Some kind of mumbo jumbo going on in the master bedroom, Alexia had no idea what the sisters were up to. There was a blood transfusion, she knew that, but that was not uncommon, the sisters shared blood, among other things. There was something of each sister in them all, so you could be pretty turned around if you were being passed around, as some were, with progress reports from sister to sister. It made a heart-bond to the family, and the heart of this bond was always Kristian. Laurnet wanted to know what had become of the male who had nearly broken her sister's back, and Alexia figured the guy was lucky the way things went down.

Laurnet nursed Kristian with the tyranny of a mother; a love learned from the hard work, responsibility, and sacrifice Kristian had made for her sisters. Kristian alternately slept and cried for two days, pain the medium of Kristian's existence, like pleasure, they breathe one another's faith. She had grown up with pain that had become her mother of invention. Crises made her a visionary, using the trauma of childhood in a breakout, out of herself and out of the roles prescribed for a Good Girl. Other than Alexia and the sisters, no one really knew Kristian; she didn't share herself with anyone until they became her desires, and then was bored with them and gave them away. But Alexia had come to Kristian as a baby, really, at fourteen, and so she was something of a sister, in the innermost circle, but outside of it as well, and she knew how Kristian's mind worked. When she was coming up through hard times, she was sustained by ambition alone. Everyone thought she was so successful, a genius, they worshipped her, but there were failures no one knew about. What made her career was, if a job fell apart, it never freaked her like it did others, she took it in stride and built new plans at once out of the ruins of the old. It made for a power Alexia found irresistible, that she aspired to, that she had never seen in a woman before, except for maybe Maggie Thatcher.

It was understood a Destroyer like Maggie would be destroyed; it was the way of things. But wasn't Kristian a Destroyer? She had destroyed others, and all the morality and gender rules, and was forever destroying herself to remake herself. And if a Destroyer was to be destroyed, then what was to become of Kristian?

What the others didn't know, except for the sisters, is that Kristian had never killed a woman before; all her marks had been men that were a pleasure. And it was pleasure bending every Kim that she romanced, and afterward it killed them. Gender-bending was not a hatred, but a hobby. Kristian killed the very good and the very gentle and the very beautiful boys impartially, and if a man were none of these, he could be sure she would kill him too, but there would be no special hurry, and she would not bother to change him in that Amazon future she was making for women.

Somberg opened her eyes to the young virtuoso who was beyond progress reports. Sitting boylike, one knee crooked, gazing at her with blue-eyed predictable innocence that was anything but that. A little knowing smile, hair curled around her ears, and those eyes, the pale blue of a Norwegian winter sky that was the wind she rode in on. The beauty was in and of herself a spiritual retreat.

"Laurnet sure knows how to do it with imagination," Alexia said. "And Isabella's about to go out of her cowboy mind."

It was ultimately, always, the path beyond the inextricable bounds of pain: others. Somberg entered now, the pain vanishing as she pictured it: Laurnet piloting *Pequod* with Isabella's breath at her neck, insisting that she receive the high calling of personal sanction of a lost soul in Ireland—which is to say that Isabella wanted to do the mother. Laurnet at the controls, smiling to this one-sided dialogue with the calm of a woman on a desert oasis.

"What's Laurnet up to now?" Somberg took the fresh clouded drink Alexia offered. She took a good numbing sip; it started the world spinning backward.

"Oh, she's found some twisted mountain road in Ireland! Said, 'The Irish really know how to build a death trap!' "

"Sounds like the Irish." Somberg reached out to give Alexia's hair a casual stroke. So blond. She loved to muss it. And Alexia, with her little natural breasts and long, narrow limbs, loved to be mussed with. In a classic white calfskin leather jacket, collar up, gold zipper and buttons gleaming. Black crocodile belt and top scooped to impossibly soft skin, the honey of the Caribbean sun. That generous golden mouth frosted in Toast of New York.

Alexa's placatory tone was raised to entreaty. "Laurnet says the road was built for the age of horses. She says it's *'perfect!'* She's flying the plane while Isabella reads the mother's medical records . . . looking for God knows what."

"She must have an in with the family doctor."

"A nurse. Laurnet arranged it all yesterday."

"Yesterday?" Somberg looked to the burning moon and tried to remember yesterday. All she saw was a flickering candle flame.

"Yeah, while you were out, on whatever they gave you. Laurnet said, *'You have to know a mark to do a mark.'* " Somberg smiled to hear herself quoted by her sister. "So we got the mother's medical records. And Laurnet's juiced about her rental. It's a *Volvo!*"

"Oh, really?" Somberg brightened, and now noticed the lovely bouquet of tiger lilies on the seat beside her. A note attached, from the baby, her youngest sister.

"We used one in Austria," she said, sipping the illicit drink that could tiptoe into the past, improvised the present, make a swinging drunk of the future.

"Heard about it. That rock star. What was his name? Lestat?"

"No. That was Sydney. I'm talking *Austria.* Not Australia."

"Oh, you mean the blackbird thing, right?"

"Petrels, dear. Known as the storm bird."

"Petrels, right. Laurnet said something about that. Who was it . . . a journalist or something?"

"TV reporter. Or rather, *television personality.*" Somberg laughed at the absurdity of it, plastic hair and pancake makeup called personality. She sipped, gliding in the jet stream. "He was doing a series on a prominent industrialist. Supposedly polluting the environment. We were brought in to maintain decorum."

"Had to look like an accident?"

"Hmm. The media would be all over anything that happened."

Alexia tilted her chair so the moon shone blue on her face. "Is that better?" she asked?

"Much. Thank you, dear," Somberg said, admiring not the moon, but the lovely lethal. Did an ambassador's bodyguard in Vienna last year. Held his face as she kissed him, and Somberg could still hear the neck crack. A sound akin to biting into a stalk of celery that Alexia loved. The heavily armed man slid to the floor without a decibel of warning, in what resulted in a tragedy for Austria, the ambassador with his eye on the presidency. "It had to appear as an accident," she said, memory changing direction, from Austria to Australia, "but it had to be horrid, to satisfy the client. You know how irritating the sleazy, slimy press can be."

"Difficult combination. Chance and horror."

"Yes, but he had this red Volvo. It was like a gift from the gods! We don't often get a mark strapped into one." Somberg smiled onto a yellow-tinged moon that tasted like wormwood. *Are there petrels in Ireland?* she wondered. Not that it mattered, Laurnet never used the same technique twice.

"There are *so many ways* to do a mark," Somberg said, raising a Waterford crystal glass gleaming with a 24-karate gold rim. Gazing into eyes equally exquisite, and in the showcase phenomenon of the drink she saw the fine-boned blond face beaten to a pulp. Both sides bloated out of recognition. Bruises blue and yellow about the eyes. One side of the mouth ridiculously swollen, the battered thing speaking through a hole on the other side, as frightened as a cornered rat, but fighting back with the bewildered story of a father's tantrum. The trained ear catching the choked fury in the confused voice. Confused not about the beating, but trying to explain the love-hate. It was that courage, getting beyond pain to grapple with truth that inspired a passing nouveau rich woman of sometimes ill-repute, of machismo herself, to heroinism. A great courage deserves a warm place to live, a hot cup of tea, a gentle light, a soft, clean bed in which to sleep, a welcoming plant in the window that grew with the healing of an adolescent and an iron lady in need of caring. "Too bad," Somberg mused to the beauty, self-healed, "the way men are so attached to their guns. There are so many ways to do the work. They've no sense of *art.*"

"Art? Or heart?" Alexia replied caustically.

Somberg emptied the glass, in a wheeling sensation. Seeing the Australian TV personality flying down the rocky switchback of a mountain, reeling in a Volvo filled with birds pouring through the rear armrest lowered to the trunk. The trapped bird's scream more frantic than the trapped screaming man. Ripping at his face. Clawing at the eyes open wide in yellow red-threaded puddles.

"But I'll tell you this," Somberg said to her beautiful moon that reflected her light, "learned it as a child: when you run into a problem, *finish it off quickly, before it finishes you.*" She gazed into the absinthe that was now a puddle of yellowy eye threaded with blood, and she drank down the eye, and for just an instant heard the gunshot again and saw Daddy vanish into the hay. She touched the hair as blond as hers and kissed the lips as wide as hers and looked into eyes a clearer blue than hers, and kissed Daddy good-night with Alexia opening her mouth wide. The air wild with cosmetic scents and perfume and body emanations and secrets of strength and survival and splendor that only Somberg knew. A love, like a memory, that was hers, that was only hers. Those eyes so blue, so richly blue, only she knew the truth of Alexia's gender, a femme that had climbed to the highest tier from where you could see Daddy lying bleeding into the hay. "When things go bad, they frequently keep going bad," Somberg said, losing the golden glass, finding sweet golden lips, drinking deep.

She was at peace now in sleep in the joys of her powers, and Alexia shut the window blind onto the moon. Others never saw her like this, in despair. They saw only the predator. The infallible. The mosaic, the painting. The outside. Never the wounded shell. Never the rubble that she would rebuild into legendary splendor, as soon as she opened her eyes to feed those who waited.

Far beneath the surface of her sleep, in the wondrous world of the deep, the great white whale of pleasure swam on. There were nursing mothers in the watery vaults, floating on their side, and some of them were sisters. The newborn spiritually feasting from them, drawing nourishment that made them almost more than mortal, nearly immortal, so great was their size and strength. The nursing mother's gaze fixed idly on the female and male world, seen from eyes on opposite sides. A soul-experience that a once-broken child caught as a fever of dying, then to see again. Alexia had nursed, and knew truths about girls and men, most of which mounted to silliness, theater that was not nearly as interesting as sisters.

Nowhere on earth was there a union as separate and together as sisterhood. It was sometimes a pathetic arrangement, as last month when Kristian ran off with the "Garden of the World" idea that was entirely Laurnet's but would likely never happen if big sister didn't steal it, making an ass of herself. To live in the cusp of three international sisters is a tedious back-and-forth. There is strength to gather. And there is the melee.

There had been the lunch at Tramontana in Paris that was to be spent talking business. A clique of femmes and sisters turned somehow, Alexia couldn't remember how, into a psychodrama. A public fight. A scene. The baby locked herself in the bathroom. Laurnet and Kristian yelling through the door. Alexia tried to refrain the yelling; tried to negotiate a reconciliation; they only yelled at her. She retreated feeling ridiculous, an accessory to a crime she hadn't committed. Management called the cops. Alexia back in the foray, she and Isabella seducing the three cops so the three sisters could continue. The baby was coaxed out and all was well, until someone started pounding on the table to be heard. Someone broke a wineglass. Someone smashed a plate. The cops laughing, everyone in the restaurant the sisters' co-dependent audience with Alexia getting up the money for bail when the prima donnas got bored with going crazy, kissed and made up, drove off drinking a bottle of Blue Nun, of all things. Alexia had no idea where the Blue Nun came from. Turned out to be one of the cops's.

It was like that. Sisters fighting in love. No one was closer and no could hurt more. They would break up and not speak to each other, but you knew there was no chance that they could break up for real. They belonged together. As soon as one needed the others, they were there. Like Laurnet, at the controls of *Pequod* while wounded big sister sleeps, double skunked on the killer drink. It was more than a marriage, sisters. It could not be encouraged, and could not fall apart. They now each worked alone, but were always together, and whoever took on the one, took on them all. Blood was bliss, and a hellishness to be feared. Like a legend.

23

"*STANFORD!* WHY THE devil do you have a team prying into entry cards? They worked all bloody night!"

Trent glanced up from files strewn over his desk. Graham was in the door, wearing his tough guy expression. Pink jowls going red. Hand on hip lecture style—a Churchill trademark. He was in navy, also Churchill, tie artfully awry, to fit in with the boys.

"That's *overtime*, Stanford!"

"Right," Trent replied in a tone of gravity that supplemented Graham's firing squad mode. "Afraid it's related to Brighton."

"Look here, Stanford, this department operates on a budget "

"Certainly, sir."

"*A budget*, Stanford! Allocations from Parliament."

"I'll keep that in mind."

"See that you do!"

It was a tricky gauntlet Trent was running, career in hand. The PM authorization allowed him to spend Graham's budget at will, and all the poor sod could do was protest. When the Fox, Sweeney, and the Pope were netted Trent would again be subordinate to Graham who was well aware of his standing at Number 10, on the lookout for some noble deed to expunge the blot of the Brighton bombing. He needed the spectacular. And he was overdue. However, he had the text prepared for his speech to the press. For that shining hour! A few minutes would do. One winning arrest. Or hope the IRA would be successful on their next Mrs. T venture, it'd suit Graham perfectly. To have *that woman* replaced before she replaced him.

"Found *this* on Burnett's desk." The door groaned as Graham reclined against it, waving a fax transmission like a flag. "From the FBI. About a Dana Jenkins of Dayton, Ohio."

"Came in yesterday," Trent said, rocking back in his chair to glance at the jaded pigeons eyeing him through the window. "It's what the boys were working on last night. Thought I'd fill you in when I had something concrete."

Graham set a pair of spectacles on his nose in the careful, self-conscious way of people who had just started wearing them. He paraphrased as he read. "Seems Ms. Jenkins never applied for a passport. Has never been to Ireland. And never made a passport application for her son. They'll advise if there are further developments." He paused, looking over the top of wire-rims that Trent thought made him look quite a bit like the guy that shrank people in *Dr. Cyclops*, only Graham was on the dumpy frumpy side. "How can this possibly be related to Brighton, Stanford?"

"It's complicated, sir."

"Oh? Let's hear it."

Trent swept a hand over the enticingly arranged strew of files. "Afraid it's a bit of a mess just now." He watched as Graham took it in. Just the sort of mess he loved to poke his nose in, grunting and snuffing and rooting around. In search of Teflon. Folklore. Quicksilver. "If you've a moment, I'll fill you in . . . but I don't have anything conclusive."

Graham didn't need to be asked twice. Parked himself in the guest chair Trent had ready for him, a comfy throw pillow for the back the way he liked it. Graham arranged the pillow. Read while Trent closed the door; dropped a rolled towel at the threshold for the pesky nonsmokers. Lit a Cohiba. Watched over Graham, always efficient at paperwork. The commander flew through the reports on Vogler's acid margarita. *"Frightful!"* he said. Next were Taylor and Jimenez, Graham hooting as he read, telling Trent the same would happen to him if he kept smoking. Now Heydrick's glass-seasoned beef. Graham, a celebrated beef eater, looked up with a flare of pain in his face. *"I believe that's the most god-awful thing I've ever heard of!"* Then Rostov and his Dobermans. Now the others, reading with a grimace, unaware of the Definite Integral connection, the reports copied onto Interpol forms. Finally Graham thoughtfully compared the sketch of Sterling to the ice woman to Nordstrom to the Dana Jenkins passport photo. Trent paced as he reviewed a summary he had prepared on Danny Moore, this the tricky part, to enlist Graham in Jessica's dreams.

Problem was, Jessica was on the wrong side of the camera. She did not live in the pulsebeat of tabloids. Wasn't a sex queen or a movie star or politician or any other unrepentant American vulgarity. She had no fantastic energy. Nothing to slobber over. She was neither great nor near-great, either of which would have had a favorable exchange rate with Graham. She was only a mother in need. Desperate, but that would never fire grandstanding Graham. Desperate must be packaged as intrigue. That Jessica's case had, oodles of it, though she was not fully aware of it.

"I say," Graham grunted over the scatter of files, "this is a dizzying business. Let me get this straight: You believe this ice woman is the same who did *all* these oral killings, who you think is Nordstrom, living as Jenkins, who you believe has kidnapped an American child under the alias of Sterling. Correct?"

"That was what I thought," Trent said, smoking.

"Was?"

"There was the problem of height."

"Ah, yes. Nordstrom was shorter than Ice Woman."

"And shorter than Jenkins and shorter than Sterling."

"So, Nordstrom didn't fit."

"Right." Trent dropped into a facing chair. Took his time; kept it simple. "That's why I contacted the Swedes. The insurance company sent me this." He pulled an express envelope from under the pile, producing it like a magician's trick. Graham spent a moment reviewing the insurance applications of Peter Julius Nordstrom and Kristian Mary Somberg. The attached photos gave the appearance of blond-haired blue-eyed twins.

"Note that Kristian Somberg," Trent said to the window ledge of listening pigeons, "is the same height as Ice Woman and Jenkins and Sterling."

Graham verified all four heights. He gave a grunt. "Jolly good, Stanford. Now, what's the point?" he demanded roughly. "I fail to see what any of this has to do with *Brighton*."

"Ah, well, here's what I make of it." Trent unlocked his gaze from the window and swung around to face Graham, saying, "She killed him."

Graham drew his shoulders around him, the confusion on his face almost comic. "She *who*? Killed *who*?"

Trent smoked a moment, playing it out. Life nothing but a stage. "Somberg married Nordstrom," he explained to the pigeons, "killed him in a boating accident, which was not an accident, then assumed his identity and collected the insurance on herself."

Disgust seemed alarmingly genuine in the pigeons who blinked and ruffled their smoky gray feathers.

"But Nordstrom is shorter," Graham protested, wide forefinger thumping the insurance application.

"Right. But after the explosion there was damn little left of Nordstrom. Insurance companies don't verify the dimensions of the *living,* only the *dead.* I suspect Somberg was sitting down whenever she met with the insurance adjusters as Nordstrom."

"She, that is to say Somberg"—Graham's chin tripled as he looked, bewildered at the sketches—"may be living as a man? As Nordstrom? But using the identity of this woman Jenkins?"

"Not quite. I rather doubt Somberg would live as a man." Trent fiddled with the cigar; he liked the feel of it in his hand. Feel was everything. Feel helped him think. "I'm beginning to get a feel for this woman. I suspect she hates men."

"Oh, God! *One of those!*"

Trent's cigar glowed, then faded. "Or I may have that backwards," he said, his eyes skating off to the pigeons regarding him curiously. "She may *love* men." He smoked on that, and added, "She may love them a great deal."

"In what way?" Graham probed.

"She may have a weakness for their feeble will."

"Feeble will?" Graham cried.

Trent laughed, entertaining himself for a moment, winging it, like a pigeon. "It's not an uncommon trait in beautiful women, to love easy marks. She may know their mysteries—most men so anxious to be known. She may love the pushovers. May love the ones with a *will* even more. After all, a vampire loves their prey, don't they?" Graham looked at him with a combination of doubt and resentment. "She kills men," Trent said, more certain, "*because* she loves men. Because we kill what we love. And most importantly because she has consumed all their secrets, and so they no longer gratify.''

''Sounds like you're reaching, Stanford.''

''I suspect,'' Trent said, in mid-flight, but going slow, ''Nordstrom was one of her early kills. But not her first. Too sophisticated to be her first. But too risky to be the work of a pro. Knew what she was doing when she selected Nordstrom. And note how young she was when they married.'' Graham frowned at the insurance application. *''Sixteen,''* Trent said, glancing at Graham, who was now intrigued. ''If she was experienced then, she had to have started as an adolescent. Made a million off Nordstrom. Somewhere along the way, picked up an oral fixation.''

''First-rate *sicko!''*

''Whatever she is,'' Trent said to the pigeons pressed close to the glass as if listening in, ''she's now a *professional.* I suspect we'll hear from her again.''

Graham rooted through the files, mulling it over. He seized one. Attacked the pages. Then slammed it down. ''This can't be the work of *one* woman,'' he said.

''That's what I thought.'' Trent rested his Cohiba in the desk ashtray. ''Her description doesn't fit all the hits. Even taking into consideration a makeup kit. But the *technique* of the work is the same. Interpol,'' he said, making no mention of Parkinson at MI5, ''suspects a seven-figure assassin in each of the hits. It would appear she does two a year. Collects a few million. Does God knows what to entertain herself the rest of the year. Whatever her hobbies are, I'd bet it's related to her love/hate for men.''

''So,'' Graham said, lifting a ballpoint, pointing to sketches as he went along, ''Somberg became Nordstrom?''

''Briefly.''

''And Somberg is the ice woman assassin?''

''Almost certainly.''

''And Ice Woman killed *all* these others?''

''I suspect she has accomplices. Perhaps more than one.''

''Then . . . Somberg became Jenkins?''

''Briefly. For expediency.''

''And she's also this Sterling? The kidnapper?''

''I suspect so. Yes.''

Graham put the sketches and pictures in sequence. He glowered at them. Filled himself with a robust breath, in the face of evil, not daunted for a moment. ''Fascinating business,'' he said. ''But I fail to see how any of it relates to *Brighton.''*

''It's actually very simple, sir.'' Trent crossed a leg, delivering his rehearsed lines with a firm, decisive tone. ''In searching for the child, we uncovered the assassin. That's why we're running an entry card search for Jenkins and Somberg. All entries into Britain in the last six months.''

Trent watched Graham consider his bait.

''I don't understand,'' Graham said. ''You're searching for the *child?* Or the *assassin?* Because the child is an American problem. Why the devil were you searching for the child?''

''Oh, but we're after the assassin,'' Trent replied, slipping the question, but giving him the scent. ''You see, Sterling, who I think is Somberg, was sighted in *Ireland.''*

A small smile greased Graham's lips. The smile of a portly old bloodhound who might have a way out of Mrs. T's doghouse.

"At St. Mary's Cathedral in Killarney," Trent said, taking up the cigar again. "A priest there, Father Shanahan, identified her. Said he spoke to her." He drew meditatively on the cigar, and watched as smoke raftered lazily to the window. "Odd thing is, Father Shanahan has gone missing. We're told he's at a funeral in *Belfast*." Graham's smile widened. "A funeral for a *Mahoney*. I checked the records; a Tomas Mahoney was buried yesterday."

"And you suspect Mahoney is IRA?" Graham asked, cutting Trent off, taking the bait.

Trent lifted open palms. "I'm just shadowboxing here. I don't know what to think. *You* have all our sources over there. It might help if you'd *shop the network*. See what turns up in Belfast."

Graham peeled a stick of peppermint gum. He chewed on the problem. Now making notes as he chewed. Trent sat smiling at the handsome pigeons that with their gift of flight could peer into any window. So many windows available to pigeons. Every window with a story, and he was grateful for the pigeon company, and wished they could advise him, to help him sort this out. He knew that Mahoney was IRA, dug out the bulletin on him last night, but didn't know how Mahoney was related to Shanahan. Graham could find out faster than he could, and with Graham busy, he'd be free to search for Somberg. Find Somberg and he'd find Danny. If an entry search turned up blank, he'd check on Shanahan next, but he wanted to get Jessica out of Killarney. It was highly improbable a priest was IRA, but if he were, and if Somberg came to Killarney to meet with Shanahan, then Jessica was in very deep water.

Graham stacked the files. He stood, peering down his long nose at Trent. Took a breath and swelled himself up till he looked about five hundred pounds. He adopted his stance of smoldering hostility, hand on hip, and all the rest, though he was neither smoldering nor hostile. He was quite intrigued, thank you.

"The whole thing is a bit *irregular*, Stanford. The child, there's the rub. He's an *American* problem. I'll ring Belfast. My people are up to scratch; you can be sure of that. They may not be visible, but they're at the forefront of things. If this Mahoney is IRA, they'll know him, top to bottom. But you do understand, your authorization extends *only* to Brighton."

"Right. Wouldn't dream of using it for anything else."

Graham kicked the towel out of the crack under the door. He swung it open. Cuban smoke spiraled out. "It's all iffy, Stanford. But we'll have a go at it. But we shall want *credit*."

"You can have it all, if you like."

"Don't be bloody silly. I'll share."

He let the old boy turn to leave, take a step. "By the way," Trent said, ever so casually, "you wouldn't happen to have heard of a *Gorgon*, would you? Alias for some underground type? Anything along those lines?"

"Gorgon?" Graham rounded sharply in the doorway. He frowned. His lip curled out. He considered the question. "Only Gorgon I know is from the Greeks. You remember, the bitch, *Medusa*. Had hair of snakes. Turned men into stone if they looked into her eyes.''

''The first femme fatale,'' Trent offered.

''That's the one!'' Graham's bear-trap memory clicked in. He was on a soap box now, doing a lecture for the pigeons. ''Was originally a beauty—I've always had the notion she was something of a teenage temptress. Stupendous little kitten. Or maybe a good girl who was prime, lusciously prime. Ravaged in a temple. Raped by a priest.'' Graham sighed, tragically. ''Cursed to become a damn monster. Winged, she had the power of flight. Golden scales protected her heart. And there were those eyes. Gorgeous eyes. Seductive eyes. Men made lousy choices in sight of those eyes, none ever the same again, changed in a way they couldn't know— or if they knew, couldn't resist. Turned to stone just the same.''

Graham mulled all this over for a moment, then on a wave of tutelage added, ''Actually, there were *three* Gorgon sisters. What were the names of the other two?'' Graham looked to the pigeons, counting them off on his enormous fingers. ''There was Medusa. And Stheno and Euryale,'' he said, nodding. ''They were immortal, but Medusa was not. Though they all had wings and the golden scales. All killers. Caused serious mayhem. Unfeigned. Unbridled. Everyone terrified of them. Lived on an island, somewhere, no one knew where. Only the sister's nymphs knew where the island was.''

''Medusa was poison,'' Trent summarized.

''Oh! No doubt. Poison for men. Women, well, they could look into those eyes. They must have been breathtaking.''

''*Three* of them, you say? You're certain of that?''

''Stanford, you were deprived a *proper* education.''

''I know it. But I struggle on.''

''Yes. Three of them, I'm sure of it. Made quite a name for themselves. There's never been a trio of sisters like them since.''

Trent worked on the smoldering cigar, considering Chimera Enterprises, Limited. The bogus company Sterling passed off on Jessica. A Chimera was a cruel parody. A foolish fancy. But it had a second meaning. A Chimera was a killer. A nightmare. Head of a lion, body of a goat, tail of a serpent. A bloody fire-breathing she-monster. It too was from the Greek myths. Was this proof that Danny was in the hands of a game player, and assassin, and she told Jessica as much in their first meeting? This is what seized Trent, Chimera, not Medusa, dismissed as Graham's ramblings.

''Of course, you know who took Medusa down . . .''

Trent looked up through a cloud of smoke.

''Perseus!'' Graham volunteered.

''Right. But ol' Perseus had a little help, didn't he?'' Trent said, taking up the teacher role. ''There were winged sandals and a magic wallet and, as I recall, a cap that made him invisible.''

''Well, you did do a bit of reading in Ireland! Yes, and the gods gave him a shield, as well, that was from Athena. Hermes, the guide and the giver of good, supplied him with a sword. His mother was a beauty herself, for the longest time Danae was locked in a house of misery. Married a fella—his name slips my mind— who taught Perseus about the Gorgons. Put him onto the scent, as it were. He had these gifts and an enormous courage, Stanford, rather like you.'' Graham gave a sardonic smile. "Headlong. Foolhardy, people said. No one in his senses would have taken on that warring bitch. But he had balls. Passed all manner of test, a journey through the twilight land, and whatnot. He took down Medusa, not unlike Thatcher, I'd say." Graham stood a bit taller; sharped his shoulders and proudly proclaimed: "Yes, Perseus was *the man!*"

Graham favored Trent with his camera-ready smile. Fancied himself a Perseus. Always had. Big targets his thing. Stanford a bit too gung-ho for the work. Took a tactical man. Like Graham.

Trent seemed not to hear a word. Sheer Graham fascination. The Wicked Witch of the West. Returned to the Planet Dog. A woman wheeler-dealer amid the ancient male bastions. Now taken the form of Thatcher, sassy, brassy, capable and competent. A Medusa back by popular demand. The power of women to castrate all men, how Graham saw it. How men loved the stone-turning myth of Medusa. How they talkety-talked-talked-talked about Thatcher. All bird song. Proof was the pigeons, all in a flutter, they suddenly took flight. As if they knew who Perseus was and had set out to carry the word. Medusa pure fairy tale. What was real was the reference to Gorgon. Probably nothing but Russian code for one of their ghoulish hitters. What would tell the tale was not myth but fact. Who was Mahoney? What was Shanahan doing at his funeral? Still, the other did intrigue. Trent glanced up to see Graham leaving.

"Commander."

Graham glanced back.

"What become of Medusa? You said she *wasn't* immortal?"

"Why, Perseus decapitated the bitch. Lopped her head off with that sword. But he had a hell of a time doing it!"

"Right. Thank you, Commander."

24

JESSICA PICKED AT her pork roast, pushing the peas around her plate like a bully. She lifted her feet into the empty chair where Danny should have been sitting. Her feet were sore and her thighs were sore, but it was a good soreness that reminded her of Trent, who only last night was in her arms and tonight seemed a million miles away. She had spent the day canvassing Killarney, showing a picture of a lost little boy to every soul in town, and she didn't want to think about it or how beat she was. To put a good face on it, she thought of it as *elegantly wasted.* Certainly she had been that last night. Elegant with Trent. Wasted by Trent. She smiled at the memory, and tired to recall how she had come to finish the day at a window table of the Black Velvet Pub. It had appeared to her as a haven for a damsel in distress, and she wondered again what had become of her life. She hadn't planned any of this.

Each day in Chicago her downward spiral got worse, with a cold rage coming on, and there seemed to be no end to the sorrow. Pit had saved her with body and soul concotions of exercise and Beethoven. And Hayashi had saved her with his quiet understanding. Then there was Trent. She had set out to find Danny and seemed to have found love instead. But you can count on love to leave you in desperate straits, which it had. She was well into the day before she realized how much she needed Trent, a need that was annoying but perfectly normal, and that was good, and by the end of the day she was thoroughly strung out. Going primal in Ireland. She found herself at the Cathedral lighting a candle for Danny and wondering about God, who seemed to have changed colors, she couldn't invoke His presence. He was called by ninety-nine names as in ninety-nine beads on a rosary and she had counted each and every one and the number of her invocations had been innumerable and still Danny was out there, somewhere. Though he had been here, in Killarney, and that seemed as unreal as everything else.

There was a crushed feeling in her stomach that she was now trying to fill with pork. An emptiness where hope used to be. Betrayed by a damn fool who had believed she could find her son and was only now coming to grips with a lost world, and so it was indifferent to a lost boy. A cold cynicism was creeping over her, and now she tried to fill the emptiness by pouring chablis into it, watching the shadows lengthen and sink into Killarney brooding black against a deepening blue sky. The twilight was animated by shapes and silhouettes. Across the street a tall woman came down the walk, her *café au lait* coloring made golden by a street lamp that had just come on. Jessica took another good long drink of wine and called for the check. She didn't want to attempt that snaking Gap road in the dark. The world was snake enough.

Shanahan walked in bloody meditations, Marline at his heels, from the church kitchen to his office, reading the messages laced with gossip. Made it to his Gothic desk, at least that put some distance between him and her endless litany, and for a moment he forgot Belfast. Sipping tea, Marline's shrill came through the depths of his exhaustion as the rabid chatter of a broken man whose red-eyed submission still stared him in the face.

"The Fitzgeralds had their baby. Their *fifth* boy! Debi is fine, but Paddy is a wreck."

"Aye," Shanahan said, closing his eyes against the scenes of the black arts. " 'Tis agony to do and misery to watch."

He stared with unsteady concentration as Marline fanned out her messages across his desk. Gone for three days and now she was swarming him with her pink message slips. His head in a torment, tongue swollen with thirst. He needed more than tea to offset the shrieks in Belfast made the worse by needy, annoying people who he couldn't abide, and he wondered why he put up with Marline?

"And Liam O'Malley was picked up for public intoxication. *Third* time this month! That one will never sober up."

He nodded agreement, lowering the teacup into a drawer. Splash of Black Bush. The whiskey fumes as sweet as salvation.

"Jon O'Reilly was seen round town with Kathy Bishop. Putting on airs she was! And him with his grand talk."

Shanahan closed his eyes and drank the spiked tea, his mind in his whiskey, Marline's trill lifting, and without trying he was returned to dear, old Belfast. In memory it played as strangely fantastic, phantasmagoric. The single bare bulb swinging in the basement, so the room took on a sea-motion. It was as though the animal screeches were not coming from a man but from the slidings and coilings of the shadow over the wall. The shadow, like the screams, spellbinding. Tomas Mahoney, shirt peeled away, dangled upside down like a drape of raw beef. The feet hung from heaven, frantic hands suspended above hell. The thin shadow of the switch rose over the ceiling, to come down in a low whistle that made the shadow writhe on the far wall like some inverse puppet of a manic creature. Old hickory bit into flesh, once, twice, thrice. The back now marbled in blood. As always, Shanahan summoned strength from prayer that he now gave to Mahoney's eyes that scampered like trapped rabbits in their sockets: "The earth shall tremble at the look of him: if he do but touch the hills, they shall smoke!"

The chilling cruelty continued, a dreadful fascination, thick-limbed Mahoney turned into a sling of red traitorous meat. The two vibrations of patriot and priest going on together with the bloody screams. The patriot breathing in rasps, with pain in his rushing arm. The priest with agony in his heart. Flogging until the sound of denial was whaled clean away. Pain coming into Mahoney's brain like a drug, a few applications later the traitor was singing like an altar boy. Shanahan, sheened in the sweat of the righteous, listened to the Judas confession.

Shanahan's eyes rolled back from Belfast to settle upon Marline. It was all the invitation she needed.

"*Heavens!* What a week!" She continued, elated. "The phone wouldn't stop ringing!" She romped through her pink messages as the father romped through the forest, populated with grotesques, freaks and lost souls.

The soul of man is a forest. A dark vast forest spiked with sunlight. Wild life lives in the forest. As that primal forest that terrified the world-conquering Romans. The dark forest out of which the white-skinned hordes of the next generation stormed. Who knows what will come out of the soul? Shanahan was finding out.

In the forest there was the spiritual and the sensual, in which all must suffer, to die and disintegrate and be reborn. Shanahan heard and did not hear Marline's tales of temperance and frugality and industry and order, and above all chastity. He was in the transition of the far-driven soul, almost over the border. In the great continuous convulsion of disintegration. Old Hickory rising and falling, in a pitch higher and higher, as in a man's shriek. Nerves beginning to break, the man beginning to die. A man must be stripped, even of himself. This disintegration could only be a galling, ghastly process to a priest; though a woman who had been raped by a priest might see this process in an entirely new light. Same process. Same changing. Same ecstasy of vision. The difference being pain and beauty.

There was a delight, be it sadomasochism, in changing others.

Though Shanahan feared he was becoming more scientist than artist. Flogging and watching. Then listening. He had taken Tomas Mahoney in. And when Mahoney betrayed, selling out to the Brits for his thirty pieces of silver, it was Shanahan's duty to bring him down. Upside-down, as it were. Witnessed by the others. This pretty boy made into the ghastly that would romp in dream. When it was over, the patriot put his switch away and the priest lifted his cross. He gave the miserable soul last rites. What remained of Mahoney was tied to the tracks, his family spared a traitor's disgrace. The Brit train did the rest, that was as it should be.

A man can be broken by pain or beauty. But all men must be broken. The breaking a heightening. The result is mastery of your fate. Father Shanahan felt himself on his way, though not quite broken. In his self-torture, self-lashing, lashing his own white, thin spirit. The patriot lashing the priest. Who loved it more? Patriot or priest? Hard to say.

"Oh, and that nice American mother came by," Marline gushed. "She'll return tomorrow. And did I tell ye that Jon O'Reilly—"

"Hold it." Shanahan looked up through vague, unfocused eyes. "What American mother?"

"Her name is . . ." Marline fumbled through her pink notes. At last she found it. "Jessica Moore."

The migraine came at once, like one of Marline's long darning needles. A gleaming spike of pain driven through Shanahan's ears and deep into his brain.

"She's *here?*" he gasped. "In Killarney?"

"Aye. Staying at Cullinane's Thatch she is."

Shanahan saw the shadow of old hickory coming down in a high, sharp whistle. He flinched at the scream that if it hadn't been in the basement would have brought windows open in bleeding Belfast.

"She seemed *rushed!* Not polite. But then, she *is* an American, ye know. Been soliciting all over town. Showing a photo of her lad and a sketch of a mystery woman. Who's the woman?"

Mahoney's scream was hideously amplified in Shanahan's aching head. "Holy Mary and all the saints," he muttered, though he did not intend this to be a depiction of the mystery woman.

"A *man* from England let the cottage. But I don't know his name, not yet. And I heard—"

Shanahan's black eyes lit with fire. "*England,* ye say?"

"Aye."

"And when did *he* arrive?"

"Why, I don't know. But she came in yesterday morning."

Shanahan fell back in his chair as the grip of the headache strengthened, and now he was tied with belts at the wrist with his arms spread-eagled waiting for the switch. Except it seemed his head was being crushed inside an inquisitor's lovecap as well. The cap tightening with pain. Why had she come? What would she find? What damage could she do? Who was this Brit? How could she know a Brit? Was she searching for the lad in England? Had she sent the lad's picture to the schools in England? Wasn't Thatcher's visit to Grantham just days away? The flogging questions wouldn't stop.

"That's all, Marline. Thank ye."

"But I've more messages!"

"Tomorrow morning."

"But I've not told ye about Mary Flanagan! She wrote from Gibraltar. Said you'd be welcome to come any—"

"*Marline!*" He caught himself snapping at her. That was not his way; that was the patriot. The patriot would take old hickory to her. "Tomorrow," he said gently. He helped her from the chair. "Everything must wait till tomorrow," he said, leading her to the door. "I'll be out the rest of the day." He shut the door behind her before she could say another word.

He locked the door, as if to keep what out? The mother? Had to keep her out if patriot and priest were to survive in one man. And now he paused before the black hickory crucifix on the wall. Marveling at this cross on which he had been placed. Its beams, the love of God and the love of Ireland, bisected at his heart. The mother like nails in his palms. Pinning him. What was he to do? How could he stop her? Could he kill a mother searching for her son? The Gap such a lonesome place. Nothing but sheep there. The sound of a shot would fade away into the black mountains. No one to hear it, except his soul. He winced at the migraine and took his car keys and went out the back door.

Somberg wore a Chanel velour robe that with the hood up gave her the look of a black monk, as that black monk that could vanish before your eyes in the Chekhov short story of the same name. The monk-like robe was her way of playing with the tumultuous rape that she wore lightly now; the robe gorgeous before the blaze in the studio fireplace where she plotted her escapes. On the desk were two flight plans. One from Grantham, England, to Copenhagen, Denmark. The other from Dundee, Scotland, to Bergen, Norway. The courses plotted through airspace that lay beyond the range of British radar. The first was a primary route, the other the backup. She planned options for uncertainties that came with every job; the work of the artist was to take the unexpected and turn it into the creative, preparation made it easier. The future, Somberg knew, existed first in imagination. It was her finest weapon.

The pain in her back was a kind of uncontrolled passion, and she accepted it and did not struggle against it. It was unworthy of her attention. Emotions were always dangerous and faithless; in the days prior to a hit she avoided all influences over her.

There was Kim's kill to come, a planned influence, a pleasure of the highest order, that of a creator. The brilliant soap-opera intensity—if all went well— of Kim's male demise would release the tension. It lay in her as a humming power cable that she respected. The way to overcome tension was in *the heightening, the flow, the ecstasy.* The great white whale of pleasure! She would follow it anywhere. The gratification of the obscene. The outrage beyond diminishment. The search for ever-increasing thrills could distort if run to extremes, she had seen it happen to her mother, never aware she was overcome until she was lost to her own mayhem. It was a risky game flirting with depravity but not being stalked by it. Still, there was nothing, nothing like the wild chase.

And here was the beauty now, calling in a glow of love from the balcony. "Kristian! Eric wanted to say good night."

She invited them down, her two pleasures. Her adored son and her newest creation in a black pullover. Looked genderless but it was Donna Karan. Kim such a pretty baby in demeanor and carriage that he couldn't pass as a boy on the street to save his life. What with his hair in a swing-cut, and the fresh romanticization of his smooth Polynesian complexion. None of it as a performance but an experience lived. With no conception of his change, and that was the thrill and mastery of it. To do it unconsciously. Intrinsically. All of it so tantalizing it inspired her tyranny.

Floating down the stairs, he smiled, lovely smile, but not as pretty as his pout. She was looking forward to his pretty pout of perplexity. It would come tomorrow. She laughed thinking about it. A soul in the throes! In the crisis of love. How could he do anything but love his demise when he was to be his very own dream girl? An oppressed spirit soon to be freed! The feminine self. To begin in tomorrow night's gala, a limited-run disaster. It was all showbusiness. Kim Lee to go down like the others. To come out a fashion statement, a desirable mien, a hipster, a junkie for the feminine scene at first, a bit of a nut at first, you never knew, since they were caught between two lovers. Male to be left as roadkill that would appreciate in value over the years. Female to rise from strange fruit to a new soul music! A femme the very image of God Herself. All fun! Some called it gender-bending, but that wasn't quite right. It was mind-bending. That was the thrill.

Her son came galloping pony-style across the studio. In his footed Superman pajamas, once loose, the fabric taut at his legs, and the realization that he was growing was a bit overwhelming. A thing she had assumed would happen but she hadn't yet imagined it. A future that was coming whether she imagined it or not. He leaped into her arms in a cry of, *"Mama!"* and for a transitory enchanted moment she held her breath in the presence of an overwhelming rush of feeling, glistening for a moment as it rose within her. The boy so happy to be in her arms, as though she held all the wonders of the whirling universe in the cup of her hand, not a doubt in the tender worship of this child who was nothing less than her great orgasmic dream of creation from the Savoy Hotel. It came over her darkness and was as that first dawning in which the burnished gold finger of God slid over the dark waters enjoined in the secrecy; turned to a sunglade; all the waves whispering together in that forever mystical impelling that brought forth light and land and all that dwell therein, in that strange spectre known as life. Such was the dawning of love in Somberg. It rose from the depths, not as a monstrous white whale, but as a gentle child. Only a child could do it, give that wonderous phenomena that was none other than the great pleasure that had long eluded her, suddenly hers, now snuggled in her arms, and she was hapless before it.

"Can I have some chocolate pudding before bed?" he asked, curled into her lap as cozy as a little forest animal.

"Did you eat all your peas?"

"Uh-huh."

"And your pork roast?"

"He ate it all," Kim said.

She took a judicious moment to consider the request, letting excitement build in pleading eyes aglow in firelight. Those eyes like two big blueberries set in freckles. His hair tousled like golden wheat. She was aware of his growing dependence on her and found she reveled in his devotion that was almost as deep as the unsounded depths of mother and child. Depths that had been known to swallow even the most professional of women. It now occurred to her that perhaps the hypnotic intoxication was not all his.

"All right. You may have a *small* bowl."

He started to bolt from her lap. She held him, squirming. It was the best part, always, always, always, the battle of wills.

"And what do you say?"

"Thank you, Mama." He gave her a hug, careful of her bandaged arm. A bite received from a very bad dog named Winston.

"You're welcome," she said, and kissed his cheek, as soft as love itself. He ran into the dark with that sentiment, profound beyond feeling, swelling in her in a kind of wind that fanned off pictures long since put away. Blowing through her mind. A similar scene a lifetime ago. Kissing Daddy good night, then a skipping dance to bed, while Daddy applauded with delight. The wind blew a whirl of pictures inspired by her son's unexpected, incalculable sentiment, and in among the rush were terrible, awful haunts. All part of the wonderous phenomena of intrepid memory, such pictures hitherto revealed only in candlelight. Something in her twisting out in horror to that hapless object otherwise known as Daddy, in that apparition of life that was, at times, almost real. He was real, wasn't he? A breathless spectacle in a barn somehow conveyed wondrously unknown before her, with out touching her, though Daddy had reached out to her, she was now certain of that. Magnificent, actually, how the mind's eye was blind to it, in that dilating dominion of mother, so that other than what was in the record, it never actually happened. It was a well known fact, that in no way was attributed strictly to her, that that which we love we kill.

"Brush your teeth after the pudding!" she called after him.

"I will!"

They started up the stairs, the pair of pleasures, and for an instant she had a terrible sensation, a quick stab of premonition, that she would never see her son again. A morbid chill ran up her spine, splintering her crazily, throwing her open, so that in that instant she was a throbbing lump of flesh and fear. Quickly she recovered the ground beneath her, never one to worship the fires of emotion, only a mother's low, guttering, unenthusiastic candle flame that dipped and sputtered and blinked in the eyes, to lick back the past into the shelter of darkness.

"Good night, love. Sweet dreams!" And then to her creation: "I'll catch up with you later, darling." Kim smiled, and with no trouble at all, Somberg could see Melissa Brooks in the smile.

She watched until they vanished into the gallery that joined the main house. She picked up her compass and mechanical pencil to return to the flight plans; the pain in her back like the fire, snapping and crackling, drawing her eyes from her work to a girl dancing before the fire for her daddy, who loved her very much.

Jessica had a little too much wine and not enough supper and was struggling with that left-hand stick. She passed the cathedral and turned onto the road that led to the Gap, flashing through a tunnel of trees; the car flattened the hill and came out of the curve with the lake behind her and the sky waxy red, the mountains swallowed in the oncoming night. She braked but barely slowed and pulled sharply through a turn with no brake on her emotions as the seriously seductive specter of Trent rose. In the dimness of the car glistening hands unclothed her while she drove. Dream naked in the dark behind the wheel, she felt the glide of his cheek on her breasts and belly and buttocks and thighs, and far down inside her she felt a stirring and the sudden force of wanting him all over again. She was driving a little wild but hardly noticed, the Volvo sliding around curves, the brake line oozing fluid every time she touched the brake. The pressurized line was blistered as if by an overheated engine, Jessica was just that, flush as a young girl as again she opened her thighs to this Englishman. A lovely little quiver in her lips. It was not the driving experience.

She turned at the clutter of road signs in the form of arrows pointing every direction but up, which is where she was headed, and never saw headlamps tailing her through the snake turns. Kate Kearney's Cottage rose on her left. A green phone booth in the car park. She touched the brake, thought of stopping but slid past. She'd call Pit in the morning, just now she wanted to get back to the cottage and dream some more of this extraordinary man who was inside her again, his hands clasping hers, their fingers twined. "We're bound for parts unknown," he said with the smallest smile. She took a long, languorous deep breath. From the cliff edge she saw the sun setting through dust that blew up out of the twisting road that treaded down into the Gap where they had loved, and in the setting sun the dust appeared as blood blowing in the wind.

Girls are entitled to their dreams that should not be muted or muffled, but should become part of their emotional experience, and Jessica was reminded of that as she slid the car down into the Gap, with no thoughts whatsoever of the car. She did not know, for instance, that Volvo was the first family sedan with a rear center armrest that could be lowered to access the trunk. It was designed for Swedish families to stow skis in the car. Took a minute for a skilled technician to replace the armrest. Took less than that to change the #7 and #12 fuse in the wall panel near Jessica's left leg. And the catch on her seat belt had been replaced, but there was no way to tell this, or that the trunk was a hive of bees.

They were not your garden variety of bees. They were larger, and somewhat angular. Their coloring a mixture of brown, buff and ochre that provided good camouflage against the tawny undergrowth of the high rolling plains of Yucatan, Mexico where the bees were known as *"la tormenta secreta,"* the secret storm. The toxin from most bees is very mild, causes swelling as the toxin's enzymes begin breaking down the tissue at the point of the sting, while other bee venoms are more virulent. The tag of "killer bee" given the sub-species of the Yucatan bee was not quite fair, more legend than fact. The human fatalities on record were few, and those only because they were allergic to the hemotoxic of bees. The lethality of the Yucatan bee remains clouded in exaggeration and conjecture, but this is without a doubt one of the planet's premiere bees.

The males were giants among bees. Elongated, their bodies a lance shape, the male instinct was to attack the prey in a "combat dance," a form of pre-aggression. They whirl in an aerial song, rubbing, poking, even stroking the victim. The amorous males were larger, more frightening than the female, but virtually harmless. The female follows the male, in something of a mating ritual, the male's twining courtship session with the victim is brief, but tantalizing and critical to the forthcoming attack. The victim is braced for assault, blood high, skin taut, pumped, as it were. The female, identical in color and pattern, though her tail tapers more sharply into a stinger, is attuned to light and scent. She comes in the morality of a hurricane. The female needs only a split-second contact with the bedizened prey to deliver her venom more accurately, and deeper into the tissue than any bee, other than an Asian species not available on such short notice. Big sister had said she wanted the American mother to go down in a "frenzy," so the Yucatan bee was selected, otherwise

Laurnet Jalou would have used one of the two hundred snakes she kept in Kenya. But then, it was said there were no snakes in Ireland.

The bees had been gassed with halothane, but were now wide awake, Jessica winding down through the road that looked to her like the high road down to hell, perilously perched above the bog she couldn't see in the deepening shadows. Laurnet, tailing in her car, had only to touch a remote and the now mechanized armrest lowered. A crack. Enough to allow one or two bees to escape.

Jessica turned down into the Gap road with the cliff edge to her left with the bog below and all to her right the sheer, black, knotted rock face of mountain. She put the love story of Trent away to focus on the driving, feeling the car slide a little on the steep dirt road, but it wasn't much and she felt safe inside the shoulder harness of her seat belt. Flipped on the headlights to chase back the shadows that provoked the gloom that was as real and dark as the shadows and would, she knew, always be part of her landscape until she was reunited with Danny. The mental wards were full of people who succumbed to those shadows, many of whom needed only to experience Beethoven that was an inoculation against the gloom, like those shots that could save you from bee venom.

She whistled it now, the brave tiny tune of the seventh symphony that began on a flute, as light and feel-good as a child, only to encounter darkness, but emerged fearing nothing. Didn't need a CD, she knew every beat, the symphony a roar reverberating over the high walls of the Gap, in her mind louder than a factory whistle, and so she didn't hear the buzzing, not at first, but she felt an odd itch behind her ear. A feathery tickle tracking across the back of her neck. Her hand reached to give it a scratch. Then realized it was alive. She crushed it under her hand. Felt it still fluttering, still alive. Now a bee rose over her shoulder, in the car it looked huge, and for an instant she froze.

"Holy fucking shit," she whispered, seeing a ten-year-old girl fleeing from a swarm of wasps. Running to the Beethoven seventh in full swing, the girl in a kind of rapture of fear, all tingly in her her hands and legs and between her legs, until she fell. Now pinned to the garage floor, wasps whistling down upon the howl of a wounded animal. Crawled under a dirty old chair. Only to find that's where the wasp had come from, their nest on the bottom of the seat. She lay there, impaled by wasps that wouldn't quit. It felt like she was on fire, her whole body swelling like a balloon shot by a blast of helium. Except she wasn't floating, she was sinking. Now her father trying to pry hands from the chair. He lifted her into the car. The shot at the hospital had saved her life and she was told never to play near a wasp nest again. *Not wasps. Not yellow-jackets. Not bees,* Jessica thought as she lashed at the huge striped thing diving for her face, swatting it as she pulled the Volvo through a sliding turn in the Gap road, and the Beethoven seemed to leave her at her scream.

"Goddamn!" Jessica swatted at another one that came out of nowhere. She hit the brake and it sank slowly to the floor, making her knees go weak. In her mind she knew something was wrong with the brakes, but all she could think about was the burly bastards buzzing around her head. For an instant she stared in fascination, couldn't help herself, they were her *worst* fear. It was as though her fear had traveled

to new frontiers to draw from the darkness of her gloom, to make from it these fickle, bulked up, fearsome, otherworldly bees. "Where did these things come from?" She didn't hear her thin, warbling voice over the rushing in her head with a warmth flowing into her cheeks at the delicate crawl of a fiend up her ear. She lashed at it. It fluttered away. Why didn't it sting her? The pair whirled before her eyes, so terrible she lost the transition of rational thought for a moment, her eyes following them to the back of the car. She saw the armrest lower. Did it all by itself. Spookiest thing she ever saw. A dark cloud came swarming out of the trunk. Jessica's mouth went dry as the cloud spread over the ceiling, growing like a living thing.

She pulled through a turn and hit an electric window switch. The back window didn't open. She tried another one. Nothing. She tried them all, beating on the switches—"*What the hell*!?"—as a hot wire burned into her left hand, burning very deep, an intimacy in the sting below the surface with pain already spreading up her hand. She shook her hand. "*Shit!*" The tiny bee flew away, cool and sassy. She struggled with the damn British stick that didn't want to shift. Something hit her neck. Her eyes went wide at a bright flare of pain that brought a flash like a still jump on film. A newborn screaming his lungs open. Tiny hands flaying before her, glazed bloody in the miracle of birth. She knew a kind of crazy exhilaration in the swirling cloud, the predators accompanied by Beethoven that made a musical euphoria of the terror, easily the worst and best of her life. And there is nothing better than the worst, unless it's the best, like Danny. But she refused to panic, in the mess of her life she hung on to the steering wheel, though it seemed she was going faster.

Headlights splashed over black mountain coming up in a rush. Jessica pulled on the wheel and mashed the brake. It oozed down as the car slid around a guardrail kicking up a long river of sparks. A dry, metallic taste in her mouth. Now the thought came in loud and clear: *Something the fuck is wrong with the brakes.* She mashed them again, harder. The pedal went to the floor. Now that she understood the cause of the speed she was gaining, she could not shake the terror. She tried the windows and tried the brake but now there was something in her hair. Something crawling over her scalp! She swiped at her hair. Huge bees flew out. Like the damn things were making a nest in her hair! Or teasing her. Why the hell would they do that? But why in the hell didn't they sting her? For a second, she thought she had imagined being stung, and swatted at the cloud overhead. Her hand came back throbbing.

Her hand, hit twice, was a sorry spectacle of pain. It began to swell before her eyes. She saw it as a shapeless lump of raw meat. Looked like a cartoon. And didn't she belong in a cartoon? Hadn't her life become a big joke? She saw Bugs Bunny slam himself with a hammer, Danny laughing and applauding and shooting her with his finger gun, cheering as mama fell. "*Great! Do some more!*" She tried the door handle, as if she could jump and not kill herself. The electric locks were fused shut. In the rearview mirror, red sunset dust was boiling up behind the runaway car gaining speed. The females, junked-up on halothane, were in a nasty mood. In the pleasure of their trade that was the *swarm*. The prey was now overwhelmed by fear, blood up. The confines of the car made for a bee-fest, the swarm hideously amplified in a violence the bees themselves could feel through the air. They dropped on the prey now, the males abandoning the chase, leaving it to the terror of the family and their feminine wiles, that was the instinctive piece-by-piece kill. They would sting it until it stopped moving. Then they would sting it some more, until it was dead. They were not inclined to separation, the only survival was escape.

Jessica slid the car around a curve, leaving an abrasion on the rock wall, over-steering and now deflected off the guardrail and she glimpsed the dark bog looming below. She was searching for the hand brake when they came, the black cloud raining down, and she let out a scream of *"Oh, Jesus!"* as the volley of pain came up her arm and up her shoulder and it seemed to come out the top of her head. Through a squeezed face of pain she saw the damn road that kept falling and twisting and wouldn't quit. Her eyes fell from the road to her arm. It was covered with bees. *"Fuck!"* She shook her arm, as though it were not a part of her, as though it were an object, like a towel or shirt that she could snap in the air with this amazing host of bees lifting like a haze. They circled and came for the other arm, drilled now with a bolt of pure white pain that slivered her eyes. She screamed and shook herself free. She slumped forward over the wheel with shoulders pulled around her to protect her face, the pain all over her like a thing that had been crouched in the dark silence, waiting since Danny was taken.

Her eyes fell on the hand brake. It was between the seats, she cursed herself for not seeing it sooner, but now bees were in her shirt. Crawling in her shirt. *"God-fuckingdamnit!"* She beat at herself as they nailed her to the seat, Jessica stripped by panic to her very soul, in a state of nakedness, feeling like an old thing that needed to die and disintegrate, that must be gradually broken down before anything else can come to pass, so many stings she couldn't separate the pain from the shrill of the hive that grew around her head as the car seemed to shrink. The car going flat-out down the mountain that swelled in the windshield. She pulled another wicked curve and tried to escape the seat belt. It was locked and wouldn't release. She pumped the brake and tried to shift down—*"Goddamn British cars!"*—the muscle in her calves flickering crazily like they were about to give out. Crawling up her chest, the bees were stinging as they crawled up her chest. A band of fire inside her shirt as if the fuckers had crawled into her heart, and it was then Jessica knew she was going to die.

It came to her in the sharp curve just ahead that she rushed around, and it came in the stinging in her ears that was her own stinging of pain that would not let her go. It came to her in the twilight just beyond the cliff, she felt as though she were at the very edge of eternity. And the assurance of death came to her as fear that as she faced it, it was gone; it slipped away from her as easily as a nightmare slips away from a woman who awakes, cold skimmed and gasping from its grip, who feels her body and stares at her surroundings to make sure that none of it ever happened and who then begins at once to forget it. And it was then, in that instant of letting go, that the Beethoven returned, the heroic seventh coming out of the blinding stars of pain in her eyes, and her hand fell on the emergency brake. She pulled hard on the hand brake, too hard. The road began to spin. Headlights sprayed over the mountain wall. In a billow of unscrolling dust she saw Danny in a silvery helmet of horns, holding a silver gun aimed at her heart. The bitch squatted behind him, steadying the gun, her finger on the trigger. The bitch was calling Danny by a name. What was it? It was beyond Jessica, out there in the stars of pain that exploded

in the roar that came in Danny's laughter as she was shot again and thrown backward, into a spinning, the Volvo spinning out of control, shattering the guardrail,
now sliding off the cliff edge. And to Jessica it seemed the sense of falling would
never end.

25

HEIDI HILTGEN WAS waiting for the beauty, Alexia and Isabella escorting the dear
arm in arm into the salon, as if the little one might make a break for it, but there
was no escape. Was there anything more delightful than the folly of man? Heidi
thought not, and she took it out on every one of them that she changed.

She, and Heidi called them *she* from the moment they entered Kristian's arms,
was led through Corinthian columns and hanging baskets with flowers dripping.
Girls in rose satin gowns, heads in curlers turning and smiling. Conspiracy in the
air. Paranoia on the beauty's face, which made it more thrilling for everyone. The
little one was in sunshades and denim, trying to look macho, like maybe a ranch
hand, creaking forward reluctantly, like a *Cat on a Hot Tin Roof,* and Heidi thought
that vile Tennessee Williams would enjoy this. It was empowering work, changing
men. It was Heidi's life, her livelihood, and though it felt shameful and degrading
to a male it was, in fact, the opposite. It was freedom and self-discovery. Emergence
with Ishtar. The grace of inevitability.

She was taken to a room with a massage table, Heidi waiting there. A weight-
lifter, her blond hair was cropped close to her handsome head. Silver-blue tank top
and shorts, limbs that had the gloss of new copper pipe. She said something in
German to the girls, they snatched her shades and ran away laughing. She yelled
after them, but it was too late, Heidi closed the door.

It was drivel believing femininity belonged only to girls, it was the nature of all
of Ishtar's creatures made in Her image. A kind of beauty that had meaning, that
lay below the surface in the deep of the male, otherworldly, you might say. The
unraveling of a man was woman's infantilizing privilege, gals had been doing as
much for millions of years, and it was not crazy, but the purest distillation of everything good. This child had all the physical features required: the large eyes, small
nose, full lips, small jaw, and delicate bones. The skin was glorious. Hair gorgeous,
as were the lashes. The beauty was blushing. Why couldn't a boy enjoy being pretty?
Doesn't a male feel the magnetism of the Goddess, so electric. Heidi could feel it,
ordering her to strip.

Kristian had first hired her as an *au pair* for her sisters, then children who had
lost their mother, gone to the sanitarium for a long season. Heidi was a big-boned
German, resilient, with a presence that commanded attention. In time, she became
Kristian's aide-de-camp in the conquest of a golden young Moor in Geneva. He had
to be taken without disrupting Kristian's marriage. It was decided to bring him in
in the guise of Heidi's female assistant, so the lord of the chateau wouldn't know.
The lovely boy was kept in lipstick and skirts that made him more accessible to

Kristian, taking the blooming, blushing Moor at will, and Heidi thought this a pretty impressive swindle of the husband. Though the boy was so petrified by the venture, the hugeness of his need often required Heidi to relieve him of the enormity of the feminine appeal.

Heidi came to the light of Ishtar by way of Mother. She took the girls to the sanitarium by the mountainous lake once a week, and the experience immortalized Mother. Her eyes as violet as that peaceful lake whose character she took on sitting beside the waters telling the girls how the world was made, who ran it, and how it should be run. She had Laurnet hold out her lovely long arm. Time was as long as her arm, from shoulder to fingertip. The length of time that God was said to be male was as long as her hand, from wrist to the tapered nails Heidi faithfully buffed before every visit. In the entire rest of time, as long as the girl's arm, God had been female. It was an historic fact proven by archeology uncovering her deity that extended around the world.

In those visits, Mother taught the survival and revival of the Goddess as supreme. The girls learned the customs, rituals, prayers, and symbolism of the myths as well as the evidence of the temple sites and statues of the worshipped Goddess that extended back to earliest history, beyond the Neolithic times. She took the girls back to those times, to live through story in a society that venerated a wise and audacious female Creator. She was a warrior, a hunter, a markswoman, a leader. She was the Great Goddess. The Queen of Heaven. The Lady of the High Place. The Celestial Ruler. Among the great towering Babylonians, she was called Ishtar. She was depicted sitting upon the royal throne of heaven, holding a staff around which coiled two snakes; on her seal was inscribed, "Lady of Vision." And the knowing of Ishtar changed the girl's entire perception of themselves. It changed Heidi.

It was Mother who suggested Kristian's awe lamb, the young Moor, might be happier converted to the feminine. An evangelical light burned in Heidi's eyes. It was a chance to save a soul. The boy would emerge seeing the world in a light and language above the murky understanding of common men. Kristian gave Heidi full charge of the Moor who was from the lineage of the Libyan Amazons, to be cultivated into femininity that he might experience Ishtar and serve Her. As Man should serve Woman.

Heidi was careful how, when and where she broke him, and in those early days, he was fraught with crises at this turning. He learned the dark shape of Heidi's wide hips and pointed breasts in the corner of his eye. A firm hand quite suddenly under his chin. Taught to speak so the simplest syllable sounded soft and exotic. Taught how to dress. How to walk. How to sit and smile. And above all, how to serve. Taught to believe and worship the female deity, and his existence was hugely exhausting; Heidi was relentless. A longing penis needed attention, and got attention, but only in the context of the Goddess. "Let your body in to Her, let Her tie you in, in comfort," Heidi taught the solitary boy who was then still perfectly sane.

He had been a stranger in his own life. Imprisoned, as all men were in their bullying and belligerence, so they could not find the irrefutable path, and were incapable of following. But Heidi fixed that for the lucky Moor. A sexual sorcery came over him, and Heidi was surprised how even the simplest acts, going to the boutique, for instance, was such an inexplicable rising that he had to be relieved in the fitting room. Wasn't this striking, strong-boned reaction to femininity proof of repressed veneration of the Goddess? Hadn't men scrawled Her image on their cave walls, and now on their billboards? Didn't men worship Beauty? It was natural and instinctive, though they were blind in worship.

She kept after the Moor until the male in him was undone and he was at home in the feminine. Until it was his, now her, nature. It was to the Moor as the arterial strike of a vampire, as if the blood were sucked from his veins, replaced with the exotic to find the phylum of his nature. Clothes were the least of his change; he was effectively dismantled, his thinking changed. She was now elegantly courteous, sensitive to others, to feelings and senses, humble before the Goddess and woman and man alike. So luscious, so lustrous was the Moor, Kristian's husband twice made passes at the lamb, until his tragic boating accident that left Kristian with the magnificent chateau. Heidi was of a mind that all boys should spend a period as girls, living in the other divine world in which they were as delicate as a piece of crystal too fragile to touch, until you were ready to take them. Boys schooled by women to serve women, if even for a short time, a year or two. They would all be better lovers, better men, if they chose to return to being male.

And so it began, the great gender venture. Two femmes a year were selected from a population of 2.5 billion males; the chosen rare indeed. Nominees accepted from friends, a dossier submitted to Kristian, who made the selections. The science of personology was consulted. All candidates fourteen to twenty-two, born on August 25, 26, 27, 29, or September 3, 11, 13, 19, or February 22, 24, 25, 28, or March 6, 10, 14, 17. Most femmes were raised by their mother; most had one or more sisters; all had to have inordinately high IQs. The selection process narrowed further by physical attributes, charm, craving for approval, smoldering insecurities, a history of endless love affairs, an innate predisposition to serve, all types of emotional diversions were viewed as a plus, an exhibitionist nature was a premium since so much of feminine life is a performance, beginning with makeup. The finding of the perfect femme candidate was a riddle, as was the making of one. It was game, as well as benevolence.

Homosexuals and drag persons were not accepted, it would have ruined the pleasure of turning, however a natural affinity for men did surface in training, a girl naturally attracted to men. In time, lost girls were accepted as femmes, in keeping with Amazon traditions, their point of departure different from boys, though all ended at the same place, in a solidarity before Ishtar.

Mother suggested the fine gold chain at the ankle as a token of femme bondage. They did not use whips and leather restraints; instead they freed the male of restraints, using only the whip of passion. Their turning was not so much a work of the body, but of the heart. Kristian gave each a necklace of icy diamonds that made them sumptuous, and they would never feel alone again. The tattoo was Heidi's very own idea; she mastered the blood art to engrave each beauty with a similitude of the femme's individual awakening, and it would stay with her through the times of great passion. The butterfly became the mark of those spoiled by pleasure.

There had been fifty-six femmes, some were retired in the hands of assorted keepers, forty-two in current service. There were a hundred and thirty-six in the patriarchal Amazon network; the waiting list for a femme was six years. Rotation was once a year on average, an allowance paid, femmes collected a lovely nest egg. Hypnosis was used, and the occasional drug if a catalyst was needed to induce transition. Male femmes received estrogen B+ injections, a female hormone which enhanced erections. Cosmetic surgery was an elective, and was not always needed. Physically and metaphysically they were reconstituted as androgynous beings, the highest echelon of maturity, passing through two stages: the ultra feminine, or taming; the feminine, or bitch; before reaching the skillful mixture of gender, to serve as sister operatives.

As careful as screening for acceptance was, and the vigilance in remaking the psyche into female potency, there had been one or two casualties. There were always tears, so healthy, but the weeping had led to nervous breakdowns on seven occasions. Eventually the Moor was lost, though not entirely, she came to reside in the sanitarium with Mother, which in retrospect all felt must have been the work of the Goddess, the young Moor as Mother's reward. One femme had hung herself after only a year of service, but she was French, who were given to emotional abandonment. There were always rival suitors that were not in the Amazon network; miracles were arranged and they disappeared. One femme had been kidnapped, the lost lamb in Mother's prayers until she was found by Kristian, taken by a man in Venice, an incurable romantic, the femme spoiled useless and she had to be retrained. One fell in love and married her patron, the New York triplex apartment given to the sisters in exchange, and one too tempting beauty was murdered in Colombia, land of the infidels. Otherwise, the wizardry begun by Mother, Kristian and Heidi was going spectacularly, four beauties a year walking the gangplank to be swallowed by the great white whale, that number was expected to increase, so that by 2000 there would be some two hundred femmes in service, as gorgeously androgynous as a Maxfield Parrish painting, with no exceptions.

"A salon is a magical changing place where real miracles happen," Heidi said to the naked beauty she appraised with the burning eyes of a true believer. Such large dark eyes with heavy lashes. Pouty lips. Perfect complexion flushed by fear "Do you believe in miracles, little one?"

She was speechless, her erection speaking for her, beginning to stretch. Heidi knew how much the erection loved her brisk tone. She was laid on the table, bottoms up. Heidi spread and flattened atrophied limbs dieted model thin. She was clasping the edge of the table and she began there, uncurling fingers, massaging the hands. Up downy arms, watching the flesh bead, to a slender neck, working a tautness there, then down the bare shoulders undeniably feminine, they might look lovely in a halter, following the slope of spine, palms sliding around a narrow waist and flair of hips, rising to the swell of his sweet dimpled bottom.

"You're lovely, truly lovely," she said softly, touching the wetness forming between the legs, just like a girl. She left her pale handprint on the golden ass, treasuring the shiver that ran up the spine, about to come-hither to God.

"It's normal and natural to want to become what you desire," she said, icing the bottom with hot honey wax as if she were a cake. "The more you love beauty, the more you will serve it." A strip of muslin was embedded in the wax. "The more you serve it, the more you will love it."

There was a quiet terror about this one that was absolutely delicious. This a sacred rite. The male caterpillar in the final cycle of life about to come to an end. Heidi to free a soul from archaic male superstition, the beauty so lucky to be saved. She ripped the muslin away to a high scream that everyone in the salon heard. Heidi continued, ignoring the pleas, pleasantly ruthless in her work, and like Ishtar, Heidi worked her over head to toe.

The Prokofiev *Piano Concerto No. 3* was well into the second movement, pounding away like an insatiable hard-on. Heidi's hands playing over the long, curved, now silky body. The concerto and her hands swirling fear into passion, the heat so intense, as if the virgin were about to combust. She rolled her over, the beauty blushing in intense nakedness. Caressing the breasts, two flowers blossomed at the tips of her breasts, and as Heidi massaged them in oil, the nipples beaded like ripe mulberries, it was all Heidi could do not to bite them. Her hands melting skin that burned beneath her touch in sacred submission that was the female's secret, the erection in a panic, Heidi would not touch the panic. This alone, the lack of touch, was enough to start a slow shudder that ran up through her as the breasts rose and fell, with a color mounting so prettily in her cheeks to stay there like the warm flush of sexual success. The dream nearly realized, ripped for years in the heart, males with no idea how they longed for the female, and Heidi would not betray the arrival of death, she left the erection swaying, polishing the smooth molasses skin that gleamed sinfully in oil. And Heidi loved the beauty, as she loved them all, truly, dearly, with devotion and the assurance that she had saved their souls.

"Butterflies begin in an ugly cocoon," Heidi told her as she wheeled the tattoo cart over. "They crawl on their male bellies, but grow into winged flowers! Flying gems. Ishtar's perfection."

She readied her tools to burn her signature on the femme. It was impossible to predict the outcome of this metamorphosis, there were so many esoteric factors. Fluctuations of character, foreign cultures, and maturing phases with those they served. In the years to come they might be a nymphet beauty, or a true world explorer, a phenomenon of the sullen and troubled, or the nature of Ishtar, wearing a sheen of elegance. A femme could become anything, but they were never the same. There were always problems in the new life, but they now had a worldwide family. They knew so much more about them, and could shape the first critical year. Risen from shame, born of fire. The pretty-baby would fear glory would vanish at midnight, into a pumpkin and rags, but they were never changed overnight, and so the simple salacious admiration of their young supple bodies would not end, and they would not go blindly along as the unreliable male, but with eyes wide open as females that are the connoisseurs of wonder that is the nature of the Goddess.

"Butterflies have frail bodies," Heidi said, rolling her abdomen onto a high pillow, "but no backbone, so a butterfly can't be broken. Their pretty wings pump air and blood through their veins. Their forte is *hiding*. They love *disguises*." She allowed her hand a smooth greedy drag over the arched right cheek of the femme's perfect ass. A girl on one side, a boy on the other. An iron lady could have your cake and eat it too. "Do you understand the butterfly's purpose, dear? Did Kristian tell you?"

She lay speechless, perfectly still. She shook her head. Heidi tsked. Kristian had been too busy playing mother.

"They *serve* the flowers," Heidi explained in her precise, absolute English. "They drink their sweet nectar, helping the flowers multiply by flying from flower to flower, carrying the precious pollen. Laying eggs in the seeds of the flowers that bring us more flowers and more butterflies.''

This was not gratuitous instruction, but a job description, at those transient, disguised operatives at the Abbey Library, and at St. Mary's Cathedral. Father Shanahan saw the same faces, but never recognized them. Not all femmes were operatives, the third level only, but all played a vital part of cross-pollination in the worldwide Amazon network. The carried ideas and aspirations that christened the launching of projects shared jointly, as the femmes themselves. They gave of their hearts that went on and on after they were gone, to make all into one. The butterfly's power was that they were not powerful, but lithe and of feminine air, nearly impossible to catch, attested to by many a broken heart.

Now Heidi began the work she loved, the blood and cut of a butterfly, each an original. She had done a gorgeous red-spotted purple, a superior zebra swallowtail, so many luscious American coppers; there was a lavender *Morpho rhetenor,* very pretty, found only in French Guiana; a sumptuous, delicate pearl-white Chinese *Cyrestis rusca;* a temptress turquoise Mexican *Strymon damo;* a pair of golden *Terias hecabe* in India; in the Alps, the classic *Lycaena hippothoe;* and several species of the painted lady that dominated the young culture, ''the champion migrator.'' The rose-blue-amber, black-veined beauty she was doing now on the lower right cheek was a kallima; it lived exclusively in Asia.

There was the brush of Alexia's kiss at his cheek, and Kim was left alone in the hall of the Ruben Hotel at the door of a suite that opened slowly. Drawn into the dark on the Prokofiev that was trilling up his spine. A living room of candles, maybe a hundred burning candles that had no scent, so it appeared as if he were entering a house of fire. Lacy shadows of ficus trees over the ceiling; a profusion of flowers about a brothel's scrolled chaise. No one else, save the great gold gilded mirror erected beside the chaise that gave back the dark and the hundred fires lit in a heart that burned for the shadowy girl before him. And beyond her, the moon rising into a mauve sky with a single star.

Somewhere a clock softly chimed in the fiery display, and it would be today until it was tonight but tomorrow would not be today again for the first time ever. Tomorrow would be a new day never lived. He tried to remember a big goal he had. Wasn't it related to education? And didn't he once want to buy something? What was it? A car? An apartment? It didn't matter. Whatever it was was gone. Whatever secret issues were enshrouded in taste and aspiration and its desperation that was the way of a man, so fine and powerful and full of airs, could not matter now.

He felt like maybe a guy who's been shot and crumples to the floor like a suit of clothes slid from a hanger, his head emptying itself onto the floor like a leaky wineskin, only it's not blood pooling there but thoughts and he has something to tell himself and isn't telling. Like the last daybreak after a dream that turns out to be life and you wake confused with one thing running into another, trying to recount the dream and cannot. You try to think of your bank account, your business, reputation, your cool, your stuff, and you can't remember any of it, with some kind of fear growing upon you; and above all the stuff you can't remember, one thing stands out predominantly and penetratingly: the thought that you're dying. Kim was there, going out of a life grown wearisome to him, into that other one which with every passing month had grown clearer and more desirable to him. And looking back as he died, he found none of the things were the way he had expected, and he wondered if he had ever learned a damn thing in his life.

He was right there, at the bottom of his mind with the dark and the fire repeating over and over again in the mirror that held his gaze, unable to stop staring at the shadowed girl, unable to run away or do something to suppress the gathering fears against which he felt helpless, with all his recollections and thoughts interwoven and jumbled in his brain, until she called his name. A voice that commands uncommon strength, a strength for which he was grateful, upon which he was content to draw, because dying ain't in any boy's plans. And in her voice all the summer days were no longer gone, and the light was no longer passing out of him. And someone—what was her name?—knew that this was going to be great, just great, feeling pleasantly nervous but very confident.

A light bloomed above. His lips parted in amazement at the girl in the gold-framed mirror, and Kim could not speak.

"Just look at me," the Breaker whispered from the dark in a line that Kim knew by heart, "that's how you are and I did it and there's nothing you can do now. You've been changed."

Her reflection was suddenly before him, and he was blessed to look at it. The geometrically perfect face with its tanned bronzeness, so golden and frozen and still as a statue. The fine bones of the cheeks and the straight nose and the rise of the genius forehead. Such a shiny blondness to her that no boy, and no big goal, stood a chance. Her expression as blank in the dark mirror as the mirror itself. Her eyes holding him from faraway, and in the dark they were not blue, only in memory were they blue, and he couldn't know if he was turning to stone from memory, or from his love for the dark that in was in her eyes. Both still as statues. He of stone. She of glass that looked onto the quiet lovely girl.

The Breaker was at his ear: "Men are lost to everything but their work. They are staked and fixed and unchangeable, and they believe themselves unshockable. But men do not have the power and they never did. Women have the power, but won't act on it."

The light of a hundred fires drew shadows over her china-doll cut with dark bangs to her lush eyes, her hair swingy to the back where it was shaped like a bell, tapered to the base of her neck. She was in a pearl Oriental silk robe and three-inch pumps with a delicate gold chain at her ankle. Kim knew her name. What was it?

The Breaker: "Years go by and nothing ever changes with men. They know only the things that are not possible. The completely destroyed and heavy things. The dull, colorless and safe things. They enjoy only what smacks of conventionality, and they cannot, not to save their soul, deliver themselves from the deliberate."

She seated herself on the chaise, sitting very still inside herself, with Kim's life on hold. She crossed legs that gleamed with light, folding her hands in her lap. She lifted her chin, considering her neck, slender and smooth. No way to tell. There was her soft shaded face and lovely rose mouth. The brows were feathered, dark eyes shaded, cheekbones exquisite. In the Oriental robe, the cleave was unmistakable, pushed up out of a lilac lace bra and Kim could not escape the capture of this beauty whose visage held him tight with its refinement, and even austerity. A girl marbleized and highlighted, no surgical enhancement needed to make him weak forever. It seemed to have happened overnight, he would not have believed it possible. And he almost knew her name.

Behind him, the Breaker: "There has never been and will never be a starlet, a mogul, a visionary, an ostentatious artist lacking in the intoxicant of sex. It is intrinsic to all power. And if you've got it, and you have, dear, you haven't got half enough."

A delicious quiver went down her back as a platinum diamond collar was clipped around her neck. She could not take her eyes from the diamond dazzled blaze, their myriad colors as the prisms of her emotions not afraid of commitment, of trusting, of total acceptance of her now sometimes impulsive, temperamental, always changing complexities. Her heart racing with the Prokofiev that had been her pulse and his preparing since he first heard it, and now the heart that beat to the concerto was hers. She was found and he was awaiting sentencing on charges of monotony, not to be mistaken for monogamy which she had no intention of heeding.

The Breaker: "You can never escape what you love and what you love is me that you have become so now you love you as you love me and you were always coming to me. You're mine. You belong to me."

A yellowy dangerous absinthe was passed. She sipped the devil drink slowly, a little tremor at her lips preparing for a laugh, with eyes wide and dark and beautiful. A secret in those eyes that could be found in the cool wormwood drink that was death that was nothing but selling out and, honestly, he didn't stand a chance. She drank some more to take away his grieving, and there was no question about it now, she would not be a virgin much longer.

"Melissa."

"Yes, ma'am?"

"Do you remember what your purpose is?"

It came back to her, the name and charge given in internecine midnight kisses in which his will bled in a wine-drug that was a veil for a nightly wedding whispered by sneak femmes that she now repeated as her vows: *"To give the best you've ever had. To give you what you want, when you want it, as often as you want it."*

A light of triumph came into Somberg's eyes which were now blue in the mirror, delighted with this lovely mystery she herself did not know. No one knew her. She didn't know herself, but she would.

"That's perfect," Somberg said. "Tomorrow Eric will remember his assignments just like you."

For the space of a heartbeat Kim was back, having served as witness to this wedding. He was there but had been away and could not tell where he had gone. He felt he had a grave mental illness, and it was love. In love with this foxy, suggestive, retooled and infectious dream that he had become, so he was caught inside his romantic afflictive dream. But Melissa Brooks was not a dream. She was real. And this eager prelude-Melissa was real. She was him.

"And after Maggie," Somberg said, "we'll have a holiday at my island outside of Martinique. You'll learn the art of massage."

"Yes, ma'am," she said.

"You can swim with me."

"I like to swim."

"Dance with me," Somberg said, no longer the Breaker but the Sensualist, stroking the brand new girl. "Mix drinks for me."

"I love to do that."

"Talk to me, if that's what I want."

She nodded. "I can learn to do those things."

"You will learn, dear. You'll learn to give a manicure. Oil me for the sun. Exercise with me. Draw bath water. Turn down the bed. Make yourself pretty. Read law if it's what I need."

"Yes, ma'am," she said to the cobalt eyes in the mirror.

"And, of course, I'll have *guests* for you to entertain."

She felt like silk and she was going to be a great lay for a long time, and already Somberg hated to give her up to her baby sister. She stroked her back, blond face beside her Asian face in the mirror that was everything. Most men do not love women. Men love their image of women, which is not the same, a far cry, maybe a rape, of women. A man can only love himself, and a man loves his dream girl. It was a cruel message, but true. Its proof was the wordless fuck. A wordless fuck is a dream fuck that may be a girl he saw on the sidewalk this morning, or in a magazine—men love clip-out art—or some heavenly beaver from a wordless episode in his past, such as Melissa Brooks. Men believe in love. Many men believe they truly love. Love not to be confused with need. Or want. Men want plenty, but not nearly as much as women want. And so the circle was completed in the mirror, to cure men of the fear of flying, Somberg turned them into their dreams who want as a girl wants and, finally, the dears were free to love and love well.

Femmes were an evangelical experience for Heidi. A heartland enterprise. A connection with Ishtar. Not an alternative value; but *the* value. So glorified was its fanfare and promise that the notion of termination didn't occur to her full-fledged exuberance, gentle and affectionate, and absolutely ruthless, so Heidi was the perfect sergeant-at-arms.

To Somberg, femmes were the practicality of a great fuck. To fuck well you must love, and males could only love a dream they became. The miserable male acceptance of surrender was followed by a true grit birth of a fuck-loving female accompanied by sacred silence. Femmes were pleasure first, a male death second, and that was pleasure, too. Many of the female femmes had known the worst imaginable violations, and Somberg set them free, in a victory of sorts that gave her a savior quality that was true, wholesome, and worthy of imitation. The whole of it, female and male femmes, in keeping with the airy spiritualness of religious ritual that was the past that would make the future, the feminine to rule again.

"Gender is such an amusing game," Somberg said, stroking her, watching those little titties rise, amused at how she loved to be treated like a piece of property. "It's so much fun when we cross those lines made by others. Never underestimate the thrill of the forbidden, darling."

"Oh, it's a blast. A real headtrip!" she said laughing. This was not jargon, she was living it. It was as real as the bridal wreath beside the mirror that held her fascinated gaze. "But those lines are fading fast." She gave a little tilt of her head and let her hair swing. "I'd say the balance of power is changing fast. Women seem to be getting the upper hand!"

"Darling, *we* have always had the power, but men didn't know it. And your knowing tells us something about you, doesn't it?"

They laughed in a way they had never laughed before, and she was amazed at the fluidity with which love occurs when you let go.

There were three souls in the room, two were born of air and flying, and one was sea-born and dying. Kim was in pitted conflict against the sea and it felt like he had fought against it all his life, always in an unspoken fear kept like a weight inside. The hell of it was—he was only just realizing—girls weren't afraid of it. In fact, girls loved being fucked. He was afraid of it for his pride, and afraid of the event, and afraid of strange results. All religions are inclined to fear and strange superstition, male was a religion, and as much as he hated to drag God into this, he couldn't deny he had worshipped Beauty all his life. Problem was, his religion had a hopeless, hapless hard-on, and he couldn't stop the Miracle that was getting up this minute to stand suggestively before the demon mirror while Kristian fondled her sweet ass.

That Prokofiev concerto was in his head with the speed of it in his blood, Kristian opening his robe with hands of air gliding down silken skin. Teasing girl-hard nipples in a bra, the concerto like a wind that blew everything sideways in his head, like he was a water droplet sucked up in a storm, her hands exploring matching bikini panties and the girl-smoothness of his crotch. His religion tucked away, hidden under a bushel where it could not shine, in a maxi pad pulled between the cheeks of his heart-shaped ass rolling at Kristian's thrilling touch. It was everything the Miracle ever dreamed, total betrayal of his faith, his own heaven or hell right here on earth, judgment for what he could not say. God help him, but how he did love it all, the concerto mounting to clouds, and now he had a terrifying thought: any woman could be doing this to any man, and it didn't matter what she-he clothes they wore.

This was Life and Death. Night as black as Erebus which a man must pass through before he reaches Hell. A hall of light above, faint but now growing brighter. He stood motionless and stupefied before the Miracle in the mirror, losing strength and spirit, had been for some time, like in that salon of changing, girls watching his turning, all of them loving it. Unless something was done for him soon, he would be a dead man within a week at the rate at which he was sinking. But he could not stop Kristian from fondling his ass, and could not stop the Miracle from loving the touching, and Kristian in a strapless black satin bodysuit, breasts pushed up, the high cut legs edged with lace that matched the lace of her black stockings. His religion was in a dreadful state, growing worse, the incarnation of stone and for the life of him, he could not touch it, tucked away as it was. It was not his to touch.

The devil drink was passed. Cool and bitter delicious in her mouth, and the beauty thought it a shame it was illegal, and if they were going to make an absinthe illegal, they should make the Prokofiev No. 3 illegal, because it was a dangerous mind-bender once you were in it. Or, rather, it was in you; in her airy head like hung fire. She and Kristian touched each other completely, she very vulnerable to Kristian, and it was as if she had fallen in love with her for the first time. Right now she was so happy, but even as her robe was taken away, she knew this could not last. He had icky fantasy dreams but she was a realist and knew life was short, too short to waste on fear or doubt or someone else's silly rules. He could dream, she would live. And she drank deep again, loving Kristian's ravenous hands, like Aphrodite, like Catherine the Great, like Cleopatra, like Thatcher and like Medusa, with something electric in the air as beauty was stripped.

"Don't be afraid of what's inside you, dear," the Sensualist said softly, kissing her diamond-pierced ear. "All things in the universe are changing, and you have changed. Let go, that's all. Trust and let go of the struggle and be one with the Goddess."

A moon had formed at the edge of the night, and she stood in its blue light wearing only diamonds at her neck. Kristian was on her knees in an oral fix, with Kim's male hope restored, but the beauty knew Kristian would never do this for a male, and now the creative mystery had begun. Before her wide eyes, shadows danced in a hundred shafts of candlelight that rose and stuttered and bent from side to side, licking back the night. Electricity seemed to be the first, intrinsic principle among the feminine, random flashes of lightning in Kristian's blue eyes. The lightning continued incessantly for some time, and it was all she could do to stand upright in the darkness of the mirror, in the irregular and blinding flashes in her very own dark eyes. A tongue of flame probed lasciviously. She rocked in her heels. A candle point grew upright, solid and still. Stroked very gently, watching in the mirror as she was taken into perfect male ecstasy that sent her female transplanted heart into frenzy, a shuddering through his whole frame. Then the perfect stillness. The darkness, which was almost palpable. Not a word spoken. She stood lavished in the hundred flames as though waiting for something to happen.

The head job was all in the art of killing that was serenity. That was the way to harness the power, and that was the way to use the power, in serenity. Somberg loved watching him fall apart. This was her kick and what she was hooked on. Really enjoying life as the Thunderer; the overlord of the two naked elements, fire and water. She laughed and fondled that ass again, kissing the beauty for a long time, and the waters rolled off her in purity.

There was a candle for every femme, and of the many beautiful faces in the burning lights, no face but this one contented her. She wanted him more than anything. Loving the many looks in these Asian eyes; the beauty wistful and wondering; he looking like he was ready to hurl herself off a cliff. He soon to be lost, and he wouldn't be able to remember his own name. Two different people with the mind a welter of contradictions, the odyssey of the gala a few hours away, the undoing into his dream of Melissa Brooks—no one can find peace of heart until they return to the dreams and convictions of their youth. The gala was to be played as community theater, but her femmes were not amateurs. A kind of song about it all, like grand opera that like Wagner was conducted in a custom theater that was Somberg's world at large. All in the search for the perfect fuck, whose mind and body were equally fuckable. She loved to save femmes from themselves—the males had to be taught how to live—and once saved, she would snatch up their heart and run away with it, to love and keep it in a velvet lined box with the others. Like Mary Shelley, authoress of *Frankenstein,* who kept her poet's dead heart in a box on her vanity, Percy forever hers. Somberg was the same. She was Woman. She had to possess.

They shared the drink, gazing into one another's eyes. They embraced in long drunken kisses. Drunk on seduction and Somberg could keep on with this insanity for the rest of her life, this exoticism of Amazon origin that was every woman's right, as it was every woman's past. Using neither bitchness nor servility, but a dangerous romance to now change him in such a way that he would never be able to pretend this had not happened.

The drink and kisses peeled the beauty like a navel orange, the shell of her soul over the floor, the sweet fruit so pretty on the scowled curve of the chaise, to be devoured one juicy piece at a time. The bottom round and firm as an orange, with its aspiring butterfly. A gorgeous tulip mouth longing for one more kiss. But serenity would not kiss her lips, kissing instead her throat and one of those priceless nipples and down the smoothness, loving the warmth and hardness of her back. Loving her more than the others which was how Somberg always loved them. The legs spread wide, the butterfly arched high, so she was utterly naked and terribly open and greatly cherished. Gender made no difference in what was to come, it would be the same female or male, taken without mercy.

"All truth goes through three stages," she said, kissing her hot neck, fingers in love with the bell-shaped tapered hair, so happy and swingy, so perfectly feminine. "First it is ridiculed. Then it is opposed. Finally it is accepted as self-evident."

Now she took the organ that like the devil drink was illicit; it made women the equal of men. The laws not to stop notions, but in case the organ became a national craze. The bodysuit unhooked beneath, with one long curved end slid inside Somberg, the other rising up between her legs. In the stretch black satin lightly boned, she had never looked so blond. The lamb trying to come to terms with this, gazing to the moon, that spotlight that sways the sea-born, the hot burning moon in which one could lose his mind. Somberg put a fond arm around the pretty baby's waist, controlling her loss of control. The sleek young limbs a little bit shaky of the awful, awesome monster that would bring the red red blood. All virgins bleed. Blood the mystic power. Her head over the side of the velvet chaise, sexy hair dangling down. Light played about her face with candles and stars burning upside down, so it seemed as though all the world was turned upside down. Lying helpless, but not hapless. Massaged and coaxed and cooed into letting go, and as she succumbed, sliding smoothly, so smoothly inside with nothing frightening or demanding, as if this were nature, and the sudden hardness of it actually seemed to stop the breath in the body.

She did not love the beauty as a man, men have no idea how to love; only a girl knows how to love, a girl who has been fucked. Gently, ever so gently, in a radiance of power, power always a thing acquired, Somberg took the baby watching in the gold mirror. Rocking her sweetly, killing him cruelly with effortless control in the aching heat, with Prokofiev going mad over the tantric cries. She was dwarfed, feeling so small and insignificant and helpless next to the enormity of the world which was that appendage that drove with a power that commanded. She had been aching for this since teased with a finger in a swimming pool on their first date. Caught in strong urges that had made such a mess of him, the young must be careful, so careful of what they possess, lest it possess them. And Somberg brought real heart to the part, in a euphoria, possessing this smooth-blushed torrid body so that it was clear, perfectly clear in the driving force, that from now on anything can happen, anything goes, and there would be those to answer to for years to come. Already she loved it, fragile and delicate and needing someone in a way he never needed, and in the needing she knew in her soul, the female was supreme and always had been.

The lovely tulip lips were making pleasure noises in whispery undertones. As Somberg kissed her, she drank from the kiss with a fire-flying fluiditly. She was overwhelmed, powerless to stop a love that was coming, Somberg loving her deeply, so very deep and sure, taking strong hold so she would know she would never be let go. To come to terms with a feminine nature, in a coming that in love the beauty instinctively held so they all peaked together, in smoky ripplings and gleamings of the exquisite agony that took her to a place called obsession where he found the peace of the possessed.

26

"GOOD CHRIST!"

"That hurts?"

Jessica glared at the doctor. "Like hell!" she said.

"How about this?"

"Oh, *shit!*"

"Bend the legs."

"*Damn!*"

"Aye. Nurse, note that she has full articulation."

Jessica sat up in hospital bed, blinking at the crucifix on the facing wall. Out the window it was night, but she didn't know which night. She knew Danny's name and knew she was from Chicago and that Danny was missing. In dreams, all through the night, the little flute of hope played; she had been asleep but Beethoven's Seventh was wakeful and decided and could not be stopped. There were stings all over her body and she had been in a car wreck, but she didn't know how she knew that. The doctor looked like Mr. Potato Head. Short and plump with a dark curling mustache on a round face. And there were the round little glasses to make the image complete. The spindly sister nurse, a real iron, stern-looking woman, stood fatefully by Dr. Potato Head's side, making notes on a chart. Jessica was about to give the doctor the third degree when a priest came through the door.

"And how's our patient this evening?" Shanahan asked.

"She's a bit *irritable.*"

" 'Tis understandable, considering."

"Nothing broken, but she may have a slight concussion. She's rather sore."

"And we're lucky she's not allergic to bee venom anymore," the nurse quipped, long finger rapping her chart, reading from records faxed in from Chicago. "Must have outgrown the allergy."

Shanahan peered down on her and introduced himself.

Jessica stared up at blackbird eyes. Deep eyes, a fiery black. The smile crooked, like he did not quite have credibility with heaven. The Father was not what she had expected. On the phone, his voice promoted the image of a buttery round priest with a fringe of white hair. The man who stood before her was gaunt, tall, with a long, furrowed face. A strikingly photogenic face.

"Do ye recall what happened, child?" Shanahan asked.

Jessica was spell-bound by the drama in the face before her. There was much to reckon with in Father Shanahan.

"She's a bit confused," Dr. Potato Head offered.

"Do ye think a stroll would be in order?" Shanahan asked him.

"I'm not *budging!*" Jessica declared. "It hurts to breathe."

The doctor gave Shanahan a left-handed look out of the corner of his eye, stage play, perfectly Irish. He was not IRA. He was a sunshine patriot, a bit gun-shy, which made him cooperative.

"I think a stroll would do her fine," he said to Shanahan. "Ms. Moore." He smiled his Potato Head smile. "We'll look in on ye later. I'll give you some time with Father." Then he signaled the nurse and they stepped quickly from the room, leaving Jessica staring up at a face that but for the love of God would be truly frightening. She mentally framed and shot a portrait, one side of Shanahan's hollowed-out face cast in light, the other in shadow, the fascinating black eyes cavernous.

Shanahan returned to the chair beside her. He had been there all night, waiting with her, a revolver under his cassock should the perpetrator of the car wreck return. He had watched her in her sleep, and listened to dream mumbles. A woman in a mad, frantic hunt. The reddened bee-stung face made her look wild. And wild she was; a very sight of sights to see, wide eyes still consumed with panic; the wildness made her all the more lovely. Splintered body and maddened heart. Fearless as fire, and as reckless. Obstinate. Weren't all American women? He knew something of her soul history, having held her hand over the phone, and through the night as she called to the lad. She was at peace with her own conscience, if not with all the world. It was more than he could say for himself.

"Do ye recall driving into the Gap, child?"

The Gap. Yes, she remembered the Gap. Running through the night rain with Trent. Seemed they had been running all night.

"Ye were driving on that narrow ribbon of road."

"What *time* is it?" she blurted out.

" 'Tis half past nine."

"What *day* is it?"

"Saturday. End of April. A green and muddy month in Ireland. But then, most months are green and muddy in Ireland."

She looked to the ceiling. She knew the pattern of cracks there better than any other fact in her life. The disembodied face of the nurse floated on the ceiling. She had a syringe. Giving a shot Jessica didn't remember feeling. When was that, yesterday?

"Do ye recall the bees?" Shanahan asked.

"*Bees!*" Jessica jumped at the memory. "There were *dozens* of them! Seemed like *hundreds!*"

"Aye." Shanahan nodded, steadying her sway. " 'Twas frightful."

The bees suddenly seemed to be coming out of the ceiling. She couldn't see them, but she would hear their swarm for the rest of her life. "Where did they *come* from?" she cried.

She looked up at him with eyelids heavy, eyes filmed over and blank as glass, dilated from drugs that added to her lostness, and the profound impact of the father's face. Without that spiritual get-up, he would look like some battle-scarred soldier. But there was the soft, suffusing Irish voice. Already she loved the voice.

"Let me help ye up, child." He reached for her with a bony hand.

She flinched.

"The doctor says ye need exercise," he said as the good responsible man of reason, forethought, intrepidity. He drew closer. They appraised each other. She didn't trust that saintly crooked smile. "I'll help ye walk, Jessica Moore," he said, peeling back the sheet. "And while we walk, we'll talk."

She rooted deeper into pillows, clutched the sides of the bed. Bees humming in her head. "Where did those fuckers come from?" Now she remembered the brakes that wouldn't stop. "What happened to my *car?* Nothing was working!"

"Ye took a bad jolt in the car wreck. Ye need to walk to clear yer head. Not far, just down the hall a bit."

Shanahan removed pink slippers from his robe. Jessica stared at them. What was a priest doing with slippers in his pocket? The beginning of a real alarm stirred as he put the stiff new slippers on her feet. Why was she letting him do that? Now a scrawny arm around her shoulders. He eased her yowling out of bed. A wave of dizziness and Jessica grabbed ribs that were like fish bones. She stood holding him for a second, trembling like an old woman. Cold air rushed up her gown to turn her back to gooseflesh. Could he see her bare body? The mad humming of the bees made itself into the shape of a tune humming inside her head. That damn Irishman singing "Danny Boy" in the airport again. She fought back tears as Shanahan cloaked her in a blanket, wrapped around her shoulders. But even with the blanket, she sensed he could see right through her. She felt that when they spoke on the phone. A man acquainted with sorrows. He helped her find her balance and shuffle to the door; she caught a whiff of whiskey and mouthwash.

Down the hall, in a flat-footed hump-shouldered walk, she pried at Father Shanahan with questions. He told how the car dropped into the bog, a miracle it fell backward, seat protecting her spine. He told her it was God's grace he happened to be in the Gap but did not tell her he had been waiting there to spirit her away. He heard the accident and called for help, he said. As he spoke, Jessica saw red welts on his spidery hand. And there was another sting on his ropy neck. She walked on down the hall, as if against a current, Danny's flyers swirling around her in the flooding car. A buzzing at the top of her head with a brightness behind her eyes. A shatter of glass. A sensation of being lifted out the window. A black robe floating on the water and she sailed away from the Volvo half-sunk in the bog; the gray buzzing cloud spiraling into the darkness seeping in to eclipse the scene.

"I'm *beginning* to remember!"

"Ye may wish ye could forget," he said softly.

"You *saved* me!"

"No, child. 'Twas the hand of God that saved ye."

"The car was flooding, I remember that. I guess if the bees didn't kill me, or the fall, the water would. But *you* saved me from the flood. I *know* you did."

He snatched a Psalm from his bag of Psalms and delivered it with show, to celebrate, to dazzle, and to keep her walking to the door: "The floods are risen, O Lord, the floods have lift up their voice: the floods lift up their waves. The waves of the sea are mighty, and rage horribly: but yet the Lord, who dwelleth on high, is mightier! Thy testimonies, O Lord, are very sure: holiness becometh Thine house for ever."

"Thank you," Jessica said, nodding to the words as they rang in her broken heart, and now suddenly, uncontrollably in tears: "You don't know how true it is! The waves and the sea and how they rage horribly. It's like that, a flooding every day."

"I know, child," he soothed. "God help ye, I know."

He led her to the back door, using all his skills to calm her. To heal her. To tie a loose cannon to the deck. To get her safely into his camp. He opened the door onto a cold night. Clouds ghostlike against the black sky. At the curb, a rusted old Datsun. The once-brilliant green paint faded, the frame leaning drunkenly to one side, passenger door open invitingly.

"This way," he said.

"I'm not going out there!"

" 'Tis my motorcar. Ye'll be fine."

He started her forward.

Jessica grabbed the doorjambs. "I'm not going *out there!* Not dressed like *this!*"

"It's all right. I've yer clothes in the car."

"My clothes?" She turned on him in a panic. "What are *you* doing with *my* clothes?"

"Come"—he said with his bent smile—"we've not much time."

"Where are we going?" she pleaded, wanting to trust him.

"Where we can talk."

"Talk? About *what?* Talk *where?*"

"Where ye'll be safe."

"Safe?" Her head was buzzing again. She saw moths as a swarm of bees dive-bombing out of a floodlight and she cringed into his black arms. "Safe from *what?*"

"Have no fear, child," he said with eternal reassurance. "I'm taking ye to a field office of the Irish Republican Army."

"Oh, Jesus!"

"Aye. *He* is with us," he said. And the shock allowed him to ease her from the door and into his car.

The elevator doors slid open. Trent weaved through a maze of work stations and so many potted plants it might have been an Ecuadorian jungle. Through a succession of corridors. Men hunched over computers. The boys working late tonight. Something going on. Ducked into the dwarfish kitchen for tea. Actually found a clean cup. On his way back to his bunker when suddenly Graham was there. Ham face grinning. Like some poet, changing hues before his eyes. Hand on his shoulder, now steering him into a conference room.

"I *know* why you were in Killarney!" Graham announced, slam of the door adding to his drama. His round, happy red face looked like that of a tuba player in a

German band. Trent had never seen him so jolly. What did the missus do for him last night? From the looks of him, it looked like it went on all night. "I've already sent a team to shadow them!" Graham trumpeted.

Trent trying to catch up, reclined against the plastic-wood table, steadying a bone white cup and saucer. Just came in from a nap after pulling an all-nighter. "Them, you say? In *Killarney?*"

"We'll net them in one tidy bundle!" Gleeful eyes zeroed in on Trent. "The Fox and Sweeney! And, you'll be pleased to know, I've alerted the Security Committee and notified the PM."

A sip of tea to buy time. Trent still waking from dreaming of Jessica. Not pleasant dreams but nothing he could recall. Woke with a sense of urgency, irritated she hadn't called. Left word with Pulaski to have her ring the office.

"You notified Mrs. T of what?" Trent said, trying not to make it sound like a question. Bad form to show you're mystified.

"Sent the news by messenger just now!" Graham beamed. His second in command, Frances Pym, tapped on the window set into the door. Graham ignored her. "But *how* did you know about Mahoney?" Graham asked, dropping into a vinyl-leather chair. "Who put you on to him in the first place?"

Trent sat down, not sure how much Graham knew or to what extent his own disbelieving spirit still demanded proof of what it knew, that Jessica was in danger. "Well, sir, I—"

"Never mind! Not priority now. The *assassin* is priority now!"

The cup of tea paused before Trent's lips. Steam curling at his nose. Looked through the steam. "Somberg?" he said.

Graham laughed and all of him shook. "Oh, she's a *plum!*" His breasts swelled with a voice that lifted with eyes to the ceiling, as if thanking his lucky stars. *"A real plum!"* he shouted with the boyish enthusiasm he brought to all disasters.

Trent used a game-show smile. "Sir, what *exactly* did you come up with on Mahoney?"

"Why, he's IRA! News came in this morning. Fortunately, I *always* come in early." Pym tapped the window again. Graham glanced up at the rapidly rising aspirant. Pale face powdery in a broad-shouldered gray suit, looked like one of Graham's. Brown hair cropped like a boy. Graham pointed to his watch and held up one finger. He leaned forward in a tone of conspiracy. "They're overcontrolled, you know," he said, glancing back at Pym. "And right on our heel."

"How's that, sir?"

"The *women.* They're taking men over. Taking over our clothes, our haircuts, our jobs. I tell you, Stanford, the world is going to hell in a pair of trousers and a bra!" Graham was on a roll, high on tragedy, his bigotry electrified with the rest of him.

"Mahoney," Trent pressed.

"Yes, seems Mahoney was working for us. Hush-hush. Deep cover. You know the routine. We put a warrant out on him—weapons possession—so the muckers would take him in. Had him in one of those IRA splinter groups. Belfast underground. Riffraff but canny men. Though Mahoney wasn't too canny. No real awareness. Nothing but tittle-tattle. Warmed-up leftovers. Telling us what we already knew. Never delivered the goods. Someone leaked. We lost him."

"You lost him? How?"

"*They* picked him up. Turned him inside-out with questions, I suspect. We photographed the funeral. Bloody cold bunch they are! Take a man down, then bring flowers to the widow. They were all there. Fox, Sweeney, and this Shanahan. My boys said the whole lot is Republican!"

Trent blinked, faced point-blank with it, what had provoked his turbulent dreams, the one circumstance he most deplored.

"So, you think the Pope is—"

"That's right! A bloody priest!"

Trent watched him over the rising steam as he sipped his tea. Trying to keep emotions out of it. Trying to decipher the meaning of it all. Danny was taken by an assassin. She was sighted at the cathedral. To meet with the Pope? About what?

"My God, man, don't you see?" Graham lifted his eyebrows and kept them way up on his forehead. "Shanahan is the Pope and he met with this man-killer bitch to—"

"Right " Trent nodded. "But the question is *who?*"

"Why, I should think that's *obvious!* Who would the IRA pay a million-plus to kill? Don't know where they'd got all the money." Graham grinned up at Pym pacing the hall. He held up another long finger, waggling it at her. "But they always manage, don't they? No, there's no stopping them when they really want a thing. Armed robbery. Bank heist. Whatever!" He winked at Trent and said, eyeing Pym tugging at the skirts of her jacket, "I was speaking of the IRA, not the women."

Graham laughed a low, sweet chortle. Trent smiled, tolerant but not too kindly, his mind wide awake now, racing ahead.

"I've sent a team out Killarney way," Graham continued. "I'll have something for those sniveling reporters now! Solve *Brighton* and *Neave* and bag a *seven-figure hitter* to boot!"

His grin sparkled as if onstage. Faust, rolling about in the tangle of his life. Holding his enormous belly. Tiny bubbles bursting merrily in his head at the very thought of royalty!

"I'm sending Pym over to Buckingham Palace straightaway." Graham's lower lip curled out at Trent as if at a bad taste. "I say, you look a bit *stale*. Might need a fresh shirt, old boy. See if I can't get an immediate appointment. Break into his schedule! Won't be put off! Frightfully sorry, do pardon me, and all that, but this is *priority!*"

"Sir—"

"Don't you worry about a thing, Stanford. I'll handle this." *Like Mr. Lord God Almighty Winston bloody Churchill,* he thought.

The night had been too long, and the day was coming on too fast. Trent shuffled back over the circumstances that were beginning to look like proof. Had the IRA hired Somberg? But something was missing. Out of tune. Why hadn't Jessica called?

"So where are the Americans on this?" he asked.

"The *what?*" Graham looked at him as if he'd spoken Chinese.

"The child, sir. *Danny Moore.* What did your report have to say about him?"

"The *child?* Didn't say a bloody thing about the child! Why would you consider him at a time like this? He's not our problem. I should say he's nothing more than an amusement to this Medusa."

Out of the riot in Trent's head, from a quiet corner, Graham's announcement repeated itself. "Buckingham Palace, did you say? Graham, I'd have thought we'd meet Mrs. T at Number Ten."

"Thatcher?" Graham's happy face curdled into a fatuous leer. "The target's not Thatcher! They wouldn't try *that woman* again. Not after Brighton. With security *doubled?* You think they don't know that? Why, they've spies in our own office." His fist pounded into a soft open palm, the fist aching for a spy to roughen up. "Certainly that's not why they hired this *oral-fixated bitch!*"

"*If* they hired her," Trent said softly, wondering why Graham would exclude Thatcher entirely. Seemed an error in judgment. So excessive as to almost appear intentional. As the work of a spy.

"You've been on Brighton too long, Stanford. You've become bunker-minded. Bogged down. Caught up in superfluous detail, like this *child.* Can't see the forest for the trees!" Graham gave a bright smile, squinting, as if into a room of exploding flash strobes. Graham in his heyday. Graham caught up in a potboiler. Graham already reading his reviews. Stardom can change the people around you, he knew that and was prepared for it. "An amusing notion, though," he added. "Medusa out to tag the Iron Lady." He couldn't restrain a base grin. "Women are rather harsher on other women than we men, you know. Subject to certain, shall we say *jealousies*? Imagine what Medusa would cook up for the Old Girl."

"I think that's a question worthy of serious consideration," Trent ventured. "I'd say it's the *first* question that should be addressed. *How* would she hit Mrs. T?"

Graham never heard him. He was on his feet, hand on the door, grimacing as if ready to bull through it. "I'll run all this by committee, but I'm sure they'll agree. There can only be one target for this man-killing bitch who must defile her victims. The *obvious* target. The symbol of Great Britain's *virility.* The Prince of Wales!"

He swung open the door and Pym was on him in a flash. Trent took a minute to finish his tea, looking at the acoustical ceiling full of holes. How often we do see what we want to see? Find what we need to find? Jessica looked at the sketches and saw the same face. Graham needed the spectacular and found it. It appeared the sketches were related. And the Mahoney connection suggested Shanahan was the Pope. This was not an overwrought heart speaking; Brighton and Danny were linked. He glanced back at Pym studying Graham with a judicious superiority as he unloaded his tale. *Why take the boy?* Didn't make sense. Not the work of a professional. What kind of woman was this? Charles her target? Didn't seem to fit her. Trent knew; he half-knew; then he knew nothing again.

"I'm so happy!" she sang in this exotic foreign country with its bizarre customs and a difficult new language. Living there required practice and many changes, but she was willing to learn. She rolled her eyes and glanced down her lace gown to where her penis was tucked into the maxi pad, pulled up between her legs. "And so *hard*," she whispered to her maker.

"But you no longer have to be hard to be happy!" Somberg said and kissed her soft cheek, a hand on that perfectly gorgeous ass, now with her butterfly signature on it. She had the fragrance of lilacs. Totally attentive, filled with fresh desire. Her sister was going to love her twin. What a birthday gift! The fuck of the century! Nothing like it, making love to yourself.

She was sent down the elevator and through the lobby alone. A beautiful gliding form, self-consciously graceful. The manager glanced up to see this bird-boned girl in the soft drama of black lace. He returned her addictive smile and almost called after her, but it was a trifle embarrassing to ask this young woman to verify her sex. Wasn't that the *boy* who checked in yesterday? She was the perfect image of the boy, though tongue-tied, but so pretty. So glowing, she looked as though she had just lost her virginity. The lonely beauty floated through the front door and to a waiting limousine. The manager, who had a reputation for vigilance, pulled the passport for Room 740. With the girl's smile still suspended in romantic memory, he checked it against that of Kim Lee. Their faces were identical. The manager shook his neat white head and looked speculatively at the door, wondering if it wasn't a typo, the "M" under "Sex."

Father Shanahan's Datsun rattled through the dark alleys while Jessica stared at a Killarney the tourist never saw. Gone was the Disney beauty. The back side of the town looked like an old woman, rose blossoms washed from her cheeks, her complexion cracked and peeling, blistered into warts, a grime lodged in the broken mortar joints that grinned at Jessica like rotten teeth.

She pulled herself into chocolate-colored jeans. Loosened the hospital gown, wriggled into a blond turtleneck as pain cycled up her back and stabbed into her neck, giving the night a fog that was not there. She looked vacantly at Father Shanahan.

"Why are you kidnapping me?"

"I'm not kidnapping ye."

"All right. Why are you taking me for a drive?"

To stop you from interfering in that fine Thatcher murder, the patriot thought. "To shield ye from another attack," the priest said.

"So, the bees were . . .?"

"Not our doing."

" '*Our,*' " she said. "Now what does that mean?"

He didn't reply. He parked the car. She took her herringbone jacket as he helped her through the back door of a pub. A note on the door: "Closed for Repairs." She entered a lukewarm haze of neon beer signs. The fragrance of whiskey rose as a vapor from creaking floorboards awash in sawdust, as if to soften for the tourists the blood-and-glory outfit that resided here. Complete with costume. Six men in sweaters and corduroys stood footed in long shadows, considering their dazzling reflections in a gold-speckled mirror. Cheeks and eyes made greenish by the glow of a Guinness neon sign that tinted the brass-topped bar on which they leaned drinking stout. They glanced her way as she passed through dark beer-stained tables and chairs. She looked at the tin-plated ceiling gleaming with firelight like an oven. And now here was the sweltering heat of the peat fire.

Shanahan positioned a wing chair in front of the fire, easing her into it saying, " 'Tis my favorite chair. My thinking chair."

The faded burgundy leather chair was wide and warm, and she sank with relief into its soft comfort. She was drained and empty, an emotional wreck. Shoulders hurt. Legs hurt. Fingers hurt. Her jaws ached from clenching her teeth. Stoned on some kind of dope that seemed to make the fire flicker in slow motion the way all things move in Ireland. She had lived too long in pain, denied the nourishment of all that is happy and hopeful; living in the past, without the power to make her future, like Ireland. It was a life therapy could not fix, this extensive bout with the bogey man of depression that would leave her comatose. In firelight, Jessica saw something of the bogey man, dark and brooding. She closed her eyes against Father Shanahan who she could not understand, and now memories tumbled back in pieces, sometimes whole pieces, sometimes fragments, but the theme of every remembrance was Danny.

27

"ARE YE SLEEPING, child?"

Danny was in bed beside her, his arm around her, kissing her ear. She held him tight and thought he had come to her bed because he had a bad dream. She heard someone calling from far away, and now she knew she was dreaming. The rarity of Danny translated by dream was only some monologue with herself, a kind of masturbation of the mind, felt so good; an attempt to solve a murder of love in a court that made no sense. The court of dream. She was pleading her case before the ruthless judge. *Exhibit No. 1, your Honor: my everlasting dream confessions. I am seriously in love with this child, and I'm probably on the verge of a nervous breakdown if I haven't already passed it, and now that I think about it, I know I have.* Why was she in a court? Why did she have to defend herself when it was she who was shot and left for dead with her son held by the bitch? Now the court was gone and it came to her faintly, the little flute in Beethoven's seventh, the happy tune of hope riding over the exploratory hunger of dream that never ended, with that faraway voice louder now, calling over the heroic seventh now in full swing, the whole symphony giving back the tune of hope, so grand!

"Child, 'tis time to wake."

Her eyes opened to a skeletal face of white hair and black eyes. Her sleep had lasted only minutes but seemed like hours.

"Have a sip of this." Shanahan gave a her glass of golden Irish whiskey. She tried it. Felt like she swallowed a flame.

"Ye look frightened." The Father pulled a chair up, sitting down beside her in the glow of the fireplace that radiated warmth over cold despair. "Don't be frightened. We will watch over ye."

"Who is 'we?'"

Shanahan took a moment to baptize his throat in drink. She glanced to the bar, where a hostile audience was eyeing her. As she looked at them, their eyes went to the ceiling. And she looked up to the see the glimmer of fire over the tin-plated ceiling.

"We are those of us committed to the Irish struggle."

"The Irish struggle? I thought you were a priest."

"I am a priest," he said in the art of confession. "A servant of God who is *also* committed to the cause of Irish freedom. Are ye familiar with our struggle?"

Firelight flickered over his fascinating hollowed-out face, and Jessica found she could not stopping looking at him. One side of his face was the state of misery, the other was bliss, together they evoked wonder. "England still has part of your island?" she said, speaking to the misery. "Belfast or something?"

"Aye. Ours is a struggle that has lasted eight hundred years. In 1921 we freed all our people but those in the six northern-most counties. Taken by an army eight hundred years ago. Held to this day by a Brit army. But what is time to love? 'Tis only sorrow and fury, the balance between them the making of a killing force."

"You're not a—" Jessica caught herself and stopped.

"A terrorist?" he offered.

She nodded and took another drink.

"Well, now," he said, " 'tis a slippery word, *terrorist.* The definition of which hinges on your point of view. Was George Washington a terrorist? Patrick Henry? Or that hothead, John Quincy Adams?"

"Gee, I don't know; I always thought of Washington and the others as *patriots.*"

"Aye. But the only difference between patriot and terrorist is *winning* and *losing.* The killing is the same. Had Washington and the others lost, they'd have been hanged. Ye'd know them today as terrorists. Their names would be a curse. Their story forgotten."

"I never thought of it that way," she said, feeling a kind of delicate horror unfold beside her. Caught here in an ancient war. In purposeless pain that she knew well. But Ireland didn't amount to a hill of beans next to Danny. Couldn't really afford to care about Ireland, past or present. What did he know about Danny?

Shanahan looked away to an American map above the fireplace. It was pummeled with hundreds of stickpins that flagged hometowns of tourists who had stopped in for a pint. Wanted to hear a tune on the pipe and fiddle. Catch the brogue in full flower. Maybe find somebody who believed in fairy people. And right they were, the fairy people did exist, one sat beside the lovely Yank now. He frustrated the hell out of the Brits, the way he went missing whenever they searched for him. Shanahan smiled at the thought.

"What would ye Yanks do if Maine, New Hampshire, Vermont, Massachusetts, Connecticut, and New York were still under the Union Jack? Would ye sit and hope that *someday* John Bull would surrender them? Or would ye do as your patriot fathers did? Would ye slaughter the redcoats from behind bricks and trees? Murder the bloody Brits till they packed it in and headed for home? Gave the whole thing up as a bad show."

Jessica glanced down to his black boots, scarred and cut.

"There is only one language the Brit understands: *violence.* They never left anywhere on their own. Not America. Not Israel. Not India or Egypt or Iran or Cyprus. And he won't leave Ireland, not until it becomes too costly to stay, too painful to abide."

"So," Jessica said, taking another shot of courage. "Do you kill people, *Father* Shanahan?"

"The enemy dictates the method," he replied coolly.

"Then you're—" She swallowed a big lump in her throat. Had the bitter, coppery taste of fear. "You're IRA?"

"I'm a member of the Irish Republican Army," the priest said, the name rolling deep and sacred into the night.

Jessica stared. "You *really* kill people?"

"There are some things in life worth killing for," he said, looking at her closely. "Some things worth dying for."

"Like my son," Jessica heard the Irish whiskey say.

Shanahan looked straight into her. "Would ye kill the bitch who took him?"

"In a New York minute!"

"Aye," he said, seeing the fire in her eyes. "Our grand poet, Yeats, called it a 'terrible beauty.' "

They lapsed into a silence. Looking at each other with the knowledge of what they shared. Jessica and Mother Ireland. Danny as the six northern counties. Stolen with violence, mother left for dead. And Jessica wondered, *Would Danny still be hers if she didn't recover him this week? Would he hers if she didn't find him this year? Or in ten years? Or in eight hundred years?* Love was a thing, she knew in her heart, that time did not touch. What was wrong eight hundred years ago was wrong today. The only way to make it right was to return that which you took. Would the bitch return Danny? Jessica knew better than to put stock in dreams of fairies. Though she had a sense of fairy people, made accessible to her in the pub. Felt almost as if they were blood relations, she and Ireland, mothers in a tempest, aching for their children.

"So," Jessica fumbled on. "*Who* is this woman who took my son? You know her, don't you?"

She sensed the tension more prevalent than ever. An almost visible aura of tension filled the sweet whiskey-scented air, the muscles of the Father's firm jaw tightened visibly as he leaned into her chair and whispered, "She's a contractor."

"What does that mean?"

"She's a *specialist*. A problem solver."

"And what problem was she contracted to solve?"

The patriot hesitated. Took a dip into the whiskey.

"She's an assassin," the priest confessed.

The pub started a slow spin. Jessica closed her eyes. She saw the sketch of the ice woman. Dana Jenkins. Nordstrom. Now Sterling in a pew in the cathedral, her arm around Danny, laughing as she called after Jessica, *"Run, Mommy, run! But where are you running to?"* It seemed that she had run headlong into the IRA. From out of the whirling dark she asked, "*Why* did she take Danny?"

"It was her own doing. We knew *nothing* about it. But the lad is safe. On that ye have my word."

"Your word?" she snapped back, too fast. "As a *priest* or as a *terrorist?*"

"As a man of God. The lad is *safe.*"

Jessica gripped the chair arms to stop the spinning. Voices calling to her. Like a mother calling for her son. Frantic voices. A voice like a prayer. Now angry. Shouting at her to *do!* She was just sitting and out there her son was growing up without her, and she hated herself the way Hamlet had hated and waited. Why was she thinking of *Hamlet?* How could she think of such things in an Irish pub? She pushed *Hamlet* away. Still she sat. It seemed she had been sitting for years with the fury building. But that was not true, in that time she had been working her ass off to reach Danny, but getting nowhere. Sitting, sitting, sitting. On the very edge of combustion. Waiting for the bang. One day the world would hear it. *"This is crazy!"* she shouted, feeding on the Irish fire in her glass. "He's just a baby! What good could it do to take him?"

"I can't tell ye the why," Shanahan said, keeping his cool.

"Go to hell!" she shrieked. Suddenly out of herself. The tempest no longer in the teapot. Felt wonderful. So Irish. Control blown to hell. Shanahan reached out to her, but Jessica shied away from him. *"I don't believe you!"* she cried. "I don't believe any of this! Where is Danny? How do you know he's safe?"

"I know where he is," Shanahan said softly. "I'm going to—"

"Where? Where is he?"

Shanahan shook his oblong head. "I can't—"

"God damn you!" Hands curled into fist. The whiskey and the pain drugs and the fire lashed out at him. She hit something. Maybe his face. It felt like stone. Somehow she wasn't surprised.

He grabbed her wrist. "Listen to me! *You—!"* He raised a hand to strike her, eyes like red coals socketed hot in his skull. "I've put the whole operation in jeopardy by telling ye this much," the patriot hissed into her ear. "I *can't* tell ye another thing! Do ye understand? Not another thing!" He caught himself and released her, the black misery coming over him. "But I've been in a turmoil since I met yer lad," the priest admitted, calming and becoming sonorous. "I knew then we had erred. We should have *never* brought in an outsider. We must do our own work."

"What do you mean, *'work?'* " A knot of tears in her throat. Suddenly tired. She was so very tired. When was it going to end? When would she see him again? Would he be grown? Would he have forgotten her? Or would she never see him again, or hold him, or tell him how much she loved him, how she ached for him every damn day, but never let go of the love no matter the hurt? Couldn't let go. Now she wondered if she'd be dead and buried before this was over. The Irish tenor singing again, high and sweet, that song of a father's grieving love. *"But come ye back when summer's in the meadow, or when the valley's hushed and white with snow, 'Tis I'll be there in sunshine or in shadow, Oh, Danny boy, oh, Danny boy, I love you so."* Tears were sliding down her reddened cheeks. Her hazel eyes shimmering white with tears. And then Pit was there, she could somehow feel his arm around her, his low, commanding voice inside her soul: *Don't you ever give up on that boy, Jess. No matter the hurt. Don't you ever give up.*

"Things have gone wrong in this," Shanahan admitted, "and the biggest wrong is what's been done to ye and yer lad." He took a good, long drink. It tasted like remorse. It had the exact taste. All his life he had been a man possessed by a roiling, twisting soul, like a blown, dark cloud never at peace. Caught between God and Ireland. But now, as he looked into the eyes of the weeping mother, his two faiths united in a truth. He found the words for the truth and gave them to the unrelenting Irish fire. "Freedom is worthless if it comes washed in the blood of the innocent."

"Danny!" Jessica cried. "I don't give a fuck about Ireland! Do you understand? *Where's Danny?"*

Shanahan looked at her, his eyes coming back from afar, and he knew what he had to do. The priest spoke to her now, reciting a good Psalms: "The Lord careth for the strangers; He defendeth the fatherless and widowed: as for the way of the ungodly, He turneth it upside down."

"What are you talking about?" Jessica said, staring at him, his face radiant. He had changed. He was suddenly someone else.

"I'm going to put it right," he said with assurance. "No matter what. I should have done this from the beginning."

"Done *what?* I don't understand!"

He smiled at her and the smile was not crooked but shone straight as the sun. "I'm going to fetch yer lad," he said.

"Fetch him? From where?"

"I cannot tell ye. But I have seen him. I spoke to him. I met his eyes that would not let me go. By Monday ye shall be reunited. Ye shall return to Chicago, the lad at yer side. So help me God."

Something went wild in Jessica. In rapture! Her spirit way up high! Church bells peeling in her heart in a wave of joy that she imagined was something like the savage glee that all Ireland would know if the British were to announce the return of the six lost counties. *Peace!* She was at last to be whole again. But it seemed impossible and she was terrified to believe in it. She sank in the chair. Color drained from the pub, turning black and white, now fading, all contrast lost. She closed her eyes and wanted to let go but could not. She mumbled, "I want to come with you."

"Ye cannot," he said, all tolerance and sweetness. "Things must come to pass, as I've said. Ye are to stay here. *Sleep.* Soon enough he'll be with ye and all will be well. Perhaps ye'll think more kindly of me when ye're at home in the love of the child."

"I don't know whether to believe you or not." Jessica floated in a Volvo filling with water, swirling with stinging bees, bits and pieces of the past floating around her, faces about to take shape, voices about to speak. The Father lifted her out of the car. She saw the bees stinging him. He had taken on her pain to save her. "Don't know if I can trust you," she said to the dark.

"And do ye trust the *Englishman?*"

"Englishman?"

"The one who let Cullinane's Thatch."

"Trent." Jessica smiled in her almost-sleep.

"Aye, Trent. Is he in the service of the queen?"

"I hope so," she said in the grip of a love affair that like all love affairs was timeless and without sequence. And now she was beside him, dripping and wet by their fire, naked in his arms.

"Does he know about *Thatcher?*"

"Yes," she replied. "He knows about Brighton."

Shanahan took the whiskey glass from her hand.

" 'A terrible beauty,' " Jessica muttered.

"Aye," Shanahan said. "A terrible beauty is to come."

He kissed her lightly on the forehead in gratitude for the gift of his found soul. "Good night, child," he said, priest and patriot united. "God go with ye. May it go well with ye always."

* * *

Trent returned the gold receiver to its cradle which sat on an eighteenth-century desk. It glowed with morning sun in the garishly red damask silk room. He looked about the lavish room as though lost. A refrain in him that would not quit, even in Buckingham Palace: *Why in the devil hasn't she called? Why can't I reach her?*

Last night he had rung the Garda in Killarney, asked if an officer would run out to the Gap to check on Jessica. The call was passed to a Sergeant Duffy; he gave Trent another number, asked to call back tomorrow. Trent had just spoken with him. Duffy had checked on Cullinane's Thatch. Jessica was not at the cottage, and it was evident she had not been there all night. He said there was no sign of the Volvo, and Trent assumed she had taken a room in town. But the sergeant had made inquiries. Rang hotels and B and Bs. Jessica was not registered in town. Duffy suggested she had moved on in her search. "Perhaps to Cork," he said. "Or maybe out Killorglin way. You might try there."

It was possible she was following a lead. But wouldn't she call? And there was something in Duffy's voice. What? False? Knowing? Too pleasant? Where was his concealed hostility for the English? Why had he volunteered information about the car? How did he know it was a Volvo? Had he checked the rental agency? Was the good sergeant just being thorough? Or was there something left unsaid?

A ridiculously tall door, cut as if for giants, swung open. Graham in his Sunday best, a smart royal attaché waiting behind him. *"Stanford!"* he hissed with a florid face. "The prince *is* waiting. If you don't mind?"

Trent left the phone but not the worry. Apace with Graham marching after the attache, ever the obedient servant. Down the corridor, great vault with its armorial bearings. High and mighty enough for either of England's queens, Elizabeth or Margaret.

"Medusa is an extraordinary business, isn't she?" Graham said, nodding to a report in Trent's hand, a background the Swedes had put together on Kristian Somberg. "Raped by the priest fits the myth, I'd say. Did you see the bit about her *father?"*

"Right." Trent gave an absent nod, glancing at the personal history. Why not call Jessica's neighbor in Chicago? What was his name? He may have heard from her. "I'd say she has a thing for fathers, be they natural or spiritual," Trent said, turning pages to gaze at a photo of the priest hacked to bits, sprawled in a narrow confessional, the kill done with the ugliness of emotional illness. No composure. No artistry. Not the style of the killings he had found, defined by a woman's creativity. *Feminine Mystique* would be the title of those global hits. *She's Come Undone* is what came to mind, looking at the priest, his eyes turned back in his head. Hacked with a sword. Same killer? He thought probably not.

"He's going to ask about the Rubens Hotel," Graham confided in a muffled tone. "IRA claimed the credit this morning."

"Right. Heard about it. Bring me up to speed."

"The bomb was planted behind the laboratory. Same feckless bomber who did the Grand, I'd say. You know the Rubens was on the bomb calendar found on the envelope in Glasgow."

"Yes, but it was published in the paper, wasn't it?" Was Sergeant Duffy lying through his teeth? But why would he? "It could be anyone, Graham. An IRA copy-cat."

"Why would they bother? Then ring the radio station and claim the mess in the name of the IRA?" Graham gave a muffled snort.

"Right," Trent said, still thinking of Jessica. Have to run over to Killarney but couldn't very well walk out on Charles.

"Only *one* dead," Graham said, passing Trent another file. "I notified next of kin myself. Sincerest regrets to a mother in Honolulu. Victim a Harvard boy. One Kim Lee. Not much left to identify, flesh melted in the blast. But the hotel manager knew him. Or rather, knew the *dress.*" Graham gave a haughty laugh. "What a pretty way to be found. Caught in women's clothes! Awful shock for the mother. The dress, that is. But the sisters didn't seem surprised. Their pet, I suspect. No personal effects to send them. Couldn't very well send his dress, could I?" Graham laughed again. "So I sent the passport. Testament of his presence."

Graham went silent as they approached gilded doors.

Trent leaned into him, looking straight ahead, voice dropped to a conspiratorial mutter. "Bit of a gamble, seeing only Charles on this. If we miss and *she* hits elsewhere, could be the old heave-ho. Both of us shot at dawn. I'd send this Medusa report straight round to Number Ten."

"The prince, Stanford! Forget that woman. It's the *prince!*"

He called them to the fire, where he stood at the mantel with his glass of whiskey. Duffy reported the London call, and though Shanahan couldn't imagine how the mother had come to know a C-13 agent, it was evident that Brighton had made its way to Killarney. He now ordered the Fox and Sweeney to the isle of Gibraltar.

"Ye're to report to Mary Flanagan," Shanahan told them. "She has a safe house there. The grace of it near-criminal. Lay low. Mary will harbor you till the trouble has passed."

"Ah, well," Dessie Quinn said, turning to the men gathered around, "that's the way of it, is it? Punishment for our crimes." With his youthful, sharp, foxlike features he smiled up at tall, square-shouldered Sweeney. "A bloody *holiday and a tan!*"

Sweeney said nothing to the quip. They simply could not get anywhere at all without reigning that stuff in. The wise-cracking was but fleeing from the intense and honest.

"And what about ye, Father?" Duffy said. The sergeant was a tough-looking man in a blue Garda uniform with a heavy gut made of beer muscle. "Ye can't stay here with that *Brit* coming, which he's sure to do."

"Did he frighten ye, Sergeant?" the Fox goaded.

Duffy shot the smirking kid a split-eyed look. "Ye should have heard him on the phone," Duffy boasted, his pale slab of face gleaming like his oiled dark hair. "Why, I could melt butter in his mouth with all his *heart-longing!*" The men laughed, egging him on. "Oh, he's a *whiner* that one is! The poor lovesick Brit devil sounded all *warm and weepy!*"

"Let 'im weep!" one of the men called out.

"Aye, but he'll be coming round to fetch her soon enough." Duffy nodded to Jessica asleep in the chair behind the father.

"He'll be fucking coming to fetch *ye*," the Fox shot back, "when he finds ye have *her!*"

"I'm ready to play his game. I'll make a lovely home for him in the bog!"

The men laughed like playhouse gods, and Shanahan waited till the play died. He caught the eyes of young Sean McShane standing troubled and anxious in his cap. "At dawn on Monday, ye're to meet me in yer Cessna at the airfield in Grantham."

McShane nodded with a frown of perplexity. He was not one to ask questions. His talent thrived on flying through the storms.

"*Grantham?*" Duffy blurted out. "Why England, Father? Why not go to America? Stay for a season in Boston with O'Grady."

Shanahan waited a moment in the shadows of the fire. Didn't Samson slay the Philistines of Ashkelon? Didn't Gideon destroyed the Midianites? He shall lay waste to the British. "I've given my word," he said with the firelight gleam in his eyes. "I'll make it good. I'll fetch the stolen child," he told them, "send him back with McShane, then do that British Jezebel meself."

Duffy half-laughed, looking around at the others. "*Ye* will kill Thatcher?" he said, staring disbelievingly at the father.

"Aye. Who better? I should have taken the job in the first place. 'Tis my right, my country; 'twill be an honor. Thatcher, damn her," Shanahan mused. "Don't know how she escaped us at the Grand. History was to be written that day. And now...." He downed the last of his golden whiskey, finding there the prophet Habakkuk. " 'The vision is yet for an appointed time, but at the end it shall speak and not lie: though it tarry, wait for it, it will surely come, it will not tarry.' "

A narrow wind complained as it ran through the alley while the men exchanged silent glances, wondering if the funerals and the coffins had been working on the priest's mind. Had he borne too much for too long and borne it alone? Had his Irish sense of tragedy taken him at last? Sweeney watched him toss a peat brick to the fire that licked it up, the pretty flames dancing over the tin ceiling, glinting back orange upon the men like hell itself. The men of Killarney knew their priest as a patriot like the men of old. A hard man who came to count on the world being hard. In his sixty-six years the patriot had never fired a shot or drawn a knife or so much as thrown a punch for a cause other than Ireland. And in his forty-two years as their priest never ceased extolling the virtues of righteous violence against Brits who had forfeited the right to live by being in Northern Ireland. It was not only justice but wisdom to gun down the British terrorists. They had often heard their priest quote Christ, " 'I have come not to bring peace, but a sword.' "

Once settled on what the priest believed to be the moral course, the patriot could be utterly unscrupulous in its pursuit. The patriot never regretted an act committed for Ireland, though the priest grieved for the children lost. Not all agreed with violence, the IRA outlawed in Ireland, but agreeing was not to be confused with authentic loyalty and admiration.

But not all were dazzled by the fire of the priest. "Father, what difference does it make?" Sweeney asked in his big quiet voice. "They'll just find another Thatcher, or a thousand more."

Shanahan did not reply immediately. He lifted the bellows and worked the fire, taking his time. "Random killing achieves nothing but the world's scorn," he said to the fire. "It's turned us into jackals that hide in a dark that has come to live in our souls. We achieve nothing by taking children and civilians, by the hundreds, by the bloody thousands. And yet, murder begets murder," Shanahan said to the fire. At his hands, smoldering coals began to blaze.

A terrible beauty. "Vengeance is our work, not God's. The one we seek is the one who begets murder," he said as he rose, his fury a tight fit in the pub. "Thatcher has sowed the wind," he thundered. "Now let her reap the whirlwind!"

The men stood in silence as Shanahan's thunder rolled away so there was only the wind prying at the door, strumming against the windows, sharpening on the building, the wind itself a terror that the world could not stop.

"Fine," Sweeney argued against the wind. "Then let the bloody *contractor* do her. Thatcher will be just as dead."

"But by whose hand?" Shanahan flared, flushing to crimson. A fist pounded the mantel, making his whiskey glass jump. "Don't ye see it, man? If it's not our finger that pulls the trigger then there's no honor in it."

"Honor?" Sweeney scoffed. "There's no fucking honor in death! We've not entered this to *die,* father. But to *live* free."

"Look at this woman," Shanahan said, pointing to Jessica in the shadows. "She's been shot and wrecked in a hundred ways. But still she goes on. She keeps searching. Keeps believing! And what do we do? We 'break stone,' as Yeats said. That's all we do with our bombs. We kill the wrong ones, die for the wrong reasons."

"I don't know, Father." Sweeney looked speculatively into the fire. "Maybe none of it will ever make any difference." He turned to the men around him. "Maybe the Brits will never leave Ireland. Maybe it's just a banshee's cry in the wind." And now to Shanahan: "Maybe ye've lost yer mind."

"My *mind!*" Shanahan roared. "I lost my mind years ago! 'Tis not my mind I'll go to England to find. 'Tis my *soul.*"

Sweeney went silent and then nodded, making a brief show of penitence. The Father, as always, had it right. The living must be done with the soul. The men stood tight-lipped, listening to the wind, something tight wrapped around their hearts, growing tighter within. They waited for some safer vision, but it was not coming. The father put the bellows away. He took up his drink and stepped back to the shadows to tuck the blanket tighter around Jessica.

"She *is* our story, don't ye see? Our lost hope entombed in her heart. She would sing our story—I have seen her singing with her eyes—even while her heart is breaking for her lad." Now his voice almost floated on the air rarified by the sweet whiskey and the peat fire, never taking his eyes off Jessica as he recited the old Psalm: "By the waters of Babylon we sat down and wept: when we remembered thee, O Sion. As for our harps, we hanged them up: upon the trees that are therein. For they that led us away captive required of us then a song, and melody, in our heaviness: Sing us one of the songs of Zion. How shall we sing the Lord's song: in a strange land?" Now to the men, with tears standing in his eyes: "If I forget thee, O Jerusalem: let my right hand forget her cunning. If I do not remember thee, let my tongue cleave to the roof of my mouth: yea, if I prefer not Jerusalem in my mirth."

He had them weepy eyed, every fierce man, and the love of the mother eased their hearts. She had become something of an icon in her gentle sleep, and it didn't seem the gentleness could reemerge as fire. So little of women did the men of Killarney know.

"No one is to enter this pub," Shanahan said with a sideways glower to Duffy. "Make a cot for her; she can't sleep in a chair. McShane will fly the lad back to Killarney. Ye're to meet him. Then drive mother and child to Cork; see them onto a plane."

"Aye." Duffy stood there, sad frown for the great father, his departure now realized, gathering speed, Duffy's placatory tone raised to entreaty. "And should the *Brit* call back?"

"Dance with him. But tell him nothing."

"Oh, I'll make *him* dance!" Duffy shouted to an accompaniment of relieved laughter at this well-timed joke. The sergeant marched on. "He'll dance a fine jig before I'm through with him!" There was more hearty laughter followed by a hollow silence.

"I expect to see all of ye in mass," Shanahan said from the dark. "Sweeney, ye and Quinn come early. We'll pray together."

Sweeney started to protest but knew his mind was made up a long time ago. The priest had taken a lifetime to mastermind his candidacy for martyrdom and there was no dissuading him now.

"How will ye do it, Father?" Duffy asked.

"Ye *really* won't return?" another said.

"Not till Judgment Day," Shanahan replied, knowing exactly how he'd kill Jezebel, but wondering how he'd do Gorgon.

"And ye'll give yer life?" Sweeney said, knowing he would.

" 'Tis not mine to give," Shanahan retorted. "Never has been. Out of my hands. All in His." He was ready for this end and felt himself lucky he was allowed to choose the how and when. "Light a candle for me," he said. "And one for Ireland, as well."

"And this is yer final lesson?" Sweeney asked his teacher.

"Aye. Stand and kill. Kill the ones that kill." Shanahan stepped out of the shadows to give them a final dose of the light in his eyes. "I'll save the lad," he said softly. "Then put an end to Margaret bloody Thatcher once and for all. I'll carve her not as a dish for the gods, but hew her as a carcass fit for hounds."

28

SHE WAS RAISED from the dead. She didn't know she was dead but she was and now she was alive. She was a mystery to herself and Melissa was astonished, so now the living of every day was the discovery of herself. She was no longer a boy and not a girl, but she knew them both and recognized them as the thieves crucified on either side of her, neither of which is the self. She could love the thieves, but she dare not trust them. Trust only the self.

She rolled the ladder over to the volumes of Dostoyevsky and began handing the heavy books to Alexia. She passed down *The Idiot, Crime and Punishment, Devils, The Brothers Karamazov,* and Alexia stacked them on a trestle table. Melissa took down what looked and felt like a lightweight, *Memories from the House of the Dead.*

"Ever read this one?" Alexia asked from the library floor of Warnock awash with boxes, movers hustling in the hall outside.

"Can't say that I have. It's about prison, right?" She only guessed that, seeing the loner behind bars on the cover.

"Yeah, and it's not what I'd call pretty." Alexia smiled up with pale blue eyes and boy-short white-blonde hair, and a golden tan from having spent a week swimming with dolphins in Florida. "Dostoyevsky was in prison, you know."

"No shit."

"Yeah. Political thing. Went down for what he believed." She spoke with a slight Aussie accent, a Norwegian based in Sydney but always on planes. "This book," Alexia held up the thin book, "made the others." She was referring to the fat stack of classics on the table. "His books before *House of the Dead* were a kind of escape from prison. But he got over that in this book and you might try it because, really, you're from the House of the Dead, you know?"

"As a guy, you mean?" Alexia had some kind of high-powered consultancy job and Melissa found her fascinating. An exercise in independence. She was said to be great pals with Giorgio Armani, who gave her clothes. She wore them like a guy; she was never worn by her clothes. Had she been a guy? Melissa wondered.

"Sure. Male is a prison experience. Thing is, after *House of the Dead,* Dostoevsky became a great novelist because he *let go* of the shit that happened to him. That's when he could get into his thing: characters. Made them fascinating. Powerful, actually."

"And then came *Crime and Punishment,* and *Brothers,* and all the rest." Melissa knew those books, they were famous.

"Right. The key to those classics is a theme he bagged after *House of the Dead.* Made all the difference. Made his work fun."

"Which is . . .?" Melissa looked down expectantly from the ladder to the boyish pretty face into yoga and meditation.

"Murder, murder, murder, murder!" Alexia sang, and they both laughed, knowing it was true, having been murdered themselves.

"His killers weren't mindless brutes," Alexia said, loading the Dostoevsky into the box, labeling it "Heavy Stuff." "They had a philosophy. It's what keeps life from being a drag, you know?"

"Sure," Melissa said in a blackberry velvet top and jeans. A bit dressy, but she was really into velvet. "Have you read this one?" she said, handing down a Kurt Vonnegut, *Player Piano.*

Alexia smiled on the thin little volume. "All about pleasure, dear. I guess Kristian told you about pleasure?"

"Pleasure is the essence of living," Melissa recited.

"You got it. And pleasure is *contributing.*" Alexia dropped the Vonnegut into a box with a framed snapshot from a vintage car race she and Kristian's baby sister did from Paris to Peking in which a Chinese big shot, with a security guard who carried an elephant gun, was crushed by his own car. Changing a tire when the brake gave. Mashed his windpipe, made an eggshell of his skull. Grizzly death but the Chinese wanted it that way, and for them the work had to be done with great decorum. "In *Player Piano*," she said, supplying the sweet with a missing link in her training, "the people who are depressed—the nutcases—are the ones with all the leisure time. The elite work. Work is fulfillment. And that's proven true in our experience. We all work. Not because we have to, but because *giving* is fulfilling."

"Gotcha! Kristian told me: *you must give to receive.*"

"Actually, that's Sankhya. Hinduism." Alexia packed the set of D. H. Lawrence books in with the Vonnegut, though most people wouldn't put the two together. Fact is, they both wrote philosophy in the guise of entertainment. "You *enhance* yourself by giving. It's a reverse selfishness. By giving, you come out ahead."

"So, really, by giving yourself to others, you can't lose."

"Right on."

"So, giving is the way to pleasure."

"That's right. Giving *is* pleasure."

It was a little confusing, Melissa didn't understand it all, caught in a kind of hypnotic intoxication. Change had not been a quantum leap, but rather a gradual reinvention of Kim by Kristian. Though, actually, it was Kim who invented his future by way of his dream. A boy should be careful with the power of dreams, lest he become what he dreams. The old Melissa was dead, as Kim was almost dead and going fast, with the new Melissa a force to reckon with.

She had entered the London Symphony gala last night as two people in one black lace Valentino dress. A ballroom of lavish music. An opera of voices! So many gorgeous people! Kristian as a queen in satin ivory with high ruffles at her neck, steering Kim's dream girl, showing her off. She taking the heat of men's stares; Kim in a panic, but she already something of a junkie, loving the effect she had on men. Yapping away, drunk, not on champagne, but on people. Out of herself and into the good family-oriented folk from Thatcher's solidly Conservative England. Taking introductions to men forgotten on the spot, a thing that would have made Kim sulk for days. The gala a passion play, Melissa welcomed by her new extended family, many of whom had flown in for the night.

There was Robin. Small, blond, perfectly English: huge blue eyes and tiny tits. She lived in Chelsea with Carly, CFO of some worldwide financial company, their stock just split. And Zoe, dark, sultry, tall and voluptuous; will extract your whole life story in five minutes of meeting you. With a fabulously rich woman, Aurora something, from the South of France, great pals with Kristian. And the aid to Senator Klein, Clarissa, a fluffy blond, says whatever comes into her head. These were first level femmes with a schoolgirl charm, like Melissa, and Lili, an elegantly waifish brunette. Witty, bubbly with enthusiasm. Wrote children's books out of Hong Kong where she lived with Lady Sophie, an art dealer; married, she was always taking Lili on tours of India.

Then there were the cool ones of the second level. Social pretenders. Swingy bobbed hair and tits jutting out. Among these was Eve, at 34, the grande dame; Shakiar exotic looks; slim figure but no hips. With a fancier, Margarito Duarte, they had a villa in Rio. And Anna, petite, waist-deep jet-black hair. Multilingual with an encyclopedic memory. A mimic, really funny, lavishly cared for by a Peking couple, the Yatsens, totally hip communists. The most striking had to be Yalinda, redheaded with sculptured Russian cheekbones. Makes eclectic films in Paris. Currently lives with a lady Hollywood producer; has a Chanel and Prada habit she's trying to break. And brown-eyed, long-legged, natural blond, Tamara from South Africa. Wears belts as skirts to show off. Outdoorsy, but European chic; lives between Paris and New York with an anonymous drop-dead gorgeous executive headhunter, a man, or so he appeared.

There was, of course, Alexia and Isabella of the third level, the magnetic ones; they know how to use their erotic muscle. They were joined by Nicole, very black, very tempting, very English. Tall with short hair, great face, into French rock 'n' roll; she secretly lives with a famous American talk show host, so she knows every-one. And Nicole's best pal was there, Natasha. A Japanese-born Italian of Russian extraction. Long bronze hair. Cool, enigmatic. Lives in nocturnal New York, London and L.A. with Nina, CEO of a telecommunications conglomerate, a sophisticated lesbian feminist. They were year-round skiers, went wherever there was snow; Mel-issa wanted to go with them, like maybe sandwiched between them.

Melissa had expected the network to be ridiculously bright, like Amazon super-women, but there was no real sense of celebrity about them. They were all very nice people of all nations, there was a sense of business as usual about the women. It seemed silly to think of them as some international wheeler-dealer syndicate that would bring down the ancient male bastions, though they were all women who wielded power. The men in this group were much the same, their only embellishment were the femmes. These creative capitalists were mixed with the hierarchy of English establishment clustered by degrees of wealth, and to this pond were added long-necked fashion models, and wholesome young men who looked harmless, they made not a ripple in the pond. Melissa let herself be steered through gossipy little circles, eyes opened to Kristian's global perspective, with the Kim in her pretty much mute, until a ghost came gliding out of the past. A tall, raven haired beauty with a raffish red smile. Kim's heart stopped when Kristian announced, ''You remember Lucinda Chambers, don't you, dear?''

For a woman wronged, the past is never over, until the wrong has been properly changed. They had met at a Christmas party at the Honolulu Yacht Club. Kim, about to enter Harvard, was there with his mother who didn't know but had heard about the trim, elegant woman who possessed the self-assurance of a London estate heiress. Said to be patently eccentric. Had a reputation for ''odd intensities,'' and secretaries. Some said lesbian. Or bisexual. Kim was enticed. A woman in her forties, she had tits and a great accent that made her every syllable into a command. As a lark, he hit on her, then bolted in the middle of a graceless pickup line to chase after an aspiring fashion model, Melissa Brooks.

Lucinda Chambers owned many beautiful things, self-integrity her most hard-earned possession. She remained undiminished by the pubescent insult, jilted before her friends for a frivolity. She accepted this turn, pretended to ignore it, and chose instead to get even. This gorgeous, slim Hawaiian boy was obviously a lover of beauty; he had, Lucinda learned, an addiction of sorts. There was an obsessive love life, a memorial to his desire to please. He was said to be generous, sacrificed to work for the common good. He accepted misfortune, believing it somehow a con-firmation of a higher state. And his birthday was 26 August. Kim Lee became her nominee. She drew up a dossier, ten odd pages in a buff folder, and submitted the darling as a femme candidate.

The only real escape from a wronged woman is death, and Kim was dying now. Lucinda gushing on about the Valentino gown! It must, Melissa imagined from her half of Kim's contorted mind, be the *coup de grace* for Lucinda to receive Kim as an *objet d'art*. A functioning femme. It was emotional justice, he had bolted after a fashion statement, only to become one. A desirable mien. Lucinda gazed into familiar now lavish eyes, and a kind of voltage slammed into Melissa, boosted by madness, a beauty elixir. She was, she knew, a person split. A gender speed freak, flashing at the speed of light from dream to reality, only dream had become reality.

Reality an emotional disaster. Chronic hysteria a breath away.

The air in their reunion was charged, and Kim felt other eyes regarding him with peculiar intensity. He glanced around. Robin and Zoe had their hands over their mouths, their cheeks reddened. Eve and Yalinda whispering like thieves. Anna turned away in a muffled laugh. Nicole and Natasha were smiling brightly, and their giddiness blew through him. He looked to a fine gold chain at his right ankle, Kristian put it there after their love that still burned, and he could feel the pricks of Heidi's tattoo like the stitches of a new soul. He was wrecked. Felt like an idiot for having messed with Lucinda. He saw himself as a boy in a woman's straightjacket. Miserable. Depressed. A female grotesque. He was ugly, homely, plain. Not interesting. Not gifted. A loser. He could never be pretty, but in defeat he was never closer to the soul of Woman whose Goddess was erased two thousand years ago. They did not believe they ruled on high, and so they did not.

Melissa felt as if Lucinda could see right through her velvet gown. As if she were standing naked before her Maker, wearing only panties, her hands crossed to cover her bare, beaded, hard yearning nipples. The Kim in her did not want Lucinda to see what had become of his breasts, and Melissa loved it all. She loved the goose-pimply shame and humiliation, and she loved Lucinda's power that was that of the female, now Melissa's for the taking.

Melissa was redeemed with Lucinda, so very grateful for her; Lucinda smiling on the struggle going on for the same gorgeous, blushing face. The glamorous English woman kissed burning cheeks and promised they would meet again, she was to attend a holiday in Eden, Kristian's Martinique island. At this, the pink color in the baby's cheeks intensified. Melissa in the ride of her making, a mixture of prettiness and demonism, a femininity that had found its rightful place in her heart. Loving Lucinda's power to exploit. A birthright so deliciously wicked! A girl's natural gift.

"I never caught on to Nietzsche" Melissa said, "Philosophy was always over my head," she said, reaching infelicitously to the top shelf to bring down the books that looked dreary.

"The strong are destined to conquer and the weak to perish. You start there with Nietzsche, and women should know." Alexia took the books as Melissa passed them down the ladder. "He said the secret to bagging the greatest fruitfulness and the greatest enjoyment from life is to *live dangerously*."

Melissa laughed at this, thinking of the gala. If it was an indication of the future, she would never stop being reinvented.

"Dangerous is like the voodoo of this family," Alexia said in her denim chic duds. "Kristian, and the sisters, and all of us, try to stay on the edge in some way. There's real power, moxie when you're out there on the edge, you know?"

Melissa said nothing to this but it would it come, as it had come to Kristian, the sisters, Heidi, femmes of many nationalities who all spoke risk fluently. It came from that springlike matron, Mother. They had ceased to worry about what they appeared to the world, to take on a smoother, prettier, less ordinary life, to find the undiscovered truth of self. What Alexia did not give the baby, that was two steps beyond her, was the Nietzsche diamond of Alexia's mischief: "For others do I wait . . . for higher ones, stronger ones, more triumphant ones, merrier ones, for such as are built squarely in body and soul: laughing lions must come."

They filled boxes with Hemingway, Joyce, Faulkner, everything by Le Carré, and the magician, Gabriel García Márquez. Somberg and Company saw further because they stood on the shoulders of giants. Down the ladder were passed Doctorow novels, the present composed in the past, in the audacious lure of evil.

"Why are there so many novels?" Melissa asked, sending down Herman Hesse's *Siddhartha,* "if Kristian is into philosophy?"

"I think it was Aristotle who said fiction is of greater philosophical importance than history. History depicts things as they are, but fiction shows what *might be,* or *ought to be.*"

"Or *will be,*" Melissa offered, sending down the Anne Rice vampire series, a whole slew of them. Someone was possessed.

Alexia boxed the blood-suckers with Ayn Rand's *Atlas Shrugged* and *The Fountainhead.* Anne and Ayn. The doomed vampire without a trace of light; the heroic being whose happiness was the purpose in life. Alexia figured if you dropped the books in a blender, hit Puree, you'd get Maggie Thatcher, or Kristian Somberg.

"Now here's one I'm surprised to find in Kristian's things. Gandhi! What's he doing here?"

"The thing about Gandhi is"—Alexa had to climb the ladder to take the books that were well-read by everyone, especially six India male femmes, jewels all, devastating beauties, undetectable from their Indian sisters, and there were several— "Gandhi was a man and a *liver.* Into the moment. In our time, all our value systems are being feminized. From Wall Street to Washington to Hollywood. It will spread, all over the world. And it's Gandhi who really defines femmes. He said, 'We must *be* the change that we see in the world.' And I think that's what we are, *the change.*"

"So," Melissa said from high on the ladder, "you think guys' are becoming obsolete?"

"No. I think women will change them before that happens. Some of them are good fucks. And guys' can't help but change when the world around them changes. They're being feminized now."

"And will they all become femmes?"

"God, no. Most guys would make hideous girls! Girls don't want guys in dresses. Girls are happy to steal guys' clothes and guys' power, but they want femininity to themselves. And, hey, the Marlboro Man looks good in bed! Right? So he'll be around. But the dears are wrestling with phantoms, in an emptiness that a ballgame will not fill. So the male temple will come crashing down around their ears, because it's lost its foundation. Kings and presidents will cave in to women, to become nothing more than a tampon or a celebrity fuck. The last male likeness has been carved into the mountain. The giant men are artifacts of the past.''

Alexia watched the beauty take this in. All of it rich with interruptive possibilities for one being reinterrupted herself.

''I'd say we're in the book of Genesis, some sort of beginning in a new Eden to be made by the girls. But the nature of power *is* self-destructive,'' Alexia said with a knowing grin. To know three sisters was to know self-destruction. ''In time, women will become the men they wanted to get rid of.''

Melissa had only this morning surfaced from the storm of the gala, that lightning strike that triggered her character, so she was not just some pseudonym dream. And now the last daylight was dying over Kim, ransacked by feminine winds, to soon disappear, to leave the battlefield of the heart to the victor. But there were still murmurs coming out of the male rubble, insistent in knowing Alexia's gender. She flew around London on a black Harley Davidson—male. She was a mountain climber—male. A sometimes hip jewelry designer—female. But nowadays girls rode Harleys and girls climbed lots of mountains and guys made jewelry, and some very pretty guys became jewels. Alexia looked deliciously female, so to Kim her body parts were greater than her whole but still, damn it, there was a certain machismo about her, so a guy feared his luscious, lusty cravings. Alexia was as undiscernible as the future.

''So, Alexia,'' Kim said in a voice of suppressed excitement, ''what's the truth? Are guys losing their ass here? Are the girl barbarians at the walls?''

''The truth is, guys are dreamers and girls are realists. At fourteen a girl faces her physical features, accepts her limits and learns to make the most of it. Guys all live in the illusion of their looks, they all think they're the lizard-king.''

Alexa was sitting with her legs crossed on the trestle table, gazing up with a come-on smile, Kim teased higher into delirium where Melissa lived, but couldn't stop wondering what was between the legs of this prototype of the future?

''The truth is, guys are chronic emotionalists, and girls are autocratic. A girl holds out against an insult to plot revenge. A girl's vengeance takes a long, long time. It's her role. But a guy will punch, stab, shoot, bomb the hell out of the fuckers, and maybe think about it, while he's sicking the dog on what's left.''

High on the ladder, imagination heard not a word. Kim gazed into Alexia's eyes and saw girls marching in skintight miniskirts and thigh boots, trampling down shaved skinheads, the last great exaggeration of man. Femmchismo. The aggressive, seductive, very hungry sexual ego of woman. It had been asleep for a while, but it was not erased, and looking into Alexia's sure smile, Kim made a gallant effort to believe he had the conviction to resist it.

''The truth is, guys are silly romantics and girls are rolling thunder in love. A girl has no illusions about romance, she knows it's play, plays it for all it's worth, ends it clean. Guys can't cope with the end. They make a big flipping deal out of it. They hang on, get pissed off and worked up. All guys fall hard.''

In Alexia's pale blue eyes, Kim returned to a swimming pool. Kristian's hands went down his back again, cupping and stroking his fine ass. He felt her slowly part him, with a gentle probing finger now inside. Found his prostate. Massaged it in a circular motion. He'd remember every detail for the rest of his life.

''The truth is, guys are serial monogamists, and all girls are propagators of affairs.

Girls are always adopting some airy new cause, another massive feat for the psychic system. While guys just watch another ballgame; married to the one or two concrete things—usually their work—they'll drive at till they're dead.''

In dreams in which he lived, Kim had fallen off the ladder. Alexia's perfume mingled with the beckoning steam from between her legs. She took his face and pressed it to her panties, rubbing up and down on either side of her distended kernel. He put his mouth to it and in worship dragged his tongue in one long Melissa-velvet stroke from her ass to the top of her swollen clitoris. How many times had he done that for Kristian? He couldn't recall. She had to be like Kristian, they looked alike. Alexia had to be a girl.

''The truth is: guys are cheap liars; girls are true liars. Guys lie when they lie and a girl will see through his lies every time—unless it's a lie of the heart. But a girl begins her day with a lie; hair, makeup and clothes are a put-on lie that doesn't come off until the end of the day. Girls are artistic liars, and their greatest lie is the ridicule of guys as bare-faced liars.''

The pool was no big deal. Being on his knees was no big deal. Wearing velvet and a silk camisole and matching panties was no big deal. Casanova had done as much living in a harem as a girl. Made him the world's greatest lover! Hanging onto the rolling ladder, Kim took heart. But there was a difference between loving women and loving femininity, and Casanova didn't love death. He didn't have an exploitive, self-serving Medusa to keep him in her harem.

''And the greater truth is: knowing that the portraits of guys and girls that are hung in our heads are not true, and what is true about guys and girls is changing every day.''

All his life Kim had believed beautiful girls were a special glamorous race. They were not like the others, and certainly not like him. In velvet and satin, lips glossed in divine wine, he knew it was not true. Beauty was a lie. It was learned and put on and it would not last. And in the end, beautiful girls were only people. It was the saddest discovery of his life. It was like dying.

There are prisons and prisons, and sometimes one must enter one to escape another to get out of the House of the Dead. Kim had escaped that male house which was more than most guys could say. But there was no redemption and no escape from Kristian, and Alex knew it, no hope for a boy who gives himself away to a woman. She will take everything he is and everything he will ever be; a woman is entitled to her nature, and to her satisfaction. To place the personal woes of one small male before a woman's pleasure is to deify the whole of the universe. It was laughable to think Kim would be spared. His afterlife had arrived: he was born again as a femme. The luckiest boy alive, he belonged to Kristian.

It was a tight fit, Gandhi and Rand and Rice in the same box, but Alexia made it work. She had read and she knew the most erotic part of the body. The mind. It was all women needed, a few absurd physical details, tantalizing curves that transcend the boundaries of reason, and men's minds, most of which they already possessed. The future would be a hothouse of vigilante justice. Girls with a couple of thousand years of cruel irony to get off their chest. As for Kim, Kristian had his mind a long time ago. Had him mind, body and soul. She could have taken him any time but was saving him for Thatcher. To do them back to back, a pretty baby and an iron lady. Alexia sealed up the box of books and labeled it, ''Heavy Stuff.''

* * *

The Destroyer watched them waltz in the gala, the star of the night and Isabella. A fashionable couple. He in black Valentino lace; she in a tux. His hair swingy and adorable; her hair cut boy-short. Melissa breathtaking, one of the very prettiest girls; Isabella a handsome, self-sufficient, womanly man. The pair enjoying a natural rapport, nothing to suggest gender-reversal, or the danger to come. They looked like a little romance, smart, solid, possibly falling in love, gliding in a flourish through designer gowns and the necessary tuxedos that played the virtuous roles.

The most exciting thing about the star was that she didn't mean to be exciting. And she didn't know she was the star. She didn't know she was rocket-propelled; they all were, after she did them. They were not an imitation of life; they were the real thing and whatever they were before simply disappeared, after awhile. Passive traits were revered in the males; an imminence in the eyes was the girls' power. These existed before she picked them, so that they were never alienated from their true self, and that it worked so well proved again that gender was nothing but a parlor game.

"Gender is art," the Destroyer said to Alexia at her elbow. "Breaking the rules enhances the art, if done with grace."

Alexa stood at the edge of the dance floor, watching Isabella cut her teeth as an operative, sweeping Melissa into position.

"Girls break gender rules every day." Somberg smiled on the gorgeous scene, bearing one vulnerable soul. "Done so gracefully, it's common. Trousers as natural as mascara. Nothing sexier than a woman in a pin-striped suit and nothing else, thank you. Men *love it*. In sensual transition the world is changed."

It would be like Maggie's Irish War. An undeclared war. There would be no high-velocity shell holes blown into men. No hurricane of bombs and rockets. No bullets kicking up dirt and stone chips a few feet away; no whistle of mortar rounds coming down again. No ordnance of any kind, save seduction. No one would give an order to grease the male race. Kill it. No maggot-eaten corpses stacked up like cordwood. No door to hell cracked open to give the dears a glimpse. No one sworn to murder you, so there was no enemy, though they would all be bushwhacked just the same.

In Vietnam, 2.8 million men served. In this war, 2.8 billion women served. This war, like all wars, would never be over until every man who fought in it had died or surrendered. To be sure it was a war, coming down now, and the beauty of it was, men don't have time to think very much when the bullets are flying.

"You can really only create against something," Somberg said, smiling wide as Isabella floated by, the nymphet in charm-school posture. "Against others. Against yourself. Never do what people expect. As soon as you make people happy they expect more of the same. Call it *style*. The worst thing. Art never *follows* style, it *makes* style. If you cannot be followed, you cannot be caught."

Melissa had made some pretty discoveries about herself, at the expense of that benighted boy on the dance floor fretting in the Valentino gown. The changes were dynamic, in keeping with the Goddess, but the changes were about to be destroyed. It would be done again and again. This fresh destruction was also natural, the cosmos one continual destruction of itself to remake itself.

"With each destruction of a femme discovery," Somberg said, smelling the lavender shampoo in Alexia's hair, "their psyche is transformed. What comes out in the end is the effect of all those discoveries. We succeed by *destroying our art.* This is natural, least we become connoisseurs of ourselves, instead of others. It is they who continually remake us, we are reborn in each femme.''

"So you'll never grow old," Alexia said with a snicker.

"Not in five thousand years," Somberg replied with a sharp Medusa smile, and in the smile she looked, as many said she did, like Lauren Hutton. But Alexia had met the most beautiful woman in the world and the feature that most resembled Kristian was not the exquisitely boned face, but the hands. Big hands. Strong hands. Hands that had no sexual conscience, no fear; the hands of scuba divers, women who explored the deep, and so they were not pretty, but only Alexia noticed Lauren and Kristian's hands.

There was little attempt to teach femmes, because males could not learn. The best lessons were realized; the glamour of life the instructor. The near-miss experience impressed boys; the impending emergency was effective for girls. The loaded gun approach—a male technique—was never used. The purest distillation of everything kindhearted, supine, and cruel was best, so that no one was ever petrified, except in those ways they were meant to turn to stone, needing attention, and they got attention. Womanhood at large was working in much the same way, and the more it understood about how it worked, the better it would get. The safest way to communicate a woman's change was through books; a man would never know. If a man were told he was dying and the only cure was a four-hundred-page book, he would die before he made page one hundred, and when he expired, he would be watching a ballgame. The lady's books had been coming under various authors, their muse and endowment, the sisters' network. There was a new awareness within women, a new assertiveness, a fever for freedom. Part of women-in-training, a war of the masses, never extreme, never frightening, small changes in something ongoing, big enough to drown the entire male race. A reverberation of voices, to begin to take focus in one theme, the return of the Goddess, at the turning of the new millennium.

On the dance floor, Isabella maneuvered through the tamed horde in what was akin to a pirate attack. A perfectly ridiculous destruction meant to be ghostly and maddening for a boy unschooled in the dignity of a lady. And in sexual gameswomanship, for that matter. If these lessons were taught by men, the dear might be pistol-whipped. Or smacked about, good for a few cracked ribs. Or maybe a series of well-placed kicks with a heavy boot, not enough to castrate, just severely bruise the testicles. Being a lady Kim had offended, he would keep his hardware intact for her use—this being the difference in a lady's retribution: *pleasure.* Though there was much more than Lucinda Chambers in the fanfare to come, there was the Destroyer's pleasure of a male death.

"There's no distinction between combat and perversion," the Destroyer said in weaponspeak to her heartbeat beside her. "The best attack is a combination of surprise and speed."

Kim was running a temperature, he was sure of it. He had felt languid and cold ever since Lucinda, and just knew his plum devilish lips had lost their color. He was out of himself, somewhere else, momentarily untethered from the gala, with Melissa on a fast track with Isabella. But now he was back, creeping laboriously in the waltz. Isabella edged them into the center of the dance floor, then into a stately turn, and he was spun into a passing couple. Slammed into the broad back of a well-dressed man. Kim started to give Isabella hell, when the man turned in annoyance. Kim found himself before big hands and wide-set eyes. The man standing over him. He took in the Valentino gown and Kim couldn't look at him, he looked instead at the man's shoes, gleaming with the blazing lights. Ready to bolt in utter terror, and might have, in spiky pumps, but for Isabella's grip on his elbow. Finally Kim's eyes rose, to a straight nose projected sharply above a trim mustache. A smile broke out. That wolfish smile liked what he saw, and for a second, calm and lucidity abandoned Kim, afraid the guy would ask for a dance. He had never danced with a man. Only femmes.

The heat was upon him and Kim was certain he had a fever. The guy flashing a heartthrob smile, apologizing in a deep Welsh accent. Postcard people sailing by in formal wear, women smiling amiably at the gown, nodding their approval. It was maddening! The guy's eyes cut over to Isabella, in some unspoken macho understanding of the accident, and he must have been satisfied Isabella was a guy because the eyes swung right back to Kim, and the smile leaped back to his face. A hot grin. Now purring with more apologies, a chorus of them. They went on and on. Along with the whitest smile in the world. A tingling ran down to Kim's toes with a Melissa dream in his head: dancing with Kristian and a big muscled black dude at a disco, sandwiched between them, Kristian's hands on his waist, rolling his pelvis into the dude sort of strumming against him in a leather vest and washboard torso, in bulging, low-riding 501 jeans. He had forgotten the dream but it came as a magnesium flash, with this Welshman still staring. How did girls get out of something like this? After all, *the guy had a date.* Kim glanced around for help, but Isabella was gone. Vanished. She left him marooned with the Welshman grinning like a fucking Melissa dream.

Kim was vaguely aware of the guy's date, caught a glimpse of dress and dark hair. Then she peeked, like on tiptoes, over the guy's shoulder. Sparks of silvery white jumped across the ceiling. It seemed every blazing light was turned on Kim, staring at a china-doll cut that framed a face in the same plum devilish lips and smoke eyeshadow. Same feathered brows. And was that his Valentino gown she was wearing? Kim looked to the guy with a new terror, understanding why he was grinning. His date, still obscured behind him, was wearing a similar outfit to Kim's. And the guy wasn't the only one who noticed. Beautiful faces full of smirking, polished, boiling teeth whirled past, admiring Kim, then the date, then the eyes came back to Kim with a catastrophe in the making, he could feel it, heaven about to crash. And now the Surprise pushed past her date to take a better look at the Accident, and Kim's heart stopped. He knew it had. Stopped dead. Face to face with his dream girl, Melissa Brooks, who looked like his identical twin.

Reality and dream merged, with Kim standing very still, not quite believing his eyes. Staring at Melissa with his pretty mouth agape, in dazed horror as he went further and further away from his dream without taking a step. It was impossible for this to be Melissa. What was she doing in London? How could she be wearing a Valentino gown? How could he be wearing a Valentino gown? His brain felt light and unmoored inside his skull, the gala seemed to be stalked by mayhem, an electric sizzle came into his blood with dreams blowing through his head. He was not quite there, not quite anywhere. In a dizzy, disconnected sensation; his hands, with shocking pink nails, had no relation to his wrists. They were no longer his hands.

Now in his head came a birdhouse symphony of shrieks, cries, caterwauling, trills, shouts and pealing laughter at the fool. An absolute fool who had loved a dream, when he could have been loving a girl. A fool till the end, he held out against his eyes, refusing to see the stupefied onlookers, clinging to dream until at last reality defeated him, squeezing in, an unfettered, head-turning shriek of a real girl's disbelief. *"Kim!?"*

The orchestra conductor was startled by a scream that sounded like murder. He glanced down from the stage. Twin girls stood in the middle of the dance floor with a crowd forming. Dazed by the stupefying event, his conducting slowed. One furious girl circled the other, taking in every detail of her frozen twin whose hair and makeup was identical. Disaster and uncontrolled excitement parted the crowd into conversational bouquets around the girls. Words flew between them like kisses. A hint of intimacy and vengeance in the air! The one beauty was accusing the other, she trying to explain herself with a hand that looked frozen, stoney, like the hand of a corpse, all the color drained from her face, while the other one was scarlet. The pretty babies obviously knew each other, they looked like mirrors in matching velvet and lace gowns. Half the orchestra stopped playing, and the conductor gave up on the waltz. He stood and watched in the carnival atmosphere that had overcome every pocket of the immense ballroom.

Whispered rumors gusted up to the stage, vacillating between various lurid fantasies. Had the one girl copied the other's dress? Was there a man involved? Was this a crucible of love? The girl's heated exchange implied this and more! Now a laughing blond woman in an exquisite pearl gown took the girls in hand and led them from the floor, and applause erupted as the dazzled crowd parted to let the star pair pass with everyone abuzz. Finally the truth circulated up to the orchestra, someone called out: "It was all a promotion!" Shameless grandstanding and typically *very Valentino!* As brilliant and professional as a job could be.

In the Warnock library Alexia and Melissa were taking down Kristian's Salvador Dali pictures that were a hermetic language for femmes. They were: *La Main, Paranonia, The Disintegration of the Persistence of Memory, Three Young Surrealist Women Holding in Their Arms the Skins of an Orchestra,* and *The Esthetic Is the Greatest of Earthly Enigmas.* As they prepared the paintings for shipment to Martinique, Alexia's clear, short nails drummed time to Rachmaninov, while Melissa hummed the Prokofiev, pink nails in a flutter. The difference between them was heard in the masterpieces that were of efficient service to Somberg. Music is a template for the soul. It resides in the heart and is carried in the veins; one may make themselves in music, and one can be remade in music.

The Prokofiev *Piano Concerto No. 3* Melissa knew as a sweep of emotion; it never had its feet on firm ground. It is the tempest; it suggests wildfire. It's impulse, unstrung, certainly box office, somewhat demented, opening up to the sun and speed-winding. It is an icon of insanity, its potential awesome. It is primal emotion, a potboiler that comes in three installments that never gives the listener a fucking break. It's excess and more excess; addiction is its nature, as in a flight of the feminine. It's conspicuous consumption, pounding, clingy, cruelty, a torment, it goes well with whips and chains and handcuffs, straitjackets and temper tantrums. It is at once longing and exile; exile from the self, longing to be. It is the single desire. The hot tomato. Lust and love eclipsed. Never easy, the Prokofiev is practically impossible to perform, some first timers insist it refuses to be performed, a piece of music that is not performance but a journey. Few succeed at it. Prokofiev meant it that way. The playing of it is detached bewilderment, eccentric, weird, but very proud and always, always, very pretty. It is music near the truth of a woman's soul; it is unpredictable, all about the huge and beatific and so it is beyond understanding. The continuous feed of the Prokofiev is a string of firecrackers without end. It is the train wreck in the making.

Rhapsody on a Theme by Paganini, composed by Rachmaninov, is delicate, in so many variations that it speaks the truth. It is a provoking shell game of desires and changing moods, the perpetual persona. It is of so many appetites it's baffling. From the very beginning it is witty, wise, and glamorous; it is a Milan fashion show with many, many looks, ever expanding, very expensive and very resourceful. It is amazing quickness indifferent to cynicism, tougher than truck wax. It's fun. An enlightenment, it creates, then recreates boundaries in air, and though it appears random, it is function and form. An agenda clear about what it wants and what it expects. Its many themes are never gluttony, never greed; it enjoys itself one changing piece at a time, knowing its own worth. As a piece of razzle-dazzle intuition, it is always mischievous. Looking, always looking for what it would recognize as part of itself to be used to remake itself. It uses all things, and so it is privileged. In a word it is: luxury. The work of genius, it accepts its good fortune on its face without further reflection.

The two classics were used to rescue and identify; learned as life by the femmes, though Alexia thought of the Prokofiev and the Rachmaninov as where women are, and where they are becoming.

In the library, the Rachmaninov smiled on the Prokofiev. Alexia's smile without repression. Without being harsh or ironic. A smile that said to Melissa, been there, done that.

Now from the fireplace mantel Alexia took the Salvador Dali illustration *Tres Pico,* known to her as the *God of the Garden.* The picture depicted a plantlike God of blooming foliage, veined in vibrant colors, a muscular-looking God crawling with caterpillars and winged butterflies, one of which the God held to anxious lips, about to devour it. The face was of a happy man, but between the God's legs bloomed a lily, opening out like a lover's lips.

Melissa had seen the Dali before, but it meant nothing. Now wearing a tattoo of a kallima, she saw in the picture a luscious game of sensuality and shame and power, all nourishment for the God of the Garden. The picture summoned what Kristian said after their love: "The more you eat, dear, the more you want to eat."

In a mystery Kim was released from Melissa, in long-overdue tears that did not fall, gazing at the eloquence and amiability of the Garden God about to devour a pretty blue butterfly.

"If it makes you happy," Alexia asked, "why are you so sad?"

"Jeez, I don't know." He helped wrap the priceless Dali in a gauze sheath. Kim was all at once depressed, just came over him. "What happened to Melissa?" he asked.

"Who? Melissa the dream? Or the model?"

"Yes. That one."

"Oh, the truth blew her to pieces."

"So, she won't be coming back?"

Alexia resisted a laugh. The newborn femme was changed and frightened; it made them a little raucous and there was no relief. There were the male backfirings from all the craziness, you could see it come over Melissa's face returned to Kim. The lost look was gorgeous, batting those lush lashes. It was all Alexia could do not to devour her on the spot. Instead she gave a hug and the baby fit nicely in Alexia's solid curves that looked best swimming naked. She was not voluptuous, the body not dynamite, but she moved with a wholeness of being that began at the balls of her feet and extended to every long limb. She was unified and graceful.

"You have Melissa's passport, don't you?" she said.

"Uh-huh."

"And her driver's license?"

Kim nodded, he figured she had been blown away. This morning her Gucci bag was beside the bed, ID in it, and the pictures of Melissa Brooks were a sort of confession. Like most guys in love with themselves, he had picked a dream who looked like him. And now he looked like her. And now he was wearing her fragrance, Allure by Chanel. *Difficult to define. Impossible to resist.*

"Don't worry, dear," Alexia said softly. "It will all come in time. It's the grace of inevitability."

She was adorable when she turned pouty, those perfect lips begging to be kissed. Lips that could kiss and eat, or so Alexia had heard. And it seemed to Alexia there were two words in the silence of her pouty tulip lips: Do me.

Melissa Brooks had been told the gala was a prelude to a Valentino assignment. After the shocker, the spectacle of Kim in her gown, she was taken to the Rubens Hotel, told she was to meet the famed designer who was to explain the evening's performance. That was the last time Kim saw his dream girl. She was now a kind of pride and sorrow. A murder mystery. An emotional center for a dream grownup into the real and demanding and exploratory. Kim now a little deserted, an isolated boy who would, from time to time in the rock and roll of femme translation, return, but the duration of it would lessen each time in half-shadow and silence.

"There are so many questions, I know, love."

"There's so much I don't understand."

"About what?" Alexia slid an arm around the velvet honey.

"Oh. About what happened to . . . you know."

"You must be careful with yourself," Alexia said, her stroking hands with so many wicked habits. "Don't ask too many questions too soon. You remember the way out of little depressions?"

"Depression is why the elite work," Kim replied, Vonnegut's *Player Piano* coming back easy. "Work is *fulfillment*. Fulfillment is giving. So we all *give*."

"And giving is pleasure," Alexia said, pinning her to the wall, the wrists held above the head. She struggled and dipped her face and gave a little cry in the cruelty of surrender as Alexia took those lips, kissing her deep, a kiss of belonging. A pretty baby to be taken with the Dali to the island of Eden and fucked until it was her second nature, until she craved it in the name of God. A destiny made when a boy let himself be picked up by a seductive, older woman. In such circumstances it is all irrevocable decided in a matter of seconds. It was a well known fact that had stood the test of time, there was only one way to escape a Medusa, to cut off her head, never looking into her eyes. But it was too late for Kim, in those eyes he had been taken to that other country.

"Gotcha!" Alexia laughed and gave a wink of ice blue eyes.

The *God of the Garden* was sealed in a crate to be hung at the banana plantation in Eden. The wonderful wonder beckoned, and Alexia took her velvet hand and led her away in the knowledge that we are not made of goodness or evil so much as we are made of will that we may exercise to make ourselves, or to let go. To give, or to take so we may give, which is what Alexia had in mind. She had read her books well, and was not female or male, but a Nietzsche laughing lion that had arrived. Alexia was Somberg's dream girl.

29

SCHOOL HAD NEVER been in session on a Sunday, and that made it doubly exciting for the children and impossible for Kea to keep them at their desks. The pink walls were lined with parents and grandparents telling stories of their years with little brown-haired Goody-Goody Maggie. And Mr. Higgins was there, waving and smiling, quietly consulting with two Scotland Yard agents whose solemn eyes never left the cake on the front table. This was the day before the Big Day. The biggest day in the 100-year history of Huntington Tower Elementary.

Kea had been there for hours, making everything ready; the children's best work now mounted on the bulletin boards. She had not been there alone; she was joined by two toxicologists from Scotland Yard. Gray, very solemn men. Their tone and manner very businesslike. Made Kea feel like the country was in good hands. They cut a thin slice from Linda's cake and took a sample of her homemade Elizabeth Shaw chocolate mint icing. Cake and icing were immersed in test tubes, Kea watching out of the corner of her eye, fumbling with her work. their mood so austere, made her nervous. The grayish chemicals never changed colors, and they told her the children would be free to decorate the cake. Well, of course they were going to decorate the cake! What had they expected, that they were going to poison Mrs. Thatcher?

It was a crazy assumption. They'd all eat the cake. Anyone who tried to poison it would be poisoning all the children. Kea thanked the men for their permission, but they didn't leave. They remained with the cake, cake bodyguards, she supposed, watching it with grave, hesitant faces. Like it was some albatross.

Linda arrived before the children, to ice the cake, now that it had passed inspection. She set out all the jars of decorative icing. Each was tested by the men in gray. Lemony Yellow. Peek-a-Blue. Pumpkin Orange. Spring Leaf Green. Snow White. Apple Red. They were approved and now sat on the table beside the cake with a lovely flower arrangement Linda made for the occasion, her special gift for Mrs. Thatcher. Bleeding hearts. Of course, the gray men had to poke around in them. As if the vibrant red flowers might be lethal! Kea thought they went a little overboard.

Now the airbrush and opaque projector were rolled into position above the sheet cake gleaming in chocolate. The children squirming with excitement, and as Kea joined Linda at the front she was given a hero's welcome! The applause spontaneous. Kea let it go on for a minute, until the demonstration began to get rowdy. She held up a hand for quiet. The first-graders fell silent, though some of the parents were still acting up.

"Thank you, *everyone,* for coming to school on a Sunday!" Kea said. She turned to the men in gray, in the back, watching over them all. "And we want to thank the nice gentlemen from Scotland Yard who helped us make the cake for the prime minister."

There was another round of applause, and you could just see the men in gray cringe, their faces granite-hard. Kea understood the importance of their work, but why couldn't they smile?

"I know you're *all* ready!" Kea said to the children wriggling in their seats. She turned to Linda, calm as a lake on a summer's day. "Are we ready, Mrs. Anderson?"

All Mrs. Anderson had to do was open her generous arms, and the children came running. The old classroom rocked with shouts of glee and the stampede of little feet. Kea joined them at the table while Mr. Higgins and the parents circled round. Gray men watching from behind. Mrs. Anderson switched on the compressor. It began with a mechanical complaint. A sound like *rurr-rurr-rurr.* Then faster, *rur-rrurrrurr!* The whirling had the children dancing.

"Now, class," Mrs. Anderson said. "What we're about to do is exactly what you did when you made the cake for Mr. Higgins. Do your best work. But what's important is, whenever doing a big job, relax and enjoy the *pleasure* of your work. Are you ready?"

The ensuing cheer left no doubt. The voices rose and rose in what was already a mountaintop experience! Kea wondered what Mrs. Thatcher would say about Linda's smart cake? Kea twitching inside her skin just thinking about it. Where did Linda find the courage?

A picture was slid into the projector; Kea held her breath. A caricature of Mrs. Thatcher was now beamed onto the cake. The Prime Minister had a huge head and a bouffant hairdo, a big red smile and a tiny body in a navy suit, waving the Union Jack.

The room erupted in applause! Even the gray men were smiling! It was cheeky, but respectful. Perfectly British. Thank God, they loved it. Kea sighed and smiled at Linda with relief.

"Mrs. Anderson, you've outdone yourself!" Mr. Higgins called.

"Just think of what the media will say," Kea added, still amazed at Linda's boldness. "We might make the *Times!*"

"Oh, I should think so," Mrs. Anderson said with a smile.

The children queued up, taking turns at the airbrush, with everyone contributing. Tracing the Thatcher image with icings shot through the airbrush, misted by a vial of concentrated toxin, *Helleborous niger,* concealed in a welded cavity of the compressor. There was nothing to suggest the toxin, and the children took their time, doing a meticulous job. When they finished, the Maggie cake gleamed in all the colors of death, and even the unsmiling gray men were impressed, the designer cake made by children was, like Mrs. Anderson, fun and beautiful. Yummy, actually.

He sat opposite her desk. The thin blind shadow striped his hatchet face and hawk nose and the dark brows drawn thunderously together. He looked to Allison like he was robotic. His camouflage tunic sported three rows of fruit salad decorations. The trousers stuffed inside jackboots polished to a killing gloss.

The intercom buzzed twice. No need to answer, Allison knew the code. "She'll see you now," she said, and opened the doors. He walked ramrod stiff past her, face set in the cement of a man who feels nothing and goes right on feeling it, and as she closed the doors she recalled what her Irish grandfather said about the Strategic Air Service. He called them "killing machines."

Her gramps was a very old man, a former fisherman, he still had the yellow slick, and the cap and pipe. His face, especially his cheeks, were raw and chafed from the winds that had burned his skin so the sparse silver bristles poking out gleamed. Years ago, he had been lucky enough to find jobs for his sons in England, so his grandchildren grew up under the Union Jack, though there was nothing lucky about that. A soul ache, but an economic necessity.

He just showed up at her door one day, like an idea of the heart. Dropped by for a cup of tea, he did. Her beloved gramps. There was a warm buoyancy in the air that made Allison feel young in his presence, and she remembered what it was like to skip home from school, she could hear as much in his melodious brogue.

He spoke of his father who defeated the British in the glory days of Michael Collins, "God rest his soul. 'Twas unlucky Collins had to settle for less than the whole of Ireland, but that's still possible, lass." The fat, sweet part of Ireland was free. Though in the North, no one could escape the terrifying British presence that was like a harsh, tenacious sea wind that carried with it the seeds of madness, as recorded by certain writers who had learned their lessons in Ireland, some in wee Killarney, escaped to other settings, none as pastoral, to return to Ireland only in print.

He spoke of Bobby Sands. Not so long ago arrested on weapons possession. Sands demanded recognition as a prisoner of war. Went on a hunger strike. Nine others joined him. Allison was working at Number 10 in those days, she watched as Mrs. T ignore the Geneva Convention and refused Sands POW status, deaf to pleas from clergy and politicians around the world. All Ireland rallied for Bobby, and in the North he was elected to Parliament. But at Number 10 it was business as usual; Mrs. T didn't budge. After forty-six days the grisly end finally came. Bobby Sands, a British MP, died like Airey Neave, in a steel cell. She let the Irish, all of them, starve to death. And in those days, Mrs. T was just peachy keen.

Her gramps scrutinized Allison without pity, without saying she stood by and did nothing to save the lads, then won her over with the eloquence of an old master. All the world was water, he said, inside and out. Wheezing shifting seas. Much of it bruised gray under strained wet light, this notably true in English waters where the waves were of the hue of slate. As in gravestone gray. There the sea emerged as a negative in which light things were made dark, and dark things light. Photographic negatives could do wonders to distort truth, or free it. For there were places where the English sea glowed, transparent with light. " 'Tis a beauty to behold! Makes an old grandfather proud!'' He spoke in a casual way of a priest, a mate, who had asked to peek at the PM's calendar. He had lent a special handbag for the purpose, camera inside.

Allison sat very still, with the unexplainable presentiment that something was about to happen. She asked him about this. Her gramps laughed his irresistible laugh and said that only poetry is clairvoyant, and he was no poet. Then he changed the subject.

There was a time when Allison would do anything for Mrs. T. Steal for her, pray for her, kill for her. But Mrs. T had an ego that obliged her to top everyone in sight. She hammered people until their loyalty was flattened to be made as hard as she was. After her gramps left, Allison felt him following her around the house with hostile stares. Not long afterwards, she took the handbag to work. The miniature camera built into the base made it easy to copy the appointment calender. Allison exchanged the film for a sense of redemption. Her gramps loved her for it. It was the only false move she ever made, and the only one she would ever make.

Allison looked up from her desk as the black glistening boots came back through the door. The boots marched past her desk. The SAS commander with a file in hand. Allison imagined the commander would do anything for Mrs. T. Steal for her, pray for her, kill for her. "The SAS is an efficient system of justice,'' her gramps had said. "Judge, jury, and executioner all in one.''

The plane came in low over Killarney. It banked and glided onto the oil-blackened runway. It taxied to the terminal. Trent popped the door and trotted to the car park with a leather grip. He took in a gray Ford. John Lowry sat at the wheel. The youth, like the car, a colorless operative whose creaseless face had not one remarkable feature. Reminded Trent of young Geoff Duncan, the Oxford boy-agent blown to smithereens at the Grand Hotel. Didn't need that guilt trip again.

"Any sign of Jessica Moore?'' Trent asked as he dropped into the passenger seat.

"No, sir. I've looked everywhere for her.''

Lowry watched Trent open the grip. He took out a Beretta 93R. It was no pop gun. Not the melodic compact model that Lowry had been issued. Big, black, square; the 93R made a terrific roar.

"When did you last try the Gap?'' Trent pulled the clip of the automatic and checked it.

"Just now,'' Lowry said, eyeing the shiny titanium rounds. He had seen them only once before, in gunnery class. The instructor had pulverized a demo car, shooting all the way through it. "The cottage is still vacant. She wasn't there all night.'' To Lowry, Trent appeared devoid of emotion when, in fact, he was seething.

"Have you spotted the Pope?''

"Not since mass. Seems to have vanished.'' Trent inserted the clip. Lowry wondered what the hell was going on; explosive rounds were strictly against policy. But then, they weren't in England. "Not to worry; the priest will turn up.''

"Right. The question is, *where?*'' The Beretta vanished into a shoulder holster. "Let's have the keys,'' Trent said.

Lowry hesitated. He had wanted to drive. And he wanted a go at the Beretta, and whoever it was intended for, and that would be no surprise. Titanium rounds could mean only one thing: IRA. Reluctantly he surrendered the keys.

"Right. Out you go."

"What?"

Lowry looked at him in disappointment.

"Take the plane back to London," Trent said.

"London?" Lowry cried. He just got out of London, for once. He looked over to the plane, then back. Studying Trent's face. But there was nothing to see. Only his cold burning eyes.

"Come on, man. *Out!* I'm short on time."

Lowry stepped out of the car. He stood there for a second, wearing the expression of a man tossed back to the sea and told to tread water. His mouth opened to form a response, but wisely he said nothing. He slammed the door, that was all he could say.

Trent slid behind the wheel and left a streak of rubber on the pavement. Normally he didn't carry the 93R, and normally he didn't fit it with armor-piercing rounds, but earlier in the day he had rung Pit Martin in hopes he had heard from Jessica. The call had been forwarded to Chicago Homicide. Martin had been found in Jessica's condo, a detective reported. Shot through the mouth. "No idea who's responsible. No prints. Kitchen wiped clean. Been trying to reach Moore," the detective said. "We know she's in Ireland, but no one seems to know where."

Trent had made the call about the time Graham heard from a customs officer who had spotted the Fox as he entered Gibraltar by ferry from Spain. Graham alerted Thatcher and was in high spirits when he told Trent *he* would close the Brighton case, the Neave case, and dispose of Somberg in short order. "By Tuesday," Graham declared, "I'll have Mrs. T eating cake out of my hand!"

The SAS, Trent learned, had been sent to Gibraltar, and so the outcome of that was determined. Brighton appeared to be over, with the exception of the Pope. Trent immediately took leave. Went home. Had a single Black Bush. Went to a certain floorboard in the attic. Retrieved the titanium rounds. Took out the 93R. Dropped it all in the grip and hired a plane for Ireland.

He was now steering though narrow streets, his eyes probing the walks. Tight wad of rage coiled in his chest. *Use it; use it. Don't let it use you.* There was the inevitable stroll of tourists along the pretty shop windows. Trent drove on, but part of him lagged behind, gazing into a shop window where he could renew his memories of a girl who sold her life to chase her heart. In the shop window, he could see all the way across Ireland to where she stood on a castle on a hill overlooking the sea to England. It did not surprise him to find her there, midway between their different lives. He had always thought their time together was more than a stratagem for finding Danny. He told her so. He knew something of what happened to him since their first meeting, and he feared not finding Danny as much he hoped they would. Fear as great as hope.

He passed O'Flaherty's Pub. Sign in the window: "Closed for Repairs." Turned at the corner. Scanning faces. The oral kill proof enough, Somberg had been to Chicago. Killarney would be her next move. Drove on, peering into windows, talking to himself aloud: *"Jess, what in the devil have you gotten yourself into?"*

* * *

She was tumbling inside herself. Tossing between grotesque reality and a depraved recurring dream. She had never found Danny. He had grown up with the bitch who renamed him until one day, in a strange way that only dreams can be, she found herself before the bitch's front door. She rang the bell. A boy of fourteen answered. She didn't know the boy. The boy didn't know her. She had to ask if the boy was her son. The boy looked at her as if she were dead. Such a strange, spooky look. Compassion roared with rage, trying to find Danny in the astonished surprise of the young man before her. Next thing Jessica knew, she was in some bizarre courtroom. Being fined by a judge for having seen her son. She was forced to pay, Danny having signed an instrument that said he did not want Jessica as his mother, he wanted the bitch. The bailiff walked her from the courtroom as if she were a criminal, dangerous, capable of anything. Jessica looking back at the bitch's face, twisted into a frozen snarl of a smile, her hand hooked into a claw on the shoulder of the precious boy Jessica did not know, the guttural voice of the bitch sounding as if it were coming through a big mouthful of cotton. Calling the boy by a name. What was it?

She woke with a jerk. Holding on to herself, shaky and cold. She lived in a cage in the great middle of the world that roared around her. She was imprisoned from everything and everyone, even herself, in this pursuit of her son. As she slowly gathered in her surroundings, she realized that *this* was not a dream. It was real. She looked around and realized she was in a pub. Shanahan gone. Her four keepers at a table behind her, playing cards.

In the deep chair, she felt as though she were in a dark cave beside the river of doubt. She had always thought the worst thing was to have your child die. But now she wasn't so sure. What was worse was for you to die to your child. Time, time, time, Jessica knew, was ticking away. Danny growing further and further away with every passing day. In the chair, Jessica was dying.

She pulled herself from the chair. She tossed peat bricks into the fire. *Amazing how even the earth burns in Ireland,* she thought, feeling her heart on fire. Fanning the flames with the old Irish bellows, handsomely designed, red leather with scrolled brass trim, she found she wanted to spread the fire. She wanted to burn something. Burn someone. If necessary, she'd set the whole world on fire. It began that simply. With a thought. It grew.

She stood staring, transfixed by the flames, hearing Father Shanahan in her insomniac sleep. Didn't she overhear him saying something to the others about Trent? Was Trent coming? But as she reached for that remembrance she heard him talking about killing Thatcher. Had he really said that? *Margaret Thatcher?* She knew he had and knew he had left to get Danny and tried to remember where he went. It was on the tip of her tongue, caught up in layers of sleep, and she couldn't bring it all the way back but couldn't extricate herself from it. The Father was going to burn Thatcher. Is that what he said, burn?

Her thoughts fluttered away, as though on a butterfly. She slumped into the chair worn soft with age. She felt undressed and not in good company. She was a spectacle. All that manic energy. A woman's energy. People would come from miles around just to see her go crazy. Some artistic urge did not want to disappoint. She gazed at the fire that warmed and fascinated her and would not let her go, trying to remember the voices in dreams, as though dreams and voices had become some parlor game played in her head.

The evening was silent and secret in the mist that came creeping through the wood where Shanahan stood in an open grave, black muck piled in a mound beside the hole. Sweat streamed down the heavy creases of his dirt-smeared face. He had been digging since mass, shirt and trousers a wet tangle on his gaunt frame. At his feet lay a half-buried wooden cask. He need only to unearth the cask to achieve his fate that he did not doubt.

He bent double and seized the cask, face screwing up with the effort as he heaved it from the grip of the earth. He lurched out of the grave and placed the cask atop the altar of dirt beside his pickax cross; there he rested, breath coming in ragged gasps.

It was the mother—he knew that now—she made the difference. Prior to the coming of this lovely female he was numb to the world, as if he had lost his capacity for suffering, his skin grown thick and reptilian cold, as a Father's skin can, so pressed is he with the burdens of the world. He had learned to live with the rage but in taking on the mother's suffering had reacquired his own sense of pain, and now was wholly changed. Changed as surely as if he had crawled up out of the muck to sprout wings and take flight over the years of torment and suffering. In his time, he had given his enemies torment and suffering in return, while administering grace for those caught in torment and suffering. All of it a vicious cycle without end. Always at odds with himself, the holy man and the violent man. Father and Devil. But since taking on a woman's spirit, this mother, the counterparts of him had come together in a holy violence that were now the beginning of the end.

The end was to be Ireland's quest for freedom, and in this sparkling dream, he took in the good air, gazing at the wood as if he had never been here before, as if he hadn't buried this same cask here years ago, a life entombed for this day of resurrection. The mist rolled over his eyes. He saw the mystery of eggs and half-opened buds and half-unsheathed flowers, the green things of the earth seemed to hum with greenness, and he saw it all and felt it all for the last time and the first time as a whole man.

The plan was simple enough. The cask, crude as it was, held a surprising work of truth. He would sneak into the marketplace, the global England, with the terrible beauty poised in the melancholy interior of the cask. He would be a huge success! He knew this and did not doubt it because he had dreamed it. Be it a dream of devil or father or induced by a feminine spirit of the mother; it hardly mattered. He had seen it, that and the cask was all he needed.

He put on his robe and tied the purple sash. Now priest and patriot knelt together as one in the charge of the events that as music would come in time, eyes turned to a pink-flushed heaven for the prayer. His voice lifted and rang out over the lush wood: "May the blessing of God be on this holy estate, this precious emerald isle set in a ring of silver sea. This earth of forest green and smooth skin of tender grass. This breed of fairy people, this farm of pubs and country of lakes, of moods and shadow and night, of medieval charm, this little world of crumbled castles stained by the blood of kings o'er which half-mourning skies forever hang. This land of the horse. This flowery vale! This best kept secret. This splendid deception with its sweet arias and its golden voice. This lovely mother to all nations. This cradle of misted rock where opportunity is born dead, on a diet of stone and fish. This country of the nearly famous, this perch so near the sun where the inevitable never happens. This fulcrum of history. This crucible of the heart. This piping, strident voice! This bantam republic, divided but never lost. This garden cemetery, this refuge from all storms. This first love, this promised land, this brooding seat of poets and painters, this loss for words, this Ireland!''

He had played in the wood as a lad and it was here his ashes would be strewn, and now, as he looked about, it seemed as if the buds and unsheathed flowers had all blossomed. A round moon hung above the sawtooth silhouette of mountains with the lights of Killarney shimmering on dark waters. He hoisted the cask to his shoulder, feeling its weight as if it were a cross, feeling the Thatcher death it held as redemption. No longer torn between the work of God and Ireland. A man complete. One force united. No pain. No anguish. No sorrow. He felt only the fire, God's holy fire, Ireland's fire that rested on his shoulder. He took in one last look, then passed out of the wood and into the deep of night.

THIRD
MOVEMENT

30

TRENT STOOD WITH the sheep under fading stars. From the top of Purple Mountain he could see their cottage, its white face bare but for a yellow square of window. He had waited all night and had seen Jessica's face in the stars that lent his aching heart assistance in the long wait, listening to the emptiness of the Gap, watching the road that came out of the mountains and threaded through the glen. The sheep hid behind the boulders until they realized he was as helpless as they. One by one they showed their wooly faces, coming around to the windward side where they could smell him, where they could wait with him through the night. Now, at the first light, the flock was gathered round, grazing near his feet. His quiet persistence spoke volumes to the sheep.

When he couldn't find Jessica in Killarney, Trent drove to the Gap. Saw the gash in the railing and a scar of blue paint on the mountainside. Climbed down to the bog, found a slick of motor oil. Dead bees floating on the slick. The food at the cottage had gone untouched, lamps full of oil. He had called St. Miranda Hospital, cursing himself for not having done it sooner. Records confirmed a Jessica Moore had been treated and released, but they refused to comment further, referring him to a Dr. O'Conner. He called. O'Conner was on holiday. The towing service had not seen a Volvo. The Garda acted astonished and had no record of Trent's calls. Finally Trent rang Sergeant Duffy at his private number.

"*Good God!*" Duffy exclaimed. "An accident in the Gap?"

"It appears that way," Trent replied from the public call box at Kate Kearney's. "You've no idea where Ms. Moore might be?"

"No. I've not seen her."

"And no idea why the railing is broken?"

"Well now, that happens with some frequency. 'Tis a mean road at the Gap. Made for beast, not man. We *encourage* jaunting cars."

Trent examined the dimpled face of a golf ball found in his leather jacket. "Any idea why Ms. Moore was at the hospital?"

"No, no. But I'll begin an *immediate* investigation!"

"I thought we had *already* begun an investigation?"

"Aye. But not of a *formal* nature. But I'll get right on it. This is Monday. . . . Why not ring me on Tuesday."

"Tuesday, you say?"

"Aye. *Late* Tuesday. Or first thing Wednesday."

"Right," Trent said, prizefighter fist trying to flatten the golf ball. "And would you have any idea where Father Shanahan is?"

There was a pause.

Duffy came back, terse and stiff, "I should think ye'd find Father at St. Mary's. Why would ye be wanting to see *him?*"

Trent waited a beat. *Let him sweat.*

''Actually, I've something to confess. How about Dessie Quinn? Or Padraic Sweeney? They're missing as well. I've been looking for them for some time. Can't seem to find them anywhere.''

The long silence confirmed he was talking to the IRA.

''Well now.'' Duffy laughed. ''How would ye know those buckos?''

''I've never actually met them. Just missed them in Brighton last fall. Should you hear *anything* on Ms. Moore, would you drop by the Gap? I'll be staying at the cottage.''

''Of course,'' Duffy growled. '' 'Twill be my pleasure.''

Trent lit a lantern in the cottage and climbed the mountain, but Duffy never came. Spent the night repressing fear that wanted to shriek. Was she dead? But if she was dead, why the cover-up? Duffy said to call on Tuesday. Was Charles to be hit Tuesday? But Thatcher was the one they hated. And why strike at Jess? What difference would her death make? And how did the death of Pit Martin tie into all this? The answers were beyond him, concealed in a dark he couldn't penetrate with the little he knew. The one lead he had was Duffy. *Get to Duffy and perhaps I can find Jess,* he thought, *and resolve the Charles-Thatcher question.*

Trent came down the trail worn smooth by the sheep who did not follow him, but looked after him climbing down their trail, and as the sun came out of the mountain it cut through the mist that hung over the waters with the glen taking on a new color. He reminded himself again, *Use the rage. Don't let it use you.*

In his Datsun in the car park of the Grantham airfield, Shanahan watched as the firmament unscrolled into a blistering red-violet that ignited the mist, and for a sweet moment there it looked as if all of England were on fire. A Psalms came with the fine vision: *My soul fleeth unto the Lord: before the morning watch, I say, before the morning watch.*

Now young Sean McShane came out of the fire, trying to appear as if he were not running from the Lear. There was no reason for his haste, but perhaps if the young man hadn't run, he wouldn't have found the courage to walk. Shanahan rolled down his glass, unaware of the silver Rolls-Royce parked at a restaurant across the street. A tall, dark figure sat in the Rolls, listening on headphones, elongated snout of a parabolic mike aimed at the little man standing stiff and anxious at Shanahan's open window. The exchange came in crisp and clear.

''Did ye have any trouble?''

''No. The job is done, Father.''

''Splendid. And do ye recall *all* I told ye?''

''Aye. 'Tis simple enough.''

''But should she come with the *lad*—''

''I know, Father. She won't burn if she has the lad.''

''Good, good. Now, go on. Lay low in your Cessna. I should be back shortly. If I fail to come, she will.'' Shanahan took a wad of bills from his pocket. He forced it on the lad who did not want to take it, but he had no need of currency where he was going. A hand out the car window, he made the sign of the cross. ''God go with ye, Sean McShane. May it go well with ye always.'' Their hands clasped in a grip as tight as the tie that bound them, the blood of their forefathers in that grip. The Father gave him a Psalms of benediction to take home to the divided others.

"Behold, how good and joyful a thing it is: brethren, to dwell together in unity!''

McShane turned to leave, headed for his little plane parked on the tarmac. He turned and shouted, *"Send Thatcher to hell!"*

"Aye," Shanahan rejoined, his spirit up high. " 'Tis a grand day for Ireland! All glory be to God!''

As McShane vanished into the soft burning morning, the parabolic mike was withdrawn, the figure in the Rolls waited.

Shanahan watched the last of his disciples part but would not allow himself to reflect on the loss. There was a time to think and a time to do and now the thinking was done for a lifetime and all that remained was the doing. It had been a long journey he had taken to this good end that would be a display of Irish devotion the world would not soon forget. To bring down a bloody Godzilla was a feat worthy of his life, he imagined by midnight he'd be on the front page of every newspaper in the world. Not his story, but Ireland's to be told in the commitment of his monkey life.

He had come by ferry into Britain, and as he was a priest the customs agent gave the car only a cursory review. He drove from the ferry through the land of the Bard who was the only good thing to come out of England, so many well-turned play lines taking flight as he drove, the Father freshened in this joint venture with Shakespeare, a chartwork for the future. Hadn't the titan dramatist taken on the kings? Julius Caesar. Macbeth. Antony and Cleopatra. The Henrys and Richard III. All truths in their time, swelled in the act of the imperial theme. It was what the Father was about, this time honored lightning strike of the mighty. And though he be an imperfect speaker, he was bold, and this cannot be taught or memorized but is as a calling. The Father smiled on the foul and fair day, *Macbeth* in the shrewd air as he made his way to little Grantham, thinking of those three wild witches, such lavish spirits; a man could learn a thing or two from witches. There is no more fascinating instrument of truth than darkness.

In the rusted Datsun, Shanahan reached to the back and yanked out the rear bench. A coffin-shaped wooden box and a silver Colt revolver hidden underneath. He removed the lid from the box. Red sticks of nitrobenzene lay in neat rows of cotton. One of the twelve sticks was missing.

He lifted a coil of black wire from the box. The wire had a rubber detonator pad on one end, about the size of a Band-Aid, a female plug married to the opposite end. Shanahan slid to the passenger seat and removed his cassock. Scarred boots fell to the floor. Black trousers came off, leaving him in white boxer shorts and black knee socks, exposing gaunt, pale legs roped with cords of muscle that looked added as an afterthought. A sock was pulled. He peeled the adhesive from the detonator pad, attached it to his heel, and resocked the foot. As he dressed, he ran the wire up his sock and up his pant leg and out the waistband.

He lifted a canvas vest from the box. Looked like a hunter's vest slotted with shell loops that encircled the vest front and back. And now with reverence, as though it were an act of the sacrament, the old alligator-hide hands slotted the nitro sticks into the wide loops of the vest and named them as he clipped a strand of wire to each: "Matthew . . . Mark . . . James . . . Peter . . . Andrew . . . John . . . Philip . . . Bartholomew . . . Thaddeus . . . Thomas . . . Simon.''

He pulled his arms through the loaded vest and zipped it up. Took the wire from the vest and the wire from his heel, tied them together but did not make the connections. He slid into his robe and behind the wheel, lifted the flask, though the whites of his eyes were marinated with drink. All was ready. Shanahan switched on the engine. The Rolls Royce quietly trailed in his rumbling wake as he drove into Grantham reciting a Psalms. "O Lord, Thou hast searched me out and known me: Thou knowest my down-sitting, and mine up-rising; Thou understandest my thoughts long before."

Danny watched a Thomas the Tank Engine cartoon while his New Mama tucked a white shirt into his gray trousers. She knotted a striped tie, sharpened the crease in his pant legs, and checked the part in his hair.

"Mama," Danny said, looking about the breakfast room. "I can't find my favorite belt."

"I have it," she replied. "I was working on it last night."

"Oh, good. I was a little worried."

"There's no reason to worry, sweetie. Today is the—"

"I know; I know!" He rolled his eyes, a thing learned from his Old Mama. "Today is the Big Day."

Somberg took the black leather belt and threaded it through his belt loops. Clipped the square brass buckle, which housed a miniaturized radio detonator. She checked the buckle to verify the safety was engaged. She'd arm the device after she dropped him at school. She made herself a cappuccino, sitting at the round breakfast table graced by an arrangement of firecracker flowers.

"Are you looking forward to meeting Mrs. Thatcher?"

"Yeah," he said, and dropped into a chair to finish his bowl of Froot Loops.

"Are you *excited*?"

"Yeah. I guess so."

He had a sense of peace about him. A sense of place. She watched him genially spread marmalade on his toast. There was no tremble in his hand. His color high; his voice clear. Most adults would be an emotional wreck at this stage, about to pull off the biggest hit of the century; Maggie about to get her just desserts.

"You'll get to shake Mrs. Thatcher's hand."

"And eat some cake!" Danny said with a toothy grin.

"And do you think you might give Mrs. Thatcher a hug?"

"Sure. If I hear a little whistle or something."

"You're so calm." She kissed his forehead, feeling her heart skip a beat. There was something magical about him that delighted and alarmed her. It was one thing for a mother to rename her son and to use him in a murder of his favorite parent, she was not the first mother to do such a thing, but it was something altogether different to strap a bomb around his waist, and it gave her second thoughts. Was she ready for this? Could she give up her only son for her career? Wasn't that what Jessica had done? Somberg found herself hesitant. And the hesitation surprised her. It was unlike her. But he couldn't be more ready on this, the dawn of his first kill, six years younger than she had been when she started. "Calm as a professional," she said, smiling with pride, knowing Maggie would love him, he looked just like her. She and Maggie so alike.

* * *

The heavy old spotted face had a two-day growth of silver whiskers, turkey-gobbler neck sagging, hair in white tufts, eyes closed in sleep. He was medicated and expected to sleep through the morning. Trent returned his chart to the footboard, sat on the hospital bed, and dialed the number. His stomach churning with the bell ringing on the other end of the line. He calmed love's spasms as a familiar gruff voice answered.

"This is Dr. Kaye," Trent said in his mother's soft Donegal accent. "I need to speak with a Sergeant Duffy."

"Aye, this is he," Duffy said, annoyed. "Who's calling?"

"Dr. Kaye. I'm a physician at St. Miranda Hospital."

"Kaye, is it? Don't know any Kaye!"

"I'm from Cork," Trent said, watching the sleeping eyes that rested in puffy shaded hammocks. "Subbing for O'Conner while he's away. He told me to call you if *he* came."

There was a pause as Duffy considered the bait.

"If who came?" he asked.

"Ye know, *that Brit.*"

"The Brit? He's *there*? In the hospital?"

"Aye. I've sedated him. He's fast asleep."

"Ye say ye sedated him?" Duffy barked a laugh. *"The Brit?"*

"Aye. And I hope he's the right one."

"What's his name?" Duffy asked warily.

"Said his name was Stanford."

"Well, *pigs will fly!*" Trent heard Duffy shouting the news to someone; then he came back, excited but still skeptical. "You say he's there? *Sedated*? How?"

"Came in this morning." Trent let a tremor of fear into his voice. "Asking questions, he was! I offered him files. Something I pulled from O'Conner's desk. While he was reading, I stepped across the hall to pharmaceuticals. Slipped him an injection. Into the neck. Hit him before he could get out of the chair."

"Merciful God!"

"Did I do the right thing? He's *not* a patient, ye know. I mean, I've no one's *permission*. Perhaps I should call O'Conner. I suppose that's what I should do. I'll call—"

"Easy does it. Ye've done grand!" There was a pause while Duffy spoke to the side, then, "How long will he be down, Kaye?"

"Oh, another thirty minutes."

Duffy roared. "Not full of piss and vinegar now, is he!"

"No, sir. Sleeping like a baby he is," Trent said, looking at the parched old bushy face beside him.

"*Like a baby!* Grand! Are ye in O'Conner's office?"

"No, sir. I've moved him to a room. Room Two-thirty-six. And just one of ye come. I wouldn't want a scene. We'll put him in a wheelchair."

"A *wheelchair!*" Duffy cried, announcing it to the world. "Be right down, Kaye. *Stay there.* If he wakes, give him another shot. I'll put this Brit on a grill and get some answers out of him!"

Trent rang off. Hung a battered leather jacket on the door. Buttoned a white coat borrowed from the laundry over a sweater and jeans. Straightening his Dr. Kaye name tag. He took up the end of the broom handle he had sawed-off in the basement. The homemade nightstick stout enough; it would likely do the job, considering the surprise it would be. Now he lifted the sheet over the old man's face. Had a look of tragical sobriety, like the old bugger needed a stiff drink. Trent wished he had one.

Allison combed her bangs smooth and shiny and straight and almost touching her sad brown eyes. She gazed into the mirror and saw the Queen of Downing Street, asking, "Who is the fairest of them all?" A silent rivalry had always existed between Mrs. T and the Queen. Sometimes it seemed as though Mrs. T, like Napoleon, had crowned herself. She had taken up the royal "we" whenever she spoke of herself, as if she were a queen. And how she would love to have a monarchy. To have the title Her Majesty.

Allison put her comb away, silently reviewing the day. The Americans were coming at nine for the conclusion of the summit, and she knew how the contest would be played. Her Majesty would begin with tea in the White Drawing Room; she would serve the tea herself, forever gracious, easing everyone into a feel-good mood. Gathering impressions, turning into flirtations. Bringing the Americans mentally erect. They would attempt to discuss basing their Trident missiles in England. Her Majesty would casually touch her coiffured hair and reach into her arsenal of smiles, put on the elusive one, then comment on the nuclear disarmament rally in the park outside the window, toying with the Americans like a cat with a mouse. Knowing her opponent was where Mrs. T always began; and in this case, she was especially lucky, she knew their timetable. She knew they had to leave by noon, and she'd take her sweet time, watching them soften and quietly go to pieces with time running out. Then she'd draw the Yanks wriggling to her point of view. Eventually they'd offer trade concessions, and only then would she allow the missiles into England, which was what she wanted all along.

When it was over and the Yanks had left, Her Majesty would storm into the study. Allison would listen to her endless litany of dissatisfaction and listen to her contemptuous gloating. She would fetch her tea and her everlasting Elizabeth Shaw mints and shower her with praise. Under praise, Mrs. T would act impassive, non-plused, unfazed, when, in fact, she was diamond-bedazzled by the drugging and beating given to the strung-out Americans. Her smile behind closed doors was chilly Cheshire cat, with a touch of the risqué. Something sexual in Mrs. T's tyranny. No one knew the woman like she did. Mrs. T was the hardest, the cruelest, the most alluring and the most predatory of all prime ministers.

In the mirror, Allison saw her narrow face flushed, bent down with parentheses set like clamps around her small mouth. She was astonished. Didn't know what had come over her. She let her lips curl into a faint smile. Adjusted her snow-white shirt, letting poisoned hate drain from apple-red cheeks. She had kept herself small for so very long, too long, her voice low, her steps short, her emotions compressed into the perfect secretary who Mrs. T relied on, and with a reluctant breath she returned to that self. Freshened her mouth in Soft Spoken Rose. Put her comb away and fluffed out the bow of her ruffled blouse. She reminded herself to hide her dark

icy hate. In this she must be like Mrs. T. She must never show her true feelings.
No one must know. Not ever.

From somewhere in the pub came the buzzing of a neon light that sounded like the
buzzing of bees trapped in a car. Like the yellow-bellied coward trapped in her head.
Jessica pushed herself out of the Father's chair and stood by the fire with a feeling
of vertigo coming over her. They were going to *kill* Trent. She heard the cop on
the phone. He was talking to the others now, planning the killing. Father Shanahan
was gone to pick up Danny and she was was to wait for him here, but how could
she let them kill Trent? She had to save him, that much was clear. The question
was, how?

She glanced around the pub. No way to sneak out, the front and back doors bolted.
One of the men was stationed next to the picture window, watching the street. The
others were at the back table with the cop, their guns on the bar. She took an
inventory of everything that could be used in an escape. There was the cot. The
blankets and the chair. The fireplace mantel was littered with beer mugs and a deck
of cards and a box of matches. On the hearth were a set of fire tools and a leather
bellows.

She tried to force a plan, working herself into a frenzy, her mind skittering from
one ludicrous scheme to the next. The more she worried the more morbid she became, and she kept worrying till she was sick with worry, and finally, after she was
exhausted, an idea came. A C-13 agent might say it was crazy, but it was the only
thing she could think of. She visualized it as if it were a shot in her studio. Seemed
feasible, if only she had the guts.

She waited with the tension building up inside her, until she couldn't wait any
longer. Felt like her bladder would burst. She had to use the bathroom, which meant
she had to set her plan in motion. *Don't think of the whole thing at once,* she told
herself. *Don't think ahead. Don't worry ahead. Don't think about Danny or Trent
or Thatcher. Just do it. Do it one step at a time.*

"Ah . . Excuse me," she called out.

The man by the window looked up.

"I need to use the powder room." She stood there trembling by the chair, which
was good; it looked like she really needed to go, which she did. "Is that okay?"
she asked.

He nodded and returned to watching the street.

She moved quickly through the tables glowing green in neon light with the bee-
buzzing louder in her hear. Moving the chairs, opening a path for her return. She
rounded the bar and stepped into a short hall and into the ladies' room. An odor of
decaying excrement and God knows what else. The glum of the Irish really showed
in their tacky bathrooms. They were morose. She sat on a frigid china bowl, trying
to do it, the stench of the bathroom overpowered by one even stronger, the unmistakable reek of fear.

That done, she pulled herself together. Peeked out the door. All clear. Ran across
the hall into the liquor cabinet. Scanned the shelves, feeling like she needed to pee
again. At first it didn't look like they had any; then she spotted a two-liter jug of
Everclear on the floor. *This is crazy, crazy, crazy!* She cut the thought off and

grabbed the jug, wrapped it in her herringbone jacket, then cradled the jacket under her arm. She practiced, trying to make it look like she wasn't carrying anything. Yeah, right, like the damn Everclear jug didn't weigh a ton. They'd spot her a mile away. She tried not to go mental, after all, this was the easy part. Stepped lightly from the closet. Peeked around the corner. A skinny silhouette in the window, sunlight spilling in behind him, churning with dust and maggots and atoms, her brain automatically measured the light. The watcher turned. She leaped back, so fast her breath left her, nearly dropping the damn jug of Everclear; she caught it sliding out of her jacket.

She waited, listening hard.

No feet approaching.

After a long moment, she risked another look. *What the hell will you say if he catches you with the Everclear?* She cut the thought off. She'd cross that bridge when and if she came to it. It was negative to think of such things, wasn't it? Or was it planning ahead? She wasn't sure. The man had returned to watching. A scream in her head, *Go! Go! Go!* Through her chair path, terror prickling up her back. Moving too fast, she made herself slow to a walk. Dropped into the big wing chair, slid the jug of Everclear under the seat, covered it with her jacket. Waited a minute. When her breath was almost normal, she rose and tried to act natural as she stole the matches off the mantel. Easy as pie! And now a few peat bricks tossed into the fire to make it all play real. Using the bellows, she coaxed the red embers into dancing flames. It was almost fun, playing spy; she could see why Trent did this for a living in Berlin. Back to the safety of her fat cowhide chair, bellows in hand. She was shivering, but it wasn't from the cold.

31

TRENT POSITIONED HIMSELF behind the door, his broom-handle nightstick in hand. Cautioned himself not to strike *too* hard. He wanted the Garda bugger talking, somewhat reconditioned perhaps, but not in need of the hospital's services. Footsteps down the hall. Now the door swung open. There were shiny boots and a dark blue coat with shiny brass buttons, the big greasy head before him and Trent checked his swing. The sergeant had the thickest neck he had ever seen outside of a zoo. In a split-second change of course, he slid the weapon into a back pocket and took a step off the wall as the heavy cop spun around and asked, "Are ye Kaye?"

"Aye," Trent said to the horse-faced Irishman, whose dark eyes were smoldering with suspicion. "*Dr.* Kaye."

Duffy looked him up and down. Trent sensed a wave of dislike come off him. He offered him a lovely smile.

"Ye look like a cool customer," Duffy said, unarmed, except for those lugubrious shoulders and arms. The flattened nose and cheekbones, the ears curled upon themselves like blossoms, spoke of negotiating talents exercised in alleys, or the proverbial smoke-filled back room, Trent had been in a few himself.

"Hey, I'm scared as hell," Trent replied in his mother's hearty brogue. "Mind you, I had no right to *drug* this man!"

"Ye had the right and the might of *Ireland!*" Duffy bristled with authority. "And that makes all things right." He turned to the sheeted figure in the bed. "Is that he? The Brit?"

"Aye. He's under our power now!" Trent measured those arms. A lot of meat there. But the man was three inches shorter.

"Would ye listen to this doctor's oaths?" Duffy said to the sleeping figure. He stepped round the wheelchair and stood at the bed. Hands on wide hips, grinning down at the captive with Trent as his side. The Irishman smelled of Guinness, peat fires, pipe smoke, lanolin, and boot polish.

"Will ye be asking him about that American woman?" Trent asked, the urgency in him something he didn't control.

Duffy glanced back, flat, dull face turned down in a frown. "Ye're a terrible one for galloping ahead, Doctor."

"Just curious."

"Ye stick to yer medicines, Kaye. I'll stick to mine."

Deep pink wrinkles on the back of the neck where it met the blue shirt collar. The clean-shaven, square jaw with the permanent gun-blue shadow of beard. Strength in the jaw, sinew throughout the throat and neck. Trent focused on a spot just behind the right cauliflowered ear, looked like it had been hit before. He waited until Duffy lifted the sheet and, in the instant's hesitation the haggard old man gave him, brought the broom handle around in a high, fast swing, just as the horse face turned and he missed the soft spot. The broomhandle gave a sharp crack, splintering on the greasy skull. Trent left holding a shattered baton in his hand, not quite what he had hoped for. An instant there, both of them staring at the baton. Duffy didn't collapse. Didn't bellow in pain. He only blinked.

"Shit," Trent hissed as Duffy pivoted with an uppercut that sent the bed swinging away in a blur. The fluorescent light in the ceiling rolled past, Trent catching a glimpse of that arrogant flat mouth abruptly widened to reveal anger and bad teeth. The room grew faint behind waves of gray. Trent pushed up from the floor. Duffy hit him again, knocking him to his knees.

A gasping moment there when the room was swinging sickeningly sideways with the bulky figure above him, the Irish voice already hoarse and panting. *"I'm gonna beat the living Jesus out of ye, Brit!"* A sudden shower of wild, heaving blows, and the ceiling seemed unnaturally bright to Trent. Duffy riding him hungrily, his fist with the hardness of stone, Trent surrendering the shoulders but keeping the face and chin tucked, gazing at the floor as a red mist rolled in to fog-soak the linoleum. Ears ringing. The Irish screams coming in like fractured bells peeling out of tune.

He reached out for the footboard, ducked another windmill that whistled past his ear. Now hauled himself up. A hammer hit him in the vicinity of the head, and he went down again and tried to get up. Didn't have any legs. He lay on the floor in the recovery position, while Duffy dealt him a couple of angry kicks to the groin with black comets streaming in Trent's head.

He had the bedrail again, about to climb again, leaving the ribs exposed for another menacing blow. The gruff voice coming with extra authority now. *"I'll carve me name on yer balls, ye fucking Brit!"* A click of steel, very distinct, brought back the training from somewhere, a mystery in the sliding, rolling room, and Trent's focus improved and his breathing settled with self-discipline once more. He glanced up. Light gleamed on the blade. The flash brought his instincts alive. The training did all the work. Blocked the stab from his knees. Both hands around the thick, hairy wrist. Twisted it cruelly. The blade right at his face, but with both hands he brought Duffy down, off balance. Hand to the face and into those murderous Irish eyes. Lovely shriek of pain and another twist of the wrist as Trent hauled himself up by a fleshy ear, trying to rip it out by its roots.

They danced a little jig with the knife between them, and he could feel Duffy tiring, the face pale, the lips hardened, but the fire in the eyes gone to smoke. Still, there was plenty left in those shoulders. An Irish bellow and a blind swing as another hard hammer hit his ribs with Trent gasping. They slam-danced into the wall, the horse face wet and hot against his. The bully lost his knife. The steel gave a merry ring as it hit the floor. A quick foot kicked it away. And now a blow to that saddlebag gut that slowed Duffy a step. A step was enough. Trent summoned all his fury into a flattened left chop that cut to the base of the throat and Duffy's scream came out like that of a pygmy. Now to put him away, had him by the wrist rotating clockwise, sliding up behind him, Trent using his height, yanking the thick, meaty arm up to its highest arch, provoking a good belly roar from the Irishman.

Trent pivoted with him as he tried to dance out of the hold, did a fine jig while being twisted, bent double. What to do with him? Trent looked around. Found a friend. Now the black greasy head rammed into the radiator. A moan. Backed him up and rammed him headfirst again. This time an awful basso sound. And again. Sweat streaming off the fat of the neck with a sag finally coming into the shoulders. Trent kept ramming him until he knocked the radiator loose from the wall, until Duffy's grandiose weight went limp. Trent walked him backward, dropped him into the wheelchair.

The room still swinging, and Trent drew a stabbing breath, hand on his ribs. "Duffy, you sonofabitch, I think you cracked my damn ribs."

But the sergeant didn't answer. He was slumped in the chair, one arm dangling, color drained from his face streaming with sweat and blood from a broken forehead. Found the pocketknife under the bed. He took Duffy by the roll of flesh at the back of his hot, wet neck, index finger and thumb applying the pressure, pricking the sharp blade into the tender flesh of the limp underarm.

"Make one move and you'll never use this arm again."

"*Who* are ye?" Duffy rasped in a blowtorch breath.

Thrusting rage into his ear, Trent seeing the broken railing and the oil slick in the bog, *"Where's Jessica Moore?"*

"Don't know." Duffy shook his head like a horse.

"Oh, yes, you know. And you're going to tell me."

"Fuck ye," Duffy muttered, eyes fluttering, starting to close.

Trent drove the blade deeper into the underarm, and the bulging bloodshot eyes came alive. "There's a good fellow," Trent said, and stuffed a washcloth into the open mouth. "Hold still now. Breathe through your nose." He pulled his belt and cinched the good arm to the chair. A bloody towel to wipe the horse face pretty. Blue gauze mask around his mouth and nose. Grabbed his leather jacket, covering the Garda uniform with the sheet. In the bed, the old man was nodding in a sleep that was invincible.

"If you make a noise or in any other way attempt to escape, I'll put this knife into your throat. You'll drown in your own blood. Do you understand, Sergeant?"

Duffy's broken head fell back. He groaned.

"Lovely," Trent said, rolling him out the door. "Now, you and I are going to find a place to have a probing conversation."

With the knife concealed under the sheet, Trent rolled Duffy down the hall and into the elevator.

32

DUFFY WAS STRUGGLING and muttering like a dreaming dog when Trent wheeled him out of the elevator and into the cold basement. Down the hall the kitchen staff was preparing breakfast trays. Trent rolled Duffy down the long corridor, looking for a place where they wouldn't be disturbed. Passed abandoned gurneys, considering a storage room and a roost of trash bins.

"Where's Jessica Moore?" he asked, removing the gag.

"Never heard of her," Duffy said in indignation.

"You're lying."

"Won't talk, Brit. Can't make me talk!"

"Oh, I don't know about that, Sergeant," Trent said in the tone of a man proposing a jolly family game. "We English have a long, *sanguine* history of interrogation. The *inquisitor* has always been our role. Schooled in timely applications of *pain,* we know how to pause between blows so the agony of the last fades *just enough* to allow the dread of the next before it arrives. How to offer hope that turns false to bring a man down. How to interrupt screeches and gurgles and guttural syllables. These, my Irish darling, are not taught, they're second nature to us English. We can extract information from the face. From knees. From finger joints and nails. From cheeks and teeth and eyelids and sex organs fried over a Bic lighter. Mind you, I don't speak from experience, but word gets around, you know."

Duffy squirmed in the chair. Trent pricked his neck with his knife and continued working the mind, easier than the body. In his previous incarnation with MI5 it was acceptable wisdom that a drama merchant could be as compelling as a savage interrogator.

"The game can be played crudely as a *pummeling* rifle butt used in the field. Cruel as *caffeine* under the skin. Or if you've the niceties of *pharmaceuticals,* done with sodium pentothal in a vein to depress the will. If one has the time, which you don't, Sergeant, a prolonged state of *sensory deprivation* is always effective. Velvet glove over a steel fist, that's the English way. But, of course, I'm not *entirely* English, am I?"

"Ye're a fucking Irish Judas!"

"Too loud, Duffy," Trent said, tsking and looking about. "We'll have to do something about that."

He stopped in front of a walk-in freezer and considered its possibilities. Dumped the doctor coat. Donned his leather jacket.

"Call me a Judas if you like, Sergeant. But just now I have only one country. Her name is Jessica Moore. You *will* tell where she is. I've no qualms whatsoever about suspending the rules of civil destruction on her behalf. Or her son's behalf."

Duffy watched as Trent zipped up the jacket. The collar turned up round the neck.

"Are you familiar with the science of cryonics, Sergeant?"

"Go to hell, *Judas.*"

"Actually, it's a great deal like hell, freezing, that is. Burns like the fires of hell." Trent snapped open the freezer door. A draft of vapor swirled out. "I did a science experiment when I was a lad," he said, parking Duffy in the cold swirling cloud. "Froze a half-dozen goldfish and brought them back to life"—Trent gave a sprightly laugh—"till they died hours later. But not before I won the blue ribbon!"

"Never going to talk!" Duffy shouted in what was now a surly voice. He looked about. There was no one to hear him in the empty corridor echoing with the clang and clatter of the kitchen.

"Sergeant," Trent said close to his bleeding ear, "if I can bring goldfish back to life, I can make you *talk.*"

Duffy looked up at the wide stainless-steel door that stood open before him like an invitation into a reverse hell. "Go fuck yourself, Brit," he retorted, already shivering.

Trent rolled Duffy through the snowy cloud. Parked him beside a pallet of hamburger meat. The big door fell shut behind them. A garage-size freezer of white walls lined in steel shelves racked with boxes. No truffles from Paris or Salzburg pastries from Vienna or Peking duck from China. The fastidious boxes held the functional and the efficient. Fish. Carrots. Corn. Peas. And the always thrilling cauliflower. In the back, several sides of beef hung from the ceiling, the carcasses frozen black.

Trent yanked off Duffy's cover sheet. "Would you care to know the temperature, Sergeant?"

White plumes burst from his wide flared nostrils as he screamed, *"Let me fucking out of here!"*

"I know you must be curious." Trent squinted at the frosted thermostat. "It's twenty below zero Celsius," he announced.

"Don't know where she is!" Duffy shouted to an audience of the frozen and the broken, waiting to be consumed.

Trent turned the thermostat all the way down. A numbing jet of cold began to howl from a fan in the ceiling. Took a seat on a case of ice cream, crossed a leg, and watched as a spasm of cold oscillated up the policeman-blue pudge of Duffy's belly.

"I had to build a special dry-ice freezer for my goldfish," he said by way of history that was true. "That's the tricky part to cryonics. One must *flash freeze* the subject."

"I won't talk!"

"You can keep them *frozen* as long as you like—"

"Who are ye?"

"—but the *thawing* must be expeditious or—"

"Are ye really C-thirteen?"

"—the blood will *crystallize* and—"

"How in the bloody hell can she know an antiterrorist!?"

"—induce cardiac arrest. I believe that's what happened to my goldfish. Cardiac arrest." Trent watched as a fleecy coat of frost spread over the blue Garda uniform. Frost began to grow in the oily waves of Duffy's Irish black hair, black as Trent's hair.

"Sergeant."

"Aye?"

"Would you care for some ice-cream?"

Fifty-three years prior to Lincoln's assassination at Ford's Theater, the British prime minister Spencer Perceval was gunned down before an astounded House of Commons. A few years before Columbus stumbled onto America, Edward V, the thirteen-year-old child king, was smothered with his bed pillow. Tenacious security is the principal reason there have only been only two British heads of state assassinated in five hundred years, that security the work of the Special Branch of Scotland Yard.

A team of sixteen Special Branch men had spent the night at Huntington Tower Elementary School, disassembling the grade-one classroom piece by piece. Chairs and desks were inspected, books turned out of their shelves, light fixtures examined. The floor was sounded for hollow compartments. Blackboards and bulletin boards removed. The drop ceiling was dropped, torch beams pried into every crevice of darkness. The world globe taken apart. Even the fishbowl was drained so the gravel bottom could be checked.

When the detectives finished, a pair of bomb-sniffing dogs went through the disjointed room, touching every object with their judicious muzzles. The animals' superior olfactory sense detected no explosives, and the men went back to work, reassembling and returning every component to its proper station, using Polaroid photographs. Kea Marten arrived at eight o'clock with a bouquet of jonquils and never knew her classroom had been inspected.

As a final precaution, two men were posted at the door while the children entered the classroom. Books and lunches examined by the men, not the dogs, as was normally the case. The dogs, due to an incident that had occurred in town the week before, could not be used. Once in the classroom the children would not be allowed to leave, and no one allowed to enter. Scotland Yard was confident there would be no guns or bombs at Huntington Tower.

How many times could a musical theme be repeated so it was unique in each variation? How many times could a kill be enacted so a technique was never duplicated? How many times could a femme be enthralled and transformed but never the same way twice? The simple made intricate and complex by ravishing modulations. It was one of her obsessions, *Rhapsody on a Theme* by Paganini, Piano Concerto No. 1 by Rachmaninov rolled through the Turner Studio, the concerto so loud it rattled the skylight. Somberg lounged on a chaise, eyes closed, inside the genius concerto that gave the impression of rambling improvisations but was, in fact a taut structure of variations on a single theme, as she was herself. Rachmaninov did it twenty-four times. She had nearly equaled that number in kills, and surpassed it by four in femmes.

The clear shape of the theme lived within Somberg, at times delectably lyrical, some passages frightening, some whimsical, all constructed with exquisite care, all encapsulating a wide variety of moods and melodies derived from the original, as she was from her mother who had given life to three extraordinary daughters. As the music transported her through the many variations, Somberg reviewed the kill, experiencing it in music that was not Mother's; that would be the Prokofiev. The Rachmaninov was Somberg's alone, a trimming of the soul. She knew Scotland Yard had dismantled the classroom, knew *exactly* how they had done it and how they had made it appear as if they had not done it. The Yard's operations manual for VIP security was forwarded by Nadia Roerich, a director with the KGB, and avid femme patron. And she knew the children would pass into the classroom without being probed by the dogs, thanks to a certain German shepherd she had sardonically named Winston.

Winston was a remarkably large dog, Alexia had found him in Edinburgh, easily room for another German shepherd inside Winston. Winston had been turned loose in quiet Grantham one evening last week, rushing down the street in his wolflike loping stride. A bedlam of howling and whitened eyes that spoke of a reckless depth of torment suffered from a savage Scot. Mothers snatched up their children, fleeing for their homes as Winston, sides heaving, black mouth pleated with white teeth, devoured his first victim. After they caught him, Winston was put to sleep, a blessing in light of his battered past, but not before he had the delicacy of Mrs. Whitelaw's plump calico cat. The story ran in the *Grantham Gazette,* referencing Scotland Yard's use of German shepherds to inspect all those in striking distance of the PM, set to visit a Grantham classroom next week. The challenge was easily arranged, child's play for a Pied Piper. The Yard was forced to bow to the swell of parental protest, insisting the children not be subjected to the jaws of dogs "like that fanged beast!" Scotland Yard could withstand the attempts of Whitewall to tamper with its security policies, but could not stand against a horde of provoked mothers. Mothers, as the cows in India, were sacred.

The rhapsody ended in a featherweight snippet of the theme, Somberg smiling upon the viper's bugloss on her desk, the flowers a good luck gift from her African sister, Laurnet, as lovely and lethal as the cake sitting at the school, waiting to kill Maggie. If perchance the cake didn't reach Maggie's lips, there was the explosive belt that, thanks to mad Winston, was in the classroom, undetected by the dogs. Somberg had learned years ago there was simply no obstacle invention could not overcome.

Jessica asked her captors for a pen and paper, telling them she wanted to write a letter to her son that she could give him years from now so he'd know something of what she had endured in waiting for him. They obliged her. She began the letter, though she knew if she were to write of the rambling improvisations of the struggle for her child it would take the form of a single theme, heartache, every word exact in its ascendant to emotion, in its depiction of agony, and if allowed to run its course would be the length of a complex, relentless, obsessive novel. Jessica did not have that much paper, or that time, and besides, hers was the business of pictures, not words.

She pretended to write, chomping furiously on a stick of gum she had taken from her purse, chewing the nervousness right out of her head. A glance to her captors. The one far across the room watching out the window. The others playing cards at the bar. She slid forward in the chair, body shielding her movements, turning the bellows upside down. Plugged the brass nozzle with a wad of gum, big enough she could pull it off in a hurry. She opened the accordionlike lung and, using the pen, drilled a hole into the top of it. Rolled the paper into a funnel. Inserted the narrow end into the hole. Now she opened the Everclear; the fumes rose in a cloud. Quickly, thinking only of Trent, who had to be warned of the Irish, she poured the flammable liquid into the leather lung.

She poured the jug empty; the Everclear sloshing and heavy inside the bellows. The hole in the lung she plugged with a lump of gum. The job done, she sank into the depth of the chair with the bellows, the matches beside her. Now she had a flamethrower.

33

THE COLD HUNG like a cloak of ice around Duffy's shivering body. His breath had powdered his face clown white. Lips blue. Teeth chattering. The evaporator fan howling in his head as it dropped the freezer into bitter temperatures. Duffy had his fat and Trent had his leather jacket that had begun to feel thin, and the one was almost equal to the other. One defiant, the other determined, both so stone Irish, unaware they were freezing at virtually the same rate. Trent had begun stomping his feet to keep the circulation going, trying not to feel the cold. He leaned down to thrust warm words into Duffy's frozen ear.

"Where is Jessica?"

"Fuck off, Brit!"

"You're getting light-headed, Sergeant."

"Fuck ye!"

Trent peered into lost eyes, lashes dusted white. "Very soon now you'll lose your sensitivity to light, Sergeant. You'll begin to see curious shapes and silhouettes, as if the cold has a soul itself and the soul is breathing in you, taking possession of your mind. When things dim to twilight, you'll know you're freezing."

"Won't talk," Duffy said to the hanging sides of beef.

"I won't let you die, Sergeant," Trent said, kneeling at Duffy's side, holding his pulse. "I'll wheel you out of here and listen to you scream. The thawing will burn like *fire,* but I won't feel a thing. And after you thaw, after you burn, I'll bring you back. We'll do it again and again until you *talk.*"

Duffy squirmed in his chair, his body locked in cold. *"Won't talk!"* he shouted over the howling blizzard. "Can't talk," he muttered to the pale brush strokes of a new dawn.

"You're on the verge of delirium," Trent said soothingly, but the freezer was beginning to gray around him. "Where is Jess?"

"No." Duffy shook his head viciously.

"Where is she?"

Duffy stared and Trent followed his eyes to the sides of beef, but somehow they had moved. They seemed to Trent to be a great distance away and he could barely see them. Trent stood and stamped his feet harder, faster.

"Her car went over the cliff. *Why?*" He pressed the heat of the word into Duffy's frozen ear. "Why did her car wreck?"

"Bees," Duffy mumbled, feeling a cold stinging on his face.

"Bees?"

"Aye." Duffy's fat face lunged forward, white and desperate, searching for what was stinging it. "Bees in the car!" he cried.

The rage was in Trent now, rushing over him. He imagined the fright, the help-lessness, the panic of an attack of bees in your car. He caught a glimpse of Jessica's face in the whited terror that now possessed Duffy. He took Duffy by the frosted hair and tipped the head right back with his mouth open, like a head at the dentist, with the throat exposed. He had the knife. It would be no trouble to cut his throat.

"Where did they come from? The fucking bees?"

"Don't know! Didn't do it!"

"Who did?"

"Don't know! Wasn't us."

"Who is *us?*"

Duffy's bloodied head twitched in Trent's hands and he knew he could do any-thing necessary to make him talk. Do it without compunction. Problem was, the stinging cold was closing on Trent. Over ears and fingers and toes. Hadn't counted on this, assuming the cold would attack and break Duffy before it touched him.

"Who is *us?* IRA?"

Duffy's face relaxed somewhat. The bees were leaving him now. Flying away. The stinging subsiding, going numb. He would take his leave as well, before too long.

"Is Father Shanahan IRA?"

"No!" Duffy shook his head now crushed between Trent's cold hands. He would never turn on the Father. Wouldn't. Couldn't.

Trent gazed up at the sides of beef and saw sides of Duffy on the meat hooks. Stupid fear frozen on their blue-white faces. He blinked. And now they were sides of beef again. *Who is breaking whom? Is that why he's grinning? Is this fat-insulated sonofabitch breaking me? Is he warm inside all that Irish fat?*

Trent let go of his face. He came around to the front of him. He braced himself on the arms of the chair. He leaned down into the Irishman, into his face. "Is Jess all right? Is she hurt?"

"Fine," Duffy groaned, breath smoked palely in the cold as if he burned with some inner fire, like maybe whisky siphoned from his veins. "She's fine. Cold and scared, but fine," he said, speaking of himself.

"*Where* is she?"

The blower kicked off. Deathly quiet at twenty below. The quiet cold seeped through muscle and grit and into the brain that it numbed before it killed. Trent glanced back. Hanging from the ceiling were black Duffy corpses frozen solid. And now he knew he was losing it. In deep shit here. *Need to get out of here while I can. Can't wait on this sonofabitch much longer.*

"Is *Shanahan* IRA?" Trent shouted against the cold, stomping around the wheel-chair, beating his arms about him, as cold as if he stood in shirtsleeves.

"No. Can't. Won't talk."

"Shanahan is the *Pope!* Right?"

Duffy's blue mouth worked silently, as if the cold were at his throat, freezing words before they escaped traitorous lips. He was sedated by the cold and glad for it. He had done many foul things in his time, broke a few arms, broke a few rules, he had even managed to break a few hearts, but he had not broken his oath to the Brotherhood. To do so was a death far worse than cold.

Trent pulled the knife and cut the belt. His hands red and burning as he warmed Duffy's pale hands, cold as frozen goldfish. A giant goldfish in the wheelchair. Its heart beating slowly, slowly, laboring beneath the fathomless fat where the heart was still warm, and Trent doubted he could outlast Duffy's heft.

"Where is the Pope? *Where,* damn it!"

"Won't. Can't."

"*Where is Jess?*"

"No. Can't. Won't."

"Danny? Where?" Trent seized the frosted coat lapels and saw the theatrical-looking white hair and parched face that resembled his own. He turned ruthless, shaking the man in the wheelchair, as that good man in Jessica's flat had been rousted to death. He lay the blade of the knife to Duffy's fleshy throat. The cold steel opened it instantly, as though seeking the warmth within. Happened almost as if on its own. With no trouble he could sink that blade deep to take more than blood now trickling from a one-inch wound, he could sever the throat and feel the warm rush of air coming up from the lungs. The dark things are like idiots in the cold. They have a mind of their own. The cold becomes its own master, deaf and blind and ridiculous.

He yelled now, trying to raise some serious hell, some heat. "C'mon, you son-ofabitch! Tell me! *Where?*"

Layers of ice, thin as tissue paper, had built up around Duffy's lips, which hinged open. A gray tendril of breath leaked out. Trent in a panic. Shrieking! Coming unglued. Shaking Duffy as if to shake the chattering teeth out of him. Shaking him till the tongue was protruding from the mouth and the eyes were glaring, filled with rime and frozen around as with the blur of tears. Or was the blur from his own tears?

"*Tell me. Tell me!*" Trent looked around the enclosure of the room and saw an elevator. He felt the car sink queasily beneath his feet with a shuddering working up his legs at the torture of the motor high above making a grinding sound, like the grinding of the teeth of a madman. He heard the ping of their arriving and the asthmatic sigh of electric doors. Their descent ended, and he knew dear, depraved Dante had it all wrong. Had it reversed, in fact; as in gender-reversed. Hell was not fire. Hell was cold. Wasn't all of space cold? A black freezing wasteland without end. And if hell was cold, then heaven was warmth. The Earth was warm.

Now, not trusting himself, he put the knife away. He shouted in a drawling, side-of-the-mouth slur. *"Where the fuck is Jess?"*

"Pub," Duffy mumbled.

"Pub? *Which pub?"*

"O'Fllaaaaa—" Duffy's heavy face wrenched as he realized he couldn't speak. Couldn't form the word. "O'Flaaaa—"

"Where, damn it?" Trent shouted over the evaporator fan that had kicked back on; hell whistling in his ears. "Where is she?"

Duffy's mouth did a slow, painful twist, and Trent thought he could hear the skin crack in the cold. "At pub," Duffy muttered.

"Which fucking pub? *Where?"*

Duffy looked up into the cruel and magnificent face of Death. All was confusion, one thing blending into another with the colors fading into a cold whiteness in which there was no sense of taste or touch or smell or heat, everything fused into one nothingness. He wanted to rise out of the chair but could not. Couldn't move his arms. Or his legs. He wanted to turn his head but couldn't even do that. This was the deep down exile from the Self. The cold sinkhole of gloom, harsh and even ironic. Death had the face of a handsome Irishman, but the voice of a damn Brit. And wasn't that just like Death, to tweak you into the ultimate despair?

"Where? Which fucking pub?"

Duffy's compression faltered, than sputtered back to life. "O'Flaaaaaherty's." Duffy said to Death.

"In Killarney?"

Duffy nodded, his face a living waxwork, unable to change expressions. Trent noted this and noted that he felt fine. No stinging hands. He wasn't even cold. He assumed his shivering had somehow warmed him. He glanced at the glazed stainless-steel door. *Found Jess. She's at O'Flaaaaaherty's Pub. Should I go for more? Should I go for what's behind Door Number Two?*

"Somberg!" Trent shouted. "Why did she take Danny?"

Duffy sat silent and rigid. Trent tried to shake the question into him but found he was too stiff to shake Duffy. Found himself in stocking feet, caught on some shattered ice field, feeling the terror that was the worst kind of terror, the terror of the trap between his Irish heart and his British mind, the catastrophe of ambition leading him on, and he could not prevent it, through jagged spikes of ice, the blowing cold overtaking him, here where there was no subterfuge, where he had run amok among the shards of his life. Was he Irish? Or was he British? He was a man divided against himself. Only a whole man could go on, into those Arctic blue eyes of the beast that was as a sea of ice that turned men into stone. He saw himself enter a ghosthouse. Walking its grim corridors like a haunted man. Carrying the sword that must be used to lop off the head of the stylish beast, this the only way to end its hold, to kill the thing. But could a divided man do it? A soul divided was some serious hell, he had known it all his life, and sensed he would have to choose. Between what? Ireland and Britain? Or the beast and Jessica? In the back of his mind, he knew the true authority it would take to do the beast, seeing himself in a kind of school that would be the last word of his future, and he cursed himself for what he knew but did not understand.

"Where is the Pope?" cried the Britishness in him, pressing for more. It was the bent of the British. *To take.* To take what was not given. The whole Irish problem was there. It could only be resolved by doing the reverse. *To give back what was taken.* In the cold Trent could see it clearly, simply, as a child lost in hell.

"No," Duffy muttered. "Die first."

"Somberg? To do the Prince of Wales? *Prince Charles?*"

Duffy looked up to Death, and an infinitesimal curl of a smile formed on his blue lips. Death did not know it all.

"Aye," Duffy slurred through his arch smile. " 'Tis the fucking prince."

"Damn! Graham was right!" Trent lurched from the wheelchair like a man who just been shocked. "I could have sworn it was Thatcher!" he said to the chair. He got behind the chair, put a shoulder to it, pushing with body and legs hard with cold, heavy as iron weights as he shoved the chair anchored in ice. "Jess, what the hell have you gotten us into?" he yelled at the burning cold in his brain. Had to find O'Flaaaaaherty's Pub. But, God, what he wouldn't give for a cup of tea! Hit the door handle. A swirling snowy cloud rose from the warmth beyond. He pushed the chair through the snow, smooth as cake frosting below his feet.

34

JESSICA STARED WITH insomnia eyes into the fire. She had an eighty-proof hangover from Father Shanahan's tea. She had dozed awhile, then woke in a panic, grasping for some urgency she could not quite reach. Every time thereafter she attempted to return to sleep she found herself in her darkroom with Danny committing her murder all over again. The scene replayed with the persistence of a psychic message too dangerous, too painful, and Jessica shrunk from it. She was comforted by the authentic smell of peat that hung lightly in the air. The earthy fragrance ascended from the quiet sizzling fire that like her dream kept burning all night.

The makeshift bed had gone untouched, she preferred the big cozy cowhide chair worn soft by the chronicles Father Shanahan had authored in its comfort. His narratives as those ancient myths of gods and beasts were told orally. Shanahan practically sang them, as he had sung to her in his enchanting voice, honoring her with his promise to retrieve Danny, and it seemed she had heard him in her sleep telling the tale of a death foretold.

She had been to the bathroom twice in the endless night, the "latrine" the Irish called it. Made it sound like something in a jail cell, stunk like that, and wasn't she held in something of a cell? With armed guards. No way they'd let her go. Her confinement was unbearable but part of her nutty condition, having sunk into the quicksand of the Father's tenderness and she wanted to believe he would return her baby. She asked herself for the millionth time how all this had happened. Why wasn't she at home with Danny? What had she done to deserve this? The question was familiar and took her back to a gray Chicago morning with no sun. A path lifted to a hill that Pit assaulted in his chair, Jessica jogging beside him, complaining as she went. Same song: *Why me?*

"Life's got nothing to do with deserving," Pit said, spinning his chrome wheels as fast as her good legs could run. "That's some nursery rhyme you were taught as a child."

"But what did I do to deserve this?" she said, huffing up the hill, fighting against it all as she went. "I know I should have given Danny more of myself. And I will, but—"

"That's the ticket! You *will*. It's gonna happen."

"But did all this happen, did I lose my baby, because of that wrong? Because I short-changed Danny of my attention?"

"Oh, Lord, no. Right and wrong are from the same book of nursery rhymes as deserving. We want to believe in right and wrong because the world is easy that way. Black and white. It's a thing we teach the kiddos, but real life doesn't work that way. Never did. What in God's name was right about slavery? But it was right at the time, if you lived in the old South. A slave who ran away was wrong. When caught, he was punished. Worse thing they could do to a runaway was take his kids, and they called that right. Same as the bastards who got my kids; they're right and everybody goes along with it. Right and wrong is an insignificant trinket to the complexities of the heart. It's a lighting effect, right or wrong; we can rig it anyway we want. Right and wrong is an attempt to make life simple, so you don't have to think, just follow."

"I hear you," Jessica said, pounding up the hill, keeping up, not sure where they were going. "I hate your loss like I hate my own. Falsely accusing you of sex abuse was the same as using Danny to shoot me. Aimed at the heart. Meant to kill. Then for your son to be taught that you were dead. . . ." A morbid fear crept from Jessica's heart to her throat. Did Danny believe she was dead?

"Yes, and those nickel-plated bastards believed they were right when they did it. And to this day, they'll swear to high heaven they're right about all of it."

"Sounds like *greed* to me," Jessica said.

"Oh, it's monstrous."

"I guess they call it *love,*" Jessica said, wondering if Danny didn't love the bitch that held him. "And they have to make you out to be the monster, so it won't look like *greed*."

"That's about the size of it. There's only one truth in this world," Pit squinted up at her, a legless, childless dad rolling furiously. *"Power!"* he thundered. "That's as good as Gibraltar, by Jesus and Christ. You can set a royal mess straight with power, like the power of a story, 'course it'd have to be a dilly to get anyone's attention. My story would have to be told as a mother, since we don't feel for fathers like we do for mothers. Though they feel the same. Pain is no respecter of gender."

And now in the pub Jessica couldn't get rid of the dream that had the power of story that she did not yet understand. Every time she closed her eyes she was returned to the darkroom shooting, and she wondered if Danny had been taught that she was dead? Was this the message in the hard-working dream? Wouldn't Danny believe she was dead, since he shot her? Didn't he see her fall? Jessica had the frightening certainty she was dead to Danny, and whatever had compelled the dream, was compelling her to escape. To warn Trent about the Irish who were planning to kill him. To tell him of the plan to kill Margaret Thatcher, Father Shanahan's voice echoing from out of sleep, and she wondered if she'd ever sleep again for the rest of her life. Not unless she escaped. She had to do this for Danny. She didn't understand that part but trusted it.

She turned up the collar of her blazer and slid to the edge of the chair with the bellows flamethrower at her feet. She picked it up. Her hands were slick with sweat, and she wouldn't think about the right or wrong of what she was about to do but only of Danny and Trent and how to save Trent and how to spray the fire to make a wall of fire that the Irish couldn't cross. Now she looked over the greenish neon-lit pub. Her path to the front door was obstructed with chairs. *Gotta weave through those,* she thought. *And remember to work the bolts on the door.*

Her feet spread wide as she lifted the heavy sloshing weight of the flammable Everclear. *I can do this,* she told herself. *It will work. Pull the gum off the nozzle. Aim at the fire. Pump; turn; keep pumping. Then run like hell.*

Father Shanahan considered the height of the brick wall and wished for trumpeters to march round the Warnock estate and blow the walls down as had been done at Jericho for those long ago children of Israel. He drew the sterling flask from his robe, took a pull on the hero drink, deadening the migraine beating in his temples like the snare drums of a Brit prime minister's funeral cortege. Now came the riderless black horse, jackboots reversed in stirrups, iron-shod hooves pounding the cobbles, pounding in his head, reverberating in pain. *Clip-clop, clip-clop, clip-clop.*

He finished off the flask in the grip of a vision in which he saw Thatcher who held Northern Ireland, and Gorgon who held the lad from America, as mother and daughter. He took up the long-barreled chrome-plated Smith & Wesson .45. He left the car behind and as he approached the red brick wall with its high wrought-iron gates that appeared to be insurmountable, he called upon Jehovah, the God of wrath and vengeance. "O Lord, my God, Thou art my strength and salvation which teacheth my hands to war and my fingers to fight. Open to me the gates of Thy righteousness that I may deliver the lost. Let the wickedness of the wicked come to an end, and let the evil speaker wither and burn in Thy fire, and in the name of the Lord will I destroy them, daughter and mother, the heirs of the demon who in their snare hold the fair lad and the good land. Lift me on angel spirits, and make of Thy minister a flaming fire! Blessed be the name of the Lord forevermore."

He had driven Thatcher's parade route with the streets lined in bleachers and he knew where and how he would take her. He had seen her arms as candles with the skin of her smooth face shiny in flames. The Iron Lady twisting in the heat that in a millisecond consumed her, blown to smithereens, nothing but blasted and black lines on the ground where she had stood, her remains scattered to the winds! He had only to climb the gates and kill Gorgon. In saving the lad he would redeem his soul, then meet that good fiery end that would take Thatcher in a tempest. He looked to the trail before him and called again on Psalms: *With the help of my God I shall leap over the wall.*

It wasn't easy climbing the iron gates in his bulky dynamite vest. His robe snagged under his boots, but he pulled himself up, scaling till he reached the gold-spiked lances. The black-and-white Tudor rose ghostlike out of the misted chestnuts. Shanahan saw the flaccid Union Jack that dangled from a mast. A gun-silver Mercedes parked on the circle of the drive. In his mind he quietly slid through a window. He searched the house and found her at a vanity, painting her whorish face. There would be no quips, no final stinging lines. There was a time to talk and a time to kill, and he would give the demon only the instant it took to see his reflection in the mirror. From the gate he saw the heavy bullet slam into her skull, spraying hair and chips of bone as her body was thrown out of the vanity chair onto the carpet. He would not give her last rites. He would stand over her and listen to her perfumed voice as she lay calling his name through a mouth of broken teeth, beautiful face destroyed, body jerking as if in the thralls of passion, but not enough to require another round.

He pulled himself over the lances, careful not to prick the dynamite, his old back bent double. He gripped the gate to steady a swoon, swaying at the height. Raised his boot and in turning, stepped on a fold of robe with the chestnuts and Tudor pitching upside down in his shriek of *"Jesus!"* as he fell.

Life is a steely visage when hired by one of the offshoots of the IRA. Somberg gambled on O'Grady, who was solid enough, but his sidekick, the devoted murdering priest, was on the lunatic fringe, and together the dynamic duo were something of a romantic comedy. Knowing screw-ups were practically an Irish birthright, Somberg brought in her baby sister, ostentatiously qualified as a mole, to keep tabs on Shanahan in the critical days preceding the hit. She had shadowed Shanahan since Killarney, and reported to big sister from the Grantham airfield where Shanahan's disciple had planted a bomb. This was no surprise; nor was his appearance on the monitor of the front gate camera, protocol was hardly the fashion of the IRA. Somberg was racing through the gardens with a 9mm Glock when he fell. She found him hanging from a lance, his cassock pulled over his head, his feet, a meter from the ground, were beating at the air like frantic wings. He looked like the biggest dope in the world. The ludicrous revolver on the drive. She picked it up. She peeked under the robe and smiled up at his bloodied face.

"Good morning, Father! Dropped in for a cup of tea?"

He gazed down on the frightfully independent woman. "Holy Mary and all the saints," he moaned.

"Thank you, Father. And I do have a whole array of saints. Femmes, I call them. Hardened hellions devoted to their Mary."

"You're no Mary," he shrieked. "You're a *witch!*"

Her laugh rang in Shanahan's ears as a Thatcherite thrill. She lifted his drape of robe to take a better look at him. Acute surprise was not within Somberg's emotional makeup, but for an instant she was speechless, staring at the vest of nitrobenzene.

"Father Shanahan!" she called in a chummy voice. "Did you know you're wearing a dozen sticks of dynamite?"

" 'Tis not a dozen," he muttered. "Judas is missing."

"Whatever were you going to do with all that hell?" Somberg considered the question. She saw the wires at the waistband of his trousers. They ran down his leg. She pulled off the boot and found a pressure-sensitive detonator on his heel. Plain and practical, classically Irish. Except they usually didn't sacrifice themselves. That was more like an Arab. Irish bonfires of conviction did not burn that bright. The Irish were foxy; bomb and hide in a hole.

"Oh, I get it! You were going to shoot me, then, what, go to Maggie's homecoming parade—let's see; how would an Irishman do it?—you'd embrace her as she passed and stomp your foot!" She laughed again, enthralled by his ambush. "The nitrobenzene would take you and Maggie hand-in-hand through the pearly gates! I can just see it! What a pair that'd make for Saint Peter!"

"Go to hell," Shanahan snarled.

"Yes, dear, but not today." She smiled up at him, loving the sight of a priest hanging from her gates. A gift from God Herself, his robe identical to that of the raping priest of youth in dear old Stockholm. Visions danced in Somberg's head. "I'd shoot you, Father, but the explosion would alert all Grantham. You'd be all in the trees! That'd be strange fruit, wouldn't it?"

"Strange fruit indeed," he groaned.

Managing the unforeseen was the mark of the professional, the whole point is to anticipate, but only in nightmares had she hoped for this. She luxuriated in this dream. Her *own* priest. Whatever would she do with him? The girl in her could think of a hundred things, unfortunately there were time constraints. She covered him with the automatic as she cut him down. He landed in a heap on her drive. Shanahan wobbled up on wonky legs. At gunpoint she led the hopeless priest through her garden, dribbling blood over a bank of wild blowing thyme and oxlips and nodding violets. So romantic! So Shakespearean, really, in jolly ol' England, full of surprises.

Trent stepped out of the public call box. He strolled past the tourist office, just another Brit admiring the little gem of Killarney. Glanced into shop windows, pretending to be fascinated with the handwoven sweaters, while scanning the fog-soaked street reflected in the glass. Looking for nothing, seeing everything. He had just leveraged the full weight of his PM authorization against the Yard and the Royal Navy. Never heard Graham howl so loud. The old boy sounded like a stuck pig. It didn't seem such a terribly excessive request. After all, the *HMS Hermes* was in the Irish Sea, cruising for port. It was a slight inconvenience for the aircraft carrier. A scrambling exercise. But it wasn't as if he were calling for an air strike on Killarney. "Just need a taxi," he told the admiral aboard the *Hermes*. "In a bit of a hurry."

Taxis were lined at the curb that he passed with the drivers studying him with a bold curiosity. But that was nothing but Irish spurning for tourism and Irish adoration for the tourist dollar, the soul of Ireland that it could not escape. It was at the center of his thoughts, *escape.* The loss of a son is nothing to trifle with. It is a serious onslaught of the soul. Testing all impulses and motives and capacities and weaknesses. Something primitive at work in Jessica's relentlessness that could never be restrained. There was the prevailing fear that must be denied, but did simply still exist, that you might never see your child again. See being the least of it. Love being the whole of it. It was a primitive honor, to prowl through the depths of unfathomable emotion beyond any earthly reason to find that love that was never lost but had been taken. So there was the plague of the black thoughts of hate. A brooding ferocity. Starving out love. Jessica had the fever and there would be no restraint and no significant relationships until she found the boy. It might go on ten years. It would to Jessica be as a day. She would go through many Trents, wearing each out in unprincipled tenacity that must deliver. A kind of unscrupled love that would leave the corpses of a battlefield of friends and family and men with the best intentions behind her. Taking a sort of strange pride in sorrow. The longing, the exile, the deep-down defining depression were Jessica's and she would not escape them until she recovered love. By hook or by crook. As in publish or perish. Her resolve would go off the charts and beyond the fear of never loving Danny again. No fear can stand up to hunger. And so Trent searched for her, this savage with the desperate grief, in the full knowledge that he must recover the child to fulfill his own need which had become Jessica. He looked for her in the blind whiteness of the Irish fog that was none other than love.

He found O'Flaherty's Pub easily enough. In the middle of everything, corner of New, High, and Main Streets. Silhouette in the window. Cardboard sign tacked to the tomato red door: ''Closed for Repairs.'' If under repairs, why was a man watching the street from the window? How many ''repairmen'' were in there with him?

The lady at bakery was so very nice, offered him a jaunting car to the Gap of Dunloe as she filled a sack with pastries. It so happened her brother had a service that gave tours through that primitive wonder that had forgone the preservation of appearances to give the absolute face of Ireland never marked with civility. Trent thanked her kindly, and assured her that he would pay the Gap a visit, soon. He carried the pastries up New Street. He was invisible in the cloying fog. He knew the lads must be hungry if they'd watched all night. A pastry might hit the spot about now. Something for the cause. A small contribution from those who silently serve, as Trent had since he met Jessica and was drafted into her cause. He would deliver his gift, to fetch a look inside the pub. And now he breathed in the sticky pall of the ground fog, keeping out of the sight line of the window to rehearse his lines, comforting bulk of the Beretta under his left arm.

Jessica got the match ready in case the fire flickering in the peat did not work. Cold sweat slid down her ribs. She felt almost hypnotized by the sigh of the slow burning fire of no more danger than a fairy princess sleeping in a fabulous castle. She made herself forego the hopeless fable that waited for others, the hopelessness and waiting so easy to slide into. A state of mind that made attack inconceivable. She had an instinct to wait for Danny. Hopeless about warning Trent of the Irish. Hopeless about her daring plan, and about a ruined career, and the shipwreck of her life that in the air of absolute hopelessness was the smashup of every life that ever hit bottom from where we must *let go* of our hold of the deadly hopelessness to believe. To do. *Action!* was the language of the living. Something, anything, must happen; she felt it in her bones. She would make it happen. She would do it now. Somewhere she could hear a baby crying, wailing, choking and crying some more. A baby in her imagination that was nothing but the crybaby of the world. And, again, she heard that small flute melody of true, unfailing hope from Beethoven's seventh. It would not be repressed. It swelled, with the full symphony, to drown out the crybaby, and those louder voices of pestilent reason.

Sure, the Irish had their guns, but they were at the far end of the pub. They seemed miles away. She had surprise on her side. And, besides, they wouldn't shoot a mother, would they?

She watched as the man in the window came across the room to speak to the two card players. *C'mon!* Pit bellowed in her heart. *Quit stalling! Where's your guts, girl?*

In my cold belly, she though. That sounded chicken shit and she immediately overcame it. *I can do this,* she told herself. *It will work. Pull the gum off the nozzle. Aim at the fire. Pump; turn; keep pumping. Then run like hell.*

In those words, repeated again as a charm, an incantation, a summoning, some fierce brooding character took possession of her. Of immediate hostile intention. Unexpected, wild, and as violent as the Irish themselves. It would take that to escape them. She would fight fire with fire. And hardly breathing, she pulled the chewing-gum plug from the brass nozzle. A roaring and beating in her ears like the sound of the ocean as she pointed the heavy sloshing bellows at the fire with a wave of love spilling through her, steadying her aim at the low glowing coals. She said a prayer and shoved the billows handles together. A fat stream of Everclear shot out and exploded in a white-hot flash that made her jump.

A second there when Jessica was thunderstruck. Red coals all over the hearth with a warmth flowing into her cheeks. It worked. It actually worked! And then came a frenzy of feet and she did not panic but steadied herself and pumped another stream of Everclear and kept pumping, hosing Everclear halfway across the pub, staying well ahead of the flame so it wouldn't feed back into the bellows. In the fireplace the peat was now burning like a smelting furnace, as though it had been cut from the flaming bog of the Irish soul, choking, blistered, desperate under the loss of six counties to the North. The flame tasted the straight alcohol, licking it up in little tendrils of low blue flame that skipped over the sawdust floor, excitedly gulmping liquor like some drunken man. The fire shallow at first, an unstable fool, the flames seemed to stagger and lean, looking around as though familiarizing itself with its surroundings. Growing upright and steep, pointy flames in peacock blue tinged with green, the very fire of the Irish spirts, Jessica could see as much, what's more, she could feel fire in her veins. Gorgeous flames! Leaping for the ceiling. Sawdust and Everclear burning like some mother's napalm.

She kept pumping, turning as she pumped, watching as tables became a shimmering turquoise-yellow wall. Two men running toward her. Mouths twisted open. Jessica aimed the bellows at a pennant of flame. Pumped hard. A rill of Everclear shot across the pub and through the flame to became a turquoise river of living fire that streaked in a spooky *whoosh!* sound, its flaming tongue licking for the bar. Mirror and liquor bottles exploded! Colored glass danced in the air! A Kodak moment with all the colors reflected on the tin ceiling already roiling with ovenlike heat. Then the breaker box blew and dropped the pub into darkness, jagged sparks raining like the white-hot spits of hell over her captors in retreat, and Jessica was then no longer a hapless mother. She had never been spiritless, anemic, her imagination run to ground. She had never cried in a window seat on a bleak frigid day. She had never lost a night of sleep. Never arose in despair. Never cringed before a storm of anguish that came from nowhere in the middle of broad daylight. Never screwed up her eyes to heaven. Never shook a fist at God. She had never been stripped naked of her dignity and was never reduced by her wounds. She rolled her eyes over this burning, illuminating, fitful fire, that seemed made of her very emotion, so overpowering, but now with a touch of control, with a purpose, and she was in that moment, awe-inspiring. Terrible. Deadly. The whiner vanquished forever, finally fighting back in bewildered wonder to this pent-up, mysterious frenzy to which she now woke to, that was nothing less than the visage of herself.

She felt a sudden urgency come over her, that was not unlike the humming of angry bees coming out of a hive. She dropped the bellows and ran through choking smoke. Running in the dark—she hadn't planned on that—with hands outstretched, shoving a path through the chairs. She glimpsed the front door and a sly grin curled—she had done it!—just as a chair leg seemed to reach up and catch her. She went down hard, hands first, sliding over the sawdust floor. A red mist in her eyes, that was now a red gleam as she crawled up to her knees. Her head swimming in the heat that she saw rolling off the ceiling like the froth of heaven. She must have hit her head, she decided. For a second there she saw the smoke rolled back as clouds to reveal the Cleveland Symphony, Pit in a frenzy as conductor, doing exceedingly well for himself directing Beethoven's seventh. The supreme energy of it vibrated all the way to her feet and helped her fight off an intense blackness that wanted to overcome her. *"Damn it!"* She pushed herself onto her feet with a shriek with the swirling now in the very air she breathed. Choking air. Jessica sidestepped a table, mowed down two chairs, glancing back through the iridescent waves of heat that showed, beyond the wall of fire, the dark columnar shapes of men. Their tirade of Gaelic coming in loud and clear, along with the hiss of fire extinguishers.

She made it to the door. Unlatched the top bolt. Easy as pie! The bottom bolt jammed. She shoved. It wouldn't budge. She kicked at the damn thing. Suddenly the face of the door shattered into splinters. She dropped to the floor as another fusillade raked above her head, and this time she heard the gun and her scream. It seemed impossible anyone would shoot at her. She was so *right* in her cause. But now she saw the muzzle flashes through the flames, but in the dark still couldn't work the bottom bolt of the door that seemed to be beating from the outside like a big drum. She heard her name called. The calling went on with the effect of silencing her efforts. She realized it was Trent calling. She yelled in return. The door burst open. Light streamed in.

She never saw him. She saw only a hand. She grabbed it and was pulled up into the light that shone now on a gun that erupted in a loud staccato burst of thunder in her ears! In the afterclap of Trent's Beretta all sound in the pub ceased. She stumbled, and then fell out the door. Legs shaking from the gunfire. Now running with an urgency unlike anything she had ever known, the guns still erupting in her somewhat deafened ears. For an instant it looked like all of Killarney was going up in smoke. God, had she somehow set the town on fire? She cut through curling fog and through cars and across the street with Trent yelling behind her.

"Shit! Jess, slow down a little!"

She eased off a step, and as he came out of a cloud she took one look at him, in that leather jacket, with his hardened face, the danger in his eyes, but with a crooked smile, and her heart went romping down the street. She knew then that she couldn't live without this man.

"This way," he said as they approached an intersection.

"What? I can't hear!" She pointed to her ears.

He grabbed her hand, pulling her with him around the corner. "Are you okay?"

he asked. She nodded, couldn't stop her smiling. He was gorgeous in the fog. Some kind of leathered animal running through fog. A prime specimen. Very alert and grave. The sinewy muscle in his face and neck glazed in dew. His stride long and so very smooth that something in her wanted to just stop and watch him run. He would run forever in that fog with her running beside him. "What the hell is going on?" he shouted so she could hear with her shot ears. "Where did the fucking fire come from?"

They ran past the bank. Past the deli, its clouded round window giving back Trent's reflection as a shield in which she saw the features of the monster who took Danny. But as she looked, the seemingly mystic reflection appeared not to be Trent but a grownup Danny. As though he were running into the next millennium. Jessica shuddered at the sight of it, seeing the Beretta in Danny's hand.

"I did the fire!" She shouted so she could hear herself, and she couldn't stop the brag in her voice or the crazy exhilaration through the terror rolled together with the love into the wet fog so dense it seemed like they were standing still when, in fact, they were running flat out. "I had to escape. To save you."

"Save *me?*" Trent stared at her flushed face with the wind in her hair. His hand at her waist, steering her across the street. "How did you manage to set the pub on fire?"

"Never mind that. Trent, they're going to kill Thatcher!"

"You mean Prince Charles," he corrected, running smoothly beside her, hand on her back now, very sure of himself.

"No. *Margaret Thatcher!*"

"No, it's Charles," he insisted. "Come on; the car is this way." He pulled her into an alley, and they vanished into fog.

35

SHANAHAN WOKE AND tried to remember passing out. He had a concussion that had induced a bloody migraine, this one a real vise-gripper. He felt like a piece of dung, in a general state of dizziness and nausea. He tried to move and couldn't. Bound to a bench in a bleacher like the ones erected along the street for Thatcher's homecoming. The bleacher in a balcony above a studio. Pleasantly Gothic, with the most ostentatious woodwork and gables. His eyes followed a beam that supported the balcony and ran above the studio. A sculpture hoist hung from it, casting the shadow of a hangman's noose over a marble bust of Thatcher. He was left to stare at the likes of the woman he set out to kill. Splendid.

In his throbbing head, a sweet Irish tenor was singing "Danny Boy" in a quivering voice. And now his mission of rescuing the lad came back to him. He had done a grand job of fucking it up. He recalled climbing the gate and falling, and the Beast who took him prisoner, the bloody harlot. Merciful God! What had become of him? All his manful talk of murder, now taken by a woman. He pulled at the ropes, but was tied like a damn pig bound for market. He gave the Thatcher bust another look. White marble, it sat on a pedestal next to a handsome desk of ball and claw feet, fit for a king. Or a queen, as the case may be, the bloody harlot. There were grand sofas, filled with goose feathers, no doubt—he felt like a damn plucked goose—with a creative disorder of scaffolding about, the shelves with cans of paint. Looked like lacquer. The patriot in him, ever the cool customer, reckoned the bomb that could be made from all that lovely lacquer. Enough there to send this overdone English manor house to hell. It was a shame he was tied.

Suddenly Gorgon was there. Smiling up from the foot of the bleacher. Blond hair and blue eyes set off by the black she was dressed in. Carrying a bouquet of bridal wreath. Well now, what would she be doing with that?

"Welcome back, Father. Did you have visions of the walking dead?" Shanahan wouldn't look at her face. Long legs ascended the bleacher. He saw her twirling his silver revolver on a finger. "I see you don't understand *'the walking dead.'* But you will."

She was standing before him, with those looks soft enough to melt butter in a man's mouth, the harlot. Her full, ripe breasts swayed before him, so close he could kiss them. Or bite them, but he was gagged. He closed his eyes against temptation. But she was waiting for him in his dark. Sun blond hair and dark feathered brows framing those eyes of such an extravagant blue. The tenor singing high and sweet when he looked into those eyes he could not look away from. It was God's gift to the Irish, to turn suffering into music. And now the tenor singing "Danny Boy" was accompanied by harp and accordion as he opened his eyes to her blue gaze fixed upon him. God rest his soul, they were fetching eyes.

"You appear confused, darling. Do you remember the gate?" She sat down beside him. He was still in his dynamite vest but it was now buckled over his robe with the rope around his shoulders and waist so all he could do is sway before her. "You fell and I cut you down and brought you into my home like the Good Samaritan. Then you passed out like a young virgin. You are a *virgin,* aren't you, *Father?"*

She was speaking to him out of the mist of his concussion. He felt a sickness that was like a giddiness of high altitude. In a cloud of Shalimar perfume. He drank it in, groping inside himself, unprepared for this. And wasn't that just like Satan, to pose as a tempting beauty? And now he knew where he was. The throne room of the Devil. With its high Gothic vaults and that claw-foot desk and the grand fireplace big enough to skewer a man in. He called on Saint Patrick! He called on Saint Jude! He called upon Psalms: *Thou shalt not leave my soul in hell: neither shall thou suffer thy Holy One to see corruption.*

"You're in the gallery of the Turner Studio. Built for the man himself, Joseph Turner. His students sat where you are and watched as he created masterpieces of light! Now you'll watch, dear. Or rather, listen. I've set up a speaker so you can hear as my masterpiece comes down, Father. After all, I know how priests love to listen to secrets in the dark. *Listening* is your thing."

She laughed as he grumbled in his gag, unable to say a word. She stroked silky white hair. He tried to pull away. She put her arm around him. She held him in his ropes. Stroked with fingertips that were at once florid and terribly raw to the priest. Brute sensual torture. And the more Shanahan suffered, the more Somberg loved it. She had been had by a priest, but never had a priest.

"Love your gun, dear," she said, fingers caressing the long barrel of the weapon.

"So big and silvery! Like a toy, really. I think you're just an overgrown cowboy at heart. It's a shame I don't have Eric's cowboy hat, it'd go perfect with the gun!"

He fell right in, eyes wide shut. Swallowing every insulting word. Doing everything that is expected of a five-star sucker who was terrified of Beauty, right down to the trembling, rocking with rage in his ropes, now shuddering like some awful blind man in a first attempt to walk. She continued to stroke him, her very own priest, and watched his horse-face redden, his breath clogged in his throat. Her fingers entering that territory where there were rigid boundaries and ideologies, now up for grabs. She placed the bridal wreath in his lap. It felt like he had gone rigid.

"I won't be using a gun today. Not my style, darling. Won't need a gun. Maggie will soon be immortalized along with Lincoln and the Kennedys and Martin Luther King. Just think, they'll call her, *Saint Thatcher!*" She smiled at the hot revulsion in his Irish black eyes. "I think sainthood is in order, after all, Thatcher is the *greatest woman of our age.* Just ask any of her PR agents!"

As she laughed, he snatched another look at that marble bust, a pleasure to see Jezebel turned to stone. The sculptor had posed Thatcher with that cool insolent smile rarely turned to the world. The Iron Lady appeared relaxed, dangerous, lethal. Like the woman who taunted him. Together they were everything that had gone wrong with women. There was no welcome in Ireland for the likes of these two. Holy Mary and all the Saints, why didn't the demon just plug him and get it over with? Why toy with him? God knows he would have executed them, both the Iron Ladies. But would you look at him now? Ravaged by the abuse of Beauty with his courage cringing and his sanctity at stake. His flesh on the verge of succumbing. Rising to her. He damned himself for what he could not stop. He lifted his Psalms from a ravaged soul: *Try me, O God, and seek the ground of my heart: prove me, and examine my thoughts.*

"Maggie was a revolution," she said, fingers trilling down his thighs, traumatizing her priest. "She single-handedly changed Britain from a give-it-to-me welfare society to a do-it-yourself entrepreneurial nation. Rather like you, don't you think, Father? You *do it to yourself,* I bet. But what you want is for someone to *do you.* Socially, Maggie did what Marxism never could, made the pompous upper classes irrelevant without bloodshed—a womanhood thing, unthinkable to Irish menfolk, to change without bloodshed. And it's fitting Maggie should die without violence. After all, it was *her* method that inspired my method. It's like fashion, darling. I match the method to the mark. They often aid and abet their own death. I find pleasure in that. Can't explain it."

With the concussion, Shanahan was barely holding it together, she was more dangerous than any explosive, leaning over him as she spoke, his flesh alive at her caressing, rippling touch. "Maggie and I are alike in *so many ways.* Direct. Opinionated. Strong-willed. Women in an all-male arena. Maggie rewrote the rules, to make history, not follow it. A woman of vision! Of conviction! Of self-powered flight! Maggie had wings, of a sort. She had eyes that they say could turn her opposition to stone. We share the same assets and failings, almost as if we were sisters. She's hardly family, but her plight has been that of all women, bare-knuckled survival, most of us emotional desperados, Maggie was no different, not even particularly bright—a gawkish intellectual at best. Maggie simply refused to be denied, the woman was *willful,* and for this she will undoubtedly be given an honorable place in world sisterhood. Honestly, Father, I couldn't possibly let you kill her. Thatcher must be taken by a woman who is her *equal*.''

She hovered before him; she seemed to crowd around his head. He was heart-sorry O'Grady had ever hired her, this Gorgon. In his concussion-blurred vision, her wild blond locks, loose and teased, appeared like snakes. And didn't she have wings? Didn't a Lear jet have wings? She was invulnerable in her wealth, her heart protected as by golden scales. In the name of the Almighty, he now knew who she was. Why, O'Grady, the damn old fool, had hired Medusa! Cajoling, full of sexual innuendo, her beauty a hidden hell, reprehensible, grandstanding, a killer to be feared, she had all the traits of the ancient myth resurrected in those blue eyes that as he gazed into them turned his flesh to stone. God help him, he loved it. And wasn't that like Medusa? To love her while she destroys you. Did Somberg have two sisters, like Medusa, Shanahan wondered.

With the tidiness of a planned death, she slid her hand under his robe. She grasped the erection in his trousers. To add to the effect, she took up his revolver, finger on the trigger, barrel at his temple. She did not conceal her delight to the priest caught between two deaths. ''I've a confession to make, Father,'' Somberg whispered. ''I've *always* wanted to rape a priest.'' A smile for his gaunt, sweaty face gone scarlet. ''I know what a horror love would be for you, which makes you *such* a temptation.''

The bloodlust of the patriot rushed through the veins of the priest who before he left the airport planted a bomb in her Lear. Shanahan looked into her eyes and saw saw the explosion to come. Pink and gray and coal black nitrobenzene waves bil-lowed through the fuselage and engulfed her in an inferno. Her eyes aglow with the preternatural light of the damned! Twisting tongues of fire sucked the oxygen from her lungs in a wild little cry! Shanahan himself could feel the heat, positively raging, until at last she convulsed and gave it up like something broken, smashed to pieces, a woman done, unable to make a sound or move, sprawled in a kind of ecstasy, consumed by his holy fire. Hail Mary full of grace.

''But unfortunately,'' Somberg said, ''I just don't have the time to fuck you today.''

Sculptor's strong hands held his struggling face. She branded with British Red Coat lipstick.

''Don't worry about your rescue.'' She flipped open the chamber of the revolver. Dumped the rounds into her palm. ''The Yard will swarm Warnock soon as Maggie and the walking dead begin to fall.'' Wiped the gun clean. Left it on the bench beside the bridal wreath in his lap. She trotted down the bleacher, and paused at the door into the house. ''England, not I, will be your bride in a marriage to come. Presided over by a judge. All of England will watch! A shame Maggie won't be able to attend, I know how she'd love to be there, you being the one who took her beloved mentor, Airey Neave. Unfortunately,'' Somberg sighed mournfully, ''I'll miss your trial. But you may consider your magnificent cowboy revolver my wed-ding gift! I'm sure the prosecutor will find a use for it. Trace it to some victim of your Irish wars—which will not be me, dear.''

She watched him wring helpless in his bonds, hellish babble erupting from his gag. ''Good-bye, Father. See you in paradise!'' She laughed and blew him a kiss, then vanished through the door.

He knew he should be after saying his prayers, but could not turn to God for the sight of her blue eyes, gazing after her long after she had gone. And then there was only Thatcher down below, set in stone, as though she had looked upon Medusa's eyes. Folly began to sink in upon him. Not just the folly of being bound with nothing to look forward to but days of internment and trial, but the gargantuan folly of the violence that had resolved nothing. The waste of all it, ah, that was the crime. The only redemption was the lad. He would give anything, anything, including his life, he'd gladly give his life to *save the lad.* That's what he promised the lad's grieving mother. It was his only prayer and hope, other than the sweet hereafter. And now the damn singing in his head, the piping, strident tenor that menfolk instinctively detest. And those two bitches, Gorgon and Thatcher. *Fuck 'em both and feed 'em to the flames of hell,* he thought. He harked to the old tune, "Danny Boy." How to save him from Medusa? Ah, but the Lord works in mysterious ways. Father Shanahan's black eyes rose to heaven. "Let the ungodly fall into their own nets together," he prayed, "and let me ever escape them."

36

THE FOG WAS stacked thick between the trees on the narrow, crooked road. Trent was working up and down the gears, foot never touching the brake, driving fast, as people do when they're being chased. Fighting doubt rekindled by Jessica, about whom he had no doubt. Threw a glance her way, all the questions of life answered in a well-loved smile. He hated to intervene in her escape high, the fire shine in her eyes a sex-positive wave, otherwise known as "do me," quite impossible just now, and there was doubt to settle.

"Shanahan was to retrieve Danny from Somberg?"

"That's what he said. He'd kill her, then Thatcher."

"You're sure he said *Thatcher?* Not the Prince of Wales?"

"I *know* he said Thatcher." Jessica gripped the door handle as Trent heaved into a turn, no explanation for his wildcat driving. Jessica snatched a breath. "He said he would 'carve her not as a dish for the gods, but hew her as a carcass fit for hounds.' "

Trent frowned. "That's *Julius Caesar.* Only he reversed it. Caesar was to be carved as a dish fit for the gods." But now he saw the Irish twist of the phrase, which like Patrick Magee's palm print, was never intended to be read. "He said *today?*"

"Yes. Today. That's why Sterling was hired. To kill Margaret Thatcher."

"Right." Trent wouldn't dispute the last point, not yet. "Her name's not Sterling," he announced, pulling through another sharp bend. Should he tell about Pit? Or the report the Swedes sent on an adolescent who shot her father? He thought not, not just now. "Her name is Somberg. Kristian Mary Somberg."

Fire radiance was transformed into a startled expression. "You mean Nordstrom's wife?" Jessica asked.

"Right. We have you to thank for her name. You found it back in Dublin. Remember? Somberg killed her man, assumed his identity to collect the insurance. Gender-reversed herself, you see. Quite a payoff. I'll explain it all later. Shanahan said . . . ?"

"He said she, Somberg"—the name sounded strange on Jessica's lips, far from the fury she associated with Sterling—"was hired to *kill* Thatcher, like I said. Only now Father Shanahan is going to do it. Evidently the Irish really hate Thatcher."

For a sickening moment Trent was reminded of the news flash out of Gibraltar. You could pretend to live as if you didn't hear such things. As if the government had a right to gun down unarmed civilians in the street. It was the way most people would handle the news. Except for the Irish. Problem was, he was Irish. In his mother's home country; her blood hot in his veins and he had to be careful not to compromise his British decency. An Irishman might be inclined to turn a blind eye, let the Brit PM be hit. Whether by Somberg. Or Shanahan. Or both. More the merrier for Ireland.

The car shot over a hill and dropped them into a billowing wall; for a moment there was nothing but milky mist and he was driving on Irish instinct. Trees flashing past, fogged as ghosts. Limbs hung stiff and heavy and empty, extended out to the road, as hands from cuffless sleeves. Trent saw varnished faces. Wounds bubbled with flies. In the foggy glimmer, rummy eyes stared at him, mottled the color of rotting fruit. They lined the long road, a harrowed featureless kinship of British corpses, mouths open in the same silent chorus. In the perpetual freeze of sorrow. They appeared and disappeared. The car ran on, stirring a whirl of wet dead leaves. In a state of horror deferred, Trent suspected the target was, as Jessica said, Thatcher. Confirmed his suspicions. But why would Duffy say Charles? And Graham was parading Charles. And everyone else in the office believed it was Charles.

"Where was Shanahan going? Did he say?"

"Well . . . I think he said Grandam."

"*Grandam?*" Trent shot her a glance. "In *England?*"

She nodded.

"Jess, there is no Grandam in England."

"Well . . ." She shrugged. She threw up her hands. "It was something like that!"

" 'Something like that'? My God, Jess, you're talking about the assassination of the British—!"

"Could you slow down a little? Why are we driving so fast?"

He slung the car gracefully through a bend, one eye in the driver's mirror. *Steady, steady,* he told himself from the thin ice of his composure. "Grandam?" he said, without the sharpness in his voice. "I wonder; could it have been *Granton?*"

"Sounds close. I was half-asleep, you know."

"Asleep? Christ, I thought you said you heard him!"

"Well, I heard him in my sleep."

Staring at the road, he restrained his shout. All she could think of was Danny, he knew that, couldn't fault her for that, had no conception of how heavy the intelligence was she was relating. Like news of an invasion. Scotland Yard holding its collective breath, while one slightly fogged American mother sorted through her dreams. A recital to be heard all over England.

"Not Granton, right, how about—?" Suddenly he was in grammar school. Shipwrecked in geography, never his best subject. Peering at a map in his textbook. "How about *Grantshouse?*"

"No. I don't think so."

"Grantchester?"

"No. I'm sure that's not right."

Names of English towns flashed by in the fog. He tried to catch them in midflight. Using phonetics, now a game show host.

"Thatcher's hometown is Grantham," he offered.

"That's it!" Jessica shouted, so loud Trent jumped. "I *know* that's it! He said *Grantham* at dawn on Monday."

"At dawn?" Trent gave his head a shake. "Dawn?"

"That's what Father Shanahan said. *'Dawn.'* He told someone to meet him at dawn, but I can't remember who."

Patience, patience, Trent reminded himself. Now softly but firmly, "Jess, it's almost noon now."

"Oh, shit. Is it really?" She looked out the window. No way to tell the time in Ireland; nothing ever changed in all that fog. "Well, hell, is today Monday?"

"Right."

The fog was breaking up, coming at them in sudden patches. A rolling country unfurled through a gauzy curtain. Trent giving her a ride on the stomach elevator as the car flew down a hill and up the other side, her whole life this way since Danny was taken, but the speed couldn't be helped. Something, Trent supposed it was love, knew her next thought. In burning the pub, had she burned her only link with Danny? She had said Shanahan would bring Danny to the pub. Had she, once again, chosen someone else, this time Trent, over her son? He could see it come over her, a new terrible sense of failure. Shattered the peace of the ancient green country lost to her eyes that saw only Danny. Shrieking tires as they careened round a bend didn't help; the tires speaking for her. He took the moment to fill her in on what he knew about Chimera, and the odd bit about Perseus. As though the myths of old were never over and were told again by the ancient mute stones, the legends made into lives. It all fit so well, one had to wonder if the whole of life wasn't decided long ago. Or maybe like crazy Monet, God just kept painting the same picture over and over and over again; always in a slightly different light each time, in each age.

"What about *Danny?*" she said in a state of low hysteria. "What are we going to do? Father Shanahan said he was going to *bring Danny to the pub.* And now—"

"Don't worry, love. We're going to England to find him." He rested a hand on her thigh, the warmth of her body mingling with his own, if only for a moment. In the mirror, headlamps were made into bonfires by the fog.

"England!" Jessica's voice zoomed upward. *"How?* Father Shanahan said Danny was coming *here!* To Killarney! If I'm in England, how will—?"

Trent held up a hand as if to stop traffic, now using the hand to pull through a turn. "*If* Shanahan recovers Danny, we'll come back for him. We'll come back with a bloody army. But just now we've a problem we need to elude." He looked into the mirror. "How many do you count behind us?"

Jessica whirled around. *"Oh, shit!"* She watched as a caravan rolled over the belly of a hill. She counted the cars coming fast. "One, two . . . three!"

"Right." Trent returned to the work of the driving. The other would happen all by itself; it always did. He had a fresh clip in the Beretta, with more to spare. But he would prefer, just now, a 20mm Lahti. Lovely if he had one mounted to the back of the car. Jess could drive, he could pop shells at the boys. One of those immense 20mm rounds would make a smoking wreck of an engine block. "I saw someone pointing us out as we left town," he said by way of explanation. "Didn't take them long to catch up, did it?" He gave a smile meant to infuse courage. Jessica seemed immune to it. "But then, they know this road better than I. Fog was unlucky. Could have taken this faster if it hadn't been for the damn fog."

He gave the smile again. Her confusion only increased.

"Trent! What are we going to do?"

"We're going to England, as I said."

"*How?* Is Scotty going to beam us up?"

"Something like that." He stabbed the accelerator, eating up a straightaway, glancing back at the cars rolling through the wild country. "And I sure as hell hope Scotty arrives on time."

The motorcade crawled through the crowd-choked streets of Grantham resounding in cheers, echoing off the charmless low brick buildings with the sky aflutter in red, white, and blue. Allison was in the last car, as it turned a corner she had a good view of the Queen of Downing Street in a navy suit. Her Majesty standing in an open convertible waving with both arms.

They passed a three-story corner building. Faded sign above the door: "Roberts's Grocery." Her Highness waved at her childhood home, the second-story windows with neighbors throwing confetti to Alf Roberts's little girl. She was frozen there for a moment, arms in the sky, her lacquered hair gleaming like a blond helmet in the sun. Tender, bright flakes of confetti fluttered down though the streamers like the downy feathers of doves, and that only made the irony worse. A banner stretched over the street. Allison read the letters as blood red: "Welcome Home, Maggie!"

Allison would have sold her soul to escape this hour, and she supposed in a way she had, in a suicidally indiscreet relationship with an Irish poet, now shot dead by none other than the woman who was receiving the adoring, not to say obsessive, admiration. The news from Gibraltar had come over the radio without warning. They had been en route to Grantham without Her Highness who came in by chopper and Allison, in the company of others, absorbed the shock with the economy of emotion that characterized the PM's staff. The party in which she traveled scarcely spoke of the news. They spoke instead of changing hair-dos and hair-don'ts. In their way, they were all offshoots of Her Highness; a solid lot that believed only the strong survived. If you were Irish and you had been shot down unarmed in the street by the SAS, well, dears, it's tough titty. It was not murder. It was a policy decision.

Allison felt like a traitor in the anger that kindled in her. It was more than anger, it was disgust that quivered in Allison's stomach. It seems Allison had become a truly independent woman in her opinion of the slaughter of unarmed Irish in Gibraltar. Three were dead: a woman, a man by the name of Sweeney, and Dessie Quinn, who the radio announcer said was known as "the Fox." Shouldn't such an ostentatiously qualified breach of ethics, such as murder in the street in broad daylight, be the animus for speaking up? As in being forthright. As in one loudmouthed assistant suddenly out of control. Wasn't it her *British* patriotic duty to express her outrage? A new steely visage seemed to be taking possession of Allison. Steely perhaps, but it was not iron.

The execution-style murders in Gibraltar were made all the more spectral by the blur of the parade. The faces that surrounded Allison strangely alight. Cheering! Waving! Laughing! Calling the name of the Homecoming Queen! The grocer's daughter took a bow. Allison saw a grinning Jekyll and homicidal Hyde, she wore one smile in a public light, and another in the dark of manslaughter.

The little Grantham band marched on playing "Rule Britannia" sourly out of tune as home folk took up a chant: *"Maggie! Maggie! Maggie! Maggie!"* Allison thought she was going to be sick. It was made worse by her silence. Still, Allison gambled on.

Jessica squeezed her eyes tight against a memory of the sound of grating steel and sparks slinging off the guardrail with the bees closing in. She tried to think only of Danny as Trent sent the Ford sliding down the Gap Road. Danny had to be in Grantham because that's where Father Shanahan went. Grantham! Where was it? Suddenly she had to have a map. Had to see it. Had to touch it. This place where Danny was. She opened her eyes to the gash in the rail, but instead of seeing herself plummet over the side, she saw a jet fighter way down there in the glen. It sat next to the lakes with its long, pointed nose like some hummingbird that had dropped down out of the sky. And that must have been how it landed because there was only the narrow, twisty dirt road. The high-tech fighter looked as out of place in that wild, blowing canyon as a color television in a Neanderthal cave.

Trent, driving hard, slewed out of the mountain and bounced over the stone bridge. Jessica's head hit the ceiling and she came down hard as they slid onto the road. The next thing she knew, the nose of the plane seemed to swell in the windshield, Trent saying something about a taxi to England. She saw a pilot in the cockpit. Blue helmet and mask. She stared in wonder at the jet fighter, so unexpected, but then that had become her life.

The Harrier's howl rolled off the canyon walls, reverberated over the lakes so the roar was overwhelming. The primeval setting and the roar got the better of Jessica's imagination, provoking an image of the savages that dwelled here ages ago, just the other day. They lived in companionship with nature, with the trees and seas and hills and stars that became part of an animated world of stories told round the fire. The stories were of gods and heroes, of love and abomination, always on a great scale, overloaded with sentiment, often of an individual quest. The tales gave spiritual aid against the darkness that lurked in swamps and woods, and in the hearts of wild men. In ancient times, the darkness roared.

What was redeemed from the stories was not the pretense of the tale, but the idea only. They threw a kind of light into the thoughts of the listeners. Within the living stories was a secret opening through which inexhaustible energies poured into the soul that then and now held the germ power of the higher spirit. The quest for fulfillment, for self-revelation, the tricky passages through detachment and transfiguration that each person endures, were found in the stories. In myth lay the magic rite of the hero that could only be achieved at a cost of pain and grief that now Jessica heard in the Harrier roar that had the sound of a beast! She saw herself as the beast. The roar was her rage about to take flight. Her feelings not to be denied. Somberg. That was her name. It settled on Jessica's tongue in a fury Trent could not hear sitting beside her, though the world would. "Somberg." The bellow of it, Jessica saw, sent the savages scurrying for their caves. She felt a little nuts, a little off-kilter, no telling what she would do next. The mother had come from barely holding it together, now to a roaring, flying beast that set pubs on fire.

"There's only two seats!" she shouted over the roar. "Who'll be left behind? We have to have the pilot, right?"

But there was no time to answer. He slid the car sideways in a cloud of dust, blocking the road. Now she was out the door into the roar that shredded the air as if peeling her ears inside out, and Jessica covered them with her hands. Trent scrambled up a rock and up the silvery wing glaring with sun. He pulled her up. Now she could see the cars that had been following them were now swerving down the Gap Road. Making a long cloud of dust. Trent yelled something, but she couldn't hear him. She yelled back, but he couldn't hear her, and left her to run over the spine for the cockpit. She followed, in a duckwalk, balancing with both arms, nearly sliding off, the whole plane trembling with power. Trent dropped into the cockpit. He waved her in. What was she supposed to do, sit on top of him? She decided that must have been what he was yelling. She inched forward, went feet first, sliding down to straddle Trent's lap with the glass canopy coming down behind her. It was like they were crammed together in a roaring, trembling phone booth about to take off. But how? There was no runway!

"Don't touch that!" he shouted into her ear, pointing to a red lever on the arm of the chair. *"Ejection seat!"* He pointed to the sky. She nodded with her legs tight around him, riding him, loving the solid feel of him vibrating under her. He put on the helmet and spoke to the pilot and now the engine spooled up to an ear-splitting screech. She saw the cars race out of the mountain and down into the glen. Were those guns out the windows? Were they shooting? She couldn't hear a thing. She turned to ask Trent how the hell the plane was going to take off without a runway, and he was looking right at her, smiling, face stubbled in beard, flushed with color, about as enticing as she had ever seen him. She was overcome. She kissed him, holding his face in the helmet; totally crazy, kissing him with barbarians pouring out of the mountain.

Trent gave the pilot a thumbs up. The engine shrilled and the trembling in the floor started up her feet and up her legs and up, flowing deeper and deeper until she was one perfect concentric fluid of feeling. Caught there in a sensation coming in such good measure, she felt a little swayback, so unexpectedly tender, her nipples rising and it was a little unnerving in Trent's presence. She closed her eyes with the slow shudder working its way upward into a little flame that started tight and compact, but in the low good vibrating increased into a kind of rippling and spreading. How had this happened? Where did this come from? The whole world roaring with the blazing feathers of flame melting a stonewalled heart, her soul on fire with a sound in the roaring like someone laughing. She shrieked, *Oh, God! What's happening?* She looked down to see it was Trent laughing, holding her with the trembling about to drive her out of her mind. The engines spooled up louder, then they all went up together, straight up in a vertical liftoff! Jessica's world rocked. The rush skyward made her bowels go slack, it sucked her breath away. Shoved hard against the muscle of his pelvis with the ground falling into sky that came down around her, the engine screaming so shriekingly, the little muscles dancing in Trent's cheeks, and already she was being pressed into a second coming. They leveled off, hovering at the top of Purple Mountain, the flame inside her running into a brilliant exquisite point that melted her all molten inside. She sobbed and kissed Trent as if something terrible had happened, and in the look in his eyes she knew, they were changed in some provocative way. She did not shy from the change or the high, but redeemed it as pleasure.

Wooly sheep were fleeing over the blowing mountaintop that was at Jessica's fingertips, if it weren't for the glass canopy, she could reach out and touch it. She laughed at the sheep who from a safe distance huddled, staring stupidly at the screaming, flying thing, that to Jessica was the gloriest of exploration.

"Destination, sir?" the pilot squawked in the headset.

"Grantham, England," Trent replied.

"Grantham?" the pilot asked, astonished.

"Roger that, and I need to contact London with a flash message."

"Thumb the green toggle on your console. The *Hermes* will patch you through. They're Storm One. You're Foxtrot Four."

"Roger."

"You might want to hang on, sir. I've orders to vacate Irish airspace ASAP."

Trent placed Jessica's hands on the yellow hand grips. Her smile widened, the pulsing power now quivering through her arms. What had she done to deserve this? Below them, Irish barbarians looked up openmouthed from the road, hair flying in a windstorm rippling the lakes a slate gray in the green skirt of meadow with purple-black mountain all around. The cottage was at the end of the road. A little white square of stone with a thatched roof

"Storm One, this is Foxtrot Four," Trent rasped into the face mask. "Priority transmission for Scotland Yard. We've a Bravo Black Omega alert in Grantham, England. I repeat, a Bravo. . . ."

The pleasure overcame the grief and misery, and Jessica was glowing with health and well-being as though she had been fucked four times a day. A break in the storm that demanded nothing of her, a treat that reminded her this was the way to live, and she could almost sense her ordeal was over. It didn't last long. She felt herself moving and climbing, slowly at first, and then she was fused into Trent, their weight doubled in seconds as they rocketed up into a shrieking high-g climb with their ears popping. They were banded together looking down on a green and quilted land stitched in squares of stone, that before their eyes shrunk and flattened into an island, that turned into an emerald in the sea, and the jewel shrunk to a memory as they flew into the sun.

37

ABOVE HER THE heavens were violet-colored and below the Earth was hooded in billows of cloud hung above the sea. Fibers of light crawled through the cloud like luminous eels. As she watched, the clouds contorted into monstrous forms, twisted, coiled in places, to evoke images of supernatural combats. Jessica was a mile high, eavesdropping on Trent grappling with Commander Graham scrambled to a helicopter bound for Grantham. Trent was now insisting with competitive firmness on a point, he looked up anxiously at Jessica straddling his lap as if he hoped she would corroborate his point. She nodded, not really knowing what they were talking about. Trent had drawn her a map on the back of his card, Grantham was just above and to the right of London. Jessica tried to imagine the place where Danny was. She had few emotional resources left, and nothing would come. She took solace in knowing she was on her way. We only know how to use what we have, and she had done that, with what little power she had, and it had put her in a Harrier that flew at the speed of light and landed vertically, something akin to those winged sandals of Perseus who lopped of Medusa's head.

Trent signed-off and lowered the mask on the flight helmet. She saw his look of disgust and the hopelessness was immediately on her again. "Well," she said, as he just sat there like a sex object. "What did he say?"

"He said"—Trent gave an acrid smile—"Mrs. T would be informed of my 'theory.' "

"Theory!"

"Right. Said no one would believe there are *two* IRA assassins working the *same* target at the *same* site on the *same* timetable."

Jessica looked to the clear, cold blue sky domed by the glass canopy. Was God up there? "But I *heard* Father Shanahan!"

"I know, Jess. I gave him the Julius Caesar line. He said it 'wasn't relevant.' " The harsh smile again. "Thatcher's people will be briefed. But you have to understand; in England there are those that remain medieval, ancient, perhaps even prehistoric."

"Graham, you mean?"

"Yes, well, it's not just Graham. After all, one doesn't shut down a Thatcher media production based on 'theory.' It'd be like setting a china vase before an oncoming train."

She let out a gasp. "What did he say about *Danny?*"

"Graham had the school check their enrollment. There is no Danny Moore in the class. No Jenkins. No Nordstrom. No Somberg."

"Damn it!" she shrieked over the bawl of the engine that now seemed to take on a frantic note, murmuring hollowly inside her.

"Jess"—he slid her hand from the ejection lever—"everyone has been alerted.

Our boys turned the classroom inside out. There are no explosives. No sign of anything unusual. They've your description of the Pope—''

"*Father* Shanahan, you mean.'' She glanced at him with a quick flash of anger that surprised him.

"Right. If he's in the vicinity, he'll be apprehended.''

"Yeah, sure. And what about Danny's picture? Have they shown it to the teachers at the school?''

"I mentioned that. Graham said, 'Smashing idea. But I haven't *fax* capacity from a helicopter, have I, Stanford?' ''

The engine became a monstrous snarl. Jessica couldn't escape it or the pressure building up. "What's Thatcher doing in that classroom?'' she asked the blue sky.

"I don't know, Jess. Mrs. T's a politician. I suppose she's pressing the flesh. Getting her picture taken. Whatever. Why?''

"It just all seems so—'' The bawl of the engine was now very loud. It filled the world. And how small a thing it was, Jessica thought as she looked down on it. "Trent, don't you think it's *strange,* Thatcher going to that first-grade class, and Danny is *exactly* that age? Father Shanahan said he was going to Grantham! I mean, am I nuts?'' She looked to Trent. Her eyes wide. She looked a little nuts. "Or is this . . .'' Her voice trailed off.

"Jess.'' He held her hands. She felt him trying to soften what was to come. "Look; Graham said Charles is at Gloucestershire. Our people have him bottled up on his Highgrove estate.''

Her eyes left him to flee out the canopy to the cold heavens; now they came back to him. "So?'' she said.

"Right, well, Graham was wondering if Father Shanahan might have said *Gloucestershire?* Instead of Grantham?''

"Trent! He said *Grantham!*''

"Right. But you did say you were half asleep.''

"I *know* he said Grantham.'' She glared at him and didn't know him. Didn't know herself. Shattered somewhere back there, maybe when they broke the sound barrier. Maybe when Somberg broke her by shooting her with her own son. "You don't believe me, do you?''

"Jess, I've *always* believed you. Can't help myself. But there's a lot at stake here. An Omega Alert is something akin to yelling, 'Fire!' in a crowded theater. Except the theater is Great Britain. You can't know all the people that are put into motion.'' There was a heat in her hands; she felt almost feverish. Her head tilted, her eyebrows raised. Was there a God in heaven? "I thought the *Julius Caesar* was the clincher,'' Trent continued. "But several people at the office commented on the *similarity,* you see. In Grantham and Gloucestershire. You are *certain?*''

She looked out over the boundless distance of space, staring into the sun-white gleam of the canopy, into the rock eye of pain, she could see, its line, its form, its silhouette in the strobe flash of a '50s living room set. The Devil sat on a cushy sofa, arm around Danny, playing a game of mother that never would have happened had Jessica not helped her. She had done it. She had been played the fool. Now she had to find a way to undo it. It was not just that Danny was lost, Jessica was lost too. "She knows how to get her way with people,'' she said to Danny standing in the starry glare, holding a big silver revolver leveled at her chest.

"Who?" Trent asked, "Mrs. T?"

"She has this great sense of style," Jessica said, her voice just above the engine rumble inside her. "Of refinement. People admire her. Really, it's adoration. And she's magnified by all that." Jessica reflected on the curvature of the Earth, hating to admit how much she had liked Somberg when they first met. She had seen her as a mentor. She had wanted to become like her. Had she? Jessica wondered. "On the one hand, she's hypersensitive; doesn't take criticism well." She recalled how difficult it had been to direct Somberg. "But then she has a very hard core. *Tough*," she said to Trent, who nodded understandingly, assuming she was speaking of Thatcher. "Gives the impression she could withstand anything. Any kind of attack. Mental or physical."

Below, the clouds twisted and coiled to shatter the sunlight into broken shafts displaced by the Earth as it turned. "Revenge is a *thing* for her," she said.

"Yes," Trent replied, thinking of Thatcher and Gibraltar.

"That, I think, was part of why she shot me. Shot me using Danny. Because he loved me. That may not make sense to you, but a woman understands it." Jessica thought Pit would understand it. He knew the variousness of a woman who smiled and smiled and no one knew she was a villain. His son held captive by the lie of a regal family. If only there was a way for Pit to reach the boy, to speak to him, be it as a ghost that could penetrate the great lie.

"She wanted Danny," Jessica said, coming to what she could not admit before. "She wanted him the way a woman wants a Gucci handbag. Or a Rolex watch. Or a suit by Armani." She saw Somberg's arm around Danny, helping him steady the revolver aimed at her heart. "The truth is, she's very seductive. Danny liked her. He loved her allure. She inspires that." A white flash threw her into the back wall of the darkroom again. She bounced off, the flame in her side. "She knows how to use affections. How to extend them, how to withdraw them. You could see her doing that."

"That's quite a power."

Her eyes returned to Trent, trying to push back the picture that kept forming at her lids. Danny rollicking, laughing, as she stumbled forward, her arms open to him, bleeding inside the robot suit that was nothing but her damn career. "She won't make many mistakes, Trent. I hate to say it, but she seems invulnerable."

"Oh, I don't know, Jess. I've heard as much about Mrs. T. People say she's invulnerable. But don't you believe it. And even if no one can touch her, people like that will destroy themselves. Their strengths turn on them. They lose by excess. Nothing new, been going on for millions of years. And it'll happen again."

"You think so?"

"Oh, I think the dog will have his day," Trent said, smiling his smile that was only with the eyes. " 'Foul deeds will rise,' " he said, " 'though all the earth o'erwhelm them, to men's eyes.' "

"Is that from *Julius Caesar?*"

"Not quiet. *Hamlet.* A ghost story about a lost father, but it works for mothers as well. " 'For murder,' " he recited, " 'though it have no tongue, will speak with a most miraculous organ.' "

Jessica gazed down upon the Earth as if she were not part of it. She was outside it, riding above it in a rhapsody of words. Hamlet was not the only one who knew something about sorrows and flashes of merriment. And bloody deeds. Hamlet, she recalled, worked in pictures, a bit like herself. He caught the conscience of his enemy with a play. Told one story to the audience, but spoke in a different tongue, in murder's tongue, to the guilty who were the whole reason for the play. The play was the thing for Hamlet.

But she didn't want to think of these things. Life was down there and she wanted to be part of it, no matter how it hurt. She wanted to share it with her son. "I've been living in the dark house for so long," she said from a darkroom spinning around her.

"It's not having *been* in the dark house," Trent answered her softly. "It's having *left* it that counts."

She lapsed into silence, wishing only that it was over. She just wanted Danny so they could get on with their lives.

"We're on our way," Trent said, holding her hand, giving her as much assurance as he could. "If Danny is at the school, we'll find him by and by."

"By and by is easily said."

"Yes, well, by and by is about"—Trent looked at his watch—"forty minutes."

Jessica didn't hear him; she had long ago taken off her watch and time had lost its hold on her. She looked to the clouds boiled up like monstrous ghosts, like a father's ghost, his son lost to him. The image dredged up lines from *Hamlet;* she hadn't thought of it since high school, but every word came back with a new meaning. " 'Tis now the very witching time of night, when churchyards yawn and hell itself breathes out poison to this world: now could I drink hot blood, and do such bitter business as the day would quake to look on." Jessica smiled, grateful for the telling lines as they closed on the school and the bitch who held her son.

In her head she listened to Paganini's themes from behind the wheel of the Mercedes purring in the drive of Warnock Manor, while in the passenger seat Melissa's pink nails kept time to Prokofiev. It was that good time when the story was written and was now to be played out for the world. It was the opening of the door. A final synthesis of heart ripened down to its most intimate details that from the inception had only one purpose. Somberg didn't think of the details of the plotting begun like the best stories, with only the end in mind. And she did not think of that either. She sat quietly within herself and listened, to everything.

On the console between the seats was a radio that broadcasted Kea Chieng reading *Peter Piper* to her class. The children were in hysterics each time Kea repeated the rhyme faster and faster with the PM's visit just moments away. Kea's voice was picked up by a fiber-optic microphone sewn into Danny's shirt collar, relayed to a receiver in his belt, then beamed to a transmitter concealed in the piano in the adjoining music room.

"You know what I hope?" Melissa smoothed out the deep purple velvet of her skirt that slid very sexy over the stockings that, in the matching pumps, made her legs simply glamorous. She was so very lucky in that she had the limbs of a girl, though her spirit was still somewhat in mayhem between genders. "I just hope Thatcher eats that cake," she said, trying to be chummy with Kristian.

Somberg's eyes never left the horizon. "How likely is it," she said in a tone of indifference, "that Maggie won't eat a cake made by *children,* iced with her *favorite* chocolate mints, served in her *former* classroom on her school's hundredth anniversary while the English *press* takes pictures?''

''Well, she *might* not eat the cake,'' Melissa added gamely and tried not to sound so demure. But it was difficult with her lips glossed in Pink Flush and her cheekbones blushed with her brows softly arched, but you didn't really see them for the bangs that touched her wide-open dark mascaraed lashes. In her bobbed haircut, she looked like a china doll, but tried not to feel like one.

''All I have to do,'' Somberg lifted the electronic detonator from the dash, ''is press a button. Eric will hear a low whistle. There'll be a five-second delay, long enough to hug her, then—''

''Maggie will be barbecued!'' Melissa let out a wild peal of laughter. Somehow the reckless sexual obsession of the feminine riled a euphoria for death. It was all so powerful. ''By the time they find all of her charred limbs—''

''We'll be sipping Chateau Lafite Rothschild in Copenhagen.''

''I just hope it doesn't happen because of Eric, you know? I love Eric and I hope Thatcher eats the damn cake.''

''I don't have hopes,'' Somberg said dispassionately. ''I only have plans.'' She turned up the classroom broadcast, as if to turn down the femme. At this stage a femme was lavishly complex, their sexual energy enormous, a breathtaking fuck, you never knew what was going to come out of the box. You might get *Lolita*. *Pretty Baby*. *Rebel Without a Cause*. You could get *The Exorcist*. Or some version of *Taxi Driver*. They were often combating personalities living in both genders, unpredictable, therefore a nuisance on a job.

Melissa settled into the quiet, but she wondered if anyone had checked Kristian for a heartbeat lately? She had her game face on. Looked like she was made of iron. Kristian was nothing like her baby sister who came in from Chiang Mai last night, Melissa got a peek of her. She had Kristian's eyes, very blue, but slanted and sharp. High, round Mongolian cheekbones that were exquisite, with a strong lantern jaw and that Oriental solemnness about her. The more Melissa studied her, the more she realized how she looked like her. Their wedge cuts the same. Why, they could be twins! The both of them Kim's dreamgirl. Alexia said she was only fifteen, and that was, like, unbelievable, she looked years older, so mature, the most fascinating womanly-man Melissa had ever seen. She was an inspiration, made you want to get over those adolescent femme voyeurisms that were fruitier than a fifteen-year-old.

It was Alexia who told Melissa the secret of her future in Chaing Mai, and in a graceful, fluid, frenzy of masturbation, she simply disappeared, like into another time zone. Kim took over, writing about Kristian's gorgeous baby sister in his diary. The secret Casanova diary was hidden from Kristian, never easy, hiding a diary from God. The lousy thing was, Kim hid it from Melissa. When she returned from that faraway place, his diary was gone. She had no idea what the goofball was writing about her! They were it seemed, more and more, two separate people, something that started way back when, maybe before Kim met Kristian, Melissa didn't know and didn't care. She just wanted to be one. Her true self.

From the radio came a burst of applause. Somberg smiled at the ceiling like a concertgoer who knows the music well. The applause was followed by Kea's suddenly shaky voice. ''Mrs. Prime Minister! Welcome to Huntington Tower Elementary School!''

"This is it!" Melissa joined in the children's clapping.

"Welcome to hell, Maggie," Somberg whispered with dark sweetness to the Irish saints.

"Thank you *very* much!" Margaret Thatcher replied through the continued applause. "We're so very excited to be here!"

"This is a big day for our class, Mrs. Prime Minister," Kea said, her voice trembling with excitement. "We've a surprise for you, but first, the children have a presentation to make."

Somberg groaned. "I wish they'd dispense with the crap and get to the cake."

"We have to learn to be patient, Ms. Assassin," Melissa said, mocking Kea's African voice.

Somberg's smile faded. She turned and glared. "Would you shut the fuck up?"

"It was just *a joke!*"

"This is not amateur hour."

It took only that for Melissa to abandon them, cruel, really, how she vanished to leave Kim in the lurch. "I'm sorry, Kristian," he said with atonement.

"This is the quiet, calm majesty of death," she instructed with spiritual reverence. "A truly personal art."

Kim, whose passive and active traits differed in expression from Melissa's, gave a bow. As in the deepest experience, which he was, in the deep of dreams in the velvet dress that was Melissa's sweetness and strength and his alienation from his male self. The dress an immanence in the eyes of the fickle beholder. The dress a death. Like the world, stardom death coming down now. Everything planned, under control, except for one slightly gender-tipsy femme who was excess, excess everything, a loose schizoid on the deck.

Allison stood next to the bulletin board while the cameras tattooed the classroom in strobe flashes. The front of the room a thicket of microphones and camcorders that bathed Her Majesty in the light of a dozen suns. Allison had seen it before. Stage 10 at MGM. Real life choreographed into a charade. A sound bite for the evening news. Mother Maggie encircled by adoring young faces who ooh and aah over a woman who had made herself a character in her own overblown myth entitled *Iron Lady*. It was all so cheesy. So silly and colossal, as myths were. The wonder was that anyone believed it. But then it was a world accustomed to TV miracles.

Allison thought it a shame there weren't cameras to record the slaughter of the three Irish at Gibraltar, and wouldn't it be something if when Madame Tussaud did Maggie for her wax museum, she portrayed her as a seductive killer. It was extreme exultation and a sort of consciousness, being on Thatcher's staff, gradually devoured, the life sucked out of you in your anguish of extreme love. But everyone asked to be sucked. And everyone began in love. So perhaps Maggie should be preserved in wax as a vampire. Madame Tussaud worked in the realm of power, who has it, how it works, and how it is making history. It was said that her next wax figure was to be none other than the distinguished, disintegrating Fidel Castro. No one knew the mind of the mystic, always serviceable, strict Madame Tussaud, but it was rumored that the tender woman was preparing a place for the Dalai Lama in her museum. And Allison thought she detected a geopolitical theme in Ireland, Cuba and Tibet. They shared sister struggles against superpowers.

The teacher presented a book signed by the children, and Her Majesty turned it into an Oscar performance. She had learned to read in that *very* classroom! A book *very* much like this one! She recalled a story about a spotted dog, Tip, and his kitten friend, Mitten! Allison watched as the children ate it up like chocolate, stealing glances at the yummy cake waiting in the wings.

You learned to read, Allison thought, *but never learned to feel. Learned to win but never learned to care. Learned to get elected but never made a friend you didn't use until, no matter how much they loved you, they had to turn on you.*

A cute American blond boy and a prissy little girl presented Her Majesty with roses, blood-red beauties, like Thatcher herself, concealing long, treacherous thorns. *If only they were lilies*, Allison thought. Not that she would do the woman in, but wouldn't it be justice? But only if she were gunned down in the street.

Shanahan sat in the bleacher and listened to the classroom broadcast that came from a studio speaker. Thatcher's voice had been distant, tangles in the rustle of clothes, but then the lad rose and walked to the front of the room in a flurry of static, and now she came in clear, the regal quality unmistakable. The boy had to be standing right next to her. Shanahan shut his eyes. Unsure what to pray for, he asked only that the lad be spared.

"I'm Annie Fowler," a frail voice said.

"How do you do, Annie?" Thatcher replied. "What a *lovely* pink dress! And you *must* be Eric!"

"Yes, ma'am. I'm Eric Anderson."

"How do you do, Eric?"

"I do fine! Thank you, ma'am."

Shanahan nodded, same lad he had met in the cathedral. Only now he spoke without a stutter. A bright, clear voice. Trusting.

"Eric," Thatcher asked deliberately, "I understand your name has *something* in common with America?"

"Yes, ma'am. I'll show you."

Shanahan heard a screech of chalk. The lad asked Jezebel if she could find his name in the word *America*. Shanahan lost the thread of the conversation, his mind returning to Gorgon's taunt. What did she mean by the walking dead? How can one be walking but dead? Living but dying but not know you're dying? He lifted the phrase to heaven, asking for a revelation. *The walking dead.*

Somberg leaned into the speaker, listening with her face undressed. The children applauded as Thatcher drew a box around *Eric* in *America*. Somberg had never been applauded. Her unsigned masterpieces had never received recognition, and that was one of the differences between them. Maggie needed an audience. Needed acclaim. Maggie had to rule, but Kristian had only to lead. She had found her place, her sweet circle where she was adored, even worshipped. Her dominion. Her opera in which she wrote all the obsessive characters from the inside out. She wasn't driven by opinion polls, didn't crave that reassurance. Politics was living inside a script, being possessed by others, while she possessed others. And politics was conventionality, the essence of Maggie, while she rejected anything that smacked of the common. But the poison in that was that she could lose her capacity to enjoy the simple pleasures. Like her son. She and Maggie shared that, they both had children. And both had a smart, solid, sturdiness. The opposition found an unexpected strength. Nothing accidental about either woman, both self-sufficient, and that was the breathtakingly lovely part of them. Other women, such as Kristian's two sisters, might be freewheeling, footloose, nubile girls at fifteen, and especially at eighteen. Thatcher and Somberg were, in their time, grace and elegance beautifully embodied in a career, comfortable in the certainty that self-love justifies any consequence.

"Christ," she muttered as the Thatcher applause continued, "you'd think she had just completed a heart transplant."

"The children are nervous," Kim said with a schoolboy excitement. This was his first real kill.

"I *know* they're nervous." Somberg was aware of dualism in the car. Melissa now Kim. The beauty flickering like a light bulb not screwed all the way in, though she had been screwed last night.

"That's why they're clapping so hard." Kim twirled a gold bracelet on his narrow wrist. Felt like a manacle. "And I'm a little nervous, too!"

"And I can tell you something else about my name," Danny said in a talkative burst. "When I separate the letters and add an I, it reads I AM ERIC A."

"How very clever of you, Eric," Thatcher cooed. "Now, I believe we're ready for the cake."

"You're not supposed to know about the cake," Danny said. "It's a *surprise.*"

The classroom exploded in laughter.

"Well, I confess, I *heard* about it," Thatcher said. "I had no idea Elizabeth Shaw mints could be made into an icing!"

"Yes, ma'am. My New Mama said it'd be heavenly!"

"Did you hear that?" Kim gasped. "He said, *'New Mama!'* "

Somberg's smile turned to stone. She picked up the detonator. She snapped back the shell that covered the button. Something she could not deny thought of her lost baby, swallowed in the fire of her professionalism. How many mothers had made a similar choice? Career over family. Wasn't that Jessica Moore's folly?

"*God!*" Kim shrieked. "What are you going to do?"

"Just relax, dear. I'll handle it."

"Jesus, Kristian! You're not going to—?"

"Would you shut the fuck up!"

The Creator's fury scared Kim right out of himself, into that erotic gray zone. And now pretty-baby sat a little taller, a sense of harmony returned. "Yes, ma'am," Melissa said in the calm of an actress. So much of being a beauty was an act, most girls knew this, as did the great composers, Prokofiev and Rachmaninov.

Allison watched the jackals circle, snapping Her Majesty as she cut the cake. Now serving the plates. It was absurd the way they took pictures of every little thing she did, as if it would be her last. It seemed to Allison that they were just waiting for it. Praying for it. Always at the ready. Hoping for a lightning strike. For the crack of a high-powered rifle with a fist-sized hole erupting out the far side of Thatcher's head, like it did Kennedy, a double handful of brains blown out the front of the skull with the Iron Lady going down, slain in her own blood. That was what they were waiting for, not the service of a cake.

Her Majesty beamed before her red plate of chocolate cake. And now the teacher cut an extra piece for Denis. It may have been for Her Majesty's husband, the man behind the great woman, but Allison knew she would be the one to tote it back to Chequers, their next stop. Allison watched as Her Majesty's fork slid below the calorie-loaded icing to take a bite of cake. She did that all the time. Dipped a spoon beneath the cream to eat the custard. Slipped a fork beneath the sauce to eat the fish. One of her many weight-watching tricks. The lady had so many tricks, and one of them was the myth of the good-girl. She had, even from her first days in this classroom, elected herself to recognition of herself. And so she was something of a loner. A rule breaker in her quiet, determined way. She was good, yes, but to herself. She did it in the way she ate the cake now, prudently sliding the fork beneath the icing. Maggie had been something of a thief no one ever saw. A good-girl that was to become a thief of hearts.

"Mmm!" Thatcher smiled amid a lurid series of flashes. *"It's wonderful!"*

I hope it sours in your iron belly, Allison thought, seeing her doubled over in a sequence of violent retchings. Blowing a jet of Elizabeth Shaw chocolate mint cake over her royal blue suit. In that moment, Allison had a sense of the prophetic. Though she had no idea the cake was lethal, or that the all-for-love scenario in which she gave the PM's calendar to her grandfather had made the cake possible. She did it and didn't know it was done. Problem was, she was on the only one who could have done it. The PM's calendar was her exclusive domain. Only Allison would know the PM was coming to Grantham months in advance, in time to enroll a child in the school; Commander Graham didn't see the calendar until much later. A poison cake would hang Allison, though treason was not an executable offense, as, say, being shot down in the street in cold blood. It was merely life in prison without parole.

"Won't you try some of the icing?" the American boy asked, drifting closer to Her Majesty. He looking up at the great one. *"Please!"* he said, as if begging for his life.

Allison grinned. *You've been caught, for once! And it's about time!* She smiled on the boy who begged better than a politician. He had learned to plead more with the eyes than with the lips.

Somberg rested her finger on the detonator button. She leaned into the speaker, a deep crease in her forehead, cracking like an internal earthquake across her brow. *"Eat it. Eat it. Eat it!"* she fumed. "Eat it, Maggie. Eat it and die."

Danny watched the nice PM lady raise the bite of iced cake to her mouth. She licked the fork clean.

"That was a *big* bite!" he reported as if in sleep, hearing the Brahms waltz as though it were floating through the room.

"I believe this is the *best* icing I've ever eaten!" Thatcher beamed and promptly took another bite, smiling for the cameras as the sweet death melted over her taste buds.

Danny quietly counted her bites, and when she ate the whole thing he reported that, never hearing himself muttering. Then it was suddenly over. The PM hugged him, and then surprised him pie-eyed by giving him a kiss. Danny's face turned warm in a burst of strobe light as all the cameras exploded at once, the light oddly familiar, and in that instant saw his Old Mama behind a camera. *"Great, Danny! C'mon! Let's try one more!"* He dropped his plate. His mouth fell open. But when he looked again, his Old Mama was gone. But he was certain he had seen her, if only with the heart.

"Thank you so very much for letting us be part of the hundredth anniversary of Huntington Tower," Thatcher said in her goody-goody voice that she had learned in that very classroom. "This has been an experience we'll remember for a long time. The cake was *wonderful!* I'll never forget it. Good-bye, children!"

Danny waved as the PM drifted away in another blaze of light, and he watched very closely, photographers filing past, but his Old Mama wasn't there. Though he could still feel her in a place where she had never died, and that place felt like home.

Somberg released the maternal breath she had been holding. The professional allowed herself a smile, and she flipped the protective shell over the detonator. She slid it into her pants pocket. The death of her son had been only a few quick breaths away, that would have been horrid, the work of a devil woman, but then how many times had Jessica killed the boy by ignoring him? The danger was now past and he was hers, all hers, she'd never have to use him again. Though there was a truth to motherhood that went unspoken, even by assassins, that those who are tamed are used. So many children walking around feeling small, insignificant and helpless compared to the enormity of the world, in which all people are children. The only hope was for the child nobody wants; the child who breaks the rules. Like Thatcher. Like Somberg.

"What a fucking head trip!" Melissa cheered, her glossy lips shining and shining. "I can't believe it's over!"

"Not quite." Somberg planted a kiss on that lovely mouth. Drank her in, tasting her, beauty's incarnation nearly complete. So many ways to kill a male, it almost exceeded sanity.

"Ding dong, the witch is dead!" Melissa sang sweetly, high on murder. Somberg permitted herself the ghost of a satisfied smile. The most exciting thing about a newborn femme was that they didn't mean to be exciting.

"You mean, she's one of the *walking dead*," Somberg corrected.

"Oh, sure. But let's get the hell out of Dodge. I don't want to be around when the Brits find out what that means."

"There's no rush, dear. We have plenty of time." The Mercedes glided into the street, Somberg smiling to herself in celebration of a double-kill. Maggie and Kim. They were done simultaneously, each in the practical, illicit, step by step vigor that led to the enormity of death. Kim was now the sumptuous little kitten, the teenage temptress, the fashion model object he once lusted after. Melissa about to enter her luscious prime, good for three or four years. Her now supple, youthful, feminine smooth, feminine soft flesh was made all the more delicious knowing that she was, though it had not yet occurred to her, the walking dead.

The virginal sweetheart loomed unexplored, sleepwalking, in every beautiful boy. Brought out by simple salacious seduction. Kim's death, as Maggie's, was internal, a work of the heart so it was more pleasurable than any external kill, such as a heartbreak or a gunshot. The nymphet that Melissa had become was to be made into a reliable asset, though she was not that yet. At this point the femme was a phenomena that made lousy choices at everything, you tried to make all their choices for them, until they learned, all over again, how to choose in their new reality.

"There are now minute time-release granules of poison in Maggie's stomach," Somberg said, lips pursed to hold back a grin as she drove down tree-lined Dickens Street with so much emotion.

"God, that's *so* fine. How long till she drops?"

"Depends on metabolism and weight. The toxin strikes children quickly. Which is why I built an immunity system in them."

"By poisoning the class with the other cakes, you mean?"

"That's right. The volunteer mother's snacks, cookie treats, the cakes, they were all poison building up enough immunity so the children won't zone out and cause a panic today. Eric's immunity was fortified beyond the others. But as for Maggie, the toxin will remain dormant until mixed with her digestive enzymes."

"Cool. How long?"

"Hmm. It'll take an hour or two before the granules' protective coating begins to erode."

"And then what?" Melissa was on the edge of her seat, feeling rare and beautiful. Nothing like a victim.

"It's a new toxin. My youngest sister cooked it up. She calls it *Helleborus niger.*" Somberg smiled at a parody on their sister, Laurnet, the African. "It's Latin for the Christmas rose."

"Love it!" Melissa said, clapping and laughing.

Somberg drove on to the school where she would pick up the star of the show, her son. The boy had managed to nab a kiss from Thatcher. He was something of a thief of hearts himself! And like Melissa, Somberg was so juiced, she did not feel like a victim.

"Once ingested, then secreted into the body, *Helleborus* alters the protein structure," she said. "An internal war begins. Starts with a burning sensation and a rise in heartrate. Panic speeds the process, the *Helleborus* now in the circulatory system. Then it really gets ugly. Inducing spasms. Facial contortions. Profuse sweating. Hallucinations are common."

"Oh, God, that's, *so* wicked! And right now Maggie is, like, hunky dory, right?"

"She's fine. She has no idea."

"When, in fact, she's about to go to pieces!"

"That's about the size of it."

"Poor baby. I can't wait! And you know what?"

"What, pet?"

"Shanahan would give his front seat in hell to see this!"

"No doubt." Somberg was delighted to hear music in Melissa's breezy cool. She was the perfect gift for the perfect baby sister that had contributed the perfect toxin. She smiled on the gift. "You're enjoying this, aren't you, dear?"

"Oh, Christ, this shit just blows my mind!" Melissa gleamed, all polished up with kisses. "I'm, like, tripping out here!"

"Yeah?"

"Oh, yeah!" Melissa looked up to trees joined in a triumphant arch, twinkle bells of sunshine glinting through. A Casanova diary the furthest thing from her mind. It was never on her mind. It was on Kim's mind. "I mean, you gotta appreciate what an explosive situation this is. Maggie has a *time bomb* in her belly!"

Somberg grinned. "Fitting for an IRA kill, don't you think?"

38

THE HARRIER SANK vertically through clouds like an elevator and Jessica saw the school first as a matchbox that grew to a shoe box and then to a red brick building. She wanted to pull on the ejection lever and catapult herself into that school. The bottom fell out of her stomach as they dropped faster. Trent's lips were moving, but all she heard was the engine howl as thunderous as the gunshot in the darkroom, the afterclap of which had never ceased. The last time she saw Danny he was murdering her.

At the treetops there was a great blast of air with the dead winter grass swirling overhead in spikes of dusty sunshine that made the blue sky glow. Hovering there between earth and sky at the cusp of landing a keen sensation came over her that what would surprise her most when her search for Danny was over and years in the past, was the way in which she would end up understanding her own life. The revelation was abruptly interrupted by the solid thud of the good earth and then everything stopped moving except for her head that was still flying.

The canopy hissed up. Jessica uncoiled from Trent's lap and stood up and stretched the tightness out of her insides that was like a long night without sleep. She slid down a silver wing, an eagerness on her face. Restless, questing eyes took in the school. Windows blank; it appeared empty. Trent was saying something as they walked quickly over a play yard trampled into paths by little feet, but what Jessica heard and could not escape was the happy shout of Danny's play as forceful and presumptuous as a dream.

"Did anyone spot Shanahan?" Trent called to a grandiose man waiting on the walk. He wore a smug smile and a snug gray suit. He waved, a big, fluttery wave, as if welcoming them for a holiday.

Graham would not stoop to shouting. Nothing to shout about. He waited till they joined him, the privileged couple, jetting in on a Harrier. He viewed Jessica with a judicious superiority, his truculent precision covered by a smile that would not let go of him. She was lovely, that explained much, but hardly a member of the society to which the use of a Harrier belonged. But then there was Stanford's PM authorization. Graham hoped she was impressed with the joyride, because it *most definitely* would cost Stanford.

"The Pope was never here," Graham said in his plummy voice of jubilation. He gave an exultant smile, then led them up the walk to the school.

Jessica wanted to charge ahead, but restrained herself. She remained at Trent's side, matching Graham's stride that to Jessica was slow, laborious, plodding. She ready to get out of control. Her insides a slippery mess. She had come thousands of miles, through the depths of despair, through amusement-park mood swings, through fire, to have finally found Danny's school. She knew it was his school, no matter what they said. The bitter illusions of past leads were suspended in a hope that was brand new! She saw their reunion played out in a joy she rehearsed every night in her head. The photo illustrator imagined she would see him first, in the classroom, then Danny would see her and let out a yelp to come running into her arms. She knew it was foolish, but could not restrain the urge to picture a happy ending.

"And Somberg?" Trent asked, breathless.

"She wasn't here either," Graham said. "The whole thing was a wash. Afraid you missed on this one, ol' boy."

Graham held the door. Jessica didn't a need a door, she would have gladly thrown herself through a window. She stepped now into a hall of scuffed floors and walls in abstract gray. The school spooky quiet. Not a child in sight. Her face over-intense. Her breath squeezed out of her chest in short bursts as she looked up and down the empty hall. Where was everyone?

"Which way to the grade-one children?" Trent asked.

"The children?" Graham frowned. His lower lip curled out disapprovingly. "Why, the children are gone, Stanford."

"Gone?" Jessica shouted. She gave Graham a look of both annoyance and anxiety. She turned to Trent. Heart in her mouth. Ready to burst! He held up a hand; he would handle this. She waited and forever extended for another moment.

"School was dismissed after the PM left," Graham announced. "But not to worry, her visit was a *smashing* success!"

Jessica made a sharp, exasperated sound.

"Glad to hear it," Trent said. "But Jess was rather hoping to look for her son, Danny. Don't believe I introduced—"

"Yes, of course." Graham extended a wintery smile to Jessica.

She took in the stiff white collar and striped tie. Thick limbs, doughy face, soft double fold of chin. A red carnation in his lapel. Looked like he was dressed for someone's wedding.

"Heard all about you, Ms. Moore." Her hand was swallowed in his fleshy grip. She shook it in a fever of impatience. "Terribly sorry about your troubles. Trent's kept us apprised. Seems we've *all* been working on your case for some time."

Suddenly she wanted to belt him in the mouth. She was flaring at anything, spoiling for a collision. Where was Somberg?

"I asked the teacher and principal to stay." Graham rolled his lordly weight to Trent. "You'll need a *report*. There'll be queries, you know, about the enormity of this alert. And all its frills." He glanced out the window to the Harrier sitting in the play yard like some giant toy. And wasn't that the way Stanford had used it? But that would come out in the debriefing; it would take the form of a firing squad. Stanford shot down with his PM authorization that every time Graham thought of it, inspired a smoldering hostility. "Though I suppose congratulations are in order, old boy!" Graham said brightly.

"Congratulations?" Trent asked.

"Oh, haven't you heard? The SAS bagged the Fox *and* Sweeney in Gibraltar.

Savages to the slaughter! Heads for Mrs. T's fence post, I should say. Think of her as a female Kurtz." He chuckled at that one, a splendid touch of the literary. *Heart of Darkness*. He knew all about it. Fancied himself as the good Marlow. Mrs. T as the hungry, foreboding, head-hunting Kurtz. Thing about Kurtz was he had the *faith*. Could get himself to believe anything. He was an extremist; the ground you inherit with a heart of darkness. Graham smiled on Jessica, a Mickey Mouse American, so she would know nothing of darkness or a book composed up the river, "in the greatest town on earth." He continued, speaking to Trent. "That leaves only the Pope, doesn't it? Should net him straightaway. If not here, over there. I've a team waiting in Ireland."

Trent cut his eyes to Jessica. *Hang in there*, his eyes said.

"No more need for a PM authorization," Graham said with his smile. "Not with Brighton sewn up and all *this* to explain." He looked again to the shiny fighter. "Afraid the mayhem your alert brought on was a strain on everyone. *Including* the PM." Graham nodded to a door down the hall. "The teacher is in one-twenty-one. I've transport back to London. You may have my wheels." Graham bestowed Trent with a ring of keys. "It's a hired car," he said. "To be returned to the airport. Ms. Moore." The jolly smile rotated back to her. "All the best in the search for your son."

"Thank you, Commander." She had him in her sights now. Eyes lasered in on that smirk. If only he weren't Trent's boss, she'd let herself turn scary. Scary was right at her fingertips. She had every right to be scary. She had a heart of darkness; she had read Conrad's book too many times. She started to give the Commander a piece of her mind, just a small piece. "Danny was—"

"Unfortunately, our department can no longer be available to assist you, Ms. Moore. However, we do have a *Missing Persons Bureau*. I'm certain Stanford can help with the forms."

Jessica looked to the ceiling. She prayed for strength.

"Stanford, we're all *relieved* you missed on this one!" Graham clamped a hand on his shoulder in the role of literary scholar, or intimidating manager, or level-headed leader, he couldn't decide which. "I'm sure your Somberg character—a real genie, I must say—will turn up . . . *somewhere!*"

"Right. Question is *where?*"

"*I'll* resolve that in the morning. *Early* in the morning, Stanford." Graham gave Jessica a parting nod, gentility part of his mastery of hardy skepticism. "You'll find the teacher and principal waiting for you in room one-hundred-one" he said, then went up the hall with a sanctimonious swagger.

"What an asshole," Jessica said, seeing surreptitious signs of an Orwellian character in Graham. And wasn't room one-hundred-one where the Ministry of Love tortured poor suckers in that dark novel, *1984*?

"He's a gargantuan dichotomy of C-13," Trent said, arm around her, leading down the hall.

They walked fast through the serious hush in the hall. The school silent as a morgue, but Jessica heard voices. A child's laughter. And someone calling over the laughter. Calling with her arms wrapped around Danny. Calling from that dark jungle in the heart of Jessica, calling in Somberg's head-perfect tone: *"Run, Mommy, run! But where are you running to?"*

* * *

Pacing at the wall of windows, Trent's footsteps matched his frustration. Going too fast, slowing his questions to the principal while watching Jessica in the back of the empty classroom. She was chomping on a stick of gum. In a nervous despair. Her eyes darting around the brightly decorated walls. Now her gaze settled on the platter of cake crumbs on the teacher's desk, with the principal perched beside it. White head and rosy cheeks and a three-piece suit with a polka-dotted tie. Teacher in a Saxe-blue skirt and ivory blouse. Trent caught the small African woman looking at Jessica in a peculiar, cautious way. As if she knew her.

"You were in the classroom all day, Ms. Chieng?"

"Yes, sir," Kea said, turning from Jessica to Trent.

"And, Mr. Higgins, you were . . . in your office?"

"Heavens, no! Not *today!* I was all over the school today!"

"Did you see a tall man? About sixty? Gaunt, wrinkled face?"

"Well, let me think. . . ."

Jessica stood before a painting on an easel. A field of splashy spring flowers done in the same style as the watercolors pinned to Danny's bedroom walls. Samples of children's script were mounted on the bulletin board. One of the pages seized her eye. Wide loops in the *g's*. A high swirl in the *s's*. Her hand traced over the big cylinders of the capital *B's*. She was returned to a rainy Sunday morning, the two of them nested in pillows in her big bed. She felt her hand on Danny's as they formed his first script letters. Now she read the name of the sample on the board: "Eric Anderson."

"You know, I believe I do recall a tall, thin man," Higgins said in something of a drama. "Do you remember him, Kea?"

"Was he in his sixties?" Trent pressed.

"Yes. I'd say he was. Wearing a dark suit."

"*Where* did you see him?"

"Right here," Higgins declared.

Trent stared at the jolly little man. *"In the classroom?"* he said with visions of Shanahan dancing in his head.

"Standing right there." Higgins nodded to where Jessica stood near the back of the room. And now he laughed playfully and said, "He was the Scotland Yard toxicologist who tested the cake!"

Outside the windows, clouds didn't create a darkness, not even a dimness, not precisely, but the quality of the light had changed since they had arrived. Jessica stared at a jungle gym that stood out in a dreamlike, steely relief. She saw Danny climbing. Could hear his pirate laugh! And she could not repress the darkness that came over her as she thought of Somberg with her son, the lines of Joseph Conrad's classic coming back to her as she turned from the window to walk on "in the mist of the incomprehensible, which is also detestable. And it has a fascination, too, that goes to work upon her. The fascination of the abomination—you know, imagine the growing regrets, the longing to escape, the powerless disgust, the surrender, the hate."

Jessica tried, but found she could not suppress the darkness. She dropped into a child's desk and watched Trent at work.

"Mr. Higgins, do you realize the severity of this—"

"Oh, pooh!" Higgins cried. "We've had a simply *marvelous* day! Everything went as planned. We'll remember this day for the rest of our lives!" Trent received the benefit of Higgins's thrilled and saintly smile. "The game's no longer afoot, Agent Stanford. All the players have gone home." Higgins glanced down at the platter of cake crumbs. "I only wish I had a slice of this *unbelievable, unforgettable* cake to give you."

Trent peeled his leather jacket to cool the anger. Rolled the Beretta into the jacket so it wouldn't intimidate. Set them on a chair, gazing at the empty cake platter.

"Tell me about the cake, Mr. Higgins. Who made it?"

"Why, the children did! And you should have seen it. Iced it with a caricature of Mrs. Thatcher. And she *loved it!* Rather cheeky, actually. There'll be pictures in the *Times* tomorrow."

"And Mrs. Thatcher, she *ate* some of the cake?"

"Devoured her piece! Of course, we all had a piece." Higgins turned to wink at Kea. "Actually, I had *two* pieces."

"No, you had three," Kea said, poking his soft pudge.

"Well, who could blame me?" Higgins grinned, thrilled to be caught. "It was *heavenly!* Mrs. Anderson outdid herself!"

"Mrs. Anderson?" Trent asked, leaning against the blackboard. "I though you said the *children* made the cake?"

"No, the children did the *decorating*. Mrs. Anderson did the baking." Higgins sucked in his stomach, instinctive whenever he thought of those blue eyes. "*Lovely woman,* Mrs. Anderson!"

39

TRENT STOOD BEFORE the blackboard, weighing a stick of chalk as he considered the remains of the cake. Higgins had said several mothers suggested it after seeing a newspaper photo of a similar cake made for him. Seemed innocent enough. The toxicologist had tested it. Though at the time no one was aware an oral-fixated assassin had been hired by the IRA. But did he know that as fact? Wasn't the Somberg-Shanahan link assumption? And hadn't Duffy acknowledged the target was Charles? The sergeant's shuddering voice in the freezer was compelling. But Jessica was insistent. Shanahan had said Somberg was hired to kill Thatcher. And as if that weren't enough, Shanahan was coming to kill Mrs. T as well. Fine; where was he?

Then there was Graham, staring down with that fatuous leer that did not believe in Somberg as the profound menace. The idea of woman as predator was, Trent had to admit, an odd one. After all, men were stronger, which implied a woman's kill would not be physical. If a woman were to kill, it would be with magic, with conniving. And didn't the cake support this? Trent had read the Gorgon files and knew Somberg had hit Jessica, and still, woman as killer was a stretch. He was compromised in this, being a male, needing this last bastion of the strongman to in some way leave women inferior. He realized this was true—but would never admit it to Jessica—and pressed into service his gender bias, a partner with reason in this witch hunt, a sound notion supported by myth.

"Mr. Higgins, how did the newspaper find out about your cake? Did *you* call them?"

Higgins brooded. He turned to Kea perched on the desk beside him. "Who informed the *Gazette*?" he asked her solemnly.

"Linda Anderson called them. I believe she was acquainted with someone on their staff."

"Anderson?" Trent asked. "The parent volunteer?"

"That's correct," Kea said.

Trent took a moment to mull over this.

In the second desk in the third row, Jessica had returned to the darkroom. She was waiting for Danny and in the C-3PO suit that gleamed silvery in the dark. The door opened. Danny stood in the glare with Somberg behind him. Jessica started to bolt from memory into the gift of darkness, of conscious blindness that had saved her broken heart, but she made herself endure it. She felt again the excitement spinning around inside that tin-can suit. In the sorcery of her Halloween surprise. She saw Danny holding the big gun, and now saw what she would not allow herself to remember. A helmet of horns. As silver as the gun. She lurched forward, in robot cadence, her trick or treat exchange with Danny twined now with Trent's interrogation of Higgins.

"Hel-lo, lit-tle boy. Is yo-ur na-me Dan-ny?"

"Mrs. Anderson did the baking. Did she frost the cake?"

"No! I'm Eric! And I have a gun!"

"Yes. She frosted it and the children decorated it."

"And the frosting was? What? Chocolate?"

"Why, yes. It was made of Elizabeth Shaw mints. Mrs. Thatcher's favorite candy."

"Oh, de-ar. I do not like gu-ns."

"And how did you know that, Mr. Higgins?"

"Pardon?"

"I want a treat!"

"How did you know about Mrs. Thatcher's favorite candy?"

"Sor-ry. I do not ha-ve any tr-eats."

"Well, we all knew. That is to say, it's common knowledge."

"Give me a treat, C-3PO, or I'll do a trick!"

"But I believe Mrs. Anderson suggested the frosting."

"Ho-w a-bout a ki-ss in-stead?"

"It was such a sweet idea! And the PM loved it!"

"Give me a treat or I'll shoot you, C-3PO!"

"Mrs. Anderson. She's from Grantham?"

"Ca-n't hu-rt me. I'm ma-de of ste-el!"

"Mrs. Anderson is American. From LA, I believe."

Jessica saw Somberg cock the hammer of the gun. She took a step, opening her arms as Somberg sighted on her heart.

"How long has Mrs. Anderson volunteered at the school?"

"She's been with us since, oh, January, I believe."

"Wo-uld you li-ke a hug Danny?"

"No way! I want a treat!"

"I understand the Yard toxicologist tested the cake?"

"They were here on Sunday, when the children decorated it."

"And did he test the Elizabeth Shaw mint icing?"

"Bye-bye, C-3PO!"

"Absolutely! I witnessed it. Some sort of chemical test."

"And the toxicologist approved both cake and icing?"

"Certainly. Then one of your people stayed with it overnight in my office. I say, it's getting late. Are we free to go?"

"No! Pl-ease! Do not sho-ot!"

A tongue of flame stitched the dark, and Jessica hit the back wall with a roar. Bounced off. A burning in her side. She looked down the narrow darkroom to see Trent at the blackboard, and as he dismissed Mr. Higgins he stepped away from the board and she was left staring at a child's handwriting on the wall.

I AM ERIC A

Everything was coming at Jessica at once, crammed together and howling through a narrow tunnel of memory that was not really memory but some kind of dream. A dream that on every despairing, desolate night had obsessed her. A dream like all dreams, with mythical powers, with secret strength that she now drew on to hear in darkness what she never could in the rational light of the day. *"Hel-lo, lit-tle boy. Is yo-ur na-me Danny?"* Now came his reply in her head. *"No! I'm Eric! And I have a gun!"* She found herself, not in dream, but standing beside the desk in the old classroom, galvanized by memory, trembling, pointing to the blackboard with a finger that to anyone looking on might seem silly, meaningless, irrational. Pointing in compulsion, in the spiritual rebirth of self found in the unmistakable hand of a boy that she had taught how to write his name. He had done that for her, and she couldn't speak. Couldn't get the words out. The deceptively simple work of Somberg could not outwit flesh and blood and need that had, in love, extracted the killer memory when it mattered.

"Jess? What in the world?" Trent stared, stunned by the most god-awful expression he had ever seen. Looked as though she had seen a ghost. "What is it?"

She came forward in a black light. Her legs made of iron, she could barely walk for fear of falling apart. "Danny wrote that," she said, still pointing. "He wrote it," she said in a sob that was both relief and dread. *"I know it!"*

Trent unlocked his gaze from her face and swung around to read the board. The letters square and straight. Hardly looked like the scrawl of a crime victim.

"I don't understand," he said, shaking his head. "How can you know *he* wrote that?"

"The darkroom!" she cried with Higgins gawking. "I remember now. He called himself *Eric!* He said it just before he shot me." From her face poured an expression of such tornhearted affliction that Trent could have believed she had just been shot. "Don't you see?" she pleaded. *"Danny is Eric."*

She was drawn to the spot where Danny had stood writing that name, though she was blind in the process, in a depth of darkness that no one could know until their child is taken away. The riddle Danny had left her, thrashing around in her head. She felt him there in the silence waiting for her to find him, and the despair that welled up in her, in a surge of sorrow that brought with it such joy, the whole of it some kind of panic, was a *force* coming around. It was the point of departure from the darkness, and she could not know if or how she might save Danny, but there was no question, she had saved herself. No longer a victim, she was now a mother again. Jessica took her first nurturing breaths in the helpless confusion, with all the world turning into the light.

"What's going on here?" Higgins demanded.

"Ms. Chieng," Trent said, turning quickly to the teacher. "Does Mrs. Anderson have a little boy?"

Kea stared at Jessica. She knew that face. "Yes," she said, her dark skin shining, unable to take her eyes from Jessica.

"And the boy's *name?*"

"Eric Anderson."

"He wrote that," Higgins said, nodding to the blackboard.

His mind racing, ticking through the possibilities, Trent forced a calm into his tone, needed facts, not emotion.

"Ms. Chieng, could you *describe* Mrs. Anderson?"

"Well, she's tall. Very attractive."

"Pardon me," Higgins interrupted. "May I ask—"

"*How tall*, Ms. Chieng?" Trent pressed.

"Quite tall. As tall as you. A blond. Very blue eyes."

"*Blond?*" Jessica asked. "*Blue eyes?*"

The shine went out of Kea's face. She struggled for a voice. "Her eyes are a startling blue. I believe she's of Scandinavian descent."

Jessica turned to Trent with a fever in her eyes. "I know it's her," she said, though Jacqueline Sterling was a brunette with green eyes. "I know it's her," she said again, touching the chalked message Danny had left behind. He had been here. *Right here!*

Trent eased her into a chair. "Easy now," he murmured close to her ear. "We've a *lead*. But we've not found him. Not yet."

"What's going on here?" Higgins demanded.

Trent looked at the cake crumbs. It was perfect. Death made by children. He said to Higgins, "Your Mrs. Anderson is not who she says she is. And I suspect the cake is lethal."

A low, awful moan escaped Kea.

But Higgins didn't hear the teacher, he was now and always seeing Mrs. Anderson as divine. She had invited him to Warnock Manor for tea. He remembered the tea and biscuits and kissing Mrs. Anderson but did not recall barking like a dog named Winston for Mrs. Anderson's amusement. And he did not recall hounding the PM's advance team, insisting that the children be asked to make a cake for Mrs. Thatcher like the one made for him. He remembered only those blue eyes that blazed with hypnotic light. He saw those blue eyes now as an open-eyed dream. Lovely Mrs. Anderson was the enlightened thinker, her revelations were deliverance. She was the unbearable likeness of God Herself. Higgins knew this but didn't know how he knew it. He knew God was female, Her name was Ishtar.

"Now, wait just a minute!" Higgins sprang forward. "Wait just a bloody minute! *Our* Mrs. Anderson is the *finest* parent volunteer in this school! She has served this school selflessly. Why, she's the stuff dreams are made of. And as for the cake, *your* people tested it and it passed. Passed with flying colors!"

"They were mistaken," Trent said, and reached for the platter of cake crumbs.

Higgins leaped in front of him. "I refuse to accept this, this, this *hoax!*" Higgins howled, standing erect, arms akimbo. "You're *terrorizing* us, sir!"

"They *did* test the cake," Kea offered.

Jessica looked up at the blackboard again. "I AM ERIC A." "No, you're not," she whispered, hands curled into fists.

"Step aside," Trent ordered.

Higgins bayed, "Mrs. Anderson would *never*—"

"Your Mrs. Anderson is an *assassin*," Trent shot back. "That much I *know*. I believe she was hired by the IRA."

"Sir, you are mistaken!" Higgins jabbed an index finger at the towering man. "Mrs. Anderson is the sweetest, kindest, most loving parent I've ever known!"

Jessica caught Kea staring at her. A quality of nervous despair in her face. A knowing.

"Do you have a class photograph?" she asked the teacher.

"*Who* is this person?" Higgins demanded.

"She's the boy's mother," Trent said. "We believe Eric Anderson is Danny Moore, kidnapped from Chicago last October."

Kea laid a hand on her breast to still a racing heart. She saw the honest, unflinching portrait of Eric in this woman's face, and Kea derailed herself for not having trusted her instincts. She knew there was something wrong with Linda Anderson. She was too good to be true. "We had a picture made last month," she said and began to rummage through her desk. Couldn't stop her hands from shaking. "It's in a file. Somewhere."

After a moment she found it. An eight-by-ten glossy. She showed it to the American woman, a picture of herself and her eighteen smiling students standing on the front steps of the school. "This is Eric Anderson, right—"

It took only a glance. So strange, his face among the English schoolchildren. "*Right there*," Jessica said, cutting Kea off, pointing to the second face on the third row.

Kea could not restrain her stare, in a kind of daze of horror as like a fugitive, the truth settled in. Kea had not managed her classroom, she had, in fact, been thoroughly managed. And Eric, and this lost mother, Kea's heart went out to them both.

Jessica took the picture from the teacher, and it dropped her into a chair. He was a stranger in that gray British uniform. His fun mop of hair was gone, cut short, it was combed in a way she'd never comb it. Combed smoothly over his round skull, in a ruler-straight part. He had changed, she felt, in a million ways. The eyes were somehow dimmed. The freckles faded. Smiling as though his real smile were imprisoned behind constricted lips. Her heart was breaking as she realized that her baby had grown, and not just taller. He was older. Wiser. Somehow sad. A leanness to his face, the softness gone, already on his way to adulthood, having been through so much. A frantic scramble in Jessica's chest, but it was far too late, time having overtaken her, Danny's childhood lost and there was no way to get it back from the bitch who took him. Jessica had put her watch in her desk drawer, hidden all the clocks, put the calendars away, now awakened from the sleep of grief to stare, transfixed, at the cold terrible cruelty of time.

A quaking was working all through her and it wouldn't stop. Working itself into a killing hate, Jessica caught here in the outrage that she wouldn't know her own son if she saw him on the street. Kristian Somberg did that. She did it with pre-meditation, knowing exactly what she was doing as she did it. And now the fury drew Jessica out of her pain. Mean things, she had learned, know no rules. Mean things get away with murder. Mean things thought that they were invincible, but Jessica no longer believed that, not inside the electrically massive hate. A new luminosity in her eyes. A true power. The power of undaunted conviction that could not wait to write its story. It needed only opportunity.

"We've got to get this cake tested again." Trent picked up the platter of crumbs as carefully as if it were a bomb.

"Oh, for Christ's sake!" Higgins pleaded, as a good guard dog hypnotically trained. "The bloody cake *was* tested!"

"Right. I don't know how she did it and I can't explain it and don't have time to argue. Where's a telephone?"

Trent glanced at Jessica. A silence about her as if she were composing a piece of writing. She lifted his jacket from the chair beside her. She looked to him with tears standing in her eyes, her lips hardened, her jaw set in such a grim lock that one wondered whether she would ever speak again. It was the face of a woman who would not give away her secret cradled in her arms.

"Mr. Higgins," Trent repeated. "The nearest *phone*?"

Higgins sighed grudgingly. He stirred slowly from the desk, feeling a fool but not quite sure why, and already it was too late, granules of *Helleborus niger* like a hundred tiny eggs in his belly, waiting to hatch into death. "In my office," he moaned with his beauty-blind eyes that could not look away from Mrs. Anderson. "I'll take you there," he said, and started for the door.

"And we need one other thing," Jessica said, following them out the door, with the good solid weight of Trent's Beretta in the jacket in her arms. "We need the address for Mrs. Anderson."

40

THEY WERE CAUGHT in traffic, looked as if all of Grantham had declared a holiday and had taken to the narrow streets. Kim felt like a prisoner in their slow escape that didn't seem to concern Kristian listening to *Rhapsody on a Theme* by Paganini, as Melissa smiled in the windshield of the tree-darkened avenue. Smiling from that changed world, Kim now accessible to their joint psyche, but on the lunatic fringe of the female, not what he had bargained for when he fell for Kristian. She had made a comedy of his obsession with beauty, and the joke was on him. He was well on his way to becoming "adjusted," as Alexia had said, but he was just now at odds with himself. Melissa felt beautiful; Kim felt demonized. This dynamic duo in a contest for a flickering heart split between two personalities, in a game made by Kristian, the String Puller. Pulling someone so lovely out of Kim, that had she not existed in Kim's dreams, Kristian would have invented her.

Kristian was man's greatest fear, a truly independent woman. So independent she could toy with the visage of men. Ancient male bastions were her playground. Men had for ages insisted that women learn how to behave. Now Kristian was teaching; Kim learning that he was someone else. A true game, especially funny when played on Americans who thought they were so sexually swift, when, in fact, they were so uptight. Her pursuit of gaming and gilding the lily, so to speak, gilding the penis, to be more to the point, was not emotional illness but a flight of the boundaries that kept life safe and boring. Kim understood this. He was artistic expression. And it was difficult to mind, in the tempest of the temptress.

After years in the male trenches, Melissa rose in flight, on colored wings. She was the embodiment of his monstrous notion of female desire. Amazing the smallness of space she had left him, squeezing him into what was meant to disappear. Kim knew he had been particularly susceptible to all of this, having had so many crushes on girls. It was as though all the girls he never fucked had come together to make a bonfire of his sanity, to put him in a kinderwhore dress, sheer horror. Why is it that trousers weren't horror for women? How huge these thoughts had once seemed to him, and how quickly Kristian had subdued them. Continually relieving him of the hugeness, till he felt almost detached from it. No more fantasies to masturbate over, that was male; the dream thing was the real thing which was life; this was female. He felt as though he were dancing with his femme self in the Rainbow Room, but he was no longer leading. His reflection in the glass left no doubt, he had come a long way, baby. Nothing more serious to Melissa than how she looked, that left Kim in despair. Her telltale heart inside, pounding to be heard. She was quite a star turn.

Melissa was searching for more immediate, ecstatic and penetrating modes of living. Penetrated the best part. Simply loved it. She wanted everything because that's what a girl does. And she cared about everything, while Kim feared how perilously close he was to not caring at all. Deserted, isolated, Kim was alone in a dream that could no longer be repressed. His personal problems didn't amount to a hill of beans to her, she luxuriated in his loneliness, sorrow and exile, and in his repressed longing for Ishtar. At night, Melissa, as Ishtar, reigned supreme.

At night she dreamed of clingy ensembles. Of itty-bitty miniskirts and glass slippers that would, most certainly, be three-inch heels by Prada. Of necklaces bangled with diamonds that shone like her eyes; diamonds a sense of style, so important. He was lost and had no idea where he was headed, but her future had been agendaized. Melissa wanted long, swingy hair that she could twist up and pin for an elegant look. She would be surgeried into Barbie-dom, she wanted implants, real cleave, not the nubblings of a girl's bosom that were like kiddie-porn. And she wanted Lucinda Chambers, for starters. Lucinda, having conscripted Kim after he jilted her, was panic for Kim. Melissa would do for Lucinda what Kim never did, fulfill courtship, Melissa with so many shameless appetites. A work of the mind and body. A nice disorientation. A free-fall through gender. Men and women were susceptible to the seductress that had the power of the kill, Melissa knew how to play each, a romantic operative that was at once a full-fledged member of both genders. Her first tantric victim to be Kim, caught in the beauty that was no illusion, that smiled back at him from the windshield where these previews of coming attractions played.

Kim glared tragically at the choked street, imagining the hell that would come down once the British learned what they had done. But the new breezy, creative part of him knew Kristian had planned for the traffic. The poison wouldn't kill for a while yet, everything under control. Eric was in the back telling about the kiss Thatcher gave him. Kristian would, as she watched the road, turn from time to time to see the sunlight falling with romantic affection upon her son. His happy voice seemed to compel them into the future, Kristian breathless as she listened to him.

Kim coiled the boy's explosive belt and put it in Kristian's purse along with the Glock with the laser sight. The new part of him was anxious to learn how to use the Glock, but Kim wanted no part of it. The tree-darkened avenue gave way to open road and Kim gave the kid a Game Boy to keep him busy so they could talk.

"Aren't we going the wrong way?" he said, his eyes swiveling to the cars left behind. "Don't we turn on Dickens, to go *home?*"

"We're not going back to Warnock, darling."

"We're not?" His voice slipped a little. Or perhaps it had slipped a lot and he only heard a little. He suffered selective hearing. "If we don't go home, how will we get our luggage?"

"Alexia picked it up this morning. It's onboard the Lear. Our things to be blown all over Grantham, for effect. We have Father Shanahan to thank for that."

Kim didn't follow this, but it didn't matter. What mattered was his diary left at the house. How could he get it back if they weren't returning to Warnock? His mouth went dry, thinking about what was in his Casanova diary.

"But this isn't the way to the airport either," he said, feeling a ratlike intensity crawl into his cool.

"We're not going to the airport, dear," Somberg said with the thrill of a disclosed secret. "We're changing cars outside of town. Alexia and my youngest sister are waiting for us."

A cheer and a little organ tune rose from the hockey game as Eric scored a goal. Somberg grinned, recalling how her sister went crazy last night. Kim the perfect birthday gift: a twin lover. Kim's likeness to her sister the reason he was chosen. When her sister made love to Melissa, it'd be making love to an alter ego, gender-reversed so there was the enormously appealing energy of breaking all the rules. It'd be like screwing herself. Kim was to become a huge smash, runaway hit! When he loved her sister, it'd be like making love to his female self, speeding his duality into a true giving soul. All of this planned from the beginning, which is to say, from Melissa's beginning. Timing critical in loving and dying and in being born. And in escaping. Somberg checked her watch. Running a tad late, but there was plenty of time yet.

*   *   *

The Mercedes glided onto the motorway, leaving a cloud of German luxury fumes in the face of Grantham. Kim divided from himself. Should he tell about the diary? Or blow it off?

"What kind of car does your sister have?" Kim said, smiling tensely at Kristian, trying to hide his secret. "And where are we going, after we change cars?"

"She has a Rolls, dear. A silver cloud. You'll love it. And we're going to Scotland where the Gulfstream is waiting."

"The *Gulfstream?*" Kim's voice skittering, as though trying to betray him. "What about the *Lear*, at the Grantham airport? It's back there." He turned to watch Grantham fade behind them.

"That's right. And Shanahan planted a bomb in it early this morning. Nitrobenzene. A single stick under the pilot's seat."

Kim's panic increased. "I don't get it. Why *two* planes? And if you knew about Shanahan's bomb, why leave it? There could be a bomb in the Gulfstream! Shouldn't we go back to Warnock? You could interrogate Shanahan! Eric and I could wait in the house." Once in the house, Kim thought, I can get the diary. But where did I hide it? He tried to remember, but it wouldn't come. He couldn't get past a flair for fascination with the girl in the windshield.

"Calm down, dear," Somberg said, turning her dolphin smile on the beauty, her cheeks flushed with worry, not like Melissa, more like Kim. "This was *always* in the plan. Since our inspirational session at the Savoy. Remember? And remember our debate back in Geneva? Now do you now know why I exposed myself in Grantham?"

Kim didn't want to remember Melissa's days of breeding. But something within him was all eagerness to please. "Because they'll never look for someone who's *dead?*" she said softly.

Another round of gay organ music and applause as Danny scored another goal on his hockey game.

"You're coming right along, dear," Somberg said to the still somewhat incoherent, though genuinely talented beauty.

"But how could you, like, *know* Shanahan would do a bomb?"

"It's why I took him down at the cathedral. To ensure his *hate*. You know how big lugs are when they hate. Mindless. All ego. Then there was *greed*. I'm sure Shanahan believed he could save O'Grady millions with a bomb at the end of the job. That was the advantage of working with the Irish."

"Because they're predictable?" Kim heard Melissa say. It sounded more like his true Self. He fought it off.

"Very good, dear. Yes, men are predictable. A bore. The same every time. The Irish bomb. No *art* to their work. Emotion their greatest weakness," Somberg said as the wiley programer. "It's said that women are the emotional gender, but don't believe it. It's always easier to move men *emotionally* than intellectually, and it's by emotional means you can influence them to *action*."

Action, the word rang in Kim's head as alarm bells, and he tried to think about his Casanova diary. He sank deeper into the leather seat. He could lounge in it forever, breathing in luxury. His mind traveled back to the night, spying on Kristian's sister, astonishing how she looked like his dreamgirl, the perfect image of it.

He was as tall as her and as thin, they had the same lush hair and the same sexy cut, their features alike, only her face was more intriguing, with those blue eyes. He imagined Chiang Mai that he envisioned as happiness. A secret country of the exotic, with new customs and a difficult new language. To live there would require practice and many changes, but Kim was willing to learn. And wasn't he in a new country? Practicing new customs? In a new emotional language? In the female experience. He could live this whole other life better than he could live his own. He was already in love with Kristian's baby sister, fighting the self-destructive force that wasn't exactly sane, that was part of most every male.

"So," said that other version of himself, the dream he would become, "Shanahan knew about the Lear jet you leased?"

"He didn't know it was leased. But, yes, I mentioned it to O'Grady after hiring a pilot who looks like me—at least in a topcoat. He'll fly the Lear. One of Shanahan's boys is waiting at the airport for my arrival. The beauty of it is, the IRA will claim credit for my death, and the press will eat it up."

"Oh, they'll love it!" said the part of Kim that came out of the makeup bag. "Maggie and her assassin, dying the same day!"

"Isn't it just perfect?" Somberg couldn't restrain her smile. "The justice of it makes it credible, you see. People are always quick to believe what they *want* to believe."

"So, there'll be no search for you, since you're going to be blown to bits!"

"I'll become a phantom." Somberg winked at Beauty, who was no longer a phantom. "Men always struggle against their enemies, but Maggie would tell you to keep your enemies close. They're often your best asset, dear, the use and destruction of them a *pleasure*. Really, Shanahan was indispensable."

Melissa revealed a huge beatific smile and mischievous mien for her Maker, but Kim's male thoughts were wired to the hum of the engine. It took them further and further away from the diary.

Somberg watched as God's sunlight ran over the country before the moving clouds. For three thousand years men had been telling the great lie, proclaiming God male, while worshiping the female. They drew Her on their cave walls, and on their billboards. The savages adored Her. They knew Her as Beauty. She was affection and lust and electric energy. They thought of Her as the mistress of civilized society, but the savages had it wrong, society was Ishtar's paramour. The coming millennium would be Her vindication. She would be more than idolized, she would come to be experienced, and not by a slight fragment of humanity, but as the life force within the liveliest of people. It was a mere few thousand years since She reigned, though in all time past, for millions of years, She was recognized as the supreme deity. The guiding principal of love and understanding. She was long suffering. Better than the worst things that had happened to women in those few years of her absence. She endured all things. She was the hope of all things. She spoke in the tongues of women and angels, and those rarities recast in Her light. These creatures happy and healthy, now often so chatty, trusting in their experience that was not enslavement, but the full realization of the unlimited Self.

"The coolest thing," Melissa said, feeling foxy, frisky, juicy, "is that I feel so changed! So *brand-new.*"

"Change is a good thing," Somberg said, "maybe the best of things." Her smile did not reveal the clock ticking in her head. Calculating digestion time. Traffic time. Flight time to Denmark.

"It's exhausting and painful and a little bloody."

"Yes. Change is often like that."

"It's what I've always wanted but didn't know I wanted," Melissa said to her reflection in the windshield. "I love it and know I'm only an apprentice, but I won't always be."

"Apprentice allowance claimed."

Somberg glanced in Melissa's direction, sitting pretty but frightened. Hands twisted in her lap as if by opposite hemispheres of her brain. Her mouth chewed convulsively on itself; the voice with a bit too much urgency, on the frantic side. These were the hot flashes of those schizophrenic episodes that were part of growing up and out male. The change was occultlike. Vampiristic. It came in physical frenzy; as Melissa merged with Kim he would, at some point, be completely undone, as in any vapid love affair, and she would achieve maturity. To join the sisters' cadre of secrets, all once secrets to themselves, now only secrets to the world, except for those choice few with whom femmes were shared. Each confused, wobbly-kneed, lust-driven babe progressed at her own pace. Convergence with Ishtar was harmonic but getting there was a trip, mild schizophrenia, nothing to be alarmed about. There had been the Nanette Saint event some years ago; the femme who hung herself, but the French were so erratic. One never knew with the French. Spurting oddities of underlife were the norm, little pyscho-gender entanglements, but a full-blown schizoid was rare.

"I suppose," Melissa said, a tad pale, breathing in snatches, "it's only interesting the first time you do one?"

"You mean the first time you do a Thatcher? Or a femme?"

"Actually, I was thinking of *myself*," Melissa said softly.

"Oh, it's always intriguing, darling. Each birth like each death is unique and creative and therefore empowering."

"I'll say! You could just, like, *OD* on it!" Melissa took a cigarette from her purse. She started to light it, then paused. "I bet some femmes, like, go over the edge. I mean, I could see how it might happen. It's like there's no boundaries any more. No rules. Not in gender. Or life. Before you were so *vulnerable,* so naturally feminine, whereas guys are so *protective,* but in this state of, oh, call it nakedness, you're so *free!* It's easy to evolve into an Alexia or an Isabella, cool and sassy, if you just let go. I feel so—"

"Don't you ever talk on other subjects?" Somberg glanced to Danny, absorbed with his game, he didn't appear to be listening. "Perversion is dull and old-fashioned. I didn't know that people like us keep up on it."

"Really!" Melissa laughed silkily, as though in the Garden of Eden. "It's overrated. It's just a way of life, you know."

A cheer and a little organ tune rose from the hockey game as Danny scored a goal. Now the tree-darkened avenue gave way to open road and Melissa cracked a window and lit her smoke. Her lush eyes swiveled to the town left behind. She looked away, and then back to Grantham. The cigarette began to jitter between her pink lips.

Somberg gave her a close look. "Is something wrong, dear?"

"Well, actually there is a *little* something wrong." Melissa's wide eyes met Somberg's for an instant, then trailed off toward the town. "You know that apprentice allowance you gave me?"

"Yes."

"Well, I think it's time to claim it. I, but I shouldn't say I, I mean, Kim, which is to say, *he* forgot something."

"Oh?" Somberg now looked at her in a peculiar, cautious way. The way you look at people you suspect of madness. It was in the voice. It had lost its soft register. It came out throaty, kind of double-clutched, as though caught at something. "What have you done, dear?" Somberg said, rather severely.

"Me?" Melissa barked a nervous laugh that was on the verge of Kim. "I haven't done a thing! Really. I refuse to be part of this. But I think *he* committed the cardinal sin."

"Darling, there's only one cardinal sin," Somberg said with her patient smile, ever the teacher, "and that's *mediocrity*."

"No, this is a little worse than that. I, uh, I really think we need to go back."

There was a quality of nervous despair in the femme's tone, and that was all wrong. Somberg felt a touch of panic, just a small hot spot. But it would grow. "Go back *where,* Melissa?"

"To Warnock. He left something there." There was a sudden tightening in the car, as though all the air had been sucked out. Melissa gave an artificial laugh, part female, part male, part pretty schizophrenic. "It's something that belongs to him that he's been *hiding* from you," Melissa said in a tattletale tone.

Somberg's smile stretched to the limits of her patience. "What is it, dear? What are you talking about? Speak up."

"It's, well, it's a, uh, a diary."

Another computerized cheer rose from Danny's sphere of the car, accompanied by the merry organ tune, Somberg already looking for an exit. The next one was five kilometers down the road.

"A diary?" Somberg said with the absolute calm of Mission Control when the rocket is on the launch pad and about to blow to smithereens. "You recorded *what* in the diary? Be *specific*."

The Creator's voice was as sharp as a slap that sent Melissa whirling off into where Kim did not know. He woke to find himself terribly induced. In some sort of socialization process learning to separate his identity in the transition of a femme. All part of emulating and nurturing which, really, he loved and didn't mind not having the upper hand, and in most cases, he knew, this almost mechanical process moved right along. Which would explain his sudden stiffness from being caught in the misogyny that was behind the diary, wherever it was. Kim didn't notice that he was afraid, he had been frightened for so long, frightened but enchanted.

"What was in my diary? Well, just about everything, I guess," Kim said, somehow accusing himself. "I wrote about what I felt and how I changed, how much I loved it and about Alexia and the rest."

"The rest?"

"Uh-huh."

"What do you mean by *the rest?*"

"Well, you know, the other femmes, like me."

"Don't tell me he used *names!*"

Kim saw blistering blue eyes that delighted him in a way he could not put into words. "It wasn't like, you know, *a list,*" he said, knowing he was running smack into Kristian's pleasure trade that was privatized, the source of those generous favors and great revenues and even greater pride, so it was her only vulnerability. "The diary is like, my story. But to really enjoy it you'd have to know Casanova's story. I mean, we were both great lovers, right? Both in a harem, of sorts. So I wrote out my favorite things about each femme. How she turned me on. How I would fuck her. How she would fuck me. Just, oh, guy stuff, you know? And, yeah, there are names in there. And where they live. And who they live with."

"You betraying little *fucknuts!*" Somberg shrieked.

"Hey," Danny shouted from the backseat. "Could you guys cool it up there? I can't hear my game when I win."

Somberg checked her Rolex. Forty minutes since the cake was served. There was just enough time to go back, pick up the damn diary, change cars and vanish. She calculated the odds, trying to assess the damage, her whole enchanting world threatened.

"And there's a lot about you in there," Kim volunteered, in full participation with his own certain destruction. But then, he had been participating in his destruction all along, so it was only a question of which way he would go. By feminine wiles. Or by the way that was beyond reason, in the face of the Creator. "And the Geneva chateau," he added. "And the New York penthouse. And the Hawk's Nest hideaway in Evergreen, Colorado. And your sugar plantation in Martinique." His voice skittered on him, but he struggled on. "And some fantasy stuff about your two sisters and where they live and your mother in the Swiss sanitarium—"

There was a shriek of tires and the stench of burnt rubber as Somberg slewed into the oncoming traffic. Danny was slung across the backseat. "What's going on up there?" he cried, trying to pick himself up from the floor. "Are you guys *crazy* or what?"

Somberg snapped out of the power turn, accelerating to top speed in only seconds. Returning to Grantham.

"Melissa!" Somberg called her back, giving the beauty a dose of her eyes as she picked up the car phone. "Where *exactly* is the fucking diary?"

41

"IT'S NOW EVIDENT," said Trent, pacing before the wall of windows in Higgins's office, phone in hand, talking to Graham in a helicopter, "that Somberg *is* Mrs. Anderson."

"Mrs. Anderson, you say?" Graham shouted over the stuttering brawl of the helicopter. "Changed her name *again,* has she? Let me get this straight. You say this woman who may or may not be a man, who is supposedly Somberg and Nordstrom and Jenkins, who is either a kidnapper or an assassin—or is she both—can't quite recall—is now a hell-bent parent volunteer at the school who has poisoned the PM and God knows who else. Have I got that right, Stanford?"

"Graham, you make it sound like—"

"Like tricks, Stanford. Like my Uncle Benji's magic show. Such a clever little man, with the children anyway. Could pull a rabbit out of most any hat."

"This is not *magic*, Graham. Nor is it *tricks*. But you're on the right track with the children. They've all been *poisoned*."

"Well, of course, they have, old boy. But I'm having a tough time making it out, you see. I'm a suspicious chap, some say. It's my nature. And my profession, thank God. Records say your Somberg is one thing, you say she's another. Then another. And another."

Trent let out a curse as he tumbled a pile of books stacked on the floor. Higgins, the principal, the persona of authority, was himself so unbound by rules. His office a pig pen.

"Difficult to keep up with the rabbits," Graham continued. "Got any more in your hat? Any more chaps Somberg toppled? Beside the lot you showed me? *She's* a trickster. Doing some as a black, blue-eyed beauty. Others as an Oriental with blue eyes. And now we have the Somberg at the school. Classic Nordic beauty. More my taste, I'd say. Like cake, love it, actually."

Trent turned from the chaos of the office to the window. He stare at a dim reflection of himself massaging his forehead with his fingertips. "Graham," he said, trying desperately to preserve a tone of composure, "I'm telling you, we *must* call an alert."

"No, Stanford, I don't believe that's what you're saying. I believe what you're telling me is you're trying to make an ass out of me *again!*"

Trent looked into the clouds looming on the horizon, throwing the town in shadow. Tragedy coming with Spielberg effects. He said it softly, very slowly, putting bit into each word. "Graham, the PM has been poisoned."

"You're coming in loud and clear, Stanford. And didn't I hear this tune earlier today? First we alerted Prince Charles."

"That was *your* operation."

"Then *you* called an alert at the school."

"With damn good reason! But that doesn't—"

"And what, pray tell, was the reason for the *Harrier?*" But before Trent could respond, Graham fired back, "I listened to you once today, Stanford. Bought it then. Created a god-awful row at the school. All looking for a double hit when *nothing* happened. I assume that's your intent now. Have me call *another* asinine alert with the intent of seeing me off to retirement. Have your eyes on a promotion, do you?"

Trent gazed at a wall of framed pictures. One shot stood out. Ms. Chieng and the children presenting Higgins a cake done as a cartoon of the principal. A happy lot. All poisoned. Trent tried again, restraining his impulse to shout.

"Listen to the *facts*, Graham. The woman we now know as Mrs. Anderson *is* Somberg, her description verified by the teacher and principal. Somberg is a seven-figure pro. Why would a pro with an oral fixation steal an American child and enroll him in the very classroom the PM is scheduled to visit? Why would she make a cake for Mrs. T? Using her *favorite chocolate mints?* Why?

There was no reply. Only the clatter of rotor blades.

"Jess has *positively* identified Eric Anderson as her son."

"Nonsense," Graham said. "She identified a photograph."

"Commander, would you recognize a photograph of your son?"

"Won't wash, Stanford. This alert is premised on *conjecture*. On bloody sketches and photographs. Where's motive? Where are the players? How does the Pope fit into this? Where's your Somberg? I've about decided she's a figment of your imagination. She is your *very big* secret. Faithfully documented. Heaps of files. Not a whiff of her whereabouts in your files. Sweeping through the male world like a cholera epidemic. Like some dark clone of Mrs. T."

Why was Graham being so obstinate? Sounded as if he knew the cake was poison and wanted Thatcher to die. Trent thought again of the escape of the Fox in Glasgow and his foreboding of the arrival of this day. "Graham, you read the cases yourself. You said—"

"How could they afford her, this man-eating Thatcher-like beauty of yours? Where does the IRA get the *millions?* They'd have to knock over every bank in Ireland! And since when does the IRA hire *women?* And not just a woman but a *tart!* Can you picture it? The IRA asking a tart to do what they couldn't? Admit to a tart they don't have the balls to do Thatcher? The IR-bloody-A?"

Higgins's desk was awash with red and blue bunting. Trent perched there, in the remains of the Big Day; he let his body slump in frustration. Holding his head in his hand, he continued, restraining his Irish temper. "Motive is simple enough, Graham. There's eight hundred years of motive. The Pope is most likely an intermediary; the IRA proper may not even be in on the hit. This could be independent." On the far wall, a Thatcher campaign poster smiled down on Trent. Maggie's piranha smile. "God knows Mrs. T has her enemies. Money is easy. America is full of it. As for Somberg, I'm on my way to find her, just as soon as you *call the fucking alert!"*

"And do you have a hard address, Stanford?"

"Yes, for Chrissake! *Warnock Manor."*

A long pause, then Graham came back with a sunny voice. "The cake is simply too elemental, Stanford. Sounds as though it were cooked up by some housewife deprived of a life. Hardly the work of a seven-figure hitter. Hollywood would never go for it. No drama. No show. She should be in a high window with a rifle, we all know that. And digest this, will you? If the bloody cake is poison, why isn't everyone dead?"

"*What?"* Trent stared at the handset.

"The PM, the children, the teacher, the principal. Everyone in the classroom had a piece of that cake. If it's poison, why haven't they dropped over stone-dead?"

"*I don't know,"* Trent said between clenched teeth.

"They're not dead because there's no bloody poison!"

Trent took a breath, counted to three. Now softly but firmly: "Graham, I've sent the cake crumbs by Harrier—"

"Crumbs!" Graham laughed. "That's all you have, *crumbs!"*

"By Harrier to Poison Control," Trent finished. "But the problem is, we're running out of *time."*

"Won't do it," Graham said stubbornly. "Not based on *supposition*. If you find this Somberg, call me from the car—"

"There's a phone in the car?" Trent leaped to his feet. He looked around for Jessica. "I thought it was a hired car?"

"It is, but I left one of our new portable phones. Call if you find her. I'll send in a team to apprehend her. At that time, I'll be prepared to put an alert at *your* disposal. *If,* mind you, you find her. Otherwise, put your thinking cap on, dear boy. It'll take something more than *sketches* and *photographs*."

"Will you at least *notify* Thatcher?"

In the telephone receiver, Trent heard silence. Punctuated by the menacing throb of the helicopter.

"I'll call her," Graham came back, "but I'll make it clear this is your doing. *Strictly supposition*."

"Right. I'll ring you from Warnock Manor." Trent rang off. He shouted for Jessica. Where in the devil was she? She had been waiting beside the desk, holding his jacket, when he began. Now there was only an empty chair with a note.

Gone to get Danny.

Love, Jess

42

MR. HIGGINS'S 1951 apple red MG roadster was pinging and coughing and threatening to die. While Trent and Higgins weren't looking, Jessica had lifted the keys from the principal's coat and taken Eric Anderson's enrollment card. It listed Warnock Manor as his address. It was set in a gold triangle as a historic landmark on the map she fished from the glove box. She had followed the map through the traffic-choked and wrong-way streets. Fighting the left-handed stick, having to pump the weak-ass brakes before every stop. Trent's black Beretta was nested in his jacket on the passenger seat. She lifted the heavy polished weapon. It had a cool balance in her hand, like the gun Pit gave her for Christmas and she could hear Pit coaching her. *A gun's like a camera, Jess; you use a two-handed grip. Point the business end of the pistol at the target and see only what's in the sight. Don't think; just aim. Let go a half-breath; then gently squeeze the trigger and hold that baby steady as it kicks into your palm.*

Jessica took note of the safety. That and the feel was all she really needed to know, though she wished she had time for a little target practice. A chance to pulverize a few Somberg sketches. Jessica preferred to think of Somberg as a sketch. She didn't mind shooting a sketch. Had shot hundreds of them. It had been a pleasure, shooting out Somberg's eyes that were not blue in the sketch, but blue in her gunsight.

The light changed, the old MG pulled choppily up the hill, a faint quaking all through the car and all through her. She was sitting stiffly, searching for street signs. Knowing if the cake was poisonous, Danny was poisoned, and she couldn't wait for Trent or anyone else. It wasn't playing hero. And it wasn't Somberg. She wasn't going after Somberg, she was going after Danny, and there wasn't time to wait for anyone else. Jessica told herself this repeatedly in the traffic that slowed again, unlike her rapid heartbeat undiminished by the calm she forced on herself. The idea of killing gave her an ache. She wanted and dreaded it, that was the truth. Felt a little like a nutcase, and felt a mammoth strength. Her eyes went from street to map to the Beretta.

Gives you the heebie-jeebies thinking about it all, don't it? Jessica was in her own private world, hearing Pit in her head, feeling his presence in her heart, and she didn't give it a second thought. She listened as if he were in the seat beside her. *I know you're scared shitless, but all you need is the hate. Now is the time for that. The hate can do this and none of it was ever your choice. Once she took Danny you could either give him up or take the road you're traveling on. She chose this way and it'll be horrid and bloody, but you'll be fine. You've earned this and paid for it with pain, and God knows it's necessary. The hate will take care of it all, and don't you worry about a blessed thing.*

She was stuck at a light behind a bus. Feeling small in her low, little car. The bus emitting noxious fumes; poison mixing with her pinwheeling emotions. And Danny had eaten poison. Danny had poison in his stomach. She breathed in the bus fumes wanting to feel the putrid poison. She wanted to feel abused and angry, and now, in the fumes, it felt like her brain was bubbling. She checked the map, then the street sign. She was on T. S. Eliot Boulevard, in her dark house, with everything stacked up and going nowhere. Nothing but a swarm of taillights ahead. Like a swarm of bees! She knew panic again, seeing Somberg in every red glowing taillight. Somberg so tall, so powerful. On Eliot Boulevard, Jessica felt hollow and leaning and stuffed with straw.

The light changed but Jessica didn't, Pit's voice riding on a chorus of horns. *Say, Pegasus, what you waiting for? Isn't this what you prayed for? A chance to nail this bitch? You gotta get that self-damning doubt right out of your head. Anyone that doubts themselves is poverty-stricken. Doubt will make a Wasteland out of you; self-belief enables you to write large whatever you are. You gotta believe, girl. Gotta trust in your Self whole hog.*

Jessica gunned the car into the gridlocked intersection; she considered herself, thanks to Pit, a survivor from the catastrophe of doubt that was ominous. She laughed at herself. She struggled with the big, heavy wheel, searching for the turn that had to be coming up soon. Now here it was, Charles Dickens Street.

She took a left at an old curiosity shop, entering Dickens. Passing a great, bleak house, she slowed, but it wasn't Warnock, the sad mailbox bore the name of Nicholas Nickleby. She drove on, not in old England but at the Chicago firing range, the Pickwick Club, gunshots ringing in her ears like a Christmas carol. Pit spoke in irony of "our mutual friend" as she shot the sketches by Boz, blowing Somberg to pieces with the blood cool in her veins. When they were done, Martin Chuzzlewit who ran the club gave her the sketches as a Christmas gift, though the pulverized Pickwick papers might inspire; he said he too knew something of hard times. She was back on Dickens Street, a novelist once a mystery to her, his stuff so juiced with emotion that she never understood, though she now saw her life as a tale of two cities: the triumph of style that was a beauty, and the pathetic shell burned in a revolution of fire. She survived the fire. It made iron of her. She was an Iron Lady. Now here was a crossroads with no signs. Which way would Dickens go? High road? Or low road? She took the low road, turning at a copper field, into great expectations thinking only of the boy she carried in her heart. On Dickens, she saw Danny as something of an orphan, an Oliver Twist who had made the desire to feel contagious. She was now that, a blaze of feelings.

In this paradise of emotion, Jessica drove without drawing a breath, Danny before her in that school picture. Clean cut with both ears showing. A stranger. Older. Taller. More mature. A boy renamed. Remade. Reprogrammed. All in the name of a woman who he called mother. Jessica's whole private world of pain sliding into brutal reality: her son belonged to someone else. Danny might not even know his own real name, or his own mother. Jessica hoped she was a fugitive loyally tucked away in a corner of his mind. She drove on, down the heart-twister of a road, her jaw slumped, shoulders hunched, her eyes peering out from lowered brows, as if about to lunge after some unseen enemy. *All you need is the pain and hate and Trent's fine Beretta,* Pit said beside her. *Don't feel or think or remember a thing. It's behind you and the only thing that matters in the whole wide world is that boy. Use all the past and don't you let it use you. Take it all out on that lady waiting in the house with your boy. Take her out and it'll all be over.*

She slid the MG into a stop in front of a red brick wall. On the other side of the high wall lay Warnock Manor. She pulled into Trent's leather jacket for good luck. Took the Beretta. Climbed out of the car, her heart a small knot as she glanced up the street at Father Shanahan's rusted Datsun. She didn't know what to make of that. Was the Father here? Did he have Danny?

Wet chestnut leaves were stuck to the iron gates that stood open in invitation. Down the snaking drive, the great house rose into a sky massing for rain. The Tudor elicited the image of a white beast crisscrossed with black scars peering out at her from dull, impassive windows. At the foot of the house, a Mercedes sat on a circular turnaround. The wind high and wild in the trees, a pennant of black fluttering from a lance atop the gate. Jessica stared at it. Was that part of Father Shanahan's robe? Anything religious lent itself to archaic superstition. Some dark doubter in Jessica deciphered the remnant of robe as the flag of defeat.

She refused to be carried off by her own dramatist. She made frightened hands useful, checking her equipment in the calm of the professional photographer. With a snap, the Beretta clip fell into her hand. It had silvery bullets she had never seen before. *Think of 'em as pretty Christmas presents,* Pit said in her head. *This bitch renamed your son and poisoned him with lies; she's worthy of your hate and deserving of her death. You're a lover and love can never kill; you get love mixed into this and it'll get you killed. Now is the time for the Hater. Hate understands what you have to do. Violence is the only language when language fails. You could talk a blue streak to this deceptive bitch and it wouldn't change a thing. Don't mix words with her. Just do the job.*

Jessica snapped the clip into the weapon and started down the drive. Now feeling a rashness, something headlong. Discovering a distinct appetite for pain that had became her maker. With a happy impertinence, she readied herself to inflict it on Somberg with its customary perversity. *You know, Jess, that '39 Mercury of yours would look real sweet on a London street. Top down. You and Danny and Trent cruising. That's what you get if you do this well. No hesitations, honey; that'll get you killed. Give this bitch a chance and she'll blow you to smithereens. Don't aim; just point and shoot. Don't hesitate and for Chrissakes, don't love. Just do and do it well and live on with Danny; everything else will take care of itself. Trust that and yourself and your good hate.*

It started to rain. Big drops, well-aimed. The drops burst around her in shallow explosions. Jessica walked on thinking only of Danny with the gun in her hand as easy and natural as a camera.

43

DANNY WASN'T SURE about ghosts. He pretty much figured they weren't real, but Warnock Manor was a spooky place with its tall windows and tall doors, so tall you could barely reach the knobs—and once he got stuck in the bathroom because of that, had to yell his head off before Melissa heard him—and even taller ceilings. The ceilings weren't flat; they were kind of rounded on top. The whole place echoey. Like a cave. It could be a lonely cave too. Even lonelier without all his toys, since the mover guys came and put everything in a boat that was going to where Danny couldn't remember. The old house was definitely spooky at night, with its monster shadows that tonight were very angry. Shadows running up and down the hall like ghosts.

"Don't worry, Kristian!" Melissa squealed. "I think I know where it is."

"You *think?* Why in the hell don't you *know?*"

"So much happened this week! Let's try the drawing room."

"*We looked there!* Stop and *think!* Where did you leave it?"

They were looking for a book that Melissa, sometimes known as Kim, had left behind. She hid it somewhere but couldn't remember the place, and Danny understood how that could happen. There were a lot of good hiding places in this house. Though it was too big to be a regular house. It was more like a castle. But not as big as his New Mama's castle, which was a real-life castle far away, but he couldn't remember where. Remembering was not his best thing. And evidently Kim was having some trouble with it, too.

She stood in the middle of the long hall, the main hall, the "corridor," it was called, with his arms cradled against him and his elbows in his hands. Her legs were kind of trembly, and his face was very white, like she had swallowed something. Like maybe a pill that didn't go down the right way. Now she ran into the gallery to look, with his New Mama right behind her with her eyes kind of squinted as if she ate a bite of pain. Danny followed them into the gallery, wishing Melissa would get her act together.

"I kept it in the gallery once," Melissa said, looking around at empty walls, the pictures gone. "But it's not here now."

"Why didn't you keep it in the same fucking place?"

"Because it was, oh, just mine, you know?"

"I don't have time for games!"

"I moved it around a lot so you wouldn't find it."

"Where did you put it *last?*"

"Well, I've been moved around a lot, too, so it's hard to remember. Really, it's Kim's fault."

Danny followed them back into the corridor. Melissa looked up and down the hall as if she was looking for someone. His New Mama put an arm around her. She seemed to understand. She said something about an addiction and an allure. For a moment she was nice, and it seemed to help Melissa who was more herself.

"All right, girl. What does it look like, this diary?"

"It's androgynous. The paper very artful. The paper is—"

"What does it *look* like?"

"It's blue on one side, pink on the other. There's a lock—"

"Never mind the damn lock! Did you try the dining room?"

Danny craned his head to see the picture of old Lord Warnock. He imagined smoke rolling inside those eyes, the chalky fingers reaching down to grab Melissa and shake that diary book right out of her. Melissa was a strange one. A girl who played at being a boy and had been a boy for a while but had had switched back to being a girl, and Danny liked her better this way. She seemed to like it better, too. But she had been screwy lately and now this. Big trouble. *Running late!* But help was on the way. He heard his New Mama on the car phone to her sister who was coming with Alexia, but was a long way off yet, and Danny kept looking at that picture of Lord Warnock, wondering if there really were ghosts in this old place. He had pretty much decided there wasn't such a thing as ghosts until today, when he had seen Old Mama in the strobe flash. He didn't tell anyone about that. About seeing her or about the sudden stab of sadness. A hoping that hurt real bad but was a good sort of bad and a hope he had all but forgotten. Like there was a hole there, something dug out and missing, taken by a spook. So maybe there were ghosts. Good ghost and bad ghosts. But he didn't want to think about it.

"All right," his New Mama said to Melissa. "If it's not in the dining room—"

"I remember now! It's in either the kitchen or the studio."

"You call that remembering? *Which is it?*"

"I'm pretty sure it's the kitchen. I know where I would have left it if I left it there. Don't worry; I'll look there."

"Jesus! Melissa! Pull yourself together, girl. We'll check the studio. *Where* in the studio?"

"Under the sofa. Or hidden in the paint racks. I kept it behind whatever color matched how I felt. Changed every day."

Danny ran behind his New Mama, whose face was narrow, with her lips tight and hard, holding his hand hard so it hurt. Like she wanted to hurt somebody. He knew she had a gun in the purse that hung from her shoulder so it was right under her arm. He had peeked inside there once and touched that gun. It was very cold. It had a special red flashlight on it. The gun was for robbers, his New Mama had said, and he knew no robbers would ever mess with his New Mama. He saw her fire that gun in the studio, and from up in the balcony she shot the hearts out of the cards so far away he couldn't hardly see them. But that and the gun was their secret. They had other secrets, but he sometimes had trouble remembering them, but that was okay; his New Mama could.

They were running up the stairs. His New Mama shouted down, "We leave in ten minutes *with the diary!*"

"I'll find it, Kristian; don't worry!"

"Meet me in the corridor. Should Alexia come in, send her out. I'll drop anything that moves in here. Do you understand?"

"Yes, ma'am!"

"Christ!" his New Mama screamed at the window of rain.

"Melissa's a little crazy today," Danny said, trying to keep up. She was taking the stairs two at a time now.

"Yes," his New Mama said, "but we'll fix that, later."

The phone tweaked. Trent swerved into the oncoming lane, passed a lorry, swerved back to his lane, and grabbed the phone. Graham's breathless voice was choked with the thrill of disaster.

"Your Harrier has arrived, Stanford. We've tested the cake crumbs. The tests were *negative.*"

"Negative?" Trent whipped the car around a slow rumbling van. "You're certain of that, Graham? *No poison*? Perhaps they should run more test."

"Yes, I am certain. I wouldn't say so otherwise, would I? But the PM and I have decided to call an alert anyway."

"Come again? Is the cake poison, or isn't it, Graham? Are we landing or crashing here?"

"What we have here in London is not toxic. No doubt about it. But it seems the old girl has laboratory facilities at Chequers. She tested her piece of cake—"

"Mrs. T has a piece of the cake?"

"Yes, and it's decidedly toxic."

"Shit!" Trent got a throaty roar out of the hired car, laying on the horn as he shot through an intersection. "Mrs. T is certain about this?"

"Of course. Isn't she certain about everything? She says it's in the sweetener. The frosting. Seems we only have cake here."

"But our people tested the icing, Graham! At the school."

"Yes, and the toxicologist is right here, breathing down my neck. He swears cake and icing are clean. And the old girl hasn't worked in a lab in thirty years. But she's *adamant.*" And then in a lower voice he added new drama, "And she believes her *secretary* is party to the conspiracy. She's put her under house arrest. Did it herself, I hear. Knocked her out cold. With one blow, I suspect."

"Which secretary?" Trent peered through the rain-blurred windshield. In the middle of a national crisis and he couldn't stop thinking about Jessica. Why the hell did she take off like that? Bullheaded. All Americans were. The harder you push her, the more she stands still. If you want her to stay, she leaps into the fire. "You're not talking about Allison?"

"Right, Allison. Astounding, actually. Allison has always been such a contrite girl. Something of a saint, I thought. Might be nothing more than a squabble between the girls. You know how they can be. Jealousy raises its ugly head from time to time. They can't wait to be the damsel in distress. But where's the white knight? Not many white knights about these days. So the women come up with their own concoctions, in search of the knight. Now we have a cake that's supposedly bastardized with poison. Yes, well, we are standing at *full alert,* Stanford. The chief Whip at Number Ten. Cabinet pulled in. You know the routine. Sending a squad of SAS your way. For your Somberg character.''

Trent was stuck behind a wall of fenders waiting on a light. The sky dark as sin. He hoped Jessica was caught in the same mess. Why would she take the Beretta? Did she even know how to fire an automatic? Graham was right, there were no more white knights. The women were rescuing themselves, damn them.

''What about an *antidote* to the poison?'' he said to the phone.

''A helicopter is retrieving the PM and her cake,'' Graham fired back. ''Toxicologist onboard. They'll analyze the toxin in flight. I'm told there are thousands of poisons, some without antidotes. But I don't know why, *if* it's toxic, it hasn't kicked in yet. Where are the dead? Good thing is, I'm told, the old girl had lunch just before the school. They'll be bringing that up on the helicopter. The cake with it, if you know what I mean. You say this Somberg person is at Warnock Manor?''

''I've no any idea. But I'm on my way.'' The light changed, but the traffic stood still. Trent shot the car over the walk, through beech trees, pushing hard; now the trees sank away from him like a retreating army into the mist. The white knight slewed back into the street, ahead of the pack.

''Give me the ETA on the chopper!'' Trent shouted into the phone, checking the map, looking for the turn, praying that Jessica got lost.

''Say fifteen hundred hours.''

''Right.''

''And, Stanford, if you net this Somberg, you're at liberty to use *any means within your disposal* to extract the particulars of an antidote from her mind. Or, as far as that goes, anything in regards to this cake business.''

''It'll be my pleasure,'' Trent said, and rang off, driving flat out through an open stretch of road, the speed sharpening his fears. He recalled the horror catalog Somberg had compiled. All hard, violent men. Jessica had her legacy of pain and her resolve. There was her fiery escape at the Irish pub. Had the guts. But how could she think that she could take on a pro? Now the sky fell in. Rain obscured an approaching intersection. He squinted and tried to read the road sign. Honked and gunned and slid the car into Dickens Street, shouting at an empty passenger seat, ''Damn it, Jess! What the hell have you gotten yourself into?''

In the Turner Studio, Somberg tore out the sofa cushions. She checked the chairs and rifled through the discarded canvases. She was leaving prints, and that would have to be resolved. She went through the desk and end table. Wouldn't allow unreason to take hold of her; time was becoming a factor, her instincts weren't flashing—there was still time. She checked on Eric, playing his Game Boy on the sofa, the child an addict. Now she started in on the scaffolding. Climbing into the shelves, digging through the cans of paint and lacquers. Labels warned of a high concentrate of solvent. Highly explosive. Low flash point. She should have had it all hauled out, but liked the creative feel of scaffolding, a sense of a thing under construction as she plotted the Thatcher kill. But it was to be finished by now! They should be on their way to Scotland! Melissa said she kept the diary behind the color that matched her feelings. Climbing and digging, Somberg saw only red. Magnesia Violet. Pepper Red. Burnt Sienna. Red Earth. Scarlet. Red Violet Lake. She climbed down and started on the next one. The back wall of the studio was lined in scaffolds. This could take forever. Now she glanced to the balcony, recalling Kim reading in the bleacher. Somberg took the Glock with her, but to keep her hands free, she left her purse in a scaffold of paint. If she couldn't find the diary, she'd use Shanahan's fine vest of nitrobenzene. All that lacquer might come in handy yet. She'd barbecue Warnock Manor and the damn diary with it.

Heat was ticking under the hood of the Mercedes. Jessica checked the interior and found a purse. A Gucci, naturally. Long, slim and elegant. It appeared to belong to a young girl. Inside there was new makeup, maxi pads, a fresh pack of Virginia Slims, a handsome alligator skin Dunhill lighter, a rabbit's foot key ring, which was rather boyish, and a passport. The passport showed a picture of a sweet young thing, Melissa Brooks. Jessica wondered, again, if Somberg wasn't gay. She dropped the keys into a pocket, glanced to the back, and froze. On the tan leather rear seat were three funky toy cars. Red, yellow, and blue.

She picked up the cars she'd bought Danny in Montreal. "How the hell did these get here?" It was more a realization than a fear at first, but it was on the edge of fear and became fearful very quickly when she remembered the cars had been on Danny's easel when she left Chicago. "You bitch! You've been to my home!" She thought about that for a second. "You've been there and returned since I left!" she said, staring at the toy cars in her hand.

She dropped the cars into the leather jacket pocket and ran up a flight of steps. Found herself before a door. A huge thing, it towered above her. She tried the big center brass knob. It was locked. Her hand went to the pocket for the keys but found the toy cars instead. They brought a swarm of Danny memories accompanied by tears. *Time to put all the blubbering behind you,* Pit said, right beside her. *You've been through all kinds of damn dismal suffering and you're in the right and that doesn't mean zip-a-dee-doo-dah. Being right won't change a thing. Power is the ticket! One bull's-eye in Somberg's skull and this is over; it's as simple as that. Now you hunker down and give yourself to the good hate. That's contrary to all the Sunday school teachings you ever heard, but it's the truth and that hate will save your ass and you gotta use it right now.*

Anger brought its own vividness. The smell of rain coming in the cool before the first drops fell. Thunderhead loomed in the sky, black and swollen and edged in golden light. The big brass doorknob gave back the distortion of a woman who looked waifish, dope-sick, the Beretta heavy as a camera but balanced in her hand. She snapped the safety off, pulling herself together, taking the rabbit's foot key ring that slid easily into the brass knob. She took a deep breath and drew on the hate as she turned the knob and pushed open the door. She moved quickly into the foyer, her heart in her throat, making it hard to breathe. Momentarily blind in the dark and now a figure was waiting on the far wall. Jessica leveled the Beretta at it, about to fire when to her left another figure appeared. *"Shit!"* The room wheeled as she pivoted in a blur with her finger tightening on the trigger, her eyes preparing for the muzzle flash, not unlike a strobe flash, but now she glimpsed a gleaming metal chest and eased off the trigger. She pulled the door open. Daylight spilled onto four suits of armor that stood on the wall. There were no knights in the armor. The eye holes in the helmets stared black and vacant. She was alone.

She ran, not as a victim, but as a predator, up the long corridor lined with portraits of haughty English lords. The surge of adrenaline in her limbs, the deep nearly fatal bullet wound a throb in her side. She pushed into a drawing room, the Beretta extended in a two-handed grip. Thin light seeping from leaded-glass windows. Walls of carved oak paneling. Silk sofas and hemp chairs, but no Danny. She released the breath she was holding.

Something in her keeping to the wall in the hall. Inched up to a bar of light falling from a doorway just ahead. Doorways were the worst, she was so exposed in a door. She moved quickly into a dining room. Marble table and upholstered chairs. Columns fluted into the ceiling. Like maybe it was left from the age of the Greeks; the room, like the great, strange house, Jessica felt, of icons and myths. No sign of a child in the room.

She slunk out of the door and down the hall with a sparkle in her eyes. A bad chemistry in this house, shadows looming and large and she kept glancing back over her shoulder, as though she were stalked by mayhem. An odd pressure in her ears, something a little jumpy, a little electric in her nerves, squeezing in on her. She decided it must be *craziness!* in the air, but at least it wasn't depression. She rolled into a library of bare shelves and bare walls, and she could just make out the clean rectangles on the walls where pictures had hung. She stood very still for a time, not quite there, not quite anywhere, staring at vacancies where pictures had been, her face waxy with sweat as in her head dream-reels unwinded, little dream fragments of Danny. A library is such a powerful, willful place. An arsenal, really. And a dizzy, disconnected sensation came over her, broken by a distant slamming noise. A prickly heat pressed against her face, her mind wired to the slamming that went on. Kitchen cabinet doors closing?

Now it stopped. All was silence. Jessica breathed a little easier and found she was praying. A shadow passed in the hall. She went comatose against the back wall. The fast shadow had passed so soundlessly, it could have been a ghost. She would have liked to believe in ghosts just now, but believed in Danny instead. That was no ghost. The heat and tension now in her fist and forearms and in her fingers curled tight, too tight, around the hot Beretta as she slid to the door. Took a breath. Peeked around the doorframe.

An attractive girl with dark, bobbed hair was striding down the hall. For a moment, Jessica couldn't move. Then she moved all at once, heart pounding in furious broken rhythms, as if sliding around loose in her chest, now lodged in her throat. She pushed herself on, up the hall. Hate ran heel-to-toe, closing on the girl with the Beretta leveled at her back. Slipped in behind her. A Hawaiian like the L'eggs panty hose model. But she didn't have the walk of a pro, hands brushing at the skirt of a very sweet dress, the sort of thing a teenager might do. She started to turn, and in one move Jessica shoved the gun into her back and clamped a hand over her mouth. Hauled her kicking and mumbling into the drawing room. Shoved her against the door. Jessica's voice like a blade at her diamond-studded ear. "Scream, bitch, and I'll kill you."

The Silver Shadow Rolls-Royce turned the corner just as Trent shoved though the Warnock front door that he left open, his right hand braced for a chop. To be without a weapon was anathema, like going vampire hunting without a cross. He hated it like he hated Jessica being loose in the house; her car out front eclipsed his hope that she had gotten lost. In the foyer, the knights stood as a medieval armory. He reviewed the selection of weapons. Lances. Poleaxes. Broadswords. He gave one of those a go. Its weight was astounding. Somberg could empty a clip into him before he could bring it round. From a suit of armour gleaming white, he eased a saber from its scabbard. Light along the long sweep of its curved surface scrolled in delicate rosettes, the ancient blade buffed to a pristine shine. An inscription on the handle: *"Hermes, the guide and the giver of good."* Not near as heavy as the broadswords, it had possibilities. You could skewer. You could pin. You could spindle or gash or decapitate. Trent returned the saber to its scabbard, sliding it into his belt.

From a neighboring suit of armor, he pried a morning star. A wooden handle attached to a meter of chain. Lovely blue steel ball radiating with gold and silver spikes. It too came with an inscription, in Latin: *"Astree Sacrum."* To the goddess of justice. Trent cocked an arm and swung the beater-ball in a circle. Arms and legs exploded! An amputated knight at his feet. "Charming," he said, and took it with him, up the darkened corridor, light gleaming off the oscillating spikes. Now if only he could avoid Jessica shooting him.

44

"SPREAD YOUR ARMS." Melissa did as she was told.

"Spread your legs."

Melissa complied, nipples hard to the door, and she couldn't stop her giggling. She knew she was in the grasp of Kristian's youngest sister to whom she was become a gender-bent twin, and Melissa could smell her perfume mingled with the heat of her body. She smells, Melissa imagined, like a Chiang Mai marketplace with a great mosaic of faces where you are anonymous, your history lost. She smelled like food carts of sushi and cages of wild-eyed rabbits and wonderful massage oils you can buy right on the street to step forever out of your life, to open like a blown cloud. She smelled of an ancient Zen garden, yes, Melissa could see it, and burning incense and mind-bending opium and rich French lesbians with the fiendish complexities of so many new languages to learn. The hand cupping her mouth let go. Melissa kissed the hand.

"I'm a little hopped up right now!" she said in a rush. "I mean, I know we're to become, like, twin lovers. Right?"

"What the fuck are you talking about?" Jessica spun the girl around. She braced the Beretta under her chin. "Where's Danny?" she said into the lush eyes staring as if at a ghost.

"Danny?" The threat of the gun splintered the beauty crazily and Melissa left in a gust. Kim felt as if he had been snatched out of a dream, dropped into the present and he was trying to catch up. "Danny? Oh, you mean Eric?"

"No. I mean *Danny!*"

"He's in the studio," Kim said to the woman who was the true walking dead. A woman twice killed.

"You're Melissa Brooks, right?"

Kim swallowed and bobbed his pretty head.

"Who the hell are you to *her?*"

"I'm Kristian's lover," he confessed.

"I knew it! She's a dyke!"

"No! You don't understand. I'm—"

"Is *she* in the studio with Danny?"

Kim nodded. "Yes. I think so."

"Is she *armed?*"

"Of course."

Jessica tried to think. Wait for Trent? But what if Somberg escaped? But it wasn't Somberg she came here for, was it? It was Danny. And what about the poison? There was no time to wait.

"C'mon." She pushed her captive out the door, Beretta at her back. "You're going to take me to the studio."

Kim was frog-marched up the hall, a panicky thrill in his blood, he had never been mistaken for a girl before. He had no idea where all these women had come from. His life was suddenly populated with aggressive women. Up the curving staircase rippled with light from a window blurred in rain, and Kim didn't know which was worse, the lady behind him or the lady before him or the lady within him that all his life he had loved and denied and could never escape. And it occurred to him now that perhaps that was how Kristian had captured him, by his denial of the feminine.

Jessica stopped them on the landing.

"Which door?" she said to the pretty baby.

A tapered pink nail pointed to the last set of doors at the end of the long hall.

"That's the gallery?"

"Yes. But I don't want to go!"

"Is there another way into or out of the studio?"

"There are delivery doors, but they're welded shut."

Jessica tried to think over the fire in her head, her mind a melting pot of rage. She tried to forget about the anger. To stick to the plan which was get Danny and get the hell out of the house. But she had the feeling that something was not quite right.

"The only way to Danny is through Somberg," she said, not so much to the girl but to herself. "Fine. That's the way we'll go. Tell me about the gallery. What does it look like?"

"The studio is about the size of a movie theater," Kim said with his eyes closed, not wanting to see himself in a dress. "The gallery is in the balcony above it. But instead of seats, there's a bleacher."

"And those doors down there, they enter into the balcony?"

Kim nodded.

It sounded to Jessica like her studio in Chicago. Except for the balcony. The plan simple enough. Slip into the balcony. Catch Somberg in the studio and take her out. But wouldn't Danny see it all? Wouldn't he see his mother as a killer? She would deal with that later. She started them up the hall, past empty rooms.

"Where is Somberg? *Where* in the studio?"

"I don't really—" The shrill of a telephone stopped Kim. A breath-holding shriek. It echoed silvery and insidious through the hall. A frantic ringing and Kim looked around desperately for the source. He saw Melissa Brooks in a bedroom mirror, and when the phone stopped ringing, he was gone.

"All I know," Melissa said cooly, "is the priest is in the bleacher wearing a damn bomb."

"*A bomb?*" Jessica whipped the girl around. Beauty delivered a raffish smile, it pierced Jessica's confidence like a knife blade. "A bomb?" Jessica repeated, her mouth gone dry, she could hardly get the words out.

"Oh, it's a humdinger, honey. A bunch of dynamite sticks."

"Don't fuck with me!"

"Mmm." Melissa pursed his pink lips. "That would be tempting."

Jessica slapped the smirk off the bitch's face. But it popped right back, like some model that didn't know how to quit, that couldn't get enough of herself. Jessica knew the type. That lived in mirrors.

"You're exactly the type of doting bitch I'd expect from a woman who steals boys."

"You don't know how right you are," Melissa said with her crafty grin, riding on Jessica's outrage. "But not everything is what it seems in this world."

Jessica, sustained by the memories of Danny, pushed the girl on, into a strange country. "Shanahan?" she said. "Where is he?"

"He's tied to the bleacher, in a vest of dynamite." Kim gave a trilling laugh, shaking her sexy hair. "The old fart was going to do Thatcher with it. But it's enough fucking dynamite to blow the whole house to hell!"

Now Jessica knew why the Father had never made it to the school, his Thatcher bomb perched above the child he came to save. He had failed and he was IRA, experienced at madness. Fear came through her confidence like a ravenous grass fire, all rose red and smoky gray. Her confidence going up in smoke. But Pit was there to ease her disheveled heart. *You know what ol' Hayashi used to tell me? I was a boy, standing on the edge of the pool, too damn scared to swim, and ol' Hayashi said, "He who thinks of consequences cannot be brave."* Jessica smiled at the sight of it, strange how she could see it as if it were her own memory. She assumed this was the first signs of a breakdown and hurried on.

"C'mon!" Jessica kept pushing the girl up the hall before the fear swallowed her whole. Kim marched, glancing back.

Melissa walked fashionably, loose-limbed, with an androgynous swing. "You're going to get your head blown off, pretty mama,'' she said, smiling back over her shoulder at Jessica.

"Oh? I don't think so. I have Somberg's lover, right? And Somberg's lover is going to do what I tell her.''

"I seriously doubt that.'' Melissa touched her pretty hair. And the more she touched it, the prettier she felt. "You're dying for it.'' she said with shrill and vile. "And Kristian will give it to you, honey. Believe me. Kristian will give it to you good.''

"Believe *me*.'' Jessica hissed, Beretta at the nape of the bitch's neck, marching her down the hall until they were outside the double doors. She stopped the girl with the mascara and the natural blush and the glittering vanity. She listened hard. All was quiet. A madness in the air. It was enhanced by the brute loveliness of the model before her, striking a pose, as if for a photograph, as if mocking Jessica's career that was also a brute loveliness. Jessica pushed the smartmouth to the wall, pinning her shoulders. "Mum's the word, honey,'' she said with the gun and her lips at the girl's diamond-pretty ear. "We're going to play *Let's Make a Deal*. And you're going to stay with me *every* step of the way. Just get comfortable with my gun here.'' Jessica wheeled the girl around, stepping behind her, holding her by the throat, the Beretta at her skull.

Melissa tried to pull away, but Jessica held tight.

"Be cool, pretty baby. Be *smart*. Do *exactly* what I tell you, and maybe you won't get your hair messed up by a bullet.''

Jessica took a moment for a deep breath, finally letting the suffering go. It came in a fury of sleepless nights and lonely weekends and grotesque holidays that she hated. There was that crushed feeling in her gut, waiting for her with the emptiness of disbelief and all the rest of the misery that had become who she was. Exhausted. Pissed off. Moody. Depressed. Guilty because she let it all happen, helpless to fix any of it, feeling all along as if she had somehow abandoned her son, Jessica could see it now. She had plunged into the deepest gloom. Anchored in bed, in such suffering and despair she couldn't move. Sad. Poisoned. Feeling old, so old she didn't care anymore. A drunk in the gutter of her bed and she couldn't get up. Days stretched into cold fatalism in which there was no feeling, she just went on living, no meaning to a world without Danny, and so all experiences were equally pointless. Jessica saw the wreckage of her life, the destruction by her career of the mother who was not glamorous, not successful, who was reduced to the demented home-maker and so she had no value. It all came crashing down in the pill-popping loss of Danny, and defeat bled into her bones. The pain was bloated and purply black, an ugly thing that she had become and could not seem to escape.

It was all compliments of Somberg, and now, without even trying, the hate came, all by itself. Hate blind to all reason. A growing, bleeding, breeding obsession. A power to be channeled, that could achieve, that was greater than Jessica was and the hate knew no limits. It came like a blazing malaria through her veins. She wanted to scream at the delicious burn of it! She gave herself to it, feeling it grow, hate pushing through her fear. Whistling up into her brain. The nerves all tingly in her hands and fingers with the hate flaring in her eyes till she loved the very act of hating, until she was one Iron Lady. And Jessica found she hated Somberg as she loved Danny. The hate was as mature as the love and as fierce and as witless and as miserable and as powerful, but she wondered if the hate was stronger than the love? Who did she want more? Danny? Or the bitch who held him?

And now in a perfect ecstasy of rage, already looking for Danny, Jessica shoved Somberg's pretty baby into the balcony, Beretta at her skull.

45

JESSICA STEPPED INTO the balcony and the first thing she saw was Shanahan in a dynamite vest. He was halfway up the bleacher, tied to a bench, she saw him in side view, his face reddened, sheened with sweat. Somberg was behind him, her back to Jessica, attaching wires to a telephone. A black automatic with what looked like a flashlight attached to it was on the bench beside the shell of the phone, Somberg's eyes on her work, and for one precious instant, Jessica had her. But as she leveled her gun sight on the back of that blond head, she caught a glimpse of a boy in the studio below. Her heart leaped in love, and Jessica couldn't help but turn to glimpse Danny. In that split second Melissa shrieked "*Kristian!*" and when her eyes swung back she was staring into a red laser beam from the gun now in Somberg's hand. Unbelievable how quick she was.

For a transitory bewildering moment, she was locked in a stare with those blue eyes. No heat in those eyes. They glared back in a hypnotic gaze and Jessica felt herself turn to stone, the nerve run out of her like some girl run home to mama. The sharp circle of red laser sought her face and Jessica quickly pulled in behind Beauty trying to squirm away.

"I take it you're no longer allergic to bee venom, Jess?"

Jessica wanted to say something clever, but words failed her. After all those nights of raving at this woman, now she was mute with fear. The laser slid over her arm around Beauty's neck, and Jessica yanked her arm back, holding Beauty by the hair. She glanced again at Danny, couldn't help it. She saw him for only a fraction of a second, afraid her heart would burst. He was seated on a sofa before a fireplace, so big you could walk into it. He was playing a Game Boy. There were stairs before her. Run down the stairs and he'd be hers! Run down the stairs and she'd be shot dead before she reached the studio.

"He's a wondrous child." Somberg smiled into the wide eyes as they came back to her. "I never realized what an obsession a child can be. I don't know what's come over me."

Jessica got a good look at the lunacy of the dynamite vest. A red wire in Somberg's hand ran to the rust-colored sticks. Father Shanahan smiled his crooked smile, his eyes turned down to the bench. And now she saw beside him, a big silver revolver. There was a sudden burning in her side where a bullet had been lodged. Was that the same gun she was shot with in Chicago?

"I never use a single shot," Somberg said with a calmness that unnerved Jessica.

"Always two to be sure. I don't know what came over me, Jess. I must have been enamored with the child. Or was it motherhood? Difficult to distinguish, isn't it, dear?"

Still Jessica couldn't find a voice.

"Motherhood is a busy, noisy, jumbled, ridiculous love. An all-consuming love. Some women never recover themselves." As she spoke, Somberg twined the red wire around the bell of the phone. "Children are an addiction of a sort. All you are, all you've got, all of everything. It begins infectiously, for most of us mothers, in the exquisite beauty of innocence, though there is a certain self-destructive bent at work there. Mothers talk about their lost babies swallowed up by the children they have become when, in fact, it's *they* who are lost and swallowed up. Happens so easily, you scarcely know it until you're gone." She tied the red wire to one of the sticks of dynamite. "I've been somewhat lost in Eric. Professional instinct compromised. Came to me just now, as you stepped through the door, in what alcoholics refer to as a 'moment of clarity.' I can't allow a sweet obsession to compromise another venture."

Jessica tried to think over the whirling in her head. What was Somberg saying? Was she going to kill Danny?

"I have something you want!" Jessica suddenly blurted out, too desperate, too shrill.

"*Want?*" Somberg smiled, twisting wires together on Shanahan's detonator pad, keeping the laser pinned to the sliver of pale face peeking out behind Melissa. "I *take* everything I want. Isn't that right, Melissa, dear?"

"I have your lover!" Jessica shouted. It came out as before, in a doleful voice, mingled almost with a sob.

"My lover?" Somberg arched a brow at Melissa, who glowed for her. The luminescence of the laser now stabbed Melissa between the eyes. "Watch closely," Somberg said to Jessica. "I'll show you love. How does that line go?" She flashed a Hollywood smile. "Love means never having to say you're sorry."

Melissa staggered back from the red beam in her eyes, pushing Jessica to the wall. But she did not speak, she had not been spoken to.

"But, wait!" Somberg turned to Shanahan. "Didn't God so love the world that She gave Her only son?" She smiled on the red-faced priest. "What could be a more appropriate manifestation of love?"

Jessica saw the laser beam slide away from Beauty and over the low banister and down the stairs. It reached out across the studio to pin the back of Danny's skull.

"*You fucking bitch!*" Jessica shrieked, and now she was ready to kill. Didn't need the gun. Could tear her throat right out of her neck. She leveled the Beretta at Somberg, gripping the Beretta tight, but the damn thing wouldn't stop shaking. She never had this trouble on the firing range. But this wasn't the firing range. This was nothing like the firing range.

"Drop the weapon, dear. I can always get another son. You know that, Jess. You helped me take yours. Remember?"

Jessica had a clear shot at her. *Pull the damn trigger!* she screamed in her head. But what if she missed? Then Somberg would shoot Danny. Jessica was dying to pull the trigger. Never wanted anything so bad in her life. But did she want Somberg more than Danny?

"Now means fucking now, Jess. *Drop the gun!*"

The balcony seemed to dim as she lowered the Beretta. She set it on the oak floor. She kicked it away as instructed. It slid spinning to the bleacher a few feet away. Beauty stepped away and Jessica was left standing alone, never so tall or so wide, sweat trickling from under her armpits and down her sides. Naked in defeat, she hated herself as much as she hated the bitch.

"Much better." Somberg grinned, beheading Jessica with a mock broadsword of red light. "Come. Sit here." She pointed to a bench in front of her. And now to Melissa: "Did you find what we were looking for, dear?"

"No," Kim said with his love of shame. "It wasn't in the kitchen. It must be in the studio. You want to me to go look?"

"That won't be necessary. Stay put for a minute."

The bleacher had six tiers. Jessica sat on the second, in front of Somberg, forced to watch the spectacle of Danny as a cheer erupted from his hockey game. She was feeling suddenly empty, as if she had given blood. She knew she was going to die. She'd be shot with the same gun used in Chicago and her struggle and everything she had endured, that had broken her and made her stronger, would now all end.

"Hands behind you, Jess. I'll have to tie you with Shanahan's gag."

Jessica obeyed, her hands waiting at the small of her back, and Somberg smiled at the twitching fingers of the wiped-out waif. This long-suffering romantic character, now the guest of honor at what had been a problematic, but still promising affair. Somberg's life had taught her to measure dangerous time; she had learned to control the burn to urgency. And though this was getting a bit near the bone, there was still plenty of time. Somberg knew the granules of *Helleborus* had begun to dissolve, but the victims would assume it was indigestion. When eventually it was diagnosed as poison, the authorities still wouldn't know the source. The cake, having been tested by the Yard, would be the last thing suspected. All was well, unless Jessica had somehow managed to unravel the hit in her search for Eric.

Time now dictated priorities. She left those lovely hands dangling to return to the bomb. Once the detonator was wired to the phone they'd be on their way, the diary to go up in flames. That left only the man in the house, who she knew wasn't armed. Her sister had called, saw him enter with bare hands cocked.

"How in the world did you find us, Jess? Through the school?"

"School? What school?" Jessica said. "I was in Ireland. I came when Father Shanahan called."

"Oh? A Beretta is a *lot* of popgun, Jess." Somberg tied the positive detonator wire around the hammer of the phone, a bit difficult with only one hand, the Glock leveled expectantly at the door. "Where did you get the Beretta, dear?"

"Father Shanahan. We met at the hospital. He took me to this pub and gave me the gun. Called last night. I'd have been here this morning, but I thought he said Grandam, England."

The phone connection finished, Somberg began wiring the electronic detonator. Fixed to Shanahan's vest, it was the size of a fountain pen. Looked Czech, but was American. California Pyrotechnics, model 31. Quality stuff; she wondered what Shanahan was doing with it?

"Who's the man coming to see us? Friend of yours, Jess?"

"Man?"

"Hmm. Tall. Dark. Drives a Ford."

Somberg ran the blue wire from the brass bell of the phone to the detonator. Now she ran a series of dummy wires into the phone and detonator; always disguise the simple as complex, to discourage heroes.

"Oh! That's *George*," Jessica said. "My boyfriend. He's a stockbroker in London."

Somberg laughed at that. "Jess, you're a terrible liar. But whoever he is, he should be easier to manage than that half-man." She twisted the positive wires together, red from the telephone hammer to the red of the detonator and the red that coiled around the vest, spiked into the eleven sticks of nitrobenzene. They were Dupont. A smelting furnace packed into every stick. She set the open telephone on the bench and began to unknot Shanahan's gag, she needed it to tie Jessica who'd make an exquisite shield for George, or whatever his name was.

"Half-man?" Jessica said, thinking only of Trent. She had called him her boyfriend. Was he her boyfriend? She supposed he was. She had taken her boyfriend's gun and now he was somewhere in the house and she wondered if he was unarmed. Only the woman with the brains of a gopher would steal a cop's gun to go after the devil alone, that's what Pit would say. "I don't know any half-man," Jessica said. "Who are you talking about?"

"You know, that legless, childless father in Chicago."

Jessica felt a sudden stab of fear. A steely spike to the heart. "*Who* are you talking about?" she said, her voice trembling. "Not Pit?"

"Yes, Pit," Somberg said jubilantly. "That's the one! What a mess. I left him all over your kitchen, dear."

Jessica's mouth went suddenly numb. Felt like she had a dental injection. Her upper gums frozen, and it seemed her tongue had disappeared down her throat. "What are you saying?" She tried to control the panic eating at her brain. "I talked to Pit just last . . ." She tried to remember when she phoned Pit last, but it wouldn't come over the blood rushing to her head. It brought a morbid chill. Was Pit dead? She couldn't imagine a world without Pit. She racked her memory, when had she talked to Pit last? She realized now she heard from him only moments ago, in the hall.

"He left gore all over those lovely pickled pine cabinets of yours, Jess. He was *difficult.* But then some fathers can be."

Tears stung Jessica's eyes. It was impossible to believe Pit was dead. Somberg had to be fucking with her head. But there were the toy cars; the bitch *had* been to Chicago. And there was Pit's voice in her heart that Jessica would never have listened to if she knew Pit was dead because she didn't believe in spirits. The balcony seemed to shift out of focus and go blank with the terror that for months had steadily devoured her and had now taken the Great Heart. Pit was the best thing in her life, except for Danny below in the studio, playing his game, the damn thing cheering as she tried to think, trying to find her way to, what? What had Beauty called him? Eric? Jessica again saw the handwriting on the school blackboard, I AM ERIC A. Danny had to believe he was Eric to have written that. And being Eric, would he know her? Would he know her face? Her voice? Did she still live in his heart? Or was she killed when he fired that gun at her? Was she dead to Danny, as Pit was now dead to her? Murdered by Somberg.

Something came over her that was maybe the spirit of Pit, or maybe the ecstasy of rage that was in full meltdown. Jessica turned to see Somberg's gun aimed at the door, her other hand unknotting Shanahan's gag, and Jessica never thought about what came next; it came all on its own. It was as though another person had stepped inside her, climbing in a wild rush up the bleacher with the good hate surging in her veins, burning in her veins. As Somberg looked up, Jessica drove a fist into that immaculate face, and the look of Somberg's stunned surprise was worth anything! Jessica hit her again with blood coming out of the nose. And now she launched herself at her with the strength given only to maniac rage, one hand going for the gun with the other beating the living Jesus out of that face that had haunted her dreams. Somberg dropped the gun to steady the phone, sliding a finger between the ringer and the naked wire that if they touched would detonate the bomb. Jessica took the opportunity to hit her again. She looked for the gun, what had become of it? But when she turned, Somberg was not where she had been. It was almost supernatural how fast she was. Jessica couldn't find her and then was hit in the back by a blow that felt like a baseball bat. It drove the air out of her lungs, knocking her off her feet. Jessica managed to grab a handful of blond hair as she fell.

They tumbled into the bowels of the bleacher in a scramble of arms and legs. Speech like cats! A blond face grotesque in rage. Laser blue eyes that didn't blink before Jessica's impending blows. A hand reached out for her neck. Jessica managed to bite the hand and tasted salt and dug nails into the hot eyes with something tearing at her nose and at her ear, but now she saw something on her back and hit whatever was there as hard as she could. The scream was like an animal screech! Jessica hit the back again with Sobmerg bellowing and reaching to steady the phone that had begun to fall. Jessica couldn't understand why Somberg kept grabbing the telephone, but she took the opportunity to pound that wound again. She beat on it until it appered splattered with blood, her top creamed with blood, like the mess of Jessica's heart in which she had lived out her life between mood swings and crying jags. She had reeled lurching from her darkroom where she was shot, to a global search for her son, and now, on the bench before her, she saw a big silver revolver. Was it the gun Somberg had given Danny to use on her? Jessica couldn't extract herself from the hope that it was. She snatched up Shanahan's gun. She pulled the hammer back as she came to her feet. It was perfect! It was Karma.

Somberg rose from the bleacher, tall and blond. Jessica held the big gun on her; it trembling in her hands. Gooseflesh ran up her spine, staring into the eerie calm of those eyes. No fear in those blue eyes. Somberg's charm, beauty and style had made her seem invincible, and Jessica had once believed it. She believed it no longer. She believed in herself. She would give as she had received. Seeing Danny holding a gun on her, laughing in a helmet of horns, Jessica aimed for the bitch's heart and braced herself for an enormous recoil that might take her the rest of her life to get over. She could not stop herself. She squeezed the trigger.

There was only a metallic click as the hammer fell on an empty chamber. Jessica stared disbelievingly at the gun.

"You surprise me, Jess," Somberg said, smiling as though she were proud of Jessica. "I didn't know you had it in you."

Jessica pulled the trigger again. It landed on another empty chamber. She tried it again. And then the balcony went white as Somberg knocked her down the bleacher.

Her ears were ringing to a thousand bells, all out of tune. Her body light and fragile, Jessica lifted onto a bench with the ceiling rising and sliding overhead, its outlines smudged as if in heat. "Did you think I'd leave a loaded revolver beside an IRA madman?" Somberg sounded far away. Jessica saw only Nordic bones and hideous hair like snakes. "Try that again, Jess, and I'll blow your brains out in front of my son."

One side of Jessica's head felt crushed, her body hovering on the bench, and now it just took off in flight. Flying away on a clear spring day, the air so smooth, like glass. Something ticking steady, steadily in her ears, might have been her heart. Loving the clouds and blue sky, and now a long, low circling over a field of new grass and wildflowers and Madame Monet's long white dress with her son rising from the grass behind her. The only gratification remaining from her Danny vigil was the pleasure of crying, and now Jessica began to cry so quietly it was only behind her eyes. She felt dead, but hope would not die, and she clung to that Monet vision of herself and her son, she would be faithful to it until the end. Her hands were yanked behind her, tied in panty hose.

"Ye did grand," Shanahan said beside her. "Just grand!"

"*Melissa!* Go downstairs. Get Eric. Jess has persuaded me; we'll take him with us after all."

Kim clung to the door frame staring at Kristian as though it were he who had been kidnapped, and it only just now, in the terror in her voice, occurred to him that he could have left her any time. His eyes fled to the studio of scaffolds shelved with lacquer. Looked like some soundstage for a play. In his gender-bent head, the third raging movement of the *Prokofiev Piano Concerto No. 3* was playing as some buccaneer and his heart could not escape it or his budding breasts and his new bottom; for the love of God, Kim could not stop the demented concerto or Melissa's devotion to it.

"*Kim!*"

"Yes, ma'am," Melissa said, born again in those inexplicable eyes, so purple, so blue, so violet, so otherwordly.

"When you bring him up, dear, cover his eyes. Make it like a game. I don't want him to see his Old Mama."

"I understand," Melissa said, luscious and lustrous. "She's going to die, again."

At the door in the hall, Trent peeked around the pretty girl at the madwoman. She was tying Jessica's hands. He had expected something violent and obnoxious and bitchy; as some dark clone of Mrs. T. Vampiric. Hot-blooded. Like a tyranny of personality disorders. He was surprised at her very cool beauty. Somberg was compelling, actually. She had a haughty mystique. Jessica, now bound, was in a quiet desperation, ravishing in her intractable sorrow. Her zapped-out mind, Trent supposed, must be barely bounced on the edge, as she was, on the edge of her bench in the bleacher, staring with Somberg out into the studio at Danny. The two thwarted, distorted women seemed to infuse one another.

He readied the morning star. The radiant spikes glittered in the gloom of the hall.

The Beretta was on the floor at the foot of the bleacher. The best he could hope for was to distract Somberg long enough to retrieve the weapon. He would have to unleash the morning star with extraordinary care, he would have one chance, and one chance only. He left the saber by the door, freeing his hands and his mind, forgetting what was at stake, concentrating on what must be done, and the speed with which it must be done.

He waited until the pretty baby started for the stairs, and then he came through her, driving her face first into the floor with that hellish spiked ball spinning at his side. As she fell, he unleashed the morning star at Somberg. It flew quickly and effervescently as a comet. In that instant he heard Somberg's first wild shot with the balcony streaked in laser, and just before he dove for the Beretta, he caught the stultification of Somberg's face, as if that morning star had come whirling out of another time, like perhaps the age of the Greeks. Trent rolled once across the floor as Somberg released another burst from the Glock that in the balcony sounded like artillery fire. He came up with the Beretta. On one knee before the bleacher, targeting the lunatic already shielded behind Jessica. She was lightning quick, even in disaster, Somberg's right shoulder frothing blood. But she had not lost her cool, she was already shouting down to Danny that everything was fine, just fine, one of the guns accidently discharged, nothing to worry about, they would be leaving soon.

Trent could not look at Danny who was behind him. He remained a magical boy, a fairytale never seen. A mythic child made of Jessica's limitless love.

"Let her go," Trent said to Somberg who had the Glock braced at Jessica's head. He took solace in the shoulder, slathered and dripping, it looked as though Somberg had been mauled by some beast. "Just let Jessica go," Trent repeated, trying not to see Jessica's eyes widened at the gunfire.

"Drop your weapon or she's dead," Somberg said in a low, guttural voice, so Danny could not hear.

"No problem," Trent said, speaking to those striking eyes enamored by pain that had to be excruciating. Would it reach her head? Trent hoped it would. "Just let Jessica go," he said. "I can shoot you and you can shoot Jessica. But it doesn't have to come down like that. We can talk about this. But I won't leave until you let Jessica and Danny go."

"If you so much as flinch," Somberg hissed like a viper, "I'll fucking execute her."

"No one is going to flinch and no one is going to shoot and no one will die here today." Trent watched the blood ooze from her shoulder, the color draining from her face. He drew on everything he knew about the woman, to keep the blood flowing. "There are no amateurs here," he said appealing to prima donna airs. "No crazies or bomb throwers or dreamers. We're all *professionals.* Just let Jessica and Danny go and we'll be on our way."

"No way, hotshot. Eric and I are going home."

"Ah. Home, is it?" Trent said, relying on his gabby Irishness. "And where might that be?"

She did not respond. She held Jessica by the throat, the gun at the base of her skull. Jessica sat very erect, in a charm-school posture. Trent would not look at her, he watched Somberg's eyes in flight, calculating the odds and the options.

"Home," he said, drawing upon one of her great natural gifts. "Well now, that wouldn't be home with father, would it?'' He smiled very slightly. ''We know how he was shot *in the barn,*'' Trent said, drawing from the report the good Swedes had sent him.

''Oh, the barn, is it?'' Somberg mocked him. Red lips skinned back to a spittled grin. ''I thought perhaps it was *Maggie* that brought you here.''

''I know, you had no choice,'' Trent said with a tiny stroke of tenderness. ''Had to do it. But it must have been rough, I mean, your own *father.*''

He was waiting for her to fall apart. The bleeding would help her along, the life running out of her. But the great renown of a problematic family was another sort of life, Trent bled it.

''He beat her, we know. You really had no choice. Had to save *Mother.* That's what she told you, right? Always do as Mother says, right? A flawless plan, if you ask me. After all, a child wouldn't be prosecuted for murder. A murder Mother didn't have to commit. But how did she persuade you to do it?''

The blood was running warm down her ribs, a slow trickle so the wound couldn't be as bad as the pain, though Somberg couldn't afford to look, her eyes fixed on Jessica's beau who held the Beretta with the calm of a cop. She welcomed the old familiar pain back, and it rapidly passed all previous bounds. Pain enhanced her senses and she could hear again the roar that echoed through the barn, as if it happened only moments ago. She saw her father hurled back into the hay in a candlelight dream that was never a dream. He lay dying in her mind in shadows of smoke. A grimacing psychopath joined him in the candle shadows. Mother was once a woman of such candescent beauty and excitement, a creator, an original, now given to compulsive imitation. In a sanatorium, swimming on the floor, hideously laughing. ''We are all female fish!'' Mother cried out. ''Men more female behind their faces and voices than anyone knows or than they know themselves!'' She swam on, dear, fragile Mother, possessed with raging intuition.

''Amazing shooting for a twelve-year-old girl,'' Trent delved, extracting what Mother's candle had blinked away. He paused as the blood wept from the mangled shoulder. ''Father was shot not once, but *twice.* Once in the belly. Once in the heart.''

The pain radiated from Somberg's wounds, from a torn shoulder and a torn heart. It seemed to fill the world that flickered in dream fragments unwinding in her head. She saw the dazed horror of her father's face as his only daughter shot him with his gun. A portion of his vitals horsekicked out his back into the barn. Now she stood over Father, he lay as limp as a broken bird. She turned to Mother who nodded. Then she shot him again to clap shut the calls of this lesser creature who swam away into the darkness beyond the candle that Mother had used to help her sleep at night. And after the barn, Somberg moved with determination across the surface of her life, by and large she had been able to avoid the past. Somberg, by the force of her will, made a life never dull or ordinary, not only for herself but for her two sisters. Always keeping ahead of the past. Never easy with a hereditary demon at their heels. Insanity in beautiful women is not all sweetness and light, but fucking ugly and it made Mother horrible, though the struggle to overcome a sickness could make you great.

''Then there was the priest.'' Trent glanced to Shanahan. The morning star lay beside him, gold and silver spikes glistening in gore. He was using it to cut his hands free. "The priest was your next one, wasn't he?"

"Mine? No. He was not my work." Somberg stared into a flame, low and guttering, unenthusiastic. The problem with dream candles is that they just keep burning, the flickering points like silent metronomes dancing all night. "No," she said to the black hole in her soul that the candle had left. "The priest was not my work but my mother's. She did for me what I did for her."

Trent watched the blood well from the nasty wound doing its work. Her head-thumping would soon become nausea that would slide into vertigo, her world would tilt at a skewed angle, a bit more skewed than it normally was. Then he would take her. All he needed was a little time, mother and daughter tangled in a family history of father-killing that no amount of kissing would ever really fix.

Jessica's hearing was coming back now, her ears ringing from the shots that for the longest time would not stop, the terror still twitching in her hands. The barrel of Somberg's gun was behind her right ear, Somberg pressing it so hard against the bone that it hurt. Felt like she was trying to push it into her. The woman's hot breathing at her neck, their bodies squeezed together and Jessica could feel her every heaving breath. That and the blood spattering the wood bench let her know Somberg was wounded. She was making small sounds of suffering, so faint no one else could hear them, but Jessica could, and what's more, she could feel them, so they shared the pain as they had shared Danny, who was seemingly oblivious to everything, playing his hockey game in the studio below.

She had Somberg's Glock at her ear, while she stared into the black orifice of Trent's Beretta. It seemed that either the man she loved or the woman she hated was about to kill her. And it seemed she had been caught here since her son was taken away. The tormented victim, trapped between love and hate.

"Danny's behind you," she silently mouthed to Trent. Now his eyes touched her briefly in a cruelty of hope, both her men, Danny and Trent, before her for the first time. It was a moment made by insanity. The desperation, idiocy, neediness, largeness, loudness and selfishness of the standoff could not be grasped by the sane mind. Long ago she was just a photographer, a single mom getting by. She had been that in that order. And if by God's grace this ended well, with Danny, that would all be reversed. Never would she put career before the love of her life, the tears coursing down her cheeks, drama heightened now by the call of a boy that for the first time in a long time did not come from a dream.

"Mommy! *What* are you guys doing up there?"

"*Danny!*" Jessica started to leap to her feet. Somberg shoved her down hard. "I'm up here!" she shouted to him.

"I'm hear, dear!" Somberg said, shouting louder.

Danny looked up to the balcony with a frown of perplexity.

"Mommy?" he called in an uncertain voice.

"*Yes! Danny! It's me!*"

Somberg clamped a hand over Jessica's mouth. "What, Eric?" she called down in the voice of authority.

"Who are those people up there?"

"Oh, they're just ghosts, dear. The old house is haunted. You know, I always told you it was."

Danny threw his head back and laughed.

Standing near the door, Melissa was fascinated by the double Mexican standoff. The Brit and Kristian with Beretta and Glock. And the two mothers cheek to cheek, appealing to the child with something far more powerful than a gun, love. Which one would win the boy? Which one would die? It was a game Kim would have been oblivious to, that Melissa found thrilling and riveting, like her new life that had made Kim prettier than his dreams, his hysteria acting as a beauty elixir, all but wiping him out.

"Keep playing!" Somberg called to Danny. "I'll be down in a minute." And now to Beauty: "Take off your heels, darling."

"If she moves," Trent said, glancing to the frivolous girl, "I'll drop her."

"No, he won't. If he takes his gun off me, I'll blow his face out the back of his skull." Somberg looked straight into the eyes of the femme and said, "Take off your shoes, *Melissa.*"

Kim heard the voice of the Breaker, but Melissa heard the Sensualist in whose eyes she was complete. Those eyes spinning his head around in a sad confusion that was the whole story of being a male. Melissa kicked off her heels. It was difficult to tolerate Kim who was not one of Kristian's wunderkind creations, and so he was so easily awestruck by Beauty and never saw the disorders or maladjustments or the gifts. He never understood that all men had the optional feature of being female, it's their spiritual nature. The offspring of these split-personality tantrums was the release of a memory spinning in the sweet blue of Kristian's eyes. Melissa snatched it up, singing: "I know where the dairy is! It's behind the orchid paint in the scaffolding. Should I go get it?"

Somberg restrained her smile. The diary was in the scaffold with her purse that held Eric's explosive belt, the remote in her pocket. A new color came into Somberg's face, the happy color of a woman who had refused to accept the limits of her own conditions, who continually confronted the limits and so tolerated the pain to live beyond it. This was the end. She knew that and knew she'd go on without Eric. She did not feel sorry for herself, but rather, bent close to Jessica, her lips at her ear to impart the secret. "*Most people get what they really want,*" she whispered. "*They become what they perceive themselves to be.*"

"What are you talking about?" Jessica cried, seeing only the painting of Madame Monet with her son rising out of the spring grass behind her.

Somberg smiled on the smashed-up woman, and the sadness of her whole story. She never despised Jessica as Jessica did her. In fact, she rather admired Jessica. They were a lot alike. And it seemed, as she recalled their first meeting, that was something Jessica wanted. We must choose our mentors with a sympathy for their pain that will likely become ours, and always be careful not to become their victims. A lesson too late for Jessica.

"Do you know the definition of magic?" Somberg said to Trent.

"Careful, Brit!" Shanahan shouted, one hand cut free, untying the other. "She's a demon from the fiery pit!"

"You're going *nowhere,*" Trent told her. She was showing just enough face. He prepared himself. One titanium round to her skull, pivot left, drop the girl, then right to Shanahan. "I'll take you down or take you out, Somberg. But I'll *not* let you go." He made it sound as though he meant it, as though his love were not before him, bloodcurdling tears shining in her eyes.

"Magic," Somberg said, gently releasing Jessica, a hand into her trouser pocket for the remote detonator, "is when the audience watches the right hand, while the left performs the trick."

Trent tried to read the blend of agony and joy in Somberg's eyes as she gazed down on Danny. It was a parting look. What was she up to? Then he saw a magic box in her hand. A remote for what he didn't know. He was about to squeeze off a shot when Somberg kissed Jessica full on the mouth.

"Good-bye, darling. Love your new haircut!"

Trent had her in his sight, with the power of life and death in his hand, a god about to deliver a lightning strike, when at the kiss Jessica shrieked and leaped to her feet. She became cover for Somberg standing now, aiming the detonator at the scaffolding in the studio that was a combustible showpiece. Eternal seconds of delay, but Trent couldn't fire for Jessica's flailing, and then there was an explosion in his ears. The studio gone a dazzling white. Same as the sun in the sky. Hottest day in the history of summer. The heat intense with his scream struggling on through the overbearing swelter that hit him in the back like something solid. He was pitched off his feet, suddenly mortal.

Jessica saw a pylon of flame leap up from a scaffold in the studio. She saw Trent thrown into the bleacher with a face that looked as if he'd been electrocuted through the penis. Her eyes flew to Danny. He dropped his game, mouth open in a silent scream as the scaffold near the stairs mushroomed into pretty pink flame. A bone-deep shudder shook Jessica with no breath in her lungs. The surreal nightmare in brilliant rainbow flames. A terrible beauty. She stumbled down the bleacher, shrieking at Somberg, the blood-lust pushing through her fear, ready to kill. The Beretta was at her feet. She picked it up as Somberg and Beauty ducked out the door. And now she would choose. Danny or Somberg? Love or hate?

46

JESSICA DIDN'T HEAR herself screaming. She didn't see herself shove Trent out of the way. She didn't feel the scalding heat of the orchid pink fireball blooming over the stairs. She saw only Danny with his wide-open mouth shrieking a cry heard more with the heart than the ears. She had started down the stairs when Trent caught her by the arm and pulled her back.

"Let me go!"

"Jess, look down there." Trent pointed to the lower flight of stairs, smoldering and smudgy. "The fucking stairs are on fire!"

"I don't give a shit! Danny is down there!"

Jessica broke loose and started down the blazing stairs and again, Trent wrestled her back. A wind of heat on their faces as she struggled in his arms. From the banister Jessica saw the fire as some shining, shocking symbol of the dark, making a flaming pyre of the scaffolding, devouring each in succession, the flames feeding on the racks of lacquer, sopping up paint to explode into gelatinous rainbow flames. Danny was opposite the fire, near the fireplace. He was safe for now, but Trent doubted whether in five minutes anyone would survive the heat, the air already hot and noxious. Soon, the entire studio would go up in flames. And then there was Shanahan's vest. What was the combustive temperature of nitrobenzene? They had used it once on the Wall in Berlin. In memory Trent saw a label on a crate: "Keep in a Dry Cool Place."

"*Let me fucking go!*" The heat was infectious, Jessica felt it as a furnace glowing deep within her, burning in her fingers curled into fists, and in the cords that stood out in her neck. It bubbled up her throat and she could not speak for the hate of the bitch who she could just kill, and the love of the boy she would gladly die for. She had died, in the difficult days and impossible nights, alone without her child, living with a crushed feeling in her gut, exhausted, pissed off, anxious, profoundly depressed, and now to come here, a thousand miles from all of that to find Danny, only to lose him to a fire? She couldn't bear it. Wouldn't bear it. There had to be a way. She tried to think, her mind racing, but all she could seem to think to do was to run to Danny.

She was going nuts in the terrible glamor of the flames and turned, finally, to Trent. He was about to speak when suddenly Father Shanahan was there, babbling about the fire of the devil's throne room and a flight of demon angels he could fly above.

"There's no way down!" Trent shouted at the old Irish fool. "The stair was the only way."

But Shanahan was insistent. Jessica could hardly hear him for listening to Danny's cry for help. She saw Shanahan's bony finger point to a support beam that ran across the studio above the fire. A sculpture hoist hung from the beam. Below it the marble likeness of Margaret Thatcher smiled onto the hellish flames.

"I'll go," Shanahan said. "Don't touch the vest. Lucifer wired it to the bloody phone. Looks booby-trapped to me."

Jessica glanced back to the bleacher. The bulging vest of red dynamite sticks was on an upper bench. Her eyes followed a mess of wires to the phone, and now she knew why Somberg kept steadying the phone in their fight. The vest could be exploded by a phone call. In her head a pulse began to hammer and for the first time Jessica understood the reigning madwoman. Somberg was at once simple and grandiose. The whole world was hers, anything and everything to be used in the pursuit of her dreams that ran rampant through her every action. When would Somberg call? It would take only that to explode the whole manor house, and for what? What did Beauty say? Something about a diary? Jessica ground her teeth together madly. A diary was of more value to Somberg than Danny.

The shouts of Trent and Father Shanahan turned Jessica on her heel. The men wrestling with each other, Shanahan trying to pull away, but Trent wouldn't let go of his arm, the priest was to be arrested. Trent yelling something about about the Grand Hotel and the assassinations of Airey Neave and Lord Mountbatten.

"Are you out of your mind?" Jessica grabbed Trent's arms in a hug that freed the Father. "Let him go! He can save Danny!"

Trent was arguing that he could save Danny, after he cuffed Shanahan. He produced a pair of cuffs, from where Jessica had no idea, but he was already too late, the Father was climbing atop the banister. He stood up wobbly on the low banister wall. Heat billowed in his cassock. He looked to the beam just below. It was a good wide wooden beam that ran the length of the studio.

"Wait here," he called to Jessica. "I'll deliver the lad, as I promised ye at the pub."

"Be careful, Father!" Jessica reached out to him. He bent down, a bony hand squeezed hers. She looked into the leatheriness of his gaunt face for the last time. He gave her a little wink.

"I've no need of caution, child," he said with a sure smile. "The Lord God is with me. I'll see you in Ireland, one day." He turned to face the flames, and a Psalm came to his lips. "Praise the Lord upon earth: ye dragons, and all deeps; fire and hail, snow and vapours: wind and storm, fulfilling His word."

Trent tried to grab for him just as he jumped. He caught the beam dead center, teetered, then found his balance. There was a sound like wind in the trees that swirled about him as he duck-walked through heat rippling like the shimmering drapery folds of paradise. Below, he saw small young flames run over the floor to the lad turning in circles before the great fireplace, a fireplace Shanahan had been studying all day, praying for deliverance. He had no idea it would come like this, but who can know the mind of the great Creator, or the multitude of ways in which He works?

He reached the sculpture hoist. It held a stout burled rope. He sat on the beam, reeled out the length of the rope, but it fell short of the floor, dangling above the bust of bloody Thatcher. He could climb down and drop to the lad, but once on the floor, there would be no way to reach the rope to climb out of the flames. The lad saw him now, looking up with his innocent face filmed in sweat that gleamed the colors of the fire. He gave a desolate cry that tore at the heart of the Father who saved the lost in the name of God and killed the Brits, wherever he could find them, in the name of Ireland. The gargantuan dichotomy was laid to rest in the lad, ten thousand evocations of penitence for blood spilt found comfort in him. To save the lad, Shanahan knew in his enlightened-savage soul, was to somehow save himself.

Shanahan looked to the ceiling where grasping hands of fire crawled, snapping and crackling and promising death. "I will give thanks unto Thee," he praised, "for I am fearfully and wonderfully made." Gradually his vision cleared and he saw the host of Irish saints gathered and waiting. He needed only to be shown the way. He had prepared all his life for martyrdom.

When the rope fell short and Danny cried out, Jessica bolted again for the stair. Trent was now struggling with her, trying not to feel but to think. If he let her go, she would be consumed. A staggering, twisting, burning candle of arms and legs racing for her child. If Danny were to die in the fire, she would never live again. If they could not save him, it would be better to leave her to die with Danny. But how could he leave her? Trent knew he could not. And so it seemed they were all headed for tragedy with no way out. It was a shame, after all Jessica had been through, using the thread of a lead to swing from one hope to the next in a love that never gave up. And now the answer came to Trent.

"*Swing!*" he shouted in his mother's Irish tongue.

Shanahan looked up from the beam.

"Swing down and snatch him up!" Trent called.

"But the bloody rope is too short!" Shanahan called back.

Trent looked to the studio. There was a desk. If Danny could stand on it, he might be within the arc of the rope if Shanahan were teetered to the very end of it, reaching down.

"We'll get him to stand on the desk!" Trent shouted. Then he told the priest how he must tie himself to the rope of the hoist.

Shanahan pulled a bitter grin and nodded to himself. He understood now. He'd have to fly like one of Lucifer's angels in the fire. He pulled up the rope. He took it with him, skittering back along the beam in the relentless heat with flames above and below. The flames were beautified and embellished by the memory of the demon and Shanahan knew had he not been tied to the bleacher he never could have looked into those blue eyes. Eyes as hypnotic intoxication, as fine and gentle as organza. She held him captive as she had many men, with her eyes alone, and he felt himself grow as hard as stone. She was often irritating, certainly destructive, a legend of elegiac poetry and he saw her now in the flames, this Medusa, soothing into sensibility the irreconcilable absurdities of his life so that the pretty flames that were her legacy were as the hot kisses of Satan. She called from the fire. Something in Shanahan wanting to fall for her, the fiendish temptation.

But he did not fall, and as he neared the balcony there came a succession of explosions, like Irish bombs, as another scaffold of lacquer went up into swelling flames that leaped to the ceiling in fantastic colors. He saw it as the froth of hell! But now the balcony was cut off. There was a wall of fire before him, the air flaming up to purple, licking at the great skylight. Through the flames he could see the mother wailing in the arms of the Brit. And still he did not despair but believed in his destiny. He would swing as sweetly as Joyce sang, Joyce self-exiled from Ireland to become an Irish saint.

"I'll throw him!" he shouted.

"What?" Trent called back.

"I'll swing down to fetch him, then heave him through the flames. You must catch him in your arms!"

"Right." Trent gave a wave of acknowledgment to the Irishman who tied to the rope would never escape the fire. It was just. He would go as he had sent others, Neave, Mountbatten, in flames.

Jessica was rocking back and forth, moaning as she watched the Father return with the rope. Then when the scaffold blew, she and Trent were driven back to the bleacher. She stood on the bench where Somberg had placed her, a captive again. She had a cheek in either hand and was twisting the flesh as if it were dough. She caught a glimpse of Father Shanahan staring at her through the flames, his mouth working, his eyes dark holes. She never heard what he said. And now Trent had her yelling. They called to Danny. They had to have him climb up on the desk. She screamed in outrage and despair, her voice struggled on through the heat. Trent and Jessica shouted together. "*Danny! Up here!*"

Danny looked up from the little corkscrews of flames dancing around him, he thought he saw the ghost of his Old Mama up in the balcony. She called him by his old name. Her voice came from a long way away and it hurt him inside, but it was a good hurt and he could see her face now in the balcony, he loved face all shiny with tears. And now he knew there were ghosts in this old house, knew it all along. He listened carefully and did as he was told. He ran to the desk and pulled out the drawers, climbing them like shelves in a bathroom closet. He had always been a good climber and waved to his mother's ghost from atop the desk where he knew he would die and become a ghost himself. He was not as afraid of the fire as he was afraid of dying. Hadn't he killed his mother? Hadn't he shot her dead? Something in him knew it. He did that. But as the ghost returned his wave from that world where the light was mostly violet, he saw the ghost did not look angry with him. It was a good ghost.

Jessica stood in shoes that felt stiff and hard, as if her feet had changed shape while she was standing on the bench. She watched the Father stretch the rope as far as it would go. His mouth turned down in a sneer at the effort, pulling on the heavy coarse rope, getting everything out of it, like a good story. A dark vein in his broad forehead pulsed like a fuse as he used his crimson sash to lash his left hand to the end of the rope. In this way he could not let go, no matter the fear, and Jessica imagined the fear was ravenous out there in the fire that she saw as snakes switching and lashing over the ceiling. The pink-to-purple snakes swelled on the air that was now so hot it seemed the heat went right though her and out the other side. But the Irish Father looked madly exhilarated. His white hair roiled in the heat of the wind, his gaunt cheeks glowed with hectic color.

The desk stood as an island above a sea of flames that to Danny felt like little hot needles pricking his soft skin. The ghost called to him again, and as he looked up he saw a blackbird flying down out of a ceiling of fire, long black wings fluttering out behind him. He seemed to be reaching out to Danny, this great blackbird with white hair and the skeletonlike face of the priest Danny had met in church. Only now his face had a rosy light that Danny felt inside, and he felt sure that the angel-blackbird was coming to take him to his Old Mama who was waiting in heaven. And Danny reached high, on tiptoe, as high as he could reach.

Jessica saw the Father sweep down over the burning floor. She saw his right hand strike Danny and her heart slammed two violent beats—it looked as if he knocked him off the desk! They were lost in a gout of flame and she never heard her shrieking or her prayer but God must have because just then she saw them again, they were together, riding the rope to the ceiling! Danny was like a lamb in the crook of the Father's long arm, he was holding the boy close and Jessica couldn't breathe and couldn't turn away and couldn't stop the trembling that came over her whole body with her life at the end of that rope suspended at the apex of the swing. It seemed to Jessica that they hung there for an eternity, then they started down through the wilting heart of the flames.

Jessica was clinging to Trent, holding his arm so tight, her fingernails were white-going-on-purple, when the terrible heat exploded the skylight. A storm of glass rained down like glitter with the ceiling coming alive with fire snakes feeding on the lacquer and fresh air. They swarmed in evil S-shapes through the rafters, hellish things breathing fire, growing to a hideous size. In her mania, Jessica saw a hatch-head rise on the biggest snake, it had the look of Somberg, glints of violet and vermilion in its eyes. Jaws of fire opened and a pink tongue licked down the rope. It was right at Shanahan's face. The Father looked up and shouted something at it, and Jessica watched in wonder as it recoiled, whipping upward, leaping out of the skylight to bellow at God.

They were sailing back, rising now through a vaporous wall, with Trent cheering Shanahan. *"C'mon, you Irish sonofabitch!"* He pulled Jessica from the bleacher to the banister. She had to have his help to move. She took a shuddering step to the fire that was flailing like the arms of a flaming psychopath over the banister. She now prepared herself to catch Danny to be thrown through the fire. Her heart was hammering and her arms felt weak as she lifted them. How could she endure this? Then a presence came over her and Jessica did not doubt it; it was confirmed by the force of all his character. Jessica felt Pit slip up behind her. He embraced her, his huge arms around her, girding her arms, and she wept a little and smiled a secret smile, and the small, hard knot in her stomach relaxed. She *knew* it would be okay. Pit gave her that feeling.

The Father rose up out of the flames holding Danny. Jessica saw him through the fire, swinging up to her, her baby with his gorgeous face and his hair flying. He was *so* beautiful, infusing her with an anguish and suffering that reached a pinnacle then, Jessica thought she would explode! She saw the Father kiss Danny on the head, his long Irish face twisted, preparing to launch the lad as they flew up to the banister, but twelve feet shy. In that instant the Father met her eyes, his voice thundered in her burning heart: "O give thanks unto the Lord, for he is gracious: and his mercy endureth forever!"

Trent shrieked, *"Do it now!"* and Shanahan pitched Danny headfirst into the flames that engulfed him as those days of boy-madness that had possessed Jessica and remade her into iron.

Jessica's wild heart slammed inside her chest, she saw only the pink-to-purple flames, and then he came flying out of the fire like some kind of Bat Boy to crash into her chest. The sky seemed to crowd around her head, the earth buckled. Jessica found herself on the floor, her head thumping and buzzing, Danny sprawled over the top of her, a boy dropped from heaven. She touched his face, her fingers not believing the softness there. She touched his hair. She kissed his hair. She looked into his blue eyes blurred in her tears. Jessica hugged him and Danny smeared purple paint on her face and on her arms. Crying and shaking, she held his hot little hands, her hands not believing their touch.

"Do you remember me?" she asked, terrified of his answer.

Danny looked up at his mama with a goofy smile. It was the strangest thing because he didn't feel dead, this felt more like heaven, so many feelings coming back in a remembering he had all but forgotten. "I love you, Mama," he said. "Where you been?"

The Silver Shadow Rolls cruised down the motorway. The pain was unspeakable, and so Somberg did not speak of it. Her sister, the baby, was beside her at the wheel, Alexia in the back, leaning into the front to care for her, showing Melissa how to arrest the bleeding. Blood was not a thing to be shy of, it was a nuisance, makes a job messy, though it can contribute to the art and always to the pain. The tribal philosophy Somberg had taught Alexia was now imparted to Melissa, functioning the best way to teach, on the job; it is potent and powerful.

Alexia had followed them out of town in the Mercedes that was left on a side road, the car set on fire so prints were purged in the same fashion Warnock Manor would be. Alexia was such a beauty, her skin and her hair so fair, brought that Dylan song to mind, *Blonde on Blonde*. Somberg smiled on her inspiration as she fussed over the shoulder, she had her own vitality and charismatic charm, and Alexia would undoubtedly write her own stories in the years to come. Alexia was merging into the largeness of family to find her own place. There were two calls to make, Alexia made the first one, ringing Somberg's look-alike pilot standing by in Grantham.

On the Grantham airfield, Sean McShane waited in his Cessna with the Father's money burning in his pocket. It made him sick to take the money of one who ministered to them for such a long time. He would do this job well, and now here came the Mercedes into the car park. Through binoculars, he could see a figure in an overcoat and hat emerge from the car, matched the Father's description. The bitch, no doubt. She was alone, the lad was not with her. Sean followed the figure as it ran from the car to the Lear parked on the tarmac. Now he took up the detonator. He was some distance away but knew the flue detonator would work, same one the Father used on Mountbatten. Sunk a boat, now it would sink a plane.

It would be a footnote to history, the woman who killed Margaret Thatcher was killed herself, and wasn't that the way of the world? Death begets death. Sean waited till the Lear was a lovely silver bird rising into the sun. He touch the detonator. The sun exploded into a fireball, scattering the remains across the sky, like funeral ashes on the sea. Perfectly Irish.

In the Rolls Somberg swallowed a pill that would control the pain but would not betray it. The shoulder wound was horrid, but the pain was an old friend and Somberg did not fear it. For now, she disguised it by mockery and raillery to keep it in contempt and reduce its stature, and in time she would release it in tears, in a sorcery learned from Mother. She was the centrifugal force of the family, Mother unified the sometimes disparate sister factions and themes and scenes and settings, her oral history a best-seller with the jigsawed family that was now more than sisters. Mother's reminiscences and loony-bin insight, a rare poetry, smoothed into sensibility the sometimes serrated edges of sisters and those who loved and served them. Her memorable life was the faith of Ishtar, a part of the family mythology, as it was a part of all history, and would in Mother's incandescence be transformed into vitality for the world at large. The dreary development of womanhood was to be reborn in the mighty and inexhaustible possibilities of the the wise creator, the one source of universal order, the reigning supreme deity that was and always had been a woman. These things Somberg looked forward to, Grantham, England already a memory.

There is no restful haven for an unquiet mind, Mother taught this by example. Each daughter founded her own haven in homage to the fatigue that was inevitable and the culprit that had wounded the family's great natural gift, Mother. In the unhurried, healing days of Martinique, Somberg knew she would come to think of Eric. The light at her sugar plantation was like a revelation and there she would live through the inevitable days of melancholy in which she would recall her once-upon-a-time son. It would make her glad to relive the hard work, responsibility and sacrifice of being a mother. She would not fake the healing, the pain was a vital part of her integrity. It was the pain that governed most people, the trick was to learn to get over it, to the one and only thing of consequence: pleasure.

Just one call left to make. Somberg hesitated. Jessica, she knew, had come a long way. From a regular girl, normal and well-adjusted, sometimes the sensitive artist, to the sad victim with outsized and oversized emotions, to conquering her vulnerable soul that was in danger of becoming the psychotic nutcase. Women of no less stature than Mother went over that edge, into the compelling, ravished, zapped-out cult of the crazy women. Jessica had something of Mother's eyes that believed in miracles in a world where such things were, as sisters knew, still possible. The future existed in imagination, and if you dream, you could dream it, and had the courage to believe in your dream, you could create it.

Jessica had believed in such dreams that were unthwarted by her torment that she had overcome, Mother would love to meet her, and so it was a shame this last call was necessary, but the diary could not wait. In need of a muse, Somberg played the *Prokofiev Piano Concerto No. 3,* Mother's favorite, then tapped the number into the car phone. It rang only once.

Danny and Jessica and Trent ran through the corridor roiling in smoke like the waves of the sea. Danny felt like he was swimming though deep water. It felt kind of wonderful. And a little crazy. They burst through the front doors. The rain had stopped. Clouds echoed with the throb of an SAS helicopter. Now Danny saw soldiers jumping out of the helicopter as it came down in the street. The soldiers running down the driveway! Danny stopped on the porch. His eyes gobbled it up. "What the heck?" he said. But there was no time to explain, his Old Mama took his hand and pulled him from the house, running over the estate with a kind of trembling in her that could Danny feel but like so many things, did not understand.

They ran through the high chestnuts, with Trent shouting at the soldiers, waving them back. Something was alive in the air, Danny knew it. It was shimmery and brilliant and very precious. It was the gleam of danger that the mind knows whether you do or not. Learned from attitude as from anything said. An attitude his New Mama had instilled in him; an urgency in his veins that was forever his, that is the state of being able to do anything. He would forget many things, but Danny would remember these powerful feelings made unforgettable by what happened next, when the phone rang in the Turner Studio.

Trent pulled Jessica and Danny behind the great trunk of a chestnut as a golden sheet of lightning fired through the windows of Warnock Manor. The black-and-white facade exploded, ripping the roof off, sending it flying over the estate where Danny was tucked under Jessica with Trent of top of her. When the shelling debris had stopped, Trent peered out at the shroud of pink and gray and coal black smoke that rolled away from the convulsing bowels of the house, as though it were a living thing struck dead. But was all dead that was in the house? Trent suspected it was not.

Father Shanahan was dangling from the rope when Trent saw him last. There was Jessica and Danny's reunion, and when Trent looked again, the priest was gone. The studio floor was a hell of flames, the empty rope of the sculpture hoist was still swinging, burning like a fuse, but there was no sign of the Irishman. Trent's eyes flashed over the fire. What the hell happened to him? There was no time to look again, but as he was hurrying Jessica and Danny out of the balcony, Trent saw the smiling bust of Mrs. T was gone, as if it had been snatched up by Irish spirits.

Trent stood now and looked over the remains of Warnock Manor. The wing that had been the Turner Studio was vaporized, only the tall, wide chimney was left standing. Trent considered it for a moment. In the logical sound spirit of his Irish mother, he would not search the chimney, nor would he suggest that the soldiers do so. Shanahan had, after all, saved Danny. Trent told himself the vanishing of the old priest was Irish magic. He heard such tales when he was a boy. For lack of a better explanation, Trent would report Father Shanahan dead. He hoped he would stay dead.

His report would only be filed at Number 10. It would become one more myth in that clouded kingdom, excluded from the future, safe from the voracious appetite of a sensation-loving world. It was Mrs. T's way, there would be no one to criticize or mock or disavow what never happened. No screaming headlines in the *Times*. Only a picture in the back pages of Mrs. Thatcher smiling down on a cake iced with an amusing caricature of herself. Flocked around her were a gathering of children, one of which was an unidentified boy said to be from America. The caption would make no mention of the death of the school principal attributed to a heart condition or that the teacher and the children had had their stomachs pumped. Nor would there be any mention of the injection all had received to counter a toxin they were never told about. The truth of the day at Huntington Tower Elementary existed only in those who had lived it, a truth safe with those few who would never forget.

On certain nights, for which there was seemingly no reason, Jessica would wake gasping in the thick, suffocating blackness. And sometimes in certain lights, as in gray times when sunlight is seeping through the shades and all things are outlines, she would be consumed by a panic that would slip its hood over her mind and draw her back in time to an extravagant effulgence of misery. When attacks came, she would sometimes lose all sense of the reality of what was happening, in a terror that she could not shake off, for which there was no blunt chemical corrective. In those times, she was taken back in her history to that hugely exhausting place. To that heart of darkness where she was confronted by the limits of her endurance, and then pushed beyond that endurance into what she never believed possible, and still, all the while, though she was scared shitless of never seeing her child again, Jessica in memory as she did in fact, never lost the dream. In those times of swoony horror, as in the days of helplessness, she hung on.

Jessica for years would have problematic mental health until she taught herself to listen to her own soul music. She heard the music in her wide-open gaze of the past that she could not shake off, in which she felt like roadkill, and in the music the loss of a child's years that could never be restored became a legacy she actually appreciated over time. In every great woman there is a madness that is fueled by suffering that drives a multitude of directions; it is in the quiet soul that peace is found. From this place Jessica settled into the dreariness of normal and happy, to prize that gift that she would never lose again. It was not the loss of the child that was found which she treasured; it was the loss of Self found after the child was found. This was the gift.

Jessica was holding Danny when a sheet of paper came floating down out of Warnock Manor, riding on waves of heat. She reached out and snagged the page as it fluttered past a pyre of burning debris. It was a flyer with a photo of a lost boy, an artifact from the tyranny of the woman who took him. Jessica read a caption that was once etched on her heart: "This Child Is Missing."

"No, he's not," she said, squeezing Danny tight. "He's home. We're both home."

Jessica wadded up her flyer and tossed it to the fire. They watched it burn to ash and blow away into that twilight land of legend where heroes flew on winged sandals and had a magic wallet, Athena's shield and the sword of Hermes, the guide and giver of good. From the moment she threw that flyer away, Jessica began her life again, to love her son for the rest of her life. She rocked her baby in her arms. "Everything is going to be all right," she sang softly. "Everything is going to be all right." And in the sweetness of her song, it was.

In his Old Mama's arms, Danny watched Warnock Manor burn. He saw smoke curl ghostly from the old spookhouse. It drifted out to him and he breathed the smoke in, like breathing a ghost, and he smelled like a boy who had been cooked right inside his clothes. The smell of the smoke was very powerful and it would stay with him as a feeling, with a memory of phantom faces in the smoke. Of the many faces he saw, the one he loved and was most angry at was the beautiful face of his New Mama. Why did she teach him his Old Mama was dead? Why had she done that? Why did she have him shoot his Old Mama? Or did he imagine that? But he knew he had not.

Danny did not understand his feelings, but would not forget them or the burning of the haunted house. They would remain like the groves and graduations of a fingerprint that do not change as a boy grows into a man. The quiet undertaking anger of having been used to kill his mother would sleep in the deep soul, to command a stillness, an awe. One transparent-blue morning it would rise, and in rising, it would hunt. It's a fact known and chronicled in many ancient tales, those who suffer beatings and bruises, those who are hunted, will become the hunter. The hunt being the only escape from the haunted soul. Danny was the son of Jack of London, a boy who had inherited a call to the wild.

The Rolls-Royce took her away from the pain, through the changeless green country, and she tried not to think of the child. But she thought she could hear his very quiet voice. And she could not stop seeing him in flames of supernatural pallor. She did it. She had burned him alive.

She turned from the awful to consider the saber Melissa had snatched as they left Warnock Manor. She drew it from its scrolled scabbard. Light gleamed along the long curved sweep of its blade etched with lovely rosettes. The scrolled inscription gave it a fantastic romantic character. A sword like this, she knew, would have been used to dismember assailants, it could decapitate, and was still perfectly capable of cleaving someone in two. Buffed to a pristine shine, it was so keen and silver, the blade blinding, and for a moment Somberg glimpsed Eric in the gleam of the blade. The boy shellacked with the high gloss of destiny, and she looked at the blade in a peculiar, cautious way. It gleamed with death, as terrible as her love.

Somberg put the saber away, and with it the ghastly thoughts. She was wounded, the wound was unsightly and as ghoulish as that truth that follows love. Love is the last attainment of extended consciousness, infinite consciousness. A conscience is the one thing she had not planned on. Love is the fitful flight. Love is a mental illness. Love is thunder-fire. She saw him in the fire; she saw him burn, and her heart burned with him. She had hunted down the greatest pleasure, and having found it, killed it. And there was no peace in it. But love was dead and she was safe and that was the way with love. We kill what we love, or it kills us.

She rested in the smooth sleepy beat of the big engine, under the peace of all that English sky, in a magic air of beauty that surrounded her, there are benefits to a life gone wrong. There were no apologies to offer, she had loved and her blushed heart was possessed. The sudden fit was over and she resigned herself to what was possible, such as the Garden of the World. Soon now she would be back aboard *Pequod,* soothed by the vesper hymns of the devoted. The ship would convey her to other places in other times, flying through the feminine air, above the masculine sea, in the search for pleasure in the voyage of the strangely fantastic soul.